Dark Tide Rising

- UnderVerse -

Book 7

Jez Cajiao

Table of Contents

THANKS

Well, where to start this time? Its currently mid-afternoon for me, my wife Chrissy is out collecting our eldest son, Max, from his school, and I'm working, a fairly normal occurrence admittedly.

This book was a bit more of a fight than many of the others to create, having had such a break from the UnderVerse, I love the realm though, and couldn't wait to return.

The Omnibuses are finished now, and hopefully you'll have enjoyed the differences in them, as well as the overall polishing and work that went into them, and you're now ready for the second season to begin!

I'll warn you now though, there's a cliffhanger ahead, and that's for a very good reason, books 8&9 are coming next year (I'll be writing them anyway) and they're going to reveal an entire new arc, so get ready, because there's loads to share with you yet!

All of this, however, hasn't addressed the reason I'm here.

I need to say THANK YOU to Chrissy, Geneva and Kristen, for keeping me more or less sane during the events of the last few weeks, and for taking so much on your shoulders so that I could focus on just writing.

I need to thank Emily, because she's had to do, redo, and then redo again all her hard work in the omnibuses, when errors were found, and confusion abounded. She tackled it with good grace and was kind when she could have quite rightly called me an asshole.

I need to thank Wayne, partially for his amazing work in the rerecords with the new content, and partially because it amuses the shit outta me knowing he's going to have to read this out, while thanking himself. Heh.

I need to thank my Beta team, who've worked magic catching typos and errors, Scott, Shawn, Spencer, Richard, Keith, Denny, Kat, Chris, Ben and Neil. Thank you, you wonderful, crazy buggers.

I also need to thank Chrissy again, and my family, Max, Xander and Meemaw more than most, as the last two weeks have been hard, I've been fighting to fix things, and as such I've not been around when I should, and wanted, to be.

Thank you all

-Jez, 08/11/2022

UNDERVERSE SYNOPSIS

Note: All character details, maps and spell/ability details are on World Anvil:

https://www.worldanvil.com/

This requires an account to access, but a free one is fine, once logged in, search for 'UnderVerse' and the covers should show which is mine.

BOOK ONE:

Jax is working a dead end job, in a semi-stable relationship, and searching for his missing brother, while plagued by dreams of the UnderVerse. This terrible alternate reality is where he, and his brother Tommy, are pulled against their will on occasion. When in the dream they inhabit artificial bodies and fight to protect abandoned villages and more, standing between the inhabitants of the Old Empire and the creatures of the night.

They awaken back on earth once the threat has passed, or they've been killed, with their injuries following them. While they heal at a tremendously accelerated rate, it still requires days to recover, and in that time, they hide their injuries, lest they be locked away for self-mutilation.

After one such session, Jax decides to come clean to his GF and explain everything. Badly injured and bleeding heavily, he arrives at her home, only to find her in bed with another man. He loses control, half beating the man to death, and having his skull shattered in turn by her, using the baseball bat he'd bought her for self-defense.

Jax comes to in the hospital, chained to the bed, and is interviewed by the police and warned he faces a significant jail term. While alone and contemplating this, an unknown doctor slips in and assures him it has all been taken care of, before drugging him.

When Jax wakes up this time, it's to find himself restrained, again, but on an airplane heading to meet 'the Baron Sanguis'. A lawyer assures him that should he carry out the reasonable requests of his new employer, then not only will all legal concerns be a thing of the past, but he will find his brother as well. Jax accepts, warned that refusal means death, and meets the Baron, an inhuman monster who admits to being an interplanar traveler, and a member of the original nobility of the UnderVerse, the Realm that Jax and his brother dream of.

To be free and to find his brother Jax must travel to that shattered Realm, and open a stable portal back to this Realm, as the mana here is simply too low in concentration for the portal to be held open for more than bare seconds. Alternatively, a portal from that side, to here, would be secure and enable the nobility to return with servants and forces intact, ready to reconquer their home.

Over the next several months, as Jax is trained for the 'little task', he discovers more about the past of that Realm, including that the voice of madness that occasionally speaks to him, and that he'd written off as himself being mad to some degree, is actually the voice of the Eternal Emperor Amon, a fragment of His soul being all that's left, clinging to the genetic line.

Amon was murdered, by the Baron, His son, and others of the nobility, with the aid of the God of Death, Nimon. In the process, and as his price for this, the followers of the other nine greater gods were purged and their temples cast down. Leaving the God of Death, who dragged one of the moons down to impact the Realm, with a powerful enough surge of His 'aspect' (death) that He managed to banish the other Greater Gods.

Jax grows to hate the Baron, but has nothing left in his life beyond his missing brother, and so takes the opportunity, training heavily, before facing eleven other nobles' choices in the arena to 'earn' the right to go to the UnderVerse. He wins, barely, and trades the remains of his opponents and their personal items to their sponsors, in exchange for several magical artifacts, before passing through the great portal.

Once on the other side, and having made a deal with an opposing noble 'house' for access, he finds himself in a ruined tower. The Great Towers were bastions of the old Empire, powerfully magical, self-sustaining and intended as entire self-contained cities. At half a mile wide at the base, two to three miles high, and sustained by their own mana collectors they acted as garrisons and secure imperial bastions in places of danger.

The Tower that Jax finds himself in, however, was never inhabited fully. It was finished, intended as a research and security station, but had only a skeleton crew when it was assaulted by a SporeMother. The SporeMother, a multi-limbed monstrosity of legend, flooded the defenders with undead and possessed creatures, birthing DarkSpore creatures, parasitical clouds that could puppet flesh, turning the unprepared defenders into attackers, claiming the Tower. The few remaining survivors, beleaguered on all sides, ordered the Tower's controller Wisps to shut the entire structure down, sealing the Wisps themselves away, and preventing the creature from being able to feed on the mana of the Tower to grow stronger, expecting that the Tower would be assaulted and retaken shortly by the Imperial Legion.

Then, before reinforcements could take the Tower back, the Cataclysm came. Seas and mountains rose, islands vanished and the creatures of the deep and of nightmare were set loose to roam. When Jax arrives at the Tower he finds it dark and silent, populated by the ancient dead, with only occasional more recently killed adventurers scattered here and there. He also encounters Sporelings, immature SporeMothers, hidden in the portal chamber, fighting them and locking himself away in a side room.

Jax uses one of the spells he gained, resurrecting one of the Sporelings he killed to form a companion to fight alongside him. Using his new companion, Bob, and his weapon of choice, a bastardized naginata, Jax proceeds to clear the Tower partially, discovering the 'Hall of Memories' and its sleeping Wisp, Oracle. He is gravely injured, and alone, Bob having perished in the fight to enter the room, and when he awakens the Wisp takes the chance it unthinkingly offers, to use some of the stored knowledge of the Hall of Memories, in the form of spellbooks, to enable him to defeat the undead outside the room.

Unfortunately, all magic he has accessed so far has been through books such as this, impressing outside knowledge across his brain and damaging it each time. This final spellbook is one too many, and results in scarring, internal bleeding and more. Jax is dying and Oracle, the newly awakened Wisp, bonds herself to him in an attempt to save him, gaining access to his manapool and enabling herself to cast the needed healing spells to save his life.

Over time Jax recovers, and with Oracle's guidance, reawakens and names Seneschal, the Wisp that controlled the tower, reactivating the mana collectors and beginning the basic repairs the Tower requires, as well as awakening the Goddess of Fire, Jenae. This awakens the SporeMother, now ancient and decrepit, but still powerful. In the fight that follows between Jax, Oracle, the newly reformed Bob and the SporeMother and her minions, the Eternal Emperor Amon makes contact with Jax, guiding him to use an artifact recovered in the Tower earlier. This Silverbright potion (Dragon's blood) transforms his weapon from a standard construction into a basic magical, but evolving, weapon. Jax kills the SporeMother, but is gravely wounded. Over the next day, as he is healed, the companions clear the remaining sections of the Tower, and find the creature's nest underground, along with the remains of the Golem Construction Cradles or Genesis Chambers.

They also find the Wisp responsible for the golems, name him Hephaestus, and take the time to reclaim the single working Genesis Chamber. This begins the construction of the most basic of stone golems to protect and rebuild the Tower. In the process, HeartStones are uncovered, a magical way to send a memory, as a method of communication. Most are long drained of mana, but the fragments that remain make it clear that Barabarattas, lord of one of the two nearby cities, has been trading slaves to the SporeMother in exchange for Sporelings, hoping to raise a captive army of SporeMothers.

The Wisps sense an intrusion higher in the tower and Jax explores, finding a group of slavers, heavily armed, using their slaves to loot an old armory. Jax attacks when seeing a child beaten, killing the slavers, with Oracle's help, and driving off the two airships that had been docked on the balcony. One is damaged and crashes in the courtyard below, while the other escapes to land at a nearby lake to effect repairs.

The freed slaves pledge allegiance to Jax, and while they rest, he takes one of their number, Oren, the captain of the crashed ship, down to the courtyard. He discovers that they were pressed into service, and had no desire to work with the slavers. The remaining surviving crew swear as well, and inform Jax that there is a third ship. This is the warship that was enforcing the City Lord's will, and it was still incoming, having stopped to raid a village along the way. Jax and the slaves use the weapons they have, the remains of the damaged ship and subterfuge to lure the warship in to land, while Oracle disables their engines.

Jax and Bob, aided by some of the former slaves, fight and kill the soldiers aboard the warship, capturing the crew, freeing a group of slaves taken from the villages and locking the crew in those same cages. Jax formally claims the Tower as his, and through the right of blood, having found that he is an illegitimate son of the Baron Sanguis, and therefore noble in his own right, he begins the right of Imperial Succession.

Barabarratas, like all nobles remaining in the Empire, with no Imperial House to swear to, had been unable to lay claim formally to the Imperial Throne, but once the succession has begun, sees a way to claim the throne. He threatens war against Jax, unless he surrenders. Jax, being short of patience and self-control, as well as occasionally being an asshole, in turn declares war on Barabarratas and his city of Himnel, taunting him before leading his people in a wake. The end of the book comes to Thomas, Jax's brother, languishing and injured in a jail, before being sold as fodder, the lowest caste of soldier, to the Dark Legion of Nimon.

BOOK TWO:

Thomas fights his abusive jailor and draws the eye of a Paladin of Nimon, who grants him a chance to prove himself. Thomas is happy to take that chance and prove his worth in battle to escape the rank of fodder.

Jax awakens with a hangover, the wake having gone well, and proceeds to set about trying to repair the Tower. Two of the new recruits, now citizens of the Great Tower, Oren the Dwarf airship captain, and Cai, a Panthera humanoid with a skill for organization, assist him. Teams are formed for hunting and defense, with a personal squad geared around Jax. This is formed from ex slaves who are determined to never be cowed again. Lydia leads them (mace and shield, heavy armor), with Jian (dual wielding swords), Arrin (mage), Cam (Axeman), Miren (archer), Stephanos (archer) and Bob. Jax and his new team go to try and capture or recruit the escaped second airship, but upon arrival at the lake, find the ship deserted.

They are attacked as they search by small four-armed amphibious creatures known as the 'Mer'. In the course of the fight, Jax realizes they are young, ranging from a young adult, to a child, and they were attacked by goblins prior to Jax's arrival, attacking him in pre-emptive self-defense. The young ones are joined by older, more experienced warriors, who agree to a truce at first, and then request help to deal with the nearby goblin horde.

Jax agrees, and three of the Mer join them, assaulting the goblin camp. In the course of the fight, Jax saves the life of one of the Mer, the oldest of the younglings, and upon clearing the ruin, and rescuing the surviving crew of the airship from them, claims the land as part of the Empire. In the process, the goblin cave is revealed as a buried outpost, complete with basic golems, which are claimed and returned to the Tower.

The Mer village remains neutral, but several of their people join Jax, including the youngling, Bane. The leader of the Mer that join the Tower is Flux, an accomplished adventurer, and he supports Bane's desire to be Jax's bodyguard. Several of the older Mer decide to join the Tower, many of whom are skilled, but crippled. Jax heals them, magic being increasingly rare in the UnderVerse since the fall of the Empire, and his abilities and the knowledge stored at the Tower are revealed as being incredibly valuable. The rescued crew join Jax, bringing their ship and joining the resurgent Empire.

The older banished Gods are awakened, and Jax has a disagreement with one, Tamat, the Lady of Assassins. Using a draconic legacy from Amon, Jax manages to beat Her in Her weakened state, before being forced back by Jenae, who begins the process of spreading the worship of the original Gods again. The Gods are weak, but They have abilities They can grant, and information from the past that is relevant. Nimon is unaware They are back.

Jenae, after an earlier disagreement with Jax, helps him to find that his brother was recently in the city of Himnel. Oren and the others implore Jax to free their families, to bring them to the Tower from Himnel. He agrees, pausing only long enough, to have his body inked with tattoos, guided by Jenae, Ame, a Mer runesmith, and a tattooist named Renna.

While attempting to find a hidden entrance to the city, used by smugglers, Oracle, who has fallen in love with Jax, and he with her, is captured and taken deep underground by the Drow, a race of Dark Elves that are scouting the city for an unknown reason. Jax catches some of them, and in a bout of frantic insanity, imbues his body with sufficient mana that he gains a new ability 'Mana-Overdrive' speeding his movements and strength up, but it is short lived, and results in a 'crash' afterward. Jax uses this ability to kill two of the Drow, and then, driven mad by Oracle's capture, pain and fear allows his darker side to come out as he tortures the Drow for information.

Bane calms him down, hides the body from the others, and guides Jax back to himself. Jax's group, now including Barret, a former soldier and a member of Oren's ship's crew, dives underground, hunting the Drow. Over the underground trip, they meet Ashrag, an ancient Cave Spider, who remembers the Empire, and despite her monstrous appearance, was once an Imperial Citizen. Jax resurrects ancient Oaths, claiming them as his own at Amon's direction, and passes out from the mana drain. This convinces Ashrag and, after fighting a group of her brood, she swears allegiance. She agrees, on the condition that Jax free the tunnels of the Drow who view her kind, and their bodies, as a great delicacy.

Jax eventually leads his team through the various dark places, and finds Oracle, captured by the Drow leader, a Drider. The half woman-half spider, has several smugglers held captive and fights the group. Jax is triumphant, but Cam dies at the hands of the Drow. Oracle is freed and the smugglers are mainly compliant, save their leader, who ends up making a comment that Jax disagrees with pointedly, and dies.

The last few Drow fight a retreat, until they are killed by a new threat coming the other way along the tunnel. The three newcomers slaughter the Drow, then, after a tense standoff, are revealed to be Imperial Legionnaires. The Imperial Legion has been dismissed and derided since the Cataclysm, slowly dwindling in numbers and through several bad apples in leadership, have become outsiders in their own homes. They are disliked and disrespected by the locals, even as they march out to fight the creatures that nobody else can.

The Legion is falling apart, its members lost and despairing, until Jax resurrects the Oaths, and finally a chance at a future is given back to them.

The three scouts, Yen, Tang and Amaat swear to Jax, and reveal that they are even now, below the City of Himnel.

BOOK THREE:

Jax leads the group to the surface, fighting off a group of local thugs who attempt to hunt the Legionnaires, and eventually reach the Arena and Arena Master Mal, one of the local leaders of the Smuggler's Guild. This is the man Oren had recommended as the best choice of an ally in the city. At the same time Jax is in the process of capturing a small group of Djinn, who offer allegiance in exchange for freeing their captured clan mother from the Skyking.

Mal agrees to help, for a fee, and introduces his team; Soween, his right hand, Jay his muscle and Josh his mage and Soween's husband. While Jax is resting, and about to finally get some 'private time' with Oracle, who can assume human form and size at will, Mal receives a message from the local crime lord, the Skyking. He demands Mal turn over the 'Legion' having discovered that it was Legionnaires that killed its people. Mal refuses, and instead, to gain the time they need, arranges a series of arena fights with the 'captured' Legionnaires, including Jax, and betting games.

While Mal makes these arrangements, Jax and his team visit a local healer, intending to get some of the deep seated injuries to his brain that are slowing his ability and level growth addressed. Along the way, Jax is surrounded by the enslaved, seeing the casual cruelty of the people, the way that nobles laugh and stroll, while slaves on the verge of starvation carry their bags. Amon sees this and their twinned rage escapes control, resulting in a temper-tantrum of epic proportions, leveling a section of the city and freeing the slaves, while also releasing Amon to face Jax inside his own mind.

Jax manages to defeat Amon, but in the process, discovers that he's had an unrecognized parasitic inhabitant all this time. He tears it free, gutting himself in the process, and only survives through the intervention of his team getting him to the healer, and the divine help of Jenae.

The Legion, having lost contact with their scouts, and seeing the devastation in the city, send a small, but elite team out to investigate, and with their help, Jax is returned to the Arena. The Legion settles in to protect him.

Jax is drained by the healing, and Centurion Primus Augustus, one of the four Primus of the Legion, fights in his place in the Arena that night, slaughtering all thrown against him.

Jax awakens and meets Mal and the others, works to integrate himself with the Legion and meets the non-human members of the shipyards who've been brushed aside by Barabarattas and his kind as 'sub-human'. They are recruited, and a plan formed. Rather than escaping with everyone through the hidden Smuggler's Path and robbing the city for the Tower's needs, a new more daring plan is concocted.

The airships are built in the shipyards, and Himnel's greatest weapon is under construction, the battleship. Currently it's a bare structure, open to the elements, but under the plan, additional volunteers are brought in, and the battleship is sealed up, and made, minimally, airworthy. The Legion are contacted and given orders, in three days they are to capture the shipyards.

Having little alternative, and no love for the city, as well as a legitimate authority encouraging it, the Legion agree.

Jax fights and recovers that night and trains, dragging Grizz, the Legionnaire into his group, as well as Yen and Tang. The next night, after the fight, he leads his team to raid and rob the Magical Emporium, a golem secured shop. The presence of the golem leads Jax and the others to discover a hidden section below the main shop, unknown by all. They realize that long ago it wasn't a shop, but a golem repair and construction facility. The golems are claimed, the construction facility below ground being ordered to begin repairs and construction, while golems there are used to repair ancient mining golems, which are sent to the Tower, burrowing underground. The rest of the golems are sent to wait in the river for the assault on the shipyards.

The following night the Arena fight is 'fixed', but Jax, with the help of his team, wins, and they launch the assault. Combining the assault on the Skyking with the one on the shipyards, Jax and the small Legion team, along with his own, take the Skyking's tower, killing them all. Halfway through the fight, when confronted with the rarely seen Anubai, a heavily magical species, Jax activates his trump card, his Tattoos. Rather than being decorative, they are in fact magical runes enabling him to channel mana through them, helping him to turn the tables on his foes.

In the fight, they capture the first of the airships circling on 'overwatch' over the city. To capture the others, Jian assumes control of one of the ships and accidentally, being unfamiliar with the controls, fires a giant fireball at the tent city of recruits around the Dark Citadel of Nimon. Jax, as the leader of the group, is blamed and declared Apostate, and a holy war begins.

The ships are brought under Jax's control, and return to the shipyards, to be crewed by his people. In the following confusion, Jax is hit in the head and injured. The ships flee Himnel, having stolen the vast majority of the city's manastone store, which are needed to power the engines of the ships.

Without stones, Barabarattas is unable to give chase, and the ships head out to sea, hoping to leave the impression that they're not from the Tower, and as Jax had ordered. Unfortunately, Nimon is aware of the truth.

The Dark Legion attacks the stragglers leaving the city, and their latest recruit, Thomas assists in killing some of Jax's Legionnaires. Jax awakens when they are far out to sea, close to the Sunken City, a flying city from the old Empire that crashed into a seamount. He confirms the orders to land there, to make the ships secure, and then to make for the Great Tower. He also finally gets some 'private time' with Oracle.

BOOK FOUR:

Jax meets the Legion leadership, Prefect Romanus, and Alistor, his right hand, as well as the crew of the battleship and many of the refugees. While in transit, Jenae informs Jax that knowledge he needs is lost in the Sunken City, and he vows to find it. Jax is still recovering, but by the time the ship lands, along with its much smaller escorts, at the Sunken City, he attempts to meet the two local parties from both Himnel, and its enemy city Narkolt.

Both are found to be led by 'nobles' but Himnel's is using slave labor, as well as being offensive, and suffers an 'accident' involving a sword. Narkolt's group are slightly more respectful and are given 24hrs to come back and discuss their intentions. The remaining guards from the Himnel group are given the same chance. As part of the discussion Jax uses an Imperial Ability, freeing the city of the souls of the unquiet dead that were condemned to roam it eternally, granting them their peace.

Once this is realized by the nobles, they ignore Jax's warning, and lead their people into the city's depths, searching for loot and artifacts. Jax orders the Legion into it as well, then leads his team in. In searching the depths, they are trapped by a landslide and explosions, set off by one of the nobles from Narkolt, and are forced into the depths.

Jian uses one of two books Jax gives him at this point and summons a demon to assist him, although it becomes clear the demon cares little for anything but gaining its own power. In the search, they are attacked by a group of feral Gnomes, explorers trapped long ago by the undead revenants and worse. These Gnomes were forced into a small pocket that, with typical gnomish ingenuity, they made into a livable space. They were then enslaved by a Skinwalker and its controlled Leviathans, forced to give their water and more to it, leaving them a water source heavily contaminated by metal, to drink and to raise crops from. The result is that the Gnomes essentially are driven feral, regressing and attacking each other. A small group is preserved as best as they can, while the greater population succumbs to madness.

These mad Gnomes attack Jax and, in the process, he and Oracle heal one of them, at least partially restoring his mind. Giint is broken by the things he's seen and done, and joins Jax, not knowing what else to do. The remaining feral Gnomes attack, and are driven back, as Jax and the team attack the Skinwalker and its pets. Jax wins the fight, but the Skinwalker, unbeknownst to them, is inside the creature they just killed, and escapes.

Back with the Dark Legion, Thomas, wounded from long ago injuries, is offered up to the Dark God, allowing His blood to mingle with Thomas' and regaining his magic, as well as sparking to life a dark seed, as he begins to fall in love with Belladonna, his squad leader.

Jax uses an Essence Core and gains the ability of flight and increased mana regeneration through meditation. Jenae reaches out, informing them that a hidden force is incoming, led by the Drow, with captive SporeMothers. Jax orders Oracle to go to the fleet resting overhead. They are to leave immediately and fly at full speed to the Tower to defend it. Jenae makes it clear that the Gnome's original ship, while hidden, is still usable, but the DarkSpore the SporeMothers could release would result in massive casualties if the fleet doesn't leave.

A small number of the Gnomes have been swayed by Giint and wish to join Jax, agreeing to lead him to the hidden ship. He leaves them to prepare, attacking the nearby camp of the undead, led by a necromancer from Earth, a previously sent through 'volunteer'. Bartholomew the Lich, or 'Barry' as Jax refers to him, appears and traps the team, only to have Lydia, in a burst of desperation, seize the hidden power of the Valkyrie, turning the tide of the battle and beginning her own ascension. Barry is killed in the fight, and Jax, when he recovers the rest of the loot from the vault, also awakens a slumbering Wisp. Jax, his team, and the Gnomes race to reach the ship, receiving injuries along the way, but reach it just as the enemy arrives overhead.

The ship is powered up, and the Wisp is permitted to bind itself to the Gnome's ship, gaining control. They use explosives from the Gnomes to free the ship of its hidden location, and then fight their way out of the Sunken City.

One of the enemy ships crashes in the fight, releasing the SporeMother and leaving it behind, while the others follow. In the fights that come, Jax and his team are badly injured, and Stephanos dies, killed by a Drow. Just as all seems lost, Mal appears, flying his own ship and driving the Drow back, having left the fleet to come and help.

Jax and the others start to recover, only to have Jenae reach out, informing them that Nimon has dispatched His Dark Legion, an advanced force, to make a portal close to the Great Tower, and plans to assault it. With that, Jax orders Tenandra, the name the gnomish ship's Wisp has chosen for herself, to get them to the fleet with all haste.

BOOK FIVE:

Jax transfers ships. Along with his team, and he orders the fleet to land as soon as they are over land again, cross-loading the most skilled Legionnaires and his own team onto a small number of the fastest ships. He leaves the fleet under Romanus' control, and names Augustus as his heir, in case anything happens. Miren, Jian's lover and the surviving archer of the team, quits, unable to keep going.

The faster group flies ahead, securing the Tower and using the majority of the stolen manastones to repair the structure in a massive burst of magic. The next few days are filled with training and meetings as Jax tries to get the Tower's structure, both physical and command, established. Then quests are given by the awakened Gods, and as the Tower is secured. Jax raids the other locations in the path of the oncoming Dark Legion, determined to prevent them from uncovering the golems that could make a massive difference in the upcoming confrontation.

While these are being stripped, Denny, a Legion trap smith, takes an advance force and sets up an ambush for the approaching enemies. Jian's demon rebels and is banished, leaving Jian weaker and furious. He turns to the second book on demon summoning, and heartbroken at the news that Miren has run straight into the bed of a Legionnaire, binds a succubus, Sehran. When Jax finds out, he and Oracle question Sehran, but permit her to stay as a part of the team on a trial basis.

Thomas, unbeknown to Jax, is a member of the closing Dark Legion, and on a side mission, discovers he has a rare gift. As a Dark Berserker, his own nascent power as a berserker is corrupted by the dark gift.

Jax joins Denny and the others, and the trap is sprung, annihilating the majority of the Dark Legion, and Jax, after injuring Belladonna, is beaten back by Thomas. The pair fight each other, unknowing, and Jax escapes, setting off a magical attack that kills several of Thomas' friends in the process. Jax and the Legion take their airship and fall back, while the Dark Legion flee and Jax proceeds to clear local sites of interest.

A hidden interloper, Ronin the Bard, is discovered in the Tower, and joins Jax's team, bringing knowledge, music and a little magic to the team. The Arbuton, a sentient tree, is found living atop one of the old outposts, and deals are struck, with Jax sending a golem to aid the Arbuton, and the Arbuton sending Woodite, a Grove Tender, and its mate, Ha'zel, along with two guardians to assist the Tower.

In the exchange, Jax is separated from the team and dragged underground through a river, only to find a long-buried city filled with kobolds who summon their revenants and attack him. He uses his ability to free the souls of the enslaved within the kobolds' weapons, trapped and ensorcelled revenants, and strips the city of life.

When Jax awakes, having been overpowered by his ability, he finds one of the spirits waiting for him and it offers to guide him out. On the way however, Jax is contacted by Malthus, the 'Administrator of Pelath's View'. The being claims to be bonded to the city, much in the way that Seneschal is bonded to the Tower, and is alone, having been buried for long ages. He offers knowledge and artifacts, as well as a safe fallback position for the Empire should it need it, all in exchange for company. And a song.

Jax agrees, and several hours later, reaches the surface, meeting Oracle and the others, before returning to the Tower, finding that the rest of the fleet has arrived.

Thomas throws caution to the wind, determined to save Belladonna, and has her bound to his back, an IV drip botched together using a vampire's teeth and worse, to share his own blood, and hopefully the healing ability that he shares with Jax, with her. He sets off running to the Dark Citadel, as Jenae informs Jax that She found traces of Thomas... as a Dark Legionnaire.

Jax dispatches Mal and Augustus to Narkolt to try and recruit the Legion garrison there, then returns to clearing the surrounding areas. He and Amon face each other again, this time Amon comes out ascendant, and faces an ancient evil, devastating it, the village, and the land around for miles. Jax has his power torn out of his control, and has a split second to fight Amon, or save Oracle and Bob, who, as bonded companions, need his mana and health pool to live. Jax chooses them, and uses his rising understanding of magic to free them both, forcibly evolving Oracle into a new species.

Lydia faces her past, as well as her father and husband, who sold her into slavery. Jax and the rest of the team watch as she beats them half to death, then the team travels to the slave markets of the Habieen, following the path her mother was taken on to be sold. The resultant fight includes a mana-hurricane, and only the intervention of the Gods keeps Jax alive, but badly broken. Tenandra takes the ship and flies away, attempting to get reinforcements and to draw attention from Jax as he's carried by his people, surrounded by hundreds of freed slaves, into the forests.

The Dark Legion, guided by Nimon, chases Jax, who has recovered consciousness, and his people. Jax sends Lydia and Grizz to free the soul of the last Valkyrie, claiming her armor, rather than letting the following Dark Legion stumble over its resting place. With the rest of the team sent away, Jax is down to Bob, Ronin and Bane, and he sends Bob and Ronin to guide the freed slaves, sending Bane to hunt the Dark Legion's scouts.

The Dark Legion advance teams kill the slowest of the refugees, showing no mercy, and Jax makes a decision, asking for volunteers. They slowed the advance, killing several dozen, but seeing that there's no chance, with the numbers arrayed against them. Jax sends the volunteers on ahead, ordering them to protect the others, as he remains behind to buy them time.

He uses his flight ability, 'Soaring Majesty' to conduct a series of hit and run attacks, drawing the enemy to him, before folding together the most powerful spell he can, literally drawing a firestorm down upon himself, while screaming a challenge to Nimon, the Dark God himself. Then Jax attacks the Dark Legion, determined to sell his life as dearly as possible.

In the course of the fight, the brothers come face to face again, this time Thomas wins, pinning Jax to a tree with a spear, removing his helm to see the light in his enemy's eyes die… only to look into his brother's eyes.

Thomas rebels against Nimon and his weakened blood, drained heavily into Belladonna, allows him to swear to Lagoush, Goddess of Water, and he is accepted as Her champion. The brothers fight the Dark Legion together, but no matter how valiant, skilled, and dangerous, two men cannot defeat hundreds.

At the end, as they both believe it's all over, Augustus steps forward, Mal having gathered all those that he could, and brought them when he realized what was happening at the slave camp. The Imperial Legion faces its antithesis, and wins, driving the Dark Legion back. Jax is collected, and the forces fall back to the Great Tower, the refugees being shepherded by Legionnaires and airships.

Bane, however, is missing…

BOOK SIX:

Jax and Thomas have been reunited, and although the return to the Great Tower was painful, both of them being badly wounded, they have made it back to a secure location and start to rebuild their relationship.

Sint, God of Light and Order, had tasked Jax with recovering His Chosen Champion, and the airship bearing Lucian, Restun's Great-Great uncle arrives. A confrontation between uncle and nephew ensues, as Restun has spent his entire life, battling against the stigma of an uncle that was not only infected with vampiric essence, but that was banished from the Legion.

In the ensuing argument, and with the confirmation of Lord Sint, it is made clear that Lucian was made a scapegoat centuries ago to cover for the then Legion-General's excesses.

The result was an innocent man sent wandering the continent in the aftermath of the Cataclysm, battling evil wherever he found it. Lucian is elevated to Chief Justicar, and set to establish an order of Justicars to enforce the laws.

Jax and Tommy, now going by Thomas, set off and took the fragment of Lagoush, Lady of Water, to the Mer nearby. They continue on to reclaim the tools of Svetu, the God of Gnomes, long lost to the world in an ancient ruin.

The ruin, now populated by insane Goblins and Orcs, is hidden high in the mountains, taking up the front and publicly accessible section of an ancient Imperial production facility.

Jax and his team, assisted by Thomas, loot and recover the site, eliminating most of the inhabitants, and ending up with several Orcs that had been captured and enslaved, as new citizens. The production facility requires several tons of rare ores however, to regain functionality.

These ores were long ago mined by a lost mining golem, and Jax and his team set off to recover the golem, finding, in the process, a clan of Amilith. The mining golem (and the accumulated ore) is recovered, and the Amilith are left in their valley, all save two who are determined to reclaim a member of their tribe back at the Tower.

On the way back to the Great Tower, several fleeing airships are seen, also heading for the Tower, and under attack by demons. Tenandra, in her ship-body, is able to get Jax and his companions close enough to fight the demons and save one of the ships, though the others are lost.

Rewn, City Lord of Narkolt is aboard the lead vessel, having been chased from Narkolt by an assassination attempt by the Drow. Rewn swears to Jax, and agrees to relinquish the city to his control, but in the process of the discussion, is revealed as being a puppet.

Rewn has been 'guided' by his advisors for his entire life, provided a wiling harem, drink and drugs, and told what to say in public. He is utterly unprepared for the realities of life, and breaks down on learning he will actually have to work if he expects to rule in truth in Narkolt.

Bane, missing from Jax and the others since the battle in the forest against the Dark Legion, is found to have been diverted by Tamat, Goddess of Assassins and Dark Deeds, and is currently slaughtering her hated brother Nimon's priests. He rescues a trio of Dwarven women, and they assist him in his slaughtering of the priesthood, as well as their escape, as Bane attempts to return to Jax and his friends.

Rewn attempts to involve himself in the plans for retaking Narkolt, and is handled by one of his concubines, Carmen. He is removed from any kind of leadership position in the short term, while Jax and the Legion assault Narkolt.

Mal is sent ahead, along with a small team of spies, all of whom are captured on arrival, after Mal's lover Alyssa, the owner of the 'Kneeling Lady' whorehouse, mistakenly arranges monitoring of him.

The assault on the city is hard fought, but ultimately successful, and a Drow Drider, a massive half Dark Elf, half spider tears free of the City Keep, revealing the Drow presence for all to see.

In the ensuing fight, a great many good people are lost, but eventually, the city is taken, and Jax turns to mopping up. The Drow, attempting to flee from the city, use a heavily modified transport to try and collect their remaining forces from the 'Kneeling Lady'. They release an immature SporeMother into the city, and Oracle is injured. Jax loses his shit and beats the SporeMother almost to death with his gauntleted fists.

Oracle is exposed as having been changed by the spells and bonding that Jax was forced to bind her with when Amon had torn his connection apart in their last altercation.

Days pass as Jax consolidates his control over the city of Narkolt, and Rewn finally arrives, attempting to declare his ownership, and refusing to learn his place. This results in him being stripped of all rights to the city, and his former lover Carmen, now imprisoned by his hand, being raised up instead to rule the city in Jax's name.

The City interface grants a true Imperial Noble with access rights, a way of monitoring all illegal actions in the city. Jax and his people make use of this to gut the Smuggler's Guild, wiping out the majority of the corruption that has festered in the nobility since time immemorial as well.

Many of the nobles refuse to swear fealty to Jax, and are banished, fleeing with their forces into the surrounding forest. Mal is named a noble, and proceeds to name Alyssa his lady, then brings his father, Hannibal, in to finish gutting the Smuggler's Guild, using the pretense that he was banned from all the 'good bars' by them when he was declared a traitor for helping Jax.

The ancient Imperial Armory under Narkolt is uncovered, and a sleeping Elder God, the original Valspar, is accidentally set free, before being summarily killed in the ensuing chaos when the Gods lend a hand, fearing the result should such a creature regain its strength of old. The Armory contains some working facilities, and they are turned to producing golems and weaponry.

Bane arrives during the fight against the Valspar, and helps to turn the tide, before retaking his position as leader of Jax personal bodyguard.

The city manastone mine is also recovered, an ancient deposit of stones that had been continually converting the city's sewage to manastones since the Cataclysm. This fact had been long lost, and the sewage had been allowed to continue building up, until Jax and his team, literally swimming through the sewage at times, cleared it out and reclaimed it and started repairs.

Barabarratas is inducted into the order of Vampyrs by his assistant Cletus, who in turn is a supporter of Akanji, Lucian's brother. Barabarratas, seeing that his enemy Jax has claimed and secured both the Great Tower, and the city of Narkolt, changing the balance of power on the continent, makes a deal with the Dark Legion and Nimon's priesthood. In exchange for them protecting the city, he cedes some control over it to them.

As Jax and his forces prepare to assault Himnel, a Wisp colony is discovered far to the north, with several of the Wisps being captured by Himnel's forces. One is forcibly bonded to a young girl that is found to have enough of the noble Imperial bloodline. Through Nimon's blessing, she is able to assume control of Himnel, in name only. She is, however, able to command the golems in the city to fight Jax and his forces when the assault begins.

Thomas is sent with Tenandra and a small team to rescue the Wisps, while Jax, with Romanus advising, leads the assault on Himnel. The airship battle is short, the new weapons and methods of manufacturing that Jax has brought to the UnderVerse result in the annihilation of Himnel's forces.

Once the Legion is flown into Himnel's territory, they are deposited and create a beachhead, protecting the area as the Himnel army and elite forces are flown in as well.

Barabarratas orders an assault on their position, one that takes the lives of many Legionnaires, but it ultimately unsuccessful. Romanus is badly injured and Jon takes over as leader of the assault above ground, while Jax and Augustus, along with the remaining Legionnaires and his team, use a mining golem to assault Himnel from below, thinking to avoid the walls, and the deaths of innocents that would come if they were to assault the city directly.

Under Himnel, Jax and his team meet Barabarratas's secret weapon, a captive SporeMother breeding ground, along with hundreds of possessed undead.

Jax fights the SporeMothers, and eventually kills Cletus Thane, Barabarratas's assistant and handler. Several of Thomas's old Dark Legionnaire team are exposed as having been transformed into monsters to track and kill him for abandoning Nimon, and one of them is found and eliminated.

Jax takes control of the SporeMothers, and the hunt for the Vampyrs begins, resulting in several of the coven being killed off, and Alistor, the former Tribune of the Legion of Himnel, being exposed as a traitor and a secret adherent of Nimon.

In the following assault on Himnel's keep, Jax forcibly converts the golems to his side, but only after the deaths of many of the Legion. Jax and the remaining forces assault the remaining enemy forces in Barabarratas's throne room, and in the fight, Jax and Amon bond.

The Eternal Emperor augments Jax's abilities and knowledge, enabling him to easily exert his will over many of those there, and in a pitched battle, Lucian defeats Akanji.

The City of Himnel is taken by Jax and the Dark Legion, along with their surviving priesthood, flee to their citadel.

With the twin cities of Himnel and Narkolt held by Jax, and the airships as well, the Dark Citadel is gradually reduced in power, starving their forces, until after a few days of constant attrition, Nimon takes a direct hand on events.

The Arch Lich Ghastool, empowered by Nimon, leads his forces out of the depths of the ocean and assaults Himnel, Jax and his forces having deployed already before the city in the defensive emplacements they'd been preparing to fight the Dark Legion from.

Grizz is killed in the fighting, and the horror of his failure, the realization that many of his mistakes and the deaths caused by them are down to his own refusal to admit his differences from the others, drives Jax to take a final step, and to accept his power. He bonds himself to Amon.

Jax saves Grizz, returning him to life, and as a newly born Master of Mana. He then lifts into the air, slaughtering the Lich's army and the Arch Lich himself, tearing the mana that was sustaining the ancient undead free in a single act, using that mana to raise his 'Genetic Viability' overall by more than twenty percent though a single spell.

The Heliogifts, magical claymore mines, that had been hidden in the field ahead waiting for the Dark Legion's advance, are set off as the Dark Legion, well, advances…

Many of the Dark Legion elites are slaughtered in the ensuing explosion, and more are killed as Jax unleashes his own war golems, before finally unleashing a spell crafted by one of Amon's highest mages.

The Dark Citadel is destroyed, and Nimon, in a fit of rage, challenges Jax to a battle for his soul. Jax agrees, and the Gods gather round, ensuring a fair fight, reforming his armor and healing him, preparing him for the battle ahead.

Nimon and Jax have equal points agreed, all of Jax's stats are totaled, and Nimon creates a physical avatar with the same points. Unfortunately for Jax, the physical avatar has no need of such things as Intelligence, Charisma or Wisdom, being controlled by Nimon himself.

As such the avatar is physically far superior to Jax, and Jax wins only through a combination of blind luck, and trickery, thanks to his razorwire belt. Jax kills Nimon, cutting His head free, and orders that it be made into a goblet, just because he can.

That night, in the celebrations and festivities, Oracle drops the bombshell to Jax that, regardless of all the perfectly good reasons why it shouldn't have happened, including their being different species, and her having never previously had a body capable of it, she was indeed, pregnant. His life, never simple, got far more complicated

PROLOGUE

The corridor was almost entirely black, only her lack of options kept her running at top speed. The last light of the torch, so far behind her already, guttered out, and a gurgling chuckle echoed from far too close.

Morgana tripped on some of the old bones, hitting the ground and rolling. She banged her elbow and knee on the floor, cursing in the dirt and dust. The Saint Christopher necklace her mother had given her caught on a wayward finger and snapped free, falling somewhere in the darkness.

"Goddamned shithole of a...!" She panted, scrambling back to her feet and limping on. "Come on, Morgana. You can do this!" She reached into the thigh pocket on her right side, ripping the velcro and fumbling a chemical light free that she snapped and shook quickly. It bathed the wide, well-maintained, if dusty, corridor in an unearthly green light.

"Fuck, I miss my gun!" She gasped, before staggering into a halting run again, the light held in one hand, the other ready to draw a knife at any second.

One of the team had already died from friendly fire...or stabbing, in this case. The Sarge had beaten into them all that if they ran in the dark, they did it without a damn weapon drawn, or they'd face abandonment when the portal reopened.

Right now, she was seriously considering abandoning that bloody sensible rule in favor of one that maybe, just maybe, gave her the slightest chance of surviving.

The sarge wasn't going to chew her out for it. The last time she'd seen him, he was literally chewing on Petersen, biting through his windpipe and showing every sign of enjoying himself immensely.

He'd looked up at her and the other two with her and just *smiled*, even as the black veins under his skin pulsed and grew.

More of the squad lay dead around him, and one of them...

She banished the thought, shaking her head and digging deeper, taking the next corner to the right, then turning to the left. Her mental map worked wonders, even in this insane world or realm or whatever it was.

She ran on, crossing the silent courtyard; the gentle breeze that made the trees on either side of the buried city rustle mocked her as she passed.

A way out, that was what she needed!

Fuck the treasure, *fuck* the wages, *fuck* the power, the immortality, all of it! Less than a goddamn week ago she'd been facing life in prison for putting a bullet in the back of a rapist motherfucker's head.

Then *they'd* come, asked her if she wanted a new job, a new life, and a second chance. She'd taken it. Mariella had sent her the divorce paperwork already, and she'd not even bothered coming to visit her in the cell. And besides her, well...the damn cat had always hated her anyway.

Why the hell shouldn't she take a fresh start?

Now she fucking knew! She'd barely landed at the damn airfield when the boss lost his shit and killed two of his own people. He'd apparently trashed the compound, or the upper floors at least. She and the other new recruits, a handful of people that seemed all right, but weren't particularly trustworthy, had been kept in the lowest level of the barracks and told to keep quiet. The next thing she knew, others were arriving: ex-soldiers, mercenaries, and worse.

The kinds of people she'd dedicated her life to putting behind bars were turning up, supposedly the same as her. They were all led into a central atrium, given an Oath to obey—one she'd been warned would enforce itself—and when one of them had refused to give it, he'd been shot in the fucking face there and then.

They'd all taken the Oath after that.

She'd kept her head down, keeping away from the others as much as possible, until two of them decided that, as a woman who stayed on the outskirts of the group, she'd be fair prey.

They'd tried to attack her in the shower at night-time, and it had gone badly for them.

Morgana was sure she'd have won the fight. She was trained, experienced, and unlike the other two, was sober and already in a foul mood.

Instead, she'd ended up spending two hours in the officers' mess while a pissed-off captain explained to everyone, again, that the Oath was a form of geas, and that assaulting your comrades, especially when you had a clear intention of killing them afterward, would end extremely badly.

The sight of their muscles literally ripping themselves free and sending their lifeblood shooting across the room and dripping from the ceiling would haunt her forever.

That had been the worst thing she'd ever seen, until they got here.

Now it wasn't even in the top ten of freaky shit, and she had another three hours before the portal reopened to let the scouts back through.

"Moooorrrgannnaaaa!" a sing-song voice warbled. Things moved in the darkness at the edge of vision, and she leaned into the run, picking up speed, hissing as she frantically searched for anything, a crack, a hidden door, a fucking sewer grate, even!

The damn place was underground; it had to have a way out!

Stairs went nowhere, the outer wall was solid, the damn wells were dry and sealed all the way around.

A scream of pain, of horror, rose from somewhere in the distance. A voice, garbled, begging for help. Morgana turned, twisting *away* from the noise, remembering the first time they'd fallen for that trick, and the creatures that had been waiting, hidden around their mutilated comrade.

Things moved on the outer ring of the light she carried as she skidded to a halt, barely staying upright. She sobbed, the hairs on the back of her neck rising as she realized she was surrounded. She skidded to a halt and desperately searched for a way out. Dark figures skulked out of the darkness to encircle her. Thick, oily-black veins rose and throbbed beneath their skin as they stared at her.

"Morgana," the creature that was once her sarge said. "Don't be afraid, child. We won't hurt you."

"You…you ripped Petersen's throat out…with your fucking teeth!" she hissed, backing up, spinning around and coming face-to-face with another scaled, short creature with milky white eyes, wearing a tool belt.

More and more figures oozed from the darkness, and the damn outer wall behind the sarge split open like a cut in the wall, disgorging dozens more.

"We were *hungry*," the Sarge defended itself. "So long without meat…without life!"

"What do you want?" she almost screamed.

The sarge smiled, bloody flesh still stuck in its teeth.

"More," it said simply. "We want more."

"Well you'll have to fight for it," she hissed, dropping the chemical light on the floor and dragging the dagger free from her hip and ankle both, slashing at the creatures surrounding her as they stopped closing in.

"No, we don't," it said, forcing a rictus of a smile onto its face again in a gesture that was clearly meant to be reassuring. "We wish to *bargain*…"

"Wha…what?"

"Your kind like gold, gems," the Sarge said, lifting a hand and pointing as a pair of upright walking rat-like things shuffled through the crowd, only to dump handfuls of gold and jewelry onto the floor. "We will give you more, and you will open the portal, bringing others through."

"The…the portal?"

"You came through the portal. Others can. We cannot. You bring others, we let you go and give you gold." The creature said, its smile wide again as Morgana pretended to consider it.

On one hand, she was dead. On the other hand, she could get the chance to get through the portal and warn the others…as well as take some of the gold with her. She didn't give two shits about the gold, really, it might be worth a lot back home, and probably here, too, but it was heavy, shiny, and would cause as many problems as it solved.

She'd take it, though, because why not?

"Okay…but the others won't come through the portal if they see you."

"We will hide," it said placidly. "We are used to hiding." As it spoke, another form stalked through the massed group, even as more screams rose in the distance.

She blinked at it in confusion. A dusty, centuries-dead skeleton walked out of the pack, only to offer her…

"My necklace," she whispered, reaching up to check her neck where it'd broken free.

"You ran past us, climbed over us, and kicked us aside for hours, while we waited," the Sarge said, nodding its head, still with the predator's grin plastered across its face.

"You'll let me go afterward?" she asked nervously, licking her lips and not seeing any other choice.

"We promise."

"Okay," she whispered and, all around the city, the last members of her team screamed, torn apart by the seemingly innocuous skeletons laid in the corners of rooms. "What?"

"We only need one."

She swallowed hard. "How…how many?"

"We made this offer to three others," it said, cocking its head to one side. "You agreed first."

A second's hesitation…"Fuck." Morgana's voice quivered.

"Come to the portal." Sarge said happily, and the group flowed ahead, forcing her to go along with them or be absorbed.

She hurried along, desperate not to accidentally fall into the mass of creatures, only to have them all stop at once. Two from behind moved up, holding the gold and jewelry that she'd left on the floor.

"Is this not valuable?" Sarge asked suddenly. "Do you need more?"

"M…more?" she asked, wide eyed.

"Gold…platinum? Magical artifacts?"

Her eyes widened. "The last…magical weapons," she suggested, wondering if this would actually work.

It inclined its head placidly. "More will be brought."

With that, they were off again, and Morgana hurried to stay in the clear space left in the middle, desperately hoping that she might escape this.

A handful of minutes later, they were in the central courtyard again, and the portal that stood alone at one end of the tree-lined boulevard glimmered gently as they fed power to it.

"You will open the portal and encourage your kind to come through. Then, you will be set free," Sarge said.

She bit her lip, her mind frantically racing. "How?"

The group stopped dead again.

"Have we chosen poorly?" Sarge asked, its speech coming easier and easier.

"No!" She cried, then tried again. "No…I just…our portal opens from the other side."

"When?" it asked.

She hesitated, trying to figure out how long she'd been in the terrible darkness.

"Two…maybe two and half hours?" she guessed, and the power to the portal was cut suddenly, the little glimmers and sparkles dying away.

"We wait," Sarge said, standing there, staring at her, as did all the others.

"Okay," she agreed hesitantly.

Two and a half hours later, she was sitting on the floor, arms wrapped around her knees as she tried to keep her heart rate steady, using every trick she'd learned through the years as they stared at her, eyes glinting with murderous hunger.

"Here," Sarge said suddenly, making her jerk in shock, heart racing, as the group split to allow a trio of figures to march through. They were all men she knew, members of her team. Hell, one of them was Petersen, complete with the hole in his windpipe, and seemingly no worse off for it, despite the ragged hole and drying blood that coated his front.

Two of them set an iron-bound chest close by and threw the lid back, exposing piled gold and platinum, gems and more, glittering in the suddenly increased light of the cavern.

She looked upward. The mist that filled the roof of the cavern was glowing again, moving gently in a flowing pattern as it brought life-giving light to the trees and grass. The creatures around her split up, drifting away to hide in the nearby buildings as Sarge took a massive sword from Petersen and offered it to her, hilt first.

"This is one of the magical artifacts we have…the armory has many more," it assured her, letting go of the blade and turning to walk into a small recess in the wall nearby.

She almost dropped the sword, barely managing to catch it, and still the tip clanged on the ground, the cobbled stones letting loose a clear ring of metal.

"Okay…okay!" Morgana whispered, staring wide-eyed at the blade and shaking her head in disbelief at the fact they'd just given her this…this thing!

The weapon was massive, razor-sharp and *beautiful*, not to mention it damn well exuded power and was a very real threat to anything its wielder didn't like.

She shifted, hefting it carefully, and nodded to herself. It was big, hell it was *too* big, really, but she'd learn to wield it, and she'd bulk up enough that it fit her better.

Minutes passed as she stared into the silvery depths of the blade, entranced by the patterns that appeared and vanished, hints of geometric designs that faded as she looked at them, while others…

The portal flared to life, shocking her out of her contemplation, and she spun, open-mouthed, seeing her chance.

The creatures were nowhere in sight as the portal started to form. She took a few quick steps, pausing as she waited to see if she was going to be attacked, then frantically ran for it. She slowed long enough to grab a handful of the gold and platinum out of the chest, spilling dozens of coins onto the floor in her hurry.

Then she was off again, running to the portal and climbing the few short steps as it locked into place. On the far side, she saw her fellow soldiers.

She didn't slow, leaping for the event horizon, feeling gravity drag her forward, like she was being torn across the realm, hundreds, if not thousands of miles in a split second.

Then she hit the floor, the blade and armfuls of gold and gems clattering as they tumbled free.

"Close it!" she screamed. "Close it now!"

There was a second's hesitation, and the crackling colors thrown across the room from the portal went silent and died.

"What happened, soldier!" a voice growled at her, dragging her to her feet.

"Fuck, lookie this!" someone whispered, and a low whistle of appreciation rang out even as other, unseen hands reached greedily and tried to strip her hand from the hilt of the sword.

"Get off!" she screamed, kicking and shoving at them, brandishing the blade as a pockmarked, leering face got too close.

"Attention!" a voice rang out, filled with the assurance of command. Everyone straightened as the captain, followed by the fucking lord himself, walked into the room.

The captain stepped aside, and the lord walked closer, pausing as he stared down at her. His weird glowing eyes made her stomach clench in fear, as they always did.

"What did you find?" the lord asked slowly, reaching out and taking the sword from her, lifting the huge thing one-handed and eyeing it with a considering air.

"Report, soldier!" the captain shouted at her. Morgana did, her words spilling over themselves as she desperately tried to get it all out.

"An armory, you say?" the lord interrupted at one point.

"The creature said it was one of the weapons from the armory."

"And the gold, platinum?"

She hesitated, a sudden, terrible feeling coming over her.

"We saw it, Lord!" one of the others declared. "Sitting on the other side of the portal, just laid there, out in the open."

"And none of these creatures in sight?" the lord asked, getting shaken heads and 'no sir' in response.

"But…but…" Morgana whispered, eyes going wide. "They slaughtered us!"

"You were unprepared, let your guard down, no doubt." His expression twisted. "Consider yourself lucky to be permitted to live to redeem yourself."

"But…"

"Captain!" The noble bellowed, eyeing the portal. "Prepare the men, get that portal open, and secure the other side! Those weapons will come in handy, and there's always a use for more gold."

"Yes sir!" the captain boomed, snapping out orders.

"But…no," she managed to get out, her heart cold in her chest. "The other side, they're waiting! Don't you see? It's a trap!"

"Then they'll be close by, and we can slaughter them all rather than having to hunt them down!" The lord shook his head, sneering at her. "Pathetic." He gestured at her with the sword, clearly claiming it as his own. "Lock her away with the filthy gnomes. She's clearly a coward and unworthy of a place in my guard."

Before Morgana could speak again, hands grabbed at her, and she was dragged away. The last thing she heard, as the sounds of the soldiers getting ready to assault the other side, faded into the distance was a leering voice in her ear.

"Me and the boys remember what you said to us…just you wait till the Oath's taken from you, we'll be back to 'play' a little."

SEHRAN

CHAPTER ONE

"Really?" I asked, glancing up at Sint in disbelief.

"Jax, I have never had children, especially not one as unique as this child promises to be. Why would you come to me with your concerns in this?" Sint replied with a faint smile.

"Fuck." I shrugged. "Hell, I don't know, just…I guess it seemed like you were someone I could ask." I shifted awkwardly, leaning against the railing, the wild winds tugging at my cloak and making me feel even more foolish.

We were standing alone in the small cupola on the top of the Himnel Cathedral, just me and Sint, and I had to admit, we must have looked a bloody stupid pair.

He'd appeared in answer to my nervous call and had resized Himself to appear less imposing. Fat lot of good that did.

As soon as He'd arrived, the damn priests below us started celebrating, the feeling of His divine aura was that strong. Even trying to be less imposing, He was still more than ten feet tall with armor that glowed softly and a damn surcoat that had to outshine the sky with its brilliant shade of blue.

"I appreciate that, Jax. In truth, I wish that I might help you, you have done much for my kin and I since your arrival. But I simply do not have the required experience. In this, the Gods are sorely lacking," he rumbled.

I flicked a loose stone off the railing and watched it clatter across the rooftop, picking up more and more debris as it rolled down the side of the great dome.

"Yeah, well, stupid idea, I guess," I apologized, not really sure why the hell I'd wanted to reach out to Him of all…people? Gods? Beings? *Fuck it.*

It'd been less than a day since the fall of Himnel and only eleven hours since Oracle had dropped the bombshell that I was going to be a father. I was still in shock, reeling from black terror to jubilation, to depression, to exultant determination.

I'd told Tommy. Hell, we'd told the entire squad late last night, interrupting their revels with an urgent summons to our quarters. They'd come, all of them, even Ronin, who literally had to be dragged out of someone's bed.

When we'd told them, there'd been a pause, then we'd been mobbed. The congratulations, the jubilation, hell, the *confusion* had been unreal.

Thomas had been the first to ask, of course.

"How? How the fuck did you get her pregnant?" he'd said, stunned.

"Well, Thomas, when a man loves a woman very much…" Tang had started to explain with a great big shit eating grin on his face, only to be clipped by Lydia, who apparently wanted the answer to that question as well.

"We don't know," Oracle said. "Well, we *do*…" She rolled her eyes, looking at Tang, who'd opened his mouth again. "Thank you, Tang! Yes, we know exactly how the opportunity came to be for me to fall pregnant. The actual result, and the fact that I *am*, though? It wasn't planned. Essentially, it's part of the changes from when Jax saved Bob and me, after Amon accidentally cut us free."

"So…you could have gotten pregnant at any point?" Jian asked, his voice lifting in an unmanly squeak, eyes wide as he glanced from Oracle and me to Tenandra and Sehran.

"No," Tenandra assured him firmly. "Oracle's situation is unique and cannot be accidentally or even intentionally reproduced by another."

"You're safe, darling." Sehran grinned, and Jian sagged backward with a mixture of amusement and jealousy.

"No, Jax," Sint rumbled on, drawing me back to the present. I glanced up at Him, my fingers drumming nervously on the stonework. "It was not a foolish idea, and I am touched that you thought to ask for my advice, beyond that of others. However, I do have two points to raise."

"Oh?"

"First and foremost, Oracle's form is fluid by dint of her species. I would implore you to ensure this is compatible with the new life in her womb." He watched me as I considered His words before blanching.

Fuck's sake, I'd never even thought about that! And yeah, okay, we'd been careful last night and this morning with things, but the last few days?

Hell, Oracle had had the crap beaten out of her by some of the creatures we'd fought! Not only that, she'd been small, then fun-sized and full-sized I didn't know how many times.

I felt Oracle reaching out, a sense of warmth and reassurance that flowed through our bond, even as she spoke in my mind, sensing my alarm and the reason for it.

"It's okay, my love. I'd changed my size several times before I realized and have been careful since. Our child is in no danger from my size changes at this point. However, in the future? I will shift less and less." I sent my love back to her, feeling the ghost of a kiss on my psyche before she vanished again.

"Oracle says her size is okay; she can change it, but as the baby gets bigger, she'll do it less," I told Sint.

"That is a relief. The second point, however…"

"Yeah?"

"Security," He said, looking down at me. "Oracle is no longer merely the lover of the Scion of the Empire, but the mother of a new dynasty. One that will have a far greater instinctive grasp of magic than almost any other species. The combination of your own not-inconsiderable gifts and those of her kind will mark your children out as targets for those who wish to counter your ascension."

"What?" I whispered, the creak of my gauntlets closing on the railing ignored as a sudden, horrifying thought of my unborn child being attacked, filled my mind. "Over my dead body!"

"To those who would harm your child out of fear of their future? This would be more than acceptable. Jax, I simply advise you to consider your position. This child is in a position to bring about wonders for the Empire and its people and to ensure your line's continuation. While few know of its existence now, this will not last long. A secret told has wings, after all," Sint said.

"I'll tear the fucker's wings off," I muttered, getting a smile from Sint.

"Jax, I have mentioned these concerns not to rob your news of its joy, but to make you aware that the Gods are here and watching over you. We are proud of all you have achieved and will continue to take a hand in your development and that of the Empire. However, this brings us to another point we must address."

"Go on." I stood straighter, knowing I wasn't going to enjoy this. *Next time fucking call Jenae, or hell, Lagoush...fuck it, Tamat, even!*

"You managed to claim a fragment of Nimon's divinity after fighting Him; are you aware of the meaning of this?"

"Not a fucking clue, mate." I muttered.

"Then I will explain what we know, and we will learn together," Sint said. "A God has two souls. A personal soul, and a divine soul. Both acting in harmony tie us to the Realm of the Gods and this one, allowing us to move between the two easily and influence both."

"Okay."

"You, however, have reached out to the Realm of the Gods on your own several times already."

"Yup."

A faint smile twitched the edges of Sint's lips. "To do so? I can only guess that it was the influence of Amon enabling this, but now Amon is gone, is he not?"

"Yeah." I sighed. "When I woke this morning...yeah, he's gone. It's like he was waiting until I was acknowledged as Prince."

The last few days, I'd felt him going, even before the incident in the throne-room, but that had been the real turning point.

He'd burned himself up when he'd worked with me closely, helping me and showing me the reality of who he'd been and what the power had felt like.

When he'd gone, I'd felt...less? The fragment of Nimon's soul was there inside me, and it freaked me out a bit. But the coldness, the utter knowledge and acceptance of the power that I'd wielded in the fight against the Dark Legion then Nimon, that was gone now.

I felt both more and less human.

"Now that Amon has fully moved on, you are left with a choice. You may accept that you have fought and won against Nimon. You have gained a valuable breathing space for your resurgent Empire, and you have the opportunity to take one of two paths. First, you may abdicate from the Imperial Succession." He paused, looking down at me.

I stared back, totally surprised, having not seen that coming.

"If you remove yourself from the line of succession to the Imperial throne, formally, mind you, then you have sufficient right to declare a Princedom of the Empire, under Imperial Rule, for Dravith. In doing so, you remove the driving force behind many of the nobles across the realm, who even now are gathering their forces and plotting."

"But...but what about the rest of the Empire?" I asked, totally confused.

"It would collapse. The final straw having been laid, the remaining Imperial facilities and rights would be released. Those who have been unable to claim authority over the remains of the Empire would find no further impediment to that."

"Then why…?"

"This would not ensure the safety of Dravith, but it would remove much of the impetus behind those who will even now be attempting to gather forces to face you. It may help you by granting you the time to marshal your forces and repair that which needs it."

"So basically, if I chicken out now, the nobles all over the rest of the realm get to claim any and all imperial facilities and will probably ignore me, but they'll be able to make their own golems and shit, if there's a facility nearby?" I asked, the thought of what those assholes would do to anyone in the way of such prizes making my fists itch.

"Essentially. Also, those who are constrained against acting against Imperial citizens, much as Ashrag was, can attack with impunity. Any who chose to name themselves Emperor in your place would be able to, provided they had the strength of arms to hold onto it. The Old Empire would be no more, and a thousand kingdoms would most likely rise in its place."

"Sounds like it'd be a shitty deal for everyone else," I said, folding my arms. "I mean, the nobles would love it, but the people? Shit, man, this would kick off wars on a massive scale, wouldn't it?"

"Most likely, yes."

I shot him a sideways glance. "What the fuck, Sint? You know me…or at least I thought you did, that's no choice at all!"

"I do know you, Jax, but it's because I know you, that it's important that you understand your options. This would most likely enable you to focus on Dravith to such a degree that you could unite it, and bring about a secure border, enabling your people to live in peace."

"But if you're outside of my borders, then you're basically fucked!"

"Yes."

"Not happening," I growled. "Regardless of the fact that I'd have to be a *monumental* wanker to pull that shit off against the normal folk out there, there's also legionnaires, hundreds, if not tens of fucking thousands of them! They're my people, each and every goddamn one of them!"

"And that brings us to the second choice, Jax. If you are to ascend the Crystal Steps and be proclaimed Emperor, then you have to decide how you will rule. Regardless of how you will reach that point, decisions you make now will have great influence on your actions and future."

"Yeah, my build," I guessed with a grunt. "I know I need to focus more on Charisma and shit, make people more likely to accept peaceful deals, but…"

"But Amon didn't, and you and He are more alike than you know. No Jax, your build, as you call it, is a discussion for you and your advisors, not for you and the Gods," Sint pointed out.

I winced, remembering that I wasn't talking to a friend or one of the gang.

I'd been relaxing and starting to get over the whole "divine awe" situation, and the last time I did that? I ended up in a fight with Jenae.

"I'm sorry, Lord Sint."

He cut me off with a raised hand. "I do not seek your worship, Jax; my point is that this discussion needs to be about the fragment of Nimon's divine soul you claimed."

"Oh! Oh, all right then," I agreed, relaxing slightly.

"A divine soul can be shattered into ten fragments, and gaining ten fragments will enable you to ascend to Godhood, Jax. This means that in claiming a fragment of a divine soul, you have made yourself a target all over again. This time, however, you are a target for the remaining holders of divine fragments."

"There's others?" I asked, stunned.

"There are many. Once, there were fifty Gods."

"Fifty!" I swore. "Holy shit, man, there's…"

"Twenty-three of us now," Sint interrupted. "That we are aware of, at least. There were ten Greater Gods, each tied to an element of magic, ten Lesser Gods, were tied to a substrate of mana, and the remaining thirty divine aspects were free, but far weaker than those of us who embodied reality."

"So what, there were Gods of everything?!"

"Yes and no. Much of the reasons and reality of the Gods are still beyond you, Jax. I mean this not as a slight, but some aspects you cannot understand at this stage and others you simply are not ready for. Some truths are not meant for those who are not divine."

I opened my mouth to complain, and Sint raised a hand in warning.

"I'm sorry, Jax, but our time is limited. To move on, yes, there are others out there with fragments of divine souls, some are Lesser Gods, such as Illoth or Asmodeus, others are mortals who managed to slay a God and gained those fragments in battle."

"Shit," I whispered, thinking of the feeling of power that constantly seeped through to me from the fragment even now.

"Quite," Sint agreed. "There are others who are attempting to collect the required ten fragments even now. In gaining the fragment, you have become a target for those others. However, only one remains on this continent, to my knowledge, in the high elven city of Albens, also known as the 'City of Light.'"

"And where the hell is that?" I asked, getting a faint smile.

"I cannot tell you that, Jax. It is down to you to discover and explore the rest of the continent. I cannot play favorites in such things." Even as He said it, though, a little notification flashed in the corner of my vision. I popped it up, a fresh symbol pulsing far to the northwest of the continent on my map, buried deep in the forests marked there.

I mentally added a marker to it, and the symbol that Sint had blatantly added faded away. I didn't know why He'd done it this way, but I wasn't complaining.

"One point, Jax. The holder of the fragment in Albens has sworn to no longer hunt for those who hold other fragments, but should you seek her out? You may tempt her to try to take yours. I recommend you do not do this, at least not until you have reached level fifty at the minimum."

You have been given a Quest by the God Sint: Divine Is As Divine Does

The God of Light, Sint advises you DO NOT attempt this quest before a minimum of level 50.

Seek out and acquire fragments of divinity, aiding you in both your ascension of the Crystal Steps to the Imperial Throne and to Godhood.

Seek out and harvest fragments of divinity from those who hold them: 1/10

Reward: True immortality, Ascension to Godhood, 5,000,000xp per fragment

I nodded, noting the lack of an accept section, mainly because we both knew I was going to do it, and I closed the kill one that'd been flashing away as well. I'd deal with that later.

"So, what happens if I get more than ten?"

That elicited a smile. "Then you will ascend in power to the lower ranks of divinity."

"So, what, you and the others have a load more than ten?" I asked without thinking.

"In divine circles, it is considered incredibly rude to discuss this. You did not know, and as such I will forgive you this *faux pas,* but this is not something that will be discussed, ever," Sint replied bluntly. "Moving on, and to be clear, the others who are hunting fragments are unlikely to have had divine assistance to explain this. You have to make a decision with the fragment you possess."

"Sorry, mate." I winced. "Go on…?"

"Have you examined the fragment?"

"Uh, how?"

"Hold out your hand and will it into being," He started to say, before hurrying on as I lifted my hand. "NOT NOW!" He barked.

I jumped and backed up, as He shook His head, blowing out a long breath.

"Jax, a fragment of Nimon's divine soul comes with a tremendous amount of power. Holding it out where another God can take it from you is the height of foolishness, so do this later, when you've had time to think, and do NOT hold it for long. We are your allies and recognize that your increases in strength massively benefit us, and yet? Knowing that you nearly offered that fragment where I could take it?" He shook His head. "Please, do not do that again."

"Okay, yeah. Sorry, Sint," I said, taking a step back. "So, with the fragment?"

"Summon it and hold it tight, reach out with your mana, and connect to the fragment. You'll be given two options. First is to absorb the fragment. You will grow in power and gain access to some of the abilities you demonstrated in the fight with the Dark Legion and the lich, essentially gaining a form of mastery over the local manafield." He looked at me askance as He waited, seeing me struggling with something. "Go on, Jax, ask your question, but we must be brief."

"Why am I just getting access to that power now? I had access before?" I asked.

"You did," He agreed. "But that was due to linking with Amon. Amon was a Master of Mana, and He had absorbed the two fragments of divinity that He had gained."

"Wait, He had two?!" I asked, aghast. "What happened to them?"

"They were released upon His death. A faint link was all that the remains of Amon had, and even with that? When linked to your own capacity, you saw the abllltles he had."

"Fuck, yes. Right, how do I absorb this?" I muttered, holding my right hand out again, only to be cut off by Sint.

"STOP!" He barked. The force of His will shoved me backward several feet. "Jax, stop, you fool!"

"But…"

"That is the LESSER of the two choices!"

"What the fuck?" I said, eyes wide.

He made sure I wasn't about to go ahead, then lowered His upraised hand.

"Jax, this is the path to immediate power, it is true. It is one of the reasons Amon was named the Eternal, and it took Nimon's own intervention to kill him. But understand this, absorbing the fragment will regain you access to some of Amon's abilities, including greater control over mana, once you have worked to master it. That path, however, *precludes* your ascension and will prevent your growth beyond Stat points!"

I froze, the sensation of Oracle there, summoned back through the link as she felt my confusion, then the warning she was sending me as she caught up.

"Jax, if you absorb the fragment, you CANNOT ascend, and upon your death, they will be lost, the power seeping free into the surrounding realm. You understand that some places are fundamentally magical? That there are places that have tremendously powerful gatherings of mana? Well, this is why.

"Add to this, once you take the step of absorbing a fragment, your body will no longer evolve naturally, so exercise and practice will no longer affect you. Instead, should you choose to, you can bind the fragment to your own soul, and you will gain a power related to that aspect. For example, if you gained more and more death fragments, one day you could ascend and displace Nimon Himself, regardless of managing to kill Him."

"But I'd lose the ability to control mana as I had? Not generally spells, but controlling the local area and using all the mana I wanted?" I asked.

"No, Jax, you have *already* lost that. When Amon went to His rest, you lost access to His abilities. Have you not tried?" He asked. I shook my head, having known but not wanting to believe. "Try it," He suggested. I sighed, shaking my head.

"I don't need to," I muttered, the coldness that had filled me, the way that I'd just done things, not needing to think about it, just imposing my will upon reality, that came with a feeling that I hadn't had when I'd woken up this morning.

I'd not considered the ability to manipulate mana being attached to that, but in truth, it damn well made sense, and even now I realized that I'd suspected it.

"Jax, you will gain great strength from absorbing the fragment, but once you take a step down that path, you cannot change your mind. I recommend you consider the alternative well."

"Which is to become a God?"

He nodded. "You already intend to face Illoth, do you not?"

"Fuck, yes." I growled at that thought.

"Well, each fragment comes with three abilities to choose from, one of which is common to all, the others unique to the nature of the fragment, the common one is called Soul Anchor, and it enables you to create a shield around you and your target, forcing them to stay and face you. This is not to say you can simply pull one of us across the realms to fight you, but should you manage to track Illoth to a corporeal body? You could force Her to stay and fight you, rather than Her discarding it, should the fight go badly for Her."

"So you're saying I could hunt that bitch down and fight Her?" I asked, a manic grin tugging at the edges of my mouth, until Sint held up a hand in caution.

"You could, but be aware that any other who has started down this path may have taken the same! A Greater God is unlikely to accept a challenge the way that Nimon foolishly did, and we of the Pantheon of the Flame are hunting those who have such fragments in our realm. This means that others may begin to hunt for fragments here now. Again, you have made it clear to the realm that you now own one such fragment."

"Fuck."

"Quite," Sint said, shifting in His armor. "Jax, I feel I have given you little good news here, especially considering the reason you reached out to me, so I apologize. However, it was important that you learned these truths."

"Well, thanks, Sint." I forced myself to take a deep breath and put my big boy pants on. "Lord Sint," I said formally. "Thank you for your time and your generous advice."

"You are always welcome, Prince Jax," He replied then smiled, resting one large hand on my shoulder. "I understand the choices before you aren't those that you would have picked, given your life and personal preferences, but there are times when our own desires must be cast aside."

"I know," I agreed. "I'll not abandon those people, and neither will I take the short path."

"Good man." He lifted his hand and turned from me, stepping away and taking two quick strides across the cupola…and then He was gone, like a curtain had been tugged across the world. A faint shimmer, and the sense of divine presence vanished.

I took a deep breath, then let it out, staring out over the city before me.

Across the city of Himnel, ever-present smoke billowed from the chimneys of factories, the bleating of livestock competing with the shouts of people far below.

The sun peeked through the clouds of smog and smoke, and even here, high above the streets, I could smell the damn place. It wasn't just the Cloudring, although that was hazy and indistinct, even now, making it clear they were still producing their drugs.

Where Narkolt was a city of parks and formality, Himnel seemed to be in the grip of a full-blown industrial revolution. Every building that could be put into production was, and they all stank to high heaven.

I sniffed, then coughed and shook my head. I was standing above the goddamn Cathedral of Himnel, a place dedicated to Nimon until recently, and now to all the Pantheon of the Flame, and even here, all I could smell was shit and sweat.

I was damn well tempted to burn the fucking city from one wall to the other.

CHAPTER TWO

I took two quick steps back, then dove over the railing and triggered Soaring Majesty, flying up and out of the cupola, lifting into the sky.

Weaving in and out of the stacks of rising smoke, I headed for the keep and the last thing I wanted to do today, as well as the thing I probably needed most.

There was a brief second in which I enjoyed a fantasy in which I explained to Restun that, as I'd absorbed a fragment of Nimon's soul, I was now divinely unable to gain or lose points through exercise or the lack thereof.

I wouldn't have to exercise anymore!

I shook myself. Restun would insist on trying to prove me wrong, and I'd spend just as long in fighting training each day instead of exercise *and* fighting training.

It'd be all the pain without the sweet gains.

Fuck it.

I flipped over, descending to the ground as I pulled back on the ability, landing smoothly a dozen feet from Restun and jogging toward the others gathering around him for morning PT in the courtyard.

"Good morning, Prince Jax," he greeted me, inclining his head and giving me a faint smile. "I understand congratulations are in order?"

"Thank you, Restun," I replied, smiling. "Word's out already, eh?"

"Dude, you told the *bard*." Thomas grunted, coming to a halt next to me and snorting. "Might as well have had some fucker shouting it through a megaphone."

"Hey, I resent that!" Ronin complained from behind me as he staggered into place, standing at parade rest with the rest of the team. Panting and green-faced, but he was still standing.

"Did you tell anyone?" Tang asked, appearing behind him and making him jump.

"No!" Ronin denied.

"Nobody at all?" asked Bane, appearing on his other side, making him jump again.

"No! Well, not really!"

"And there we go," Thomas groaned. "Come on then, who'd you tell?"

"Nobody!"

"Really?" I asked. "So if I ordered you to tell me the truth, you'd be fine with that?"

"Well...I only told Marie!"

"And Marie is?" Yen asked, taking up station on my right with Grizz.

"One of the chambermaids on the noble level in the keep," Lio explained, joining the group after flicking Ronin's ear from behind.

"And Sashan," Arrin pointed out.

"One of the serving girls in the main hall," Cheena added.

"And maybe I mentioned it to..." Ronin mumbled, scrunching his brow in an effort to remember the name of someone else.

"Fuck's sake." I shook my head and looked at Thomas. "You're right; next time, I'll cut out the middleman and just shout it out when I give my next speech."

"Probably take longer for people to hear that way." Thomas laughed.

I sighed. "Point."

"So what's the plan then, boss?" Grizz asked, leaning back to look around Yen.

"Attention!" Restun shouted, striding up from where we all stood on the parade ground of the keep, and silence fell…mostly.

The few who kept 'finishing their conversation' at the back fell silent as a Legion Optio sprinted to their side, speaking in a furious whisper, and presumably tearing them a new asshole.

"Very well!" Restun bellowed once silence had fully fallen. "As some of you are new, I'll make this simple! I am Primus Praetoria Restun. I lead the Praetorian Guard, the most elite of the elite forces of the Legion! Some of you out there understand the level that you must be to join the ranks of this most hallowed force, others are yet to experience the *joy* that is basic tryouts!"

Those of us who'd been through this already shuddered, but some fucking lunatic at the back started to talk again. I winced as the little vein in Restun's left temple started to throb and just knew that fucker had made this worse for us all.

"Some of you are here to try out for a place in the Legion!" Restun continued, his powerful lungs sending flocks of birds scattering for half a mile around us.

I flicked my gaze to the literally hundreds of people standing side-by-side nervously on the left-hand side of the parade ground.

They were dressed in rags, or the majority were anyway, barely decent. But where their clothes were a mess, their bodies weren't. Not only had these now *ex-slaves* been healed as part of their release by my Imperial Ability, but they were also already physically fit, or at least many of them were.

Some were starved, it was true. Hell, some were undergoing regular feeding and healing even after my ability had freed them, they'd been in such a state. But most of the slavers hadn't been idiots, as much as I hated admitting that.

They'd been fed crap food, but they could work harder and for longer when they were fed regularly. That combination of regular meals and hard work meant that, once they were healed and freed, they were perfect recruits for the Legion.

Not only did they literally owe the Empire their lives and freedom, but they also knew damn well that, should we fall, they'd probably be made slaves again.

The ex-slave core of the recruits we already had were astounding the legionnaires in charge of them every damn day. Of course, we weren't telling them that, though.

"Those of you who are here to join the Legion, welcome!" Restun called. "You have the honor of being led through selection by none other than Duke Augustus, heir to Prince Jax himself!"

Augustus narrowed his eyes at Restun over the use of his formal title before wiping his annoyance from his face and stepping forward, lifting one arm. "Welcome Legion-Aspirants! By the end of the day, you will either have earned your new rank, or you'll have learned that the Legion is not for you! There is no shame in this, and both the army and the city guard have need of honest people! Once we begin, you are to keep me in sight at all times and do as I do!"

"Thank you, Duke!" Restun stepped forward as Augustus stepped back. "For the rest of you, those who wish to attempt to lay claim to a place in the Praetorian Guard, you are to keep up with *me*!" He looked around happily at the stifled groans.

"We will begin with a nice easy lap of the city to warm up. Unfortunately, we don't have the Tower to run up, so instead, we'll make do with a fast rope climb up and over the wall of the keep behind me."

As he gestured, servants in the keep rolled knotted ropes over the side of the keep, leading up to the damaged sections of the walkway where we'd killed the defenders and created a hole in the wall.

"At the end of this gentle warm up lap, you will climb those ropes, then return here for the beginning of selection. *MOVE!*" He matched word to action by leaping off the stand and sprinting for the gates. Those of us who were used to Restun did just that, sprinting like crazy after him.

The next three hours were painful, but nothing we hadn't done before, even when Restun decided we'd warmed up enough, he then led us up one set of steps to the outer wall, then down the next, then up, then down as we did a second, then third lap of the city.

By the time we reached the keep the fourth time, Thomas and I were drenched in sweat, but we were neck and neck, his massive frame making it harder for him while his sheer determination kept him alongside me…until we reached the keep wall.

I'd barely staggered to a halt, waiting for my turn to climb, behind goddamn Grizz, who was telling a story to Yen as he climbed, when a blur passed us both, jumping, kicking off the wall, and grabbing the rope above Grizz.

"And I told her…yaaaa!" he shouted as the rope twisted and yanked sideways. The dark-haired figure of Belladonna nearly sent Grizz flying free as she grabbed on, braced herself and practically ran up the wall.

"What…the fuck…dude?" I gasped to Thomas, shaking my head in disbelief.

"Fuck!" Thomas growled, shoving another aside in the queue nearby and starting to climb. "Sorry, mate!"

I hesitated, seeing the speed she was climbing, then cursed and started climbing myself. "Move it, Grizz!" I hollered up at him, making him groan and discard the showing off.

Restun grinned, pausing on the third-floor balcony to watch the sudden burst of energy and nodding his approval of the former dark legionnaire before jogging on down the stairs.

The last two hours of the daily mandated exercise was fighting training, where I'd usually be paired up with Thomas or Restun, or hell, any of a number of senior legionnaires…but today instead, it was Belladonna.

We knew each other, of course. I *was* the apostate still, after all. Also not only had I healed her and set her free of her connection both to Nimon and to the Dark Hunters, but she was banging Tommy.

So, yeah, we definitely *knew* each other, but…

"Begin!" Restun shouted.

Before I could move, I was somersaulting forward, legs swept out from under me, and I crashed face-first into the stones of the parade ground.

"Mudder fucker!" I cursed, spitting blood onto the floor then rolling back to my feet.

I gripped my twisted beak and channeled a quick healing spell into it, shuddering as it ranged through me before stripping blood free with one hand.

"Come on, Great Prince, I expected more than that," she taunted, taking advantage of the rule of no rank while we trained.

"Okay, if that's how you want to play," I whispered, lunging forward, kicking out in a low spin-kick. She leaped back, as I'd guessed she would, and I triggered Lunge.

I blurred through the gap between us, pulling her ankle back with my right hand and driving my knee into her stomach with bone-shattering force.

She half flipped over me, having been jumping backward at the time, and landed hard, wheezing and coughing blood before rolling to her feet and weaving back and forth as she tried to get a breath, facing me.

I raised an eyebrow at her.

She stared wide-eyed at me, coughing blood before raising one hand in surrender. I nodded, straightening, and hit her with a powerful heal, making her groan as bones cracked, ribs shifting and grating against each other as they moved back into their correct position.

"Asshole," she wheezed when she could breathe again. "That's an ability."

"And you struck as Restun spoke, not after," I said. "You moved before he spoke, or you'd not have covered the distance."
A quick twitch at the edge of her lips confirmed my suspicions.

"Again?" she asked coolly, and I nodded. "Abilities permitted?"

I nodded again.

"Excellent!" she said, a sudden predatory grin making my butthole pucker.

We stepped back and braced, ready. Then she struck, taking two quick steps toward me and going for the grapple. I blocked her hands, slapping them aside and dropping to one knee, punching upward, my shot aimed for her chin in an uppercut that would send her flying.

Except it didn't land.

She'd seen what I was doing and flipped over me, grabbing my wrist and yanking hard, triggering an ability of her own. Before I knew it, I was weightless and flying, *pivoting* around her, before slamming into the hard stone ground, my bell well and truly rung and my right shoulder dislocated.

I rolled, or tried to, but she yanked me around, tossing me into the air again as her ability expired. Crouching, grinning at me, she pulled back her fist.

I triggered Soaring Majesty. Instead of landing face-first on her upcoming fist, I flipped myself over, landed on my feet *behind* her. Before she could adjust, I'd grabbed her arm with my good one, twisting as I stood back-to-back, and yanked *hard*.

Her shoulder lasted for a brief second as I flipped her over mine…then it popped as well, and she snarled in pain, crashing to the floor. I cried out, too, having used part of her motion to pop my own back in.

After a second or two gritting my teeth as the shoulder settled, I leaned down, offering my hand to help her up, ready to heal her. Instead, I got grabbed by the wrist and yanked off my feet as she rolled. Sudden cold made me gasp as she twisted around, pinning me with only one bloody arm!

I tried to shove her off, but she'd braced one foot against the inside of my wrist, her leg locked at full extension and her left hand pinning my right.

Her eyes glowed slightly, the whites seeming bright as silver and the iris black as pitch. Black smoke lifted from her body, floating upward to form a haze of shadow around her.

"Give up," she whispered.

"Get fucked." I hissed, planting my hands flat on the ground and triggering Mana Overdrive, then Soaring Majesty.

The combination of the two, as I pushed off as hard as I could, sent her flying back. But when she landed, it was on her *feet*, in a goddamned superhero pose.

Her shoulder popped and twisted, flexing back into the joint, a dozen seemingly solid strands of black shadow releasing the arm and flowing back into the rapidly darkening morass around her.

I gritted my teeth and leaped forward, aiming a flying kick right at her. She flipped over me, arms and legs tucked in, even as a handful of fingers of shadow flashed out.

I twisted, landing and skidding as I shoved back in the other direction with my Ability. Dozens more strands of blackness flashed out, wrapping around my limbs like spiderwebs.

Every strand added more resistance, slowing me a fraction more and more, until suddenly her fist was flying at my face.

I yanked back, right hand rising and slapping the inside of her wrist, deflecting the punch. Then I twisted, taking a kick high on the outside of the left thigh. Fists and feet flew, and for a few seconds, I held my own, despite her greater skill and training, but then the strands made their presence known again.

While I'd been blocking and counter attacking, they'd been slipping out and attaching more and more.

I went to block a blatant punch aimed at my stomach, and they yanked backward hard, my hand missing hers entirely.

I grunted, folding up around the punch, feeling more and more landing even as I twisted and counter attacked, the strands pulling me this way and that.

Victory creased her eyes, a grin lacing the edges of her grimace of concentration. I twisted my arms, stamping down and bracing myself, even as she started to land punch after punch on my stomach and chest.

I'd released Soaring Majesty at some point in the fight, but now I used it again, pushing myself down and back, anchoring myself instead of freeing myself from gravity's pull.

Once I was no longer being dragged about, I rolled my arms back, twisting them deliberately around the strands and gathered as many as I could before digging deeper and burning my already plummeting mana even faster as I poured more and more into the ability.

Before Bella knew what I was doing, I'd gotten hold of a good lot of the strands and I pulled as hard as I could.

One of her arms was pulled back to throw a punch aimed for my face, and instead she was dragged within reach of my favorite weapon–my forehead.

I headbutted her hard, the nut landing perfectly to break her nose, stunning her. The shadow strands, no longer actively controlled, evaporated like mist before the summer sun.

She reeled backward, and I swept her legs from under her, spinning and lashing out with a punch aimed at her face…

Only to reel back as someone grabbed onto me, then another, bodies slamming into me and shoving me back and back!

I roared, grappling with them…only for Mana Overdrive to evaporate and send me reeling as the world came crashing back in.

Words were shouted at me at close range, and arms held mine, restraining me…I growled, trying to shove them loose, even as the words finally seemed to filter through the red mist of fury.

"Man, calm down!" someone was yelling at me. "Boss! It's okay!" he shouted, shifting to hold onto me by the shoulders as I sagged.

"Grizz?" I mumbled, confused, staring at him.

"What happened here?" another voice, a woman's voice, demanded

I blinked, looking across at her dully, recognizing her slowly as Nerin, *Mistress* Nerin, the leader of our healers.

"Training fight got out of hand, that's all," another voice interjected. Edvard, the new paladin-in-training of Sint stood nearby, his brilliant blue surcoat covered in splatters of blood.

Blood.

I twisted and straightened, looking over Grizz and Hennen's shoulders, seeing Thomas helping a bloody Belladonna to her feet. Thomas was glaring daggers at me, but Bella?

She flinched as she was healed, wincing as the cartilage in her nose popped and mended. Bones and more fixed themselves in split seconds and she was still grinning.

She coughed and spat a bit of blood onto the floor. "Good fight. Almost had you there."

"Yeah, good fight," I agreed, staring at her, before grinning, despite myself.

There was a definite issue with training with my squad: while we all tried to win, you didn't go all-out, or at least I didn't, because I was always worried I'd kill one of them.

While neither of us were actually *really* trying to kill the other, we'd damn well kicked the shit out of each other, that was for sure. I paused, thinking about it. She was sworn to me, after all, so she couldn't have been *really* trying, right? I knew I hadn't been trying…not seriously, anyway.

"I'll beat you next time," Bella promised me before walking off with Thomas.

"She's fucking nuts, boss," Grizz muttered.

"Damn right she is." I winced at just how many were watching us, and clearly had been for most of the fight.

"Looks like I've found you a new sparring partner." Restun stepped up and approvingly appraised all the blood. "There was a time I'd be running you the length of the city for injuring a training partner like that." He broke off as Nerin hit me with a heal, making me grunt as the spell washed the wounds away.

When I could breathe again, blowing out a long breath and nodding my thanks to Nerin, he went on.

"But thanks to the wonders of healing, perhaps I should instead be asking why no one else seems to be putting in the same level of commitment!" That last bit was said a lot louder, and as he clapped his hands together, people moved back quickly, clearly not wanting to be anywhere near such a happily beaming Restun.

I shook my head. "Restun, we'll have deaths if people fight like that," I pointed out quietly, getting a brisk nod from him.

"We will, but of those close enough to hear my words, none are so foolish to actually fight at full capacity. Nevertheless, I will be increasing the tempo of the fights. Perhaps mixing up the fighting pairs will encourage our people."

"In the Dark Legion, all ranks are fought for," Edvard said, moving in closer when Restun shifted to allow him to join us. "All fights are on until one side surrenders. It leads to many injuries, as well as occasional deaths, but…and I say this not to be offensive, but…"

"But the dark legionnaires are more vicious one-on-one than a standard legionnaire," Restun replied quietly. "I am aware of this. The average Imperial Legionnaire will take down the average dark legionnaire, but pit the Legions elites against each other? Where the Dark Legion wins is that they have more elites."

"We still won," I said, feeling affronted.

"We did, but that was due to superior tactics, equipment, in the form of the golems and our magic, and the fact that most of the surviving legionnaires are elites now." Restun settled in his stance. "We have defeated the Dark Legion on this continent through a combination of their poor leadership and our sheer insanity. Also you personally challenged their God to a duel and killed Him, did you not, Godslayer?"

"I did, well, His avatar at least."

"And yet Belladonna very nearly beat you there. In a training fight that turned into a bloody affair. You are a natural brawler, Jax, but the reason you've stayed ahead so far is because your enemies have either underestimated you, or you have had advantages, such as the Legion or the Emperor Amon backing you."

I hesitated, glancing at Edvard, who saw my look and started to leave, bowing his apology for intruding.

I gestured him back in. "Don't worry, Edvard. As I said before, Sint says you're good, so I'll trust Him," I muttered. "Okay, Amon has gone to His rest, or died fully, or whatever. He's gone, either way."

"Then you must train and train like you never have before," Restun stated. "Belladonna is clearly happy to push you as far as she can. I'll find others like her. Intaglio and Flux are willing to push you as well." He turned, calling out to Lio, who was taking a drink nearby, her opponent washing their bloody nose while she looked bored.

"Fuck," I muttered, seeing the way she perked up as Restun ordered her to spar with me next and not to go easy on me at all.

Regardless of the fact I'd kicked Nimon's fucking arse, I didn't manage to win more than one in three of the bouts with Lio. When she handed over to Flux, then to Restun?

I lost again and again.

Two hours after the fighting training began, I was tired, covered in both dried and fresh blood, and in no damn mood for the crap that I still had ahead of me.

CHAPTER THREE

"You've got to be kidding me!" I sat back in the high-backed chair and dropped the sheet of numbers onto the table in disgust, waving a buzzing fly that flew in one window away with an annoyed gesture.

We were in a private council chamber high in the keep, the godawful decorating everywhere we went in here clearly inspired by porno backdrops from the seventies, or stylistic questions like 'how much gold plating can we stick on it before it collapses under the weight'.

I looked away from the offences against good taste and glared at the offending papers again.

Cai shook his head apologetically. "I'm afraid not, Jax. The city appears wealthy, as do the gangs, but in terms of sheer physical coinage? There is less than a ton of solid platinum that we've been able to find. Almost none of it was in the city treasury as well, that held barely six tons of gold.

"Should we strip the entire city? I have no doubt there would be more, but judging from the evidence so far, including the assistance of the city's spymaster, I doubt we could do more than find the same levels again, and we'd have to fight those who hold it already."

"How much do we need?" Lucian asked.

Cai consulted his notes. "Eight hundred steel ingots, which we have or will have in a few days, as the foundry is working at full speed. Five hundred orichalcum; we have two hundred and seventy-three. There's a mine nearby, but that will take a solid month at least to produce the needed remainder. The mine is contaminated with poisonous gases, so we will need golems to do the work, and that's without providing any of the output to industry." He flipped through a few pages.

"Two hundred and eighty glass panels, that's fine, we have that, one hundred and fifty manastones—got that—and a thousand tons of marble. We've got close enough on that, or will, provided we gut a few buildings. Then there's the thirty golem cores. We have the platinum, should we be willing to smelt almost all we have to make the ingots required. As to the gold? A solid ton of gold will provide the required weight of ingots."

"So we've got enough, nearly?" I asked Cai, my head swimming in staggering numbers.

"Yes and no," he replied, shaking his head. "We have enough gold and platinum now, which was the main issue before, providing we smelt it all to make it usable. The orichalcum will take several weeks to gather, as it will need to be mined then smelted. The issue is the golem cores."

"We can make them, though, right?" I asked, clicking my fingers. The manastone mine has the blueprints to make…"

"To make the golem cores, that's correct. *However,* to actually make the cores, we need other materials, including rubies, steel, bronze, gold, platinum, and…orichalcum."

"How much?"

"To make the required thirty?" Cai asked, one eyebrow raised.

"Of course," I replied in a flat tone.

"Four ingots of platinum and thirty of gold from the stores we have, then twenty-three ingots of orichalcum, on top of what we have available."

"Okay then, we…wait." I ran the details through my mind again before closing my eyes and wincing.

"The twenty-three ingots of orichalcum are on top of the orichalcum we already have," he repeated.

I closed my eyes, leaning back in my chair and slowly bouncing the back of my head off the high wooden frame. "So, we need the orichalcum to make the golem cores, and we need the golem cores to make the golems…that we need to do the mining, which will get us the orichalcum," I asked, trying to keep calm.

"Unfortunately," Cai agreed. "We lost some of the golems in the assault, a little over a third of the war golems, in fact. The construction golems can mine, but are ill-suited to it. The war golems are frankly poor at it, and the servitors, while they can run a foundry, are both needed elsewhere and are too weak."

"So we need the mining golems."

"Correct. The mining golems, however, are at the very least three days from the mine, that's the nearest one, and another week from that point for the next one."

"We need golems, we need gear, and we need time," I summarized, rubbing the bridge of my nose. "Is that about right?"

"Again, yes and no. I'm sorry, Jax, but these are the required materials to make this at the Great Tower. Here? Without a Wisp to make the changes or the Tower's structure to adjust and help? It would take several years to construct, not to mention being more expensive."

"Fuck." I grunted, closing my eyes and rubbing at the bridge of my nose.

"Want to hear a solution?" Mal asked laconically.

I cracked one eye open and fixed it on him, dropping my hand. "Maybe," I grumbled, torn between praying for a solution and hating that it was always sodding Mal who came up with this shit.

"Tenandra, how many golems were aboard the sunken city?" he asked.

She paused, looking to me and knowing damn well that I didn't want the answer to that question.

"Four hundred war golems, one hundred servitors, thirty crafter golems, and four mining golems," she replied.

"Mal, hell, *Tenandra,* yes the golems would be fantastic to add to our capabilities. And yes, fuck yes, I'd love to get the Prax up and running. Fuck, it'd be amazing! We'd be able to rain fire down on anyone who fucked with us with one of those intact and working, but it's fucked!

"To get the golems out, we'd need to charge them, to charge them we'd need to repair the main systems of the Prax, to repair that? We'd need golems and equipment that we damn well need *here.*" Around the council chamber, dozens of people sat listening to me as I tried to keep my temper.

"I would love to have the Prax on our side. Fuck, yes. It'd be a game changer, but realistically? Where the *hell* do we start with all this shit? We've got two cities that were at war with each other only a few days ago. They're both low on food, trade goods, and more, thanks to the damn state of the war dragging on. We've lost more than three-quarters of our legionnaires, and I don't even damn well know how many of the regular soldiers and fighters."

"More than half," Romanus interjected sadly.

"More than half." I repeated. "That's literally thousands of people dead on both sides, and that's not even including the goddamned Dark Legion! Several hundred of those wankers just plain ran for it after I fucked Nimon up. We've found traces of some of them, assaults, murders, and robberies. The city Control Center showed their locations when they were inside its limits, but now? They ran for it, headed north. We know there's at least three hundred of them, and we don't have the forces to hunt them down. We've got two cities literally teetering on the edge of collapse, starvation is a real possibility, according to Cai here, and it's fucking winter in two months!"

"A little under that, actually," Mal added helpfully.

"What my boy is trying to add, Jax, in his own way, is that the Prax could be extremely valuable," Hannibal interjected quickly. "We all know that the Prax can't be saved and brought up to usable state, not in the short term, can we agree on that?"

"Aye, whatever," I muttered, taking a drink of coffee and sitting up. "Yes, sorry, Hannibal, I've a lot on my mind, that's all."

"It's fine, Jax." He smiled. "Okay, so the Prax would be wonderful to have made ready. However, it's not possible right now, but the Prax would be massively valuable, so how about we take the first steps to making it usable?"

"Go on."

"Name someone to run the repair, give them a ship, and send them to the Prax. Send a handful of golems and have them defend the group. They can work in relays and drag the dead golems up out of the storage areas, pile them all on the top of the island, and the ship can ferry them back and forth to the production facility. There, they can be repaired if they need it and recharged. Then half are set to work on the various projects we need them on, and the other half go back to the Prax and start work."

"Work on what?" I asked.

"Repairs," he said. "The Prax were battle cities, and when I asked her, Tenandra said that the lower holds were probably swamped, so they're out of reach for us. But for the golems? They don't need air. They can strip the Prax of anything usable, while doing basic repairs. Hell, if they can get the Prax minimally operational? Fantastic. If its fucked? We loot it and move on, but at least we'll have everything off it!" He paused, seeing the horrified look on Tenandra's face. "Uh, sorry about that, but you know, business is business."

"He's right," Romanus agreed after a few seconds of silence. "Golems can work around the clock; not even the hardiest legionnaire can match their pace. Give me a hundred war golems and a high enough level leader for them? I can secure the local area, and it'll save my people from being taken away from training roles. Give me six months? I'll have the first Legion-aspirants ready to fight."

"I don't think we've got six months," Lucian interjected. When I gestured to him to speak, he hesitated. "It's to do with Peleth's View."

"Then that's a discussion for later," I said, not needing that shit to be spoken about when there were so many people I didn't know well in the room.

In addition to Romanus and Jon, Augustus and Hellenica were there, Cai and Isabella, Mistress Nerin, Tenandra and Oracle, Mal, Soween and Hannibal, Hanau, Oren, and Lydia. Thomas was there as well, but the rest? We had the local army commander, Asimah, who I didn't trust, and Lars, the guard commander who I sort of did trust, but I barely knew him.

Then, I had a new member, Terra, who'd declared herself to be the high priestess of the Cathedral of the Pantheon of the Flame. She'd not been named as such to me by any of the Gods, but nobody had hit her with a lightning bolt or anything so far, either. I was willing to give her a little trust on that one, having seen her in the cathedral leading services.

Finally, there was Baant, who'd turned up at the beginning of the meeting claiming to represent the gnomes in the city. Being both a gnome and blatantly off her tits on something had already matched my experiences with gnomes enough that I'd accepted her as well.

Plus, it was frankly hilarious, because for some reason Giint hated Baant with a passion, and Baant seemed to return the feeling with interest, so seeing Giint hissing like a scalded cat at Baant constantly cheered me right up.

"In that case, perhaps I might speak?" Terra asked after a few seconds of silence. I waved to her to go for it. "The Gods are obviously interested in ensuring their hated brother's influence is expunged from the continent. Their priority, as I understand it, is to spread their worship, secure the borders of this land against incursion, and assist in the growth of the Empire. As such, I have begun to recruit for the priesthood, and have a request from Lord Darakin. As a War God, He requests the right to recruit followers directly from the new trainees. He offers to train them to be an elite warrior core."

"The God of Battle wants to make me an elite warrior core?" I asked.

"Essentially."

"No," I said, getting a surprised look from her and the rest of the table. I waited several heartbeats, until she started to open her mouth, and then I went on. "'Essentially' isn't good enough. I want specifics, I've negotiated with the Gods before, and while I respect them, my goals and theirs are not always the same. My priority is the Empire." She opened her mouth again to speak, before hesitating and looking aside, clearly listening, before turning back to me.

"My apologies, Prince Jax. Lord Darakin offers to train an elite warrior core that will become his battle priests. They will fight where the battle is hottest and will obey you beyond all other mortals. Should the Gods not have a need of them, then they are yours to command. Lord Darakin offers them to you to use as shock troops and to claim difficult locations." Terra said carefully, watching me.

"How many?" I asked eventually.

"A thousand."

"I'll give you a hundred, and they'll be volunteers from the fresh recruits. He trains and equips them, I'll feed them and provide them access to the healers and so on."

"Lord Darakin asks that you provide equipment, for now. In exchange, He will provide information on a trading partner who will be able to assist in your current issues with materials," Terra replied after a few seconds.

"Agreed, but it'll be the basic gear all recruits are getting, nothing special," I offered. The room went quiet as the feeling of a divine presence filled it.

"I agree, Godslayer and again, I offer the honor of sparring," a deep voice rumbled through the room.

I inclined my head in respect. "Thank you for the honor of your presence, Lord Darakin." I rose to my feet. "I will look forward to the day when I can accept that challenge."

"Soon, I hope." With that, the sense of His presence vanished, and a new notification informed me that I had a new location marked on my map.

I pulled it up, glancing at Tenandra, who smiled and reached out, touching my arm then releasing it, bringing up a map across the far wall.

The continent of Dravith was longer than it was across, easily over a thousand miles, north to south, and over six hundred wide at its largest point, split down the middle by a massive mountain range, one that had been large before the Cataclysm, but now…?

When the moon Ishtic had crashed into the realm, seas had boiled, and mountains vanished, plains were lifted miles into the air, and swamps became deserts. Here, not far off the coast of Dravith, the Island of Imshi, once fertile and lush, long since pacified and used primarily as a food production area for the entire continent, had cracked in two and sunk.

But where lands had fallen or sunk…others had risen.

The gentle slopes that had run down to the coast all around Dravith had vanished as the entire land lifted higher, leaving few locations that allowed easy access to the sea.

The mountains, in turn, leaped higher still, dwarfing the Great Tower, which itself was over two miles high. Mountains that were mere miles high before now reached clawing for the sky.

Hills shattered, and great chasms opened, rents in the earth disgorged creatures that had long been believed eliminated. And, through it all, the land shook, and the heavens rained fire.

The map I had was magical, and as such, it adjusted when new information was added, using the Scroll of the Arcane Eagle and my own eyes aboard the airships were some of the methods. The Gods had shared details with me, too, sometimes a single location, other times, like when Jenae had searched for Tommy, I gained knowledge of entire swathes of the land.

The map before us showed that.

The east of the map had clearly defined shapes, trees that were so carefully reproduced they seemed to emit the scent of pine and oak. The movements of the wind made league upon league of grassland and forest ripple.

The seas sparkled, and the mountains reared, snow-capped and wild. I straightened slightly in wonder that all of this, this wonderful, terrible land was mine.

My gaze was drawn to the Tower, my entry point to the UnderVerse, miles high and shining like the jewel in the Crown of Dravith as it once was.

To the east and south of the Tower, seemingly only a few miles away, was the gently pulsing red star that marked Malus and the hidden city of Peleth's View.

We'd found no trace of the people who had been exploring the city and interacting with the peculiar personality that lived there. Hell, when the ship had scouted the area, they couldn't find any trace of it. Even the destroyed village inhabited by the Vern and their pet Drach had vanished without a trace.

All we had was a map marker, and I was damn well determined that, if I had to take mining golems there on my damn back and dig the fucker out, I'd do it.

Seneschal had dispatched war golems to search the area at my order, and for now, there was little more we could do.

For now though, that wasn't my point of focus.

Far to the south were the four villages of the gnomes, two large, two smaller, according to Lucian, who'd added those details in for us. They were in the hills and forests on the far south coast. But before reaching their lands, at the foot of the mountain range that scarred the land, was a low collection of hills, supposedly the only way to reach the western side of the continent.

Airships that attempted to cross the mountains were never seen again, as were those that crossed the hills, but trade caravans *did* pass back and forth irregularly.

Now, to the west of those hills, a new bright bronze star pulsed steadily as Darakin's gift showed itself. A small, high-walled city emerged as if drawn in by an artist, rather than appearing as a satellite image the way locations I'd visited looked.

"What is that?" I asked the room in general, getting silence form most people, while Mal and Hannibal looked at each other. "Come on you two, don't leave me hanging."

"It's the City of Hobb," Hannibal said eventually. "Supposedly, it's a trade city; it buys and sells between the groups to the north, like the Habieen, the Gnomes to the south, and anyone else who comes to their 'free city'."

"But?" I asked, waiting for the other shoe to drop.

"But it's not free," Lucian stated. "It's a walled and glorified town, one where it's said you can buy anything, but that includes slaves. I've been once. I barely escaped with my life."

"Sounds like a story," I said. "But if you've been there, why did I have to hear about it from these two?" I gestured to Hannibal and Mal with a faint smile as Oracle reached out for a coffee, then settled back and intertwined her fingers in mine.

"Because I visited it last some three hundred years ago, and the bounty for my head is still active, so I cannot share anything current," Lucian explained calmly.

"Yeah, there's a few places back home in the islands that were like that for me, too," Hannibal interjected, smiling in fond reminiscence. "This one bar…"

"Hannibal, dear?" Oracle spoke up.

"Yeah?"

"Hush."

"Heh, fair enough." He shook his head and smiled at her.

"So, Lucian?"

"Hobb is a center for slavers trying to capture gnomes and anyone else they can get, trappers from the hundreds of miles of lawless territory around it, and the last point of contact before you reach the Endless Sea," Lucian said slowly. "Hobb is primarily a slave hub, but for who, we don't know. Even when the Empire was at its height, the city was there, although it was smaller then. The slaves are always bought, and there are markets, but beyond a small number that have issues and are sold publicly, the city has first refusal and usually purchases them all."

"Sounds like a place that's due an Imperial visit," I growled. Romanus nodded firmly, as did most of the rest of the room. The only exceptions were Mal, Hannibal, and surprisingly, Lucian.

"Nothing would please me more; however, you remember your experience with the Habieen?" he asked.

Hundreds of slaves had been turned out of boxes to deal with the threat of our attack, magic chains forcing their muscles into action, even as the slaves screamed in pain over cramping muscles and more.

"I do…"

"The entirety of the city is suspected to be like that, with tens of thousands of slaves."

"Sounds fuckin' brilliant to me, then," I said. "We fly over it, I use my Ability and free all the slaves, they slaughter their former masters, bish-bosh-boom, we come home with a few thousand more recruits and a fuck load of ex-slavers' wealth. We're not trading with them, not with slavers, but I'll happily butcher them."

"Except, Hobb is on the far side of the dagger, over eight hundred miles from here by land, and no airship that's been sent to that side of the dagger has returned. That includes captains who were fully expecting treachery and were on their guard," Hannibal said laconically.

"Seriously, one of those ships was sent by the Smugglers' Guild to open negotiations." Mal added. "The guy who chartered it? He took a gang of lunatics that I'd love to have had in the arena. They were lethal, and not one of them looked it. I'd have made a fortune on bets. They flew out…and vanished."

"Also, the Habieen don't come in airships, but they always want to buy them," Hannibal pointed out. "If they were taking control of them? They'd be flying back and forward in them, those arrogant fuckers."

"So what, something is hunting them?" I asked. "A dragon or something?"

"If there was a true dragon on the continent, it wouldn't be staying on that side of the dagger. It'd be ranging all the way across and claiming whatever it wanted," Soween interjected, with Mal and Hannibal nodding.

"They're right Jax, a true dragon couldn't care less about our petty borders and nations. They were allied to Emperor Amon, but NOT the Empire. When he died, they left; no one knows why." Lucian agreed.

"They went home," I replied unthinkingly. "They had young to raise, and when Amon died, and the Empire fell, the Legions that were due to protect their home…" I shook my head. "I don't know if they died or didn't go or left or what, but it was them not carrying out Amon's promise that led to the dragons leaving."

"You know that for sure?" Hannibal asked and I nodded. "How?"

"I spoke to Amon'Tuthic, the mate to Shustic, the silver dragon that Amon rode into battle. He told me some of it, the Gods' other bits, Amon still more."

"Any chance you could do a new deal with them?" Mal asked. "Just sayin', a couple of dragons on our side would be good."

"No," I replied flatly, not sure how I knew it. "The dragons might ally with us in the future, but it has to be a meeting of equals. As it is, if we go to them, the best we can hope for is that they let us leave alive. Most likely, we'd be killed and eaten for trespassing. You would, anyway. Tuthic would permit me and Oracle to leave, but nobody else. The Legion would be executed as faithless, and anyone else would be walking meat."

"*Faithless?!*" Romanus hissed.

I held a hand up to stop him. "The Legion was to protect their nests, to provide aid, and to pay a debt that Amon owed. They didn't. Regardless of why, they broke their word. Dragons accept no excuses."

"The world *ended*. The Empire fell," Augustus ground out.

I slouched back, rubbing the bridge of my nose as I tried to be patient. "Augustus, I know, all right? I don't like it either, and believe me, Tuthic is the *best* chance we have. He's the one who would merely kill all of you who set foot on his island. The others? Most likely, they'd come looking for the Empire and punish you all for breaking your word and then trespassing. I *know* you didn't, fuck's sake; I remember fragments seen through Amon's descendants' eyes. I literally saw the cataclysm more than seven hundred years ago, and I'm not even twenty-fucking-five yet, so yeah, believe me. My life is messed up enough without fucking around with greater dragons."

"So…what would you like us to do then, Prince Jax?" Cai asked, holding one hand up as more and more people started to ask questions. The conversation paused, and I glanced at Oracle, gnawing on one knuckle as I thought.

She smiled and nodded toward me. I straightened, scrubbing at my face and taking a deep breath. "Okay, Hannibal, you've got a point with the Prax. Yes, we need to loot it, no Tenandra, you can't be the ship that goes back and forth; I need you. But yes. Romanus, can you sort that? Get them moving as soon as possible?" I asked, noting the disappointed look on Tenandra's face.

"Of course. I'll arrange it today."

"Thank you, mate. Okay, looking to the city of Hobb? We need to know what the hell is going on, but you've a point that something is happening there. It's too far to go by foot, and certainly too far to expect a few thousand freed slaves to walk back. That means we need transport either way, and that means we need the fleet. Oren?"

"Aye, Jax?"

"What state is the fleet in?"

"Ah, well…" he hedged, wincing.

"Just tell me, mate."

"It be a wee bit broken. That's all."

"Oh, well thanks for the great description! Specifics, Oren!" I growled. "Romanus needs a damn ship, so does…"

The next half an hour was spent going over the damage from the battle to our ships, to those we captured, and to the shipyards.

By the time Oren finished, it was clear that, while we had enough ships to protect ourselves, we didn't have a big enough scout group to send to Hobb, let alone a fleet.

"Fine," I agreed in the end to his wheedling. "Bring the *Dreadnought* home; you'll have ten of the crafters, once they're finished, and ten of the servitors assigned to you. Cai, take care of that, please. Oren, you've a month, any and all engineers in Himnel are yours, between the golems and the engineers. If you can't get the battleship fully operational, then you shouldn't be in charge of the fleet. Hanau, help him, please."

"Romanus, step up the training schedule as much as can be done, I want a single squad of legionnaires on alert at all times; the rest are all on training. All bladesmiths, armorers, and so on are to begin mass production of legion standard armor. I need to speak to Thorn after this, but, Cai, you're to help with this, as is Thomas. We're setting up a central factory for this. It's called standardization, and what *that* means is…"

***

"Two hours." I muttered sadly to Oracle sometime later as we walked out of the stairwell, strolling under the gentle glow of the magelights. "Two goddamn hours to sunset, that's all. The entire goddamned day, wasted in that damn room."

"It could be worse," Thomas groaned, twisting at the hip and letting out a collection of pops and clicks.

"Oh?"

"Yeah, you could be the brother of the asshole in charge and have to be there as support, while knowing fuck all about anything beyond how to hit people hard."

I grinned. "Hey, if I'm suffering, so are you."

"It was explaining factory processes to the armorers that got me," he grumbled. "I mean, they understood it, but they didn't, and you know I'm going to be banging my head off the damn wall tomorrow, don't you?"

"You volunteered to go and show them how to do it!"

"Yeah, well if the other option is another day of that shit? Count me out."

I gasped theatrically. "Betrayal! You're leaving me to face that lot while you fuck off and talk to engineers?!"

"Damn right I am, and I'll probably drink while I'm doing it. Maybe stop off for a quickie, if Bella is up for it. So, what's on the list of jobs for tomorrow?" he asked as we walked down the hall toward the stairs to our quarters in the upper floor of the keep, doing our best to ignore all the pretentious crap on the walls.

"Exercise with Restun," I growled at the utter bastard.

"Getting your ass kicked by Bella," Thomas joked.

"Then, I've got a meeting with the local nobles. Got to get some of the fuckers onboard, but I'll probably have some of them hanged by the end of the day."

"Sounds fun. Then what?"

"Then I'm off to the gnomes' enclave."

"The…wait, what?!" He grunted. "Nobody gets in there!"

"I'm the Prince, and they're sworn to me, or Baant seems willing to consider it, anyway. So I'm taking advantage of it!"

"But, but…"

"She came to the meeting for a reason…and instead spent all of it off her tits, then woke up and threw up everywhere."

"Gotta love gnomes, man."

"If not for the smell, yeah. But at least that means the damn room will be redecorated…anyway! She came for a reason, and I need to find out what it is, then I damn well need to get some of them working with Thorn."

"Nice, man, anything else?"

"Wait…was this you?" I asked, nodding towards a massive portrait of Barabarattas that hung on one wall. It was a beautifully done oil painting, the colors gleaming, the fabric perfectly maintained…and Barabarattas now sported an addition. Hanging down from his forehead over one eye.

"Well, you know me, I've the soul of an artist." Thomas admitted, preening slightly.

"Is that supposed to be a dick?" Oracle asked consideringly and I snorted, glancing at my brother.

"Yeah, a piss-artist."

"Anyway! I was asking if there was anything after the gnomes?" Thomas waved away the art critique uncaringly.

"Horkesh," I muttered.

"Oh sucks to be you, bro!"

"Want to be named as the Imperial Envoy to the Spider Queen?" I offered.

"Want to be suffocated in your sleep?" He countered with a friendly smile.

"You'd die too, Oath-bound remember? The Oath would kill you, hell, you probably wouldn't be able to do it, anyway." I said waving one hand negligently.

"Worth it. You send me to spend my time around spiders, and I'll view death as a release."

"Asshole."

Thomas paused, hand on the handle to his door, and turned to Oracle and me, opening his mouth but clearly unsure of what to say.

"You okay?" I asked.

"Yeah, man. Look, bro, Oracle…congratulations, okay? You know I've got your back, right? Nothing is getting near my niece or nephew," he promised seriously, looking from one of us to the other.

"I know," I whispered, tears pricking at my eyes as I stepped forward, taking him in a tight hug. His arms closed around me, and it was like we were kids again, the two of us, knowing that we'd face the world together.

When we broke apart, it was only for him to enfold Oracle in his arms instead, carefully.

I couldn't help but smile, looking at him.

We were non-identical twins, born only a few minutes apart. We'd both been six foot two, and fairly well-built on earth, but here? We were Olympians. Hell, we'd grace the cover of any bodybuilding magazine, and the thing was, none of our muscles were the gym-bought variety.

We spent hours a day earning the muscles, true, but we also fought and bled for them, working hard every goddamn day. Now, he was broader than me, and I was an inch or so taller, but as we were both around seven feet tall? It had stopped mattering so much.

No the difference now was that I was leaner, still heavily muscled, but Thomas? He was a *beast*. He had massive slabs of muscle everywhere, earned in long, grueling runs in full dark legionnaire plate armor, the heaviest we knew of, and then on top of that? He was a berserker.

Not the 'I'm going to lose my temper and run round tearing my clothes off and fight everyone until they taser me so much I'm drooling' boring kind. No, in the UnderVerse, class *mattered*. As a berserker base class, he physically *changed*, growing taller and bigger, muscles swelling and shifting until he'd make a terminator need an oil change and go hide in the toilets.

Now, though? Seeing the massive figure straining at the seams of his tailored top, the sleeves having been cut to let his arms move more freely, gently holding Oracle? He was clearly terrified of crushing her.

She'd been surrounded by legionnaires all day. At first I'd assumed it was me they were there for; I was the Prince and Scion of the Empire, after all, and they were always around…but then I'd realized it *wasn't* for me. Well, not entirely.

She'd had legionnaires turn up, massive hard-bitten men and women who were the elite of the elite, the kind that terrified normal folk simply by walking past and made bullies and thugs swear to be good with just a single look.

They appeared with a cushion for her seat, a snack she might like, or a drink. One had come into the meeting of the council, ducking his head nervously, only to edge around the room and put a warm glass of goat's milk down at Oracle's elbow and whisper that his mother had sworn it was good for babies.

Goat's milk.

The nearest goat had been on a farm on the far side of fucking *Narkolt*.

He'd told a ship's captain what he needed, and the bugger had taken him on a fast scout all the way to that farm to buy a dozen goats and bring them back. Even aboard a fast scout, it had been a nine-hour round trip. He'd missed morning exercises and had submitted himself for punishment to *Restun* personally at the end of the meeting.

They were all like that.

Oracle had gained seventy-odd minders, and our baby now had the most determined and elite baby-sitters the realms had ever seen.

When Thomas and Oracle broke off, she kissed his cheek, then moved to take my hand again. We left Thomas to join Bella in their room, while we went to ours.

It wasn't for long. We had time to get changed and eat something before the ceremony of remembrance for the fallen. But we sat for a little bit, the world seeming totally strange as we lay on the bed, confused about everything and talking quietly.

The world had changed.

No longer were we desperately at war, running constantly to catch up. Suddenly, for the first time since I'd found my way into the UnderVerse, I had time to actually stop and deal with things.

And I *hated* it.

CHAPTER FOUR

"Are you okay?" Oracle asked after a while, and I jumped, having been staring across our bedroom and out of the window aimlessly.

"What?"

"Are you *okay,* Jax?!" she asked me again. "With the pregnancy, with everything?"

"Of course!" I lied.

She shifted around, leveling a hard look at me as I tried to plaster a fake smile on my face.

"Jax, I can feel your emotions, the turmoil in you. You don't have to lie to me."

"I'm not lying, I'm…" I paused, looking at myself, really looking at myself, and then sighed. "Yeah, yeah, all right, I am. I'm sodding *terrified,* Oracle. I don't know how to be a dad, I don't know how to deal with things like this. Fuck's sake, I spent most of my life without a dad, and the one it turns out I had?

"He basically destroyed the goddamned realm and the Empire both, murdered his father and killed millions, if not billions by his actions!" I snorted, shaking my head. "At least the only way is up, though, right?"

"Jax, you'll be a wonderful father, but is that what this is all about? You're scared you can't do it right?"

"No, not all of it," I said. "I'm *petrified* of being a failure as a dad, as a leader, hell as the prince of the goddamn Empire? If I fuck up as a dad, I could ruin his or her life. But as the Prince of the Empire? The last Prince *was* my father, and we know how he did!" I laid back, staring back up at the ceiling as tears came out of nowhere, prickling at the corners of my eyes.

"Oracle, I led literally hundreds to battle in the last few days, hell I destroyed the goddamn Dark Citadel and killed a God. I'm personally responsible for thousands of people dying, being crippled, or losing everything they own. There are so many dead that we can't even bury them all, and they died because of me, because of my choices."

"You saved them, Jax, you saved the Legion, and…"

"I destroyed it. There were more than six hundred of them a few months back, now there's less than a *hundred.*"

Tears tracked down my face as I pictured some of the legionnaires we'd lost. Dozens of those I'd dealt with every day had died, and the vast majority of them? I'd not even known their damn names.

Terr was an armorer, damn good at his job, and the half-orc Legion Chief Armorer was Thornapple's assistant. He'd been quick with a quip, with a joke, and yet serious beyond his years when discussing his craft. He'd been torn apart by spells right in front of me.

Petin, a Legion Optio, had dived in front of a blast from an Imperial Golem's manabolt to protect me. She'd died instantly, her internals becoming externals, and all because I couldn't get control of the golems fast enough.

Hell, had I been ready to control my mana, *all* mana, as I'd been capable of? I could have left them all at home and taken care of it all myself.

Instead, I'd stumbled around beating the crap out of people like the neanderthal I was.

"The worst thing, Oracle?" I said, interrupting her reassurances that it wasn't me who'd started the fight and so on. "The very worst thing? It's that I had that power. I had it from Amon, I had it all this time. Now he's gone, and there's a way to reclaim it! I could absorb the fragment of Nimon's divine soul, and I'd gain some of that power back. I could protect them. I *should* do it!" My fingers curled into fists as she watched me sadly, feeling everything I felt.

"I could regain some of that power, then I could take Tenandra and probably wipe Hobb from the face of the fucking realm alone!"

"Then why don't you?" she asked, damn well knowing the reason as well as I did.

"Because if I do? If I take the easy path to power? Then I've given up on the hard way. I'll be powerful; hell, I could end up more powerful than Amon ever was, but I'd only have a fraction of the power of the Gods."

"And that is why it is a decision only you can make," Jenae's voice whispered in the confines of our bedroom. A second later, She was there, stepping from the solid wall as if it were a doorway to another room, then casually picking up some of my bloodstained training clothes from where they'd been discarded on a chair.

She held the top, liberally encrusted with my dried blood, and it blurred, a slight cascade of dust falling free of the suddenly pristine clothing, then She placed it on the dresser and sat in the now clear chair.

"Jenae," I said, closing my eyes and shaking myself, wiping the hot tears that coated my cheeks free as I rolled to my feet, bowing to Her in greeting. "Goddess…"

"Relax, Jax," She said, a sad smile on Her face. *"I've not come until now because I knew you needed time to come to a decision. Have you done this?"*

"I have."

"What is your decision?"

"I'll take the long road," I said, unsure how She was going to feel about it, hating myself for it, but knowing it was the right choice. "I'll take the road to Godhood."

"Then I can help you now," She said, smiling at me. *"I understand your reluctance and your decision not to speak of this with your advisors, but truly? It is the better choice, especially for the Empire. As a living God, especially one not bound as we Greater Gods are to the aspects of magic? You will be able to ensure the Empire survives, grows, and prospers until you are ready to move on and ascend higher. Yes, the short-term gains of the path to power, absorbing the fragment and moving on is a better immediate option, there is no denying that, but for the long-term? You have made the only real choice you could."*

"Are you okay with this?" I asked Oracle. I hadn't had a chance to speak to her about it. Hell, I'd only just come to terms with what I knew I had to do, despite me saying it to Sint earlier. I'd spent the entire damn day listening to all the problems with half an ear, dealing with things as best I could, while the choice rolled around in my head, back and forth, over and over.

I kept seeing the faces of those we'd lost, and I blamed myself, my weakness, my slowness, all of it. I blamed myself for their deaths, and it didn't matter if nobody else did.

The decision to not grasp the power offered by the fragment for the short-term gain, made that self-loathing even harder.

It meant I was going to be weaker, slower, and frankly less than I could be. That in turn meant that others would damn well die in my place.

I felt like I was the worst kind of hypocrite, and that was the problem here, and as I gazed into Oracle's eyes, I knew she understood.

"You're making the best choice for them," she assured me as I sat next to her again, taking my hand in hers. "I know you, Jax. This isn't a personal power grab, this is you making the decision that gains the Empire the most. While it means that more will die now…" I winced, and she reached up, cupping my cheek. "…it means that far less will die in the future. Amon was the most powerful individual in the realm, but He wasn't a God. He could be killed; you won't be."

"You could still be killed," Jenae pointed out calmly. *"But as a God, you will be far harder to kill, and a mortal that attempts it, without the aid of other Gods or the stupidity of a God to take advantage of, such as you did against Nimon? You have a far greater chance to lead your people forward."*

"It just seems wrong, Jenae," I said, wrapping my arms around Oracle and holding her. "Augustus is practically a God among men *now*. I could give it to him, turn the Empire over and let him…"

"He would not be a better leader, Jax, and even if he was, he would face an uphill battle against the Imperial rights that you already enjoy. Where facilities will welcome you, they would fight him. Despite his many advantages, he is not you. Believe in yourself, Scion, Prince, Godslayer."

"Heh, thanks, Jenae," I mumbled, not really agreeing, but kinda liking the title.

"So, you said that you could help us?" Oracle asked Her, gently untangling herself from my arms and looking over at the Goddess who was sitting in the chair Oracle had been riding me in only a day earlier.

I clamped down hard on that thought, well aware that Jenae could sense my surface thoughts if I let Her, and I doubted that She'd like to know that.

"Yes Oracle, I can. I can gift Jax with a pair of quests that will assist you in the future, as well as a small blessing." She stood, striding over to me and reaching out with one hand, resting it on my head in benediction. A feeling like a hot summer's day at the beach washed through me.

I groaned, aches and minor discomforts washed away as a notification popped up.

Dark Tide Rising

Congratulations

You have received: Blessing of the Divine Flame!

The Divine Flame calls to other fragments of divinity, granting you a faint sense of where they may be found.
The closer you come to a fragment, the stronger the sense will grow.

*

You have been given a Quest by the Goddess Jenae: Fix the Fixers II

The Goddess Jenae has commanded you to search the depths of the Prax, Glorious Retribution. There are surviving Gnomes and other species still aboard that may be convinced to aid you, as well as storehouses of mundane materials for repair and refitting. Lastly, there are golems, sorely needed by the resurgent Empire and its people.

HOWEVER, there are also enemies, both new and old, that roam the forgotten corners of the Prax; tread carefully!

Recover the golems: 0/306

Recover mundane materials: 0/?

Recruit additional citizens: 0/?

Reward: Improved technological capacity in the Great Tower. Possible technological boosts to the Fleet/Legion. 500,000xp

*

You have been given a Quest by the Goddess Jenae: Secure the Border

The Goddess Jenae has granted you a quest! The Empire was forever bordered by threats, as such, each of the civilian areas were protected by border forts, outposts, allies, and more.

Reclaim and repair the border forts: 0/6

OR

Make Alliances with other groups to protect the border: 0/3

Reward: Secure borders, Allies, 500,000xp, Possible additional rewards based on performance

I accepted them both, of course. Shit, the half a million experience from each was a hell of a boost alone, and I damn well needed it, considering everything I had coming, again closing the experience down.

"Thank you, Jenae," I whispered, dismissing the screens and looking up at Her as She stepped back, smiling down at me.

"You are welcome, my Champion. Now, while I cannot help you with the actual binding of the fragment of Nimon's divine soul, I can offer advice, if you will take it?"

"Of course," I replied, frowning.

"Do it away from anyone else, somewhere private. Binding a fragment of a divine soul is no easy task, and the experience is unique for each one. Nimon's sphere of influence is death, so be ready for its touch."

"Okay, can I get a hint?"

"I have never bound a fragment of death, but Tamat has. She chooses not to come to you, however, for your own protection at this time. Once the fragment is bound, She may relent, but as it is? It is too great a temptation. She bade me warn you about removing yourself from all life when you bind it."

"I'll do that, then. Thank you, Goddess, and thank your sister for me, please."

"I will. Now, I will wish you peace with what is ahead of you." Jenae inclined Her head, smiling at Oracle. *"And my own congratulations to you both. Your position is unexpected but not unwelcome. The birth of a new race is a cause for celebration indeed."* And with that, She was gone, stepping back into the wall and vanishing as if it were a damn curtain, rather than a solid stone wall.

"A new race?" I looked at Oracle in trepidation. "She's saying our kid is that special?"

"Jax, our child has aspects of the Eternal bloodline, and its mother is a Wisp, the first of my kind to ever breed in this way. Believe me, even if we lived in a cave and nobody knew who we were, this child would be unique. As it is? The Prince of the Empire and his lover? Yes. It's special."

"My lover," I muttered. "It makes you sound like you're this week's bit of fun, like the way Rewn had his favorites."

"Well, that's for you to change one day, then, isn't it?" she replied airily, kissing my cheek and walking across the room towards the door. "Don't forget to get dressed, dear!" She closed the door behind her, leaving me to sit on the edge of the bed, staring around.

"Fuck," I said. "Now I need to goddamn wife her at some point. Well done, Jax, top man there. Made her really know how you feel."

I rubbed my hands down my face, taking a deep breath, then scrubbed at my skin again, letting loose a jaw-creaking yawn. This day was already six months longer than I wanted it to be, never mind the ceremony to come.

I moved to the mirror, staring into my own eyes and took a long breath, in and out, centering myself as best I could without actually meditating. Then I put on my damn formal clothes, a simple black and gray suit trimmed with red, none of this fancy shit, and went to join the others downstairs.

The carriage ride was short. The streets of Himnel lined with people watching us as we traveled to the Cathedral, and the silence was eerie.

When I'd grown up, I'd only ever seen two parades, one for some celebration for the queen, and one for New Year's Eve in Newcastle. Apparently, they had one every year, but I'd been so smashed by that point of the night, I'd usually missed it, or I'd been working. I'd never actually known about it until Lou dragged me to it.

This was *nothing* like that.

Where the ones on TV were all cheering crowds, and the ones in Newcastle were people holding kids up to see it while casually commenting that "it wasn't bad, but Jimmy down the road could have done that better."'

This was the complete opposite.

The streets were lined with cold stares and furious faces. People had turned out in their thousands to watch. Nobody cheered, but neither did they look sad about the deaths.

I stared at them, confused at first, and then in growing anger as I realized what was happening.

They weren't here to celebrate the lives of the legionnaires or those of the warriors of the city that had died defending it.

They were here to watch, the overall impression that they gave off one that started with the nobles spreading shit about the Legion for so long. These people wouldn't truly celebrate until the rest of the legionnaires were dead, I knew, and the monumental task ahead of me in teaching them respect made my fists itch.

I watched them as the carriages rolled by, seeing the gray walls, the filthy streets, and the sneers on the faces of the people. Narkolt has welcomed us fully, joyfully even, once they realized what we brought. No more corruption, for a start, or at least a marked dip in it, no random acts of violence perpetrated by the nobility. No more "one rule for them, and one rule for us."

The people of Narkolt took only a few weeks to go from grudging acceptance to full-fledged support.

The people of Himnel, though? If anything, they seemed furious that we dared to try and improve things.

The carriage pulled up at the bottom of the stairs leading up to the Cathedral entrance, and I stepped down. Grizz sliding in between me and the carriage, then offering his hand to Oracle as I moved out of the way, finding he'd already flipped the steps down for her as well.

Considering she could damn well fly, it was a bit much, but I understood the feeling, and I smiled at seeing the care he took.

Until an arrow slammed into the carriage an inch from Oracle's head.

"Assassin!" a voice roared.

Grizz pushed Oracle back into the carriage, shielding her with his own armored bulk, even as I spun frantically, searching for whoever had fired the arrow.

Bane appeared next to me, his voice low and worried. "I didn't sense it, Jax, not a whisper." He admitted, before letting loose with a pulse of world-sense that made people close to us flinch away.

"Find them," I ordered, my heart filled with fury, gaze moving from window to window, rooftop to gutter and more. Bane vanished, even as more legionnaires raced for the carriage, lifting shields high and forming a protective ring around us.

"Where are you?" I growled, looking to the arrow and mentally tracing it backward through the air, even as the second carriage practically exploded as Lydia shouldered her way free and leaped into the air to search from above.

Augustus was next to me in seconds, as was Hellenica, who reached out a finger to the arrow, then hissed something, mist lifting into the air then coalescing into a thick line that flowed along the trajectory I'd roughly guessed at.

"My Prince, we have to get you and the lady out of here," Augustus said as Grizz was pushed aside and Oracle stepped back out, fairly crackling with power. Her fury fed my own as Hellenica followed her tracer magic.

"We're here to say thank you to the fallen," I growled. "No asshole is getting in the way of that." I could feel the absolute rage that filled Oracle as she scanned the surrounding buildings. A dozen Legion Alkyon, led by Amaat, tore past overhead as we spoke, searching for the slightest threat.

"Then we need to move inside and trust the scouts to find the assassin while we do," Augustus stated, making me swear. He gestured for me to follow Arrin. Tenandra stepped up to Oracle's side, whispering in her ear. A few seconds later, she was nodding and indicating for me to go.

"Tenandra's on her way," Jian assured me, as I stalked along with him, hating the impression we were giving as Oracle and I walked between raised shields, up the stairs, and into the packed cathedral. "In her ship body, I mean." He clarified, as I glanced from him, to the Wisp and back again questioningly.

I took Oracle's hand as the legionnaires split, making more room for us. I half dragged her down the echoing length of the nave towards the altars, ignoring the people who were shouldered aside should they not move fast enough on their own.

The Cathedral of Himnel was a strange design, a long corridor that was filled with seating and standing areas, supposedly to meet with the various priests of the Death God until recently. At the far end of that central corridor was a massive decagon, a ten-sided circle-thingy with space in the middle of each face for the relevant God or Goddess' altar, as well as a throne which was in the process of being carved from solid stone for each to sit on, should they want to physically show themselves.

I went straight for the one that belonged to Tamat, ignoring the shadowy figure of a priest that appeared as I closed with it.

"The Dark Lady…" he said. But I kept walking, making it clear he had the choice of moving or being walked over. "Uh, wait…uh…"

"That's the Godslayer," Augustus informed him brightly, grabbing him by the shoulder and dragging him aside as I closed with the altar. "He'd very much like a word with your lady right now, so be a good boy and keep quiet."

"Tamat!" I called out, not bothering to send the usual tithe of mana to her, instead grabbing ahold of her alter physically. "That better not have been you!"

"Or what?!" a voice hissed in my ear, and a sharp ripping sound filled the air as an unseen knife carved through the back of my smart goddamn coat. *"You forget yourself, boy."*

I twisted, catching a glimpse of flashing midnight-blue eyes in the cloud of darkness that floated around me before I released the altar and dug deep inside, curling my lip at the feeling of the dagger slowly carving a thin cut through the outside of my tunic.

"Perhaps it is time I reminded you who I am," Tamat sneered until the blade hit something far harder and was shoved aside.

The hundreds of people inside the Cathedral already, nobles, merchants, members of the various forces, the army, the fleet and the guards, as well as the families of those who were lost in the fighting watched in shocked silence, unable to make out much of what was being said, but when the first burst of light came, the last words from them fell silent.

It started on my chest, a ripple of silvery scales that flowed up and out, shredding the remains of the top that had been receiving Tamat's tender care, even as my mana dropped at an insane speed.

The scales flowed from my skin, bubbling to the surface, sliding from pores and more. Where they should have brought untold agony, instead they brought release, as if my flesh had always been ready to do this. Like the sheaths that contained a claw or a nail, my skin opened, and dragon scales flowed forth.

They cascaded outward, overlapping one after the other, forming a second skin that was harder than any mere steel could hope to be. I felt more coming as long segments doubled up, growing thicker and stronger, overlapping the major muscle groups, even as the scales continued to flow.

In seconds, it was down to my feet, now encased in solid, claw-tipped boots and flowing down my arms.

My hands were wrapped in silvery gloves, each tipped with a short, stubby onyx claw. I swung my left arm up, shoving the barely seen glint of the blade Tamat had been slicing my clothes with aside in a shower of sparks.

"Remind me of what?" I hissed. "That you're my ally? Or that you're the patron Goddess of fucking *assassins,* and one just tried to kill Oracle!"

*"Watch yourself!" S*he snarled, the eyes flaring wide then narrowing as She moved in close. *"I tolerate much, boy, but if I must remind you of the gulf of power between us, I will!"*

"WERE THEY YOURS?" I ground out, and for a long second we stared into each other's eyes, a heartbeat away from violence.

"No."

"Fuck!" I closed my eyes and turned away from her, before twisting back and looking into her furious gaze, even as my scales shivered and retracted, the will to kill dissipating without a genuine threat. "Tamat…Goddess Tamat, I apologize," I forced myself to say. "An attack on Oracle…"

"Watch yourself," Tamat repeated, clearly outraged before dissipating, and I let out a long, stress-filled breath in one long sigh. I desperately wanted to hurt someone, even as I knew that this was a fight I had to leave to my people.

"Uh, Jax?" Grizz whispered, moving close and shifting until his shield was out and in place, the other legionnaires nearby doing the same as they surrounded me.

"Yeah, Grizz…?" I muttered, distracted, my mind still racing.

"You know you're naked, right?"

"What? Oh fuck my life," I groaned, looking down at the tattered and wispy fragments of clothing that were all that was left of the smart clothes I'd been wearing.

"Allow me," Tenandra whispered, stepping up and resting a hand on my shoulder. I felt a wash of coolness, then a sudden warmth, and just like that, I was dressed again.

I looked down, frowning, and opened my mouth to ask how she'd done that, when Oracle shook her head, stepping up and laying a finger across my lips.

"We can explain later. For now, either we need to cancel the ceremony, or we need to trust the others to catch the assassin and go ahead."

"We go ahead. They're not stopping us saying goodbye to our people.

"In that case, Augustus, Grizz?" Oracle said, turning to look at them both. They nodded, taking the hint.

"Legion, release!" Augustus bellowed. Instantly, the highly trained legionnaires shifted, separating their shields and breaking the turtle formation they'd automatically retreated into as I'd stripped myself. They spread out, watching everything and in every direction all at once, and I moved, striding up to, and then onto the central dais where Terra waited with several other priests.

When Tenandra continued along with me, I glanced at her, and Oracle took up station on the other side, whispering, "Go with it, I'll explain later."

I nodded to the priests, then turned to the congregation and the rows of empty helms that stood atop a series of ceremonial carved biers representing the dead.

I bowed my head to the empty helms, feeling shame over my choice all over again and hoped they would understand. Then I straightened, turning to the people who were left behind.

"Thank you all for coming. We're gathered here tonight, to honor our brave dead..."

CHAPTER FIVE

It was nearly midnight by the time I got back to our rooms, carrying an exhausted Oracle, who'd fallen asleep in the carriage on the way back from the cathedral.

I was fairly sure she wasn't actually asleep, not really, but she was cozy and content, despite the lack of bloodshed around us, and that was enough. I carried her through the keep all the way up to our rooms, with people falling silent as they saw us approaching.

Admittedly, a wave of legionnaires locking cold eyes with anyone making the slightest noise might have helped as well, but that wasn't the point.

We stepped into our rooms, Bane flitting in ahead of us, then Grizz, with Tenandra directly behind me. Yen brought up the rear, as far as anyone could tell, while in reality it was Tang, creeping along the corridor watching the world with suspicion.

I moved through the outer sitting room and lay Oracle on the bed, smoothing her hair free and tucking her in before kissing her forehead and moving out of the room.

I started to anyway, as I reached the door. Tenandra, who'd kept exceedingly damn close to me, paused, turning to face me.

"Would you like me to release you now, so you can dress?" she asked. I frowned, looking down, and hearing Bane's chuckle as I figured out what she meant.

"I'm naked, aren't I?" I asked in a quiet voice.

"Well, in the same way that everyone is naked under their clothes, you *are*."

I held a hand up. "Please Tenandra, I'm too tired for this shit. What am I wearing?"

"Me."

"You?"

"I extended my physical body across your own, forming it into a simulacrum of clothing."

"You…I…I'm wearing *you*?!" I paused, taking a deep breath and having to physically restrain my instinct to adjust myself, knowing that the cloth that was currently comfortably cradling my nether regions right now might as well actually be Tenandra's…hands. I closed my eyes and stepped to the side of the door, so I wasn't in sight of the others in the main room, before speaking in as calm a voice as I could manage. "Yes, please release me, Tenandra."

She smiled, nodded, and there was a sudden feeling of slithering, like warm silk being pulled across my skin. Then, I was standing there, in my bedroom, stark naked and facing Tenandra.

My immediate instinct was to cover my manhood, considering that she wasn't my lover…but that ship had well and truly sailed, considering the last several hours.

"I'll be out in a few minutes," I promised her, closing the door and moving to the dresser. "Not one fucking word, Bane," I warned him, knowing the bugger would be hiding there somewhere.

"I wouldn't dream of it, oh mighty Prince of the Empire," he whispered, the air filled with a light *thrum* of amusement.

"Dick."

"Yes, she's been holding yours for…"

"Bane!"

"Sorry, not sorry."

"Dic…fuck it. What did you find?" I asked, changing the subject.

"As I said in the carriage, nothing at all. Too many people were around the site, and whoever carried out the attack was well-trained and skilled at evasion," he said, the humor dropping from his voice to be replaced with anger.

"So what, we got lucky?"

"That, or they were never intending to kill anyone and wanted something else."

"Like what?" I asked, pulling my spare trousers on and sighing as I buttoned myself up. The gloom spider silk pants were amazing, a level of comfort beyond almost anything I had ever worn, and far, far better than the damn local cloths used, but fuck my life. The number of times I'd almost asked Tenandra on the carriage ride back, totally unknowing, if she could do this for me every day?

Yeah. This was an issue, and one that was getting goddamn resolved soon.

"I'd imagine it was a test, either of your security or of your responses, but I don't know," Bane answered, breaking me out of my reverie.

"Well, we'll ask the fucker once we've got them caught and nailed to the wall," I said. "You coming or staying?"

"Staying," Bane replied. "Until we know that the assassin is dead, one of us will be with Oracle at all times, if you're not."

"As long as you sod off when I get naked, fine by me," I told him, only half-joking. I really didn't want them hiding in my damn bedroom at all, but if we were asleep? What if some assassin with a climbing ability scaled the outside of the building and used some special skill on us?

He grunted something about being glad he was blind, and I flipped him the finger, leaving the room and closing the door softly behind me.

"She all right, boss?" Grizz asked as I joined the others.

I moved to a nearby couch and settled down as the others took seats around the room. "She is mate, just exhausted. Her body wasn't built for the kind of stresses that are on it right now, I guess, so I've no idea if this is something that'll be a problem moving forward, or if tomorrow, she'll be back to normal. Guess we're all learning with this one." I smiled at the others, noting the way Thomas and Bella sat side by side, Grizz and Yen, and Jian, Tenandra and Sehran.

As well as the coup…lovers, Romanus, Lucian, Augustus and Hellenica were there, Cai, Isabella, Lydia, Ronin, and Bob.

I looked to Bob, sensing something and realizing that he'd been even more silent most of the day than normal.

"Why was she attacked?" We all heard in our minds from him.

"I don't know, Bob," I responded honestly. "Does anyone?" There were a variety of headshakes and negatives, until Romanus and Lucian shared a long look, and the Imperial Justicar spoke up.

"We don't know, but we suspect that it was a feint."

"Go on," I said.

"If the assassin was skilled enough to hide from the city Control Center, which they were, and skilled enough to get close enough with a large bow, considering the size of the arrow, then they are a highly skilled individual indeed. For them to then miss? It seems unlikely. Either you have been putting far, far more points into Luck than I ever dreamed was possible, or they were not intending to kill you or Oracle."

"Then why fire a fucking arrow at us?"

"As I say, this is conjecture, but I suspect it was either a test or a warning. As a test, it would be logical to say they wanted to judge the legion's response to their attack, or to see if they could, in fact, escape from us. As a warning? Unknown. It could be anything from a skilled assassin wanting to send a message, to an attempt at proving their skills before a request for recruitment, to an attempt to warn us to leave Himnel."

"I'm seriously considering that last bit," I admitted. "I'd feel a hell of a lot safer at the Tower, but that might be what they want?" I shook my head.

"Makes you want to stay here more, doesn't it?" Thomas agreed.

"Hell yes. Well, regardless, I want the fucker nailed to the roof of the fucking keep by their balls!" I growled, shaking my head. "They might not have intended to harm us, but they could have fucked up, so until I hear a damn good reason why, they're a failed assassin, and they pay for their attempt. Anyone have an issue with that?"

"Not at all, but, in all honesty, I'd recommend we return to the Tower," Cai said, surprising everyone.

"Go on," I ground out.

"The Tower is not only a far more secure location for Oracle and the upcoming birth…" He paused before clearing his throat carefully. "Do we have an estimate on that?"

"Not a clue," I said. "A week ago, we knew it was impossible. Now she's pregnant. Could be nine months, might be an hour's time." I shook my head in disbelief.

"Then it is doubly important to ensure the location is secure. The Great Tower is far more easily secured than a recently captured city. Duke Augustus was named as the Lord of Himnel some time ago. Do you intend to do as you did with Lady Carmen and Narkolt and have him rule here, with a chosen council, or are you seeking to move the center of government here from the Tower?"

"No," I said after a few seconds of thought. "We'll return to the Tower as soon as we've got things sorted here. Augustus, are you ready to rule the city?"

"Not in a million years, my Prince." He shook his head. "But I'll do my best, if this is where you decide you need me to serve."

"I do. I'm sorry, my friend," I sighed. "Romanus, Restun, leave a secure and strong cadre to protect Augustus and Hellenica, as well as anything they need. Then begin planning things; we're returning to the Tower. It's our seat of government, and we'll damn well make it the Legion's heart as well."

"Yes, my Prince." Romanus tapped a fist to heart in the traditional salute, mirrored by Augustus and Restun.

"Cai, summon the nobles tomorrow, early. We're having this out with them and sorting the city. Plan for us leaving in two days. Romanus, can you do that?"

"I can, provided we have the support of the fleet?" he replied.

"Cai, make that happen. Tell Oren to be at the meeting in the morning, as well." I got a few nods, and I turned to Ronin. "Ronin, I know you, Flux, and Lio were intelligence gathering. They're still out searching, so give me a run down."

"The locals aren't against us," he said. "Despite the way things looked tonight, the vast majority of them, and please don't take this wrong, don't give a damn about us or the Empire." He looked around apologetically.

"They literally don't see how it affects them. A few days ago, it was Barabarattas, the Dark Legion, and the other nobles. Now it's the Empire, some new nobles, and the Legion. As far as they're concerned? It's business as usual. Yes, their lives are less likely to be ended by a random noble acting…well, like a noble. Or the gangs or Dark Legion, hell the corrupt guards and the soldiers, any of them, randomly killing them, but…they also lost their slaves."

"Their slaves," I muttered, shaking my head in disgust.

"Yeah, don't get me wrong, boss, the vast majority weren't slavers, but they worked alongside them. Foundries had slaves provided for certain jobs. Others had a personal slave for menial tasks. The lowest workers all had the fact that they weren't slaves to reassure them that some bugger was always worse off than they were.

"Most people weren't actively involved in slavery, but the entire city benefited from it. From the sewers being maintained, to the lamps lit, to the shit shoveled out of the gutters, and the ingots stacked. The butchery and having food deliveries prepared or kitchen drudges. All those jobs? The slaves are gone, freed up, and most want to serve in the new Legion."

"Good for them." Grizz grinned.

"Yes and no." Cai corrected Grizz. "The simple fact is that all those jobs were essential, and now there's an entire segment of the workforce that's vanished. Yes, when things settle down, the city will be better off, but for now? Every sector is in upheaval."

"Exactly. Then, you've got the outstanding issues that the nobility created with the Legion. In Narkolt, they hadn't gone as far, and nobody trusted the nobility anyway," Ronin pointed out. "Here, they didn't trust the nobility, but they damn well don't trust the Legion, either. Add in the murders that were carried out before you came here the first time? People *still* think that was the Legion, by the way."

"The Vampyres were literally feeding on people, and the nobility were telling them it was the Legion." I muttered, shaking my head. "Fuck's sake. How the hell do you do a hearts and minds op without the internet and so on. Any idea, Tommy?" I asked, scratching at my beard tiredly.

"No clue, bro."

"Why bother?" Bella asked.

"Because we need them to understand that we're not their enemy." I pointed out.

She shook her head. "You're putting too much effort into that. The majority don't care who you are, the louder you promise you're not like their last ruler, the more they'll look for whatever you're hiding from them. I say ignore them, get the city on its feet, and let people make their own decisions. Or, clamp down on the city and make it clear what happens when they annoy you. It's all they understand."

I flicked a glance at Thomas, who was wincing, but he nodded as well.

"She's got a point, bro. We're not like the others. Let them see that for themselves, sod the hearts and minds ops."

"Fine. Cai, can you fix the economy?" I asked.

"No." He shook his head. "I can deal with the issues as they come as best I can, but for now, we need a great many workers we just don't have if they're in Legion training. I'll get Hannibal working on it, as well as Hanau, but the simple fact is that we need those golems, and the more I look into it, the more certain I am that we need them as soon as possible."

"We need golems to mine the ore to make the cores to make the golems. Got it, great." I sighed, rubbing at my eyes. "So, Flux and the others are busy searching for a skilled assassin who was basically warning us off, most likely, who can't be tracked through the city interface, they're *that* good. The economy is basically staggering along, but about to go into freefall. Rather than everything being sorted now the war is over and I've kicked that fucker Nimon off the continent, we're worse off, is that right?"

"Essentially, yes," Cai said, as the others sat silently. "In time, we'll all be far better off, but for now, we need to plaster over the issues as best we can and work on rebuilding."

"There are some good points, if you'd like to hear them, Lord Jax?" Isabella said into the silence.

"Hell yes, Isabella, I'd damn well *love* to hear them."

"We have nearly twelve thousand people freed from slavery. They're safe, they're being fed and given the time they need to adjust to life again. Over three hundred families have been reunited so far, that I'm aware of, families that had given up all hope, and another thousand are being given support to deal with their losses."

Silence rang in the room as we all looked at each other, seeing Isabella sitting tall and proud in the middle of the room, as she made it clear to us all that the real importance of freeing the slaves wasn't the effect on the economy, no matter that it was that damn effect we had to deal with.

"Aye, an' ah've been approached by six now that ah think ah can train…ah think," Lydia added.

"What, as Valkyries?" I asked, stunned.

"Aye."

"Shit, Lydia, that's amazing news! Why the hell didn't you tell me this earlier?" I gasped.

"Because…because ah don't know how to do it." she said. "Ah kin feel the potential, an' these six 'ave all got it, but I ain't never 'ad ter teach anyone before!"

"Bollocks." Thomas grunted, shaking his head. "You taught your team, didn't you?"

"They were all learnin', just like I were," she disagreed. "Iffin ah fucked up, it weren't that bad."

"You were just defending the Lord of Dravith, you mean?" Romanus asked her. "Optio, you laid claim to the rank on your own merit. You lead the personal squad of the Prince of the Empire, and are one of the most dedicated trainees I've ever seen." He broke off, looking to Restun.

"That's correct, Prefect. The Optio is both highly skilled and extremely dedicated. Yes, she is still learning, which is less than ideal. However, the only way *any* of us improve is by learning. And gaining a dedicated Valkyrie squad would be a great strength for the Empire," Restun declared.

"Aye, except ah 'ave no clue 'ow ah'd do it!" Lydia growled. "It's not like ah can jus' start trainin' them!"

"Why not?" Jian asked, from where he sat between Tenandra and Sehran. "Seriously? Why not?"

"Because ah donna know how!" she snarled. "Ah'm part of Jax's squad, ah've no the time te be..."

"Start with the Legion," Lucian interrupted. When she paused, looking at him uncertainly, he went on calmly. "Start with the basic Legion system, if they are to be an offshoot of the Legion eventually. I understand that is your intention long-term, Jax? That all armed forces be integrated into the Legion in some form?" He glanced at me, and I nodded.

"In that case, start with the Legion training system, and add to it. so they can integrate with the Legion easily. Much of their early training can be carried out by the Legion. That gives you time to add to the training around your current position, unless you wish to resign from..."

"No!" Lydia cut Lucian off. "Ah'm no leavin' ma squad nor Jax!"

"Then, if you're willing to train these recruits, I suggest you speak to your patron and your own trainer and begin their integration," he continued smoothly. "A full wing of Valkyries would be a tremendous boost to the Empire."

"Oh, hell yes!" I said, thrilled at the possibilities. "Lydia, if you can do this? That'd be a hell of a boost."

"Well, aye, iffin yer want, but ah'll need te get tha armor and more. It were all in tha Temple o' tha Winds! Or back in tha Empire!"

"Where's the Temple of the Winds?" I asked, only to have Tenandra lean forward and rest a hand flat on the table in the middle of the room.

"The Temple of the Winds was set atop the island of Imshi..." As she spoke, the top of the table shifted and blurred as she used her malleable form to create a map that we could all see.

First, the city of Himnel appeared, then the map zoomed out, slowly drawing farther and farther upward into the heavens. The bay appeared, then the local coastline, the rivers and valleys, followed by Himnel and the great forests.

Soon, the Tower was in sight, as was the lake that housed Bane's village, then the mountains to the west and the sea on the east.

Then it paused, and a mass outlined in red appeared deep in the ocean, pulsing as it appeared, a wireframe drawing of an island with huge fields. Central roads led around a single tall mountain in the middle, and atop that...

"The Temple of the Winds," Tenandra intoned. "Ancestral home of the western Valkyries, sat atop the volcano Sanak, on the island of Imshi."

"Well fuck," I muttered. "If the fucker sank, what seven hundred years ago? What the hell do we do about that?"

"We raid it." Oracle said from the door behind me. I twisted around, seeing her leaning against the wall and smiling tiredly.

"Hey you," I greeted her as she moved across, leaning in for a kiss then sliding onto my lap and sitting back against me as she spoke.

"Hey, everyone. Sorry, this whole physical body thing is taking some getting used to," she apologized as the room greeted her.

"We can do this later if..."

She shook her head. "I'm pregnant, Jax, not dying. As to the Temple of the Winds...Bane, could you reach it?" She directed her question to one side, and Bane appeared, leaning against the wall there.

"Probably," he said. "But with an assassin on the loose, I don't think it would be wise to send me away, especially as I'd most likely need a team."

"And a ship, considering how far out it is," I said, shaking my head. "And the damn things we saw swimming in the bay? Fuck that."

"We need to get the armor," Romanus said.

I grinned. "Oh, we need to get the armor, all right, but that's not the point. I'm saying that we're not going down there, no chance am I sending my friends to swim with the goddamn crazy wildlife. Not when we've got our own leviathan."

"A leviathan?" Yen asked, before grinning. "Oh...you mean the golem?"

"I mean the golem," I agreed, nodding. "Tenandra can you show it, please?"

She nodded, frowning as she dismissed the image she'd been holding and created a new one.

This time, it was a single great creature, or so it appeared at first. It looked like a damn crocodile with fins instead of legs, a short, wide snout filled with multiple rows of teeth that could slide back from the front section, like a chainsaw in perpetual motion.

The front was wider than the back, narrowing to a thin tail with four smaller fins that could twist independently. Directly behind the head were four retractable arms that folded flat into recesses in the body, two ending in sharp, scissor-like cutting blades. The other two were larger, appearing to be designed to grip and crush their target.

From there, the body flowed back to the tail, studded with hatches and retractable tentacle-like arms, designed for retrieval of resources or repairs, depending on the situation.

And it was more than eighty meters long.

It was a true monster, made to fight the monsters of the deep on their own terms. It was huge, and was a little under three weeks from being completed by the golems in the production facility we'd claimed all that time ago.

For the first time, we had an actual need for it, beyond a "yeah, that'd be nice to have" situation, and I nodded to myself.

"Okay, we need to get that sorted out. Once that's finished, we can order it launched, then it can strip anything it can find from the Temple of the Winds."

"That's probably where that Ghastool lich dude was from, wasn't he?" Thomas asked.

I leveled a finger at him. "Good point bro. We get it to search for Ghastool's stash as well," I agreed. "Okay, how the hell do we get that sorted?"

"The production facility has a link to the Tower; Heph will be integrated into it now," Oracle assured me.

"That's a relief, then. Okay, so tomorrow we beat the nobles into place, and we make sure that's sorted, then we get any last minute details we can address. Get the line of succession clear here, then I'm finding whoever fired that arrow."

"We'll find the assassin, Jax," Augustus said. "You need to continue to bind the city to you, and the Empire."

I paused, remembering I damn well needed to do that as a priority, and because…

"Yeah, all right. I'll leave that to you, Augustus. Tip the city upside down and shake it if you have to, see what falls out."

"I will. Is there anything else?" he asked.

I hesitated, looking down at Oracle.

"You need to warn them," she whispered.

"Yeah. One minor issue," I said, before taking a deep breath then launching into a whole discussion about divine souls and the choice I'd made and still needed to carry out.

***

"So what, you've lost half your powers, and now you're aiming to be a God, because in the long-term, you'll be waaaaay more powerful?" Thomas asked sometime later, getting a groan from Bella as she buried her head in her hands.

"He's going to be a God?" she whispered. "That means…wait!" She sat up suddenly, looking at me wide-eyed. "You're going to take time to become a God, right?"

"Yeah it'll probably take me years, if not centuries," I answered, frowning at her.

"Years…" she said, smiling evilly. "I'll be able to beat a God senseless for years."

She stared off into the distance as I narrowed my eyes at her, then I looked at Restun, who was grinning as well. That evil bastard was going to find some way to make my damn training even *harder*.

"Bane, Tang? I need you to watch over Oracle. Everyone else, I'll see you tomorrow," I said, forcing myself to my feet with Oracle still in my arms.

"And where will you be?" Restun asked calmly.

I sighed, looking at him, knowing this was going to go down like a lead balloon.

"I'm going to the field where we killed all the Dark Legionnaires. It's time to bind the fragment of death."

They argued with me, of course, all but Oracle. But, in the end, I'd been warned by a Goddess about making sure that nobody was nearby when I did it, and that kinda held some weight with me.

CHAPTER SIX

I landed gently, running a few steps to kill my momentum, and enjoyed the damn silence for a few seconds before sighing. Awesome landing and nobody to see it.

I'd picked this place partially because nobody would be here and partially because what had happened only two days ago meant there would be a huge amount of residual death mana in the area.

It also stank to high heaven, unfortunately.

It was in the middle of the fields that stood between the city of Himnel and the remains of the Dark Citadel. That was currently a massive pile of rubble being worked over, day and night, by dozens of golems and over a hundred of the city guard and the army.

They were all there because the golems could move the shattered remains of the citadel, and the people could tell the difference between junk and damaged treasures.

The army and the guard were there because they could watch each other, and neither trusted the other, so there was less chance of things going "accidentally" missing.

The citadel was a little over two miles from where I'd landed, and the diamonds we'd used for defense were a mile or so behind me, while were I stood…

It was a mess.

Dozens of Heliogifts had been detonated. Discharged, shattered manastones had been filled with the power of the sun before being packed with hundreds of roughly made metal balls all around them.

They were the magical equivalent of claymore mines, and when they'd gone off, several thousand Dark Legionnaires had been passing overhead.

That had ended badly for their army, considering that a significant portion of it was shredded, reduced to an unrecognizable state, with ears and teeth being found miles away in trees.

The war golems had plowed straight through the reeling remains of the army, not even bothering to stop as they pounded the survivors into hamburger meat.

It'd been the end of the Dark Legion as any kind of real cohesive threat to us at that point. Then I'd flown past, glowing like the fucking sun and torn the citadel down in a display of pure, God-like rage, before literally sawing their God's head off and punting it.

Therefore, where I stood right now was an utter mess of shredded limbs, flesh, torn metal, and blood.

I'd been warned by Augustus, when I'd told them all where I was going, that it would need to be cleansed soon, regardless of what I did, as this much death mana would create revenants, undead, and more, otherwise.

Now, I stood there, the mud around my boots swamp-like in the way it clung to me, the earth torn and battered, and the air filled with hundreds of thousands of flies, crows, and more.

I turned slowly, seeing the imps that feasted on the terror and adrenaline-filled flesh. Here and there were darker things, creatures comprised entirely of shadow and teeth that chewed and hissed at my incursion into their territory.

"If you can understand me…leave, now. I won't warn you again," I called out, before taking a deep breath and reaching *inwards*.

I couldn't explain how I did it, but a second later, I held it in my right hand; a fragment of divinity, glowing with all the power of death.

It was small, barely seeming to fill my hand, maybe an inch wide at the base, jagged at the top and sharp. It'd been clearly shattered off something greater, making me think of a stained-glass mosaic made of shadows that radiated a terrible weight and gravity.

I held it for a long second, staring into the depths of it, aware at the edge of my mind of the sudden interest of everything nearby.

I felt the attention of the realm pulled inexorably towards it, and I reached out with my mana, a tiny thread of the energy that made me *me*, carried along with it, as my own soul touched the remnant of Nimon's.

I gasped, eyes flaring wide as my soul ripped forth, dragged hungrily into the shard. *Something* reached back, stabbing into me and taking up residence in the space that had been left behind.

I collapsed, my knees hitting the sodden earth with a splat. Then I toppled sideways, eyes wide, breath rasping as I panted in pain and horror.

The veil.

The veil between the realm of life and the realm of the dead was there, a heartbeat away from me. I could feel it, feel it in a way I'd never experienced before.

I recognized it instantly, the chill, heart stuttering nearness of true death, and I felt them all.

Thousands, no, *tens* of thousands, just in the area around me. I saw the souls of the dead, those I'd ripped from this plane and forced into the next through my actions, and those who'd long since been banished from life.

I heard their cries, their demands, and their hunger. They were driven by sadness, wrath, and regret, and they teemed around me, separated from the living by a gossamer strand of invisible silk.

They were drawn to me, pale specters lost in the cold realm of death, suddenly finding a warm bonfire of life in their midst…and they *wanted* it!

Some of the souls that reached out were desperate for help. There was a sudden cacophony of voices, most too faint to make any sense, but sounds made it through. The older the specters were, the fainter their cries for help.

The more recent dead, though? They raged, hundreds screamed in denial, reaching out to me. Spectral fingers scrabbling like desperate claws tearing at the bright bonfire of my soul, ripping shreds of energy free and frantically feeding it into grasping maws, teeth chattering hollowly.

I felt them tearing at me, and my strength seeping free, even as fresh notifications began to flash.

Dark Tide Rising

Congratulations

**You have taken your first step on the path to Godhood,
but where will it end?**

**The primary Fragment of Divinity that you accept comes with three
abilities to choose from, but choose carefully,
for this choice cannot be undone, and until the choice is made,
the fragment, and your soul, are open to the UnderVerse.**

Soul Anchor

Create a spiritual anchor between your soul and that of your target,
forcing them to remain in close proximity to you.

Note this bond cannot be dissolved, and it must end with a Fragment of
a Divine Soul attached to that of the originating Soul Anchor. Should
you lose this fight, your own Fragment will be drawn into your opponent.

Charge: 1 per 24 hours

Death's Embrace

Tear a rift between the realms permitting the soul of one who has
departed to return. Beware, though, should the returning soul have no
body to return to, they will seek to possess another, creating a powerful
and immortal revenant!

Charge: 1 per 24 hours

Lich Mastery

Liches are accepted as the masters of the Undead, but they must bow to
their own master, the God of Death! Binding your Fragment of Divinity
to enslave liches will allow you to create a soul-bond between them and
you, forcing them to bow to your will.

Note, a fully-fledged lich will be able to defend against this ability,
requiring you break their will or physical form to reduce them
sufficiently to force the bond. (Additional Fragments will increase your
power to enslave.)

Charge: 1 per 24 hours

It wasn't really much of a choice, not for me, and I forced myself to focus, to
ignore the pain, the fear and everything else to actually deal with what was before
me right now.

Yeah, the power to basically make all liches my bitches would be useful. Hell,
they could raise the dead and solve a lot of the issues I was having right now.
Buuuut, I couldn't really see ten thousand rotting corpses doing the dishes and
shoveling shit as an improvement.

A stray thought popped up, thinking I'd make billions back home by making them work in call centers, and I dismissed it as too cruel, remembering my own time in them as a soul-broken worker.

Likewise, the ability to pull revenants back through the veil once a day, essentially allowing them to possess the living. For a necromancer? Hell yes, awesome ability, capture a load of society's weakest, summon a powerful undead spirit through the veil, and suddenly you've got an immortal death knight motherfucker ready to kick ass.

For me, though? Fuck that.

I selected Soul Anchor, even as Sint had known I would. For a second, nothing happened, as more and more of the fresh dead gathered around me. I lay there in the mud and the blood, staring wide-eyed into the midnight sky and the slowly falling rain, shuddering in pain.

Then it was like the world caught fire.

An ember caught first as the fragment pushed deeper into my palm, cutting into me, widening the tear so more of it could enter. It slid forward infinitesimally slowly, and every fraction of a millimeter increased the heat by an order of magnitude.

I'd have screamed if I could, but the *power*…the fragment dug into me, burrowing through my flesh and somehow into my soul, awakening it in ways small and profound, readying me for the changes to come as I absorbed more power in the future.

The dead who'd been frantically feeding on me, attempting to tear my soul apart, wailed in fear as the tables were turned. Death mana was ripped from them and the surrounding realm.

I felt it pouring into me, gathering, compressing, *building!*

Over and over, more and more! The spirits screeched as they were dragged backward into me, clawing at each other in their frantic desperation to escape, their souls breaking apart. The death mana that kept them here, that gave them the power to feed upon me, was in turn fed upon.

When I felt like I couldn't hold any more, that the world itself was about to burst, it twisted upon itself, and my perspective shifted suddenly. What had been a vast space, a battery comprised of a huge reservoir of energy, was instead revealed to be a tiny fraction of the space I needed to fill.

Suddenly, there were two batteries, then ten, then a hundred of them, each tugging and pulling at the nascent energy of the realm, tugging free all that was aspected by death and feeding it into me, while I grew in power.

I felt the changes, the way that my body shifted, accepting and drinking in this new power, this energy, this…this magic!

More notifications bloomed, stat point increases, warnings of damage, of death, and of life! I felt it all around me, overwhelming my senses!

As I tore the death mana from the realm around me to fuel my change, life, always battling against its antithesis, surged into primacy.

The field I had laid in mere moments ago, a vast mess of torn earth, blood, and rotting flesh, entrails and organs, bone and metal, transformed as LIFE roared through it.

I rolled over, hissing in pain, feeling the magic around me going wild as the balance was disrupted and I reached out, half-remembered hints and more enabling me as I twisted the magic, desperate not to waste it all.

I found them all around me, hundreds of seeds, the remains of meals that had been left behind by birds, by animals, in the rotting remains of the Dark Legionnaires. Seeds of new life were everywhere, and I slammed the power into them, sending trees soaring into the air.

Dirt and gravel, blood and bone flew everywhere as roots dug deep, branches pushing free and twisting, reaching for the heavens. Apples and pears flourished; grapevines fit for a mature vineyard raced up the trunks of mighty orchards and bloomed.

All around me, nature's bounty filled the torn and devastated fields, and I screamed as the power tore through me.

Eventually, as the power built and built, I was forced to let go, forced to release the massive surge of sheer life. It burst outward, a supernova of overpressure that burst from me like a detonation, leaving everything behind…better.

My DarkVision let me see the boughs of the trees overhead, swaying in the breeze. The grapes swelled, the grasses and mosses buoyed me up, then tree branches caressed me. I was no longer lying in the filth, but resting on them, the air filled with the scent of fresh grass.

I gasped like a fresh-caught fish, unable to breathe as the changes tore through me, neurons firing wildly as everything morphed.

Congratulations!

**Through hard work and perseverance,
you have increased your stats by the following:**

Agility +10

Charisma +10

Constitution +10

Dexterity +10

Endurance +10

Intelligence +10

Luck +10

Perception +10

Strength +10

Wisdom +10

Continue to train and learn to increase this further.

Congratulations!

You have gained a new Ability!

**Through binding a Fragment of Divinity,
specifically one aligned to death magic,
you have gained the ability Reaper of Souls
and may use this ability once per 24 hours.**

Reaper of Souls:
The Soul Reaper is a single use weapon, used to send a soul through the Veil, regardless of their current condition. Rather than being reliant on the victim to defend against it, a Reaping fails only should the wielder's health be too low to carry out the attack: each blow drains both the victim AND the wielder.

Beware: *Deployment of a Soul Reaper must result in a soul being banished through the veil. Select your victims wisely.*

I blinked in shock, and my final words as the world grew dark around me, and I slid into oblivion were heartfelt.

"Fuck me, what would have happened if I *absorbed* it?!"

CHAPTER SEVEN

woke slowly, blinking in the gentle morning light, as the sound of nearby voices filtered through my consciousness. It was slow at first, snatches of conversation, hushed tones, words that almost made sense, but not quite.

I shifted, not ready to wake up, wanting just a little longer, and the voices hushed. I sank into a deeper slumber, the world receding until someone dropped something metal that crashed against something else.

I sat upright, brain hardwired to respond with panic and violence…and fell out of the damn tree I'd been laid in, suspended a dozen feet off the ground in its lowest branches.

"Fuuuuck!" I wailed, plunging through green and healthy lower branches to crash into the ground face-first between Grizz and Giint.

"Morning, boss!" Grizz declared cheerfully.

"Him awake," Giint added to everyone else, totally fucking needlessly.

I pushed myself up onto my elbows and looked around at the verdant grove we were in, seeing the stunning mass of fruit, the orchard flowing away in every direction. I heard the trill of birds, and buzzing of insects, the happy calls of people in the distance who couldn't believe their luck with all the free food…

And I saw Giint holding two honest to god *handfuls of steel* that he'd just banged together to wake me up.

"I hate you," I informed him calmly, spitting out some grass and random vegetation.

"Giint get that a lot," he agreed happily, nodding to me then wandering off.

"Come on, boss, let's get you up…got the dignity of the Imperial Throne to think of, after all," Grizz muttered, grabbing me under the arms and hauling me upright.

"What bloody dignity?" I asked, wiping myself down and shaking my head. "A man has a little nap, and that bastard…"

"Well, Augustus has dignity still?" Grizz pointed out.

"Yeah, well, okay, I'll grant you that. But dude, I was just having a nap."

"In a tree."

"In a tree," I agreed.

"In an orchard."

"Okay, so maybe…"

"That wasn't there yesterday."

"Okay!" I snapped. "So maybe…"

"Did he kill anyone?" Bane called from one side.

"Doesn't look like it, actually," Grizz replied as Yen called back from the other direction.

"Can't find any dead."

"No bodies over here either!" Arrin shouted.

"He conquered anyone, lately? Claimed their villages or homes?" Bane asked.

"Well there was a city a few days back," Grizz said, rubbing his chin in thought.

"Told you. Murderhobo."

"He killed a God as well." Someone called out further away.

"I hate you all," I growled, turning my back on the grinning buggers and stomped over to where Lydia was standing with her arms crossed watching me. "How long have you been here?"

"Most o' tha night," she said. "An orchard two miles wide and six long just appears, it'll tend ta get noticed." She polished a ruby red apple on one sleeve, before taking a bite as I winced.

"Damn, that big?" I muttered, shaking my head at the thought of what could have happened if I'd bound a life fragment. The resulting surge of death would have devastated the area.

"Yeah, you should see the city." She continued.

"Shit, what happened?" I winced.

"Well, let's just say that everyone's a bit healthier; that's the good news."

"What's the bad news?"

"Well, turns out that, if someone's died recently enough, then they're not that dead, after all."

"That's, well that's awesome, so I basically brought a load of people back from the dead?" I asked, stunned

"No."

"What?"

"Their bodies started freaking out. The souls are gone, but it was like the corpses didn't want to give up. There's a lot of very upset people around that had to cut their dead relatives up to stop them shaking."

"Shit, that's…" I covered my eyes with one hand, rubbing at my temples as a thousand possible side effects suggested themselves to me.

"And there's a lot of bugs, and rats, and basically all the animals and insects and so on went mad." Lydia added, glaring at me.

"Uh…"

"JAAAAAX!"

I heard a familiar voice screaming and spun around.

"Where is he!" Mistress Nerin fumed, stomping in our direction before spotting me looking around the edge of a tree at her. "You, boy! I want a word!"

"Fuck," I muttered, leaning back more or less out of sight and closing my eyes.

"Also, a lot of pregnant people gave birth early," Lydia added.

"Oracle?" I asked, eyes flaring wide in panic even as my blood ran cold.

"She's fine, but she's worn out, told me to tell you not to worry, and she thinks she's getting a handle on it all now, whatever that means," Lydia assured me, seeing Nerin drawing closer. "Basically there's a massive plague of rats and other vermin boiling up from everywhere, so the guard, the army, and the trainees are all getting a lot of practice in this morning. I'm going to leave you now. Good luck!"

"Jax!" Nerin growled, reaching out and grabbing me by one ear, then hauling my head down closer to her level as Lydia ran for it. "Have you any idea what you just did! The…"

"Not a clue," I admitted. "Nerin, that hur…"

"Not a clue!" she shrieked. "Not a clue?! The boy drove more life-aspected mana into the land in minutes than should be there in a year, and he's not got a clue!" I batted her hand free and straightened, rubbing my ear.

"I didn't know it was going…"

"He didn't know. Oh, well, that makes it all right!" she called out to the dozens of legionnaires who were sliding away and trying to look as though they'd never been there. "You just casually disrupted the realm. You made the dead walk and converted twelve miles of battlefield and terminally poor farmland into abundant orchards. You just solved half the food problems for the city, and probably Narkolt as well, for the entire winter, by accident?" The last bit was hissed.

"Well, yeah?" I admitted with a wince. "Sort of? I mean it's a good thing, right? Not the dead walking obviously, but the food?"

"NO!" she roared. "It's not good, because we don't know what effects it'll have! We don't know if life was taken from elsewhere to do this! Will the land be barren after this? Will the trees fail? Will this cause a famine next year because the entire continent has been drained of life?"

I froze, having had no clue that it could have this kind of a side effect, and I tried to explain that, but my lips flapped and no sound came forth.

"Jax…" she hissed, clearly trying to calm herself. "Boy…you wield the powers of the Gods like a child playing with a lit torch inside the village grain barn. No clue that it could bring destruction to everyone. Worst of all, you do it again and again, because you got away with it the last time!" She ended with a sigh, covering her eyes as she shook her head.

"I'm sorry, Nerin. I spoke with the Gods about this, about the fragment of divinity I had, and they recommended this."

"This?" she asked, gesturing around at the orchard. "They told you to do this?"

"Well, no, they told me to bind it where there was a lot of death mana, and when I did, I felt the surge of life when the pressure of the death pushing against it was taken away. I felt it surge forward, and rather than just let it go to waste…"

"Rather than let the mana settle itself out, you directed it into providing food for thousands," she finished for me. "Jax, for the immediate effect? It is wonderful, but we don't know what will come. Please, boy, you always manage to be in the right place at the right time, but think! One mistake, and you could be responsible for the deaths of thousands. We are all children of balance."

"I'll try," I agreed. "I didn't think, that's all…"

"Then you have to start! Do you know how many people I had to heal this morning?"

"No?"

"None," she snapped. "Not a single person. Since you decreed that we would heal any of your citizens, those who have sworn to you have been turning up at the keep, at the enclave, and at every official place between. Healers who aren't sworn to you are cursing your name over and over because people are refusing to pay them, and now you've healed the entire damn city!"

"That's good though, right?" I asked, confused. "And the healers can join us…"

"And how will they earn a living now?" she asked bluntly. "What about the fruit sellers, or those who owned the other orchards? Now that this much food is freely available, others will lose everything!"

"I don't know!" I snapped. "Fuck's sake, Nerin! I don't know, all right?!" I scrubbed at my beard with one hand.

"I'm a blunt fucking instrument. I don't know about this shit. I hit people. I hit them really hard until they stop doing shit I don't like, that's me! I don't know what I'm doing with all this crap, I just…"

"You need to learn!" she snapped.

"I'm trying! What the hell do you think I do all day? I'd rather be out fighting than dealing with this shit. *That* I can understand. *That* I can deal with. Amon didn't have to…" I broke off, stunned as I remembered that and the difference between what I'd been doing and what he'd done. "*Amon didn't have to*," I repeated. "*That's* why he had the council and the Senate, and all that shit…Nerin, you're a genius!" I laughed, grabbing her round the waist and lifting her into the air in celebration. Then I set her down gently, and turning to the others who were trying to stay out of the way.

"Gather up! We're heading back to the city!" I called out, before grinning down at Nerin evilly. "So, Nerin, you ever hear of the 'curse of competence?'"

"I warn you, boy…" she started, before growling as I walked away from her.

I shook my head, moving off and calling for the others, leading them back toward the city, even as I pulled my notifications up, ignoring her grumbling. The majority were unimportant. Unarmed has leveled by three points, daggers by one, negotiation by two, that kind of thing. Most of them were from back in the fight against the necromancer and Nimon, more than anything.

Some were to do with the city, informing me of access rights, or of production levels. I flicked through screens about morale, which was slowly climbing, and corruption, which was very slowly dropping, fecundity rates, currently enjoying a massive boost apparently, and mortality, which took an enormous dip.

I saw pages that explained details for shit I literally couldn't guess at, but that as a leader of the city, I could access at any time.

I dismissed that shit out of hand, scanning through until I found the bits I needed to see.

Congratulations!

You have killed the following:

- 1x Greater Divine Avatar, level 40 for a total of 3,000,000xp
- 4x Flesh Golems, level 1 for a total of 120,000xp
- 211x Undead Shamblers of various levels for a total of 14,572xp
- 14x Death Knight of various levels for a total of 486,345xp
- 1x Arch Lich Ghastool, Lich-Lord, level 61 for 742,411xp
- 127x Undead Warriors…
- 247x…
- 11x…
- 14x…
- 109x…

The prompt just went on and bloody on, line after line, page after page, until I shook my head and focused, condensing the description for me and my team down to the important details as I saw them.

Congratulations!

You have reached level 41 to 48.

You have 49 unspent Attribute points and 1 Meridian point available.

Progress to level 49 stands at 3,274,113/6,455,000

I nodded in satisfaction. Yeah, yeah I'd accept that. Admittedly, putting that many point into any area all at once would probably kill me from the shock outright, or cripple me, but if it didn't? I'd be able to happy-slap the next SporeMother I met into the middle of next Tuesday.

Okay, yes for this I *had* killed a God…so if I hadn't leaped up the levels like I had my dick trapped in the space shuttle's door on launch, I'd have been crying foul, but still.

Thomas was going to be soooo pissed.

I pulled up the stat sheet, frowning at all the extra details, the lines upon lines of explanations, why this was that high, why that was adjusted, and I shook my head. Nope, I wasn't having this.

The lines blurred, leaving me with just the important details left over, and a much tidier screen, cutting down my titles and class details especially was a hell of a difference. Removing the bonus list didn't remove the bonuses themselves after all, but let's face it 'Godslayer' was the kind of a title a man liked to keep on his shit.

Name: Jax Amon				
Title: Godslayer				
Class: Sorcerer II			**Renown:** Imperial Scion, Prince of Dravith, Master of Himnel and Narkolt	
Level: 48			**Progress:** 3,274,113/6,455,000	
Patron: Jenae, Goddess of Fire and Exploration			**Points to Distribute:** 49 **Meridian Points to Invest:** 0	
Stat	**Current points**	**Description**	**Effect**	**Progress to next level**
Agility	63	Governs dodge and movement.	+683% maximum movement speed	27/100
Charisma	60 (55)	Governs likely success to charm, seduce, or threaten	+500% success in interactions with other beings	97/100
Constitution	107 (105)	Governs health and health regeneration	2140 health, regen 152 points per 600 seconds	N/A
Dexterity	81 (76)	Governs ability with weapons and crafting success	+710% to weapon proficiency, +81% to the chances of crafting success	36/100
Endurance	63 (60)	Governs stamina and stamina regeneration	1890 stamina, regen 42 points per 30 seconds,	15/100
Intelligence	125	Governs base mana and number of spells able to be learned	1250 mana, spell capacity: 64 (62 + 2 from items)	N/A
Luck	70	Governs overall chance of bonuses	+60% chance of a favorable outcome	54/100
Perception	65 (55)	Governs ranged damage and chance to spot traps or hidden items	+550% ranged damage, +55% chance to spot traps or hidden items	18/100
Strength	65 (62)	Governs damage with melee weapons and carrying capacity	+68 damage with melee weapons, +687% maximum carrying capacity (+25% to melee damage and maximum carrying capacity)	33/100
Wisdom	81 (71)	Governs mana regeneration and memory	Mana regeneration: 12 points per minute, 400% more likely to remember things,	82/100

I nodded in satisfaction. There were still some details I didn't need, but fuck it, that was good enough. Now there was the really important shit to deal with, both my points and my meridians.

I pulled them up first, following Lydia's directions with half an ear as I focused on the screens before me.

PRIMARY

Brain: 1/10 Spell Cost Reduction: 5% (Primary Bonus: 1 spell slot per point)
Head: Primary Node: Additional points invested will reduce mana cost by 5%
(Note: Air Elemental Core results in increased mana regeneration by 50%, self-control decrease of 5%).

SECONDARY

Eyes: 1/10 Vision Improvement (Secondary Bonus: +10% chance to notice important visual details)
Eyes: Important details will glow to your vision. This will level with the relevant skill.

Ears: 0/10 Hearing Improvement
Ears: Important sounds will become clearer with concentration. High levels will aid in translation.

Mouth: 0/10 Vocal Improvement
Mouth: Your voice will become 10% more likely to have a desired effect on a target, soothing, seducing, persuading as required.

Nose: 0/10 Tracking and Detection Improvement
Nose: Scents will be stronger, aiding in tracking.

Heart: 1/10 Health Increase
Heart: You will gain an additional ten points of health for each point invested in your Constitution.

Lungs: 2/10 Stamina Increase
Lungs: You will gain an additional ten points of stamina for each point invested in your Endurance.

Stomach: 0/10 Sustenance Improvement
Stomach: You will gain the abilities to resist poisons by 5% and to gain sustenance from more sources.

Legs: 1/10 Speed Increase
Legs: You will gain a boost of 10% to your speed, as well as better stability over various terrain.
(Note: SporeMother Core results in a gain of 10% to your speed in darkness. Speed in daylight will be decreased by 20%)

Arms: 1/10 Strength Increase
Arms: You will receive a boost of 25% to your carrying capacity and your damage output with melee weapons.

Hands: 1/10 Dexterity Increase
Hands: You will develop crafting abilities at a 10% increased rate, along with a greater chance to succeed in crafting complicated items.

As much as I wanted to make the most of the points as I saw it, and assign a few of the meridian points to new monster cores, or hell, that angelic core that Nerin had, if she'd let me have it…I didn't dare.

Restun had been right with everything so far, and knowing that there was a damn quest that only unlocked when you were high enough, with one of each of the meridians unlocked?

I knew what I had to do.

I had four meridians unaltered and one point, as well as being only two levels from unlocking another, so it was time to focus on it.

My options were limited to stomach, mouth, nose and ears. Stomach, with a corresponding ability to resist poisons slightly, which was practically worthless to me, or survive on more random stuff, again, useful to a ranger I've no doubt, to an Imperial Prince?

Not so much.

Next was mouth, gaining me a ten percent boost to persuasion and seduction and such. Okay, I could see the use there, not so much in seduction, admittedly, as I was sorted on that front, but in persuasion? Yeah, that was clearly of use to someone in my position.

Then came nose and ears. Nose made smells stronger. That sounded like a strength in some people's lives no doubt, but I spent most of my time around the Imperial Legionnaires, and more specifically, Giint and Grizz, who seemed to be caught up in some impromptu chemical weapon experimentation, judging from the smells I was occasionally subjected to.

I decided I'd leave that for later, if not last.

Then ears…okay, making sounds easier to pick up, and higher levels would aid in translation…So far I'd been lucky in that most people spoke common, a variant of English that was a little off, but easily understandable. But as I started to travel more and explore, I was bound to encounter other languages. I'd have to take it soon no doubt.

I paused, considering one last time, then took mouth, quickly warning the others about what I was doing. I approved the change and waited.

It started as a tickle, almost like when I'd eaten too many chilies, or that time I'd had those ghost chilies, and before the real burn had hit. A twitch, and a tingle that started at the back of my tongue, and slowly spread.

It burned and tingled, going both numb and strangely more sensitive as sections of my mouth altered in tiny ways. All the while, the burn spread.

It poured up and down, flowing down the back of my throat, moving to my voice box, even as my lips turned numb, and I had to concentrate not to drool.

I tried swallowing, feeling like I had a lump in my throat, almost like I needed to be sick…and it just got worse, building and building until…finally, it settled, and the feeling slowly returned.

It felt like forever, but according to Grizz, it was only a few minutes, and I straightened again and nodded to Lydia, who barked the order to move out, as I started checking my stats over again.

There was a quantitative change when you reached a hundred in any stat, "achieving the century" as it was sometimes referred to, and it was different for everyone.

When Restun hit it in Endurance, his body had altered to the point that even hours of insanely exhaustive exercise for everyone else barely winded him now

I'd gained the ability Hyper-Cognition when I'd hit a hundred in Intelligence. Matching that to my existing Mana-Overdrive had resulted in a pairing that made me lethal even when facing a goddamn Elder Vampyr, and it'd saved my life.

I looked over the various stats carefully, evaluating my fighting style so far, and the way I lived my damn life. I could get any of them to the century, if I really wanted to, hell, my lowest physical stat these days was one of the most important for the way I fought, Strength!

I'd deliberately not been adding points there because I could increase that by exercising, and it did help. Hell, the harder we worked, the more points I gained, but…

Could I afford to wait any longer? How many months would it take to reach a hundred, when I could do it in a matter of minutes. In the fights to come, I'd need that leverage.

Doing some quick calculations and loving that they were so much easier since dropping those points into Intelligence, I worked out that if I really went all-out, I could drop thirty-five into Strength, to hit that one, leaving me with fourteen points, not enough to hit another century…hmmm.

I could instead drop nineteen into wisdom, leaving me with thirty, and then do either luck at thirty, taking all the points, but maxing me out on two new centuries, or I could do nineteen on dexterity and nineteen into wisdom, leaving me eleven to push, say…agility from sixty-three to seventy-four?

I was focusing more on the centuries I could achieve, rather than the way I fought then though.

I was a spellsword, and a brawler at heart. Yeah my class was sorcerer, but that was for Oracle, not me. What did I need?

Strength, because as a brawler, I was damn well using it heavily all the time. Wisdom, because as a spellsword based build, I damn well used my spells like they were going out of fashion, and tended to try and blast the shit out of any problem I couldn't headbutt into the grave.

Dexterity? That was my sneaky one. If I did that, I'd have a one hundred increase to my chance of a successful creation—should the potion already be viable—in alchemy. It wouldn't make it so that I could make mud and twigs into a healing potion, it was augmenting me, not changing reality, but it would help massively.

That, in turn, would make my potions better, which might save my people further down the line. Also, I was seriously wondering what the hell different abilities I'd get from those centuries.

Alternatively, I could drop forty-nine points into Intelligence.

I already had a stat of one-twenty-five. That would let me hit two hundred when I hit level fifty. I didn't know if the second century was the same, or a new ability, or hell it might tear my body and mind from each other, for all I knew.

But if it worked?

It'd give me a massive boost to my spellcasting, at least.

Amon had a manapool of over *thirty thousand* at the end. I had no clue how much of that was down to class choices, stats, and equipment, but that was his normal, as near as I could remember. On top of that, he was a literal master of mana able to pull it from the realm around him.

I decided I'd ask Restun about the second century, and if it wasn't a good idea, I'd re-evaluate. I always felt wrong putting off my levels, but the way things were right now? I needed to grow up and deal with them, not just shrug, pick whatever I fancied at the time and move on.

I flicked the screens away and picked up the pace, feeling a hell of a lot better about everything now that I had a damn plan.

CHAPTER EIGHT

By the time I made it back to the keep, the sun was high overhead, and the planned early morning meeting with the local nobility was well overdue. I'd considered on the way, if I should dismiss them all, hell, I probably should cancel it, or apologize to them, or one of a thousand different things.

I did none of them, though.

I'd reached out to Oracle as soon as we set off properly, feeling her sitting in a comfortable chair in the sitting room of our quarters, trying to help Selkie, the unstable and traumatized Wisp, and Tirana, the girl that had been raised to rule the city in name alone by Nimon and his priesthood.

I'd told her what I planned, getting a sense of agreement and relief, and she'd agreed to make sure everything else was in place, as well as work on Selkie and Tirana.

Now, as I ducked into a side room she'd arranged for me with Augustus, Cai, Hannibal, and Mal, as well as a pile of fresh clothes, I grinned at the steaming cup of coffee that Mal held out to me.

"Mate, I knew you were a good one," I told him, taking a sip and sighing in enjoyment.

"Of course I am." he agreed, before opening his mouth again, the look on his face one I'd learned to recognize.

I held up a hand, stopping him. "Mal, we both know you've got an angle or a plan to rip me off. Just for once, keep it until later; we've too much to sort today."

"You take all the fun out of my life, you know that?" he grumbled, sitting on a chair as I stripped off, hitting myself over and over with Scour as I did so. The dirt, dried blood, and who knew what else that was smeared across me fell to dust on the floor.

"I know, man. Okay, Augustus, are you ready? Is Hellenica okay with this?" I asked, and he snorted.

"I'll *never* be ready for this, Jax, but if you're asking can I do it? Then yes. I can, and she is ready as well. She's actually excited, as crazy as that seems."

I grinned at him. "I'm sorry to do this to you, mate, but it needs to be done."

"I know."

"Hannibal?" I asked, buttoning my trousers and turning to him in question.

"I'm ready, I've a list of jobs and our needs, not to mention the smugglers' hideouts. I'll make sure they're met, and the target is ready. Once she's had her wings clipped, she should be able to deal with the treasury easily."

"Good man, try not to rip me off too badly, okay?"

"I make no promises," he warned me, winking.

"Cai?" I asked, shaking my head and turning away from the older smuggler as I shrugged into my shirt, fumbling with the buttons.

"I've got the measure of them now. Where more of Narkolt's nobility were powerful and used to making their decisions as the heads of their houses with little oversight, the Dark Church and Barabarattas had purged the majority of the Himnel noble houses of that. They lived in fear of crossing those more powerful than them and took it out on those under them."

"Then they're used to being beaten and robbed by their bosses. Now we just need to scare the shit out of them and show them a better way," I concluded with a slight smile, quickly tucking the shirt in and checking myself over. "Ah, fuck it. Let's not make them think I'm taking them seriously." I pulled my shoes on and headed for the door.

When we emerged into the corridor beyond, it was silent, the waiting Legion escort warning away anyone that came too close to the room I'd been in. I had to smile at the thought of the relief the keep's staff would feel by the time I left.

We set off at a steady march, the thick carpets with red and gold drapes and tapestries on the walls muting the clicks and crunch of steel-shod boots as we closed the distance.

The last two flights of stairs emerged onto the floor that held the throne-room, grumbles and conversations carrying from the distance as we approached.

As soon as the elite guards stationed on either side of the door saw us, the crash of their salutes brought a grim, nervous silence from the room beyond, and I noted that word had spread.

The Prince of the Empire was here at last, and I looked *happy*.

Apparently me being happy was akin to Restun telling jokes, because it was freaking the locals out, judging by the way they raced for cover.

I slowed to a brisk walk outside the main throne room, and glanced around, my people closing in around me as I gave last-minute instructions.

I'd spent most of the journey giving out orders, and everything was just about ready as Thomas gave me a fist bump of support and backed off, allowing me to march into the throne room at the head of the group, alone.

Marching down the long red carpet, I ignored the assembled nobility, the rich, and the merely curious who had managed to wangle an invite to this audience.

I had eyes for Oracle alone.

She sat on the small chaise lounge that she'd had brought in a few days earlier and was flanked by both Lydia, Tenandra and Sehran, with Selkie and Tirana nearby, the last pair glancing around uncomfortably.

Oracle was anything but uncomfortable, sitting with her long legs folded up under her, laid back slightly in the lounger and smiling as Lydia said something quietly to her, the entire room watching my approach.

I diverted to her, leaning down and kissing her gently on the top of the head before winking and looking at her little escort. Between Lydia, Tenandra, and Sehran, I seriously doubted that, had the entire overdressed court decided to draw weapons and attack, it would have taken more than ten seconds to clear them out. Oracle was in utterly no danger, and that was ignoring her own power.

Still, I was damn pleased to note the legionnaires standing nearby, fully armored, as well as a handful of the elite guards who were sworn to me, carefully chosen and dressed as visiting nobles, dotted around the room, just in case.

I took a few steps up onto the dais and turned around, standing at parade rest automatically as I stared out across the sweat-stained finery and sparkling crap before allowing myself a small smile.

I waited, watching them, and after a few seconds, I saw answering, much larger smiles, clearly nervous, break out. Clearly, Oren had been right when we'd spoken about the nobility. *"Iffin yer scare 'em enough, they'll do whatever ye do, copying ye outta sheer terror. They de it wit' Barabarratas all tha time."*

That long-forgotten conversation from perhaps months ago sprang into my mind, and I saw them differently. At the time, hearing about how corrupt and self-serving some of them were, I'd assumed they were all like that. I'd thought that, if they weren't all scumbags, then they'd have overthrown Barabarratas before now, or at least tried to lead by example.

Now I knew better.

The nobility standing nervously sweating before me was the best of the city's current crop. Most of them were weak, all of them were minor nobles, or had been a week ago, or they were the surviving lower members of their noble families, their parents or relatives having proven they were untrustworthy already.

"Thank you all for joining me," I said calmly. "As many of you are aware, I was busy last night, so my apologies for being late in joining you this morning. However, the orchards I have provided on the site of the battles with the Dark Legion should ensure that life is easier for the people over the next few months."

I watched their faces as I spoke. Some quickly hid their disbelief, while others seemed pleased about the sudden change.

"Now, I'm also aware that the city has been on a war footing for the last several months, if not longer, with little thought given to the niceties, such as making sure the population is fed and kept warm throughout the winter. This will be changing, as long-term, I have been assured, it is unsustainable."

"Some of you have been complaining about the Legion commandeering your household troops, others about your properties being 'ransacked by Legion thieves.' Would anyone like to comment on this?" I asked, smiling coldly.

For a long few heartbeats, I thought one of them was going to be stupid enough to take the bait…until his wife stood on his foot and elbowed him in the stomach at the same time, doubling him over with a hiss of pain.

"I'll take it that this was a misunderstanding on your part, then. Let's make a few details clear, as you've all had plenty of time now to get used to the new, or should I say, old laws and the realities of the situation. You are all nobles at my sufferance only. You have all been interviewed by Lucian, my Chief Justicar. Several of you have stepped up to rule your houses after these conversations rendered the previous inhabitant of that role unsuitable, be that because they were called to military service, or the headsman's axe."

I paused, deliberately making eye contact with two of the younger members of the court whose parents had been beheaded immediately following their interviews.

"Now, I think you've all realized that a time of change can be painful for those who live through it, but hopefully you've noticed that it can be profitable as well. Yes, you've lost your magical items. For that, I apologize; those that are not of use to the Empire are being returned, however, while the rest will be taken off your debt." I smiled coldly. "But we'll get to that in a minute."

"Many of you here are survivors of the houses that were personally responsible for both the tax collection and disbursement of those funds and the interesting stories that were spread about the Legion." I turned to look at two of the nobles off to one side: a much older woman sat on a chair that was only slightly smaller than my own throne, and her granddaughter, who'd been making passes at Romanus, apparently at her grandmother's behest.

"Lady Rosemary Cerinbaum, do you have anything you'd like to say about this before I go on?"

"No, Prince, I do not," the older woman declared smugly.

"Excellent, then this is going better than I'd hoped. I'd expected to have to behead you before now," I replied, turning back to the room at large. "Lady Rosemary was exceedingly careful in the ordering and encouragement of the slander of the Legion, making it impossible for us to prove that she was personally responsible for the majority of it. All we could prove was that she had firmly held beliefs, publicly stated, that all legionnaires were thieves and parasites upon society. As such, the acts that others undertook to curry her favor, further slandering and ruining the lives of many good legionnaires, weren't deemed as provable to be her intention. She even managed to phrase things to such a degree that the Chief Justicar himself had to admit defeat."

"I am but an old lady that has made a mistake regarding the Legion in the past, Prince," she called in a wavering voice.

"Yes, well. You also collected the taxes for a third of the city and handed those over, less small fees and your percentage, to the city treasury. Again, we could find no proof of wrongdoing personally, so congratulations, you're exceedingly careful." I said.

She lifted her hands, shaking her head. "Prince, I am but a humble woman…"

"Yeah, no," I disagreed. "Fortunately, the advantage of being the Prince of the Empire means I get to deal with some of these issues personally. So, you say that you have been misunderstood, and that you are now a supporter of the Legion?"

"Most definitely."

"Then congratulations, *Marchioness* Cerinbaum, on moving into the ranks of Imperial nobility." I injected the mana required into the statement and smiled coldly as the notification, one shared with all Imperial citizens in Dravith, popped up. "As you're the first to admit that you were wrong in your previous declarations of the Legion and now intend to support them fully, you get to be the first in the new council of Himnel and will be responsible for ensuring that the people understand the Legion properly."

A predatory smile spread across her face, a more cautious hopefulness on the granddaughter's face as she looked from the older woman to me and back again. She was clearly less willing to believe I'd support their family.

"Your role, considering your familiarity with the tax operations of Himnel, and your desire to make amends to the Legion, will be dealing with all of the tax operations for Himnel. Once again, the Legion will receive the full amount owed, and those funds will be used to outfit them. Do you accept this role?"

"I do!" she declared proudly, her voice no longer wavering as she discarded the 'poor, weak old woman routine.

"Excellent! So, you'll be responsible for dealing with the rest of your fellow nobles and assisting them in making good on their debts. Hannibal has a list, and as the First Lady of the Treasury, he will be both watching over you and instructing you." Hannibal strode up to her, holding out a long list that she took carefully. As soon as he released it, the tightly wound scroll started unraveling and showing line after line after line of owed debts.

Hannibal had pointed her out as both the richest of the surviving nobles and the sneakiest. When Lucian had sworn blind after two hours of interviewing her that she was guilty of being behind a thousand minor crimes, and absolutely none of them could be proven, I knew I had the perfect first civil servant.

"Now, you'll also see the taxes moving forward are most reasonable. In fact, they're half those that Barabarattas enforced." Bright smiles crossed the faces of the merchants and more at that.

"As the taxes are so low, however, there's no need for all those annoying loopholes. Now, everyone will be paying their share, high or low, and Marchioness Cerinbaum will make sure of it. After all, from now on, if you don't pay your taxes, she and her house are personally responsible for paying them for you."

"What?!" Marchioness Cerinbaum half-screamed, almost falling from her chair.

"You're exceedingly skilled at hiding your income, Marchioness, so I suggest you use those skills to make sure of who is earning what. Oh, and as I said before, Hannibal will be watching you." I smiled at her.

"Now, one of the main purposes of those taxes is to support the Legion and the Empire itself, not just to make life nicer for the nobility. As such, the Empire requires that Himnel, like Narkolt, have a voice for the Legion on the council. Fortunately for you all, I have no time to fill this role myself, nor will I be remaining in Himnel. As of tomorrow, the Legion will be returning to the seat of governance for the Continent of Dravith, the Great Tower." I sat back on the throne and looked out at the gaudily dressed butterflies.

"As such, it is time for the Lord of Himnel, Duke Augustus, Heir apparent to the Empire, to take over as the city lord." I gestured to the side, and Augustus stepped forward, fist crashing against his breastplate in salute.

"He will be ruling here in my absence in perpetuity, along with his lady, Hellenica, Clan Mother of the Gueric Clan. She will be granted the Imperial noble title of Duchess and will be assisting the Duke. I recommend you do not annoy either of them." She strode forward to stand by his side, a smile tugging at her lips. The only hint that she wasn't the average noble lady that she appeared to be was the slight blurring of the fabric of her dress at the edges.

"Unlike in Narkolt, where the majority of the more powerful members of the nobility had been replaced with Drow or their sympathizers, here there was an intact council. Instead of the Drow thinning its ranks though, I have done it." I forced a smile as I came to my feet and looked out at the terror-stricken assembled nobles.

"I have eliminated the corrupt, the perverted, and the evil from Himnel's council. Unfortunately, that means that there are now only three people left alive on it. One of them is the Duke, the other his Lady, and now Marchioness Cerinbaum. Those of you who genuinely want to take the chance to apply to be a part of his council, feel free to take it up with him, as make no mistake, it is *his* council. Just be warned, he has nearly as short a temper as I do." There was silence for several seconds as I smiled at them all again, actually starting to enjoy myself a little.

"Now, a few more points to note before I let you all scuttle off and hide. First, the position of leader of the Council of Himnel. That person will receive a place as a member of my Senate as well. Those who wish to take such a role, you have until tonight to explain to Augustus why he should support you in that, and he and I will discuss it, when I damn well have time.

"Now, as promised, we come to the point of debts owed. Unfortunately, as Himnel's nobility dispensed with the Imperial Oaths of Allegiance several generations ago, only the city is responsible for the owed back taxes, so I'd imagine that's a great relief to you all." I waited as the room echoed with subdued sighs, and the majority of the crowd sagged in relief.

"As such, I have depleted the city treasury, and it will need to be refilled. Fortunately, there's an easy way to do this. The Legion is owed ten percent of all taxes collected in the city, is it not, Cai?" I called out, and Cai, once a slave sold in this city, destined to be fed to the SporeMother, stepped forward and smiled toothily at me.

"It is, my Prince."

"How many of the nobles have paid their taxes?"

"In full?" he asked, knowing what I wanted and waiting for my slow nod. "None of them."

"How many have claimed that tax from the people and therefore owe it?"

"All of those here."

"Excellent. You all have until the end of the day to pay your back taxes, or you will be in default and your possessions claimed. Should you be unable to pay, for some genuine reason, then perhaps Marchioness Cerinbaum will be willing to grant a small amount of time to you or permit you to pay the debt in another way,"

I suggested, looking over at her and seeing the naked terror glinting in her eyes as the entire nobility of Himnel blatantly marked her as their only hope. While she visibly tried to speak, nothing coming out, as she realized that unless she managed to get them to pay their debts, she'd be bankrupt instead.

"I'd suggest those of you who cannot pay, put together a proposal for her. In fact, she's going to be very busy with this, and as such, won't be available to carry on with the rest of the council business today, so instead..." I looked to the back of the room, getting a nod from Hannibal to show that he was ready.

"Those who are concerned that the situation is not fair, or that Marchioness Cerinbaum isn't carrying out her obligations correctly, may speak to Hannibal at the back of the room. He is the Imperial tax collector, after all, so he's the one who will be ordering the manacles and chains and so on." I had absolutely no intention of ever permitting slavery, but a night or two in a cell while they thought about ways they could help the Empire? Hell, yes.

"Moving on!" I barked, and the few who had started to drift toward Marchioness Cerinbaum or toward Hannibal froze, staring at me like a deer in the headlights.

"Himnel now has a great surplus of fruit, after I raised a new orchard for it. As such, I believe most of the most basic food issues have been addressed. That means Himnel is ready to move forward. When the twin cities were first created, they were set up as they are by the Empire for a *reason*.

"Narkolt was to be the shipping and distribution center for Dravith, and Himnel was to be the production and supply center, with the Great Tower as twinned defense and research. We will be returning to this state of affairs quickly! Himnel is a forge-city with hundreds of factories producing everything from cloth to keels for the airships and cannons for their decks. Production was ramped up for the war effort, but it was done *poorly*. Corruption, theft, and slavery produced a massive difference in the possible output of the forge-city. Augustus' main responsibility will be to get Himnel up and running as it was of old."

"As it was of old, so shall it be!" The legionnaires all boomed automatically, scaring the locals half to death.

"Most of you here are now panicking, thinking that you're about to lose everything. This may be far from the case, after all, those who ran the forges originally, who built for the Empire, were amongst its richest before the cataclysm. So do think on what you can bring to the table. Quite frankly, I'd be overjoyed to have more honest people join the higher ranks of the Empire, should you prove yourself."

I twisted my lips into a facsimile of a smile.

"One final point. Many of you here were involved in the smears against the Legion, personally or through your families. You *knew* these were lies. You knew it, and you did it anyway, in the pursuit of personal power. That ends now.

"The Legion not only fought and bled for you, protecting you day-in and day-out from the monsters we all know are out there, but they did it despite your actions. Lord Arent of House Bannte was found to have been both the person behind the law that the Legion had to declare the route they'd be taking when they left the city and admitted under oath that he was selling both the details for the route and the locations of isolated homesteads to slavers. He was personally responsible for the deaths, most likely, and possibly for the enslavement of Imperial Legionnaires. He did not act alone." I scanned the now-quaking people before me.

"As of today, you will all become determined supporters of the Legion. Where the shitbiscuit Barabarattas encouraged you to slander and revile the Legion, lest you fall out of his good graces, I warn you only once. Attack a legionnaire, be that physically or verbally, and you attack the Empire directly. Attack the Empire, and you attack *me*. Attack me, and I will *personally* gut you, disband your family, strip your treasuries, and salt the earth you once owned. *Do not fucking try me*."

Silence fell across the room, and I forced myself to calm, well aware of the twinning process of mine and Oracle's anger.

"Those of you who are here as nobles may leave. Merchants, step forward, as Cai and Hannibal have information for you," I said, almost causing a stampede as Marchioness Cerinbaum and her granddaughter tried to race for the doors. The rest of the nobility, seeing their best chance at surviving as nobles, or at all, gave panicked chase.

The room was empty in under a minute. Cai and Hannibal spoke to the merchant princes and greater craftsmen who had been able to get an invite. I had to smile as I guessed that the practice of people desperately trying to get into these meetings was going to be dropping a hell of a lot after this morning.

"Are you two ready?" I asked Augustus and Hellenica as Cai and Hannibal went on.

"Gods, no," Augustus muttered with feeling, quirking a smile as Hellenica smacked the back of one hand against his side. A soft *ding* as she rubbed her knuckles was the only sign she'd hit him as he smiled down at her.

"We're more than ready, Prince Jax," Hellenica assured me formally. "And thank you for the title, it…it means a lot."

"You're welcome," I said, smiling at her. "I'm sorry, both of you, for dumping the city on your shoulders, gods know it's going to be a hell of a lot of work. But you can do it, I've faith in you. Now that the local area is sorted out, and the only wars we have are with the others who want the throne? Well, it should be a while before anyone can get to us here!"

"I hope so, but…" Augustus started, only for Cai to turn and gesture to me as Baant stomped into the room.

"Shit, hold that thought, mate, I'd totally forgotten I was supposed to be at the gnome's place hours ago."

"It's fine, Jax. I'll deal with these people, no time like the present to start being the lord, I suppose." Augustus and I exchanged a smile, even as Hellenica was already moving, smoothly stepping up to distract Tirana and Selkie as Oracle and the others joined me.

We moved through the group, accepting the nods and bowing, until we reached Baant.

"Prince Jax, you wish to tour the gnomish facility?" she asked, smoothing her expression, and I nodded. "Good. But you alone; we don't permit outsiders into the…"

"Of course." I agreed, cutting her off. "But obviously, Oracle goes with me. She's my bonded partner, after all."

"Well, okay, but…"

"And Tenandra is both my transport and my advisor on technology, as well as being intimately acquainted with gnomes. She's also a Wisp who controlled a flying city, so I'd imagine you'd like her with us to answer any questions you have about Imperial technology from before the fall?"

"Oh, well, yes…"

"And Lydia is my Valkyrie and leader of my personal squad, so unless you want the entire squad to come with us, to ensure my safety, I'd imagine you'd be happy if it was just her?"

"Well, well, yes, okay but…"

"And Sehran, because I damn well said she'd be welcome. I doubt you want to make a liar out of me," I finished, looking at Baant with one eyebrow raised.

"No…no, that's fine." She sighed, closing her eyes and gesturing over her shoulder toward the door. "But just them…not that Giint…mad bastard."

"Oh no, I'd not expect you to let Giint come along!" I said, pretending to be horrified as she led us out of the room.

"That's all right, then."

"I mean, he's the Champion of Svetu, your patron God. But don't worry, when I speak to Him, I'll make sure He knows why His Champion, and by extension He Himself isn't welcome amongst your people," I went on, starting to enjoy myself. The extra ten-point boost in Charisma had clearly come with a faster damn tongue, and it was flustering Baant no end.

"When you speak to Giint…"

"No, when I speak to *Svetu*, I have to have a meeting with Him about the production facility and the new designs. After all, He needs me to recommend some more people to go and work with Him personally."

"*OH?*"

"Yeah, I've not got the time, unfortunately, so I've asked Giint to sort it out," I finished nonchalantly, making Baant go almost tomato-red in color through sheer apoplexy.

"BUT…BUT…"

"But he has my absolute trust as a member of my team."

"He can come," she growled at me, then sped up, stomping along, clearly wanting to be free of the palace before I added anyone else. I couldn't help myself.

"He's busy at the moment, I think, something to do with a divine object Svetu gave him." I thought that was what the little cube he was always playing with was, anyway. "But I'll let him know he's welcome in the facility any time he wants." The slump of her shoulders as well as her silence was enough, and I stopped at that point.

"*What's going on? Why are you picking on her?*" Oracle sent to me. I grinned, taking her hand in mine as she reached out.

"*She'd refused Giint access to the little cluster of buildings the gnomes are all holed up in apparently, the guards turned him away, but they let the others in. Not sure why, but I wasn't having him excluded.*"

"*It's because she likes him.*"

"*Shit, no. She hates him!*"

"*For gnomes it's much the same thing. Ask Sehran. Oh, and both she and Tenandra will need to siphon some of your mana, if we're going far.*"

"*Why?*"

"*Why the mana?*"

"*No, no that's fine, and yeah, they can siphon some, I mean why does Sehran know about that?*"

"*I'll let them know then, and she told me about it. Apparently, she was summoned by a gnome warlock a dozen decades back. Said that gnomes are even crazier than we think, but they make a real effort to calm it down around us. Oh! And I quote, 'they're freaks in bed'.*"

"*I don't know if I want to know what kind of shit they're into when an actual sex demon calls them freaky.*"

"*You'll never look at them the same again now, will you?*"

I shook my head, watching Baant's back as she led us quickly though the keep and out to the main parade and courtyard. A small, for us, coach waited, harnessed to a Fenris clockwork horse.

I stared down at the beautiful machine, feeling the wonder I'd experienced the first time I saw one all over again. Well, the second time; admittedly the first time the bastard had been trying to kill me.

"Holy shit, I'd forgotten about him," I muttered, stepping forward to look at the utterly still machine.

I saw after a second that it wasn't mine, the bronze rings around the eyes and the various moving sections were an electric blue on this version. The body was slightly smaller and wider, but overall? It was blatantly the same creation.

I opened my mouth to ask Baant about it, but she was already inside, making me shrug and follow after.

CHAPTER NINE

"So, the Fenris that's pulling the coach," I said, even as I reached out and in with my mana channels, feeling both Tenandra and Sehran accept the gift thankfully.

She shot me a hard glance. "Not for sale."

"You've not heard my offer."

"Don't need to. There's three years' work invested in making one, not making another." Baant grunted.

"What about the rest of your people?" I asked. "Is it a personal creation? Might someone else make some?"

"Some? Three years it takes to make one right, how many do you want?"

"A hundred."

"Three hundred years' work!"

I shook my head. "Is it three years for you to make it alone, three years for a team, or what?"

"Depends."

"Depends on what?"

"What we're making."

"The horse."

"What horse."

"The fucking Fenris! Are you deliberately trying to wind me up?" I asked, getting the ghost of a smile before it vanished. "You are!"

"You made me say Giint could come in." She shrugged.

I looked askance at her. "He's a gnome; you're a gnomish community."

"Still our homes."

"You let the others in!"

"They're not him."

"No, he's your…you know what? Fine. Giint can enter the compound, and beyond that, I don't give a shit; it's his problem. So, the Fenris." I gave up, waving the little bastard aside and moving on.

"What do you need a hundred for?" she asked.

"Cavalry. A hundred cavalry that don't get tired and can run straight through spears and so on? Fuck, yes."

"They need manastones."

"I've got manastones."

"Three years to make one…alone," she admitted grudgingly.

"Have you got any on order? Or being built?"

"Some. Most already paid for."

"Who paid for them?"

"Nobles," she said, looking out of the window, clearly not wanting to talk in the carriage.

"I'll let Hannibal know," Tenandra offered, joining the conversation for the first time. "He can compare the list of assets to the list of debtors."

"Thank you." I smiled at her, before settling back and giving Baant the space she clearly wanted. "How's the refit going?"

"It's going well. The lower decks are solid now, and the upper structure is close to being sealed. The reinforcement is solid, and the cabins are being redone. The new cannons are tied into my structure, and the engines are being replaced and upgraded. Overall, despite the pain of the original damage and the replacement, I'm proud of the changes."

"Glad to hear it."

"Not as glad as I am!" Sehran interjected. "Our new cabin is much, much bigger, and she put in a swing for…"

"And that's enough, dear," Tenandra said, taking Sehran's hand in hers and giving it a gentle squeeze. "Prince Jax doesn't need the details."

My mind had already gone off the rails at the thought of what was clearly a sex-swing, knowing Sehran, and the mental images it was conjuring, added to by Oracle suggesting that we have one fitted in our cabin as well, meant I totally missed Baant muttering something about arriving.

"Jax!" Lydia grunted after a few seconds, elbowing me. I jumped, shaking myself and looking around, groaning as I realized that not only had I totally missed that the coach had stopped and that everyone had been waiting for me to get out. I'd been lost in thought about the sex swing, and Oracle's mental images she'd been sending me, while staring absently at Sehran's fantastic cleavage.

All of those minor details combined meant I could currently pole vault out of the damn coach.

"Later," Oracle sent me, along with a mental image of her in a succubus shape that was similar to Sehran's, and a hint of a question, asking if I wanted her to change to that form for some fun.

My mind stuttered to a halt again, as I climbed down the steps and forced myself to look around the compound to distract myself. I saw the main gates we'd entered by shutting slowly on pistons, looking smooth and marvelously well-crafted…until one of them gave an almighty clatter and fell off the track it'd been following.

Within thirty seconds, the courtyard was filled with half a dozen gnomes, some locals and others clearly from the Prax, all arguing over whose fault it was and possible upgrades.

As near as I could tell, from the rapid-fire burst of swearing, shouting, and cheers, apparently they were over the bloody moon that it'd broken, as it meant they got to improve on it. Crazy little bastards.

Baant was already stomping up the stairs to one of the buildings that surrounded the courtyard, and I couldn't help myself. I winked at Lydia, pulled a handful of the little sticks of the gnomish wonderdrug out, and tossed them into the middle of the argument before hurrying after Baant as if nothing had happened.

There was a sudden pause in the raised voices, then a scramble as the Prax gnomes dove on each other, fighting for the sticks, and the local gnomes hesitated.

Then they piled in as well, and I got a shoulder-bump from Lydia as we all followed Baant, the pair of us trying to stifle giggles like schoolkids.

Once the door closed behind us, though, all the random shit vanished from our minds.

The building that Baant had brought us into was a combination office, barracks, and factory floor, with showers of sparks flying off some kind of lathe in one corner, a half-built leg of something that made the Fenris look like a child's toy dangling from a harness, and an engine for a ship being tested in the middle of the room, while on the left?

There were a series of bunkbeds, five of them stacked one atop the other, several with snoring gnomes in them. The nearest one had his, or her, goggles down, and the flaps on either side of their bloody stupid looking hat folded down over their ears…

I glanced to the side, eyeing the pair that Baant had on, even as she muttered and grumbled, pulling levers on what was either a steampunk coffee machine or possibly a weapon of mass destruction. Knowing gnomes, it may well be both.

I suddenly realized I'd never seen Giint actually have his goggles down. They were always atop his head, and it all clicked into place. The scruffy cap was strangely solid on either side, with what looked like a soft inside and a pair of goggles that had half a dozen different lenses on them, all flicked down when it was on the top of their heads.

The damn multiple lenses were so they could block the world out and sleep in places like this! Flick a black one in, and it was dark enough to sleep. Flick a clear glass one down instead, and the air wouldn't blind you when you went fast, green, and you'd see better in the dark.

Shit, it was brilliant.

These were simple, low-tech ideas that were so effective that they were everywhere for the gnomes, but I'd never noticed. And to most people? They were so crazed at the best of times that it was just ignored as another weird thing gnomes did.

I opened my mouth to ask Baant about it, only to have a mug of coffee shoved at me and got another surprise.

Baant's own mug wasn't as I'd been half-expecting, basically an espresso-sized tiny thing, considering her size. Instead, it was a proper, full-on mug that you'd expect to be the large size in any coffee shop.

The one she'd passed to me was clearly well used and assumably kept for the bigger guards I'd seen outside when we'd first passed the compound months ago…as it was fucking *huge*.

I stared at the pitch-black, bubbling liquid in trepidation, wondering if I was supposed to drink it or set it down and swim in it! The damn mug was as wide as a soup bowl and deeper than most tankards, as well as holding at least six regular cups' worth inside it.

I shrugged and took a sip, eyes widening as I tasted it. It was good coffee, well, I thought it was, at least, but the damn thing had to be at least half straight honey!

It was like drinking hot coffee-flavored treacle.

"Nice," Sehran muttered, licking her lips before swiping the mug Oracle set down with a shudder, alternating sips from one and then the other.

"It's…strong," Lydia whispered, setting hers down. Tenandra simply smiled and declined it, explaining that, as a wisp, she didn't need it.

I moved to cut off the inevitable questions that I knew were coming as Baant frowned, looking from Tenandra to Oracle and back again.

"So! You wanted to speak to me about something?" I asked. She paused, before nodding slowly.

"How did you know?"

"You came to my private council meetings and joined in as if you were expected," I replied dryly. "You weren't, but because your people are generally unfriendly at the very least, and considering how minor the meetings were, I allowed it. Also, you passed out in about a minute, so it didn't matter."

"It was boring," she defended herself.

"Fucking right it was," I agreed wholeheartedly. "So what's the issue, and what are you offering?"

"We need help," she said after a few seconds.

"Clearly, or you'd not have asked me to come." I took a seat on a chair that felt like it was from a child's play set and set my bowl of coffee on the table. "What do you need help with?"

"Breeding."

"Aaaaand that's not really my skillset. Sehran?" I suggested, pointing to the succubus, who grinned maniacally over the top of the big coffee cup.

"No," Baant said. "We don't need help…ah!" She grabbed at her head and rubbed the heels of her hands into her temples growling to herself, before opening her eyes again. "Look, we don't need help with the physical act of breeding…we're not the drow! We need help with the number of partners!"

"You're asking me to arrange a gangbang? Not really my skillset again, Sehran maybe…" I asked, totally lost.

"Ah…I think she means that there's an issue with the number of gnomes able to breed. Essentially, their group has fallen below a sustainable level," Tenandra suggested delicately.

"Oh…OH!" I agreed, nodding my head as I realized what she meant. "Right, yeah okay, well, I'm sure we can arrange a trip to the gnome villages to the south. I mean, we were considering visiting anyway…" Before I could finish, Baant shook her head.

"No good," she said. "That's why we were sent to the cities. We bred and left our children behind to be raised by our families, while we searched for more gnomes to take back with us."

"So, shit, you're saying you need to find more gnomes, or you'll die out?" I asked, getting a firm nod. I winced, thinking about how many dozens, hell, maybe hundreds of gnomes I'd killed in the Prax.

Yes, they were batshit crazy, but…

"If we do this," Tenandra said, "What could you do for us?"

"What do you want?" Baant asked. "You want the Fenris? A hundred?" She shrugged. "With enough gnomes, we can make them, but it will still take many years."

"What about armor?" I asked.

"Armored Fenris? Seems pointless, and it'd take longer, but…"

"No," I said. "I have a team of legion armorers working to develop the next generation of legion armor and weapons. They're using my own Fenris to get ideas, or they were. If we find you more gnomes, could you help them?"

"How many gnomes?" she asked quickly.

"No idea," I answered. "There were a handful that stayed aboard the Prax, deep down, but there were SporeMothers aboard when we left."

"There were at least a hundred," Oracle said, stepping up and resting one hand on my shoulder. "They were feral, much worse than Giint and the others. They refused our help, ran from us, or attacked us, but we might be able to heal some of them, if the SporeMothers haven't reached them yet."

"A hundred," Baant whispered, shaking her head. "Most villages are less than that. If you should find a hundred? That would help our people more than you know."

"Seriously, Baant, they're feral as all hell, crazy. Fuck's sake, I'm sorry, I really don't want to smash your hopes on this, but we're talking about a group of people that were so far gone they were *feeding* on each other. I literally fought and killed dozens in hand-to-hand, and they wouldn't stop coming."

She stared at me with tears in her eyes. "You might have killed my species."

"Fuck's sake." I muttered, unthinkingly taking a long swig of the coffee and nearly sending my heart into overdrive through the sugar and caffeine rush combined. "Gods, that's strong! Okay, look, I'm willing to try, we've already sent a ship." I paused, turning to Oracle, but before I could speak, Lydia answered the unspoken question.

"It were sent yesterday afternoon, should be on site anytime later today, Oren an' Romanus sent a fast cruiser, orders to get there quick and check tha situation out, with a half dozen war golems aboard."

"That's a relief then. Tenandra, how long 'til you're ready to fly?" I asked.

She smiled gently. "I'm always ready to fly, Jax, but I'll admit, things might be a little uncomfortable for most of my passengers for perhaps two days? That will give me sufficient time to seal the upper floors from the wind and weather."

"Okay, if–and I do mean bloody *IF* we do this, considering that it's the Prax, and most of the systems there, if we can reawaken them, will need either me or Augustus to go personally–" I paused, rubbing my chin in thought. "Yeah we literally just handed control of the city over to Augustus an hour ago. He can't go, so you're asking the Prince of the Empire to go do a dungeon dive for you, Baant. You need to understand this isn't a little request." I waited for her to acknowledge it.

I'd already decided I was going. The need for the golems, the constant little attempts by Hannibal, Mal, Tenandra, Cai…hell everyone knew it was a good idea. It just kept climbing up my priority list slowly that was all, until this request, and the thought of the gnomes joining us tipped the balance.

Hell, to escape all the shitty organizing and get to kill something? I'd drag my balls over broken glass to avoid a day like yesterday. No, this was about making sure the gnomes were tied to the Empire, and I was getting wholehearted support from them from here on out.

"You want us to join the Empire," she said. "We will argue in favor of joining the Empire, and your actions will speak to this, but it is a matter for the council to decide, not for me."

"You've got a council here?" I asked.

She shook her head. "The Council of Gnomes is a proud and ancient tradition; all gnomes must speak before it to make this decision."

"Even Giint?"

"Well, no. He's…he isn't a member of our villages," she replied, flustered.

"He's a Gnome."

"He needs to be a resident of one of the enclaves or of the villages, and in good standing."

"He's literally the Champion of your patron God."

"Do you want him to argue your case before the council?" she asked, changing tack.

I snorted, shaking my head. "Fuck, no, the little bastard's crazy."

"Then stop arguing for him to be allowed in, and I'll do it instead," she said sweetly.

"Okay, fine. But you and your enclave, you all help the Empire from now on, right? You help the armorers and…"

Your Quest Fix the Fixers II has been updated by the Goddess Jenae

The Goddess Jenae has commanded you to search the depths of the Prax, Glorious Retribution. There are surviving gnomes and other species still aboard that may be convinced to aid you, as well as storehouses of mundane materials for repair and refitting. Lastly, there are golems, sorely needed by the resurgent Empire and its people.

However, there are also enemies, both new and old, that roam the forgotten corners of the Prax; tread carefully!

Recover the golems: 0/306

Recover mundane materials: 0/?

Recruit additional citizens: 0/274

Reward: Improved technological capacity in the Great Tower, Possible technological boosts to the Fleet/Legion, Gnomish support, 500,000xp

"That's more like it!" I muttered, before lifting my head and speaking as I stared at the ceiling. "Thanks, Jenae!"

The flames in the various hearths around the room flared in response, then just as quickly died away.

"Okay, we've got a quest, people," I informed the others, before turning back to Baant. "You're going to help the Empire if we do this, right?"

"Of course."

"Then you get to start now. Put together a list of all the commissions you have ongoing at the minute and who they're for. If the owner is in debt to the Empire, then we can transfer that order over to us if it's something we can use. If it's not, then we'll give you a project to work on instead."

"We can do this, but if the original owner refuses, then this is for you to sort out. We are too few to be caught between the Empire and the nobility," she said, one hand unwrapping and rewrapping a small nugget of something that I just knew was going to wipe her out.

"Fine," I agreed. "Okay, I'll get Hannibal and Romanus to factor you into the plans." I paused, then grinned. "You came here to get help, basically, is that right?"

"Yes, also to make new things or improve our designs. But yes, mainly it was to get help," she said.

"But you didn't tell the locals?"

"They would have taken advantage of us. They already charged extra when we bought our people back from the slave markets."

"You didn't think we'd take advantage of you?" I asked slowly.

"No, we know you will. But the difference is that you're taking advantage of everyone equally, hammering them into the slots you have chosen for them. You seek to rebuild an Empire; we can be valuable allies and possibly more. Before we would have ended up at best as servants, at worse as slaves to the local nobility. Instead, we have the chance to be valued partners."

"And you've no choice," Sehran cut in with a winning smile. "The only way you can get the gnomes off the Prax is if Prince Jax helps you. Otherwise, you'll have to fight SporeMothers and who knows what else."

"And we've no choice," Baant admitted slowly.

"Okay, well, are you determined to stay here?" I asked, gesturing around in the Enclave.

"It is safe."

"The Great Tower is patrolled by war golems, and the Legion will be moving back there tomorrow, it's going to become the center for all training for our forces and the government of the continent. We'll be building new larger forges and more."

"Larger forges?" She perked up immediately. "The forges…we would have our own workshops? And the golems, perhaps you have…"

"There's crafter golems, war, construction, and servitor, as well as mining ones and the facilities to make more, including specialist designs." I offered. "I'll do you a deal: you relocate to there, take as many of the gnomes as are willing to go with you, beyond Giint, *obviously*, and you work with the armorers. Teach them to do…what you do."

"Are they gnomes?"

"No, they're all sorts of races."

"We can work with them, but we cannot teach them to be gnomes."

"You know what? That's fine, whatever; work with Thornapple, she's the Legion Chief Armorer, and she'll sort you out," I said, taking another sip of the insane coffee. It was sweet as treacle and so black it looked like the inside of a politician's soul, but damn, it grew on you.

"Fine," Baant agreed, smiling. "But, you have to save any gnomes you can from slavery."

"Deal," I agreed unthinkingly, as a new Quest notification popped up, which I accepted and dismissed just as quickly.

You have received a new Quest: Free my people.

The leader of the gnomes of Himnel, Baant T'Ashar, has offered you a quest to save her people. Long have the Gnomes been hunted and taken by slavers, desperate for their skills, so long in fact, that the Gnomes are now at risk of dying out as a species on the Continent of Dravith.

Find her people, free them from their unjust captivity, and Baant will join you, arguing for the gnomish villages to declare their loyalty as well.

Recover the Gnomish slaves: 0/714

Punish the slavers: 0/126

Claim the villages: 0/4

Claim the Gnomish enclaves: 0/3

Reward: Improved technological capacity in the Great Tower, Possible technological boosts to the Fleet/Legion, Gnomish support, 100,000xp

I blinked as the notification vanished, then swore and pulled it back up, seeing the massive numbers of Gnomes on it, suddenly realizing that I might have been had.

"Hobb holds many of my people, as do the remaining slave markets," Baant said, grimacing.

"For fuck's sake…"

"You wanted to see the workshop?" she asked quickly, gesturing at the half-finished constructions further down the building. "Perhaps you'd like to see them before you go, to see what we can bring to the Empire?"

I pivoted unthinkingly to look toward the hanging parts. I tried to think how to rephrase things to make it clear that Baant fucking owed us for this.

I noticed suddenly that she hadn't moved and turned my head to ask a question…only to see Baant sigh in relief then throw a gleaming black nugget of something into her mouth and chew ferociously.

"Wait!" I reached out, even her eyes glazed over.

It literally took seconds for her to slump back in the chair from the position of straight-backed, sensible leader to stoned-to-buggery Gnome.

"Yeah, I think she's gone," Oracle said, peeling back one of the now-drooling gnome's eyelids.

"How the hell did she wipe herself out that fast?" I growled, moving in close to Baant as Sehran and Tenandra started talking about harnesses, fingering the leather hanging on display, and Lydia sighed shaking her head at the little sod.

"Come on, you buggers." I sighed after a minute, giving up and shaking my head. I led them back out to the carriage…only to find that it was gone, the gates were sealed, and thanks to my chucking those sticks into the pile of gnomes earlier, there was nobody around that could still speak, beyond a guard on his break in the guardhouse.

He apologized, explaining that this was what always happened when they let someone in, and he let us out, sliding the bolts shut behind us as we stood in the street less than a minute later.

"Now what?" Lydia asked. I sighed, turning around and looking to the north.

"Now we walk back to the keep," I said. "Bane, you here?"

"He's on a break." Tang's voice came to me a few seconds later.

"So, he missed the gnomes' enclave?"

"Yeah, he was looking forward to that one. I managed to convince him to step out for an hour for shits and giggles so he'd miss it," Tang said happily.

"Okay then, everyone, remember it was utterly magical and the coolest thing any of us have ever seen!" I ordered the others, getting a low laugh before a carriage blasted past, splashing us all with mud.

"What the hell?" I growled, staring after the fleeing carriage. Its rider was barely hanging onto the roof, blood flowing from a bolt that was sticking out of his side. Then an explosion rang out from the direction he'd come, and the street devolved into chaos.

CHAPTER TEN

I spun around, as did the others, staring in the direction of the sounds and the slowly rising cloud of smoke, before cursing and sprinting in that direction.

I didn't know what was happening, but I was hardly dressed for a fight, considering the smart clothes I wore.

Yeah, I could summon my dragonscale armor, but that required a shitload of mana to keep active. Also, if I summoned it, the goddamned thing came out of my skin and shredded my clothes, so as soon as I ran out of mana, I'd be naked as well as reeling from a mana migraine.

I shook my head as the crowds grew thicker, the street packed with panicked, fleeing people. People ahead sprinted in panic in our direction. We were buffeted from side to side, until I growled, seeing Oracle twist in midair to avoid a panicked imp.

"Tang, get Tenandra to her ship, and bring the Legion!" I barked at him, before launching myself into the air, Lydia and Sehran following, even as Oracle zipped alongside me.

Tang swore, and Tenandra latched onto him, growing tiny as he leaped up, grabbing onto the edge of the house and pulling himself up to run across the roofs toward the keep.

The steady dip in my mana and health from Soaring Majesty wore on me, but as always, it felt amazing as well. I rose from the crowded streets, heading for the open sky, twisting around a vaguely familiar tower ahead. Then we picked up speed, glancing to either side and seeing Lydia and Sehran on my left and right, with Oracle landing on my back and holding on tight.

"Are you okay?" I asked.

She sent me a distracted sense of comfort. *"I am, but I don't like changing my size unless I need to, not now that the baby is growing, and the changes. Jax, we really need to talk."*

"Are you okay?" I repeated, worried.

"Yes, just…look, we'll talk about this when we get back, okay? There might be a better way to do this."

"Okay, look…" I sent, when Sehran screamed and twisted in mid-air, just as a dozen black blurs flashed past me at insane speeds.

I ducked instinctively, dipping behind a raised gargoyle and slamming my feet on the roof, skidding. With my ability, I shoved in the opposite direction, almost launching myself backward. I grabbed onto the gargoyle, twisted, and landed, checking Oracle.

She was all right, and the darts hadn't hit me, either, but…

Over to the side, the next building along, lay the pile of groaning, torn flesh that was Sehran. She'd spun to the left and had been hit a handful of times by whatever it was. Then, she'd impacted the roof of the building, her wings snapping in a series of pops and grinding cracks.

Now, she was laid at the end of a long smear of blood, gasping, and…and riddled with long black darts.

"That fucking assassin!" I snarled, glaring around, even as my fingers flickered into the forms required for Complex Healing. Tang was taking Tenandra to her ship-body, and despite her being only half assembled, she'd be here as fast as it was possible to go. But for now, it was just us.

I desperately searched until a flash of white got my attention. Lydia was ducking and diving, her great wings beating the air hard as more and more darts flashed after her.

"Oracle, keep hidden and help Sehran!"

I got a sense of *"of bloody course I will"* through the bond, then I released my spell a half second after hers. Sehran whimpered in pain as fractured bones and torn flesh shifted around to their proper places.

In the direction of the fire, I saw nothing. There were just too many buildings, too many places that the assassins could be. Judging from the barrage of darts, it had to be an Ability. Nobody could fire that fast and accurately, not with the local shoddy crossbows and…

There!

I'd seen it for a split second, a wave of distortion as a dozen darts flashed through the air, chasing Lydia. The building they'd come from was ancient, some old tower that'd been pointed out to me when we first took the city as the…

"Oh, shit!" I hissed, my stomach dropping. I threw myself over the side of the building, even as darts slammed into the roof tiles and wood around me.

I deliberately ducked as low as possible, pulling up and flashing along a street barely six feet above the ground, taking a left then a right. Chimneys and more shattered overhead, darts flashing past and hammering into the buildings on either side of me.

I took the next intersection at horrific speeds, digging deeper into my mana and health both. The doors and windows blurred as I dashed past them, the screams of the dying and injured rising into the air. I left the line of sight of the tower…and the fire stopped.

It had to be there, and that was terrible news.

The Tower of Himnel, once the Wizard's Tower, long since abandoned, and even slated for destruction by dozens of city lords over the years, was empty and had been for centuries. The lower floors were too small for the luxurious apartments skilled mages could demand, and the upper, well, they were sort of occupied already.

The top three floors of the tower looked out over the middle of the Merchants' Quarter, prime real estate. Yet, they were empty, because no matter what the inhabitants tried, the tower wouldn't permit changes of any kind.

The tables had fallen apart, the chairs were riddled with rot and worse, but the tower itself refused to let them be replaced. New tables and chairs would be crushed or dragged across the floor and hurled from the windows by unseen hands.

Screams and vicious blows would rain down on anyone who tried to remove the original furniture, despite it being utterly ruined. It was tied into its own private mana collector, so damage done to the Tower was replaced and repaired overnight.

It had been fought over for centuries after the Cataclysm, until eventually it was given up on and eventually ignored. The third floor from the top was a barracks that could house no soldiers, and the top floor a luxurious apartment that contained no luxuries, as rotten and spoiled as it was.

The placement, and the luxuries weren't the problem though…

I damn well hoped I was wrong about it, as I flew out into a deserted crossroads, only to have the first dart hit me a second later.

It was a lucky shot, considering how I was jinking from side to side, lifting and diving, but still, it punched into the back of my right leg, sinking into the muscle and tearing a wide hole, even as I rolled to the left, lining up on the tower. It seemed utterly undisturbed, apart from the bodies strewn around the base.

I felt it now that I was closer, a dragging of mana that seemed to twist the air. Shoving hard in the opposite direction, I dove to the right and spiraled into the upper floor window of a merchant's shop in an explosion of glass and wooden window reinforcements.

I hit the deck inside and rolled, swearing as the dart caught on the floor, gouging a thin line into the wood. It caught on something and made me hiss in pain as my leg jerked to a halt. My weight and the inertia of the roll tore it free in a spray of blood.

I swore, but rolled again, deliberately getting clear of the front windows before casting Complex Healing on my leg, then blowing out a long breath as the pain built then subsided, the spell causing the surrounding flesh to bubble back up and reknit together.

I checked my status, seeing I was down to a third of my mana and two-thirds health now, and popped a mana potion, one of a stash I'd swiped from the keep when we'd been checking it out shortly after the battle ended.

I didn't have many, but that didn't matter. More of a problem at this point was the fact I had fuck-all armor and backup.

"What's happening?" I sent to Oracle.

"I've stabilized Sehran, but she's furious, and apparently so is Jian, according to Tenandra. Sehran is hiding, ready to distract on your order, and Tenandra has been in touch to say she's closing on her ship-body. The engines are going through their warm-ups, and she'll be aloft in another eight to ten minutes."

"And Lydia?"

"Very, very angry," Oracle warned me, sending me a mental image of Lydia flashing around and around, dozens of darts flashing past her, but little in the way of injuries. *"She keeps getting hit by some spell that's confusing the hell out of her. Every time she closes on the tower, they hit her, and she loses all track of what she's doing. Then a dart hits, and the pain wakes her up again. I heal her, and she races for the tower, and it starts all over again."*

"Get her and Sehran ready. I'm a few buildings away from it, and I'm going in."

"Have you got your armor on?"

"Not yet. if I summon it too early, we're fucked. I can only power it for about a minute."

"Mana potions?"

"Three, plus two health, that's all I've got," I said and got a growl of annoyance.

"I told you to get more sorted!"

"Can we argue about this later, please? I really, really *need to kill something right now."*

"Well, we will be, I'm not forgetting this time, and Jax?"

"Yeah?"

"Don't you dare make me raise this child on my own."

"I love you. Tell Sehran 'now'," I said, then I took a deep breath and started for the back of the building.

I'd made it a dozen or so steps when the front of the building exploded, a great ball of superheated air smashing me in the back and sending me cartwheeling through the wooden frame of the window ahead of me.

The glass shattered, poorly made and old. Its warped shards shredded my skin, even as the flames, linked to Jenae's domain as they were, did less damage to me as Her champion.

I had a split second to see the glass coming, and I triggered Hyper-Cognition, even as I closed my eyes.

The world around me slowed as my brain sped up, the hammering of my heart seeming to quieten, as the glass tickled and cut my skin.

Then I was through it, triggering Soaring Majesty and reorienting, even as I heard the otherworldly strains of Sehran's siren call of lust. I flipped over, locking onto the tower, and rammed the world behind me, sending the buildings at all sides blurring as I accelerated at an insane speed.

I crossed over the outer boundary of the tower's fences, the rusted and filth-covered barriers loaded down with centuries of ivy and weeds, the courtyard massively overgrown and…and the air shimmered and seemed to split like a mirror shattering. Each fragment tumbled away and reflected a different reality.

Then I saw them.

A dozen tents all laid out in tidy rows, hundreds of men and women hurrying here and there, armed to the fucking teeth, guards holding the gate and the tower.

It wasn't the sad, dilapidated mess the wall of illusion had shown when I'd looked across the city. This was a proper Wizard's Tower, awe-inspiring and tall, with archers' balconies filled with troops, dozens of people racing back and forth as they tried to get what looked like rip-offs of gatling guns into place.

The top floor had wide doors that were open to the air, and on the balcony stood three people, including a man I recognized. I didn't know his name, but I'd seen him twice before, once outside the building when I'd first arrived with the Baron. I'd shouted at the baldy bastard, then hid, so it looked like the Baron was insulting him, and once when the Great Portal had been opened at the end of the arena fights.

I had no clue how he'd gotten here, but he was a fucking noble…one of the original ones, and he'd been on Earth!

He pointed at me as I leveled out and sneered. A massive bolt of lightning, green and black and weird as all hell, burst from the end of a wand he held in one hand, blasting down right for me.

I rolled to the left, flying as fast as I could and gritted my teeth, damn well hoping some of these wankers would have mana and healing potions on their carcasses when I was done with them, as I triggered my dragonscale armor.

The blast of lightning hit the ground a few feet to my right, tearing a great fountain of earth into the air and sending people flying, smaller discharges reaching out and tearing holes in his own forces.

Where the lightning hit, instead of arcing out or shocking, it seemed to leave nothingness behind, carving scattered fractal patterns in their bodies.

I felt the heat and the blast of the displaced air, but I was past it, moving too fast as I somersaulted over, deciding at the last minute that flying toward that fucker was a bad idea, instead aiming for the inside of the building.

I crashed through a downstairs window, not having time to realign and aim for the goddamn open door farther around on the right side. The glass shattered, the people on the ground who had been continuing to frantically work through the ongoing fight suddenly looked up, shocked and drawing weapons as they realized that something had gotten past the outer ring of security.

I landed hard, glass and framing for the window under my feet, and skidded across the room, passing a startled-looking woman with her arms full of bolts from a nearby crate.

I managed to stop, twisted to face her, and growled as she dumped the bolts, reaching instinctively for a hip holster that wasn't there. She realized her mistake and changed direction going for a sword she had strapped to her back.

That was a terminal mistake.

I blasted off with the last of my Soaring Majesty, cutting it after using it for both speed and momentum, twisting at the hip to bring my right foot around, whipping it across her face and shattering her jaw.

She hit the floor, neck at a hell of an angle, and stayed down.

I continued the spin, drawing back and punching down with my right fist, driving it into the back of her neck, ending the threat before she could recover…and the death's head lifted in my vision, making me hesitate for a second.

That had been…far too easy.

The sound of running feet from my right echoed for a second, then three men burst into the room, the lead one swinging a massive spiked hammer.

I stepped back, having seen the length of the haft and where he was in relation to me. The hammer whistled past my face a good six inches out of any real possibility of hitting me. Then it slammed into the wall, exposing his right side to me, even as one of his friends tripped over his outstretched leg, losing his grip on the sword he was carrying as he face-planted to the floor.

I stepped back again, eyeing the incompetent threesome, the last to arrive hanging back behind his two friends, as the lead one with the hammer yanked on it, trying to get the spiked head out of the wall.

"Fuck's sake, lads, you're a bit shit at this, aren't you?" I asked, not really expecting an answer, until one of them gasped and snapped something at the other two in Spanish.

I missed most of it, catching the words for "him" and "gold," and that was about it. But the three of them stared at me open-mouthed before rushing forward in a frantic burst.

The hammer was left in the wall, the wielder instead drawing a dagger that looked like he'd stolen it from a steakhouse.

I eyed them all, frowning, then shook my head as an explosion somewhere overhead brought me back to reality. I didn't have time for this.

"Surrender or die," I snapped at them, not even bothering to draw my naginata out of the bag on my hip.

When they kept coming, I went to meet them, a single step forward, and I backhanded Hammer's attempt at a stab, deflecting it aside with my right hand. I turned my left over and reached across in one motion, grabbing him by the chin with my thumb underneath, then ripped back the left, snapping his neck and half-lifting his body into the air as I did it.

I slapped the palm of my right hand into the center of his chest, even as the death's head appeared, driving the meat-sack before me backward into the other two with a crunch of breaking bones, and all three hit the floor.

I hesitated for a split second, then grinned to myself.

These were human guards from *earth*. They were the kind of thugs I'd grown up fighting, dangerous to the untrained, but no match for me when I'd come here, let alone now I'd leveled so far past superhuman that I was practically a different fucking species.

I popped another pair of potions, a healing and a mana, offsetting the injuries I'd taken so far and the damage from my abilities, not to mention having to use my armor. I released that as well letting it retract, and instead powering up my tattoos. Hell I was probably scaring the shit out of people even more, considering I was now running at them naked and covered in glowing tattoos.

I raced from the room, charging mana into the shield rune on my left palm and the shock and plus runes on my right fist.

The corridor beyond was a mess of half-open boxes, shattered doors and more, and two men and a woman were running down it toward me. I grinned and ran at them, seeing the stairwell behind them leading up and their faces as they gaped at my nakedness then lifted the Earth-built crossbows to their shoulders.

They opened fire, and I ran on, the five or six shots they each managed to get off slamming into the shield and shattering before I reached them.

I didn't even bother to fight them, just kept running, then triggered Lunge a split second before impacting them with my shield extended.

They went flying amid screams, broken bones, and blood. Then I was past them, continuing on before they'd even finished bouncing off the stonework. The death's head floated up out of the corner of my eye, and I didn't bother to check if it'd been one or more of them who'd died.

I ran as fast as I could, kicking off the wall and slamming people aside as they emerged from doorways. When I hit the corridor on the next floor, I blasted people aside like a bull in a china shop and kept going.

As I reached the next stairwell, I released the building charge in my right fist, reabsorbing the mana, and started building Explosive Compression.

The next two floors were much the same, running full-speed at the inhabitants as they opened fire on me, my shield shattering their bolts and doing double-duty as a battering ram of concussive force, sending them screaming out of windows, pulping them against walls, door frames, and more.

I couldn't help but grin as I burst out onto the fourth floor, my mana down to half. The litany of screams and explosions from the floors behind resulted in the group of soldiers before me already backing up. I skidded to a halt, taking a trio of Magic Missiles on my shield, actually making my mana tick up slightly as they were absorbed into it.

I grinned through the distortion at the two mages in the center of the pack, even as the second one lifted her hands and cackled, throwing some variant of a Fireball at me.

It arced through the air like a grenade, and I pushed more mana into the shield, spreading it out wider and forming a block over the corridor, sealing my side off from theirs. Then it exploded, and I laughed.

It was apparently some kind of magical napalm spell, one that coated my shield…getting its mana ripped out and fed into the shield to strengthen it, while the rest was blown back toward her own troops, who screamed in pain and tried to strip it off their body armor.

Fucking body armor!

"You're fucking pathetic, you know that?" I called over the screams to the horrified-looking pair in the middle, before lifting my right hand and showing them the gently rolling marble of bright light. "See ya," I sneered, then threw the spell at them.

It covered the distance between us in a split second, punching into a panicking soldier's face when he stepped in the way. It shattered his skull as it unfurled, sending brain matter and blood, minced tissues, and worse across the walls. The bodies that were close were violently hurled into the walls, floor, and in one case, the ceiling…before it triggered fully and ripped back inward, dragging them all kicking and screaming into the center of the hall.

The sounds of bones and plastic breaking, screams and bursts of blood, flaming arms and legs and voices begging for mercy filled the air.

I ignored it all.

I popped the top off a mana potion, my last, and poured it into my mouth as I checked in with Oracle.

"How we doing?" I asked as I waited for the spell to run out, knowing that racing out onto the top floor unprepared could be fatal.

"Sehran has taken some more hits, but she's all right. She managed to Glamour one of the archers, and he shot one of the mages in the back of the head before they killed him."

"Nice." I grinned, thinking of the confusion that will have caused. *"You and Lydia?"*

"I'm fine, staying behind this chimney. It's boring, but it keeps the baby safe, Lydia, well, she's not very happy. One of the darts managed to get into a joint in her wing and snapped the bone. She managed to land, but it was in the courtyard, and she's taking out her temper on the guards there."

"And the boss?"

"Disappeared, no clue where, the surviving mage and guard went with him."

"Looks like my break is over, then!" I replied with a grunt, seeing my mana was almost full.

"Be careful, my love," Oracle sent, along with the feeling of ghost lips kissing my cheek. I smiled, sending a burst of love and affection through the link, then leaped over the last bit of the compression zone as the mana gave out.

It looked like there was maybe one survivor…if they got immediate medical aid.

I got my head back in the game, triggering my shield rune. The next stairway was longer than the last one, taking two full revolutions. But as I ran, I felt the mana above me being driven into something, a massive amount of power being employed. I pushed harder, not daring to fly as tight as the stairway was, but…

I burst up into a dozen guards, all holding shields ready, braced together. Without being able to build real speed, when I hit them, it was me who bounced off, hitting the doorway and half-falling backward, staggering, then snarling.

The shields snapped to the side, opening a thin gap between them as they rotated slightly, and the crossbows were jammed through. I managed to brace myself, twisting and leveling my shield just as they opened fire, bolt after bolt punching into the small, protective oval of twisted air, deflecting and shattering, but they seemed endless, dozens being fired one after another.

I wedged my back against the doorway and shoved forward, triggering Mana Overdrive and Lunge simultaneously, my right hand formed into a blade of bone. I covered the few feet in a blur, driving my hand through the gap and shattering one crossbow, then grabbing the shield by the edge and tearing it to the right. I punched forward with the left, driving two others backward.

Without the cohesion of the center, the shieldwall fell apart, even as the bolts started to hit, my shield being too far to the side to protect me fully.

I took two hits to the chest, fortunately high and low respectively, meaning it was mostly muscle and stomach, rather than lungs and heart. But they fucking hurt, and I roared in pain and anger, sweeping the shield across me. I slammed more mana into the tattoos, focusing on the main Shield rune over my heart.

This one wasn't as small and directed as the palm one was. This was the main event, primarily designed for magic, and drawing much more heavily on my mana to stop physical projectiles.

I growled, shoving hard at the shield from the inside and making it bloom to full-size, blasting the nearest soldiers in a detonation of force.

They flew through the air, and the room behind them was revealed, as was the fully active goddamned portal in the middle of it!

I swore viciously, racing forward, ignoring the soldiers as the noble, with a handful of lesser nobles and hangers-on, marched up the steps. The big bald bastard sneered as he stepped back through the portal, vanishing in a kaleidoscope of colors.

The portal pulsed, then shook, the building all around it suddenly quaking…and the walls shifted, pulling in.

"Fuck!" I snarled. The last dozen or so of his people raced up the steps and threw themselves through before the portal shut down with a snap.

Mana blasted outward from the portal, shaking the tower even as the build-up of mana in the air continued.

"Jax!" Oracle screamed in my mind. *"What the hell is going on in there?"*

"Some noble asshole from my world just fled through the portal! The whole damn building is shaking," I sent back, turning round and round, trying to figure out what the hell was going on.

"Get out!"

"I can't! The damn windows are gone!"

Whatever the noble asshole had done, the windows were *literally* gone. The doors that led out to the balconies, even the one that led down to the stairwell, all of them were gone, and the bloody walls were closing in!

I ran for the nearest gap, reaching it just as it closed, and pushed against it, feeling the thick stone pushing me back, even as Oracle spoke in my mind again.

"The tower is shrinking! He must have forced the controller to use the mana collectors to do it, somehow, I'm trying to get to the collectors; if I can cut off the mana."

"Be careful!" I sent.

The soldiers scattered around the room fought to break free as well, wailing as they were forced inward with the shrinking walls.

I could possibly smash a section of the wall out with High Explosive, but the room was getting smaller by the second, and the blast from that wouldn't be good for anyone inside.

"Can you understand me?" I barked out, looking around at the dozens of men and women who had been my enemies seconds before. First one, then another, then they were almost all nodding. "Fine, mana potions, who has them?"

A single hesitant hand was raised by a woman at the back. "I saw some in a box," she offered in a thick Spanish accent, pointing off to one side. I jogged in the direction she indicated, seeing a half-dozen empty crates, assumedly that had once held bolts, then a box of health potions, shite ones, looking at the quality, then…

"Thank the gods," I muttered, tossing the lid aside and crouching. Twelve potions sat inside, nestled in the middle of perfectly formed polystyrene. "Right! Get your arses over here if you want to live!" I barked out, picking up the case and moving to the now-dead portal in the middle of the room.

"Oracle, can you stop the changes?" I asked her and got a feeling of panic but determination as she fought with something at a distance, closing as fast as she could. *"I trust you, my love, and I'll keep the walls back as long as I can."* I sent a burst of trust and reassurance to her, then eyed the buggers who moved in close.

"I can use my shield to stop the walls, but the farther out I push it, the more mana, and the shorter a time I'll be able to hold it. My people are trying to stop this on the outside, so all we have to do is survive long enough…"

"For you to kill us!" one of the men spat at me.

"You came to my city and opened fire on my people, fucknut! You attacked me; what the hell did you think was going to happen?"

"We returned to our lord's homeland," he snarled back hotly, stepping in close.

I grabbed him by the front of his stupid fucking tactical vest then yanked him in for a headbutt, knocking him out.

"Right!" I bellowed. "Anyone else? If you want to fight, I'll kill you now and save myself some mana. If not, dump your weapons, and I mean ALL your weapons, and get in close, time for a cuddle!"

With that, I popped the first of the potions, taking myself back to almost full, as I yanked the bolts out of my chest, tossing them aside and hitting myself with a heal.

I saw the looks I was getting at my casual use of both brute force to remove them and the healing magic, but I didn't have time to deal with it, as I checked them all over for weapons as quickly as I could.

I could probably hold the walls back for a short time, maybe even long enough for Oracle to take the mana collectors down, but I certainly couldn't do it while watching them all, and it'd be easy for one of them to slip a knife between my ribs when I was distracted.

I gestured them all in next to me, telling them to sit on the floor as close as they could, while I handed the box to a guy to my left.

"If I start running low on mana, pour one of these in my mouth. Once it starts, I'll go through them fast."

"How will I know?" he interrupted.

I paused, frowning. I'd gotten so used to the way that everyone just knew, that…

"I'll start looking like shit, shaking and wincing, like I've got a horrific hangover, I guess," I told him. "You buggers have a lot to learn about the realities of life. How long have you been here?"

"A day," one of the others answered. "Thereabouts anyway."

"Shit, and none of you showed up on the control system." I shook my head. "A problem for later. Right, get in close!" I raised my voice over the cracking and grinding of stone as the various blocks that formed the outer walls moved in closer and began overlapping.

I sat, folding my legs under me in true kung-fu sensei style and ducked my head, closing my eyes and gently pushing out my shield.

I slid it out over the group, forming a low dome that was as tight as I could make it and still encompass everyone. The others commented on the feeling of it, even as more warned how close the walls were getting.

I felt Oracle's reassurance, false confidence plastered over the top of panic as she worked, fighting her own battle, the others drawing close.

The walls touched the outer edge of my shield. I grunted in pain, the sudden weight of the building pressing in as in the distance stone crashed and collapsed. The floor above us fell inward, the topmost floor of the tower and the private residence of some long-dead mage tumbling down.

I groaned, pushing back as the stone slid inexorably inward. Bodies crowded closer and closer as the pillars of the portal gate creaked and groaned, offering a little protection and reinforcement to my efforts.

A glass vial was hesitantly pressed to my lips, and I swallowed, having little choice but to trust them, despite their actions, as I focused on my meditation and pushed back against the stones.

I couldn't stop them.

Not as I was, and I no longer had the luxury of the Master of Mana ability which would have stopped this in its tracks, or the goddamn Fragment of Divinity. But I could slow it, even if only for a bit.

"Jax get your shield up!" Oracle sent suddenly.

"What the hell do you think I'm doing?"

"Tenandra is firing on the collector!"

"Fuck my life!" I growled, apparently sounding particularly heartfelt as others around me grunted and muttered agreement.

The world went white as Tenandra opened fire with the new cannon, and flames and over-pressure replaced the pushing force of the walls.

They lasted seconds, then relief! The walls had stopped. Yes, they were still there, still holding us in place, trapped under multiple tons of rock, but the determined and steady pressure was gone.

I gasped, giving up on the meditation and the shield, blinking my eyes open. One of the men was holding out another potion, and behind him…

I struck out instinctively, shoving aside the thin little punch dagger the fucker had somehow concealed and watched it sink into the side of the guy who'd been about to give me the potion.

The dagger-wielder snarled and yanked it back, then stabbed at me again. My fingers stiffened into the adder strike that Restun had been drilling into me.

It was perfect for close quarters, unarmed fights, using stiffened fingers to strike nerve clusters and sensitive spots, ears, eyes, temple, and throat.

Now, as close as we all were, it let me strike him in the throat, once, my stiffened fingers collapsing his windpipe as my other hand caught the dagger, twisting until I heard the bones in his wrist snap under the force.

The next few minutes were long ones for everyone in the enclosed space, as the attempted assassin slowly died, unable to breathe.

One of his fellows tried to save him, shuffling in and trying to push around to get to his throat, planning on doing something with the dagger. But as soon as he cut into the skin, the spreading blackness that leeched free of the knife made it clear the fucker had poisoned it.

I turned to look at the man who'd been stabbed, seeing the sweating, the red flush to his cheeks, and the spreading veins of blackness climbing his cheeks. I went to work, alternating using waves of Scour and Complex Healing back-to-back as we waited.

I managed to save him, but as one of the men asked if I'd save the assassin as well, I snorted and shook my head, looking down at the slumped figure slowly asphyxiating before us all.

The next half an hour in the enclosed space was unpleasant for everyone. The nearby corpses that had shoved up against the barrier of my shield stank, their bodies bursting under the pressure and blood seeping into where we were sat. The twisted doorway of the portal that hunkered overhead occasionally let out pops and crackles of discharging mana.

When the rubble finally shifted nearby, the group tensing in fear as an inhuman hand reached under a block to carefully lift it aside, I was well and truly done with their shit.

The golems uncovered us in quick order, and I stood, pushing the survivors aside as I stalked out of the gap. Tenandra hovered nearby, half her superstructure still open to the elements and her cannons sitting proud.

Oracle was there, of course, as were most of the team, including Thomas and Augustus with a bevy of his elite guards and dozens of seriously pissed-off-looking legionnaires.

I just took Oracle in my arms, holding her for a long few seconds, then turned to Augustus as he stepped forward, looking furious about the assault in his city.

"It's nothing you could have protected against, Augustus, but we've got a massive fucking problem, and no time to deal with it. Thomas!" I called, seeing him straighten instinctively to the voice of command. "Lock these dumb fucks up with any other survivors and get your arse back to the keep to join us as quick as you can. I need them searched for anything and everything…they're from Earth."

When I said those last three words, he swore, then nodded, understanding that I needed him to do it because the locals might miss something that he wouldn't.

"Command group, I need you all back at the keep; we need a meeting! Augustus, sorry to pull rank, but…"

"Anything you need, my Prince," he replied calmly, smiling slightly before passing me a robe. "You do realize you're naked again, right?"

"Fuck's sake…yeah, thanks, man. Right, get everyone back there, Cai, Romanus, yourself and Hellenica, Restun, Oren, Tenandra, and Oracle. Fuck, better include that damn bard as well," I muttered, seeing Lydia stomping over with a crossbow in one hand. She handed it over and quirked an eyebrow as I looked at it.

"It be a hell of a thing, light and strong, but fast…"

"It's mostly aluminum and plastic," I said, shaking my head as I looked the weapon over. It was shorter than a regular crossbow, and with two sets of spinners or whatever they were called on the arms, doubling and redoubling the power of the bows. There was a long magazine that slotted in underneath, with the bolts nestled in tight, storing twenty or so at a time.

I flicked the arms, feeling the tremendous pressure they were under, and guessed at some form of spring steel that I wasn't familiar with.

"Get someone to gather them all up, as well as the bolts. The Legion flyers will love them, and the gnomes can strip a few, figure them out, and make better ones." I took another magazine and slid it into my bag, then dumped the entire crossbow in and looked at Lydia and Sehran as she landed nearby as well, moving in close to Oracle and me. "Are you all okay?"

"Aye, just a bit shocked, ah were no expectin' this…just a trip ta see the gnomes, an'…"

"And because you weren't expecting it, you weren't ready," Bane snapped, appearing nearby. "Fuck's sake, Jax, I can't take a few hours off to sleep without you destroying half the city?" He ignored the look Lydia gave him.

"There's no time for shit like that," I told them both. "Everyone aboard Tenandra, and I mean everyone who's coming!" I repeated, raising my voice and looking round at the others, getting nods from those who were needed, like Augustus, and a mocking salute from Thomas, who knew he wasn't.

Tenandra clearly heard me, shifting her patrol of the tower and pulling in close, as a crew member I vaguely recognized slid a long plank over the side to clatter against the edge of the tower's balcony…or what was left of it.

I nodded my thanks, striding across as Oracle flew. The others either followed or flew depending on their personal capabilities.

I jumped down onto the deck and moved to the side, glancing back at the smoking wreckage of the tower, as well as its mana collector. It'd resembled a stone obelisk, tall and imposing, much like the ones that the ancient Egyptians loved so much. Now, it was a smoking wreck of shattered stone and crystal, making me curse as I reflected on the lost opportunity.

In under a minute, we were lifting into the sky, the wind tugging at us as I walked around the narrow edge of the deck bracing, avoiding the massive open sections of Tenandra's deck as best I could.

I pushed the door open into her helm and control room, satisfied at improvements in here, and carefully not commenting on the fact that the cabin behind it, that was now Jian's living space, along with Sehran and Tenandra, was fully finished and looked fantastic through the open door.

The door swung shut and locked with an audible click, I smiled at Tenandra, who stood in the middle of the room, legs braced in her customary sea captain stance.

"Welcome aboard, my prince. Apologies that my body isn't quite finished, but…"

I shook my head. "It doesn't matter; you were supposed to have a few days at least before you needed to make any flights. That's not the point, though; again, you saved me today, Tenandra, thank you."

"It was my honor."

"Well, believe me, it was appreciated," I said. "Now, more importantly, how quickly can you be ready to fly, if we push it?"

"I'm ready now."

"But half the deck is missing," I finished for her. "I know. You'll be staying in the shipyard for at least another day, while I take another ship to Narkolt. Can you be ready for tomorrow?"

"I can, if I can commandeer some more help. Some systems won't be finished, and I may leak in places, but…"

"But that's fine, and yes, order up anyone you need to help." I said, feeling the powerful engines turning us as I glanced at one of the images of the outside world that she showed on the wall. "How long to the keep?"

"Six minutes."

"Thank you," I repeated, turning back to the others. "Augustus, my team and I will be leaving once we've had a quick meeting to bring everyone up to date. While I was in there with those assholes, I got some information, and it changes everything. Secure areas are anything *but* goddamn secure, if there's a portal in them. And we've got at least two noble houses, probably more, using them behind our back."

CHAPTER ELEVEN

Half an hour later, we were all gathered around the table in one of the luxurious meeting rooms high in the Himnel keep. Besides myself and Oracle, Tenandra, Lydia, Augustus, and Hellenica, we had Cai, Oren, Hannibal, and Mal, Romanus, and Restun. As I poured myself a drink, Lucian and Isabella hurried in and took their seats, followed by a flustered Nerin.

"This had better be good, boy, I left…" Nerin said, and I held up a hand, stopping her dead. She saw the look on my face and shut the hell up, taking her seat and inclining her head, recognizing that I wasn't Jax, her occasional student and therapy victim. Today, she had been summoned by the Imperial Scion, Prince of the Empire.

"We've got problems," I declared, pulling the crossbow out and laying it on the table between us all, the magazine next to it. "This is a specialized design, made in my home realm. It is clearly mass-produced and used to outfit an invading force, one that didn't show on the damn City Control Center.

"That's not even the worst of it. They were led by a noble I remember seeing at the arena fights I won to get here. That means that they have somehow managed to open a portal to get back, and while they don't have guns, or apparently explosives, they've been planning and working towards this for hundreds of years and can control the portals."

"Where is this noble now?" Cai asked, reaching out and picking one of the bolts up curiously, hefting it for the weight and then examining the tip with one finger.

"He escaped through the portal, leaving it to shut behind him, and instructed the tower to collapse. He was fine with the notion of killing more than half his guards to kill me, which suggests…"

"That he has more guards and is opposed to you personally, as well as having a pre-prepared fallback location arranged or planned." Romanus finished when I hesitated.

"Exactly. I questioned the guards, the ones who survived, anyway. Seems that not all of them were 'his' guards originally. Basically, he brought a core group of oathsworn guards and then hired a bunch of mercenaries, paying them a hell of a lot of money to give up their lives on Earth and come with him. Apparently, the choice was 'serve me or die,' so there's a lot less loyalty than you'd expect.

"They were all told they'd be swearing an oath soon, but the noble flew into a rage and sent out his assassins as soon as he realized I was here, too. Once they were off, presumably hunting me, he retreated into the upper rooms of the tower and left the oathsworn guards to command the others."

"So, was the assassin who fired the arrow at you or Oracle earlier one of his people?" Cai asked.

I shook my head. "I don't know. They could have been, but that means they weren't drawing attention; they were just a shit shot."

"The weapon doesn't match," Lucian interjected. "If the guards were using these crossbows, why change to a longbow for the attempt? Also, the escape and the original assault suggests skill and experience. These guards were apparently newcomers to the world as well as our skills and leveling system in general."

"Great, so it looks like we're back to a third party. Fuck's sake." I growled.

"Why don't they show on the city map?" Restun asked calmly.

I pointed a finger at him. "Damn good question. I'm assuming it's because the various nobles are members of the Empire, and their troops are operating under that. As such, they're not hostile to the Empire, just to me personally. Until I'm crowned Emperor, it's not the same thing. Mind you, it could be because I had a goddamn cheese sandwich earlier, I don't fucking know for sure. The one person who knew the real reasons the Imperial systems worked as they did is long dead, so we can only make educated guesses."

"Can they access the Great Tower and assume command?" Romanus asked.

"No, we closed the Great Tower down ages ago; the portal is fully offline. I'd have done the same here, but..." I shrugged.

"But too many things to do and not enough time," Augustus said.

"Basically, yeah. Add to that, I knew there was a fucked-up old mage tower in the middle of the city, but I didn't know that was where the city portal was."

"It's long been abandoned. The portals were only accessible to those of Imperial blood and authority, so when the last of the old nobles died, so did the right to use them," Lucian said with a faint smile. "I always thought it a good thing, personally, as it kept the lesser nobility from using the Old Imperial systems and further ravaging the realm."

"It was. Now it's a real fucking problem because I don't know where or how many usable ones there are. The guards who were able to talk said that the noble, Enon of House Balthus, was furious because someone else managed to get their portal open first. There was something about sacrifices, but they didn't know for sure what had happened there, either." I shrugged. "It could be that there was a goat stabbed and fuckin' entrails used to predict the future, for all we know, but..."

"Sacrifices, of course." Lucian glanced across at Hellenica and Nerin. "Is it possible?" he asked them.

I glanced from one of them to the other. "What's this?"

"Blood magic," Nerin spat. Hellenica hissed in disgust, folding her arms over herself and gritting her teeth.

"It's a horrible thing, Jax, not something any of us would ever do, so we've not talked about it, but there's power in blood," Oracle explained. "Both in fresh blood to power special runes, such as the containment spell that was used to entrap Hellenica, and..."

"And in blood sacrifices of the unwilling," Nerin finished for her, shaking her head. "It's disgusting, but it's a source of power for those who are willing to take that route."

"How unwilling?" I asked, getting a pretty damn good idea already how the Baron and his kind had powered the portal.

"Murder," Nerin confirmed. "A great deal of mana is released if a living and sapient being is sacrificed in the right way; however, the structure that receives such power usually doesn't last long. Such energy is, by its nature, destructive. As such, it is rarely used, even by those who would have no such moral qualms."

"How many would be needed to open a portal between the realms?" I asked slowly.

"Many hundreds, and the portal would last only a short time, as well as being rendered useless afterward, requiring a great deal of effort to rebuild. Or, so I would assume, anyway."

"You are correct Nerin," came Jenae's voice, cutting us all off. *"As near as we can tell, such a use is both possible and probable, in this case. However, this would be an option of last resort, as the portals would be rendered inert afterward, requiring a complete rebuild."*

"So, that cockwomble of a father of mine, he's done this?" I asked grimly, and Jenae paused, clearly considering.

"I am unsure, Jax. It is likely, but by no means certain. Should one of the noble houses choose this route, I would suspect more would as well, yet it is an act of folly in the extreme. Should their portal connect to one that was sealed, then any traveling in it at that point would be killed. Should the portal run dry of mana before a stable connection is made? It will close, and the nobles would be trapped in your realm until they could rebuild their portal."

"Falco—well, his daughter—told me that the Great Portal was failing and that it wouldn't last much longer," I mused. "Apparently, they can't replace whatever is breaking, so if that breaks, and the minor, private ones all need it somehow? Maybe that's why they did it?"

"It is possible, but I suspect not. Any Imperial citizen would have received the notification of your ascension, provided they had access to mana."

"Even the tiny bit in my realm?"

"There is more there than you believe. Mana is an integral part of life; without it, there would be none."

"Okay, so you think he saw that I was making a play for the Imperial Throne, lost his shit, and started sacrificing people, using their deaths to power the portal, and went balls deep?"

"Balls…"

"Shit, I mean he went all in, risked it all on a single roll of the dice."

"Ah, well yes. You said that Duke Enon was here, and that another had opened their portal first?"

"According to some of the guards, yeah."

"Then, once one was found to have done this, more likely than not, the others would begin as well. They bring true death for many and risk true death for themselves."

"So it's a real roll of the dice," I grunted. "I wonder how many died?"

"Probably tens of thousands to open each portal and hundreds more in transit," Jenae pointed out grimly. *"The number of deaths, however, is the lesser detail."*

"Go on…"

"Have you considered the likely result of the old nobility returning?"

"A lot of assholes trying to grab power?" I asked, then swore as my brain jumped ahead to the natural conclusion.

"Quite…" She said, then as I went on swearing, She spoke to the others. *"While Jax regains control, I will share his conclusion with you. Not only will*

they be impossible to track using the current city control systems, but many of them have valid Imperial authority which equals any other save Jax himself. And, as Scion and Prince, he does not have the authority to remove any high-ranking noble who was granted their title directly by Amon."

"So, if one of these assholes turns up at the production facility, they can order the golems to slaughter our people, and the golems damn well will!" I ground out, my mind racing through possible counters.

"Correct. However, the golems under your direct authority can be ordered to only respond to certain individuals. You are still the Prince of the Empire and hold the highest Imperial rank. While you are not the Emperor currently, you can strip a <u>lesser</u> noble of their title, should it be rooted in your territory. Enon, for example, was once Duke of Himnel. As such, you can strip him of his remaining Imperial rank, and his dukedom was stripped when you named Augustus to that position. Your father was Duke of Inneth and the Dark Marches, two territories outside of your control, and as such, you cannot claim authority over him."

"I formally declare Duke Enon of House Balthus, once Duke of Himnel, to be stripped of all Imperial authority. He is declared outlaw and is to be taken prisoner if possible. If not, he is to be killed," I said, injecting my mana into the words, before hissing in pain as my mana was ripped from me.

Attention, Imperial Citizens!

Prince Jax Amon, Scion of the Empire, Acknowledged Heir of Amon, has stripped Duke Enon of House Balthus, formerly Duke of Himnel of all Imperial Authority and declared him an outcast!

Let no Imperial Citizen offer the criminal Enon succor. Any who raise a hand against the former duke will be richly rewarded, while any who aid him will be declared anathema.

All Hail Prince Jax of Dravith!

"Right. That should help when dealing with that wanker," I muttered. "Now what?"

"We would recommend you restrict those with authority over the golems to specific individuals, as that will slow the older nobles from exerting their authority over them. Should they have a bloodstone, however, their authority will be recognized."

"Then I need to make damn sure they can't get into anywhere that holds the golems," I said. "Oren, I need a fast reaction force. It'll have to be elite guards, those with some command of magic, though, as I need the Legion at the Great Tower. They're to be dispatched to Production Facility One…Shit!" I cut myself off. "Jenae, is there a working portal at the facility?"

"Two. One is Svetu's private portal for trans-shipping, and as such is secure, the other…" There was a long pause, then She sighed. *"It is both active, and currently in use."*

"Fuck!" I snarled, "Oren! Get your ass in gear. I need the fastest ship you have ready to leave in ten minutes. Lydia, gather the team!" I barked at them both, sending them running. "Augustus, you're in command of Himnel, and until I return, the damn Empire. Romanus, support him as you would me. Hannibal, Cai, Lucian, work together and get me a damn map of Imperial portals!"

I sent other people running this way and that, attempting to deal with every eventuality, but the simple truth was that we were coming too late.

I ordered more potions, mana, health and stamina, to be taken to the ships, as well as a handful of advanced war golems, just in case, and my regular armor as well.

"And tomorrow, as we planned, Romanus, you're moving to the Great Tower," I finished.

"Jax, perhaps now is not the time for the Legion…"

"To be anywhere but around me? Hell no, I totally agree, but if I keep you close to me, if I keep you where you can support me? Then I'll gain almost no experience from the fights I'm going to have, and I will have fights. I need that experience to grow. More than that, though, I need the Legion."

"But…"

"But the Legion can't be in two places at once," I replied, again talking over him. "If you're backing me up, if you're keeping me safe? You're not training the next generation. We desperately need *those* legionnaires. Every day lost because the Legion is watching over me, we will lose ground as the nobles run rings around us attacking wherever we're weakest. Also, you'll be accepting the rank of Legion General."

"I…what, but…" Romanus stuttered.

"You're already the Legion General in all but name, and it's about time that was sorted," I said. "We should have made it formal before, but that's it."

Citizens of the Empire! Rejoice!

The General of the Imperial Legion of Dravith has been formally named!

Romanus Dominai Perival will serve as leader of the Legion of Dravith, guiding all Imperial Forces as commander to all as well as assisting both the Prince and the Heir.

Hail Jax Amon, Prince of the Empire!

"I…thank you." Romanus said softly. I glanced at Restun as he cleared his throat.

"We run the risk of losing you, though," Restun said. "Perhaps I or Lucian should go with you…"

"No. Again, you'd be a massive help, but in this situation, I need you training the next generation. Hannibal, do whatever you need to do to get me the resources to build that goddamn Imperial Academy. It just jumped to priority number two, right after me shutting down the portals and securing our territory!"

"Ah've got tha fast scout *Fury's Awakening* comin in fer a landin' outside noo; they be on overwatch since Tenandra went mental."

"Since I what?" Tenandra asked Oren in a warning tone.

"Since, eh…well ye went screamin' inte tha air all engines on full. Scared tha shit outta everyone, ye ken?" he suggested, looking nervous.

"The Prince of the Empire was in danger of being crushed to death, Oren."

"I was literally less than a minute from being a smear between the blocks that made up the tower," I confirmed before dismissing it and moving on. "Oren, I'll be out in a few minutes, but I need you to make sure that she's got enough supplies to get us to Narkolt, then on to Production Facility One."

I turned to Tenandra. "I know you're fast, and you'll be far more deadly than most others once your rebuild is done, but for now, I can't wait. Get ready, and as soon as you are, and damn well loaded with supplies, get your arse out to meet us. We'll transfer from the *Fury* to you, then we'll go to the Prax. That's the last stop before returning to the Tower."

"I understand, Jax," she said. "Do we have any way of warning the ship that we sent this morning?"

"Shit, yes…they had war golems aboard," I growled, looking to Oren, even as I knew the answer.

"Nay, laddie, te get close enough to warn 'em, we need te catch 'em, and they bin gone fer a day noo."

"Shit, but…" I broke off as Thomas walked into the room, and suddenly it all fell into place. "Hey, bro!"

He froze at the devilish smile on my face, then backed up.

"Don't try and run, you'll just end up tired!"

"What the hell did I do wrong now?" he asked.

"Absolutely nothing," I purred, taking a deep breath and injecting mana into the next proclamation.

Citizens of the Empire! Rejoice!

The Leader of the Imperial Senate has been chosen.

Thomas Amon, younger brother to Prince Jax Amon, will serve as his left hand, advising him and addressing concerns of state, politics, and Imperial matters, as well as assisting both the Prince and the Heir.

All Hail Jax Amon, Prince of the Empire!

By the time it was done, I was gasping and had a nosebleed, having used that much mana, and Oracle was standing by my side, massaging my shoulder. Someone shouted for a handful of mana and health potions…as well as a towel and hot water.

"Oh, you fucking didn't," Thomas growled, reading the notification. "You think you're dumping all this shit with the nobles on my shoulders? You know I'll just stab them!"

"Why the hell do you think I don't want to deal with them?" I grumbled, forcing myself to sit up straighter again. "But no, this isn't a 'palming off the job' situation. As the leader of the Imperial Senate, you have authority equal to the Heir. While you can't overrule me, you can do just about anything else, which means that you can also…"

"Order the golems?" he guessed, nodding and pointing at me as he clicked his fingers.

"Damn right. More than that, though, you can shut the portals down! It'll take a day to hit Narkolt and get back, or two days to do that and reach Production

Facility One, never mind getting back from there. No, I'll hit Narkolt, then head back. Tenandra will be ready by then, and I'll head straight for the Prax, while you head for the production facility," I said. "It's in use *right now*, the portal I mean, so that might mean one guy got through, or hundreds. They'll be human, though, and unlevelled, bar the leader of them, maybe."

"So, me and my team will cut the fuckers apart," he replied, nodding.

"I damn well hope so. Get in there; close the portal down."

"Jax, instead, if we lock the portal to only being accessed by your Imperial Senate, and you disband the original Senate, then any you name to the Senate can use the portals. Then we'll have the ability to travel from the Great Tower to the production facility in one step. Or, once you have the Prax portal online, we can start shipping manastones in to connect up and charge the golems," Oracle suggested, and I nodded.

"That's a better idea. Sorry, Tommy, do that please. Lock access to the portal connection down to just the Imperial Senate for now," I ordered. "Okay, here goes nothing. Fuck, I wish I could see their faces when I do this."

I paused as the door opened, and I nodded my thanks at the serving girl who brought in a steaming bowl of hot water, a towel, and her companion brought three mana potions.

I had the water set aside, popped a mana potion, and nodded to Oracle, who smiled and took ahold of a second one, popping the top and holding it ready.

Citizens of the Empire!

The Old Imperial Senate is forthwith declared obsolete and stripped of its power and authority.

The New Imperial Senate, led by Thomas Amon and including Cai'Amanth a-Ull, the Imperial Consul, Legion General Romanus Dominai Perival, and Imperial Chief Justicar Lucian D'Aquitaine, will replace the Old Imperial Senate, with all rights and powers intact.

All Hail Jax Amon, Prince of the Empire!

I winced, shaking my head and coughing as Oracle poured the third and final mana potion into my mouth, a little going down the wrong way as I sat up and saw the world around me again, the notification closing in response to my will.

I had a sudden second to wonder if it was possible to do this, to set a notification up that would override your will and blind someone in the middle of a fight? Or would it take that into account and not let you do it?

Then I shook myself and drank the rest of the potion before scrubbing the drying blood from my face with the towel. I could have used Scour, but I didn't like the idea of doing that to my damn face.

"Okay then," I groaned, shaking myself and forcing my words out with a little more determination. "Thomas and his team will hit the Imperial Production Facility and lock the portal down to just us. Lucian, Hannibal, and Cai will locate any other portals. Augustus will get Himnel sorted out, and Romanus and Restun will lead the Legion back to the Great Tower." I looked from one to another and got a series of nods.

"My team and I will be heading to Narkolt. I'll get that portal seized and bring Carmen up to date, as well as make her a member of the Senate, I suppose. Then I'll head straight for the Prax. Getting that portal locked down and the golems unloaded just became a massive priority." I frowned, turning to Oracle.

"Can we...can Heph take control of the golems and lock them down remotely?" I asked, suddenly remembering the relay stations.

"Possibly," she said. "We could either go to the command center or..."

"Can you do it from here?" I asked. "Can you communicate with him and arrange it?"

"I can."

"Do it."

There was a brief pause as she sat back, frowning and seeming to stare into the distance, before she nodded, coming back to reality.

"Hephaestus responded. He's shutting down the production facility and the war golems on site. Several of the golems have already dropped out of his control, and he can't sense the control room fully. Now that he knows what's going on, he's locking everything down as quickly as he can. But the most he can do is limit the control they'll have and gain us some time."

"That's all I'll need," Thomas said. "I'll take my team, and we'll reclaim the facility." He nodded to me, grim as he towered over the majority of the room. I sighed in relief; if anyone could do it, he would.

The only one who didn't return my look was Nerin.

"Boy...why am I here? We both know you don't need me here, and as a member of the council, I'm of little use..."

I shook my head. "You're here Nerin, because tomorrow when Tenandra is ready, and we all set off for the Prax, you're coming with us. You're the best healer we've got by a hell of a margin. There's a fuck load of seriously unstable batshit gnomes on the Prax still, and we need them."

"You expect me to go into battle with you?" she asked. "Boy, my adventuring days are long behind me!"

"No, Nerin, I don't expect, I *require*. You'll be the difference between us having to kill a bunch of insane gnomes or rescuing them. You'll be kept in the middle of the group and protected as best we can manage." I sighed, disappointed. "Do I need to order you to do this?"

"No," she said after a long hesitation, sitting back and glancing down at her hands in her lap. "No, but my last adventuring party died, boy. When you're the only survivor, it does things to you. You damn well better make sure you don't die on me!" She pointed at me.

I smiled gently at her, finally understanding.

"It's true, it really does fuck you up," Thomas mumbled, one survivor recognizing another.

"Well, it looks like you've got another therapy victim, Nerin, and maybe one who can help you as well," I said. "Right, that's it, people! Get to work, and if you need to make decisions, time seriously fucking matters right now. You're all on my council because I trust you to make the right ones."

Mal opened his mouth to make a stupid comment, and I pointed a finger at him. "If this is a joke or an attempt to rip me off, your new title will be Lord Mal of the Smallest Manhood. Not the time, Mal, seriously!" I warned him. "Is it important?"

"…No."

"Then you can take the piss when all of this is dealt with. Go!" I ordered everyone, standing and heading to the door.

CHAPTER TWELVE

It took longer than that in the end, as things often do, but about forty minutes after getting to the ship, Thorn and the others stomped down the gangplank to the ground, and the engines built in power.

The rest of the team spread about the deck, doing last minute odds and sods, shooing sailors away from the crates of potions standing by us.

The hurried rush meant that the ship had been on patrol, with the sailors basically keeping watch for anything dodgy going on. But that was it, and they'd been expecting to finish their shift soon and go chill out.

Instead, they were carrying the Prince of the Empire and his personal team to go and fuck up someone's day, and they were powering through the mid-morning clear skies, headed for Narkolt.

"Yer checked yer armor yet?" Lydia asked me, stepping up to stand by my side. I grunted, turning from watching the houses and factories falling away beneath us.

"No, I need to though."

The armor situation was a bit awkward, currently. At the end of the fight for Himnel, and the Imperial Territory of Dravith, I'd had my armor changed by a gift from the Gods.

That was wonderful. Hell, they'd basically bonded my draconic gifted scale armor into my normal armor and made a thing of absolute beauty, but they'd also powered the draconic armor's mana needs for me in the fight, with the better sections of my original armor, the Helm of Imperial Right, and the matching vambraces altering, along with the remnants of the Faithful Service set of legion armor I'd been wearing at the time.

When Thorn had seen it, she'd gone absolutely fucking insane, practically swearing to have my children if I'd let her touch it.

I'd managed to restrain myself, just, from making any comments about anything—it'd been hard—and I'd just handed it over, keeping my helm but giving her the vambraces.

The only problem with all of this, was that for me to summon my draconic scale armor, I had to power it with mana, and it wasn't cheap.

Basically I had enough mana I could run it for about a minute, and that was all. So realistically, I couldn't use the armor the Gods had augmented for me, because it needed to sit atop something I couldn't afford to summon.

And if I did? As soon as I ran out of mana, half my armor vanished, and the rest fell off, because it was designed to go on over the rest.

Since then, she'd been working on a heavily modified replacement to my inbuilt dragon scales. The end result was a form of blackened scalemail that looked awesome.

The only issue was that it needed to be a single piece for the rest of the armor to join to it right. As such, it was both heavy and could be uncomfortable to wear for very long, as well as making me a hell of a lot slower.

Thorn had sworn she'd fix that and was working on the mark two version already. It'd be ready soon, she swore blind, but for now, I was left with two possible options: heavy but slow defense from the godplate over the mark one, as people were referring to it, or…

Lighter defense, but being mobile.

I'd taken option two, and I now had a full, brand new suit of Legion's boring old standard-edition Faithful Service armor.

I was absolutely gutted.

I had a suit of armor that attached to the top of my scaled skin. It felt almost weightless, and Sint had assured me that the power inherent in the armor would grow with me.

We'd managed to find a set of pauldrons with a similar enchantment to the original vambraces at plus five to perception, but in giving up the Vambraces of Imperial Might to Thorn to study I'd lost five points of dexterity in the deal. That was annoying, but more annoying was the fact that I'd found these in the city armory, and if my 'Imperial Right' gear hadn't been altered into the godplate, and then needed for study I could have worn them with the rest of my gear.

The rest of the armor I'd stuck with new and standard versions, bar my belt that contained my razor wire.

No more should I be scrambling for the next part of a set or swapping bits out. I had the perfect armor…*and I couldn't use it.*

I moved across to the armor stand that Thorn had set up, along with the already adjusted suit that hung on it and the underclothes, giving side-eye to the thick padding that was going to make me sweat my goddamn tits off.

I shook myself. There was no damn need to get dressed in all of that yet. Now that I was more experienced, it barely took a few minutes to put it all on, so screw sitting around for hours as we got closer.

Instead, I did the only damn thing I could do after the way things had been going of late, and I gave my armor a quick check over, then dragged Oracle off to the nearest empty cabin.

"Damn, he's not wasting any time," Jian muttered to Tang, just loud enough to make sure I heard. Tang shrugged, leaning against the railing that ringed the ship.

"Well, you know, when the kid arrives, that'll be it for his sex life…get it in while you can and all that."

"I'm going to encourage Carmen to get serious about her love life, maybe even get married," I commented loudly to Sehran as we passed her. "Maybe you could have a think about who'd be appropriate to suggest? And Sehran, just out of curiosity, can you get pregnant here?"

She paused in the act of checking her whip for damage and turned to look at Jian, squinting as though deep in thought. I flipped Tang and Jian the finger behind my back as I walked away.

"That was cruel," Oracle whispered as we stepped into the cabin, pushing the door shut behind me and taking her in my arms.

"I know," I agreed, grinning. "But so was them saying our sex life is over…"

"It's not," she said, pulling my head down as her tongue slid into my mouth, and her arms went around my neck. It was a long few seconds before I broke away, looking down at her, and admiring the view her strappy top afforded me. "Believe me, our sex life is definitely NOT over!"

"Glad to hear that," I said, sharing one more kiss. But as I felt one hand slide down my chest, over my belt, then start to tug it open, I paused and looked at her seriously. "Oracle…"

"Uh-huh?" she asked, distractedly, undoing my belt then reaching inside to free me of my pants.

"Whoa, stop," I said, springing to life in her hands despite the words coming out of my mouth.

"What's wrong? Don't you want me to…"

"Nothing's wrong. Gods, believe me, I really don't want you to stop at all…" I said fervently, shaking my head. "But you said there might be a better way to do this, to protect you and to keep the baby safe?"

"Oh!" she replied, smiling. "I thought you'd decided that you didn't want me any more now that I was pregnant!"

"I'd be lying if I didn't admit it freaks me out a little, I'm kinda worried about bumping it, or whatever, even though I know that's not right, or a tiny hand grabbing onto my cock at the wrong time…I just…"

"Trust me, Jax, even as…enthusiastic…as you get, the baby will be fine, and as to you bumping the baby?" Oracle sighed, shaking her head in dismay at my stupidity. She looked up at me then tucked me back in my pants. "Okay, let's sort this out." She moved back, taking a seat on the bottom bunk on one side of the cabin and looked at me.

"With me being the first of my kind, both as a Wisp who's pregnant and as a Wisp who's partially human, there might be a better way to do this, but it's difficult and risky."

"Not a good idea if it's an extra risk for you right now."

She held up a hand. "It's not a risk to me or the baby, Jax; it's a risk to you and the others."

"The others?"

"Others at the Great Tower, I mean…" She broke off, clearly thinking about how to deal with this, then started again. "Jax, I'm the first of a new species, but as I'm pregnant, I'm hopefully not going to be the last. Some new species are born occasionally, and they might become strong or they die out, but one that's as powerfully magical as I am, and as our child will be?" She shook her head.

"That's rare?"

"Jax, my kind were hunted almost to extinction because we were powerful and could help others. I'm now more powerful than any other Wisp I've encountered. At first with Heph and with Seneschal, I thought I was imagining it. But after meeting Selkie and that mad fucker who went into the sewers, I'm sure. I'm not just powerful, Jax, I'm evolving *still*."

She lifted her hand and lightning crackled across her fingers, tiny arcs that flared and danced as she spoke, almost negligently holding one of nature's most destructive and dangerous forces in her hand as it danced for her.

"Jax, as things are now? I'm gaining abilities when you unlock them. But I don't think that's going to last much longer."

I sat down on the floor before her, the disparity in our heights meaning we were nearly looking each other in the eye now

"I think I'm going to start to level again," she whispered.

"You can grow on your own?"

She nodded. "I've been gaining a tiny amount of experience as we fight for a long time now. It wasn't much, a fraction of what you and the others receive. But my ability to level was burned out along with the rest. If I can regain that? I'd have a bunch of levels instantly, points, class skills, and…and abilities."

She paused, looking at me and waiting to see how I was taking this.

"Oracle, this is wonderful!" I told her, feeling it as well as just saying it. After all, if Oracle could level on her own, hell, not only would she be able to increase her own mana pool, but she'd grow stronger and learn more magic on her own.

Then it struck me.

"Oracle, our bond…will it…"

"It won't break," she said quickly. "Even if something happened through the magic to break it, we could recreate it, anyway. Don't worry, my love…you'll never be without me." She smiled, and I reached out, the lightning arcs dying away as she took my hands in hers.

"So what then?" I asked her.

"Well, if this goes on then I could bond you as well. As things stand, you are the primary still. The bond goes from you, to me, but if I could bond you in turn, we'd close the link and you'd start to gain my abilities and be able to draw on my mana pool as well."

"That'd be amazing!" I agreed, before frowning. "But you said this was to do with the baby…"

"It is, but I needed you to understand what was happening first, because this means our child is even more special, and special things attract attention."

"You mean threats…"

"I do. If I can do this, I think we need to keep it quiet, or the baby will become a target…"

"The Legion…"

She shook her head. "No, Jax, the Legion are fantastic, and yes, they'll be heavily involved in its life, but…"

"But?"

"But I need more help than they can provide. I need Wisps, Jax. I need my people," Oracle said in a rush. "If we could go to the village that was raided, or to the groves and appeal to any Wisps still there, they might agree to come to the Tower. They could help me, they could share their magic, like we do when we mate. But instead of creating a handful more Wisps for the possible loss of a few in turn…they could envelop me in that power and repair the last few broken fragments."

"And the baby?"

"Would be perfectly safe, I promise. I would never suggest this otherwise. Actually, it'd be incredibly helpful to the baby as well, probably increasing their natural affinity to magic and certainly strengthening them."

"Then we'll do it," I said. "We'll reach out to the Arbuton, get Woodite and Ha'Zel to help us, and..."

"We will." she shuffled forward on the edge of the cabin bed and reached out to me, letting go of my hands and instead wrapping her arms around my neck. "But we've only got a few hours before we reach Narkolt, and we lose all privacy again, so..."

The front of her top split lengthways downwards peeling back, even as it flaked away like ash lifting from a fire. She straddled me, more clothing flaring into nothingness, and I kissed her hungrily.

"And on that note, I'm leaving," Bane whispered, and the door opened then closed, the rest of the realm on the other side as my perfect, private world wrapped herself around me.

CHAPTER THIRTEEN

Carmen was quick to summon her advisors as soon as we landed in the main courtyard. Something about her liege-lord landing an airship in a flare of backblast on her front lawn giving her a slight hint that this was important.

I'd barely made it down the gangplank when the first of the Narkolt guards made it out of the keep and sprinted at me. He went flying a dozen feet from me as Bane swiped his leg out from under him, clearly not liking the speed and direction of the sprint overly.

He hit the grass, skidding, and as he pushed himself up, found a dagger at his throat and a voice hissing in his ear.

"Stay very still,"

The others who had been racing along behind him faltered and slowed.

"Prince Jax!" a clear, feminine voice shouted, Carmen hurrying along out of the keep, her expensive dress lifted high to keep from catching on anything as she ran. "Please, I sent him to greet you!"

"Let him up, Bane," I ordered, striding across the grass towards the pinned figure, even as Oracle and Lydia landed next to me, flanking me on either side.

"Thank you, Prince," the guard gasped, reaching up and tentatively exploring his unbroken skin even as he cleared his throat to speak. "High Lady and City Lord Carmen Al'Issiat bids you be welcome in her city and…"

"And I can see and hear her; it's all right," I cut him off as Bane hauled him to his feet. "Next time, maybe don't run at me, and there'll be a better reception, eh?"

"Uh, yes, Prince."

"Good man." I strode past him and closed on Carmen.

"Prince Jax, it's good to…" She started, dipping into a shallow curtsy, even as courtiers and more following her paused to dip into much lower ones. The men bowed or dropped to one knee, depending on their species and inclinations.

"Thank you, Carmen!" I called clearly, closing the last few meters between us and gesturing for her to stand. "I'm sorry, but we don't have time for a formal audience."

She nodded, turning and gesturing to the others.

Just like that, all bar two of them were up and heading in the direction of the main entrance to the greater palace complex, splitting to go wide of us.

The first of the last two was a tall, fiery-haired woman dressed in a mix of plate and mail armor, with a greatsword strapped to her back and daggers on either hip. She had knelt, rather than curtsied, and long blue and green lines painted across her face showed as she stood.

"This is my bodyguard, Kinsahsa," Carmen introduced, and on the other side a lizard man lifted both hands to opposite shoulders and bowed from the waist before straightening smoothly. "And this is Boaba, my chief advisor. I can have them leave as well, if you…"

"No, they're fine. If you trust them this close, I'll trust you. We'll need the spymaster as well, though."

"Boaba," she said. He inclined his head to me again, then set off in the direction of the keep. "He will summon Nathaniel. In the meantime, is this better had in the keep or…"

"Definitely the keep," I said, setting off and having her fall in alongside Oracle.

"I hear there's been a little excitement?" Carmen asked Oracle with a smile, and Oracle nodded.

"More than just a bit, assassins and…"

"I mean, a bit more personally?" Carmen suggested, flicking a sly finger at Oracle's stomach.

"Oh!" Oracle blushed, clearly an intentional thing, considering who and what Oracle was. But I couldn't help but smile at the effort she put into mimicking people's expectations. "Yes, we're very excited." She accepted my gauntleted hand, squeezing as hers slid into my grasp.

We passed through the side entrance into the keep. Half of the building was still being held up by the local equivalent of scaffolding as they worked to repair the damage from the fight and the subsequent clearing out operations.

It took a few minutes to pass through the various rooms and levels, but by the time we entered the control room, one that we'd appropriated as a barracks last time we were here, Nathaniel and Boaba were waiting for us.

"My Prince?" Carmen offered, gesturing to the Command Center chair, practically a throne in its own right. Nathaniel straightened from his instinctive bow at my arrival.

"Thank you, Carmen," I said with a slight smile, noting the much nicer room, the subtle patterned rugs and the comfortable but clearly 'working' rather than 'fun-time' furniture as well. The flowers and the lack of the stench of Grizz and Giint's arses that had filled it before were a nice touch.

As soon as I sat down, the main system opened to me, recognizing me instantly. The city's systems rose before me. I sensed the details that weren't being shown as much as those that were, finding the edges of the pictures and details, and I found what I was looking for in seconds.

"They're here," I stated flatly.

"Who?" Carmen asked hesitantly.

"Some o' tha old nobles, tha one from before tha cataclysm. They found a way back."

"The old…but they'd be centuries dead," Carmen said, then broke off. "Are they descendants?"

"Yeah, they're my bastard cousins, uncles, aunts, and probably my father as well." I grunted. "I can't see them in the city; they're not showing anywhere, but now that I know what to look for, I can find the portal easily enough."

The 3D drawings were seemingly comprised of a thousand grains of silvery sand and liquid mercury, which collapsed back into the table. In its place, a map of the city grew.

South and east of the palace, on the very edge of the land marked as the Imperial Docks, long covered over by hundreds upon hundreds of houses, was a small neighborhood. In the bottom corner of that, surrounded on all sides by walls, was the Wizard's Tower.

The portal had drawn massive amounts of mana recently, and as the keep and its systems were fully functional, I knew to look for it.

I set a warning to alert if it happened again and zoomed in on the dilapidated tower, surrounded by tenement buildings on all sides.

In Himnel, they'd built up to the edge of it, but it'd been left in glorious isolation. Narkolt had gone the other way, surrounding it and basically trapping it inside a box of taller buildings, leaving only a narrow entrance in and out.

In theory, for the people who lived around it, it was a great solution. They got to use all the space. But for me? This was one of the worst possible outcomes. First, there were constructed choke points leading up to and into the grounds. Secondly, any kind of heavy spell action was going to trash the buildings around the tower.

"They've used the portal. It looks like it was in use for a handful of minutes, but there's nothing else I can tell from it. There's also been a steady drain on the mana collectors since then, an order of magnitude higher than the tower needed before the portal activated."

"So now what?" Lydia asked, leaning against one wall, and folding her arms.

"Now we go in and dig them out."

"Ah, my prince," Nathanial cut in. "Perhaps I could offer an alternative?"

This was going to be something that left me out of the damn fight, I just knew it.

"Perhaps I could send a few of my little friends to examine the area and make sure of things before you do that?" he suggested, "After all, there may be alternatives to outright force."

"These are the same cocks that brought about the cataclysm," I pointed out grimly. "They will happily release a plague, if it'll get them what they want. They literally did that on arrival into my world."

"Ah, perhaps I was not clear," Nathaniel suggested, a slight quirk of the lips as he regarded me. "I mean to send a small team of assassins in to take several prisoners and to scout the location out. They will then bring us their victims and an accurate map of the building to plot the next step."

"And when you say an alternative to outright force, you mean…"

"We slit their throats while they're looking the other way," he clarified.

"You know, I knew I liked you, Nathaniel…" Tang said laconically, tapping a finger on the sheath of one of his blades.

"Bane?" I asked, and he appeared, crouched near my seat. "I want you or Tang with Nathaniel's people."

"My turn!" Tang said quickly, straightening up. "Bane got the last fun job."

"Fine," I replied, having no interest in their games. "Tang, go with Nathaniel's people. You know the kind of weapons that those assholes had, and we've talked enough about my world that you'll recognize most things you're likely to come across. We'll be following and will meet you…"

"Here," Nathaniel suggested, reaching out to tap a finger lightly above the second building in a street near to the tenements. "This is a local bakery; they also take an occasional payment to allow us to use their back room for our more secretive activities."

"Then get things moving. Carmen, I need a contingent of your Elite Guards ready to move in and evacuate the area, if need be. Then I'll need…" I zoomed out on the map to make the entire local area visible and marked the buildings I wanted evacuated and which ones were to be filled with troops and explained the basic plan I had so far.

An hour later, we were climbing down from the coach–a surprisingly comfortable one–and into the street outside the bakery.

The late afternoon sun was hot, the air was stiflingly close and the streets were filled with people hurrying back and forth, many desperate to get under some shelter.

The bakery was larger than most and had both a side and main entrance. We were supposed to take the side one then head straight up the stairs to the second floor. But the sight of all of us, including an actual Valkyrie and several legionnaires, as most of us were dressed, meant there was no chance of us being unremarked on.

Rather than screw the bakery's reputation, I decided it was time to be all blatant and lordly. The building was all gray stone with large doors and small windows and a wooden awning that labored to stop the sun blazing in. But by the time Grizz, myself, and Lydia were inside, all the natural light was pretty much blacked out.

The head baker and his assistants were doing a roaring trade when we arrived. Dozens of people in the shop milled around, all waiting to be served. A handful struggled to get past us and out with their purchases, clearly terrified of "the nobility."

"I need a word with the baker…and some lunch," I said regally, and just like that, the door into the next room was in use, and the locals hurried through it to the side door and out.

In a handful of seconds, the only people inside were the suddenly sweating baker, his various assistants, all of whom looked like they wanted to be anywhere else, and our people.

I stepped up, looking down into the terrified eyes of a man that could barely see over the counter, even with the small stool he was standing on, and shook my head.

"Relax, you're safe," I said. "I think you might want to get your assistants to go back to work, though?"

"They…they're here to serve," he squeaked, gesturing to the door and the utter lack of customers.

"Fine, how much do you make in an average day?" I asked.

"Ah…ah…"

"Five gold, ten? Fifty?" I guessed. He squeaked, shaking his head so fast his next generation of kids were in danger of whiplash.

"About seven to eight in a particularly good day," Nathaniel said, stepping around me and nodding to the baker. "Good afternoon, Joshua, I apologize for the necessity of interrupting you so abruptly, but…"

"Here," I said, taking out a stack of fifty gold coins and setting them on the table between him and me. "I'm being all lordly and forcing you to close for a few hours while my friends and I eat."

"Of…of course!" He gasped, staring at the money.

Nathaniel winced. "We pay him a retainer, Prince Jax, there's no need…"

I shook my head. "We're going to be here for a while. There's no need to ruin his day, and this way, it's an acceptable cover. Plus, I'm damn well hungry."

"Perhaps the red onion and goga berry flatbread?" the baker stammered.

"We'll have some of everything and plenty of butter," I said, gesturing to Nathaniel who nodded, turning to the baker.

"We'll take it all in the upstairs room, Joshua. I apologize for the necessity, but others will be coming. Your story is as Prince Jax has said: he wishes lunch for him and his friends, and you will encourage that as the answer until there is a reason not to."

"O-of course," he stammered, and just like that we were off again, moving through the front, into the back, and up the narrow stairs to the upper floors.

Ten minutes after that, we were sitting on the floor or benches as Tang slid into the room with two others I'd not met before.

"It's them," he said without preamble. "There's less than there were in Himnel, but they're better prepared and will know we're here soon."

"Why?" I asked.

One of the others, who'd slid to a knee upon seeing me, replied, "Our companion, Gethis, was killed by a trap on the way into the courtyard," he replied in a low voice, cold and emotionless. "Some kind of glass shard trap. It shredded him in seconds."

"How bad?" I asked Tang.

"He was dead before he knew it. The ground is littered with them, and they're well-concealed, but…" He shrugged.

"How did it catch him?"

"It's similar to the other one, with a massive illusion set around the courtyard, probably powered by the tower. When you step over the edge of the ground, the two make everything blurry. By the time you can see again, that's it. He was unlucky in that he stood on the trap before he could see it. I was farther around the edge and saw it go off."

"Describe the layout of the courtyard, please," Nathaniel ordered his people.

"The courtyard is intact and ringed by a circular fence of metal. The buildings around it stand solid against the fence. They have a few windows looking out over the courtyard, and those that do appear to show the illusion all the way up to the roof."

"The illusion shows a broken-down and miserable-looking tower, but it looks very different inside. The tower has been reinforced, the courtyard has been cleared, and the doors and lower floor windows are closed and sealed. There were no guards that we could see, but there were a lot of bodies lying around, all apparently fallen to the same kind of traps as Gethis did. They're just lying there. Some are stinking, but most are recent."

"They've only been here a day," Oracle said sadly.

"The city be full o' homeless, even after tha army, tha kitchens, an' everythin' we offer. Some jus' don't want te be 'elped, and some can't..." Lydia said, taking a bite of her muffin.

"And they're the bodies of these homeless?" I asked the assassin and got a quick nod.

"Most likely they lived there. Many slept in the courtyard before this. Probably they were moved on and tried to come back."

"We need to do something about the homeless, if we can," I said absently, rubbing my chin. "There are soup kitchens set up and jobs available, both in the army and out. Hell, the amount of people who joined us means there's a desperate need for people to fill their jobs...but..."

"But while many of the homeless are there through no fault of their own, many choose that life. We helped those we could, Prince Jax, and those who are not ready, well, their lives are infinitely better under the Empire than they were a few scant months ago," Nathaniel pointed out. I grunted, forcing them from my mind.

"So, the tower is sealed up tight?" I asked.

"The lower floors are all closed off," Tang said. "Doors and windows were shut tight, and while there's movement behind the windows, I can't be sure what's there. The upper floors aren't sealed, but..." He shook his head.

"You can see the balconies from the ground, and the space around them has something built on them. I'd bet there's concealed archers, maybe with the same kind of crossbows, waiting for anyone flying in," he finished.

"Then we're down to either a forced heavy assault or trickery." I grunted.

"I like trickery," Bane quipped. "But you know, planning that might be beyond you."

"I can be sneaky!" I complained.

Tang pretended to cough, the word "murderhobo" still clear as a goddamned cloudless sky, folding himself around a fist theatrically. He straightened up and pretended to be all innocent. "What?" he asked, spreading his hands. "A guy can't get something in his throat?"

"Well, I'd heard the rumors about you, but you know." Grizz grinned at him.

I shook my head at their antics, opening my mouth to speak when Giint stood up and held out a small silver cube.

"You want in?" he asked and shook the cube suggestively. "This make bright light, too bright, no see anything...we walk in."

"It's a flashbang?" I took it from him and looked it over, curious as all hell. "How does it work?" I asked, seeing nothing that suggested it could open never mind explode.

"Don't!" Lydia snapped, leveling one finger at Giint. "Don't yer fuckin' dare!"

"What...?" I said, confused.

"'E were gonna set it off ter show yer." She took it out of my hand and squinted at it. "This button?" She asked Giint, being careful not to touch it as she pointed. He nodded glumly. "Good boy."

I don't know who was more surprised, me or Giint, when she pulled a small stick of his wonderdrug out of her bag of holding and tossed it to him. It was gone in seconds, and she put the device in the bag in its place before nodding at me.

"Okay, so…did we have a plan?" I asked around. "I mean, I like 'kick the door in and slaughter them all', but…"

"But It's too subtle for you?" Sehran asked with a smile.

"I can be subtle," I grumbled.

"You really can't, Jax," Oracle corrected, leaning into me and smiling. "But that's okay, because we love you."

"Thanks, I think." I leaned in and kissed the top of her head. "Is this everyone?" I asked Nathaniel, who shook his head.

"Two more were sent through the sewers and one flier. I recommend we wait for them to report in as well," he replied.

I stood up and headed to the little bench. It was laden with mixed breads, pastries, and even a large crock of freshly churned butter. "Might as well get something to eat," I suggested, "if we've got people exploring the sewers, you might not have an appetite after they arrive!"

"Point," Grizz muttered. "Remember the manastone mine? Was not fun…it was days before I could eat sweet corn again."

"Oh gods, man, you had to bring that up!" I held the local equivalent to calzone, a baked bread with honey and tomatoes as well as *sweet corn* in my hand at the time. I set it down, frowning at him as he picked it up and winked at me, before being clipped by Yen.

The confusion and nervousness of Nathaniel's team stood out to me as I joked with my squad, but I sure as hell wasn't changing the way I lived for them or anyone else.

Half an hour went by, then an hour, and finally, as we were about to give up, another of the assassins cracked the door open and staggered in, filthy, bleeding heavily, and reeking.

I hit them with Scour at almost the same time as Oracle did the first healing, then it all went wrong.

CHAPTER FOURTEEN

The figure that had staggered in the door, barely able to stand upright, hunched around the hilt of a dagger dramatically driven into their stomach, straightened up and flicked the blade out, hurling it end-over-end into Ronin, who'd just stepped up close to me.

He was wearing the lightest of the legion armors, a scout variant with a lot of leather, but the blade punched into Ronin's thigh and shattered as he screamed, going down hard.

The assassin whipped out more throwing knives, even as the filthy and covered windows exploded inward, and the pounding feet of a dozen more men and women raced toward us.

"Kill them all!" a voice screamed. My lips pulled back in a feral grin as I tossed my half-eaten wedge of bread aside, catching my helm as Oracle tossed it to me and sliding it on.

The standard legion helm was all well and good, but fuck that.

Where I'd had to go standard for the rest of the armor, at least until Thorn could make an underskin that worked, I'd kept my helm and it felt amazing since the upgrade.

It was cushioned and fit the contours of my face perfectly, settling against my skin with a cool sensation of solidity, and it barely restricted my vision at all. I blinked as one of the assassin's blades was hurled at me, fluttering end over end, and I head butted it, shattering the gleaming little glass blade into a dozen pieces that danced and tinkled across my armor, even as I slid my right hand into my Bag of Spatial Folding.

I pulled it back out with my naginata in it, glowing bright with magic, and the assassin's eyes widened at the suddenly revealed weapon.

The assassins were professionals, hands dipping into pockets hidden inside the clothes beneath their spy's cloak. But even as they started throwing weapons, we responded.

Oracle had slid back behind Lydia, who pulled her shield up and around to protect her, even as she started summoning lightning.

Lydia dragged her mace up and across the face of a figure that landed near her, sending them reeling with blood and teeth flying.

Giint was kicked in the face. He screamed and staggered back, bouncing off Jian's leg, as our team's resident warlock lunged forward, both of his blades sliding from his twin scabbards with a whisper of silk.

He parried a frantic stab with the left blade, flicked the right across his opponent's left bicep, cutting through cloth, flesh, and into the bone before lifting away as blood erupted free.

His victim screamed. Jian punched him in the face with the hand holding the hilt of the left blade, before he spun his right in a blur of motion, slashing it across their upper left thigh and cutting through easily.

His opponent fell, practically cartwheeling out of sight in spray of blood. Giint bounced back upright and screamed in abject fury, leaping over the falling figure to grab the one who'd kicked him, a kill-stick driving up and into a most sensitive area. Grinding and chewing blades dug deep, dragging more and more meat into them as the poor figure screamed and died.

Another of the cloaked figures landed before Bob then froze, staring up into the glowing eyes in horror before being hurled back through the broken window he'd entered by. A wheeze and the sound of breaking bones was all that came from him as Bob slammed his massive maul, the Ice-Drake's Revenge, into his chest.

More landed, dozens of figures streaming in, and the rest of the team went to work. Sehran dragged her whip free, flashing it out and wrapping it around the throat of another, while smiling and singing at the one who landed right beside him.

The air was filled with the tinkle and shatter of glass and the meaty sounds of impact, the wet slashes of blood fountaining across walls and dripping from the ceiling. Through it all, I grinned and leaped forwards.

I triggered Lunge, my naginata held close to the head in my right hand, my left formed into a simple finger blade, and I crossed the distance to the door in a split second.

I drove the stiffened fingers of my left hand into an assassin's stomach with all the force I could muster, tearing through blood and organs, the thin armor barely even registering a hesitation.

I gripped him by the spine and yanked backward, twisting at the hip and dragging the naginata down to deflect a blackened sword blade that the assassin behind had extended.

The figure I'd practically torn in half let loose a bloodcurdling gurgle of disbelief as I ripped a full section of his spine free, letting him fall to the floor, broken.

The one behind saw their companion fall, but when their sword was smacked from their hand by a force they couldn't resist, my left hand coming up, covered in blood and fragments of spinal tissue and bone gleaming wetly in it, they panicked.

They tried to take a step back, hitting others running upward and bumping off, before shoving back harder and harder, screaming something in a language I didn't speak.

Others took up the shout, seeing the room behind me, the blood that was literally dripping from the walls and falling from the ceiling, and the figures that stood inside, coated in the blood of their friends and fellow assassins.

They'd attacked us without warning, and only one of us had sustained any real injury so far, and that one was being healed by Yen as Oracle was currently channeling a pissed-off emperor and literally glowing with the amount of lightning she was driving into the last two figures to leap through the window closest to her.

The air beside me buffeted as two blurs slid past from inside the room, my bonds letting me know that it was Tang on my left and presumably Bane on my right as I chased the now-fleeing assassins downstairs.

That's to say they went downstairs. I simply ran at the nearest window and leaped at it, my armored bulk tearing through the thin, old boards and filthy glass like tissue paper.

I tumbled, twisting in the air, then I was landing, my insane Agility combined with my flying experience and skills to help me land on my feet…even as the first of the assassins cleared the bottom of the stairs and I turned to face him.

The figure at the front, all in black and red leather under a cloak and with a cloth mask drawn across their face, frantically tried to backpedal, only to have their leg kicked out from under them as Tang became visible.

I grabbed one that tried to stealth past me, barely any skill involved at all, just a shitty excuse for a chameleon spell, before I was slammed to the side, driven to the floor by Bane, who flipped over me and landed on the far side, twisting around as he fought something so fast I couldn't even see it.

I rolled to my feet, backing up to give Bane some room, squinting and wishing I'd kept that damn ring that let me see stealthed fuckers.

Then I grinned.

I might not have a ring that let me do it, but I still had some spells that would ruin these fucker's day.

I took a deep breath, fingers already dancing as I started to cast. Oracle floated out of the window I'd exited in an insane display of power.

The street was rapidly emptying around us, but in true entertainment versus idiocy, people had basically picked a decent distance that they thought gave them some safety, then stopped to watch the fight.

Some appeared to be placing bets.

Oracle was literally glowing with crackling power, lightning flowing through her, hair lifting and floating outward. Her leggings and little strappy top were suddenly silver and far more figure-hugging as the power crackled across her.

She lifted her arms out to the sides, eyes bright blue and white, glowing with suppressed fury at the threat to our unborn child and she went nova.

The lightning lashed out in a single stream, then two, then four, then dozens upon dozens. Some of the strikes hit fighters who were trying to sneak away, others were barely conscious, but most hit targets I'd not even seen yet, illuminating them as they crawled, spiderlike, across the walls closing in on us.

Where the ones we'd faced so far were only fifteen or twenty in number, a full dozen more were stealthed and revealed all around us. My spell finished and lashed out to illuminate more of them.

Frostfire Circle of Cleansing slammed into the floor, a ring of glowing lines rippling out like a carved line leading straight to hell. A ring of blue, white, and red light seared up from the ground all around us, illuminating the blurs that were closing in as their stealth abilities and spells tried to adjust.

Then the runes tore their way into the cobbles all around, and the spell truly began. Flickers leaked from the gaps in reality, sparks flaring into full-blown flames, flames that raced out, drawn to movement, to life and death and to anything and everything they could find inside their radius.

They flowed up walls, and they ran up and into cracks in armor.

Those who were used to my spells and the generally mad shit that Oracle and I pulled on a daily basis ignored them. They would feel only a slight tickle as the magic examined them before rolling on, flowing down a leg or leaping from a sword tip to reach another.

Those who weren't used to it, or sworn to me, though, had a very different response.

The flames seemed to pause as they found a target, double checking in some way, then striking. The flames poured into armor's joints, burning and freezing in equal measure. The frost siphoned the heat from the body and fed it to the fire, which burned even hotter, using its victim's own heat against them.

Screams rose on all sides, even as Oracle's lightning flashed out and carved great lines across the walls and cobbles of the street.

The lesser assassins ran and panicked, but the new ones—more experienced and better-stealthed flipped from the walls, leaped onto roofs, and started to run.

"Kill them all!" Grizz bellowed, repeating the assassin's cry earlier. My lip curled in a snarl of agreement.

I'd not been able to see the figure Bane was fighting before, but now? They were weaving and screaming, staggering drunkenly as flames burrowed deeper and deeper into their flesh, even as Bane expertly carved their defenses away.

I didn't have time for this shit.

The sneaky raid was over. They knew we were coming and had dispatched assassins, so all bets were off! I took two quick steps into range and slid into a low spinning heel kick, planting both hands on the ground as I dropped. Turning my back to the enemy to build momentum, I swept my right leg around as fast and hard as I could.

It hit the side of his left leg just above the ankle, flipping him through ninety degrees at a speed he wasn't expecting and slammed the side of his head into the cobbles. I flowed to my feet, brought my naginata up, flipping it over, and stabbed down, the blade sliding through the shitty mix of bullet-resistant and stealthy body armor he was wearing like a blade through fucking butter.

I felt the crash of the ground on the far side of his body more than I felt him, the blade sliding between ribs, his lungs, and his heart, glancing across the stones then back up in a spray of blood as the assassin's eyes widened, their internal organs shredded.

They fell back, and Bane stepped back, sheathing a single dagger and hitting himself with a healing spell as he blurred, then vanished, running after the nearest living target.

I spun, dismissing the already cooling meat by my feet as I looked for more. But the few who hadn't run were either being cooked, rendered down to mince, or getting systematically broken, depending on who they faced.

The only living one of them who wasn't regretting their recent life choices stood to one side with Sehran, gazing adoringly at her.

"You" I snapped, striding to him. "What happened to my people?"

"Answer him, my pet," Sehran crooned. He nodded, breaking into a smile, his mask hanging loose from his face by one corner.

"We caught them! They tried to come in underground, and we caught them, the traps…"

"How did you know about this place?" I asked, gesturing to the bakery.

"We tortured them–the ones that survived. They told us," he said seriously. "They tried not to, but we brought the lord's torturers, and they broke them."

"Motherfuckers…which lord?"

"Caiden Y'Boraz, Earl of Teinar, Lord of the Northern Seas," he said happily. "He leads us, raised us…"

"He raised you? How did so many get this good at stealth so fast?" I asked. "And when did you get here?"

"Yesterday." He smiled. "Lord Caiden gave us Pearls…he…" He broke off, eyes flickering as I started to swear.

"Fucker!" I snarled. "Sehran, keep him; I need more answers. You…how many more are in the Tower, and are there any traps or…" I broke off as blood burst from his eyes and ears, rushing down from his nose and out of his quivering mouth, as the sound of bones cracking suddenly filled the air.

We both took quick steps back, and I growled, recognizing the Oath's effects on a body as he was torn apart by his own.

"Fuck it, kill him," I ordered Sehran, orienting myself with the buildings around me.

"Lydia! Oracle!" I bellowed, getting their attention. "Let's go fuck them up!" I leaped into the air, naginata leading like an inverse falling star, glowing with magic as I arced up and over the buildings and closed on the tower, left hand extended and mana pouring into the shield rune, sending it flickering to life.

Lydia's wings beat a steady thud as she leaped after me, growling probably as much at me for leading the way as for anything that faced her. As well as Lydia's, though, the snap of Sehran's batlike wings echoed as they unfurled then beat hard, lifting her into the air behind us.

I had a split second to berate myself, I *always* forgot about her being able to goddamn fly! Her wings weren't even subtle, for fuck's sake…but then it was gone, as the twin feeling of the drain on my health and mana from flying and the shield rune met my sheer joy at the freedom of flight.

A small collection of children on a rooftop had clearly been hiding and watching the fight, staring open-mouthed in wonder as we flashed over the buildings.

The sun reflecting off our armor, the whistle of the wind, and the target before us as the illusion of the dilapidated tower fell away, and the truth was revealed.

The top of the tower was open on one side. The double doors that led out onto a wide balcony had been flung back and pinned open, leaving the top floor a bright and airy circle of stone and luxury.

Dotted here and there were crates and boxes, clearly from our world, marked and sealed, while others were laid open, crowbars abandoned on the floor nearby.

A handful of warriors surrounded a figure I'd not seen before. Tall, well-built, and seemingly in his thirties, he stood holding a double-headed glaive in one hand, the tip resting against the ground as he waited patiently for me to close with him.

A blur muddled the shadows on one side of him as a stealthed figure moved into position. I growled, knowing it was a trap.

"Lydia, Starlight!" I barked at her, "Sehran, help her, then distraction; clear out the stealthed ones, Oracle?"

"Yes, my love?" she called, her voice at once grim and determined.

"Fuck that shit up," I ordered. While she spent a lot of her time backing me up, she was lethal in her own right.

"With pleasure," she growled, slowing and casting. Lydia climbed into the sky, reaching out to the stars above, and Sehran began to sing.

I pulled ahead, pushing more mana into Soaring Majesty, then pulled upright at the last second, dropping to land on the balcony facing the noble asshat who stayed a dozen meters back.

"You are the pretender," he called, his voice clear and calm.

"No, I'm the Prince," I responded. "You're a prick, though…Earl of Cockwomble, wasn't it?"

"Earl of Teinar, Lord of the Northern Seas," he corrected calmly. "I suspected honorable combat would be beyond you, as is respect."

"Honorable combat?" I hissed. "You sent fucking assassins after me!"

"You sent them into my Tower first."

"I sent them to find out what was going on! You used a portal to invade…"

"Did I attack your territory? Did I kill anyone? Did I make a single move against you?" he asked rhetorically. I hesitated, a brief second of confusion, of doubt entering my mind. What if he was like Falco? What if he wasn't a complete knob, and he'd been waiting for me to approach him? What if…

A slight shimmer in the air, almost within reach, caught my attention, and I reacted before my brain caught up, dropping to one knee and swinging my naginata in a vicious arc around me, even as I fed fire into it.

It blazed bright red, orange, and gold, before turning a cold, blue-white as it snagged on a cloth then slid effortlessly through flesh.

Blood erupted around me, bodies falling, and I straightened back up, sneering at him.

"Honorable combat," I repeated. "You're just like all the rest."

"Kill him," he said with a sneer, lifting his right hand and closing it into a fist, the back facing toward me as light burst from a deep blue jewel set in an oval housing.

I grinned at him as more and more of his people appeared, running toward me. Then Lydia struck.

Her Starlight ability was a class one that left her exhausted afterward. Hell, she'd been unconscious after it on one occasion, but she'd assured me that after speaking with the dead Valkyrie she was being trained by that it was a case of the more she used it, the easier it'd come, and that she'd be able to control it better as she grew in power.

However it worked, the effect was amazing.

It called upon the power of the stars, be it day or night, and it channeled that light into a beam, one that she guided. As it narrowed from a spotlight to a car headlight to a beam, it grew more and more powerful. As she closed it down to the narrowest she could, barely as wide across as a can of beer, it punched through anything in its path like a politician on the way to a handout.

The beam lasted less than five seconds, but in that time, she jerked it back and forth in front of me, making damn sure the balcony was clear, and bodies, previously hidden by stealth abilities appeared, tumbling lifelessly to the ground.

In addition to the ones that had dropped stealth, others had maintained it, clearly expecting to take me by surprise. Instead, they were chopped into kibble by the beam that jerked back and forth, their blood spraying into the air as the lance of starlight tore them into individual atoms.

When it finished, Oracle reached out to me, letting me know that Sehran had caught Lydia and was helping her land. Oracle was ready when I was.

I grinned, seeing the effect the wholesale slaughter was having on the forces arrayed against me, and I spoke aloud for the enemies' benefit.

"Now!"

The air around me exploded as a bar of lightning as thick as my thigh lashed out, slamming into the leader and driving him back several steps. The gem on his hand flared into life, coating him in an azure blue barrier of air.

The lightning hit it and was absorbed, dozens of arcs flaring off, impacting the warriors around the leader and shocking them, but powering his shield instead of punching through as I'd expected.

I heard Sehran's low-level singing with half an ear as the shield faded, and I looked into the eyes of the man standing there, grinning.

"Fuck…" I muttered, barely having time to get that out, before his shield *flexed* and like a giant lens. The power of Oracle's bolt was twisted, warped, and then redirected.

"You do it like this!" he sneered. The bolt that leaped out made the sun seem dull in comparison.

Heading straight for Oracle.

I careened into its path, slashing my naginata into the stream of destructive power, screaming as it tore into me.

I was picked up, thrown into the air, and tossed head over heels. Terrible power roared through me, muscles quivering, hair crisping, and eyes burning.

I fell backward, the balcony appearing and vanishing as I tumbled over and over, falling. Glimpses of the others storming into the courtyard blurred into each other, traps exploding in flames as Yen hammered a path clear with Flamespears. Arrin sent Magic Missiles tearing through the air.

Grizz, the mad bastard, was leading a charge, his Legion Knight sword and shield held high as he screamed a challenge. Dozens of elite guards and the rest of my squad raced behind him, flames rising from the destructive blasts we unleashed. Then I hit, and I lost sight of the greater fight.

My shield had been up still, but compared to that blast, it'd barely lasted long enough to matter. Matter it did, though, as it kept me conscious.

The ground came up fast. Activating Soaring Majesty again, I burned more mana and health, my health bar flashing as it dropped like a stone.

I powered it hard, flipping myself around…and I landed in the middle of a concentration of the enemy, all drawn up and ready to face my people.

A handful of the enemy were knocked back, and one…well, when a seven-foot-tall man in full plate armor and built like an Olympian lands atop you, redirecting all the force of their fall into you, well, the best description for him, as he was wearing leather armor, was "splat."

I rose to my full height, the world around me tinged red as my health bar flashed and flared in warning. Lightning still arcing through me, grounding itself, blood streaming down my helm from the man I'd just rendered into jam…

I snarled and attacked the blurry figures that surrounded me on all sides.

I'd lost my naginata in the landing, but it wasn't far…a screaming figure was holding it for me, but my hands were full at the moment. I slammed both arms out in as wide an arc as I could, bones breaking beneath my blows.

I grabbed a wrist—the attached hand currently holding a short sword—with my left hand and redirected the stab into one of his coworkers and closed my right gauntlet over another man's face.

I squeezed, *hard*, bones cracking as he squealed. Then I twisted my hand, snapping his neck before releasing and yanking back, driving my armored elbow into someone behind me.

I dropped low, a pair of blades crashing off each other over my head, deflecting into their friends and drawing more screams.

I rose again, grabbing arms and twisting, then pulled back and head butted the tallest of them, the blade on the crest of my helm carving deep into him. I yanked back, letting loose a snap kick with my left foot and sending a screaming figure pirouetting to the floor, clutching their broken hip.

The fight was close in, dirty, and bloody…and it lasted seconds before they broke.

Thirty men and women facing a level of violence none of them had ever imagined.

I straightened up, heart hammering, and gasped as I was hit with one, then two, then five more heals as my elites and squad started casting.

In a matter of seconds, I was growling up at the balcony overhead.

Blood ran down me, dripping off my armor. I popped a mana potion, saw the immediate dip in my mana even as it filled, and downed another. Then I crouched and rocketed back up, dragging my naginata free of its makeshift sheath as I went, sending a spray of blood into the air after me as the body fell.

I twisted out from the tower, angling myself, then flew inward. The upper floor grew in my vision as I closed, and the snarling figure that stood in the middle of blackened bodies and burning crates.

The noble asshat who had blasted me from the tower had clearly been in a battle of magic since then, facing not only Oracle, but Sehran, who was using every trick in her impressive arsenal in distraction as well as the spells we'd taught her.

As I came in to land, naginata extended, an Explosive Compression was just dying away. The shield of air was vanishing again with debris raining down from the walls.

Before he could get off a counterattack, I was there, landing hard into a slide, my boots clanging and sending up a shower of sparks in and out of pools of blood, swinging for his head.

He parried it, just, the shield bursting into fragments and slowing my blow just in time for him to block my blade.

He abandoned magic, grabbing his two-headed glaive with both hands and dropped to one knee. Twisting at the hip and grabbing the shaft with his left hand, he brought the blade up and stabbed at my thigh.

I dipped the head of my naginata, catching his blade behind the head and spun. Deflecting him to the side and whipping the weapon around, I danced back from him. His counter slash barely missed as I brought my blade down fast and hard.

He blocked it, a shower of sparks flaring bright and making us both squint as we backed up, then struck again, weapons glowing with magic.

I stabbed out, and he blocked, slapping my weapon aside then dragging his down mine. The blades raced towards my fingers, only to be knocked aside as I hopped and snap-kicked with my right foot, twisting and angling my shaft down, as I tried to stomp on his haft, slamming my elbow into the side of his helm.

He staggered then planted his foot on a crate and shoved back, our shoulders against each other. I moved in turn, surprised by his strength.

He twisted to face me at the same time I did to him, locking the shafts of our weapons together as we both tried to kick and shove the other down.

He let go with the left hand, stabbing forward with that hand, heel extended under my shaft and angled up toward my face. I ducked to the side, and the bottom of my helm clattered against the upper section of my breastplate. Something hit it, a blade skittering across my vision, hitting but bouncing off the God-altered glass of my eyes.

I saw his mistake in the same second as he did, a widening of his eyes as he missed. I jerked down with both arms, trapping his arm on my side of my naginata, against my chest, then twisted my weapon.

His arm was locked in place, unable to move, rotate, or escape. It was forced out of place, then past its tolerances, using my naginata as a lever.

He screamed as the joint of his elbow was forcibly snapped loose, and I drove the flat of the blade into his face, staggering him back.

He took three quick steps, abandoning the glaive to clatter on the floor, grabbing at something on his belt, ripping it free, and throwing it at the floor.

I rushed him, stabbing, and felt the blade catch on something, cutting through thin armor, and reinforced cloth, flesh, then…

I was flying backward, the world around me full of bright light and pain as a compressed spell released, blasting me into the ceiling, then letting me fall facedown with a crash of armor.

Garbled noises and the tower shaking were all I could register. I couldn't see anything, nothing at all, until I was dragged to my knees, my helm shoved back to expose my throat.

I struggled weakly, still stunned, barely able to feel anything…until the hand holding my helm released it. I slammed my chin down, covering my exposed neck a split second before something clattered off it.

Pain, confusion, and anger rose. Determination wafted from Oracle, love, and fear, as well as belief, belief in me so powerful I could use it to power a fucking starship across reality.

She knew I'd kick this guy's ass.

She'd seen me fuck up the God of Death and steal part of His soul.

I felt it, and my rage roared to life.

I couldn't see…but so what?

I didn't need eyes or ears…

I lunged, arms outstretched and drove the blade on my helm into something. A cry of pain and anger rewarded me as, sod's law, I passed under his arm, barely nicking the bottom of his left arm with the back of the blade.

He clamped down hard on the side of my helm, driving a dagger held in his right into the side of my armor, denting it with the power of the blow, but failing to penetrate.

I wrapped my arms around him and lifted, driving myself to my feet and sprinting ahead, still unable to see. He screamed and stabbed at me, his body shifting and altering as he called upon whatever abilities and changes his essence cores had bought him.

"Left, my love."

An image of the room before me filled my mind, shady and indistinct.

I saw the edge of the balcony, the arch of the stone that lifted and flowed across the ceiling…and I rammed him into the edge of it, as hard as I could.

A few ribs broke, and he coughed, his broken left elbow banging uselessly against me as he released me in a spasm of pain. I straightened, driving a left hook into his face.

It snapped his head sideways, and I twisted at the hip. West's long-ago words, screamed at me from the side of the ring, echoed in my ears.

"Twist and pop, lad, twist and pop! Hips aren't just fer the ladies!"

Gods, he'd screamed that at me every time I'd fought. In the end, it'd stuck though, and now I did it instinctively, using every damn muscle I could to slam a fist into the dimly sensed figure before me.

His jaw shattered under the blow, my gauntlet clattering as something came loose, and vision returned as Oracle healed me.

Blood sprayed, and a tooth cracked in the fucker's perfect smug smile.

I grabbed his thick black hair with my left hand and punched him again, full in the face. His head crashed back, my left hand suddenly full of torn hair, as his head rebounded from the wall, bricks crushed by the transferred force. Stone dust rained down on us both, and I dipped low, slamming a fist into his lower right ribs, then the other into the left.

I broke them systematically, hardly even realizing it was my voice screaming my fury at him as I tracked the punches up his body, rib by rib.

I could see his face now as he twisted, eyes shifting to green, insectile slits, blood dribbling from his mouth. He blocked a punch, slapping it aside, only for me to slap his hand aside in turn. Then, grabbing the inside of his wrist and turning it, I locked his right arm in an arm bar and punched it as hard as I could, driving my mana into Mana Overdrive as I did it.

The ability flared to life, doubling and redoubling my already-impressive strength. I snapped his forearm, leaving the bones jutting free on the underside.

He screamed, then hissed something at me, the words bubbling on the blood in his mouth and throat.

I didn't need to hear them clearly.

I knew what he was trying to say.

He'd tried to kill me and my friends. He'd tried to conquer the city, or he would have, and he'd already been part of the cabal that had killed Amon and started the Cataclysm.

He'd seen that he was about to lose, to die, and he expected to surrender to me. To survive, then stab me in the back and go right back to being a shit biscuit of epic proportions.

"Denied!"

His eyes widened in sudden realization and terror.

I blocked his useless attempt at hitting me and raised my right foot, stomping down on the inside of his left leg, twisting the limb and shattering the knee.

He screamed as I drove the web of my hand, encased in armor, into his throat.

He broke off, choking, eyes bulging, and I grabbed him by the throat again.

"Can yer mother stitch?" I hissed, old memories of fights rising in my mind. "Then stitch this!" I leaned back, then drove the armored forehead of my helm into the front of his face.

Bone broke, blood burst, and he went limp as I pulled back, the instinctive headbutt somewhat ruined by the slight tug. The blade that I'd forgotten was attached came free of the deep divot it'd carved in his skull.

I stepped back farther, releasing him, and let his corpse fall to the floor. Blood burst free in a great gout to pour across the floor as I turned, surveying the ruined upper floor of the mage's tower.

The tower shuddered, and I fed mana into my words as I spoke the words the realm needed to hear.

"Caiden Y'Boraz, Earl of Teinar, Lord of the Northern Seas is dead! Surrender, or die like your master!" I boomed, the last quivers and kicks of the meat laid before me, as if he still tried to deny it…then the crash of steel echoed up from elsewhere as weapons were cast down in surrender.

The fight was over.

For now.

CHAPTER FIFTEEN

felt them coming, Oracle, Lydia and Sehran flying closer, even as the rest of the team hurried higher up the tower towards me, and I pulled up the first of the notifications, determined to get them out of the way as soon as possible.

Congratulations!

You have cleared the Wizard's Tower and have the prerequisite authority and abilities to claim this hidden location, adding it to your territory as a specialized base. As this location holds less than 10% of sentients that are actively hostile to your rule, it can now be claimed.

Do you wish to annex this territory now?

Yes/No

I selected yes, obviously, and a fresh hell of notifications popped up, showing me the other details for the Wizard's Tower, including portal controls and the illusory options.

I pulled that to the fore, even as other notifications went live, as the last beats of the shitbag on the floor's heart gave out.

Attention, Imperial Citizens of the Territory of Dravith!

Prince Jax, Scion of the Empire, has defeated Caiden Y'Boraz, Earl of Teinar, Lord of the Northern Seas in combat. His rank, territories, and possessions are returned to the Imperial Throne for redistribution by the Empire!

All Hail Jax Amon! All Hail the Prince of the Empire!

"Heh," I muttered, rereading it. "Guess that means me, then." I banished the screen, knowing that had to have pissed a few people off when it popped up, overriding everyone's wishes. As usual, I wondered how many people crashed their horse or were put off their stroke or whatever each time that happened.

"Jax," Oracle called, landing close and running to me as I banished the screens, reaching out to her. She slowed and winced, looking me up and down before shaking her head. "No," she said. "Just…no."

Her fingers were dancing and lips rolling before I had time to look down, my helm making it a little difficult to see. Then I saw my fingers as I lifted them, encased in gauntlets as they were, sticky with drying blood and the matted hair that was stuck to them.

I lifted my other hand, then looked down as far as I could at my chest…and my legs, and yeah.

I was an absolute mess.

I was literally caked in drying viscera, which fortunately flaked away as Oracle cast Scour, rolling it up and down across my body and armor.

The blood and flesh that was alien to me collapsed into dust and water, running free and coating the floor in a rough slurry that mixed with the blood and filth.

"How about we go somewhere else?" Oracle suggested brightly. I looked up at her, seeing that she was now hovering a few inches above the floor.

"The balcony," I suggested, pointing in that direction as Lydia and Sehran, who was helping to support her, landed. "I'll grab some chairs."

I strode off to one side and reached out to a chair that had somehow survived the fight practically unharmed.

Little else had.

I took it anyway, the last vestiges of my mother's teachings on good manners making me carry it across and set it in place for Oracle. Then I ruined it all and tossed my helm into my bag, then picked her up and kissed her now that I wasn't such a filthy mess.

"Hey, boss, that was fun!" Grizz called as he jogged out onto the upper floor, only to have Bane's voice rise as well.

"Oh, for the love of Jenae, we've all been fighting, and he's got his hands on Oracle already," he cursed theatrically. "Come on, everyone, we don't want to see what comes next. You know he's got no shame."

"I'm going to find you a girlfriend, if it's the last thing I do," I called to him. "Then I'm going to do my very best to make sure you've got blue balls permanently."

"I'm aquatic by nature," he countered. "I was born with blue balls, not that it's any of your business, but good try."

"Fuck's sake, Bane…*amphibious*!" I corrected him. "You've been talking to Tommy again. He could never tell the difference between those two."

"Whatever, you're still a pervert for looking," he quipped. I casually shot him the finger as Oracle settled into her seat with a sigh.

"Are you all okay?" I asked, looking around and seeing the others coming out onto the roof.

"We are."

"Aye."

"Yeah."

"My pants will never be the same."

That last one was from Ronin, who was fingering the shredded remains of his trousers mournfully.

"Look on the bright side," Tang said, nudging him. "A few inches higher, you'd be singing soprano."

"Gods, if that ever happens, don't try and save me. Just make it quick," he muttered, shuddering.

"Idiots," Lydia grumbled, stepping forward and looking me over. "Yer looked a mess before. Ah think more time wi' Restun…"

"What did I ever do to you, Lydia?" I shook my head. "I mean, really, that's just cruel."

"Uh, is this supposed to be doing this?" Jian interrupted from the far side of the room.

I pivoted, following his pointing finger to…the portal.

Sparks were starting to arc up and down it as power was fed into the portal from the far end, light reaching out in flowing lines from points of glowing disturbance on the Inside of the arch.

I swore, almost knocking Ronin flying as he barely managed to get out of the way of my sprint in time. Skidding to a halt by the portal, I slapped my hand against it and focused.

A collection of screens popped up, but rather than read any of them, I shoved my intention toward the tower controls. A new screen that I vaguely remembered popped up.

Greetings, Master of the Tower.

Do you wish to restrict access to this Portal?

Yes/No

I selected Yes, obviously, and a second prompt arrived.

Please select level of restriction:

- Fully Locked

- Key access only

- Restricted to members of a designated group

- Open to designated individuals

- Open to all connections

I chose the option to restrict access to members of a specific group and designated the new Imperial Senate only and grinned as the lights shifted.

Restrictions accepted. Shielding portal.

The light had been flickering through a dozen different colors, then more, most of which I had no names for beyond "greeny-blue, sort of." Those were overcome by a fresh, bright red light that reached out from the arch, flowing like water across the portal surface.

It closed over the entrance perhaps a second and a half ahead of the portal, completing the connection.

The portal opened, a wavering room appearing on the far side. A face I vaguely remembered from the Arena on earth stood to one side, drawn and haggard as she waved a line of soldiers forward.

She glanced at the portal, the vision of her fading in and out of focus as her eyes widened. Then she was screaming in mixed terror and fury. Her forces raced into the void, each of them blurring as they raced across the distance between us.

The first one hit the barrier. The soldier before me seemed to be running down a short tunnel. He accelerated up to a horrific speed, until at the last second, his face registered terror. A flash of light, and they were gone.

The Wizard's Tower shivered as their life force and mass was converted directly into energy and mana, then absorbed into the structure.

The tower accepted it, and I grinned, knowing she was actively fixing my new tower while she lost troops.

Another dozen soldiers were converted to energy before she could stop them. Even then, the last one that tried to stop was too slow and was catapulted into the barrier.

Once they were all stopped, she strode up to the edge of the portal and stared at me across space.

When neither of us did anything, it began to feel weird.

"Why's she doing that?" I asked out of the corner of my mouth. Oracle snorted.

"She's trying to make you feel inferior."

"Really?"

"For all their power, the old nobility were just people, and idiots," she said.

I grinned, holding one finger up to the woman in a "wait one" gesture.

"Can she hear me?"

"I don't think so."

"Someone cut that knob jockey over there's head off and pass it to me," I ordered, grinning.

It only took a couple of seconds, then Tang was there, holding it by the remains of its hair, handing it to me from "off-screen," as far as she could see.

I lifted it, turning it to face her, and gave it a little wiggle. Her eyes widened in outrage. Then I turned, lining it up just right, and drop kicked the head at her.

It hit the portal and was deflected, unfortunately, bouncing off to the side and hitting Giint, who started shouting and screaming at it, before punting it as well.

In seconds, the head was flying back and forth. I sighed, enjoying the utter outrage on her face as my team engaged in an impromptu game of football.

She'd clearly have happily killed him herself, but to see one of the elite, a 'true' noble, as she saw it, treated with such casual disrespect, that was more than she could bear.

She screamed and shouted, then cast a spell, hammering it into the portal. There was a flare of magic aaaaand that was it. The spell was absorbed into the shield, then into the tower.

Oracle moved over to one side, laying her hand on the portal, then shifting around in my mind, reaching out through me instead.

I let her, and continued to annoy the woman, waving at her and making obscene gestures while Oracle worked, before moving onto the old favorite of pretending to be Travolta in *Saturday Night Fever*.

The woman went apeshit, hurling colored light and flame at me and I couldn't help but grin.

More screens flared up then fell away as Oracle manipulated the system. The mana that the woman on the far side was pouring into the shield like water was rerouted, the room around us beginning to repair itself.

She only kept it up for a minute or so, but by the end of it, what was left of her forces that hadn't committed 'suicide by portal' had fled. She was standing there, hunched over, fingers like claws gripping the edges of the portal and staring in at me.

She'd shifted during her tirade, going from humanoid and attractive to tall and thin, haggard, with red, glowing eyes, chitinous fingertips, and pointed teeth, with a hunchback that bent her almost double. Rips appeared in her dress as she panted, losing control of herself.

"Don't do it," Oracle warned me.

"What?" I asked absently, still staring at the woman.

"She could close her side just as easily as you locked this one; you'd never make it."

I grimaced, realizing she really did know me better than I knew myself, considering I'd literally just been thinking about leaping across the distance between us, knowing she was low on mana and self-control right now.

"Even if you made it through before she closed the shield, for all we know, there are a thousand warriors just out of sight, or it's all an illusion. There might be a pit waiting for you, or anything. There's a reason the portals were never used to attack anything; they're too easily disrupted. Please Jax, don't," she said, stepping up and resting a hand on my forearm.

I hesitated, then laid a hand on the portal, pulling up the connection options.

As long as it was connected, it was drawing mana from her side and actively repairing the tower on this side, but I couldn't rely on it being safely shut.

For all I knew, there were a million ways she could fuck with me from there.

I smiled and blew the evil bitch a kiss, then disconnected it, seeing the fury and outrage as the connection failed, the vision of some room far away becoming gray and wan before vanishing all together.

I turned back to face the others, ducking as a bloody mess of a head flew past me. "Okay Grizz, you can get rid of that thing." I told him.

I turned back to the corpse and grinned, a collection of rings on open display as Grizz punted the head over the side of the balcony.

"Ronin, you want to do the honors?" I asked, trying not to think about the way that must have looked to the people below as I gestured to the body. I figured, with his examination abilities, he was the least likely to make a mistake with a cursed item.

He carefully searched the body as I moved back out onto the balcony, looking over the edge with Oracle by my side.

"So what were you doing?" I asked her quietly.

"I figured the Tower was derelict for a long time, so it could do with some work. The original layout will stay as it was, but now it'll start cleaning itself out and welcome Imperial subjects again."

"Why wasn't it doing that before?"

"It was set to only permit access to members of the Imperial Nobility or their appointed servants or the Legion. Basically, if anyone had realized the Legion could have been using this place since the Cataclysm, it'd have supported them. But for anyone else, after the nobles fled? It was deliberately forcing them out."

"Fair enough. We'll need to have some forces dedicated to keeping it safe from now on."

"They'll be comfortable, I suppose..." Oracle agreed, grinning. "Maybe make Fyre responsible for it?"

"I thought you didn't like her?"

"*Nobody* does, but that's not the point. She'd be over the moon to be free of the rest of the mages and have her own tower. I'd expect her to go massively over the top in setting up defenses, knowing she'll be the one at risk if the portal activates."

"Fine by me." I grunted, watching the elite city guards below us as they moved through the surviving trespassers.

There were still a good sixty or so of them alive, which stunned me, considering how many we'd already fought and killed. But as they sat in rows, stripped naked by the elites, their possessions set aside, I shook my head.

The sheer number of people who must have been sacrificed to get these fuckers through…

There was a clatter and creak from the alley that led up to here. I glanced in that direction, seeing a prison wagon being carefully led up as the first of the vanquished stood and were chained together before being led into the back of it.

"What do we do with them?" Oracle asked. Before I could respond, Bane was there.

"We give them to Flux," he suggested.

"Why Flux?" I asked, glancing over at where the Mer leaned against the railing nonchalantly.

"You said Flux was to build you a cadre of spies and assassins, right?" he asked, before pointing at the people below. Stripped of their red and black armor, they were all clearly toned and healthy, with a weird and complete lack of body hair, from what I could see from up here. "They're half-trained assassins."

"They're the enemy," I said slowly.

"They were, but look at them. Admittedly, I don't really get the things that you say are attractive to your kind, but when I examine them, they seem almost identical? They give off almost no scent, and while the majority have only basic training, you said that they cannot level in your world…"

"They can if they have Pearls." My mind raced as I considered the assassins who had been waiting for us outside the bakery, using their less-skilled brethren as bait.

"Then those few who were waiting have been heavily invested in," Bane said.

"Okay, I'll speak to Carmen, I guess," I said. "Right people, five minutes, and we're leaving. If you want to loot, do it now!"

I moved back to Ronin, who had dragged a table out onto the balcony to hold his treasures as he examined them. "What did you find?"

He smiled.

"A handful of items, nothing particularly amazing, but not bad." He lay a handful of jewelry out on the table nearest. "Two rings that increase stamina, two that increase Strength, each by two points."

"A stamina and a strength ring to Lydia," I muttered, picking them up and tossing them under-arm to the Valkyrie, who grinned and snatched them from the air. "A stamina to Tang."

"I hear he needs all the help with Carmen he can get," Grizz commented, elbowing Giint in the side of the head suggestively.

"And a strength to Grizz," I finished, tossing them out. "What else?"

"Necklace of Increased Dexterity, plus five that one," Ronin said, eyeing me hopefully.

"You can have it," I said, knowing that it was down to him, me, Bane, or Tang for that. As our bard, it was perfect for him playing his instruments.

"Then we have an earring of Charisma, well, its plus two to Charisma, but it's called the 'Tart's Gem'," he said, holding a crescent moon up, the shape making it clear it was supposed to be attached to the top of the ear rather than the bottom.

"Yours again…"

"Thanks, boss! And the last one is this." He held out a small statue. I took it, flipping it over in my hands and examining it, curiously.

Remembrance Lost		Further Description *Yes*/*No*	
Details:		A statue of Remembrance Lost, imbued with a single memory that can be examined again at any time, provided the original memory was captured intact.	
Rarity:	**Magical:**	**Durability:**	**Charge:**
Highly Rare	Yes	12/100	17/100

"What the hell is this?"

"They're pretty rare, boss. They're basically a solid memory, but when you make them, you can add details as you remember them, and they can be updated easily."

"Not sure what you mean?"

"They're like the memory crystals, Jax," Oracle cut in, glancing at the statue curiously. "But instead of a skill memory, they can be anything, a favorite meal, an important meeting, a secret, anything. You can store that memory in the stone, and each time you need to check it, you simply channel a little mana into the base and hold it as you relax. You'll experience the memory as if it was happening right now."

"Sounds like it could be fun," I said, thinking of reliving some of the awesome events I'd survived so far.

"It also means you can examine an event as if it happened to you…such as having a Justicar get a memory of an attempted murder, or the memories of the first person to find the body, and so on. They were common devices long ago. The HeartStones we found in the Great Tower are weaker and cheaper versions of these," Oracle pointed out.

The HeartStones were surprisingly simple, literally a small shard of crystal imbued with a memory so that you could communicate across great distances, recording a message and sending it with a courier, as Barabarratas had done. They were usually used for rich lovers who had to part, apparently, but the thought of the tiny shard and the much more carefully carved statue made me wonder at it.

"Is there any risk to me using this?" I asked Oracle, glancing at Ronin to make sure he understood the question as well. They both shook their heads.

"There shouldn't be," Ronin said. "They turn up every so often. Usually, they're hoarded by the nobility because they show what the world was like before the Cataclysm, but that's basically it. They're a memory, nothing active."

"Then let's see what was so important," I said, sitting in the chair Oracle had vacated and channeling a thin stream of mana into the base.

It took a few seconds, as I sat there and felt bloody stupid, shifting uncomfortably and feeling…off. Then all at once, the world was gone, and I was standing on the battlements of a tall castle.

The bright sunshine was gone, and instead, the red of the setting sun painted the sky as I leaned atop the crenellations of a great keep made of black stone.

"You're back again, then?" a voice called. I twisted around, seeing a smiling woman striding up to me.

"You know I can't leave you yet, Barishka," I heard myself say, my voice deeper and filled with love and regret. "A few more hours…or days."

"My lord, you *have* to go," she sighed, stepping in close and wrapping her arms around my waist. I felt my arms encircle her and hold her tight, even as the point of view changed, lifting away from her sad smile and staring back out over the rapidly darkening fields.

"I know, but it's madness," the memory said. "Our son isn't ready for this, not by a hundred years. The boy is callow and vain…"

"He's our *son*. He tries, and he's ready for more responsibility. Yes, he could be more…more," she finished lamely. "But he's desperate for your approval. Take him with you. A few weeks in the capital, seeing you not just as his father, but as a true noble, showing those who have abandoned honor's path for what they are."

She smiled at me, and I pulled her close again, kissing the top of her head.

"I'll take him and show him the difference between the House of Y'Boraz and those who defy the Emperor's will. He's our son, and I love him dearly."

There was a fuzzing of the air, and the scene changed. A much younger version of the prick I'd beheaded a few minutes ago was half-running and half-skipping to keep up with me as I rode along inside what I now assumed was his father.

We hurried across a massive courtyard, creamy marble inlaid with gold gleaming underfoot as the heat beat down upon us. I winced unthinkingly at the sight of the legionnaires in full plate all around the outer ring.

I could feel the heat, like the worst of the summer heatwaves in Afghanistan, yet these assholes hurried to get out of it without a thought for the Legion Praetorian Guard who stood at full attention in the baking sun on all sides in their black and red armor.

"But why?" the younger man whined, carrying on a conversation I'd missed the beginning of.

My host sighed. "Because it's our duty, son."

"*Farren* doesn't have to do this; he's with the rest of his family at the baths," the boy continued, only to be cut off with a growl.

"Farren is the *second* son of a *minor* house. Neither he nor any of his house will be responsible for more than a few thousand miles of territory! You   should you meet with the emperor's approval—*might* be destined for more, one day."

"But father," the boy complained again, tugging at the lacy wrist of his sleeves. "He's your grandfather; he's my great grandfather. Why do we have to call him…"

"He's the emperor, boy!" my host hissed as they climbed a handful of gleaming steps, the door before them opening smoothly as a pair of massive lord-class war golems loomed over them in clear warning.

"Watch yourself inside, Caiden. He may be our relative, but so are hundreds of others. You have to prove you should be trusted, and whining will only anger him!" my host went on as the pair passed out of the blistering sun and into the much cooler halls of the Imperial Palace proper.

The walls and floor were simple, creamy marble with brown and gold patterns, glorious chandeliers hanging from the ceiling at regular intervals and thick red carpet that ran up the center of the corridor, muffling the sound of footprints.

"Ah, Lord Y'Boraz," an urbane voice called from a side room as the pair passed, drawing a sigh before the pair turned and smiled.

"Prince Sanguis! What an honor," my host said as I glowered at the fucker though an impassive mask of politeness.

"Prince!" Caiden squeaked, dropping low into a bow that almost kissed the carpet.

"Good to see you again, nephew," my fucking father said with a lazy smile. "I feared you'd not come."

"Grandfather called, and so we answered," Y'Boraz replied calmly.

"Well yes, good to know you're still loyal and all that. And this is your boy? Little Caiden? It's been a long time, young man," Sanguis said, offering his beringed hand to Caiden, who practically fell over himself in a rush of hero worship.

Long minutes of pleasantries were exchanged, most of the time spent watching the way that Caiden fawned over Sanguis, before my host broke the conversation, insisting that they were expected and shouldn't keep the emperor waiting.

"Yes, yes. Go see my father," Sanguis sighed, gesturing negligently down the gleaming corridor. "Once he's had a look at you, we'll need to talk again, young Caiden. Perhaps a little light lunch with some of my friends would suit you more than following your father around the capital?"

Caiden practically wet himself in excitement.

"I fear there will be little time for frivolities, Prince Sanguis," Lord Y'Boraz replied, trying to keep his voice calm. "We were summoned by the emperor for a reason."

"*I* had you summoned," Sanguis corrected with an oily smile. "You and all of the nobles. It was time to have a proper gathering and to have the younger generation learn the way things will be run in the future."

"The Emperor..." Y'Boraz started to say, only to be cut off by a smirking Sanguis.

"...is waiting for you. Now, run along, nephew, and Caiden? You'll find a pageboy waiting when you leave the audience with my father. Follow him and join me and my friends."

With that, the prick turned and walked off, leaving Y'Boraz quietly fuming while Caiden stared adoringly after him.

"Father...perhaps the emperor doesn't need to meet me?" Caiden suggested, and Y'Boraz stared at his son in shock.

"He's the eternal emperor, boy!" he hissed after a few shocked seconds of silence. "When he calls, we come!"

"Yes, but he asked for you, right?" Caiden said, gesturing after the retreating form of Sanguis. "You said before that this trip would help me to make allies for my time as the head of our family, and Prince Sanguis..."

"You will become the head of the family only should I choose to step down, boy. Should you start following the example of *that* one, I swear I'll never even consider it!" Y'Boraz snapped at the young man, before looking around to make sure nobody was close enough to hear what he'd just said.

"But father!"

"Silence, boy!" Y'Boraz snapped. "We will talk later, just…just accept that not everything here is as it seems." He turned, hurrying the boy along as they joined a line of minor nobles in an antechamber. "Speak when you're spoken to and behave. I'll explain it all later."

The images blurred again, and I was now sitting in a comfortable chair, one hand rubbing at my temple as I listened to a shadowy figure giving me a report in a dark room, the fire blazing merrily as the rain lashed out of a midnight sky, battering the windows.

"…hope. He's firmly under Prince Sanguis's spell."

"Why?" I muttered tiredly. "Why of all people would he choose that snake to emulate?"

"He is powerful and experienced at seducing others to his causes." The shadowy figure sighed.

"Too powerful," Y'Boraz replied. "Grandfather knows something is wrong, but what possible reason could Sanguis have? Grandfather is known as the Eternal Emperor for a reason! The Gods themselves favor him…" Y'Boraz shook himself and sat up, tugging his doublet straight and forcing in a deep breath as he thought.

"I don't know what the foolish boy has in mind, but he's proven he's not ready to be in this nest of vipers. Make ready. After the Emperor's address tomorrow, we return to our lands. Make a report to the Justicars on all you've told me about Sanguis' plans and gatherings. It may, as we both hope, be entirely innocent, but if not? Better that the Justicars know."

"Yes, my lord," the figure said, bowing low then backing into a hidden door.

"My love, I have failed you," Y'Boraz muttered sadly, glancing up at a painting of the woman from the battlements, hanging atop the fireplace. "I still harbor some small hope the boy is salvageable, but after all I've seen, our fears are well-founded."

The scene blurred, and I saw more meetings, the tempo growing as time passed, Y'Boraz addressed Caiden over and over again, taking him back to the castle by portal, then arguments, reports, and rows.

Months passed in a flash. Sometimes the woman was there, other times several others replaced her. Occasionally, figures in legion armor gave reports or received them.

I watched the pair growing old before my eyes, and for the first time, beyond Amon, I felt sorry for one of the old nobility. His son was pulled in again and again as they tried to make something of him. He refused Legion service or magical training and refused a commission in the Prax fleet, the exploration force, and more.

Weeks became months and years, and the boy grew more and more arrogant as more reports were handed to legionnaires and Justicars.

I jumped suddenly as the scene changed again, and I saw my host clearly for the first time, staring into a mirror, holding the statue that Ronin had given me.

"Grandfather, I don't know what else to do," he said slowly, shaking his head. "I…I've tried, again and again, but I can't reach him. I've filled this statue with all that I can remember, adding it in as best I can as makes sense. I'm sorry that some sections are unclear. Had I suspected what I do now, I'd have recorded this sooner. Sanguis plots against you, and many of your own children aid him."

He shook his head, tears flowing down his cheeks as he went on.

"This makes no sense, and yet, I cannot find any other explanation. I have filled in as much as I can here, and reported all I suspect to your Justicars. They are in agreement, and by the time you receive this, I will have done what must be done in disowning Caiden. He and many others of his generation are bewitched by Sanguis, yet I know not how or why. Sanguis was once the best of us. I looked up to him, respected him, and frequently sought his counsel. Now, though? He is the venomous snake in the nursery, and despite the love I once bore him…he must be treated as such."

He went on, going over details of plots he'd uncovered, of troop movements of forces that were outside of the Legion chain of command, and of actions. While each on their own seemed innocuous, looking at the whole was quickly growing terrifying.

"Eternal Emperor Amon…*Grandfather*…I…I hope and pray that I am wrong. I have never wished to be wrong about something so much. Should I be found to be dancing on the precipice of madness and paranoia, I will happily stand down, relinquishing all my authority and rights. I fear that, in the days to come, however, not acting on my suspicions will be cursed as soundly as collusion…pl…p…urk…"

As he'd spoken, he'd been visibly sweating, in distress, but as his hands rose to his throat, and his eyes swiveled to the goblet on the nearby table, I made the connection.

Whatever the poison was, as his vision swam in and out of focus, I noted it had not prompted a notification until now. Dozens of them were popping up, blinding him as he frantically swiped them aside, falling to his knees.

He coughed, then vomited on the thick carpet, blood splashing and covering his hands, as a cry echoed nearby. Slim hands appeared, turning him over, staring down into our eyes.

"My love!" the woman gasped. "What's wrong?"

"P…p…pois…on…" he managed, throat swelling closed as he fumbled with a tied-closed pouch on his hip, trying to release an old-fashioned knot with fingers that felt like unwieldy sausages.

"My love…the message to the Emperor. Did you send it?" she asked, carefully, taking the pouch from him and smoothing his hair down as she stared into his/our eyes.

"U…huh?" he managed to grunt out, confused, eyes flicking to the pouch she was holding, but not opening, as he lost feeling and control in his body.

"Did you send it?" she repeated coldly. "Did you tell the Emperor anything? Wyvern messengers, magic, memory stones, anything at all?"

He couldn't help it. His gaze flicked to the side, and she followed his line of sight to the Statue of Remembrance Lost where it lay under a table.

"Ah, well played, 'my love'." she sneered, before climbing to her feet as foam began to fill our throat, choking us. "Well, at least I won't have to put up with you pawing at me any longer. Small mercies, I suppose." She brushed herself down. "Caiden, darling…" she called out. The door cracked open, letting in a familiar grinning face who carefully closed the door and looked down at us as the last light faded from our eyes.

CHAPTER SIXTEEN

I jerked upright in the chair as the world around me was righted, and I was back in my own body, heart thundering in my ears, hands shaking as I gripped the arm rests.

"Jax?" Bane asked. I shook my head, trying to catch my breath, the sudden knowledge that I was dying, betrayed by not only my son, but the woman I loved as well?

I looked at Oracle, seeing the horror and pain on her face, and knowing that she'd been viewing it through my mind as well.

"That fucker's lucky he's dead," I muttered, turning to look at the corpse on the floor.

"What happened?"

"Well, *he* helped Sanguis, but his father was loyal to Amon, so this shit biscuit and his mother poisoned him." I groaned, rubbing at my throat, still feeling the phantom memory of the choking, cloying foam that had filled his lungs.

"How bad?" someone asked.

"He loved his son, despite knowing he was a fucking wanker and untrustworthy, and he'd agonized over telling Amon for months, if not years, while making reports to the Justicars anyway, because that was the right thing to do. He spent forever trying to help his son and turning to his lover…wife, whatever. He'd told her what he was doing and why, and she fucking *poisoned* him."

"Why would he carry something like that around?" Tang asked, nudging the body with a boot. "I mean, it was a record of his failures, right? Of why his father was handing him over to the Empire?"

"His father was trying to save him, trying to make something useful out of him, and he was having none of it. Probably kept it because, after they ran from the UnderVerse, it was the only way that he could see any of the realm, but still. Hell, maybe he was getting off on the whole fucked-up family thing," I muttered, shaking my head.

"Now what?" Ronin asked.

I forced myself to my feet, feeling like I'd been sitting in that chair for long weeks instead of a few minutes at most. "Now we go see Carmen, then we start hunting these fuckers down. If that ass is anything like the rest of them, then they're a cancer on the realm!" I snarled, setting off toward the door.

I led the others through the Tower, descending the steps with Oracle by my side, one slender hand gripped in mine as we stepped over bloody bodies and discarded weapons.

"Prince Jax," one of the elite guards barked, jerking to attention. "Lord Tiedeman ordered that all the prisoners be taken to the palace dungeon for questioning, with their possessions sequestered away for examination by Nathaniel." He paused, clearly waiting to be told if that was right or not.

"That's fine. Flux will be working with Nathaniel, for now. Feed and water the prisoners and give them some damn clothes, but watch them carefully. If they do anything that seems suspicious, or that you don't understand, use lethal force."

"Uh…lethal…" He questioned, not recognizing the term.

"If they try to escape, or do anything that looks like an escape attempt, kill them. No warnings, no hiding them away in a fucking easily escaped-from room and going on a smoke break, okay?"

"Uh…yes, Prince!" he replied, clearly not understanding the context, but "kill them if they fuck with you" was clear enough.

"Why an 'easily escaped from room'?" Bane whispered from close by.

"Where I come from, it's kind of a tradition that prisoners are put in easily escapable locations, then they overthrow the evil Empire when they get loose."

"We're not evil," Oracle complained as we walked out the front door and into the warm sunshine.

"No, but to them? They've left their home, had their friends slaughtered in a world they don't really understand, and their lord's head was punted out of a window a while back. They're not going to be sure which side is which."

"They're also almost all identical," Oracle said, looking around as we passed a group waiting stolidly for their turn at the wagons.

Apart from the obvious differences between men and women, the vast majority of them *were* scarily identical.

They were all dark-haired, of average height, and Eurasian, well-toned, but without the larger muscles I was used to seeing with the legionnaires I spent most of my time with. Instead, they were slender, wiry and…yeah.

They were either naturally without body hair, or waxed extremely regularly.

"That's just fuckin' weird," I muttered.

"Scent," Yen said quietly, moving up to walk alongside Oracle, Lydia, and me. "We're taught in the Legion that, when we're taking on stealth roles, it's better to remove all hair from your bodies. It doesn't make you sweat less, but it means that the sweat goes quicker, and you're less likely to be smelly afterward."

"Nothing ruins stealth like being able to smell someone," Tang whispered from stealth somewhere nearby. I noticed that, while most of the prisoners stood silently, occasionally one would glance in Tang's direction.

"They're good," I muttered, shaking my head. "Thank fuck we got to them when they'd only been here a damn day."

"They could be great," Yen agreed. "They're all skilled at unarmed combat as much as armed. If I had to guess? I'd say they've been trained their entire lives for this, but only a few were given the Pearls, and the rest were trained around the clock. Once they got here, their trainers will have been sending them on quests constantly, even if just to shadow someone, leveling their stealth skill as fast as possible."

"Yeah, but in one damn *day*?" I asked disbelievingly.

"The higher levels take time to reach, but think back to when you first arrived here. How fast did you level then? You can get five or six levels in stealth in a day if you really try, and you aren't starting at a high level," Yen pointed out. I nodded, seeing it. "After all, if you thought you'd have a single day here, knowing what you do now, what could you plan to achieve, with regard to skill growth?"

"Damn," I muttered, wincing. "Yeah, I'd make the most of it."

If I were to spend the entire day in one of Flux and Lio's capture the flag games, racing across the city in insane demonstrations of parkour, I'd probably *still* level some skills at a hell of a rate. That was why they did it, after all.

That was also why I'd been doing all the exercises when I first arrived here.

The early levels were easy.

The later ones? They took years to improve on.

"I need to get back to leveling and training," I said. "I need to improve more and get some more damn quests."

"Yer do," Lydia agreed, before sighing and shaking her head. "But, an' ah hate that ah'm sayin' this, but *should* ye be doin' it?"

"What do you mean?"

"Yer the Prince. Yeah, yer always in tha front line, and yeah, that'll no' change, ah know…but the skills ye could build? Do ye need to?" she shrugged. "That's why ye 'ave us. Only so many hours in a day."

"Yeah," I muttered, agreeing as she literally said the words I constantly told myself in the silence of my head. I could improve. I could get better at everything. The issue wasn't motivation. Hell, since Oracle told me about the baby, I had even more motivation to secure my lands than ever before. It was all down to the number of hours in the damn day, and there was fuck-all I could do about that.

We climbed into two coaches and headed back to the palace, finding them waiting in the alley with Nathaniel posing as a servant ready to take care of our needs as we hoisted ourselves aboard.

The short trip back was filled with short, succinct reports, everything from the estimated numbers of the attackers to the deaths incurred on both sides, to the damage to the area and the bakery.

"Fix it up so that it's better than it was before," I ordered. "We trashed the place; the Empire can afford to rebuild it."

"Yes, my Prince…and the prisoners? I suspect they may be useful."

"Already considered that," I said. "I want them working with Flux. Round them up and get them to Himnel, and then on to the tower as soon as you can. I'm betting they'll be trained to escape and use stealth tricks, so make damn sure they're kept under lock and key until Flux can assess them." I turned to Oracle. "If he thinks they can be turned to our side and trusted, Tirana and Selkie can administer the Oath with Augustus' help, can't they?" After a moment's pause, she gave a slow nod.

"They should be able to; they're Imperial Citizens and both linked. I've been working on this and a few other things with them, getting them ready, but they don't have the 'right' to give the Oath." She paused, clearly deep in thought. "They do have Augustus though, and as your heir that should work…as well as Hellenica and her knowledge. Will we have any time in Himnel before we head for the Prax?"

"Not long," I said. "There's a million things to do and no damn time to do it."

"An hour," Oracle countered. "It'll take that long to change over to Tenandra and get any potions and supplies we need, right? If we land at the keep, I can spend that time teaching Selkie, and maybe, *maybe* we can get it figured out."

"So, get them to Flux, get them in training. As near as we can tell, they've been heavily trained to be stealth assassins and so on, they just weren't ready when we found them. Had they had a month to train? They'd have been lethal."

"A suggestion, then?" Nathaniel offered diffidently.

"Go on. Hell, man, you know you don't have to be like that, just speak," I ordered.

"Very well. then." He quirked a quick smile. "I'd suggest you send all but five to Flux, and have him take them to the Great Tower, as I believe that was your intention for the Legion?"

"Excellent. Integrate them with the Legion as trainees, send them through the same selection as the other volunteers, but break them out of the them-and-us mentality that will be inevitable if they're from another world. Make them integrate with the Legion Aspirants, then, when those with less training can outdo them at every turn, they will either break…or grow."

"Less training?" I asked.

"They move in unison, with matching weapons and armor. They were clearly heavily trained as a unit as much as individuals, yet their attributes, their stamina…physically and mentally, they are as children, without the ability to level until recently. The average house servant could beat them in almost any competition, save war."

"And you think that, when they learn that, it'll help integrate them?"

"Yes and no. When they learn their place in the realm, and have the chance of a brotherhood that is built on honor and respect? It may be enough, or it may need to be enforced by the Oaths. But either way, they have surrendered to you, and now something must be done with them. It seems a waste to spend the rest of their lives in hard labor."

"What about the other five?" I asked, curious.

"Give them to me," he said. "They killed several of my assassins."

"And you want revenge?" Grizz asked, shifting on his bench seat with a clank of armor.

"No, I want replacements," Nathaniel replied calmly.

"Cold," I muttered.

"Pragmatic," he corrected. "They need an outlet and a reason to live. I need replacements. I can manage to train and watch over five of them. More could be problematic."

"You've got an hour," I said after a few seconds of thought. "Pick out those you want and who are willing to swear, and bring them to me before I leave."

"Thank you, my Prince," he replied, hurriedly banging on the roof of the coach. It slowed, coming to a stop as we passed through the outer ring of the palace grounds. He jumped out before it started up again, carrying us on the last leg of the trip.

Ten minutes later, we were sitting in the original keep again, Oracle in my mind and Carmen by my side as the three of us worked through the systems in the command center, trying to find a way to detect the buggers, should they come again. Carmen was still trying to keep her grin under control at being not only named Duchess but to the Imperial Senate under Thomas.

It was a hell of a step up for a woman who'd been a glorified hooker for the previous city lord, but she'd damn well earned it.

After twenty minutes of searching, we gave up. There were a million possible combinations we needed to work through, the various commands seeming to be intuitive one moment then anything but the next.

"You summoned me, my Prince? Duchess Carmen?" Arch Mage Fyre called from where she stood on the far side of the room, warily watching the rest of my team.

I blinked the screens away, sitting upright "Yes." I said, nudging Carmen to take over.

"Yes!" Carmen agreed. "Apologies, Arch Mage Fyre, Prince Jax and I were busy. As you're aware, there was a recent incursion into the city."

"At the old Wizard's Tower?"

"Yes. You're familiar with the tower, then?"

"Any mage in the city is. We've all attempted to find a way to make it useful, especially given its capabilities to assist the city, yet alas it is beyond our capabilities."

"You will be moving into the tower," Carmen said. "Prince Jax has addressed the issues that resulted in it being unable to be inhabited, and we have named you as its guardian."

"I…I…thank you?" Fyre replied, stunned. "Just…like that?"

"Yeah," I said. "The tower holds a portal still, and while it's sealed to anyone who's not a member of my Imperial Senate, that doesn't mean it's safe. While nobody should be able to use it, that doesn't mean they won't figure a way around that. I suggest you make a plan with some particularly nasty traps around the portal, just in case."

"I'll send you ten of the elite guard to assist and to live in the tower with you," Carmen said. "Their role will be to assess your defensive measures and to report on them to us, as well as to raise the alarm, should anything get through."

"I…very well," Fyre said after a few seconds of opening and closing her mouth in shock. "Thank you, Duchess Carmen, Prince Jax…" She curtseyed, then hurried away when Carmen nodded toward the door, clearly wanting to escape before we changed our minds.

"That went well," I murmured.

Carmen grinned. "She just received permission to inhabit one of the most powerful locations in the land, and was told that it's hers as long as she protects it, which she would have done anyway."

"Why'd you phrase it like that with the elite guard?" I asked curiously.

"She'd have treated them as servants otherwise. Now she thinks they're there to report on her, so she'll be a lot nicer to them. Besides that, if anyone does manage to get past her defenses, I want the elite guard to spread the word, not die fighting someone who is that skilled with magic, or get caught in the cross-fire."

"Point," I acknowledged. "Okay, I think it's pretty clear we can't rely on the city command interface to alert us if any of the old nobility try to sneak in."

"No, but as arrogant as most nobles are, we'll be able to find them if they try," Carmen replied with a faint smile. "I've asked around and there were dozens of reports of peculiar behavior from around the old tower in the last day. But, as nobody was looking, nobody saw any reason to bring it to my attention."

"Then we have people look out for strange behavior," I agreed. "Anything else you need from me before I leave?" I climbed to my feet, itching to get moving, pleased that for once we were ahead of schedule, and planning on heading back to Himnel with all speed.

"One last thing, if you don't mind?" She gestured to the lizard figure standing by the door. He quickly bowed and rushed out.

"Better be quick," I muttered. The others had spent the time I'd wasted on minor local issues and playing with systems to get replacements for consumables we'd used and some replacement ingredients.

Less than a minute later, Bol was led in, and I frowned, recognizing the man. He'd been the first of those in the meetings when I'd seized the city to own up to breaking the law. He'd gained some leniency for that, working with Hannibal and Mal on cleaning up the city and disbanding his former comrades in the Smuggler's Guild.

"Bol," I greeted him.

He bowed low. "Prince Jax, Duchess Carmen," he said, eliciting a fresh smile from Carmen over her title.

"What's going on, Bol?" I asked, picking my gauntlet up from the table I'd laid it on and reconnecting it, ready to move on.

"The Smuggler's Guild, my Prince..." he said, before pausing and clearly looking for the right words.

"They're organizing against us," Carmen said, taking over the narrative.

"Bound to happen eventually," I grunted, unconcerned. "We took their stashes in the cities, arrested the upper members, and claimed their airships. What can they do?"

"Plenty," Bol replied, sighing and dropping all formality as he remembered how little I cared for it. "Look, you know there's a lot of villages out there that aren't on the maps, right?"

"Yeah?" I agreed unconcernedly.

"That's where the majority of the guild has always been. Now that you've closed the cities to them, their most profitable custom has dried up. They're building a secondary network out there, going from village to village. The nobles you dispossessed are joining them, and they've taken their guards and magic users. Essentially, unless you're moving goods by Airship, which can only carry a fraction of the food and general goods that come into the cities each day, then you take it by road. If you take it by road, now you have to pay the guild."

"Or what?"

"Or you don't get your goods to the city," Carmen replied dryly. "Caravans are being raided constantly if they don't belong to the guild. And if they do? Provided they don't break any laws, we can't trace them in the system. They just come in, and as they are one of the only caravans to make it? They've doubled their prices."

"What happens to the caravans they raid?" I asked.

"They're burning some of them, taking what they want, and destroying what they don't. We suspect the caravanners are 'buying' the looted goods from the nobles for probably nothing and selling it in the cities. It's a small team in a growing outfit who are doing the killing and burning, from what I can find out. While they'd show up on the city interface if they came too close, the rest of them are fine. Hell, most of the organization doesn't even know what's happening; they're honest wagoneers being paid to take goods into the city. It gets them around the city control system as you described it to people."

"Motherfuckers," I growled, desperately wanting to deal with it...yet knowing I couldn't. I couldn't be everywhere at once. "What are our options?"

"There's not many. Between our losses in the war, the troops we need to defend the city and carry out the guard's duties, and the training?" Carmen shook her head. "Truthfully, I could send a few squads out into the countryside, but I've done that already. They find nothing, as the locals are too terrified to report anything. In times past?" She hesitated.

I groaned. "You'd have called in the Legion?"

"Exactly," Bol said. "There aren't enough troops to patrol the area effectively. In a year or so, once the new Legion Aspirants are trained to an acceptable level, they'll be able to deal with this kind of thing easily."

"Until then, we're fucked, and our people are dying," I finished flatly.

"Well, they're avoiding the villages that have declared and sworn the Oaths...mainly," Carmen replied, before gesturing at the map she had on one table and a big red X on one of the larger villages nearby.

"That's how we found out about what they were doing," Bol said. "They raided the village and killed everyone, stripped it bare and carted it off."

"Motherfuckers," I growled. "Where?"

"Into the forest."

"Care to be a bit more specific?" I snapped, examining the heavily forested areas of the map grimly.

"We can't," Carmen said. "We sent a team of rangers after them, hoping to track them..."

"And the quest we gave them failed," Bol finished. "I was involved in briefing them. I warned them about the areas they were headed into and where our hides were."

"They're all dead?" I asked and got a grim nod. "Fuckers...when?"

"About an hour ago, while you were dealing with the noble incursion," Carmen said. "I'd not mentioned it, as I hoped that we could deal with it ourselves, but...we need the Legion," she finished, ashamed. "If we send the elite guard, then we uncover other areas of the city, in turn. We've less than forty now, since the war, recruitment to the Legion and sending ten of them to the tower."

"You need a core of skilled elite guards to protect you from assassins as well." I nodded, seeing the issue. I'd seen it in Himnel as well. After all, the sheer number of deaths in the war between the cities, then with the Dark Legion, meant we were at real risk of plagues and starvation come the winter. That was with magic being used to deal with as much as we could. "Okay, we'll leave the golems with you that we've got aboard ship, with you named as their commander. That should take a little of the weight off you."

"Thank you. In a year from now…"

I cut her off with a raised hand. "It's fine, now. If we leave things, in a year from now, thousands could have died, and with these assholes burning the food and more, there's an even worse risk of famine. How the hell did they organize so quickly?" I muttered, speaking aloud rather than expecting an answer.

"They had no choice," Ronin said. "You kicked the nobles out of the city, drove out the criminals that were smart enough or lucky enough to run as well, and a small core of the Dark Legion fled, too. They had no choice but to organize or starve.

"I'd bet they didn't plan this, or anything like it, but as they carved out a little space to survive? Becoming bandits? They'll have seen the potential to cause you problems and will have gone with it."

"They could end up causing a famine that kills tens of thousands."

He shrugged. "Why would they care? You've got smugglers–sorry, Bol–bandits, outlawed scumbag nobles, and Dark Legionnaires. None of them are particularly nice people."

"I did it to feed my family, as did most of those who stood with me," Bol said. "Those who did it for the game more than the money and power, like Mal, they got out as well, finding it was more fun to join the Empire and work within your new system. Those who survived the cull and escaped, though? They're the nastiest we had. The ones we'd not let into the city because they were animals, but we'd not trust on their own, either, because they were little better than the bandits. We sent them out to deal with the robbers and murderers, because, well…"

"Because it wasn't your problem, and nobody gave a shit," I finished for him, getting a shame-faced nod. "Fine. Lydia? We need to deal with this, but we have no time to do it. What do you think?"

Lydia straightened. "About?"

"What we do. You're my Optio, advise me," I said shortly, already sensing what Oracle wanted me to do.

"There be a ship wit' a team already sent te tha Prax. Iffin they be dead already? Nothin' we can do fer them. If they be alive? They can hold on a bit longer. They be fighters…the people in tha villages? They be getting murdered. We 'ave te 'elp them."

"Where are they?" I asked Carmen and Bol, turning back to them, as others in the team spoke out in support. Most of the group were either legionnaires or ex-slaves, and as a group, both tended to be very protective of the little guys.

"We don't know," Carmen repeated sadly. "'In the forest' is about all we can be sure of."

"Then we'll hunt them. The Legion is setting off for the Tower today." I scratched my chin. "We'll get dropped off by *Fury's Awakening* at the site of the last attack…where was it?" I asked. Bol indicated a spot on the map on a low hill at the edge of the forest to the north.

"We'll get dropped off there, then she can burn full speed to Himnel. The Legion and her aspirants should be ready to go to the Tower by then, but knowing Romanus, he'll have accidentally delayed things until he knows we're back with

Tenandra. We can divert the Legion and have them sweep behind us; the best of the aspirants can gain some experience, and the rest can wait on the airships."

"If we find them, we can use the new cannons to deal with them," Lydia suggested.

"Hopefully so," I agreed. "Okay, get moving, people. Carmen, Bol? Anything else you need to mention?" They both shook their heads. "Fine. I hope you're recruiting more damn elites?"

"Over two hundred are being trained, but if I send the trainees into the forest as they are? They'd be slaughtered, and whatever equipment we give them to raise them to the level they'd be useful…"

"Would be lost along with them. You did the right thing. It just pisses me off that this is delaying our trip to the Prax." I shook my head. "Tommy is on his way to Svetu's facility, and I'll be able to move along soon. 'It is what it is'," I quoted, straightening up.

Carmen pulled a pouch from her own bag of holding and offered it to me. "What's this?"

"An herbalist's pouch," she said. "I know you enjoy your alchemy, so…"

I glanced inside, smiling as I saw that not only was it full, but it had over a hundred empty vials in there as well. "Thank you," I said, genuinely pleased.

"It's the least I could do…considering…" she blushed, as a new quest prompt popped up.

You have received a new Quest: 'Vanquish the Marauders'

The Duchess of Narkolt has requested your aid to cleanse the local forest of marauders who are killing and looting her subjects.

Kill the bandits, free their captives, and recover the outstanding loot.

Recover the slaves: 0/41

Punish the slavers: 0/173

Destroy the camps: 0/3

Recover the stolen goods: 0/3

Reward: 10% morale boost to Imperial Territory, 100,000xp

I accepted the quest, then turned and joined the rest of the team as we left, carefully not commenting on the way Tang held back, falling in close enough to Carmen to speak quietly, while we all sped up to give him a little privacy.

As we left the keep, though, we found Nathaniel waiting, along with five more people standing on the deck of the ship under guard.

"My Prince," Nathaniel said, bowing, then staring at the others. They bowed a second later, in perfect unison. "Thank you for taking the time and for permitting this."

"It's fine," I grunted, eyeing the five. Three women and two men stared back blankly, any emotion carefully concealed behind a bland expression as they stood silently. "This is Bob," I said suddenly, gesturing as the massive skeletal figure stomped forward, standing over them at my silent request.

There were slight reactions at his arrival, a flinch from one, hastily covered, a slight widening of eyes, but beyond that…nothing.

"Bob is a summoned being, created originally from a seed of my own soul. A simple spell, but over time, he evolved, and now he's as alive as any of you." I paused at that, glancing at him and grimacing. "Okay, he's a bit bonier, I admit, but fuck it. He's alive where it matters, inside. He's also free. Should he wish to leave us? He's got that right. He damn well earned it, and even now could walk away, if he wanted."

Bob chose that point to literally walk off, and I bit down on a growl, turning to the five men and women, seeing the way they all stared at a spot an inch or two to the right of my head, not making eye contact.

"You're here because Nathaniel thinks you've got the potential to help the Empire and the realm, as well as earn your freedom again. We don't keep slaves, so your options are down to three, as you literally invaded my lands and tried to kill me." I held up a finger, counting as I spoke.

"One; you all get to spend the rest of your lives in hard labor. Think prison, rather than slavery. You'll have a nice cell, reasonable meals, and some privacy, but everything for the rest of your life will be controlled." I slowly circled them, frowning at the similarities they showed. These fuckers were literally almost identical: height, size, haircut, the lot.

"Two; we can execute you now. It's a waste, personally I'd regret that, but it's an option. Should you decide that options one and two aren't for you, well, no hard feelings. Three; you join the Empire," I said. "You'd be required to swear an Oath, probably simpler than what your old lord demanded of you, but still binding. Then you'll be retrained, given new equipment, and as you earn it, more responsibility. Make no mistake–you were trained, as near as I can tell, to be assassins and spies, literal rogues. Nathaniel here is the spymaster of Narkolt and will use you hard."

"I will, but I will also guide you, teach you, and help you to find your place in this realm," he confirmed.

I stood there, waiting. After a few seconds, I spoke, trying to suppress a growl of irritation. "You can speak."

Silence.

"You understand me, right?" I asked after another short break.

"Yes, lord," they said as one, staring straight ahead and showing no emotion.

"Which do you choose?" I asked, getting no response from them beyond a slight shifting of eyes and adjusting of shoulders. I frowned, not understanding, until Sehran stepped up, standing behind them and raised a hand for my attention.

"What?" I asked, stepping around them and frowning down at her.

"They don't understand, and they're growing more and more nervous," she said softly. "It's not a case of them being awkward, they're just…I don't know…waiting? I can sense some of their emotions, and they're really confused."

"Thank you," I said, frowning as I turned back to them, then winced as a thought occurred to me. "Oracle, could you…?"

She reached out, laying a hand on the temple of the nearest, smiling as she asked them to approve her request. The woman clearly did, as Oracle frowned, then stood for long seconds before moving to the next, then next in line, ordering them to allow her access each time.

The entire time she was there, Grizz and the others, myself included, stood with weapons at the ready, waiting for the slightest sign of danger to her.

"They'll swear," Oracle said after a few more minutes. "Nathaniel, you'll need to teach them to respond and integrate to normal life, too, and you'll need to advise Flux on this."

"What?" I asked.

"They were taken as children, those who weren't bred like cattle, and they've never been offered choices before."

"That can't be right?" Nathaniel said, clearly confused. "We make choices every day, from clothing to food to…"

"We do," Oracle agreed sadly. "They don't. They've been fed the same food, worn the same clothing, and given a number that was their identity for as long as they can remember. They're ordered to carry out actions, never asked. They're waiting to be told what they're to do now; that's why they stood so calmly once they were ordered to surrender. They literally follow any orders given."

"But that doesn't work, not long-term, right?" I asked. "I mean, they'd be great as shock troops, but they'd not last long."

"They probably weren't supposed to," Oracle said, clearly disgusted. "Their lord was happy to spend their lives, to throw them away. I think they were intended to be disposable. Heavily trained, then kept like animals, with only a few of the elite closest to him allowed to think for themselves."

"Fuck, I hate these dickbags," I muttered. "Fine, push out the Oath and bind them to us. Nathaniel, you've got a year. Train them, and explain the situation to Flux. You've both got that time; it's a penance for them, and at that point, they can ask to be released from the Oath. They can choose another role in the Empire, either as prisoners and do hard labor, or…I don't know, something else, I guess. They can't make a decision for themselves now, so we'll have to do it, then."

Oracle nodded her agreement, pushing the Oath out, then ordering them to agree to it. They did, without emotion, swearing to serve the Empire.

I hated it, as close as this was coming to literal slavery. Hell, these people, now that we knew more about them, were more like children, mentally. But…they were children who had been trained as assassins, and should I cut them loose, someone would scoop them up and use them. Better that they were protected while they were taught.

Ten minutes later, the *Fury's Awakening* was feeding power into the engines, and we all felt the gentle G-forces as we lifted into the air, slowly turning around the old keep at the center of the palace, and coming onto a northern heading as we climbed.

Oracle used the little time we had to teach a spell called 'Night's Glory', essentially a variation on my own DarkVision to the others. I had no clue where Ronin had gotten it from, but considering what a dodgy fucker he was, I decided not to ask and just moved on with my life.

CHAPTER SEVENTEEN

"Gods, I need to kill something soon," I muttered, frowning. The distant firing of the ship's engines fell silent, even to my enhanced hearing, as we moved farther into the forest on foot.

"Yer can stop pretending ta be pissed now." Lydia sighed. I glanced at her, then grinned as Bob stomped past, a fresh wreath of flowers adorning his skull as Oracle smiled and drifted over, her work done.

We were deep into the canopy of the forest, the dappled sunlight filtering through the rustling leaves overhead as we spread out. Bane was already racing ahead while Tang stayed close by, in full stealth.

"I don't know what you mean," I replied loftily.

"Yer might as well drop it," she repeated.

"Yeah, all right," I said. "The opportunity to go kick some nobles' asses after that statue thingy, not to mention those people? Yeah, I fucking need it."

"I know there's a chance they're on the Prax as well," Jian said, then shook his head. "Okay, is it likely?"

"I don't know," I said. "Genuinely I don't, but if we left the locals to deal with things while we go to the Prax, and there's nothing there? Anyone who died between us getting back to find these assholes would have been on me."

"There was at least one SporeMother on the Prax," Sehran pointed out. "That's what you said, right? That one of the ships crashed, and it was thrown clear?"

"Yeah."

"So it's been there with whatever was left alive on there, like the mad gnomes, since you left about two months ago. Rushing there is unlikely to end well. Most likely, when we get there, we'll find that the SporeMother has created a full nest, and our ship has dropped off its war golems, then turned around and is flying back to report the infestation, while the war golems hold a beachhead."

"I hope so," I said.

"And if the nobles have come through?" Jian suggested with an evil grin. "Dinner time for the SporeMother."

"Yeah, that's not really helping us, though." I shook my head. "If the SporeMother has control of the nobles, then it has control of their mages as well."

"Ah, crap."

"Yeah."

"Umm, so, Oracle, Jax," Sehran said, sidling over and putting her arm around Oracle's shoulders. "About the SporeMother."

"You can have it if we don't kill it outright," Oracle assured her, smiling.

"Thank you!" Sehran practically sang, kissing Oracle's cheek and winking at me. "I owe you both," she promised, her voice dropping to a seductive whisper as she smiled, before turning and walking back to Jian.

I couldn't help but look at her ass as she went, the damn hot pants that Oracle had introduced her to showing it off fantastically.

"She's not even trying to seduce us, you know," Oracle commented as she flew by my side. I looked down at her questioningly. "She just loves to tease. We've been talking about it, and she's absolutely loving her life. Even if she was killed now and banished back to the demon realm, unable to ever return, she'd be the most powerful succubus in a thousand years by far, and her life would be better than it'd ever been there before."

"Does she want to go back?" I asked, my voice dropping. "Jian would…"

"Not even slightly," Oracle assured me. "She's head over heels in love with him and is determined to stay for as long as he lives, at least."

"So, she's happy?" I asked, smiling as I glanced over Oracle's shoulder at Sehran, seeing her fall in beside Jian, reaching out a hand to him, the pair striding along happily together.

"Ecstatic…although she misses Tenandra," Oracle pointed out. "When it started with Tenandra, it was simply fun, and she was busy fulfilling Jian's fantasies as well. But since then? The three of them have grown much closer, and while Jian is definitely more attached to Sehran, Tenandra is important to them both, and I'd not be surprised if she attempts to bond to the pair soon."

"Can she do that?" I asked, stunned. "I thought with the ship?"

"She can. It'd be very different from the way we bonded, but…"

"Jax!" Tang called from ahead, and instantly, we were all on alert.

"Hold that thought," I said, hurrying forward to where Tang waited, crouched by the side of the trail.

"What's up?" I asked.

"Tracks," he said. "The rangers…" He indicated a handful of marks that were barely identifiable. I stared at them, working on picking out the edges, the heel, and more, and after a few seconds, got a new notification.

Congratulations!

**You have identified hidden tracks
and have increased your Tracking skill to level 10!**

Practice and learn to increase this skill further. Skillful trackers can grow in ability, until even the west wind could be traced to its home!

You may now choose your first evolution of this skill.

Congratulations!

You have raised your skill Tracking to its first evolution.

You must now pick a path to follow.

**Will you continue as you are, and choose to TRACK,
or will you follow the path of TRAP?**

Choose carefully, as this choice cannot be undone.

TRACK:

As time has passed more and more signs become obvious to you, the bend of a leaf, the break of a branch, a twist in the heel of a track, all these signs that once simply signified passage now tell their own tale. You now gain additional insight into your prey as you trace them.

TRAP:

Tracking is all very well, but perhaps you would prefer your prey to come to you? The skillful tracker doesn't follow their prey. Instead, they understand them, and they choose their ground, laying a trap that entices their prey in close.

Gain an additional 10% damage done to unsuspecting targets.

It wasn't that hard a decision, really. While the trapping boost of ten percent additional damage would be great, that required a trap to work, and when the hell did I actually make traps these days?

Yeah, I'd learned the trapmaking skill when I first arrived here, and I'd used it a little, but really? As the Prince, and soon to be, hopefully, the Emperor?

When the hell would I be building my own traps?

Tracking, though? Following these fuckers, for a start, would be useful.

I selected 'Track' and shivered as the changes imposed by the realm and mana took hold. I blinked as I opened my eyes, seeing the world shifting as new details were highlighted for me.

"Yeah?"

I shook myself, looking at Tang, and getting a snort of amusement.

"I *said* boss, you just got a skill evolution, didn't you?" he repeated.

"Yeah, sorry."

"What level?"

"Tracking. I reached level ten."

"Wow, okay, you really need some more experience with that. I'd have guessed twenty at the lowest," Tang said. "Okay, so what do you see?"

"Three tracks. Someone was moving carefully, staying to the outer edge of the path where the ground was harder, trying to hide their tracks."

"Nope," he replied, grinning. "Four people, three rangers, most likely, and a scout following them. The tracks are from the biggest of the rangers, most likely male, heavy-set or wearing totally the wrong kind of armor."

"Damn," I grumbled.

"Don't worry about it, boss." Grizz smiled. "I'm crap at tracking as well."

"You still passed the basic ranger course, or you'd never have made it into the Second Maniple," Yen said grimly. "Okay, Tang's got a point, boss. You need to hang back a bit, let the more experienced trackers lead the way."

"It be tha only way we'll learn," Lydia countered, leaning against the tree next to me and frowning at the tracks, clearly trying to make them out.

"Usually, yeah, Optio, I'd be with you on that," Yen replied. "But these assholes already caught and probably killed a trio of rangers. They're more skilled than the most basic legionnaires, and we can't afford to lose you. So, we need to have you two in the middle."

"Bane is leading the way. Tang takes the rear. Yen leading us?" Grizz asked, and after a second's hesitation, I agreed.

"Bane, Yen, Grizz, Me, Oracle, Lydia, Jian, Sehran," I said, laying out the new marching orders when Sehran started to sing softly.

It was subtle, starting as a hum, but with a glance at Ronin. He started to play a low tune as well, clearly augmenting her ability.

"What's happening?" I asked Oracle, who shrugged. But when Grizz gestured for me to go on, I did.

"Uh, then Ronin, Giint, Bob, and Tang bringing up the rear?" I finished, confused.

He gestured urgently toward the trail. "C'mon then, boss, we don't want to fall behind, right?" He suggested.

I nodded, starting off, even as Oracle gathered her magic.

"We're being watched," Jian whispered, moving in close and acting like he was offering Oracle a drink. "Staying well back, but Sehran's got them."

"Just the one?" I asked in a low voice.

"She thinks so."

"How do you know?" Oracle asked.

Jian coughed, going bright red. "Succubai can speak into their warlock's mind. It lets them talk still, when, you know…"

"When their mouths are full?" I asked, grinning and getting a cough and an embarrassed nod.

"Well, learn something every day, I guess," I said, still grinning as I picked up the pace.

"Whoever is out there is good," Grizz whispered after a few seconds. "If I didn't know they were there, I'd never find them."

"Where?"

He shook his head. "They're staying at the far range of the group. I can't see them; only the occasional move gives them away, and no offense, boss, but if you start looking…"

"I'll give it away," I agreed, nodding. "What's Sehran doing?"

Jian stepped up, as if we had no clue we were being observed and spoke quickly in a voice too low to carry, while Grizz winked and started telling a story about a bar fight he'd been in loudly enough to cover it.

I grunted, realizing we'd all started talking quieter since Sehran had detected them. I really was shit at stealth and sneaky stuff.

"She's glamouring them. She can go all-out, but it's less likely to work. As she's doing now, though? It layers over and over, gives her victim less chance to throw it off when she calls for them to obey," Jian said with a proud smile.

"How long?" I asked.

"The longer the better. Ten minutes, and she says they'll be hers forever," he said after a second's quiet consultation.

"Then I guess we need to stop for a break," I suggested, nodding to a small pool that was glimmering through the trees ahead, the last light of the sun making the shadows stretch across its surface.

Jian hesitated, then nodded, speaking quickly. "She says she can sense more life nearby, but nothing sapient. The water probably has a beast living in it, though…"

"Grizz?" I suggested.

He grinned, tugging his shield off his back and drawing his sword, then moving into the lead.

We passed between the last of the trees, coming out onto the bank of a small pond, a thin river leading downhill to the pond from the left, and the banks freshly torn-up.

"Even I can see those tracks," I commented loudly enough it'd cover anyone else as Yen spoke quickly, pretending to be looking at the beast sign.

"Tang's moving to circle them," she said in a low voice, before calling to Grizz. "Looks like a Gryce."

"What's that?" I asked, frowning.

"A Gryce is a water spirit. A bit like a nymph, but a lot less pleasant. Think Sehran's kind, but less friendly, more feral and vicious, and less picky," Ronin joked.

"They fill the water with a pheromone. It confuses their prey, like a strong alcohol, then they show themselves and, depending on the situation, seduce or beg for help, appearing like a young, attractive woman. They wait 'til you're close, then they sink their claws in, and they're a bastard to get rid of, like a leech and Vampyr had a wet baby."

"Shit, that sounds familiar. I think I used to date one," I muttered, shaking my head in disgust.

"You'd know if you had, boss," Grizz said as the water rippled and a dark-haired girl lifted her head out, looking up at him curiously.

"Damn, it's a young one," he said. She smiled at him, lifting up out of the water and totally ignoring us all, eyes only for the closest prey.

I stared at her. "So she's a…"

"Not her, it," Ronin said. "There are no males or females. They feed on anything, and despite what it looks like, that's not the creature, it's a lure. The real creature is at the bottom of the pond. It only has a beast's level of intelligence, too— enough to lure people in, but not enough to realize that we know what it's doing."

I grunted and triggered Greater Examination.

Immature Gryce

This is an immature offshoot of a gryce, seeded into a new pool before it was ready, resulting in a stunted, yet still dangerous creature.

The Gryce reproduce by asexual splitting, where a bud is split from the parent and injected into an unsuspecting creature that is then permitted to flee.

Over several days the bud grows, desiccating the host and forcing it to search for a nearby large source of water. Once the water has been reached, the bud tears its way free of the host, using the remains as an anchor to attach to the bottom of the pool.

Level: 7

Health: 150/150

Stamina: 130/130

Mana: 140/200

"Okay, so it's a lure?" I asked. Ronin nodded, his fingers still dancing across the strings of his lute, even as Grizz strode up to the edge of the water, lowering his sword and shield as if entranced.

The creature moved closer, lifting out of the water even farther, attempting to draw him in close.

Grizz smiled at it, resting his sword on the heavy plate of his shoulder and waited as it reached out for him.

The creature did look like a young woman at first: dark hair, a pretty face, a welcoming smile, and very, very little in the way of clothing.

I supposed, if I was drunk, such as Ronin suggested, I'd have wandered into the water very happily. But looking at it now? There was a hell of a lot of the view that was just wrong.

Its skin was lightly scaled, its eyes predatory, but that wasn't the problem. It was the way the gryce moved. It didn't swim or walk or anything; it just lifted through the water like it was attached to something beneath it.

It rose, almost standing free now, as the water bulged up, flowing back from something climbing to the surface, muck sliding off as the lure reached out a slender hand to Grizz.

"Uh," I said, looking at Yen, who was utterly unconcerned.

"Watch," she said. "Something like this might be dangerous to the unwary, or, you know…"

"Or you with your sex drive," Ronin added in quickly.

"Fuck me, what's gone wrong with my life when the fucking bard complains that I'm a horny bastard?" I wondered aloud, just as Grizz moved.

He seemed to barely shift his feet, but his blade was in a blurring motion, carving a sudden figure of eight in the air, along with a sound like a silk dress sliding off the foot of the bed.

"Yeah, little risk to most people who are aware, but to a legionnaire?" Yen commented, watching her lover dismember what would have almost passed for an innocent girl. "We generally get exposed to things like this in training, with someone like Restun standing by to make your life an absolute hell if you got killed."

The "girl" seemed to fall apart, its impressive chest the center of a flowing X that freed its head, both arms, and lower torso from each other in a fountain of green and brown fluid.

The creature that had been steadily rising from the shallow pond exploded into motion, a handful of tentacles bursting out of the water. The bulbous form split down the middle to expose a gaping maw of serrated teeth.

Grizz dropped to one knee, slashing from left to the right, and chopped all the tentacles off cleanly. Rising to his feet and stepping forward in one smooth motion, he discarded his shield to the left and switched his grip on the sword, driving it down, two-handed, into the middle of the creature's maw.

The blade dug deep, then Grizz dragged it back toward himself, and the creature was carved practically in two.

I shook my head as I saw the truth of it. Grizz reached down and fished some of the creature free of the pond with one hand before it could sink. The lure was more than half of the creature I could see now. Hell, it might have been three-quarters between that and the tentacles. The mouth and presumably a stomach was tiny in comparison, being blown up wide to bite onto its prey before sinking back down to the bottom of the pond to digest it.

Grizz tossed the remains onto the bank next to him, then cleaned his blade as the creature twitched and expired.

"Giint!" Grizz called to the crazy little gnome who was already sidling up. "If you find anything worth keeping…" He lifted a small nugget of the gnomish wonderdrug and waved it where Giint could see it.

Giint's smile was in danger of splitting the top of his head off as he dove into the corpse with abandon, tearing it apart before grimacing, then diving into the now-filthy water and vanishing from sight.

After a solid minute, Ronin cleared his throat. "Uh, he can swim, right?" he asked, just as a bubble popped, and a collection of fresh filth floated up.

"Not a clue. Say, Grizz…" I said, grinning at the massive legionnaire, before the water bubbled again. A hand rose, grabbing onto the bank and dragging the utterly filthy Giint after it.

He rolled onto his back, gasping for air, eyes wide. But in his left hand, he shakily raised a small, glowing essence core.

"Fuck me," Grizz grunted. "I didn't actually think there'd be anything down there."

"Why'd you send him, then?" I asked, reaching out and trying to pry it from his tightly clenched fist, before giving up and pulling a nugget of drug from my pocket and offering it to him.

He handed the essence core over, and I examined it.

Immature Gryce Essence Core		Further Description *Yes/No*	
Details:		This essence core was taken from an immature Gryce. The core, like the creature it comes from, is weak; yet, it fills you with a sense of distraction and avarice.	
Rarity:	**Magical:**	**Durability:**	**Charge:**
Rare	Yes	99/100	N/A

I considered it for a long second, then dismissed it. The vague feelings I was getting from it made me think I'd be able to improve illusion magic and more, yet when did I ever use fucking illusion magic?

I liked *fire*. I liked beating the crap out of my enemies.

Fuck illusion.

I turned as Sehran stopped singing, and saw her gesture behind us, welcoming someone, inviting them in to join us, then I saw…something I didn't expect.

CHAPTER EIGHTEEN

The figure that moved slowly out of the bushes and walked up to us, smiling nervously, was anything but what I'd been expecting.

She looked to be barely more than a child, maybe five feet tall and half-starved, and yet she also wasn't anything I'd seen before.

She was mainly humanoid looking, far more so than the creatures that served the Arbuton in the Grove, but…

> **Sylvan Female**
> The sylvan are distantly related to elves, and have a similarly long maturation period and low birth rate, but are far less interested in the realm around them, preferring to stay within their own small family groups.
>
> **Level:** 3
> **Health:** 90/90
> **Stamina:** 60/60
> **Mana:** 300/480

"A sylvan?" I asked, confused, and got even more so when Oracle turned to Sehran and spoke.

"Release her, please, Sehran," Oracle said in a tone that brooked no argument. Sehran nodded, making a sudden tying gesture in the air with both hands, muttering something in another language before 'snapping' the air between her fingers and rubbing them together as if rubbing her palms free of dirt.

The sylvan seemed to wake slowly, shaking her head as if confused. But as her eyes cleared, they filled with fear.

"No," she whispered, twisting around and about to flee, until Oracle called something in a fluting language that seemed almost musical.

The sylvan still took a few quick steps, but caught herself on a tree and twisted around, staring at us from behind it, eyes wide.

She was only perhaps five feet tall, with a small lump on either temple that looked to be budding horns, much like those of a deer. Her skin was smooth but dappled in grays and greens, with brown patterns like a tree that ran up and down.

Her arms were slender, and she had three fingers on each hand, with ears that flared out to the sides, coming to a batlike point at the top and bottom.

Her eyes were ovals of green and gold, and her legs were long, seemingly hooved and more animal than human.

Most disturbing, though, was the way she stared at us all. We weren't prey, as the gryce had looked at us, but an enemy; we were the aggressor, invading her home, and she clearly expected to be attacked at any second.

Despite all of this, she hesitated and trilled back at Oracle.

Oracle replied, her voice lifting and falling as they spoke, the language more like a collection of bird calls than anything else.

"All of you, settle down and put your weapons away," Oracle said, like the queen she was and we obeyed.

"What about…"

She shook her head. "This is important, my love. Please, sit quietly with the others, eat, and rest, but we go no farther for now." I felt the determination, as well as the pleading in her words. I nodded, not sure what was going on, but if it was that important to her, then it was that important to me, too.

I sat down with the others, pulling a coffee jug from my bag and grinning at the way that everyone else perked up. "Yeah, I know you buggers want some, as well," I muttered, pretending to be annoyed as Grizz grinned and held his cup out. In seconds, the others had their mugs to hand as well. And just like that, I was down to the dregs.

"I'm gonna have to start carrying more of these," I muttered to myself, putting the jug back into my inventory as I laid back against the tree roots with my own mug and sighed, getting as comfortable as I could in my armor, listening absently to the trills and sounds that Oracle was making and the responses she was getting.

"Where's Tang?" I asked Yen after a few minutes.

"He was watching our visitor, but when Oracle told us to stand down, he started doing laps of us. He'll turn up," she replied, unconcerned.

"Well, 'e'd better, ah've no' forgotten it's 'is turn to cook," Lydia said with a smile, her helm on the ground next to her feet as Bob slowly massaged her wings. "Gods, Bob, iffin yer had a pecker, ah'd marry ye," she mumbled, putting her head down on her armored forearms…before jerking her head back up, realizing what she'd said aloud. Her cheeks flushed with embarrassment in the dim light. "Ah mean…"

"We know," Sehran replied with a smile. "And Bob is wonderful. He doesn't talk much, but there's an attraction to the strong and silent type."

"And as to his bone…" Ronin added, strumming the lute and clearly about to launch into a silly song. He quickly shut up when Lydia glared at him.

I grinned, shifting a little to get more comfortable as Tang moved back in closer, pausing at the edge of the pool.

"Well…I'm not drinking out of *that*," he said, shaking his head at the layer of scum and blood that was floating in it.

"Giint swim in there," Giint pointed out.

Tang snorted. "Well, if that's the result, you need to have a bath more often."

"Giint clean!" Giint snapped, scrubbing his hands on the grass by his feet in an attempt to get some of the filth off.

I sighed and summoned two fountains, one for each of them, and waited while Tang refreshed himself, and Giint, grumbling all the time, started to get clean.

"So?" I asked after a few seconds.

"Bane says there's signs of a large camp ahead, no clue how many at the minute, but easily more of them than there are of us, so this might be fun."

"How far ahead?" I asked.

"The signs aren't clear. There's enough recent activity that there's at least a dozen people going through the area regularly, but that could be a patrol or some badly lost people. The camp itself is far enough ahead that he can't sense it yet, but considering it wasn't visible from the air, either? I'm betting underground."

"A couple of hours away?" I asked, guessing at Bane's range.

"At least."

"Then fuck it, catch some sleep while you can, people, no telling how long Oracle will be…"

"I'm done," Oracle interjected.

"…And I hope you enjoyed your rest, because we're back on the trail," I finished, sighing as I forced myself to my feet, brushing some fallen leaves off my armor.

"What did yer find out?" Lydia asked, beating me to it by a second.

"The nobles have a camp about a day's march ahead, with two smaller ones maybe thirty miles to the west and the south…and…"

"And?"

"And they've got more people than we thought."

"How many?"

"About six hundred."

"Shit…"

"More than half aren't fighters, but still…"

"Three hundred fighters is a hell of a number," I replied grimly. "What's the chances that's accurate?"

"Very good. The sylvan are being forced to report on trespassers in the forest, or their families will be burned. That's how the nobles' guards and the other assholes managed to catch the rangers."

"So, they were betrayed?" I asked, scanning the direction the sylvan had vanished in.

Oracle shook her head. "No, not even slightly. The Sylvan have no interest in us, not as humans and other species, not as the Empire, none of it. They don't require food as you all do…as *we* do, I should say," she broke off.

"They literally live with their trees, and have no interest in any of you. Where the Arbuton has its grove guardians and more, choosing to keep its borders free of any threat by fighting, the sylvan simply move on. Their bodies are slow-growing and are almost inedible to any creature that might want to feed on them. Their magic is exclusive to their trees, meaning they aren't even useful as slaves growing crops or anything. All they can grow is a single tree that they are bonded to."

I frowned, then noted the others nodding.

"So they're what? Neutral?" I asked, getting more nods.

"The sylvan aren't interested in us, any of us, and as there's no crossover between our needs and theirs, so they're generally ignored. Should they be bonded to a tree in an area that's being logged, the sylvan will take enough of the tree to regrow it and move on."

"And people are just okay with them?" I asked, thinking about the general shitbags I was starting to get used to.

"Mainly, yes. Occasionally, they find things like buried gold and so on, and as they've no interest in it, they usually dump it where people who are nice to them can find it. They tend to guide lost children back as well," Yen pointed out. "As a rule, most villages that find out there are sylvan nearby are counted as lucky because, if there's any interaction at all, it's generally a positive one."

"So why are they helping the…"

"The sylvan have been split by the nobles. Half the group is kept under lock and key, while the rest are forced to roam and report any interlopers. If they don't return, their friends and family are burned," Oracle said grimly.

"And what's your friend going to…"

"She's going to find other sylvan and direct them away from us, That way, she can claim she just missed us if we lose, and no others will be burned besides her and her mate if we fail and she's caught."

"Well, fuck." I grunted. "You get any details on their camp?"

"It's about a day to reach it," Oracle repeated. "They have roving patrols, mainly regular soldiers and Dark Legionnaires, but the two groups have already had fights, the soldiers coming off worse by far."

"So, if one of the groups gets wiped out, nobody will be too surprised," I finished, grinning.

"Exactly."

"Okay, people!" I called, and they all fell in on me. "Plan is, we head deeper into the forest. Oracle can reach out to Tenandra when she gets close, she was supposed to come to Himnel after all, and once our ship gets back, you know she'll be on her way. So no stress over having to march back out. But once we find the roving patrols?" I paused, looking to Grizz, who hefted his sword.

"We kill them?"

"Got it in one," I said, grinning. "They're a bunch of nobles who refused to swear the Oath, knowing they'd be outed as criminals. They ran away and set themselves up as bandits, slaughtering honest citizens. The way I'm feeling can be summed up as 'rip their heads off and shit down their necks,' so let's slaughter them all and go do something more important."

"You're getting better at the whole 'battle plan and speeches' thing, you know that?" Tang said, grinning.

"No, he not," Giint grunted.

"No, but I was trying to be nice," Tang pointed out to Giint in a stage whisper.

"Ah, Giint understand." The mad little gnome sighed, then he stuck both thumbs up and grinned at me. Widely. "Boss do good!" Giint said through the strained rictus after a few seconds, then looked around, still holding the strained smile and his thumbs up.

"This right?" he asked the group and got a round of grins.

"Fuck's sake," I muttered pointing in the direction of the camp. "Onward!" I declared heroically.

"It's this way, dear," Oracle said sweetly, taking my hand and shifting it a bit to the right.

"Fuckers."

It was an hour before Bane found us, heading back from a scout. When he did, it was with news.

"I've found a group of the Dark Legion," he said without preamble, as soon as he'd refreshed himself, the fountain Oracle had conjured dying away.

"How far and how many?" I asked, all business.

"Seven, about three miles ahead. They've set up a camp in a small canyon, only one tent between them, and a small campfire they're trying to keep hidden. One of them is on guard, the rest sitting around and eating when I saw them."

"Regular Dark Wankers, or the Elites?" Grizz asked, and Lydia grunted, clearly about to ask the same.

"Mostly regular as near as I can tell, with possibly a berserker. The one who has the tent is a little bigger than the rest, and he has the extra sliding sections on his armor that we've seen before."

"So probably a berserker, but fuck knows, really," I agreed, scratching my beard as I thought. "Okay, then, let's go fuck up their Tuesday."

"We'll 'ave to be quiet," Lydia pointed out. "Sound travels at night."

"I can be subtle," I said, smiling, and tried to ignore the groans from around the group. "I can!"

"Sure you can, boss." Grizz said, patting me on the shoulder. "We believe you."

"I hate you all," I growled, turning my back on them and resuming the march.

It took half an hour to draw close enough that Bane stopped scouting and moved in to lead the party.

The last ten minutes was both the most awkward and relaxing of the entire day, as the Dark Wankers had chosen to set up at the end of a narrow stream that had cut a path through the forest nearby at some point.

Where they'd set up was at the start of the stream where it gushed straight out of the rocks of a tall cliff. They were on a narrow bank, having broken a path up to there by wandering alongside.

That was fine. The issue was that the bank of the stream that was navigable was on *their side* of the river, trailing down from the north…while we were trekking up from the south.

That gave us three possible paths to reach them.

Crash through the bushes, crushing and breaking them all, waking up the entire camp.

Swim or walk, depending on the depth, up the river itself.

Or fly.

Sehran, Lydia, and I took to the air happily as soon as we were close enough to know where we needed to be. We took off about half a mile from the camp, with me boosting both of them up and through the heavy tree cover.

The general lack of any sight of the sky for the last few hours meant that, while I could simply blast up and through or go slowly and bend branches back, it was a lot more awkward for the other two, as they had wings that beat against and broke branches.

I got around this by having Lydia climb onto my back, flying up and edging out of the canopy then ascending up high enough that she could just let go and catch herself with her wings.

Doing the same with Sehran was a bit more awkward, mainly because she was determined to see if she could get a rise out of me. Purely for shits and giggles, but still.

I was halfway through the canopy with her hanging onto my back when she clambered up and onto my shoulders.

Before I knew what was happening, she was sitting in her tiny hotpants, legs wrapped around my neck—from behind, thankfully—and she was resting her tits on top of my head.

I'd taken the helm off because it was insane to risk hurting one of them by wearing it as I flew, and it restricted my vision a little, but that just meant she had plenty of room to get comfy.

"So…are you never tempted to ask Oracle if you can both come and play with me and Tenandra one night? I'm sure Jian wouldn't mind," she whispered in my ear. I couldn't help but groan.

"You damn well know she would say 'no,' and so would Jian," I said. "Hell, you're so happy with him, you wouldn't want Oracle and me, even if we said yes!"

"He might enjoy watching us all," she said with a shrug that did *interesting* things to my new earmuffs. "He likes watching me and Tenandra."

"Aaaand that's enough of that," I declared, forcing my way through the last of the trees and soaring fast and hard upward. She squawked and nearly fell off, then grabbed on tight with her thighs, nearly breaking my damn neck, before letting loose a little laugh and opening her wings, letting herself fall free.

I twisted around as she snapped her wings and flew up past me, her amusement and sheer pleasure at getting a reaction from me making me shake my head despite myself.

We all drifted as silently as possible through the sky, landing gently at the top of the cliff a handful of minutes later, making ourselves comfortable watching the camp below.

"Can you tell where the others are?" Lydia whispered after a handful of minutes. I concentrated, feeling the strands of Oath that bound us all together, and pointed slowly into the forest.

"There, about a hundred meters." I shifted to point at a spot in the river close to the camp. "And there's Bane."

Oracle had stayed with the others so we could still communicate. Sehran could reach out to Jian as well, if need be, but it still freaked me out not having her by my side.

"You know, we could always have a little quickie up here…just the three of us…nobody would…urk!" Sehran broke off as Lydia did something out of my sight, then leaned in and started whispering to the succubus, clearly sick of the game and ending it on her terms.

I deliberately ignored them, focusing on the camp below as a single sentry moved back into the camp from where they'd been sitting in a bush off to one side, making it harder to spot them.

A minute later, and a much quieter and thoroughly reprimanded Sehran was sitting down on the other side of me, keeping her distance from Lydia.

"How long?" Lydia asked me quietly.

"Oracle?" I asked. *"How long?"*

"Two, maybe three minutes," she sent back, along with a sense of amusement. *"What happened with Sehran?"*

"Nothing, why?"

"Jian says she's in a huff."

"Lydia had a word with her. She asked if we fancied a quick threesome up here."

"Were you tempted?"

"Of course I was, I'm taken, not dead."

"Really?"

"Nah, I'm happy with you." I sent the mental equivalent of a kiss and received the same in return.

"Okay, Grizz says we're ready."

"I love you."

"I love you too," Oracle sent.

I climbed to my feet and pulled my naginata free. "You ready?" I asked, getting nods from them both. Sehran readied her whip, and Lydia tugged both her shield and mace free. "I'll take the tent. Lydia, land as close to the wall as possible, and take the pair laid out there. Sehran, the archers."

They nodded, moving up to the edge as I looked down.

Where we'd landed, the cliff was mainly clear and narrow. The top was reasonably comfortable for us to sit on, but had we tried to climb up through the thick thorn bushes and more, it would have been a nightmare.

The Dark Legionnaires had clearly decided the same and had set up with the cliff at their backs, spread out in a semicircle facing the little path they'd worn into the valley, totally ignoring the clifftop where the three of us sat.

I took a deep breath, looked at my health and mana, ignoring my stamina as I always did, now that it was this high, and shrugged. I'd not lost much with Soaring Majesty, and what I had, well, it'd almost all regenerated now.

"Let's do this," I whispered and stepped off the edge of the cliff, falling into the night.

CHAPTER NINETEEN

The dark dickhead who'd reached the end of his shift on watch had started stripping out of his plate armor, while his replacement was cursing and pulling their boots on, still half-asleep and struggling with the cheap-ass blanket wrapped around their legs.

"Damn thing!" he snarled, finally kicking it free and yanking his boot on.

The edge of the blanket landed on a gently glowing coal, smoldering, then quickly bursting into flame as the oil-impregnated cloth embraced the end of its life in a joyful burst of light and heat.

The one going off his watch saw it and shouted in warning, causing all those around the edge of the fire to jerk awake, hands reaching for weapons with sleep-fogged minds until they saw the flame and heard the cursing idiot.

"Fucking hell, the Dark Lord's abandoned us all!" he snarled, yanking it free and turning to the water, just about to plunge it into the fast-moving stream when he paused, squinting into the depths. "Hey, that looks like…"

I let my speed build up, then flared my ability to push me upward and guide me into place instead, seconds before I would have slammed into the floor some hundred and fifty meters below.

Instead, I landed in a classic three-point superhero pose, naginata drawn to the side, gripped near to the blade, just as the supposed dark berserker dragged the front of his tent open, mouth opening to roar some bullshit about them learning not to disturb their betters.

I interrupted him. Terminally.

I took the ugly bastard in the stomach, the blade sliding through his fat, hairy belly and cutting toward his heart with all the inevitability of a politician looking for a bribe.

He gasped, eyes going wide as he tried to grab the blade, the sliding plates of his armor suddenly being exposed as necessary, not to enable the shifting of size from the berserker rage but because he was too fat to fit in regular armor. Even though it was badly fitted, it'd have given him some protection…had he not taken it off and left it behind in his tent.

I ripped the blade up, tearing through his lungs, his heart, and then twisting it and pulling back, spinning on my heel and facing the rest of the camp. Blood flicked from my naginata to splatter across the stunned Dark Legionnaires.

Their training and years of experience kicked in to tell them that immobility was death, but they were too late.

I flipped the naginata over, grabbing it two-handed just under the head and whipped the weighted base around, bringing it down into the skull of one of the men. His head snapped to the side, and he fell, stunned.

A scream tore free from the one who'd taken his burning blanket to the river, as Bane reared up and plunged four daggers into his body, flicking his blades across the tops of his legs and wrists, then reversing the strikes to carve through his victim's stomach and down his chest in eight savage wounds that spilled his lifeblood at an insane rate.

I grinned at the stunned Dark Legionnaires, only to have one of them scream in recognition.

"The Apostate!" he cried, kicking free of his blanket and diving for his sword…just as Lydia landed behind him, the crash of her armor as she landed mixed with the downdraft from her wings, sending glowing coals flying everywhere, even as she brought her mace down between his shoulders.

There was a sickening crack, and he collapsed, falling face-first to the floor and gasping, before screaming, his body unresponsive.

A woman laying next to Lydia rolled toward her, trying to take her legs out, only to meet her shield as it was slammed down, the lower spikes digging into the ground and stopping her dead.

Then Lydia lifted the shield and twisted, kicking the woman in the face and snapping her head back. She muzzily grabbed Lydia's leg, and yanked, stabbing a needle-pointed poniard into her calf and making Lydia hiss in pain before she slammed her shield back down again, edge first on the woman's elbow where it hung just above the ground. The dark-haired woman threw back her head to scream in pain, and met Lydia's mace coming the other way.

Sehran had landed a split-second after me and right before Lydia. But where I was a blur of blood and flashing naginata, Sehran landed almost daintily, her legs taking a lot of the force as she furled her midnight black, bat-like wings. She straightened slowly, tossing her hair back, her smile wide and inviting, her figure outlined in flames from behind.

Then the smile grew more predatory as her fangs were revealed, and her whip flicked out, catching one woman's wrist as she tried to draw her sword. Sehran yanked the woman forward and drove the whip's grip into her stomach, knocking her breath out of her, before grabbing her by the back of the head and yanking her head back to expose the throat.

Sehran lunged in close, fangs sinking into the woman's throat, wrapping her arms and wings around her and slowly lowering her to the ground. The look of terror on the woman's face morphed into a mixture of ecstasy and release.

A black arrow flashed out of the darkness, pinning the last dark legionnaire to a small, gnarled tree by his shoulder, drawing a pained cry then a grunt as a much shorter dart punched into his forehead, killing him instantly.

"That was mine," Tang called from the darkness.

"Mine!" Giint argued.

Just like that, the fight was over.

I examined the second one I'd hit, seeing the shattered skull, the rolled back eyes, and fluid leaking from the nose.

I could save him. Probably, under the Geneva Convention, I was required to by law. But the signatories to that document had never fought Dark Legionnaires in the realm on the other side of the universe, and even if they had?

They could go fuck themselves.

This asshole was a worshiper of the God of Death, and that wanker was on my shit list.

Every single worshiper of His that I killed weakened Him, even as each death released a little mana to Him through His aspect.

I stabbed the fucker under the chin, cutting up into his brain, killing him instantly.

I straightened up, feeling momentarily dirty. Then I forced myself to shake it off. I couldn't have left him loose nor taken him with us. After all, he'd betray us, given half a chance.

Leaving him here? Tied up, with all this smell of death and fresh blood, meat, and more? That'd mean his death damn quickly in the UnderVerse from any number of beasts.

No, I'd done what needed doing, but that didn't mean my instincts and long-forgotten upbringing didn't still rail against slaughtering a helpless prisoner.

I looked around, seeing that the one that Lydia had first hit was alive as well until Giint stepped in closer and shot him in the back of the head.

"Now Giint kill more than Tang AND Bane," the mad little bastard declared happily. "Giint deserve more gold. Giint works harder than these." He gestured at the others, blatantly serious.

I shook my head, incredulous. "You spend half your time off your face on drugs, the rest, you're either missing or killing something."

"Giint loot creatures!"

I nodded. It was a fair point.

"We all loot things," Tang said. Then he paused, clearly remembering the incident in the sewers under Narkolt. "Yeah, all right."

"Wait, you fuckers are getting paid?" Grizz asked, wounded. "I get my normal Legion pay, and that's it!"

"Really?" Yen asked, acting surprised. "We've all been on triple-plus bonuses since we joined the party."

"Yeah, man, Restun pays everyone. Maybe you should talk to him about it?" Tang suggested, trying to hide a grin when Grizz started grumbling and vowing that he would.

"Oh, that's just cruel," I whispered to Yen, who was standing nearby.

"If he's stupid enough to go to Restun with this, then it's better to remove him from the breeding cycle now." She smiled and shook her head.

"You're the one he'd be having kids with," Lydia said.

"Exactly. You think I want that level of stupid in me?"

"You've had it in you for a while."

"I meant for having kids, not just entertainment."

I turned to Oracle, leaving the conversation before it got even more personal.

The love of my life was flying over the ground between us, checking us all as she went before landing next to me and kissing my cheek as I pulled my helm off.

"You okay?" she asked and I nodded.

"I barely got started, and it was over."

She quirked a little smile before taking my hand and drawing me off to one side. "That was surprisingly quiet for you, but still we need to move on, and quickly."

"Why?"

"The sylvan. They'll have heard it, and they'll be coming."

"The…why didn't you warn me?" I gritted my teeth as I thought about us having to run or kill them.

"Because you already knew we needed to be quiet. If you'd tried to do this silently, the smell of the blood, the hormones, all of it would have drawn them, anyway. The only other choice we could have made was to leave an enemy alive behind us."

"And that's not an option." I grunted. "Fine. Okay, people!" I called out, giving up on the fucking stealth entirely, knowing that the incoming sylvan would report back as quickly as they could, anyway. "Stealth is less important than speed; there's a few hundred enemies out there, but they're broken up into patrols and more, and those who aren't are likely to be shite compared to the Legion's elite."

"Damn right!" Grizz agreed, grinning.

"And Grizz," Tang finished for me with a laugh, getting a finger from Grizz.

"Pop stamina potions if you need them, because we're going hunting! Bane, Tang! Get out there ahead. Bane finds the fuckers, passes word to Tang. He falls back and guides us to them. Let's see how many we can take down between now and daylight!"

"What if they surrender?" Yen asked. "Plenty of them will be guards who had no say in their lord's decisions."

"Knock them out, take their bags and weapons, and use whatever they have to tie them up. If they're no threat, they can be collected later and serve in the army for their crimes. If you find any who are marked as having taken action against the Empire, though, they die."

"Moving out," Bane called, striding up out of the stream and throwing his head back, water flying from his tentacles as he'd been having a drink.

"With you," Tang agreed, falling in behind him.

"Gather yer loot, you've thirty seconds!" Lydia called, and the others fell to work as I turned to Oracle.

"You still could have told me," I said.

"Jax, you knew as well as I did that there could be others nearby. We were either quiet in taking them down, or we weren't, but once blood is spilled, the sylvan know."

"Yeah, that's the point!" I said, setting off along the trail, unconcerned about loot. "I didn't know about the sylvan sensing that."

"You couldn't have taken them all down without bloodshed, and the risk of trying to without drawing blood wasn't worth it."

"I know, but still…" The conversation went nowhere after that, as the others joined us and we set off jogging back along the train, following the Dark Wankers' tracks.

It was fifteen minutes before we found the next camp, Bane locating it a mile away, hidden at the top of a small rise with a campfire blazing merrily as the idiots all slumbered around it.

Tang fell back to us, guiding us along the easiest paths and bringing us up short at the foot of the hill as we stared up in disbelief.

We didn't need Bane to lead us here. The damn campfire was in danger of spreading and burning half the forest down, and the man on guard was snuggled up against a tree, wrapped in a blanket with his head thrown back…snoring.

The sound of his snoring could have drawn us alone, but the rest of the group?

I shook my head and walked up, watching them, waiting to be attacked at any second, to find it was a trap, a trick or…

Nope.

I stopped in the middle of the camp, looking around in disgust as the others took up stations, Bob standing between two of the loudest snoring and looking down at them, a mace in either hand, raised and ready.

I almost ordered the attack out of sheer fucking annoyance, but Yen's point was valid, and I used Greater Examination on them all, one-by-one.

They were pathetic, and that was the general consensus as I read all of their details, pointing at one of them on the far edge of the camp, clearly unpopular with the rest, as the only one who was an actual criminal.

All the others were guards and conscripted locals who'd been forced into serving as their only alternative to being killed or enslaved.

"This is fucking ridiculous," I said aloud, getting a slight reaction from one of the figures, who shifted and let loose a fart that made the nearby campfire flare slightly. "Loot them, restrain them." I pointed at the one on the outer edge. "Hang that one." I paused, seeing Sehran's hopeful smile. "Fine, fuck it, might as well save the rope for tying these wankers up." I waved at her to have at it.

As she leaped atop the scumbag on the outside, I leveled my blade at the nearest throat and kicked the slumbering figure in the side.

"Wha…my turn already?" he asked sleepily, starting to sit up. I had to pull my blade back, rather than risk accidentally skewering him.

"No," I said as the rest of the camp was roused, blades resting against throats and, in the case of Giint's chosen victim, a groin. "It's not your turn to go on watch."

"Oh," he whispered, eyes wide as he stared down the length of my naginata and let loose a terrified fart.

"There'd better be a real fight in my future soon," I growled as he very, very carefully lifted his hands away from his weapons, rolling onto his front and putting his hands on the back of his head as Yen gave orders to the camp.

In seconds, they were all trussed up, tied to a tree, their own ropes around their ankles, throats, and wrists.

"This is just ridiculous," Grizz muttered, searching through their bags and pulling out a sword to show us all. "This thing couldn't cut butter. Hell, it's being kept together by the rust!"

"What will you do with us?" one of the last asked Lydia in a scared voice.

She sighed, looking over at me.

"You'll be examined, then given anything from a few years in the army to death, depending on your crimes," I said. "You're helping those asshole bandits to kill and loot Imperial citizens, but none of you were involved in the actual act, as near as I can tell." I had seen the murderer tag on the one Sehran had fed on and nothing like that on any of the others.

"You'll be left here, tied up, to be collected later by the Legion. Then you'll be given the Oath and questioned," Lydia finished for me, seeing they had meant the immediate time scale rather than the longer one I'd addressed.

"Oh…and Martin?" the speaker asked, looking over at the desiccated remains by Sehran's foot, as Jian offered her a cloth to wipe her mouth, getting a peck on the cheek from her in thanks once she'd used it.

"Martin?"

"The one she…"

"Oh." I grunted. "Murderer."

"I knew id!" one of the others mumbled around the rope in his mouth. "I fuffing knew id!"

"Well, he's paid for it now!" I said with a smile. "So, anyone want to get a chance at a pardon by telling us about the others back at the camp?"

Twenty minutes later, we were closing on the next camp, and where the last one was just shameful for the incompetence, this one was just ridiculous.

"I give up," Bane grumbled, appearing next to me, leaning against a tree and shaking his head in disgust. "*Years* I've spent training and honing my skills, and that…" He gestured up at the literal *party* that was going on further up the valley.

"You are shitting me," I whispered, watching as two people got up onto a table to dance, judging from the shadows thrown against the side of the massive tent.

The camp itself wasn't bad. Hell, it was by far the best so far, and considering its size, it looked to be one of the actual camps that were a target for the quest, considering there had to be at least sixty people, probably the conscripted villagers for the most part sitting together outside, as far as I could make out from here.

"That's a lot of people," I said grimly.

"That's a lot of *drunken* people," Bane corrected. "There's about twenty guards 'on duty', although most are fast asleep, having sex, gambling, or passed out in puddles of ale."

"And the rest?" I asked.

"Of the guards?" He pointed a few out. "Those are awake and seem disgusted by everything, but there's also some bodies nearby. A bunch of those on the far side were plotting to rob the place and run off…those two were exchanging sexual fantasies." He pointed out most of those we could see, going in a quick circle of the camp, before crouching and drawing a small map in the dirt of the forest floor.

It was dim, the light of the stars and the two moons that were up currently giving just enough light for normal people to walk into trees, as we discussed the layout, all easily able to see the map thanks to DarkVision.

"So, there's about sixty common people huddled together, trying to ignore the nobles, while the guards mainly ignore their duties and plot robbing the idiots. The nobles sit in the middle and get pissed all night?"

"An' all day, according te those buggers back there," Lydia grunted.

I shook my head again in disgust.

"Well, regardless of the locals and the pissed-up nobles, our first job is to take the guards out, and as quietly as possible. Then we can take the nobles out. Think a show of force will do for the common lot? Maybe keep them out of the fight?" I asked the group, getting grins.

"Jax, you view everything through your own experience," Jian said. "Seriously, boss, before I was a slave, I was one of the sheep out there. You get a heavily armed legionnaire, or hell, any warrior marching up and telling you to sit and be silent? You damn well do it. You look after your family and your friends, and you stay out of the affairs of the nobility. If they want to kill each other? You keep your head down and hope you don't get picked out for anything beyond cleaning away the bodies."

"Right?"

"You'd stand up. You'd pick a fight with us if we marched in and threatened you, wouldn't you?" he asked.

I shrugged.

"Exactly."

"What he's saying is that they won't want to be involved. They look to be prisoners or conscripts, if not actively enslaved; at the very best, they're servants. They'll keep their heads down and their mouths shut, especially once they see the legion armor," Ronin added absently, still looking back up the valley at them, listening to the music gently drifting on the wind.

"What's up?" I asked him.

"That song's being butchered. Mainly I stay out of things, boss, but whoever is playing that music needs to be hurt, and badly."

"Okay, so we've got a real reason to get up there now, considering the crimes against music," I quipped, getting a look from Ronin.

"Seriously, boss, you don't get it, and that's fine, but consider this, music has *power*," Ronin growled.

"Yeah, I know yours does, but…"

"*All* music has power, boss. It might not give you bonuses, but it changes your mood, makes you brave or afraid. It makes you relax or laugh. You don't know the real power of music, not until it's been used against you."

"So what, should we just send you up there?" I asked.

"Don't be ridiculous!" He laughed. "I'll leave battering the shit out of people to you folks. I'm the cheerleader here. I'm just saying be ready, something's off about all of this, and the music matters."

"Fair enough." I sighed, stretching and cracking my back as I let loose a long yawn. "How about we clear the camp out, then we get some rest?" I got nods from the others before stifling a yawn with the back of my hand again. I froze as I realized what I was doing, turning to stare at Ronin, who was playing a slow and relaxing tune.

He nodded when he saw that he had our full attention and started to play another song, still low, barely loud enough to hear a dozen feet away, yet…

The tune was bouncy, energetic, making me think of all those training montages in the movies where the hero was shite at something, then a handful of minutes later, they were kicking a kung fu master around the room, listening to a song about a tiger's eye.

I grinned as he switched to that, or the closest version he could manage, considering when Tommy and I had tried to teach it to him, we'd bumbled through most of the words and just remembered the damn chorus.

"Music is magic, boss," he said, laying his hands across the strings of his lute to silence it. "And someone's playing games with it, making people angrier than they should be." He nodded to the party as he went on.

"Watch the movements, the way people stand and dance, the crowd. I'll counter the music." He started to play something cheerful and low, and we watched the people outlined by shadows.

At first I didn't see anything, even as I heard others talking about the things they were noticing. *"They're frantic,"* Oracle whispered into my mind. I frowned, suddenly seeing the jerky movements, the weird *wrongness* of the way people moved.

"Frantic," I muttered, starting to see it now it had been pointed out to me and the music countered. "What the hell is going on in there?"

"I don't know, but, boss," Ronin said, and I nodded to him absently to continue. "Whoever that is, they're skilled, so feel free to stab them in the face at the first opportunity. If they can do this from that distance, then up close they're going to be a nightmare."

"Okay, then," I said. "Grizz, you, Jian, and Sehran head straight up the path. Literally march up to them, either side of Sehran, while she does her best to be a distraction. That should keep the guards focused on you. Ronin, use your music to help distract the guards as long as possible. The closer you can get before you fight, the better. Lydia and I will hover overhead, waiting for the shit to hit the fan.

"Once it does, I'll create two fountains. Oracle, you be ready with heals for our people and lightning for theirs. Bob, I want you to hit them from the side with Giint. Make a big show of it, scare the shit out of them. When they split to try and attack you, Bane and Tang will kill them. Arrin, Magic Missile any lone guards who are missed. Yen, FlameStrike the guards if they bunch up, and be ready in case shit goes wrong. I want a backup plan."

I got nods and smiles, then grinned back, loving the adrenaline surge that came from this shit. I kissed Oracle, then wished the others luck, taking a few quick steps and launching myself into the air, glad that this section of the forest was less overgrown, and neither Lydia nor I were inching our way through the canopy.

CHAPTER TWENTY

Lydia stretched out, flapping her huge wings, climbing into the air higher and higher as we circled overhead, Ronin's music dying away as the camp's music wrapped around us.

With helms back on, it was difficult to see much of each other's faces. But when you spent time with someone like I had with Lydia, you could read as much from the set of her shoulders and the beat of her wings as her voice.

I moved in closer, the pair of us staying as steady as we could, as Grizz and Jian marched out of the trees and toward the camp, their cloaks pulled around to cover their armor as much as possible, making them look more like Dark Legionnaires than real ones.

The guards sat up, one nudging the other and pointing to the trio, as Jian, leading the way, stepped to the side, making it clear they were escorting someone.

The guards perked up more as Sehran, her more demonic aspects clearly repressed somehow, appeared to be a lost innocent girl that was being escorted into the camp.

She was wrapped in a cloak as well. Ronin's, if I had to guess, as it was clearly too small for her.

The guards called to their friends, one kicking another who was fast asleep and getting them to stand, although most of them seemed more interested in Sehran than putting their armor on or picking up weapons.

It wasn't until Jian was less than ten feet from them, that someone noticed that the armor and helm weren't Dark Legion-issue and cried out a challenge.

By then, it was far too fuckin' late.

Jian threw his cloak back, dragging the twin swords he wore on either hip free, and activated an ability, leaping across the distance between himself and one of the guards who had been leering at her.

"Rapist," I whispered coldly as Jian hacked through his right arm then relieved him of his head.

"Murderer," I mumbled, my mana plunging as I used my examination ability over and over again, making sure that none of these men were innocent, even as Lydia flared her wings and dove.

"Brigand...Robber...*Marauder*!" I bellowed, flicking from one to another, to another. Each time I saw one, the spell brought their details up, the red flashing damnation of the Gods filling my vision.

Every single one was guilty. Every single one had attacked an Imperial Citizen, a member of my Empire.

I passed Lydia, teeth drawn back in a snarl as I flipped over, having no need to land gently, not when I could simply ram myself upward with my ability to kill my momentum.

Or better yet, I could use them to do it for me.

I landed *hard* behind them, twisting my naginata around and down as I pushed with my ability, killing my momentum and slicing halfway through the next man before he even heard me land.

I screamed, swinging the blade to the left, literally ripping it free of the first body, sending him howling to the forest floor as steaming blood flew into the air.

I hacked it into the side of the next in line, the cheap iron armor crumpling around my weapon, and I wasted no time channeling mana into it. A cloud of steam boiled out of him, along with sooty smoke as the superheated weapon refused to come free.

I planted a boot on his hip and kicked off, ripping it free, only to be hit by a shield from the left as someone rammed into me.

I staggered, shook myself, and braced my naginata against their shield, then twisted the base of my weapon against the bottom of the shield, hooking it around and yanking it aside.

He stabbed around it, his shortsword glancing off the side of my armor, passing between my side and my left arm. I released the naginata with my left hand, grabbing the back of the wrist, and yanked his hand out, keeping him from stabbing me again.

I dropped my naginata. The shield being shoved against me over and over was too close to make my weapon viable. Instead, I grabbed the top of the shield and pulled to the right, exposing my enemy.

I kicked out, left heel pounding into the inside of his right knee, staggering him, then hauled back on the shield. As it moved to the side, I took a kick in the stomach, sending me staggering back two steps.

He reset his shield, pointing his sword at me and advancing, my naginata left on the floor behind him.

I cracked my neck, rolling my shoulders as a heal hit me, topping off the tank as my health hit full again, and I triggered Mana Overdrive.

Grabbing a mattock from the floor where it'd been resting on its head beside the supports for the tent, I spun it around, grinning insanely.

He attacked. Three quick steps, shield angled, ready to take the blow from me, and clearly expecting to stab me afterward.

Instead, I took a two-handed stance, wound up, and swung for the fuckin' fences.

The head of the mattock landed square on the shield, buckling it. The shaft of the mattock snapped with the force of the impact, a cloud of wooden splinters flying everywhere as he grunted in shock, staggering backward, sword arm windmilling as his left hung limp and useless, shattered by the force of the blow.

I took two steps forward, slid my foot under my naginata and kicked it into the air as more guards closed with me, and I screamed in fury.

I heard Grizz roaring a battle cry nearby.

Sehran howled with glee as she leapt on a nearby guard, driving him to the floor from behind and sinking her teeth into the back of his neck, feeding.

Lydia had landed nearby and had her first target on his back, holding his shield over him. He lay crying out in terror as she slammed her mace into the middle, over and over again, laughing wildly.

A dart flashed past me, taking a running guard in the throat, sending him to the floor, weapons discarded as his hands came up, trying to staunch the blood.

FlameStrikes pounded into guards as they raced toward us, desperate to fight. They vanished in great gouts of flame as the forest shook around us.

Bob waded through us, ignoring the frantic fighting, beyond a single blow from his mighty warhammer landing on a figure that had been running toward the civilians.

His target collapsed with a scream, and the corralled villagers tried to draw back, making it clear they were, in fact, chained to the floor like cattle.

Bob raised his hammer high above them, to their dawning horror, then brought it down on the stump that had been driven into the ground to hold the end of their chains.

It shattered, and he pointed urgently to the forest, hissing at the cowering people before turning his back on them and laying about him with the hammer, taking down guards and assholes who boiled out of the main tent.

They were half-dressed, steaming drunk, and rabid, hacking at the air as they raced toward Bob and the rest of us. I stared, grinning at the challenge, and launched myself forward, naginata extended. Ramming it through the stomach of the man before me, then the one behind, I screamed as I lifted them, spitted through with my weapon.

I couldn't help myself, a wide grin stretching my cheeks as I threw them aside, letting go of my weapon as I did, triggering the shield rune on my left hand and the lightning concussion runes on my right, deflecting a sword with the mana shield before punching out as hard as I could at the center of their breastplate.

I felt my knuckles, the little bones in my hand, and wrist break in my gauntlet, the combination of my momentum, the force of my punch, their momentum, and hitting the center and strongest point of their fucking armor with all the force I could.

And I roared with pain, powering more of my tattoos…only to have my mana bottom out all in one go, the mana headache sending me reeling as Oracle slammed down a Frostfire Circle of Cleansing atop me.

I staggered and I heard Oracle screaming at me.

"JAX, STOP!" she pleaded.

I twisted around, my balance going, and falling to one knee, even as the flames started to repair me again, and the distant sound of music began to filter through the pain.

I heard Oracle again, realizing that she was screaming in my head, not aloud.

"Stop the music!" she begged. *"It's driving you all mad! Ronin can't help you much longer!"*

I could hear the music building, and spun around. People were going mad, properly insane! Bob stood there, calmly keeping people back from the civilians as they stumbled and headed for the forest, but anyone who was willing to fight…they were going berserk!

Guards were attacking each other, if none of us were close enough, screaming erupting in waves from inside the tent.

I gritted my teeth, the music rising, feeling the madness, the need to fight. I tore my helm off, tossing it aside, and cupped my palms, then slammed them over my ears as hard as I could.

My eardrums ruptured, and I fell sideways with a cry of pain. I couldn't hear a thing, only feel the flames tearing back toward me. Several that had been congregating around my right arm, repairing it, abandoned it in favor of my head.

I forced myself to my feet, reeling like a punch-drunk boxer, and staggered forward, trying to reach the tent, even as the flames burrowed into me, fixing the damage.

I snarled, pushing harder, picking up speed as I tried to lumber out of the encompassing circle's radius…only to list sideways and fall over as my sense of balance told me that up was actually left.

I hit the ground, rolling as I tried to make sense of the world, screams of pain and fury filling the air as my ears were repaired.

Finally, I rolled to my feet again, having made it into the tent and straightened up under a wooden table, taking it with me in a crash of falling bottles. Someone leaped onto me, taking me onto my back.

I blocked instinctively, catching the falling dagger on my armored forearm, then punching out, sending a mass of blonde hair reeling back. Furious screams filled my ears as they spat blood, then leaped onto me again, wildly slashing at my face.

Before I could react, the enemy was tossed backward by a massive, bony hand.

"Bob," I mumbled, shaking my head and frowning as I tried to make sense of things. He stabbed a finger deeper into the tent before dragging me to my feet and turning his back on me to face the screaming mess of people outside.

"Got it. Thanks, buddy," I muttered, the circle fading as it ran out of mana, and I left its radius and glanced around at the interior in shock.

"The fuck happened here?" I gasped at the devastation. There were bodies everywhere, some alive, but unconscious, probably from the drink and excessive partying, but here and there, bodies lay still and bloated, likely untouched for days.

There were naked people, having just finished or still in the middle of having sex, food spoiling on the tables and trampled into the floor, wine bottles broken and leaking, sealed, full and empty. One guy lay naked, barring his hat and ripped shirt, in a bucket-type chair, trying to figure out how to drink from a bottle of wine with a shattered and clearly sharp neck, his lips tattered and blood streaming.

Totally fine, and full bottles were mixed in around the broken and empty ones, but it was clear he wouldn't, or couldn't, simply choose another bottle.

The idiot! I shook my head in disgust, the state of the fool, ignoring the perfectly good wine there on the table. I grabbed the nearest bottle by the neck, sneering down at the figure in the chair as his lips gushed with blood, and his eyes stared unfocused at the bottle he was trying to drink from.

I fumbled to open the bottle, hissing in fury. My still healing fingers were like sausages gripping the cork.

I twisted it, then gripped it in both hands, biting down on the cork and pulling it free. I spat it onto the floor, and ignoring the shouts coming from Oracle, the buzzing of her voice inside my head growing fainter and fainter.

A crash of fighting from my left drew my attention as I raised the bottle to my lips, taking a good mouthful of wine, then gagging, spitting it on the floor as I remembered belatedly that I hated the stuff. A beer, that was what I needed.

I spotted a keg on its side in a brace nearby, a spigot driven into it, dripping steadily onto the floor. I grinned. That was more like it!

I took another swig of the wine, gagging again as I remembered that...

Something wasn't right here, a little voice said, only to be dismissed as I reached out, tossing things aside as I searched for a tankard, finding none. Instead, I tipped the wine bottle up. I watched as it emptied out atop a pile of other empties before jamming it under the spigot and turning it on, nodding to myself as the beer filled the bottle.

That was more like it. A quick drink, and I'd...do something. There was *something*, something I was supposed to be doing, wasn't there?

I shrugged, taking a long drink and absently wishing they'd be quiet out there. I was trying to think, after all!

A spray of blood splattered across the side of the ten. It was on the outside, but still, that was a mess! This was my tent...wasn't it? It was a mess, was what it was. Blood everywhere, and...and...

"You look lonely," a voice mumbled from my right. I turned slightly, looking at the elven woman who stepped up close, naked apart from the remains of a cloak around her neck and long, knee-length boots.

Her hair was short and dark, a bob that looked like straw and hacked off short, sticking out at all angles and in contrast with the smeared, yet well-applied makeup and the gold in her ears and at her wrists.

She stepped in close, reaching out, resting one hand on my shoulder and drawing her other down the gleaming armor I wore to fumble at the groin.

"You'll have to help me get this open," she whispered huskily, blatant hunger in her eyes as I grinned.

Noises howled in the distance, a buzz of outrage in my mind. But it was meaningless, and I looked the woman up and down, admiring the view.

She was filthy, grass and other stains on her, her lipstick smeared across her cheek, but I was regularly covered in blood and more, so what did it matter?

I glanced around, grinning as she fumbled at my groin, slipping to her knees and trying to free me for her mouth, even as I saw others screwing elsewhere.

The tent was huge, more suited to a damn circus from my memories, but that was the nobility, all the way. A clear section to one side with cushions and comfortable seats, all filled with people either sleeping their revels off or fucking.

The middle was dominated by three long tables, with benches and individual seats, most of which were kicked over, and the tables were covered in spoiled food, random bottles, and more, as well as the occasional body, slumped over.

Most of the time, the bodies still had their murder weapons stuck in them, and I couldn't help but laugh at that. The nobles had got what they deserved!

The rest of the tent was a mess as well, clothing lying everywhere, puddles of blood and wine, broken bottles and more bodies, and at the far end, a raised stage with a...

...A woman, slumped over, her fingers flicking stiffly across the strings of a huge harp, but she looked...she looked *wrong,* somehow.

She was barely upright, head down, seemingly unconscious, with two others dressed similar to her, all bright colors and cheerfulness, laying on the stage nearby.

One was clearly dead. The other, if they weren't dead, were having a hell of a nap, considering the way they were lying in the spreading puddle of blood that was dripping from the harp player's fingers.

"Help me."

I heard the voice and looked down, frowning. Concentration and desperation were etched on the face of the woman on her knees, and she kept fumbling with the front of my armor.

Yeah, yeah, I'd help her. I reached down and grabbed at my…no.

No, there was something wrong here. This wasn't Oracle…

Oracle.

I frowned, hands frozen as I tried to focus, knowing this name was important. The buzzing voice in my ear got louder and more insistent, even as a terrible, discordant jangle grew louder and louder somewhere in the distance.

I stared at the entrance to the tent, seeing others in silvery armor like mine fighting, one with wings battling a great big bone thing and howling as they did, while again and again, they were shocked by lightning and…

Lightning.

Lightning was important. That was what Oracle liked, and I was supposed to have used it when I was attacking the camp.

This wasn't my camp, I realized. I was attacking it! But, if I was attacking it, why was…I looked down. The woman was still fumbling at me, and the way she stared, fixated, determined to get at me…there was no love there. Hell, there wasn't even *lust*. This was need. Desperate, frantic need.

The jangling grew louder and louder as I looked around the tent with new eyes, seeing the filth, the desperation, and the way the people were fucking. None of this was drunken lust. It was animalistic and desperate.

Their faces were drawn, their eyes wide, pain etched their faces as they pushed their bodies past natural limits and continued to grind.

The air was…putrid with death, with voided bowels, blood. Hell, the entire tent was covered in spilled ale and piss as well!

I grabbed at my head, the mana migraine that had flared and then died away suddenly pulsing wildly again, and the damn *music*!

The music was doing it! It was the damn music, every single discordant beat, each random plucking of strings…made it worse!

Growling I turned from the woman on her knees, ignoring the hiss of anger as she leaped up, trying to drag me to her, clinging to my shoulders and trying to kiss me.

I started toward the door, shoving her off me, and ignored the outraged scream of fury, until she leaped onto my back, a dagger sending a spray of sparks off my breastplate as she tried to drive it into my chest.

I back-handed her, then broke her hold on me, shoving her free and sneering down at her, considering stabbing her to teach her for her disrespect.

The bloodlust rose in me, replacing the lust from before with a far darker need. I glanced about, wondering where my naginata was. That was a good tool for this, I could drive it through her, pin her to the floor, and watch her scream. I didn't have it, though, but a Fireball…

Jingle jangle jingle

Those fucking notes!

They kept going, banging around in my head and…and they suddenly made sense in the way a painting could mean two things–a young girl with an earring or an old hag, depending on the way you viewed them.

The notes made a pattern, one that…one that I knew! I could hear a voice hoarse and breaking as it bellowed out the chorus to…

"Too sexy," I muttered, recognizing the damn tune that Tommy had played over and over and over again when we were growing up. He'd taught the damn song to Ronin for a fucking laugh, and now…

Now I could hear it over the music in the tent, and the music I'd barely noticed in the tent suddenly rose, frantic, growing louder and more strident. The body laying in the blood by the harpist twitched and tried to force itself upright, pulling a flute closer in shaking hands.

"What the fuck…" I hissed in shock, before my head pulsed wildly again. I lifted my hand, and saw the Fireball I'd created in my unthinking willingness to kill the woman who'd leaped on me.

I saw the flashing health and mana bars in my vision, so long a part of me that I now felt them as much as read them, and they were dropping.

The mana was empty, and the health…it was using my life force to keep the Fireball active.

I felt the Fireball in my hand, the shifting of the spell as it was fed on life, as well as magic. I saw the shifting, growing heat of blood in the center, knowing I was feeding more into this than I should be.

I tried to pull it back, to absorb it, and pain built as the life that filled it tried to flow into my mana channels.

No.

That wasn't going to work. That'd only do more damage to me, and I was literally killing myself with this, even as others shouted and screamed all around me.

I sensed movement as the woman dragged herself to her feet, the dagger in one hand, then screamed and ran at me, the blade held high. She slashed at the air as she closed the few feet between us, and the flute started to play.

The music began to climb, and Ronin's voice, cracked and warbled, gasps filling his song…

I did what I had to do.

I shifted to the side, taking the wild slash on my armored forearm, blocking it, then shoving her aside, clearing the path.

Then I threw the Fireball right at the harpist.

It flew straight and true, hissing and popping, the flames roaring as they flashed across the space between us, only to be intercepted by a screaming, wild-haired man throwing his lover aside and leaping into its path.

It was too little, too late. The Fireball hit him and washed over and around him, greedy flames licking at the spilled alcohol, the piled bottles, the dry, oiled cloth of the tent, and the wood of the stage.

Screams rose as pain overruled the magic of the music, and the tent went up with a solid *wumph* that I felt in my chest, even as I was blasted backwards as the alcohol went up in a multicolored blossom of fire.

I landed on my back, rolling over and over down the damn hill, until a bone hand grabbed onto my leg and stopped me, leaving me disoriented, exhausted, and totally confused.

My head was practically split open for the second time in a minute as Oracle fairly screamed into my mind. I flinched with the joy and anger that simultaneously filled it.

"JAX!" She landed on me hard enough that she knocked me back onto the grass.

"Wha…?" I managed to mumble before Bob was there again, this time holding me still and rooting around in a bag with his other hand, pulling a mana potion free and practically shoving it down my throat.

"Drink it!" Oracle ordered.

"Wha…" I tried again, only to have her pull a health potion from my bag as well and wave that at me.

"Drink it!" she said again. "Quickly, Jax, we need to heal them all!"

"Heal?" I muttered, only to have Bob shove the vial at me. I cursed, taking it and pulling the cork out, tossing it aside and chugging the potion, then the next, then another Bob passed to me.

As soon as my mana leaped upward, Oracle took off, flying over me and casting the Frostfire Circle of Cleansing, followed by Healing Fountain, then she was back.

"Meditate!" she ordered, as Bob shoved two more potions at me, much weaker ones.

I downed them both, hearing the cries around me rising, the weeping, the pleading. Someone, Yen I thought, was calling out that people needed to swear to me, and the flames would heal them.

My mana surged and fell, and I settled down to meditate, feeling the compression begin as I twisted mana into the shapes I needed.

I felt the differences for the first time since I'd pulled on the mana of the realm before fighting Nimon and since I'd used the Fragment of Divinity.

The realm was no longer one to my eyes, but as my sensitivities increased, I felt the changes. The mana that flowed into the shapes I forced around me was a sudden mélange of flavors as the individual forms cried out to me. I felt the solidity of earth, and the freedom of air, the malleability of water, combined with the joyful regeneration of fire.

I felt them all, and I used them, pulling them into the structure I wove without thought, my mind existing free of all distraction in that perfect moment.

Seconds grew into minutes and more as I worked, feeling like I was a child playing with blocks, stacking them this way and that, sensing when a block was the wrong shape or texture.

I felt them all and their places in the pattern.

Then I felt the missing segments, and it all came to a shuddering halt as, for the first time, I stared at the lack of knowledge that I, and that all of us had, straight in the face.

For every space that I'd set a block, there was a gap in the pattern, mirroring it, waiting for its antithesis to be added and for the pattern to be built upon.

I looked at it, sensing that the missing sections weren't just empty gaps. They were solid as well, and yet…

They weren't filled with what should be there. The mana blocks had become solid on that side and had linked as if they were aware. They had formed the links a thousand, thousand times an hour and were making corrections for the missing sections of reality.

I stared, then reached out, sensing something as the light that shone from some of the blocks seemed to be flowing around something, giving a hint to a shape that…

"It's done!"

It all came crashing down in a split second as the world of light and magic that had filled my mind and heart suddenly vanished. Oracle was there, collapsing into my arms.

I lay there, staring up at a gently falling rain, the suddenly gray sky drizzling gently on us all, holding the love of my life, utterly exhausted by all she'd had to do…and all I could think was that I'd lost it.

I'd seen a glimpse of the reality behind the curtain, and now it was gone, and I was left with a terrible sense of failure.

CHAPTER TWENTY-ONE

I stared into the gray clouds for a long while as Oracle rested. All around me, others talked tiredly, weeping for their loss and mourning for the dead. After checking to see that my team had survived, I ignored them all, holding her and staring across the realm.

I tried to reach out, tried to reconstruct the reality I'd sensed, and I felt…nothing.

Whatever I'd achieved before, it'd not only been through the situation I was in and the frayed state of my mind at the time. It was also something that the system integrated into everything, and seemed to have missed.

I had notifications for other things, for experience earned, and for more, but after taking one look at them, I banished them all, wiping them from my mind, sickened.

In the state we'd been in, all of us, we'd fought and killed indiscriminately, apparently. There were notifications for villagers slain, experience awarded for servants slaughtered, and worse. None of it made sense to me. None of the memories were clear, and what I could remember…

It was a mess of feelings, of lust and of need, of determination and fury.

I'd screamed with the need to kill, and I'd been utterly uncaring of Oracle's claims upon my heart and my body. Only the fact that I'd been distracted had kept me from fucking that woman, had she been able to free me from my armor.

That wasn't correct, I consoled myself. I had realized and stopped. But that was only just, and again and again, I'd nearly succumbed to it.

"Hey, boss," Grizz whispered, sitting down next to me, his head hanging low. "Ummm, I'm sorry." He lay the sword and shield I'd bestowed upon him in the throne-room of Himnel next to me. "I think…I think I need to give you these back. I'm not the man I thought I was, and not the kind of a man who should wield these." I shifted, seeing the way he stared at his boots, even as tears tracked unheeded down his cheeks.

"I…I'll surrender myself to Chief Justicar Lucian when we get back, and will accept his punishment, as well as my expulsion from the Legion," he went on. The others moved in closer, all looking the same, all but Ronin and Bane.

Bob stood guard as well, stony silence radiating out from him. A sense of terrible betrayal came through our bond.

I slowly pushed myself to my feet, Oracle standing with me as I looked around at the motley collection of guards, of filthy and exhausted people in scraps of clothing, and the locals who'd apparently been kept for amusement. I looked at the camp with new eyes.

"I don't know what happened," I called out, getting everyone's attention. I gestured at the pile of bodies off to one side, and my voice dropped.

"We came here to free people and to punish those who were raiding the caravans. We came to kill smugglers and bandits, rapists and murderers. Somehow, along the way, we became the people we were trying to protect the realm from." I paused, swallowing hard as I tried to explain the shame I felt.

"I am the leader of the group," I said, forcing the words out. "I am the leader of the Empire, and I hold responsibility for this. My people are not blameless, but whatever dark magic affected us, I led you all into it, and that's on me. I'll surrender to Lucian, and seek the judgment I des…"

"No!" a voice rang out, and Ronin waved for attention. "Boss, need you all over here."

"Fuck's sake Ronin," I muttered, wiping my face with the back of one hand, then glancing around. "I will take respons…"

"Boss!" Ronin shouted, "Fucking seriously, *not your fault*, and I need you, and now!" I hesitated, before seeing the look he was giving me and cursing under my breath.

"Come on then." I sighed, leading the way over to him.

He was standing at one end of the tent, close to what had been the stage. Torn cloth, charred wood and bones, weeping flesh, and more was strewn about us. I gagged on the sickly sweet smell of charred long-pig.

The bodies were strewn all over. Some were clearly dead before this, as I'd seen earlier, but others…one shifted slightly, and I winced, readying myself to cast a healing spell…until a single note rang out.

Ronin moved faster than I'd ever seen before, the club he'd been using to push things aside with blurring up and over his head.

Then he slammed it down into the body laid half-hidden under the cloth and worse.

The blow snapped their neck, the sound of snapping bone clear even as the head was driven to one side, clearly broken, and Ronin dropped the club, cursing as he wrung his hands.

"How the hell do you people do this shit all day?" he growled, looking at his hands.

"We don't all hide from Restun," Jian muttered, shaking his head and looking at the body. "Seriously man, why did you…"

Another note rang out, then a third, slowly. They hung in the air as I stared at Ronin, stunned.

"They're dead," I said, then paused, shaking my head. "No, maybe not dead, but I've broken enough necks to know that was definitely…" I triggered Greater Examination and winced.

Athelas' Enslaved Minstrel
Once a promising young musician, Kellin Valene spent many years practicing her skills, but she was unprepared for the reality of life as a court minstrel.

When Kellin was forcibly bonded to the Harp of Athelas, her life as a struggling minstrel ended, and instead the newest incarnation of Athelas was reborn.

Weaknesses: 150% weakness to life and fire magic, 200% weakness to light magic; physical attacks inflict double damage, due to brittle bones.

Resistances: 50% resistance to death magic due to the state of the minstrel

Level: 14

Health: 174/5,000

Stamina: 0/1000

Mana: 4/180

"Who the fuck is Athelas?" I looked down at the charred body, shaking my head as the body shifted slightly, and another note rang out as the hand resting against the harp moved.

A sound like dry twigs snapping echoed, and suddenly the body was shifting, the head seemingly being dragged back atop the neck, against its own volition.

"We need to kill them," Ronin said, drawing a dagger. "Boss, I'll explain it all later, but trust me on this. They can't be saved, and the harp must be destroyed."

"Oracle?" I asked, glancing at her and getting a slow shake of the head.

"I don't know, but I trust Ronin," she said after a second. "If he says we can't save them, then I think we should believe him."

She didn't sound sure, not in the slightest, but then, none of us were as the body shifted again. It was a horrific mess, partially down to the whole 'To Whom It May Concern' nature of a fireball and the resulting fires that rolled through the tent.

The other side of it, though, was that whoever Kellin had been before they went into that tent, they'd been drained to the point of death by the harp, I guessed.

I turned, seeing my naginata standing tall nearby, still stuck through a small group of bodies, and I grimaced. Out of reach, and the suffering of this Kellin…

I reached over and pushed Ronin back, gently but firmly. This wasn't something he needed on his soul; mine was already pretty battered.

I crouched next to the body and drew my dagger as I looked into the remains of Kellin's face.

The eyes were white and sunken, the lips drawn back in a snarl or grimace of pain, and the body…hell. I didn't know how old Kellin had been, but she looked like she was in her nineties at least, and she'd not aged well.

"I don't know what happened to you, but…"

"P…le…ase," the desiccated mess before me managed to gasp out, and I took that for all the permission I needed, even as two more notes rang out.

"You need to…" Ronin called out, clearly worried, only to break off as I drove the dagger into her side, the blade glancing off a rib that cracked under the blow.

I shifted the tip around, searching, even as my eyes burned, unshed tears in them as I killed what I now suspected to be an innocent minstrel.

I felt it, the fibrous texture of the muscles and the heart, and I dragged the blade back and forth, making sure of the job. I drew the blade out, when Ronin spoke again.

"You have to take her head as well," he whispered. I shot a look at the bard, only to meet sadness in his eyes. "Trust me, boss, please."

I gritted my teeth and took hold of the back of her head, pushing the blade into the neck and sawing it back and forth. Tendons and cartilage gave up before the sharp blade, the bones in the spine sliding apart as I worked.

I freed the head entirely and pushed it free, seeing a gleam of gold paint underneath the body and reaching out unconsciously…only to have Ronin grab my hand and shake his head.

"Don't do it, boss…you'd probably win, but if you lost? The Empire is fucked big time."

I stood, grabbing a cloth and wiping the bloody blade as I glared at Ronin, forcing myself not to look at the body.

"What the hell is going on, Ronin!" I snarled.

"The cursed harp of Athelas," he said, and the others moved back almost as one.

"And what the fuck is that?"

"It's…um…"

"I swear, you tell me it's a fucking harp that belonged to some dickbag called Athelas, and it's cursed, and you'll spend the next month with Restun!" I warned him.

He nodded slowly. "It's, well it kinda *is* that…but it's a long story."

"Do we look like we're going anywhere?" I growled, gesturing around the smoking camp.

"No, but…"

"Shit," Lydia cursed, seeming to realize something at the same time Grizz did. "Sehran! Get inte tha air, search tha local area, make sure we be alone. Bane, Tang! Get out there an' scout."

Those who were named peeled off, Sehran sending those closest to her staggering as her wings beat hard to lift her into the air, Bane and Tang vanishing.

I looked at her, my brain trying to change gears, the confusion of the fight and more making my brain lag like I was trying to get porn on a dial-up connection.

Then it all clicked into place.

We'd assaulted one of the camps, and yeah, we'd won, but we'd won by basically fighting *everyone*. We were all exhausted, most of us had used our potions and more, and…

"They're coming!" Sehran called a handful of seconds later.

She'd barely gotten a dozen meters into the air, and already she could see them.

The enemy reinforcements, drawn by the sounds of fighting, the smoke, and the flames. They were coming, and not only were we not ready, but we were also in the remains of a camp we'd just assaulted, with a force that was on its last legs.

"Potions!" I barked, twisting around to eye the nearby people. They'd all sworn to me, they'd needed to, to sit in the circle of Frostfire and be healed instead of burned. "I need mana, and we need to know what supplies we have!"

Grizz moved as soon as one of the locals pointed to a chest off to one side, grabbing the top and levering it open, using the blade of his sword when it didn't want to open for him any other way.

He drove the massive blade, tip-first, into the lip of the chest, between the body and the lid, then levered upward with a great crack as the expensive, hand-lacquered wood shattered.

"Six healing, all high-grade, three mana, and…eleven stamina," he called out, even as we were gathering all the others in.

"Sixteen healing, twenty-three mana, fourteen stamina." I grunted, quickly counting all those we could find. "We've got…nineteen guards and twelve of us…okay. All the healing potions go to the guards. We've got healing spells. Anyone besides my team able to use magic?" I called out.

One of the locals who'd been chained up raised a hesitant hand before pulling it back when one of his neighbors hissed something.

"What can you do?" I asked. He swallowed hard, before whispering something. "What?!" I gestured to him. He stood slowly, hands holding each other, clearly terrified, and whispered something. "Fuck's sake, man! We're gonna be attacked in a few seconds! Speak up!"

"Necromancer!" he cried out, and several of the others who had been sitting next to him backed away, hissing.

"Fucking brilliant! Get your arse over here!"

"But…"

I shook my head. "No time for false modesty and shit. What spells have you got?"

"Summon Undead Servant, Speak With The Dead, and…"

"Yes?"

"Detect Cursed Item."

"Well, that last one would have been valuable before," I said, before frowning at the body of the minstrel. "Too much of a coincidence. Who are you and what did you have to do with *that*?"

"I'm its guardian," he whispered.

"Well you did a piss-poor job! What is it, and what the fuck happened?"

"There's no time, Jax!" Oracle said. "Sehran, how long?"

Sehran landed nearby. "There are four scouts out there, but a lot of steel and men are coming, maybe a few minutes, that's all."

"Bane! Tang!" I shouted, not caring that the enemy scouts might hear me. "Kill the scouts!" Bane and Tang would have done it anyway, but if they weren't close enough to do that, I had to think the scouts would be running now. "Sehran, can you slow them?"

She hesitated, then shook her head. "If I was rested, then probably, but as tired as I am? I could distract a few, but not many, and not for long."

"Fair enough." I grunted, before turning to the locals, almost all unarmed and huddled together, mainly farmers and villagers, from the look of them. "Lead them out of here; they'll only be in the way for the fight, and we'd have to protect them. Get them into the forest, then get your ass back here."

She spun on her heel, hurrying to them.

"You can summon an Undead Servant?" I asked the necromancer. He nodded, clearly terrified. "Can it fight?" He shook his head violently. "Can you?" A second shake of the head. "Well how the hell did you defend the harp, if you can't…"

"The barrow…it had traps and…"

"What barrow?" I glared at him.

"We're standing on it. When the nobles came, they found the entrance. They broke the traps and looted it."

"Did they break all of them?" I asked, a sudden wild hope rising that we could use the traps to our advantage, only to have them dashed.

"They broke them all, and while my 'servant' spell summons a trap-maker's spirit to remake them, it'd take weeks to just start to…"

"Well, you're fuck-all use," I snapped, gesturing after the others. "Get out of here." He nodded, sprinting after the people Sehran was leading away as I turned to the others.

"Where were we?" I asked, grimly, only to have Lydia pass me three mana potions.

"Here," she said quickly. "You an' Oracle use magic tha most." I looked around, seeing the others putting at least a single potion in their bags.

"How many are out there?" I asked, sensing his approach.

"At least seventy," Tang replied, sliding to a halt in the mud and blood that coated the top of the hill. "They're typical guard types, most of them look like even Ronin or Giint could fuck them over in melee, but…"

"Hey!" Giint snapped, annoyed at being compared to the bard, and Tang grinned.

"Can we win?" I asked.

"Against the standard guards?" Tang replied. "Easily, if we can slow them and keep them from surrounding us. If there's more? And if there's elites?" He shrugged. "Have we got a choice?"

"Not really." I looked around the camp. "Okay, you lot, grab those spears."

There wasn't much we could do, not with only a few minutes, but the guards grabbed the spears, arranging themselves as I ordered, with Grizz giving them advice.

We formed a rough triangle, the nineteen guards armed with spears and shields forming two legs of the triangle, and my team forming the base, facing the direction the enemy were coming from.

"How long 'til…" I started to ask Oracle, only to be cut off by a hunting horn ringing out, then a second one replying from the west.

"Tenandra is getting close. About three quarters of an hour," she said. "The other ships are closing, but she's in the lead and has reinforcements aboard."

"We need to hold for half an hour!" I called to our people, looking around to make sure they all got it as I tried to make it sound better than it was. "Just half an hour, and we're laughing."

The first of them started to move through the trees below, stupidly highly polished armor making it damn clear where they were, even as Bane whispered nearby.

"Got the scouts."

"Good man. How many are incoming?" I asked absently, staring at the men marching out of the forest to form up at the bottom of the hill.

"About three hundred." He informed me in a low voice.

"Might want to keep that to yourself," I whispered back, wincing.

"We'll take them," Grizz replied confidently. I glanced at him, seeing the rings under his eyes, the dark circles that screamed that he needed to rest desperately. I nodded, forcing a smile as I looked around, seeing the others were much the same.

"Of course we will!" I agreed loudly. "I'm just wondering how we split them up. After all, there's only a hundred of them, means most of the guards won't get to fight anyone at all!"

I let it hang in the air for few seconds, holding my breath and hoping.

"We'll kill more than those pretty Legion boys!" one of them called out. I twisted to see her, a grizzled older woman who clearly saw what I was doing and nodded her understanding.

"No chance!" Jian called back, joining in. "I'll beat you all!"

"Only thing you'll be beating is Sehran's ass," Tang called out, and Sehran laughed.

"Promises, promises!" She bumped Jian with her shoulder and grinned at him, before looking down at the whip in her hands. "I'll need to find a new toy for later, though."

"Shit, here!" I called to her, pulling the Corseiga whip from my bag and tossing it to her. She caught it and looked it over, smiling as she put her older leather and braided metal whip into her bag and tested the new one.

"Sorry, I've had that in my bag ages ago and kept meaning to give it to you." I admitted.

"Oh, don't you worry." She coiled and flexed the whip, a wide smile on her face. "I'll forgive you this once!"

"Have fun." I smiled, before turning to my team. "Oracle, in the middle with Ronin. Bob, move to the end; I want you to hold the left side. Grizz, far right. Yen, you're with Oracle, bombard the shit out of them," I ordered, even as I eyed the still-emerging troops.

"Lydia, Sehran, I want you to be ready. When I tell you, I want you to take off, make it look like you're fleeing, then loop around and take out any mages or the command team. Bane, Tang, get out there and slaughter the fuckers. Pick off any last scouts, then…"

"Already got them," Bane said.

"Fucker…okay, loop around and start slaughtering them from behind. Giint…" I paused, biting my lip absently as I looked around. He usually used a crossbow, although occasionally he fought with melee in close. While that was fine most of the time, from behind us here at the top of the hill, he'd not be able to see shit. "Step up and fire as much as you want, then fall back into the middle of the group. Once they get close, you're the reserve." I opened my mouth to say something else, when the little shit fired his crossbow at the forces assembling below us.

We all froze, watching the bolt as it flashed across the distance, punching through some especially shiny armor to send a guy with a gold-embossed helmet crashing to the floor.

"Fuck's sake, Giint!" I snapped. "I meant once it started!"

"You not say that," Giint pointed out sullenly before firing his crossbow again. The soldiers below broke into a sudden sprint, racing up the hill and screaming for blood.

"Shit! Lydia, give him the flashbang, he can use it when he needs it, but…" I broke off, and nodded as she indicated Grizz instead.

"Yeah that's a better idea, Grizz! Throw that into their midst when we need a distraction." I snapped, yanking my helm out and ramming it atop my head. "Get ready! Oracle, Lightning!" I snarled, even as I started dual-casting our fountain spell in the path of the onrushing forces.

The hill we were on wasn't that big. Hell, it was in the middle of the damn forest, and while some effort to create sight lines had been attempted, once the music had begun, all such concerns had been removed.

Some sections of the forest were entirely solid and others were cut clear for twenty meters or so, meaning that the buggers charging us had a choice to make.

They could run wildly, screaming and hacking at the air, as the majority were, and cover the distance between them and us easily, but without cover. Or, they could use the forest.

Those who chose to use the forest were much slower, but they were harder to see, meaning that we, generally as a group, focused on the idiots we could see.

As my fountains sprang up, water cascading down, the soldiers tried to change direction, knowing they were, at the very least, magical. They started to avoid them, then were hit by a sudden barrage of Magic Missiles from Arrin and herded back in close. He'd been holding ten golden darts ready in the air, one above each finger.

The third in line accidentally stepped in it, then cried out that "it's just cold water" to his friends. Then they ran through it.

Yen hefted her recently evolved FlameStrike and threw a single spear forward, arcing over the front lines.

As soon as it left her hands, she sagged, tugging the cork out of a mana potion and chugging it. The fact that a single spell had taken *all* of her mana had the potential to be devastating to her, considering her role in the group was magical support more than anything else.

The spell was far more devastating to the enemy, though.

It took the form of a simple javelin, about two meters or eight feet in length. It glowed a dull cherry red, like iron that had been heated in a forge. But when she released it, the simple aspect changed.

It burst into flames, the head lengthening, becoming pyramidical at the tip and sharp as the color lightened and went from a dull red all the way to white.

Along its length, as it flew, flames bloomed, rippling backwards, leaving a trail of fire in the air.

Then it landed.

It was designed to impact the ground, standing tall, but because the ground where she aimed was a little busy, it was instead caught by a helpfully upraised face.

The tip punched through the flimsy nose guard, practically vaporizing the flesh behind it before hurling the body from its feet and jutting out of the back of the man's helm, then sinking over a foot into the ground.

The end of it vibrated and quivered. The body it was attached to spasmed as the sheer heat of the weapon caused the liquids in the skull to erupt into steam. The garbled signals sent it jerking and dancing.

With the front end firmly embedded in both soil and metal, it detonated.

The blast wave rocked outward, picking up and tossing bodies aside, sending them crashing into trees, rocks, and each other, even as the haft of the javelin became liquid, flashing upward into the air to rain down in a twenty-meter radius, drenching anyone too close in a mix similar to liquid iron.

Those who survived the detonation, as close-packed as they were, screamed as the liquid metal poured inside their armor, melting through skin and etching bone.

The advance partially staggered to a halt as dozens of them died instantly, roasted in their armor. Dozens more screamed and flailed wildly, throwing themselves on the floor and rolling, trying to put the burning out.

Those in the lead kept going. Those who'd not been hit met Giint, firing bolt after bolt from his repeating crossbow while cackling madly. More bolts flashed out of the surrounding forest as Bane and Tang took the opportunity to make the most of their stealth as they passed.

Ronin hissed in pain as he started to play again, the music of his lute rising into the air and increasing our Luck while decreasing theirs. The others, Grizz, Jian, Lydia, and Sehran, each let loose with Magic Missile.

The sudden barrage of twenty missiles rocketed out, coordinated with the other casters, and took the advancing forces in the face, one missile for each.

That wasn't enough to kill, usually. Hell, it only actually managed to kill two of the charging figures, burrowing into eyes in a lucky hit then detonating. But it was enough to break them up. It staggered and shocked them, especially as it was rare to face magic users in battle, let alone an entire force of them.

Then Oracle rose above us and let loose with a bar of lighting that looked like it belonged to Zeus, punching straight through a staggering figure. She sent him smoking and twitching from his feet, before spreading it out through the standing water and discharging a handful more.

The advance was broken.

Dozens were dead. The same number, if not more, were screaming and thrashing in pain or bleeding out. I grinned as the guards with us started to cheer, sensing victory approaching, with them hopefully not having to do anything for it.

Then the enemy returned fire.

CHAPTER TWENTY-TWO

The mages were the first. A coordinated blast of fire flew out, tightened into a beam that cut left to right from the distance at a forty-degree angle.

As the ruby-red light appeared, slicing through the trees before us like butter, climbing to carve a divot out of the hill a handful of feet below the top, the screaming was hidden by the crash of trees.

Hundreds had been sheared through at once, cut off anywhere from four feet from the ground, closest to their mages, all the way up to twenty and more, closest to us. The crack as they all fell was horrific.

Worse than the sound, though, was the callous sacrificing of their own forces, crushed beneath falling trees and more as it became obvious we'd only faced the advance force.

There were nine mages, broken into trios, and arrayed in front of their forces, with the lead spellcaster standing between two others. They stood with heads bowed, holding onto their partners, acting as living batteries to power the spell.

I recognized their kind immediately.

"Drow," I snarled, seeing the smiles on their faces that the fuckers had done this deliberately.

I didn't know if the cursed harp had been their work as well, or just plain luck that they'd taken advantage of. Knowing those soft-cocked bastards and their fucking spidery helpers, I'd put nothing past them.

"Jax," Lydia said.

I shook my head. "Nothing changes. Stick to the plan. Sehran, go with Lydia, head south and loop around. Help Bane and Tang to fuck up the leaders."

"There might be more than we can take," Lydia pointed out.

"Sehran can sense them, right?" I asked, glancing over at the succubus, who nodded uncertainly. "Then only attack when I give you the signal."

"What signal?" Sehran asked, only to have Oracle's chuckle cut her off.

"When we unleash hell," she said.

"I'll keep their attention. Oracle, shield us, please," I said, before turning to Lydia and Sehran. "Tenandra will be here in less than half an hour, but if there's more Drow spellcasters, we won't last that long."

"We'll take them out," Sehran promised as Lydia stepped up and rested one hand on my shoulder, staring into my eyes.

"Ye die, and ah'll drag ye back from the grave, kicking an' screamin," she warned me.

I grinned back. "Then I guess I'd better not die."

"Damn right." She turned to Yen and Grizz. "Keep 'em safe," she ordered, opening her wings and lumbering into the sky, even as Sehran finished giving Jian a damn good kiss, grinned around at us, and followed.

"Where are they goin'?" one of the guards called, clearly scared that they were leaving.

"The advanced team of our reinforcements," I called back. "They're nearly here, and they're going to guide them in."

"Oh, thank fuck…"

I looked to the others meaningfully. The guards were on the verge of running, having seen the forces behind the mages for the first time.

Admittedly, I didn't like the sight much, either.

Where we'd been expecting a few hundred at most and that was from what Bane had told me quietly, there was that and more, as the Drow stood proud, surrounding a small group of sneering, arrogant nobles and a bunch of smugglers.

Their guards, clearly caravan workers and street toughs, were scattered throughout the first of the forces that faced us, standing side-by-side with villagers with pikes and pitchforks, eyes blank and unseeing.

There were at least two hundred of them alone, the civilians apparently forced into battle by some form of magic, and standing behind them…

There were almost a hundred archers.

A hundred professional archers, judging from the solid ranks, the formation they stood in. Bows were ready, but not yet drawn, arrows nocked as they waited for the command.

Standing behind them were rows upon rows of gleaming plate and mail-clad soldiers. Where the front of the ranks were made up of the nobles' guards, the smugglers' caravan guards, and the conscripted peasants. The rear lot were professional soldiers, and my lips drew back in a snarl of fury.

These fuckers were exactly what we'd needed in the war.

The noble assholes who had refused to join us, who had fled with their people and becoming fucking bandits, had brought troops that could have massively cut back on our losses in taking Himnel.

Hundreds had died in that fight. Hell, a force like this could have helped us in the battles with the diamonds before we even took Himnel or in facing the undead.

And instead, here they were, hiding out in the forest, waiting for us.

I didn't know how the hell they'd all ended up here, beyond thinking that the nobles must have had a reason so many of their troops were hidden outside of the city already.

The appearance of the Drow as well, *nine* fucking Drow mages, meant that there'd been a plan for them as well, beyond the fucking dickbags I'd faced when we took Narkolt, and that made me furious.

"Oracle," I whispered, the living mana batteries popping potions as their mages started to cast again.

"Trying!" she grunted. The spell snapped into place, and the air a handful of feet in front of us warped slightly as if a sudden heat haze had leaped up. She blew out a long breath. "I've put most of my mana into it, so let's hope it…"

The Drow fired again. The same spell, once used to carve through the trees, now flashed out from three points, hammering into the shield, changing it from a slight haze in the air to a sudden black wall that crackled and shook as it tried to discharge the power. I swore viciously, even as Oracle's face showed the strain as she tried to hold the spell in place.

"Don't you dare," she said, even as Grizz spoke as well.

"Don't even think…"

I cut him off. "Think? I never do, mate." I crouched and launched myself into the air, triggering my tattoos as I lifted above the wall and saw the second phase. "Fuck! Shields up!" I roared, even as the trio of laser-like beams tracked up and locked onto me instead.

They hit me a split second after my Shield spell activated, and I grinned as it took the strain off me, as well as Oracle's shield. It drained their magic into it, powering itself with their generous mana donation.

My vision was blocked by the blackness of the shield as it tried to dissipate the mana that it couldn't absorb, but I knew what was coming.

The daylight, which had just started to reappear for the others as the shield overload died away, vanished as the hundred or so archers fired. One after another, their arms blurred, and the *thrum* and slap of bowstrings filled the air.

In seconds, hundreds of arrows were flying, timed to land all at once, or as near as it was possible to manage.

I darted, holding myself in the air, hoping that my damn mana would hold long enough, even as the bastard Drow cut off their attack.

Had they kept it going, they'd have powered the shield for me, but they clearly knew that.

My own shield lightened, then turned pitch black as dozens then hundreds of arrows hit it.

I barely managed to get my legion shield out before the magical one ripped the mana it needed from me, then failed when I ran out. The screams rising behind me made it clear that not everyone had heeded my warning in time.

I was pushed back through the air, Soaring Majesty stuttering as I ran out of mana.

I landed, grim-faced, before the others, shield held up as I struggled to get the other one that Lydia and I had looted in the arena free as well.

The Legion one was well-made, strong, and light, but against this onslaught, it failed quickly, barely lasting long enough for me to get the larger, heavier one up. Then I hissed in pain as it was hammered over and over.

I glanced behind me, seeing my people had slid together, their training keeping them as safe as they could be. Each shield linked together and increased the strength of the whole.

I cursed myself.

I'd let myself be drawn up and away from the others. If it was deliberate and planned by the Drow, or just lucky, I might never know. What I did know was that I had weakened the shield for the others by keeping the person with the most bloody mana out of it!

Not only that…

The arrow-hail died off, and I bit down hard on the cork, spitting it out, then downing the mana potion, before I risked a quick glance around the shield, only to see…

"Alright, motherfuckers, my turn!" I snarled, yanking a dagger free, then triggering Lunge.

I was higher up the hill than the racing army approaching it, which meant I had a choice. First, I could follow the laws of physics and the way that spell seemed to want me to do things and go down the hill straight at my target, or…

I lanced through the air, using Lunge to fire myself off like I'd been shot out of a cannon, downward but at an angle that left me blurring through the air, before driving the dagger into an upraised face.

I'd triggered Soaring Majesty a split second after I'd used Lunge, the combination of both spells sending me through the air at a hell of a speed, my shield sending bodies flying, bones broken, as screams filled the air.

I released the dagger, hand dipping into my bag and yanking my naginata free…

Then I started to spin.

I'd thrown myself horizontal, shield held over my head at an angle, and stabbed forward with my naginata, powering it with light mana mixed with fire even as I had yanked the bugger out of my bag.

The spin was slow at first, then it picked up speed, and I had to damn well hope I was on target, as the world vanished into a scream of blood and blurring light.

I couldn't see what the hell was going on outside of my own hell of spinning inner ear and vertigo, but the slight tugging was all the resistance the cheap iron and cloth armor of my opponents managed.

Blood fountained around me, and I frantically reached out to Oracle, feeling her senses as she meshed her vision with mine. I stopped the spin and pulled to my right, all my instincts screaming that I'd fly face-first into the ground that way, but trusting Oracle.

Instead, I flashed up and into the air, a thick line chewed through the middle of the enemy advance.

I'd been aiming for the Drow as well, or better yet, their partially hidden command group at the back. But I'd missed completely, and had to be thankful with the handful of archers I'd managed to catch as well.

I arched into the sky, the world spinning crazily even as I stayed upright, and I felt the approach of Lydia and Sehran through the Oath bond, as well as a great many others.

As my ascent decayed, Oracle tugged on me gently. She could see, while my inner ear was still reeling, so I surrendered to her, a surge of love and pride enveloping me.

Air streamed around me as she twisted me around, shifting me at terrific speeds, weaving in and out. I had to grin, feeling the fluid grace that came from a creature who was as home in the air as she was on the ground, compared to a guy who had just learned to throw himself into the air and miss the ground a little.

I felt more tugging and a blow or two as lucky hits banged off my shield. My glowing naginata carved furrows though people, and Oracle guided me around for another pass.

Then Sehran screamed and fell from the air, a massive black arrow punching through her abdomen and unleashing a payload of poison into her.

I felt the fear from Oracle. Sehran was genuinely in danger, which meant Lydia was…which meant I was, too.

I took back control, falling backward and locked in on the tumbling figure, ramming mana into the ability and cutting the feed to my naginata as I raced to catch her.

Lydia was doing the same and was frantically diving, her wings beating hard and fast...

Straight into a sudden blast of ruby-red light.

She screamed, twisting and hitting a tree, the trunk thick enough and her speed high enough that she went from graceful flight, a bare three meters from catching Sehran, into a screaming, tumbling ball of pain, broken wings, and feathers.

She impacted the forest floor at almost the same time as Sehran, the pair of them throwing up great sprays of dirt and low to the ground branches.

I hissed, filled with fear as both of their profiles in my secondary vision flashed. Their health dropped drastically, and I cast Frostfire Circle of Cleansing, even as I flipped over, landing with enough momentum that I carved a furrow in the ground, coming to a halt halfway between Sehran and Lydia.

It took three more seconds of casting, my fingers twisting into the correct forms around the grips for my naginata and my shield, then I shoved downward, letting the last syllables out in a scream, as the spell slammed into the floor between my feet, barely wide enough to reach them both.

Then I was moving, barely getting my shield around in time to catch a downward strike of a hammer, deflecting it to the side to land inches from Lydia's head.

I stomped into the inside of the man's left knee, even as I slashed to my right, catching a stab from a sword wielder and deflecting it.

I rammed my shield into the man I'd just kicked, sending him staggering backward, off-balance, even as the flames spread, leaping from the circles and onto the prone figures of Lydia and Sehran, healing them.

The flames attacked any interlopers with a hissing sizzle. I sensed their approach through the dip in the mana of the circle coming from behind me. Spinning, I dropped to one knee, stabbing out with my naginata, the tip embedding into a stealthed Drow's stomach. Then I dragged it to the right, severing a chunk of his spinal cord as I ripped the blade free.

I'd cut the drain for Soaring Majesty when I'd landed, but my health wasn't high enough to trigger Mana-Overdrive, not yet, even with the flames trying to heal me.

I lunged to my feet, twisting and bringing the shield around, blocking a strike aimed at my stomach. Then I leveled the blade at a figure closing on Sehran, triggering Lunge again and blurring across the gap, skewering the figure even as the flames leaped onto them.

The next one was behind me, and I spun, practically limbo dancing under a sweeping pass of a mace. The gleaming and well-maintained head passed less than an inch from my nose as I slapped the shield into the ground, using it to bring myself upright even faster.

I straight-armed him with my right fist, the naginata clutched tight and driving him backward, off-balance. Then I twisted and rammed the shield into him, sending him to the floor.

I shucked the shield off, not having the space or the time to fight in a sensible and constrained manner.

I dropped it over Sehran, her closed eyes, gray skin and the stream of blood that ran from the side of her mouth letting me know that, while the spell might be keeping her alive, she needed a hell of a lot more than that, and fast.

What she needed was healing. To get her that, I had to kill everything that was threatening her.

The aim clear in my mind, I went to work.

I stabbed out fast, the blade dipping into the exposed throat of the figure on the floor then out, almost delicately, drawing a gout of blood with it. Standing on my right foot, I let rip with a fast, left-footed snap kick, landing in the middle of the shield the incoming man wielded.

He stopped dead, staggering back, then hacked downward, aiming for my foot. But it was gone already, and I was flowing around, the naginata held in both hands, blade dipping low and slicing through an ankle, sending him screaming backward.

I stopped, weapon in both hands and standing still in the middle of my fallen friends, waiting.

They came, hesitantly at first, but then in greater and greater numbers, moving to surround me. I waited for them, drawing my mana in close, watching as my health gently ticked up and over, the final few points filling up even as the archers drew back.

I saw the Drow watching, the arrogance and self-assurance that filled them, even as they raised hands, spells already channeled, ready and waiting.

"Surrender or die!"

The words rang out, spoken with a degree of certainty in the outcome that made them all freeze. Then a Drow started to laugh.

"You dare demand our surrender?" he called.

I grinned, unseen in my helm. "Last chance, motherfuckers." The Drow laughed on, their voices filled with sneering contempt. The nobles joined them, their voices less assured, more concerned, more going along with it. The uncertainty was felt by the troops as well, as they shifted on their feet, the creak of leather and metal as they tightened grips on their weapons or ratcheted a strap tighter here and there.

"And what makes you think we'll surrender?" one of the Drow called out.

"I don't."

"Then why ask?" he replied, sneering. "Is it for your foolish honor?"

"Fuck, no," I said, rolling my shoulders and letting go of my naginata with my left hand. Raising that hand, I pointed it at the command group, raising one finger and a thumb into a finger gun. "I just needed time for my people to get into position."

"Now," I heard Oracle say, inside my head, and at the same time, to Tenandra.

The roar of the upgraded ripple cannon was horrific, the new plasma lance ripping through the air like the crack of an angry God's whip.

What it touched simply ceased to exist, rendered to greasy smoke that floated away. She dragged the blast from left to right, carving a divot through the command group, and taking out most of the Drow in a single hit. Then the magic missiles landed.

They were fired first, but the sheer distance from her to us meant that they arrived just after the Dragon's Wrath, as Ame had christened it.

They were basically just supercharged variants of the Magic Missile spell. But frankly, they were fucking overkill.

The soldiers who were on the outer edge of the impact of the plasma cannon then the magic missiles were dead as well, either cooked through simple thermodynamics if they were too close or roasted in their armor and smashed from their feet by the exploding spells.

If that hadn't been enough, though, Oracle had kept our people up-to-date, and they were ready.

As soon as the first cannon fired, they'd started to run, counterattacking in what the guards with them had thought was a suicidal charge. At that point, the enemy couldn't even see the incoming missiles. Most of the guard stayed where they were. Several actually ran in the opposite direction, thinking to use the confusion to escape, but a handful screamed and joined my people and raced down the hill, spears flashing in the gentle rain that fell again across the forest.

I triggered Mana-Overdrive and spun, slashing my naginata around, hacking through a hastily upraised sword and triggering the slowdown of time to my senses that came from Hyper-Cognition as well, even as I winced and looked away as Grizz presumably used the flashbang Giint had made.

Something detonated in the distance anyway, and the area was bleached with an insanely white light that caused dozens of screams to rise, even as flames and a loud noise like an elephant farting rang out.

My naginata impacted, rolling flames flashing up its length, as if in slow motion. My enemy's blade shattered as my magical naginata hit a flaw, their blade detonating, fragments spinning and reflecting the light of the second cannon firing.

The soldier's eyes widened fractionally, shifting to the naginata closing on him, his lips starting to form a denial…then it was too late.

My naginata passed through his neck with a hiss of superheated flesh, even as the blood erupted into thick steam, the tip taking the nose off the next in line. I backhanded a slow stab aimed at my stomach.

The sword was sent flying, the wielder's wrist snapping. I continued around, my weapons rising and falling in a complex figure eight that avoided their weapons and shields and the thickest parts of their armor wherever possible.

Instead, it slid through ankles, wrists, throats, the underside of the arm, the inner thigh.

The world fell into a blur, but this time I was in full control. My mind raced ahead, summoning the fights I'd had, the last few months of events, and comparing them with the last week, since I'd used the gifts the Gods had bestowed upon me, and I'd used the Master of Mana ability from Amon, channeling a horrific amount of mana into myself…to raise my genetic viability.

I saw it all, my mind racing, super-charged, and I made connections I'd not managed yet, as I saw how easily I'd defeated the people from Earth. They'd been weak, compared to a leveled man from this realm, and I'd accepted that as the reason, not looking deeper.

Now, though, it all made sense.

Yes, I'd climbed in strength, of course I had, compared to the humans of Earth. But the massive jump in my strength, my speed, everything?

It'd come since I increased my viability to perfection from twenty-four to forty-two percent.

That change had literally nearly doubled my strength.

My eyes widened as I made the last few connections.

My stat sheet didn't reflect it because they were the numbers invested into me, showing movement from where I started.

If I focused on it, it'd probably update and show the difference. But for now, I had people to kill, and I was aware of the sudden gulf between where I stood and where these ordinary soldiers did.

The memory of my kicking a charging soldier, wearing full armor in the middle of his shield, and rather than going flying, stopping him dead, came back to me. I grinned inside my helm.

I slammed the naginata down, stabbing the base into the ground and stretched, ignoring the screams rising all around me, as I took a deep breath.

Then I attacked.

I slapped aside a stab from a spear with the back of my left hand, rolling the wrist and grabbing the spear behind the head. Then I yanked, hard.

The soldier staggered forward, eyes widening, until I punched him in the face.

The delicate bones in his nose, cheek, and upper jaw fractured. He let go of the spear, screaming as his hands rose to cradle what was left of his face.

I turned and threw his spear, casually, into another of them, taking him in the waist, punching through the ring mail over the groin and doubling him over with a scream.

I turned sideways as a mace flashed past, watching it falling toward the forest floor, the wielder thrown off-balance. Then I reached out almost delicately, grabbing his wrist, then twisting, locking his arm. I dragged him into his friend's path, an unfortunate bloke who was too slow to stop from stabbing his comrade in the back.

Letting loose with a back spinning high kick, I slammed my armored foot into the side of a helm. The next man peered over his shield in panic before taking the full force of the blow.

His neck gave way with a snap, and I rolled on as he collapsed, falling to the floor in a clatter of steel. Meanwhile, the last of the second Ripple Fire carved dozens more of them into bloody chunks.

I straightened up, facing dozens of men and women clad in layers of steel that my friends back home would have been unable to lift. I shook my head, seeing them hesitating.

"One more example should do it," I muttered, grinning. "Come on!" I took two quick steps towards the nearest, who backpedaled frantically, tripping over the remains of a leg, presumably blown free by the cannons.

The one next to him stabbed at my face, and I sidestepped, catching his wrist and flowing outside of the attack before kicking him in the gut.

The armor rang as I dented it inward. He doubled over, the air whooshing out of him in a great blast. I shifted, flowing with him, then kicking his right leg out with a back heel, slapping my left hand onto the back of his head, even as I pulled him forward with my right hand on his arm.

He practically flew into the floor, head-first, and I felt the impact through my boots…then I dedicated more of my rapidly dropping mana pool into Mana-Overdrive, and I pulled, hard.

I'd already dislocated his arm, ripping it upward as I drove him face-first into the floor. Hell, if we'd been on Earth, I'd have pile driven him halfway to Australia with the amount of force I'd used.

But, when I'd doubled down on my mana-overdrive, I'd powered myself into a different league.

I heaved and twisted, ripping the entire arm, still armored, free in a great gout of hot blood and a terrible scream, before blocking an opportunistic fucker who tried to stab me.

Then I beat him to death with his friend's arm.

That did it.

Grizz and the others had barely gotten through the first ranks of the unskilled soldiers and civilians when the more experienced, skilled, equipped, and frankly better soldiers behind them gave into panic.

Several of them dropped weapons and ran for it, sending the lower-ranked soldiers into an utter freak-out session.

The farmers and villagers who had been attacking seemed to wake up with the death of the Drow, tossing weapons aside and falling to their knees with screams of panic and begging for mercy.

Not all of them in either group surrendered, of course. Many held onto their weapons, and as they started to fall back, they met the stealthed duo of Tang and Bane, who started carving a path through them toward me. The panicking people broke at that, and they damn well ran in every direction.

The vast majority, though, tossed weapons aside and fell to their knees, hands on their heads in the local gesture for "I surrender."

I turned slowly, making damn sure they were actually cowed and not just faking it, before pulling my helm off and downing the last mana potion, cutting off both Hyper-Cognition and Mana-Overdrive at the same time. The world seemed to stutter to a halt for a brief second before time gradually caught up, and my mana bar started refilling.

I could see Lydia was awake, struggling to breathe through the pain, but she was moving, and her health was significantly higher than Sehran's.

I hit Sehran with the first Complex Healing, wincing as I sensed the extent of her injuries through it. She'd suffered additional internal injuries that rolled over and over with the damage the arrow embedded in her had done, the sprain on her left wrist, and the splinters and scrapes she'd picked up.

I hit her with Scour, burning it deep, well aware of the fact that she wasn't a human or any variant thereof, like I was used to healing. As a demon, her death here wasn't as final as it would be for another.

She'd be forced back into the demon realm though, and as she'd said before, she was dangerously powerful for a succubus. Her sisters would never allow her to return. It was too much of a risk that, when she did finally go back, she'd alter the delicate balance of power in that realm.

As far as we were concerned, her being banished was as good as death, because none of us would ever see her again.

All of that raced through my mind as I concentrated on her, over Lydia, sensing the poison that was even now inching its way through her system, killing off entire sections of her body.

Scour did a great job on that, erasing the remnants of the poison that had survived the flames of Frostfire Circle of Cleansing. Then Complex Healing went to work again, rebuilding her internals and granting her new strength as her body was repaired.

I shook my head in dismay, seeing the level of damage she'd been living with forever, the mis-healed broken bones, the unaligned connections in her left wing that made it grate slightly…

All things that she'd probably never even noticed. Hell, I'd lived with the minor aches and pains that were just part of me my entire life, until I met Oracle.

If I'd not had her focused on me so much, I'd have kept on going as I was. Now though, I damn well knew that others were making the same bloody stupid mistake I'd been.

I resolved that would change.

"I'm here," Oracle whispered to me, alighting nearby, one hand reaching out to rest on my forearm. I blinked, seeing her instead of the mess that Sehran was still.

I nodded, and when the spell finished, I changed its point of focus, aiming for Lydia instead.

The others moved in close, Grizz of course, being the subtle one who dealt with people the best.

"Right! All of you get out of the way!" he shouted, flapping his hands like he was shooing chickens. "Go on, fuck off over there!" He gestured vaguely to one side. "And don't run away or touch any weapons; that'll just piss the boss off." He pointed to me, shaking his head at the way that everyone started to back away around me as I ignored them. Jian pushed through, rushing to Sehran's side.

"What the hell are you doing, Grizz?" I muttered as he moved in close, taking up station and making sure nobody was close enough to change their mind and stab me in the back.

"Just getting them moving, boss, and making sure they don't grow some balls," he replied calmly, watching the world as he had my back.

"Bane?"

"He's coming. How are they?" Grizz asked in a low voice.

"Not good," I answered, shaking my head. "They'll both live, but Sehran's going to need a lot of work, and as for Lydia…"

"Will she fly again?" he asked, his voice pitched for my ears only.

"She will, but not for a while. The bones need to be put into place and healed more carefully than I can do it. We need Nerin."

"She's coming, isn't she?"

"I damn well hope so," I said with feeling, only to sigh in relief as Oracle spoke calmly.

"She's aboard Tenandra."

"Thank fuck." I noted the mess of blood and death around us. "Is that it?" I muttered aloud, pulling up the quest.

You have made progress in your Quest: Vanquish the Marauders.

The Duchess of Narkolt has requested your aid to cleanse the local forest of marauders that are killing and looting her subjects.

Kill the bandits, free their captives, and recover the outstanding loot.

You have slaughtered the main forces of the marauders, eliminating the majority of the Drow that supported them, discovering that, once again, they have stretched out a hand to poison your lands.

Recover the Slaves: 126/41

Punish the Slavers: 247/173

Destroy the Camps: 1/3

Recover the Stolen Goods: 0/3

Reward: 10% morale boost to Imperial Territory, 100,000xp

I looked over the details, frowning as I saw the massively exceeded numbers of slaves and slavers and that there were still two more camps out there.

"Is the Legion with Tenandra?" I asked Oracle quietly and got a nod. "Good. They can use the last two camps as training, then." I accepted a mana potion from Grizz and downed it, boosting the amount that Oracle had to work with in healing our people. "I'm fucking done with today."

CHAPTER TWENTY-THREE

The arrival of Tenandra, some fifteen minutes later, was a bit anticlimactic, after all that had happened, although the time it took her to reach us scared the shit out of me when I considered the distance that she'd fired those weapons.

The Wisp ship had come as fast as she could without endangering her passengers. But, when she felt the risk to me, when she sensed the numbers drawn against us, and strangest of all for her, yet most personally, when she felt the pain of Sehran, she'd thrown all caution aside, feeding massive amounts of mana into her engines, overcharging them to a dangerous degree. She'd closed the distance further as she climbed, meshing with Oracle and my senses to aid in her targeting.

After the battle, as soon as she'd arrived, her flesh-body had leaped over the side, plummeting to the ground, landing lightly through some magic of the Wisps. Then she had run to Sehran and Jian, dropping to her knees and taking them both in her arms.

Sehran had laughed, and wrapped her arms around the Wisp, kissing her and holding her tight, while Jian practically vanished under the pair.

"That's one lucky man," Grizz muttered, and I looked at him, one eyebrow cocked.

"You're one to talk…I thought you and Yen were going to have a 'conversation'?" I asked, and he shrugged.

"We did, sort of," he admitted, looking over at the woman he loved, who was speaking to a pair of villagers.

"And?"

"And…I didn't ask her."

"Why not?"

"I…I don't think she wants to," he whispered, turning so that nobody could see his face, and pretending to look back over my shoulder at the forest. "Look, boss, she made comments about knowing that the man she'd marry was meant for great things. For command, hell, she made comments about expecting her future husband to go for a bloody Optio slot at least, and we both know I'm too dumb for that. She was trying to give me a hint, that was all…"

"Fuck's sake, Grizz," I muttered in disbelief, seeing that he genuinely thought that she was saying he wasn't good enough, not that she was trying to hint to him that *he* was good enough for a command slot.

"Yeah, I know boss…it's okay though, I'm big enough and ugly enough that I'll be fine…"

"You dumb fuck," I said, the words slipping out before I could help myself.

"What…?" he whispered, clearly hurt, and thinking I was agreeing that he wasn't good enough.

"I said Grizz, 'you dumb fuck'!" I repeated, grabbing him by one massive pauldron and dragging him to one side, exhaustion limiting my already shitty ability to use anything like subtlety. "She wants you, you idiot! She wants you to know that she thinks you could make Optio! Hell, she's probably got her eye on a *Primus* slot for you, ya bloody idiot, and you think she was letting you down gently?" I shook my head. "You didn't do anything stupid, did you?"

"Well, no, not yet, but…"

"But you've been keeping your distance from her?" I asked, the last few days when I'd see one or the other and rarely both together suddenly coming back to me.

"Well, yeah, I thought…"

"Grizz, I love you like a brother, so believe me, this comes from the heart when I say you're an absolute fucking idiot. Now go and make this right," I ordered him, and he grinned, nodding sheepishly, before moving off.

"That was well said," Bane whispered next to me, and for once I was too tired to threaten him with bells or even to jump…much.

"Thanks, man," I said, glancing upwards and watching as Tenandra's ship body adjusted her angle, sliding in towards the hill that the Drow had so kindly stripped of trees with their magic.

"Are you okay?" he asked after a few seconds, and I sighed, looking away from the ship, and in the general direction I thought he was in, taking a few seconds to spot him.

"No." I shook my head. "No, honestly I'm fucking not, not after earlier in this camp, not after the things…"

"It's a cursed harp boss," Ronin said, moving around several of the bodies that were piled up and looking at them in amazement. "Damn, I wish you could have gone adventuring with me and my old group. We'd have just sat and drank beer while you slaughtered everything. Hell, you'd have put reins on the SporeMother and rode it into battle."

"Been there, done that," I muttered, straightening and scratching the back of my neck, before letting my arms drop with a grunt. "Right, this fucking harp…"

"We need to destroy it," Ronin said. "That harp was an abomination when it was made, and the Bardic College has been searching for it for over three hundred years. It's a standard Bardic Quest, one of the open quests we're given when we join, to hunt down and destroy three cursed items: 'The Cursed Harp of Athelas', the 'Flute of Damnation', and 'Big Bad Boris's Balls'. Just don't ask about that last one, okay? It's not a fun tale."

"Okay, so let's go fuck it up," I said, moving across to drag my naginata out of the soil and examining it.

Naginata	Further Description *Yes/No*
Damage:	24-40 + 104
	This two-handed weapon was built from a combination of modern Earth techniques and traditional Japanese skills, creating a weapon that is truly deadly in the hands of a skilled user. **Enhanced:** This weapon has been enhanced through silverbright and has absorbed some of the souls of its victims. **Current capacity**: 104/300 **Bonus ability:** Magical infusion: Casting your spells through this weapon will infuse it with that ability for the duration of channeling and cause X damage where X is equal to the damage done by the cast spell.

Rarity:	Magical:	Durability:	Charge:
Unique	Yes	81/100	N/A

I nodded in satisfaction, seeing the damage was up to a hundred and four on the absorbed souls already, with the natural damage of the weapon of twenty-four to forty only boosting that higher.

"So come on then, who was this Athelas, and…OI!" I shouted, seeing the necromancer who'd been so sodding useless to us earlier was trying to sneakily lead a spirit away across the hill, its ghostly form clutching a remarkably familiar looking fucking harp in its hands!

He turned, seeing us, and shouted something to the spirit that caused it to pick up speed, rushing away from us and into the trees, even as the necromancer ran in another direction.

"Bane! Catch that fucker!" I roared, before bellowing up at Tenandra as she was landing. "Tenandra! Shoot that fucking spirit!"

The order in my voice was hard and clear, the gentle pulsing of the engines as she turned, keeping her keel just right to land perfectly, suddenly changed to a powerful thrust as the entire ship pivoted, rising again, people on the decks, ready to jump down and come to our aid, instead falling to the deck and rolling as the ship adjusted, bringing the Ripple Fire Cannon on the starboard side to bear.

"Jax…innocent villagers will die…" I heard Tenandra say in my mind.

"Stop!" I snarled, reaching into myself and triggering my ability, launching into the air, as Tenandra shifted around, resuming her landing.

I passed over her decks, absently noting the way that two legionnaires were helping Nerin to her feet, and damn well knowing that I'd get the blame for that later.

Several legionnaires pointed in the direction of the forest, calling out questions as I flashed past, heading into the mess of trees, weaving as fast as I could, knowing I was wasting mana that Oracle damn well needed right now, and that others needed for healing.

It took seconds, and I'd almost given up, when a glint of gold reflected off to my right, and I twisted in that direction, turning hard.

Ten seconds later, and I was closing on the spirit, growling deep in my throat at the damn speed it was going, and the number of trees between us.

I was barely keeping up, thanks to having to weave in and out. I glanced up, thinking about going up and out of the canopy of trees, picking up speed, and then dropping back down…

…but if they changed direction I might lose them, and if I did, it wasn't like I'd be able to find tracks.

I snarled, digging deeper and flashing in and out, I had enough for another ten seconds of flight, that was it, or…

Or I could Fireball the fucker…

I might miss, and if I did, that'd be all my mana gone.

On the other hand, if I flew into a damn tree, that'd end my pursuit pretty damn fast.

I started casting, a Fireball growing in my hands. My mana dropped faster and faster; I had just enough, if I cut my flight now.

I did, literally, cutting my ability, with me nearly forty feet from the ground and flying at a hell of a speed.

I couldn't afford the luxury of getting closer to the ground, I needed the extra sight lines that being this high up granted me, but still.

"This is going to fuckin' suck," I muttered as I released the fireball, aiming for just ahead of the spirit, then angling myself as best I could as I braced myself for the inevitable.

The tree I hit was at least as thick around as I was, and it nearly knocked me senseless, slamming into it at that speed, then bouncing off, tumbling end over end to dig a ditch with my helm as I landed.

I lay there, stunned for a few seconds before slowly pushing myself to my feet and shaking myself. Dirt and pine needles fell free as I pushed myself up and looked about, plucking a few strands of previously low-hanging tree free of my armor and dropping them to the floor.

I turned to my left, seeing the smoke coming from that direction and hearing the crackle of flames. I set off, jogging over and starting to search.

The Fireball was a pretty indiscriminate spell, spreading itself over a decent area, but as I closed in, my heart dropped.

There was no sign of a spirit laid dead, which, when I thought about it made sense. They weren't going to leave a body or a pile of ectoplasm. The problem was, there was no sign of the harp, either.

No strings, no body, nothing.

I pulled up the notifications desperately, casting about and discarding skill level ups and more, cursing as another prompt popped up before I could find the kills.

Congratulations!

You have raised your weapons skill Staffs to its second specialization.

You must now pick a path to follow.

Will you continue to follow the path of MELEE, or shift to focus on MAGIC on the battlefield?

Choose carefully, as this choice cannot be undone.

MELEE:
Your fights are legend, in number and skill! Yet perhaps you could improve upon this? You wield your weapon as an extension of yourself, perhaps this is the secret for you?

Ability Learned: Recall!
You gain the ability to recall your staff to your hand in battle, this ability has a maximum range of six meters, and a cooldown of sixty seconds, costing 100 stamina with each use.

MAGICAL:
You've learned to channel your magic through your weapon again and again, over time the magical quantities of your weapon have grown in concert with your own. Perhaps now is the time to enhance this?

Ability Learned: Cast!
Casting a spell through any staff you wield is now possible, some spells may gain additional effects when you choose this path. The casting of a spell through a non-magical staff will increase the cost by 10-25%, and through a magical weapon by 5-20%

I snarled in annoyance, needing the damn screens gone, but…I made myself read them both, before selecting melee. It wasn't a hard choice after all, yeah, I could cast spells though my naginata, and they'd possibly gain something, but fuck I needed the mana more than a possible bonus, not to mention that having the damn thing fly back to my hand would be insanely cool and useful. I chose that, then dismissed it, sighing as I finally saw what I needed.

Congratulations!

You have killed the following:

- 37x Soldiers of various levels for a total of 56,244xp
- 14x Experienced Soldiers of various levels for a total of 107,530xp

A party under your command killed the following:

- 172x Soldiers of various levels for a total of 260,324xp
- 59x Experienced Soldiers of various levels for a total of 459,928xp
- 13x Drow of various levels for a total of 197,008xp
- 11x Nobles of various levels for a total of 43,121xp
- 17x Smugglers of various levels for a total of 143,044xp

Total party experience earned: 1,103,425xp

As party leader, you gain 25% of all experience earned

You have 49 unspent Attribute points and 0 Meridian points available.

Progress to level 49 stands at 3,713,743/6,455,000

Nope. No fucking specter or whatever it'd been. I cursed, knowing damn well that the harp's escape was going to come back to haunt me.

My experience was out from what I thought it should be, the total anyway, but I remembered seeing the numbers I'd killed under the harps spell, and when I'd dismissed that notification, unwilling to read it.

Whatever my experience was right now, it included the deaths of innocents, and I hated myself for that.

I searched the area carefully, including taking the time to kick some of the burning sections of the underbrush apart to be sure, but it was gone.

I waited a few minutes for my mana to regenerate, then summoned fountains, taking a long drink then using the water to put out the flames that hadn't already been quenched by the gentle drizzle.

Then I set off, walking back to the others.

It took nearly half an hour, but only a few minutes into it, I was joined by the first of the legionnaires, Restun leading them unsurprisingly.

"Hey," I grunted as I marched up to them, the legionnaires falling in around me as I stomped along, grim faced.

"I take it the chase was unsuccessful?" Restun asked, and I nodded. "Lio, hunt it down please."

Lio, who I'd not even noticed amongst the others, slapped a fist to her chest as she melted back into the forest.

"If you find it, don't touch the harp!" I yelled to the forest at large, having already lost her. "The fucker's cursed, just destroy it!"

"She's one of the best trackers we have," Restun murmured, and I shrugged.

"It's a specter, it's not going to leave prints."

"Perhaps not, but the harp is solid, it will leave broken branches and more, and should the summoner stop providing the specter with mana, or the mana provided run out…"

I nodded firmly. "Good point. Let's go have a word with that necromancer."

"I suspect we have a lot to talk about, judging from the number of your squad who have requested a private meeting with me later," Restun said, moving closer and dropping his voice.

"We do," I said, my spirits sinking even further. "Restun, what they did…I led them into that, and…"

"And you were all caught by the cursed harp," he replied firmly. "Jax, I don't know what you did, or think you did, but that harp has been a thorn in the side of the Empire for hundreds of years. It's responsible for the loss of an entire Legion maniple, and the things the survivors told us make it clear you were damn lucky to survive at all."

"I don't know what happened," I said, noticing the way the legionnaires had pulled back, giving us some space to talk in relative privacy. "I…I remember entering the camp, well, not even that. I was above it. I was supposed to make fountains for Oracle to attack through, spreading the lightning charge. Instead, I started checking the soldiers below."

"The harp is a powerful and accursed creation," Restun replied. "How long were you within its reach?"

"I don't know…a few minutes? An hour?" I shook my head. "I don't know, Restun, genuinely. I remember seeing that everyone below me was a criminal, that they'd all committed crimes against the Empire, and I…I lost control."

I paused, pulling my helm off and dropping it into my bag, looking over at him, wanting to look him in the eye and have him look in mine, have him tell me what he saw.

"I killed them," I said. "I landed in the middle, and I attacked anyone and everyone. Hell, I love Oracle. I practically worship the fuckin' ground she walks and flies over. She's pregnant with my child, and yet this woman, she…"

"The harp attacks through our desires," Restun interrupted. "From the little we know, the harp magically increases the desires of those who hear its call, and it steadily decreases your self-control the longer you're under its spell. Had you remained inside its reach for a day? You'd have attacked us on arrival, determined to protect your harp at any cost."

"I…I remember fighting," I mumbled.

"For legionnaires, that is often the greatest threat of the harp. We love to fight, to test ourselves against each other and the world, to throw ourselves into the very teeth of the enemy and carve our way through. The desire to prove yourself is strong in you, almost as strong as the need to nurture and protect."

"I didn't feel that," I whispered. "I didn't need to protect anyone. I wanted to fuck that woman, and when she annoyed me, I was going to kill her. Just like that."

"Self-control," Restun repeated. "The harp removes it and enhances the darker sides of our minds."

"Why the hell does it exist?" I asked, shaking my head. "I mean, what the hell was the point in…"

"Best to ask the bard," Restun said. "Now, I barely got off the ship before your squad mobbed me, trying to confess to their actions, so I think you need to address that. But first…"

"Yeah?"

"Look at their armor."

"Look?" I repeated, confused, and he nodded.

"Their armor is heavily scarred and damaged. The strikes matching legion training, do you understand?"

"No," I said, then I remembered. The sheepish looks, the shame on their faces, the fear on the faces of those who'd survived. "Wait…they attacked each other?"

He nodded. "They turned on each other. That all of them are still alive is either incredibly lucky, or…?"

"Or Ronin did it."

"I suspect both, but yes. You need to speak to the bard."

"I will."

He nodded and pulled back, calling out orders, clearly wanting me to take the time to think, and I did, for a few minutes as we walked.

"Restun?" I called, and he drew in close again. "What happens when you reach your second century? With your points, I mean?"

"Are you close?"

I nodded. "I could hit two I think."

"Share your stats," he ordered.

I did, obeying the voice of command.

There was silence for a minute or two as he considered the details.

I swore. "Wait, I shared it as it is, not…" I broke off, uncertain how to explain it. "I made changes to myself in the fight with Nimon. I altered my body. Hell, I changed everything, and the result isn't reflected in that screen. I don't know why, but…"

"Residual self-image," he grunted and waved at me with one hand, dismissing the screen he'd been looking at. "It's something that was in the records…although, I think I'm going to have to start rereading them at this rate, to make sure I can get them right, as you seem determined to break all of them. So…an unlucky legionnaire a few centuries back was infected with lycanthropy. She was unable to get a cure before the change went too far, and when it did, well…"

"A werewolf?" I asked, thinking of Bella and her team, until he shook his head.

"A different species, older, short and powerful, but clearly adapted for life underground. That legionnaire went on to achieve great things as she learned to control the changes and moved into the underground, serving with honor. The point, though, is that her 'screen,' as you call it, still showed her as an elf and her numbers as accurate, based on her original state."

"Okay, because she hadn't changed that much, or…"

"Because her residual belief that she was an elf and that those were her stats was powerful enough to shape the screen," he corrected. "Think about the adjustments you've made to your internal layout. To be able to exert that level of control means that…"

"That I can adjust the system internally." I shook my head. "And the changes that take place when you read the stat increases? They don't take place when it happens. They change when you read the notification…"

"And you *accept* it," Restun said. "Once you accept the details, then it changes."

"But I didn't know what they'd look like when I first got the screens up?"

"Exactly. No self-image to interfere at that stage."

"Shit, so when I update the screen…"

"Any changes that haven't taken place already will do so then."

"Fuck, so I probably…"

"Definitely, Jax. You definitely shouldn't make the change to your screen here and now. Wait until we reach the ship and the immediate issues are dealt with."

I nodded, then opened my mouth to ask a further question, only to be cut off by Restun again.

"Even considering the changes is risky, Jax, but I know you won't leave it alone. So, consider that the changes your body gains at the secondary century are cumulative. If you hit the second century in Strength only, and had hit the century in Strength alone first, then the bonus you get will include Strength alone. Should you have achieved the century in Agility and Dexterity, your second century would include both aspects."

"So if I wanted an ability that was best for say, unarmed combat, I'd be better off getting my century in strength, constitution, and agility?" I asked.

"Yes, and no," Restun replied, a slight quirk of the lips as he spoke. "There has been exhaustive examination of the results of the stats system since the Empire was founded, and still we encounter new things on a regular basis. All I can tell you is that you will gain something appropriate to *you*. Be that a personal improvement in the way you want or not, it will be tailored by the realm to you personally."

"Fuck, man, I wish I had a wiki…" I muttered, getting a smile from Restun.

"Thomas was saying something similar the other day," he said. "Such is life, Jax, but…"

"Yeah?" I asked, trying not to think about my stats, which only made me think about them even more.

"Do you feel better about the harp now?"

"Fuck, man, no!" I groaned. "I'd almost forgotten about that."

"And your stats?"

"Fuck you, Restun," I growled.

"I'll remind you of that comment in training," he murmured, and I nearly tripped over a root as my body instinctively tightened up in panic.

Then he was gone, peeling off and heading down to the left to meet another legionnaire, as I turned to the right, climbing up the hill to the camp and closing on the ship.

As I got closer, I saw Lydia, and my heart dropped, seeing her unconscious and being stretchered onto the ship. Nerin was by her side and talking to Oracle, with Sehran walking along next to her, holding Lydia's hand.

"Is she alright?" I called, hurrying up the last incline, then launching myself through the air, cutting my ability to land a few meters away on the deck.

"She will be," Nerin said. "But she'll not be flying anytime soon." She looked at me, clearly about to say something else, before thinking better of it and nodding her head in acquiescence as I turned to Sehran.

"Are you okay?" I asked.

"This is my fault…" she said.

I shook my head. "You were hit by an arrow…"

"Because I wasn't wearing armor. I dress like I do for a reason, but…" she hesitated, then let go of Lydia's hand, letting Nerin take her as she moved around to stand facing me, holding Jian's hand instead.

"I'll stay with her," Oracle whispered into my mind. I sent her a mental kiss and my thanks. *"Don't worry about before and the harp…"*

"You know I will."

"You will, but we're good, I promise. Nothing that you did under the cursed harp matters." I heard the words and felt her assurance, but I'd also come damn close to killing that random woman back there simply because she mildly annoyed me when she was under the same curse.

I dismissed it from my mind and instead listened to Sehran.

"…armor."

"What?" I asked, blinking and realizing she'd been talking the entire time I'd been speaking to Oracle. "Shit, I'm sorry, Sehran, I was speaking to Oracle."

"It's okay, Jax," she said, smiling. "Okay, so generally I don't wear armor, because I use my body to entice, to draw attention and to distract. Essentially, it draws attention, but also because, through a little magic, it draws the eye better than anything else. I've spoken with Jian about it and others in my past, but the basic rule is that things like my nipples aren't that interesting to anyone. Not really."

I blinked, then before I could help myself, my gaze wandered downward, only to be yanked back up by a supreme act of will.

"The curiosity about them, though?" Sehran said, a wide smile appearing on her lips. "Wondering if one will slip free when I do...this?" She lifted her arms above her head and stretched languidly. I kept my eyes on hers though a level of focus I didn't know I possessed. "That's part of the magic I use." She dropped her arms and straightened up, the sultry sex-kitten persona vanishing.

"So making people think they might catch a glimpse, rather than just popping them out and having them sitting on little cushions all the time with arrows pointing at them is better?" I guessed, getting a nod from her.

"Basically, it's the same with my short-shorts, when I do this..."

"And that's enough." I deliberately looked away, catching the grin on Jian's face at how hard I was having to work. "Seriously, dude, how do you get anything done?" I asked him.

"It's hard," he admitted.

"Really? Can I check?" Sehran asked, winking at him and licking her lips.

"Behave!" He laughed as she pouted.

"Yes, master," she whispered huskily, then grinned at him, clearly playing a damn game, now of all times.

"So?" I reminded her that I was there, and she turned that grin upon me.

"So, my clothing needs to be sexy still. The tease of me 'falling out' is far more effective than if I wore full armor and simply left these areas exposed." She gestured to her chest then her crotch.

"Not to mention the chafing issues," I muttered, getting a grin.

"Exactly. Well, if I were to commission some armor, but keep it sexy...?"

"Yeah?"

"Could I?" she asked simply. "I would be slightly less effective in combat as a distraction, but considerably less likely to be taken down with a single shot."

"Hell, yes," I said, blinking. "Wait, you were waiting for my permission?"

"You are the Prince," she said gently. "Also, my position on the team is tied to my performance, understandably so."

"Fuck's sake." I rubbed my face. "Okay, I think I need to talk to everyone later, but yes, by all means. Hell, Sehran, if you can still fight and help in full plate mail armor, fucking do it. I don't want to lose you."

"I think that would take a lot more work to make sexy...but thank you," she said, a wide smile appearing. "Do you need us?"

"No." I said. "I need to see Ronin and that fucking necromancer."

"Ronin's with the necromancer, Restun and Grizz," Jian said. "Bane and Tang caught him."

"Where?" I snarled, and Jian pointed off to one side, where I saw Restun stood over the little bastard, questioning him.

"Thanks!" I growled, launching myself over the side of the ship, flying across the distance between us, landing hard and sending muddy water spraying in all directions.

"You!" I snarled, glaring down at the necromancer, who went white with terror, shaking his head and looking at Restun, presumably expecting him to intervene on his behalf.

"Carl here is the son of the latest guardian of the harp, one of Athelas' last disciples," Restun informed me blandly. "He barely escaped with his life, spiriting the harp away from the Legion's Justicars after the last…incident."

"The one that led to the loss of an entire maniple?" I asked grimly, getting a nod of confirmation.

"His father has guarded it since then, living hidden away in this forest for some three hundred years, until two days ago, when the nobles found the entrance to the barrow as Carl attempted to sneak out for food."

"So…wait…what?" I asked, confused.

"The barrow that they used to hide the harp was underneath the camp the nobles set up. Carl and his father were hidden in it, waiting for the nobles to leave. Carl apparently got too hungry to wait any longer and decided to sneak out…only to be caught."

"They were going to kill me!" he cried. "They thought I was an assassin!" We looked at him, seeing the pasty skin, the lack of any muscle, hell, the general impression he gave was that if he sneezed too hard he'd snap his own neck.

"The fuck they were," I growled. "You told them what you guarded?"

"My father couldn't. His oath as the guardian kept him silent. But we could have sold it, and they'd have killed me if I hadn't."

"So you told them about the harp," I snarled. "Then what happened?"

"They sent in their guards! They killed my father and looted our home, and they didn't even pay me!" he cried. I shook my head, stunned by his stupidity.

"You *actually* expected them to pay you. Fuck's sake. Where is it now?"

"Where it'll be safe! After my father's death I became its guardian, and I'm tied to it! You can't destroy it now, it draws strength from me as much as the realm around it, and I'll get stronger!"

"What?"

"I'll get stronger!" he repeated, smiling proudly. "My spells will only increase, and I'll be able to control the harp…that's what my father never understood! You have to be strong enough to control it and…"

"And you think you are?"

"I will be!" he said proudly. "All those it killed, it takes some of their strength, and when its rightful master plays the strings that power is theirs!"

"And you think that's you," I repeated, staring at the weedy, easily dominated little shit before me.

"It is! And nobody else will ever find it, because it's hidden where you can't…"

"Found it!" Lio called, jogging over, her cloak wrapped around something. I grinned.

"Lio, you just earned a fucking bonus. Ronin?"

"Destroy it," he said flatly. "The harp twists the minds of those around it, and the longer it's around you, the stronger the effect. Destroy it now, before anyone tries to play it and this whole thing starts again."

"Anything we need to use?" I asked.

He shrugged. "A fucking big hammer would be a favorite," he said. "It's magical and cursed, but it's still made of wood…but maybe plug your ears up first?"

I nodded, looking around, then pointing at a ridiculously oversized maul that lay in the mud a dozen feet away.

"Someone pass me that please," I said, before turning back to the necromancer who appeared to be unable to speak due to sheer apoplexy.

"YOU CAN'T!" he wailed eventually. "You don't know what I had to give up, what I had to do!"

"You have to live with the knowledge that you were controlled by someone else's will? That you nearly fucked someone that you'd never have touched otherwise? That's fucking rape in my book, sunshine," I growled at him, and he shook his head.

"No! It's not!" He spat. "You'd only have done that if you were tempted anyway! That's not how the magic works, it affects your control, not desire! If you would have done something because of the magic, you'd have done it anyway!"

"Not entirely accurate," Ronin interrupted, leveling a hard look at the necromancer. "The harp was created by one of the greatest harpists of the age, but when he was getting too old to play properly, his fingers too stiff, he couldn't deal with it. He paid a necromancer to make some changes to a spell and made a deal with a demon for a dagger to hold the spell. His soul, when he had no life left in him, in exchange for the dagger being bound with the spell."

"And?" I asked, as the asshole spat and tried to interrupt, until one of the legionnaires pinned him to the floor, bending his arms up behind his back and covering his mouth with one hand.

"Apologies, my Prince. He'll be quiet now."

"Thank you. You were saying?" I asked Ronin again, and he nodded.

"The dagger held a spell, a specialized version of Soul Trap but one that instead of storing the life energy, trapped the soul itself. Then he held a competition for the greatest harpists of the land. He got them to come to him, to play the harp he'd made, then drugged them and stabbed them to death, binding their soul into the dagger, and the gems it held. Then, he put the gems into the harp and transferred his soul into it as its master."

"Fucked up story," I muttered, only to have him nod.

"Yeah, the worst part is, he's still in there." He pointed at the harp. "Because the deal with the demon was that his soul couldn't be claimed until there was no life left in him, those ten entrapped bards and harpists, minstrels, all of them, they're feeding him their soul energy, unable to move on or really die."

"That demon…" I said, grinning at Ronin, who frowned, then grinned back. "You think he's still waiting?"

"Probably."

"Think Sehran would know?"

"Again, probably."

"I'll go get her," Ronin said, a wide smile on his face. I shrugged, not wanting to know what kind of a deal he was going to try and strike.

"I don't know anything about it, but I can ask?" Sehran offered a few minutes later, eyeing the harp absently. "It doesn't smell like our magic, but the souls…" She shrugged. "It sounds like the kind of a thing the Tha'ren might be involved in."

"Go for it," I said, watching as she moved quickly, sweeping a section of the ground free and etching symbols into it, creating a ring that looked familiar.

"Is that what you did when you summoned her?" I asked Jian, who shook his head.

"I used the book. This is how it's done without it; it's like shouting across the realms. Costs a lot of mana, but it's doable without an artifact."

"Sounds like you've been studying."

"Well, we talked about what would happen if she were banished somehow. She'd be kept from returning most likely, but she'd still be able to talk, at least…"

"A sensible plan, mate," I said, resting one hand on his shoulder, as we watched Sehran work.

It only took a few minutes, but when it was done and Sehran straightened up, she was noticeably wan and tired-looking.

"Sorry, just need to recover," she whispered, leaning against Jian.

"You need anything?" One of the legionnaires offered, pulling out a mana and a health potion, offering them both.

"Thank you." She smiled and took them, popping one after the other and downing them.

"I thought you fed on his mana?" I asked, pointing my chin at Jian.

"I do, but a mana potion gives me a direct boost."

"Learn something every day," I muttered, seeing the change in her as the potions took effect, and she straightened.

"So, I'm going to call for one of my sisters, then she will reach out to the Tha'ren. They're the crafters of our realm, generally, and they'll expect there to be a cost to claim something like this."

"So, they want what? Us to name our price?"

"It's a powerful artifact, even cursed."

I shrugged. "Can you ask for some armor?"

"I could, but it'd be a waste, the armor wouldn't be fitted to me without me going back. Then I couldn't return, and none here can work the demonic metals, as far as I know. Perhaps something else?"

"Like what?"

"You needed orichalcum for the academy?" she suggested.

I nodded. "We'll take that." I smiled as, once again, the literal demon in our midst proved to be the most selfless of us all.

CHAPTER TWENTY-FOUR

An hour and a half later, there was a very happy demon back in his own realm who'd apparently been getting no end of shit from his fellows over the fact that a mortal had gotten the better of him.

Now though, he had a fresh soul that was literally steeped in cruel and evil magics for centuries, and he basically waved his hand, ordering his assistants to throw the orichalcum through as worthless, compared to the soul that inhabited the harp.

I'd insisted on destroying it on our side, which the demon accepted with as good grace as it could be expected to. It made a half-assed attempt to tempt me with another deal, then shrugged, fine with the exchange of what it considered a practically worthless metal, for a soul it had wanted for a while now.

I passed the maul to Ronin, to do the deal, and we all laughed our asses off when he couldn't lift it, before letting him play his lute to counter any sounds that escaped as Grizz did the honors.

The first blow snapped the outer body, popping gems free and destroying the magical framework that kept it together. The next two served to demolish the cursed thing, and when the demon cried out, making a strange gesture of welcoming, and then slammed the portal closed, we knew it was done.

The necromancer had gone from pleading to screaming and demanding, then threatening. Once he was released, the first thing he did was try to grab one of the nearest legionnaires' daggers. Then, when his hand was slapped aside almost contemptuously, he pulled one from inside his robes—practically a butter knife— and went for the legionnaire's throat.

The intention had been that he'd be handed over to Lucian and his Justicars, in part because the situation was so fucked up and in part because I wanted Lucian to understand exactly what had happened.

Instead, I nodded to the legionnaire, who removed the knife from the asshole then ventilated him with it.

"Was that what you wanted?" the legionnaire asked after a few seconds, looking up from the corpse on the floor.

"Yeah, he went too far when he tried to stab you."

"Thank the gods. I had a horrible moment of doubt there," he said, stooping and picking the corpse up, moving off with it as others came to collect the orichalcum.

The rest of the morning was taken up with minor issues, mainly finding the locals who had been brainwashed by the Drow and the cursed harp, getting them to calm down, to eat a little food and drink water, then sleep.

Also, we needed to clear a good section of the forest to burn the bodies, considering there were literally hundreds of them.

Some four hours later, when the rest of the fleet arrived, we were exhausted, thoroughly sick of the smell of burning bodies and this goddamned forest.

As soon as the first ships were in place, we boarded Tenandra and took off, swapping out for a heavy cruiser to take our place, then flew out to land a few miles to the north next to a large river, while the Legion deployed fully.

"So, to confirm," Romanus said in our impromptu command meeting, sitting by the river with a bottle of rum being passed around the group and Ronin lifting our spirits by playing a cheerful tune. "The Legion is to sweep the forest, take out the camps and recover whatever goods are here. The locals are to be taken to their villages, or back to the Great Tower, whichever they'd prefer, provided they swear the oath."

"Sounds good."

"And while we do this, you'll be storming the Sunken City?"

"That's the plan," I agreed, taking a long swig.

"So…are you going to take any of the golems with you?" he asked. I sighed, shifting and watching the play of the light on the water, feeling exhausted as I scratched my cheek, my brain fuzzy.

"Do you have any with you?" I asked after a minute.

"Not with us, but you took several with you when you left Himnel."

"Carmen's need was greater."

"Was it?" Romanus asked seriously. "Jax, look at yourself. Look at your team; you're all on the ragged edge. Whatever happened with the harp, and yes I'm well aware of the legends and reports of it, and I'm damn glad you destroyed it, but you need to rest."

Next to us, the indefatigable Restun sat on a log calmly. Contrasting his state with Lydia, who looked like she'd been dragged through a grinder backward…I probably didn't look much better.

"It…" I nodded. "Yeah, it probably wasn't. We thought we were hunting a few dozen bandits, then hey, it was a hundred and what? Seventy?" I shook my head. "It was more than doable. Even a few hundred bandits spread out across the damn forest and over three camps. There shouldn't have been much of an issue, especially when they had no idea we were coming."

"But they knew."

"Sylvan," I muttered. "Oracle did a deal with the only one we could find near us. That got us into the forest deep enough to take out the first of the patrols…"

"Then the blood drew them?" Restun asked shrewdly.

"We think that," Oracle agreed, shifting uncomfortably and rubbing the small of her back. "I chose not to make the others aware that spilling blood would draw the Sylvan, as I thought the increase in risk if they tried to take them all prisoner unharmed wasn't worth it."

There was a long pause when Restun looked at Romanus for direction, then eventually Romanus spoke.

"Oracle…are you the leader here?" he asked her calmly.

"Well, no, Jax is, but…"

"Jax is," Romanus agreed. "How would you feel if I made that call? To not tell him something that would have definite effect because I decided that it was for the best?"

"Well…no," she said after a few seconds. "It's not like that, Romanus. We speak mind-to-mind at times. Knowledge drifts between us; most of the time we're not even aware."

"Did *this* knowledge 'drift'?" he asked firmly.

"No."

"Then I'm sorry, Oracle, Jax…but this needs to be addressed. I understand that you are bonded, and that you are to be the mother of the Prince's firstborn. From observing you both as I have, I imagine that you'll always be a major part of the Imperial family, be that as a concubine, a wife, or Empress, but you are NOT the prince."

"Romanus…" I said, frowning and he shook his head.

"Jax, you once asked me to speak up if I felt I had to, to always give you my advice, even if you didn't want to hear it. Does this command still stand?"

"Yes."

"Then this needs to be addressed and the chain of command made clear. Please don't mis-understand, Oracle. We respect and care for you, the joy at the news of your pregnancy…well, it was universal across the Legion and the loyal citizens of the Empire. But, Jax is the focal point of the Empire. He is our leader."

"I understand," she whispered, nodding. "We discussed it at the time as well."

"And I regret interrupting the decisions we have to make to address it, but it is my responsibility to do so," Romanus said quietly, attempting a smile, and clearly feeling that while he had to do it, he really hadn't wanted to. "Do you agree that it is our role to *advise* the Prince, not make those decisions for him?"

"I do, As I say, we discussed it, just…"

"No, Oracle, there is no excuse for this. There is no 'just'. This is, at its heart, the basis of all treason, and it must be addressed."

"Treason!?" I gaped.

"When one of us decides that we must make the decision for you, that we do not offer you the information and abide by your decision? This is us deciding what will be done for the good of the Empire, instead of you. This, as I say, is the basis of all treason, regardless of good intentions. Oracle, you are the servant here, as are we all. You must remember this," he said, making me wince as I felt the utter shame that flooded Oracle at his words.

"We'll address it if it happens again," I said. "We share a mind a lot of the time, and Oracle is the woman I love. It's only right that she shares the decisions we make."

"And that is your right to decide. I'm sorry, Jax, I don't enjoy saying things like this, but it needs to be said."

"I know, mate, and thank you. Right." I clapped my hands together and took a deep breath, well aware of the feelings I was sensing from Oracle and not knowing what to do, beyond shooting her a feeling of love and trust through the bond.

"So, moving on, Tenandra has made the majority of her hull watertight, and while not all the cabins are ready, the ship is livable. Hell, we've all lived in far worse. I'll be taking her, along with my team, to the Sunken City. Hopefully we'll find our ship there, happy as can be and already loading the golems from the Prax…"

I paused, looking at the others, and grunted a short laugh.

"Yeah, alright, I don't believe that either. On the upside the ship has a complement of golems, so they'll have kept the crew safe with any luck. If not, then we'll damn well save them. Then we'll dive into the depths, secure the portal and I guess, save the gnomes and see if we can turn them to join us."

I shrugged, getting smiles from those around me at the simple description of the plan.

"Yer know it won't be tha' easy, right?" Lydia asked, shifting uncomfortably.

"I do, and I know that you're supposed to be in your room with Nerin working on your wings."

"Aye, well, she said ah needed time fer ma body ta heal up a little on its own," Lydia muttered, getting a proud smile from Restun.

"So speaks a true Optio," he said, those few words having a massive effect on her. "No legionnaire likes lying abed, wasting time that could be spent serving the Empire, when all they need is time to heal."

"True, but as you climb the ranks, you learn that a little time lost to heal right can save a lot of issues later," Romanus said with a faint smile. "You do need to rest on the flight, Lydia. I know the availability of healing magic has changed a great deal for us all, but some things, as Mistress Nerin has said, are better done in stages. She is the expert here."

"Ah'll rest, General," she said. Romanus smiled again, seemingly still both proud and uncomfortable at achieving the rank of General.

"See that you do…although, Jax?"

"Yeah?"

"I still recommend that you and your team return to the Tower with us. I could dispatch two squads of legionnaires to the Prax."

"And they couldn't claim it," I interrupted him. "They couldn't claim the Prax, they couldn't command the golems, and they couldn't shut down the portal, nor lock it out. Once I've claimed the Prax, we'll be able to use the portal to link the Tower. Once you've changed the lockdown commands on the one at your end, that is."

"Then we'll be able to send reinforcements through," Romanus agreed, sighing. "As well as golems and more. I agree it's worth it, Jax. In fact, creating a stable link that's both quick and secure between the various Imperial sites and the cities under your control is massively beneficial and something we should have considered before. The Legion can remain at the Tower and train heavily. Then, in a matter of mere hours, we can be at any point in your territory, slowed only by the trip up the Tower itself."

"Then the problem is that it's me doing it?" I asked.

He nodded. "As I say, Jax, I understand the need, and the reasoning, I just don't like it."

"I know, Romanus." I said, both of us knowing the conversation was done. Again.

"One last point then, regarding the harp, Jax. While I know you'll not listen, I feel the need to make my point clear."

"Yeah?"

"*You* were not in control before, you were under the influence of one the most powerfully cursed artifacts in the annals of the Dravith Legion, yet still, you and those who were with you managed to keep from killing the innocent. Yes, you fought each other. Yes, you did things you're not proud of. And yes, eventually you might have done those things, but you did not do any of them of your own free will. That matters."

"Thank you," I whispered, shaking my head. "I know, but…can we change the subject?"

"In a minute, Prince Jax." He said firmly, again drawing on the right to tell me shit I needed to hear, rather than what I wanted to. "Do you accept me as an authority over the legion?"

"You know I do Romanus, you're the Legion General, the…"

"And you accept me as your advisor?"

"Yes?" I asked, confused.

"Then listen and accept my advice, Jax. Let this be an end to the incident with the harp. You were all ensorcelled by a terrible cursed creation that has been responsible for thousands of deaths over the years. You have ended that threat. What is done, is done. Let it be."

I hesitated, looking around and seeing the desperate desire on the others faces at those words. I suddenly realized that as long as I held onto it, even when I was blaming myself, I was making them hold onto it too.

I took a deep breath and straightened. "You know, you're right." I declared, forcing the words out. "What is, is, and what happened is over. We'll all move on." I looked around, seeing the desperate desire to do so, warring with the individual beliefs of my squad, as I made it an order.

"Let it go people." I said firmly. "We need to move on, for the good of the realm." I said the words as determinedly as I could, ignoring the little voice inside that tried to tell me that I couldn't and that I was to blame. Some things just were better left in the past, be that an hour, a day or a century ago.

Romanus nodded clearly seeing the attempt for what it was, and accepting it as the best that could be managed for now. "So, what's your intention on arrival?" he asked, reaching into his bag and pulling out a carafe of steaming coffee, then offering it around with a somewhat forced smile as everyone crowded in.

"We'll have Tenandra examine the Prax with her senses when we get there. She'll pick the best path for us, considering that she remembers the original layout. She'll drop us off then patrol with the other ship. We'll use the golems and punch our way into the portal area, lock it to just us. Until you reach the Great Tower and unlock that one from your end, we'll go to either the original command center—we didn't reach that last time—and we'll see what survived, or straight to the golems, powering them one-by-one, I guess."

"What will you do with the golems?"

"Probably set a handful to begin repairs on the Prax, secure a small area, and see if we can get the engines rebuilt and flightworthy again. If the structure is strong enough, hell, I'd fly that fucker right back to the Great Tower. I doubt it will be though. We'll check it out and decide on site. The majority of the golems though, as we've discussed, will be sent through the portal, and put to work."

"Then we have a plan," he said. I nodded.

"Jax, I'd recommend we look at your character sheet before we go our separate ways," Restun added in.

I braced myself. "Of course."

"In the ship, with any last orders already given," he added, watching me. "You said that you had forty-nine points to assign, as well as making the adjustments to your screen. I suspect you'll be rendered unconscious at the very least by the changes, so better you are in your cabin already, rather than the others seeing you being carried aboard ship."

"A fair point," I muttered, climbing to my feet. "Okay then, Romanus, I guess this is it. I leave the clearing and securing of the forest in your hands, and make whatever changes you need to the plans we've discussed. I trust you," I said, helping Oracle to her feet, even as Restun helped Lydia to hers.

Twenty minutes later, I was sitting back in a chair in the cabin that was apparently now exclusively for Oracle and me, noting the little touches that suggested serious thought had been put into it.

The two chairs were bolted to the floor and had arms that slid aside on polished railings for example, allowing you to slide in and get comfy, then lock them closed, and the table was both fold-away and sturdy.

A little part of me wondered if Tenandra had considered the various uses I'd be putting that table to later, then gave up, knowing that she probably had, considering the way she'd run to Sehran and Jian.

The Wisps were evolving, I realized, far beyond the limits that their old masters had anticipated, and I forced myself to accept I had an uncomfortable conversation coming with both Seneschal and Heph in the short term.

After all, if they decided they wanted freedom and to move on? What did that mean for the Tower?

I forced that thought aside.

I'd deal with it, regardless. I wasn't going to take the route of the old Empire and declare that the end justified the means, not in this. I felt her hand then as Oracle reached out, resting it on my shoulder. I started, having been lost in my thoughts, and cleared my throat. Oracle knew what I'd been thinking about by the pulse of love and pride she shared with me.

"Okay," I mumbled, forcing a smile onto my face as I looked at Restun, who sat on the edge of our bed at my order. The bugger had been standing at attention when we'd started talking, even as I admired our new quarters. "Are the potions sorted? The replacements?"

"Both the replacement potions and the replacement armor sections for you all, and yes, I'll pass your thanks onto Thorn," he said as I opened my mouth. "Jax, do you want to do this?"

"Yeah," I said, wincing, having not realized I was putting it off until he said it. "Sorry, just freaks me out a little, that's all."

"Why?"

"When I first activated the Pearl…it showed me a lot, like how fucking stupid I really was." I sighed, then shook my head at the look on Oracle's face when I said that. "It's true. You know it is."

"You weren't stupid, you just…" She paused as she looked for the right words.

"I was just less intelligent than a hammer sandwich?"

"That's a new one on me," Restun acknowledged with a faint smile. "Truthfully, Jax, our baseline intelligence doesn't change hugely throughout our life, regardless of how many points we assign it. What changes is how we use it. You were never the brightest of my trainees, but you are intelligent and gifted in other ways."

"Thanks," I mumbled.

"Jax, I could lie to you and praise you as the most intelligent Prince I've ever met," he said, straightening up. "But we both know that's wasting time. Now…"

"Let's fuckin' do it, I guess." I pulled up the screens before me and focused on my stats.

"Concentrate, Jax. Concentrate on who and what you are, on the changes you have endured and more, then the stats. Search for the details that you know to be wrong and start there. Accept the changes in your mind and heart, then know that they have changed."

It was bullshit, a little part of me muttered. It sounded too much like that therapy bullshit they'd made me do in the army and when we were made wards of court.

The greater part, the part that had grown to accept this world, accepted Restun as the damn ultimate legionnaire that he was, and had no ego about knowing he was a better warrior and hell, probably a better *man* than me…that part accepted his words and started to work.

I started searching, starting, appropriately or not, at the top.

Agility: Governs dodge and movement, maximum speed, six hundred and eighty-three percent.

I sure as shit wasn't a hundred percent faster than everyone else, let alone six hundred and eighty-three…that meant I'd found the first mistake, the first part where 'me' and the system couldn't mesh.

I *was* fast, though…hell, I was *insanely* fast when I triggered Mana-Overdrive, so maybe that was what it meant? When I triggered my abilities, that was how much faster I could become?

That sort of made sense and would explain how, when I fought the Drow at first, they were kicking my ass. If they were naturally that much faster or more skilled than I was, then of course they'd win, if I hadn't cheated.

The figures though…sixty-three points in Agility. I stared at it, thinking about the average as I'd been told, being ten. Was I six times faster and better at dodging?

I'd glided through the fights with the regular transplanted humans from Earth, so maybe, but…

Regardless, I knew I was wrong. As I focused, something in me responded. A quiver ran through me, the feeling I'd get before the muscle goes into cramp, that short shift that preceded a massive altering of damn well everything.

I felt it, and rather than turn from it, I embraced it, focusing on what I knew.

When I'd first accepted the Pearl, I'd had no preconceptions, no issues that were preventing me from seeing the truth. So that point was correct–those details could have been all ones or ten thousands, and I'd not have had a scale to compare them to.

The points I'd added in until now were probably correct as well. That meant the screen just hadn't accepted the changes that were from my growth with the aid of the Gods, and that was understandable…right?

I focused on it, feeling the twitching in my muscles growing as I relaxed and *accepted* my body. It sounded fucking ridiculous, like I should be growing my hair and beard and cuddling a fucking tree somewhere, instead of gutting people who crossed me, but it worked.

The numbers started to change, only slightly at first, but as the seconds passed, I felt the quivering tightness that warned of cramp unraveling.

I felt relief, instead of the usual sudden pain. As the seconds passed into minutes, the numbers slowed and settled. I refused to look at them, not wanting to interrupt the process, and instead looked at my Charisma.

This one was a little weirder. I'd always had a level of self-assurance in public that bordered on arrogance, and I'd…well, I'd not done badly with the ladies, put it that way.

Knowing that I had sixty points in charisma and a five hundred percent chance to succeed in any situation where persuasion was an issue.

That was sure as shit *not* correct.

If that had been right? Hell I'd have been charming the nobles and more, rather than fighting the fuckers.

Now that I knew I was looking for inconsistencies, I damn well felt them. Where my Agility had climbed, and hard, this one was the opposite. The points were right, or near enough, I felt, but the five hundred percent chance?

No.

That shifted madly, warbling in and out of focus as my mind filled with images of the way I'd acted, the shit I'd put up with from people, and the way I'd responded.

Things changed, and fast.

Constitution…that soared almost as soon as I looked at it. This time I felt pain, horrific pains, as my body altered and shifted.

Hours passed, but when I was done, laid on a bed that I had no clue how I'd reached, drenched in sweat, watched over by Restun and Oracle, by Bane and Grizz, by Sehran and Lydia.

I stared at the wooden deck overhead, hearing the gentle buzz of the others nearby. I knew, the knowledge drifting from Oracle, that they'd come when they'd felt my pain and distress.

They'd come and they'd gone, they'd brought food, and they'd done basic jobs. Hell, Grizz was sitting in the corner even now, his tongue gripped between his teeth as he worked on his sword, polishing the edge.

They'd come to me and just sat there, getting on with their own lives, talking quietly, but getting up and fetching me a drink when they decided I looked thirsty, or wiping my skin, as the changes continued, and I sweated blood.

I lay there, breath coming in short gasps, staring at the stat sheet before me, stunned by the differences and knowing that, for the first time in a long time, what I saw was accurate.

None of the changes were beyond anything I could have achieved on my own. Hell, they were almost all from the genetic viability upgrade, which meant that I could start to share that with my people. I could fix them the way I'd fixed myself.

But the world had changed for me, and I could see it all now.

Name: Jax Amon				
Title: Godslayer				
Class: Sorcerer II			**Renown:** Imperial Scion, Prince of Dravith, Master of Himnel and Narkolt	
Level: 48			**Progress:** 3,713,743/6,455,000	
Patron: Jenae, Goddess of Fire and Exploration			**Points to Distribute:** 49 **Meridian Points to Invest:** 0	
Stat	**Current points**	**Description**	**Effect**	**Progress to next level**
Agility	80	Governs dodge and movement.	+700% maximum movement speed and reflexes.	54/100
Charisma	60 (55)	Governs likely success to charm, seduce, or threaten	+50% success chance in interactions with other beings	97/100
Constitution	120 (118)	Governs health and health regeneration	2400 health, regen 160 points per 600 seconds, (each point invested now worth 20 health)	N/A
Dexterity	90	Governs ability with weapons and crafting success	+80% to weapon proficiency, +90% to the chances of crafting success	36/100
Endurance	70 (67)	Governs stamina and stamina regeneration	2100 stamina, regen 52 points per 30 seconds, (each point invested now worth 30 stamina)	15/100
Intelligence	165	Governs base mana and number of spells able to be learned	1650 mana, spell capacity: 84 (82 + 2 from items)	N/A
Luck	70	Governs overall chance of bonuses	+60% chance of a favorable outcome	16/100
Perception	70 (60)	Governs ranged damage and chance to spot traps or hidden items	+60% ranged damage, +60% chance to spot traps or hidden items	22/100
Strength	75 (72)	Governs damage with melee weapons and carrying capacity	+75 damage with melee weapons, +75% maximum carrying capacity	87/100
Wisdom	88 (78)	Governs mana regeneration and memory	+1170% mana recovery, 14 points per minute,	82/100

I lay there, seeing the page before me in all its damning glory at how many points I'd been actively suppressing since my changes, I read it aloud, the room going silent as I did so. Restun spoke softly, his voice hanging in the air.

"What will you do?"

"What I have to," I whispered, finally seeing that, like the points I'd lost so many times to using the Imperial Abilities, I'd been bottling myself up when I'd been forcing myself to grow in set ways.

I needed to follow my instincts, and I was damn well going to do that moving forward.

The fight with Nimon had taught me that. We'd been physically identical in terms of levels, or points at least. If I'd not been a sneaky, paranoid fuck wanting to keep myself stocked with hidden weapons, I'd have lost that.

I'd seen what Amon had been showing me in his memories, finally. He'd not been the diplomat, nor the father to the Empire. He'd been the iron boot.

He'd stood atop the throats of those who pissed him off, and he'd stomped *hard.*

It was his people who made the Empire look so attractive to others, his diplomats who made the deals, not him. He'd gotten involved when the diplomats failed, and he'd left a scorched earth behind, smoking and barren.

It wasn't the only way, I knew that. I could, and I would, learn. But I'd not spend forever in study, that might save more lives, admittedly…or I might fail miserably and end up with my people slaughtered.

No, the more I thought about it, I wasn't Amon, and neither was I the man who'd first arrived in the UnderVerse such a short time ago. I was Jax Amon, Prince of the Empire, and it was time I damn well acted like it.

"I've forty-nine points to assign," I whispered. "I could reach my century in a load of places, or I could do it in Wisdom and my double in Intelligence. I'm at a hundred and sixty-five in Intelligence, thirty-five points there, and I've got my double, twelve points on top of my eighty-eight in Wisdom, and I've got a century, and then I've got two points left over, I can drop them into Dexterity, lifting me to ninety-two points there."

"Two centuries at once?" I heard someone whisper. "Fuck, that's going to hurt."

"Oh yeah," I agreed aloud. "Catch you all on the other side…" Then I hit accept, and started to scream.

CHAPTER TWENTY-FIVE

By the time the fractured nature of reality came back into one, finally making sense again, I was sore in almost every way. My brain had been torn apart and stitched back together, the connections between the gray lumps of flesh that made me, *me,* had been replaced with ones that felt like they were made of liquid fire.

I stared into the distance, seeing nothing as memories roared through me. I saw them all, tasting my mother's shepherd's pie, the cheap-ass ketchup that was all we could afford giving it a tartness that real sauces lacked.

I felt the cold as I shivered, naked, stripped and wrapped in a blanket, as our mother laughed and tried to get the snow off woolen gloves that were bobbled with it.

Tommy's jeans already laid on the radiator, soaked through. I watched her as she worked, smiling down at me. Then she was picking me up, hugging me to her, and I wrapped my spindly legs around her as she held me tight, her voice light and full of love calling to my brother to come and have a hug as well.

I felt her giving up her warmth to us, children who'd done *exactly* what she'd told us not to, probably ruining our clothes by playing where we shouldn't and for too long. I heard the music from her record player as she sang along and laughed, tousling our hair. She fell onto the sofa, and Tommy climbed onto her lap as well, his arms reaching out and sharing the meager heat in our cheap flat.

The howling wind outside shook the casements of the window and the ice that built up on it. The mold would creep up the walls in warmer times, and the water ran down them, and yet…it was home.

I stared into her dark eyes, seeing the hints of gray in her hair and the happy smile. I remembered the difference that only a few months would bring…her wasting away, the exhaustion that even now I could see clawing at her, the disease that she hid from us.

Hundreds more memories jostled and screamed for my attention. I held them off, staring at this one, perfect moment, seeing my mother and missing her terribly.

"This," I whispered through cracked lips, with a voice still hoarse from my screams. "This is why we do what we do."

It wasn't possible to prevent, not this. It'd already happened, many years ago, and it was impossible to stop it happening for others. No matter what I did, there would be deaths. Hell, I'd cause and mete out many of them.

No, what I did, what Tommy did, we did for this for HER.

For the sure knowledge that, regardless of anything and everything else, our actions would make her proud. We did it for a million other reasons, but at the base of them all, we did it for our mother's love and her memory.

The notifications were waiting, the world around me rising to the forefront as the memory slipped away, becoming a memory again. I stared back into the deep past instead of living it again.

Eventually, I was forced to let go. When I blinked again, I was aboard ship, surrounded by my friends and family. When I drew in a long, shuddering breath, the dampness of spilled tears on my cheeks, I felt no shame.

They'd not judge me, and the memory was too raw to be able to box away now.

"Are you okay, my love?" Oracle asked gently.

"Yeah…yeah, I am," I whispered as the memory faded, darkening and vanishing even as the final details stood out, the faint smell of cigarette smoke, the purple or brown velvet curtains…

I pulled up the notifications, hoping to get them out of the way, and that maybe, just maybe, there'd be something I could use.

Congratulations!

You have achieved your first DOUBLE CENTURY in Intelligence through point allocation, as well as your third primary century in Wisdom.

As such, you have gained a new Ability!

Mana-Manipulation:
The Mana-Manipulation ability is exceedingly rare for a mage, despite its common-appearing name. The ability to manipulate mana at its most fundamental level is the ability to interact with the wider magical world. However, rather than simply using mana to cast a spell, as most mages do, it involves the manipulation of the aspect of mana, converting Death mana to Life, Fire to Water, or any one of a thousand variations.

An expert mana manipulator can form mana into its physical form, creating manastones, yet forcing them to remain in a set aspect.

Cost: 50 mana per point converted.

I considered the details, then roamed back to the last 'Century Ability' as well, comparing them…yeah the genetic storage option was good. Hell it'd take weeks for me to build a real reserve, but once I had it, it could literally be life-saving, so there was that, a game changer, even though it wasn't immediately useful. Being able to create actual manastones, and not just the blank kind that the skillbook I'd offered to Ame so long ago taught?

That reminded me about the skillbook that was still sitting in the Hall of Memory in the tower. I needed to see if Ame was ready for it or wanted that to be given to someone else.

This skill would enable me to make manastones that were literally condensed air magic alone…I had to think that something like that would make a damn difference to the engines for a ship, or…

Or to a damn alchemist's tools! There was no need for me to make them into just a stone for whatever, after all! I could make a new mortar and pestle. Hell, I could make anything I needed out of the relevant crystal…like a fire mortar and pestle, and the effects…

I had no fucking idea what they'd be, but I was going to find out, just like I was going to find out what happened when I made a damn blade out of fire mana and stabbed some fucker with it!

I banished the raging thoughts that filled my head, blinking them away and drew a deep breath.

I forced myself to sit upright. A blanket was laid across my crotch, and Sehran, Oracle, and Tenandra were sitting the closest to me. I knew from broken memories that it'd been the three of them looking after me most of all. Even Nerin had spent more than a few hours in the room, I remembered, before glancing at Sehran, who smiled at me.

That the succubus, a literal demon who fed on souls, was one of the gentlest people I'd ever known made me smile in return as she reached over and gripped my hand, squeezing gently.

"We see all, in our role," she whispered. "We feel more than any mortal knows."

"I know," I said.

"So does Jian and Tenandra…and Oracle now, and…" She looked around, realizing that far from it being a secret, the entire room now knew.

"Thank you all," I said roughly, clearing my throat and looking around. "I bet that wasn't fun to watch?"

"Not at all," Tang admitted from one side where he leaned against the wall. "You know Restun gave us extra jobs to keep us busy when he left?"

"How long's he been gone?" I asked, not having noticed he'd left, but able to feel the slight shift of the deck under me and hear the pulsing of the engines.

"About a day."

"Shit," I muttered, scrubbing my hands through my hair and looking about the room. "You've been here all this time?"

"People come and go, most just wanted to be around in case there was anything they could do to help," Yen answered, smiling from where she sat next to Grizz, one hand toying with his hair as he lay on his back, head in her lap, all issues between them seeming resolved now.

"Well, thank you all," I said, taking a deep breath as I sat back and stretched as best I could. The bed was a decent size, but it was still aboard ship, and…I glanced down to make sure, then back up. Yup.

Totally naked, again, with only a blanket keeping me even slightly decent.

"So…my clothes…?" I asked, getting a snort from Sehran.

"They need to be burned," she said. "While you didn't lose a lot of blood, well, not compared to a normal day for us, it was enough that those clothes will never recover."

"Okay." I winced at the mental image of them having to peel me out of the bloody mess. "Sorry about that."

"It's fine!" Sehran reassured me.

"So," I looked around. "Extra jobs?"

"Restun decided that, as the top deck isn't really ready for legionnaires running laps yet, that we should all be working on our other professions, instead of being, and I quote; 'Lazy disgraces to the name of the legion'," Tang said, making little air quotes as he spoke.

"What are your professions?" I asked, having never really thought about it. I'd seen the others doing things on occasion, but never really considered it.

"*Legionnaire* is a profession," Yen corrected me, smiling to take the sting out of the words. "But we all generally have a secondary profession as well, like Armorer but at a very basic level. When you're in training, you get shared around the jobs a lot, so you can see if any appeal to you, or if there's any natural skill. Most of the time we don't really do anything else with it, but Restun is one of those who thinks if you're not busy, then you're wasting time."

"Fuck that," I muttered. "We fight all the damn time; having a day to relax now and then? Yeah, fuck that. As Prince, I declare you can have a bit of time off." I felt the mana drain starting, and I cut it off in panic before it could reach the required level, whatever that would have been.

A sudden dread filled my heart as I imagined Restun seeing I'd overruled him. Nope. Fuck that shit.

"Thanks, boss!" Grizz called, settling even more comfortably into Yen's legs then letting loose a sigh of contentment.

"So, what were you doing?" I asked Tang.

"Mainly, we all did little jobs, like checking our armor and fixing damaged straps, and so on." He shrugged, then straightened and clearly forced himself to say words he really didn't want to. "But…"

"Yeah?" I asked when he didn't go on.

"I agree with Restun."

"What?!" Grizz gasped, twisting around and glaring at his traitorous friend.

"I do," Tang declared. "Look, once we've hit the Sunken City and done whatever we do, we're going back to the Tower, right?"

"Yeah…" I agreed.

"Until we're off again," Ronin corrected helpfully, and Grizz shot him the finger.

"Well, you said that the Imperial Academy would be built as soon as possible, so if we can get some master-ranked trainers, that means we can really start leveling our skills, right?"

"Yeah?"

"Boss, look, I know Restun is planning for us to basically spend the same number of hours a day training as before, once that's done. He's evil, right?"

"Yeah, probably," I agreed, scratching my chin as I thought about it. I could totally see Restun doing that.

"So, we've got the choice here. We could either double our gains, but rather than halving our time with Restun, it stays as it is now…hell, it might be increased because he's just that twisted…OR…"

"I like 'or'," Grizz muttered quickly, clearly not wanting additional torture by Restun.

"Or…we could all look at our secondary professions, real ones. Ones that will not only get us a little extra gold for when we're old, but will get us extra points and experience," he finished, getting a thoughtful silence as his response.

"That's a damn good point," I agreed, looking around. "If you can achieve the same gains with Restun in half the time, once he declares we're all doing the same, or double even, it'll be too late. We need a plan in place early."

"You could always overrule him?" Grizz suggested hopefully.

"Yeah…no," I said after a long second of existential dread. "You could be our representative to tell him about not wanting to spend more time with him, if you want, though?"

"Fuck, no; he'd murder me."

"And that's how I feel, too." I replied flatly. "So, if you all have professions you WANT to follow, then I can tell Restun that we need to use the extra time we gain to follow those. If not…you get extra Restun time."

"Any suggestions?" Grizz asked after a few seconds, but was ignored as Sehran smiled.

"Can I take a profession as well?" she asked hopefully.

I shot her a frown. "Sehran, you're not just Jian's companion and summoned help. You're a member of the team. Pick what you want. Hell, tell me or Lydia what you need, and we'll sort it."

"I want to be an armorer," she said. "I want to learn to make specialist armors, so I can make something that's more appropriate for me, but also for my sisters, when I go back."

"That's an easy one," I said glancing over at Lydia, who nodded that she understood this was a part of her role as Optio to sort. "We can arrange for you to spend time with the legion armorers. Learn the basics, and we'll get some specialists in to teach you. Hell, anyone else have any requests?"

"I hear warlock is fun," Grizz said, before getting a look from Yen. "Not that I'd ever be looking for anyone else to join us, of course," he assured her as quickly as he could. The entire room laughed as she rolled him out of her lap.

"Physical alchemist," Tang called out. I frowned again, not having come across that one yet.

"What's that?" I asked. "I mean, I make potions, so am I…?"

"No, totally different, yet similar. It's complicated, I know. It's a bit of a rare one, probably not something we could do, but…"

"We've got a primer and an advanced manual," Oracle said in response to my glance.

"There you go, dude," I said, seeing the way his eyes opened wider. "What?"

"Uh…look, boss, a physical alchemist, they're rare, okay? I was only joking, I mean…"

"You want to do it, or not?"

"I do!" he said quickly. "Shit, I want to do that, but…"

"But what?" I asked.

"It's…complicated." He sighed. "It's all about making one thing into another, like…"

"Like lead into gold?" I asked, remembering the old stories.

"Well, yeah, but a lot more than that. Like, I'd be able to make enhancers for potions."

"What?"

"Enhancers…shit, you really haven't heard of this have you? Okay, so *Physical* alchemists are rare, and they're seriously expensive to hire, because they make things like Roses and change metals into others."

"Why the hell did nobody suggest this when we needed to get the damn things for the academy? And roses?"

"Roses!" Tang corrected. "As in the Rose of Purity, not the damn flowers."

"Totally lost me, mate."

"Physical alchemists learn to transmute as one of their skills, but it's insanely expensive to achieve," Oracle interjected. "For example, he could change iron into platinum…eventually. But the cost would probably be higher than just buying the platinum."

"It's not cheap, boss. That's one of the reasons there aren't many. Hell, the last guy I heard that could do it? He tried to go and live with the gnomes…and suffered an accident on the way when his caravan was hit by slave traders. They probably only hit it in the hope of catching him."

"So there's no other physical alchemists, and it's expensive to follow; why do you want to do it, then? And wait, you were always bored to shit when I worked on mine around you!"

"Because things like the Rose of Purity would make a massive difference! It's something you learn as time goes on, like the primer might teach the Rose of Concentration, or whatever. It'd take me weeks to make one, but once I manage it, I'd get a hell of a bump in my skill!"

"And what do they do?" I asked, still totally lost.

"They help with your potions!" he said, grinning. "Or in a forge, or wherever! Basically, once made you put one into a special flask or whatever in your potion set? Once the potion goes through that flask, the crap that's not supposed to be in there would get separated out, or the potion gets concentrated or whatever!"

"Shit, seriously?" I asked, stunned.

"Yeah, boss, and there's dozens of different ones! Each level I reach, I'll be able to make slightly stronger roses, or transmute stuff cheaper, but…"

"Do it," I said. "Even if it couldn't help my damn potions, it could help with the armorers, the blacksmiths, the herbalists, damn there's a million things it could improve!"

"Umm, could I do glassblowing, then?" Grizz asked, hesitantly.

"Seriously?" I frowned. Grizz was massive, a veritable mountain of a man, heavily built and about as subtle as swapping out a loofah for a cheese-grater.

"Well, it'd mean I could make vials that would be stronger, right? For the potions?"

"Do you want to do that, Grizz?" I asked, realizing that once again, as daft as he was at times, the heart was showing through, as he was offering to start a new profession just to help us all.

"Well, I could, yeah?"

"No, you choose what the hell you want to actually do, Grizz. You don't have to plan it for the team. We've got people back at the Tower who can do jobs as well," I ordered him. "Look, people, take the time and plan for what you want to do. Don't just pick anything. You've all earned skillbooks and memories, so when you know what you want? Tell Lydia, Oracle, or me. We'll sort it out."

I smiled at the crew, all struggling with the same thoughts.

"I mean it, people. Anything you want to do, it'll all come in handy, regardless of what it is, so don't worry about deciding right now. Tenandra?"

"Yes, Jax?"

"That includes you. If you want to use the skill memories or whatever, just say."

"I…thank you," she said after a few seconds, clearly shocked.

"It's fine. Now, how far out from the Sunken City are we?"

"A full day, or just over, anyway. We'll arrive at the Prax around the fourth bell in the morning."

"Then it's time I stopped lying around," I decided, despite the scratchy eyes and the yawn I kept blocking as best I could.

"First thing in the morning," Oracle declared. "Okay, you lot, you know he's safe, and he's already naked, so get out and go cause trouble somewhere else."

I opened my mouth to argue, then my brain caught up, and I realized that I'd much rather be naked with Oracle than working with potions.

The others filed out of the room, and I made damn sure that Bane and Tang had joined them, before I turned to Oracle, who'd clambered past me and into the gap on the bed between me and the interior wall of the cabin.

"So…" I said, getting a long smile from her. She slid under the blanket, and as I watched, the shoulders of the tunic she'd been wearing slipped down, separating and vanishing under the blanket. She was watching me, propped up on one elbow, the blanket barely covering the swell of her generous chest.

"I'm feeling very neglected," Oracle whispered, pouting and blowing a strand of hair out of the way with a little smile.

"Well, we can't have that…" I replied, sliding back under the blanket, only to have one hand press against my chest, stopping me.

"Out of the bed, and Scour first," she said firmly. "You've spent a day in this bed bleeding and more. I kept hitting you with the spell over and over, but…"

"Got it." I winced, clambering out of the bed and shivering as she hit me with the spell herself. The dust and dirt slithered as it fell from me, scraps of blood and worse dissolving into literally powder, then vanishing as it fell from me. Then Tenandra, as the ship, absorbed it. "You know Tenandra is watching us, don't you?" I asked Oracle, standing there, swinging gently from side to side.

"She can't help it. We're literally inside her after all, but she tries not to pay attention when we're alone."

"Fair enough, guess she's busy enough with Sehran and Jian anyway. So…"

"Come here," Oracle whispered, sliding the blanket back and showing me that, under it, she was naked. "Come and show me that you love me."

"Yes, ma'am!" I grinned as I climbed into bed, her arms wrapping around my neck and mine around her back, as we kissed, deeply.

It started slow, but it didn't stay that way for long.

***

The early morning sun shining through the porthole in the wall woke me several hours later. I groaned, lifting one arm to cover my eyes, blocking the light out and deciding that another hour wouldn't hurt.

Oracle shifted around slowly, the coolness of her skin against mine, and the silken feeling of her hair as she moved…

And moved, sliding down the bed.

I lifted my arm, looking down at the hungry smile on her face as she trailed kisses down my stomach, before taking me into her mouth.

"Morning!" I gasped, now fully awake, reaching down with one hand and running my fingers through her hair, stroking her scalp the way she liked as she stroked me in turn.

"I love mornings," I whispered, pulling the blanket aside and admiring the view, before losing myself in a glorious start to the day.

CHAPTER TWENTY-SIX

When I actually left our cabin some time later, leaving Oracle relaxing in bed for a bit, it was as a happier and lighter man.

I paused in the corridor outside our room, and hesitated, as I wondered where I could set up, only to hear Tenandra speaking quietly through the ship.

"Second door on the right, Jax. That one is reserved for your alchemy lab. Please be sure to choose the right, however…Lydia is the second door on the left and would not appreciate an interruption right now."

I opened my mouth to ask the obvious question, then shut it firmly. "Got it, thanks," I whispered. *Not my circus, not my monkeys* I thought to myself, moving down and into the second door on the right, momentarily worrying whether it was the right side of the hall coming from my room, or the right from the front of the ship?

I winced, the door half open as I peered in carefully, trying to make sure I didn't see anything I wasn't supposed to…and sighed in relief. I was in the right room.

It was smaller than our cabin, a narrow room dominated by the large porthole in the far wall and the benches on both sides, but as soon as I saw it, I had to smile.

It had everything I needed, including a stool that moved on narrow rails, and the table…it even had clamps, so my gear would be safe in high winds or fast moves.

"Thank you," I whispered, knowing she'd hear me.

"You're welcome," Tenandra said from all around me, making me smile as I unpacked my bag. "Would you like a hand?" Her flesh body opened the door and stepped in, making me wonder if she created the avatar out of mana on the spot, or if she'd been on her way already.

"Do you know alchemy?" I asked, as I pulled my alchemy set out.

"I've observed you working on it, and while it's not entirely in my interest, it covers a field of it."

"You have something you want to learn, then?"

"Engineering, along with Giint," she confirmed, taking a distillation set and moving around me to start to set up.

"Giint?"

"He's a highly gifted engineer…"

"He's batshit crazy," I corrected.

"That's the standard for an engineer," she countered. I grunted, attaching the tubes to their respective sections, noting the way the bench clamps shifted to fit the set more comfortably.

"Thanks," I said absently. "Okay, yeah, sure, but anything in particular? I mean 'engineering' is pretty wide-reaching."

"Structural," she said. "Giint wishes to study explosives as well. Specifically, he intends to make a special bomb, one that uses runes instead of chemicals."

"Runecrafting, okay, yeah, I'll send him to Ame happily."

"For the entertainment value more than anything else?"

"Well, yeah, admittedly, but you know." I grinned at her. "So, why do you want to help me with this? It's not really structural."

"You remember the fight I was in with Thomas? And the Dark Paladin's ship?"

"Yeah, kinda hard to forget," I said with a gesture around at the completely rebuilt body of her ship.

"They used cannons on me, and some of them had unusual effects, specifically the fireball ones, when they hit the section of the flooring where you'd spilt a potion some time ago."

"Which one?" I asked, wincing as I considered that I'd spilt enough that I didn't even know which one it was.

"One that had you cursing solidly."

"That really doesn't narrow it down."

"No, but I'll recognize it if you should make it again."

"What did it do?"

"I thought it had been fully absorbed, yet when the flames touched that section, they produced a heavy gas, one that put the flames out in seconds."

"And you think that would be useful with structural engineering?" I asked, getting a smile.

"Not entirely, although if we could soak the various sections of the ship in that potion it would eliminate some of the risk. I simply wanted to help."

"Then you're very welcome," I said, setting the last few sections in place. "Okay, first of all, just because I damn well know how many we go through, before I start anything fun, I'm making us all some mana potions." I pulled ingredients out of my bags and set them down on the table, passing Tenandra a knife, and gesturing with my own.

"So, the underside of these leaves are what we want. If you peel the leaf back, you'll see a thick upper layer; that's crap." I showed her how to use the blade, sliding it into a small ridge on the back of the leaf and cutting left and right in smooth motions.

Two hours later, the last drops of the potion were filling a vial, and I was grumbling internally at the flash of notifications again. Tenandra had left about ten minutes ago, promising to watch over me and let me know if I made the potion again, bored of the painstaking process I had to follow.

I set the beaker down with a clink, straightening up and rubbing at the small of my back, aching from spending so much time hunched over and working.

"That looks fun," Bane whispered, having waited until I was done before making it clear that he was there.

"You think?" I grunted.

"No," he admitted with a *thrum* of amusement. "It always looks boring as shit."

"Yeah well, fuck you, too," I muttered, glancing to the ten potions that sat cooling on the rack, the porthole next to them open and letting in a steady, gentle breeze.

"Seriously, though, I know we need them, but even after all the hours Tang and I have spent watching over you as you work, it just looks insanely dull."

"Thanks, man," I growled, pulling the notifications up, accepting them. and dismissing them. I'd gained a single point in skill for the effort with the mana potions, but that was it. They were basic, boring even, but they were what we needed as much as anything.

"How are we doing with potions?" I asked, and Bane paused, clearly thinking before answering.

"Sixty-two healing, sixty stamina, and now…" He let out a short pulse of Worldsense, checking the number of potions lying ready. "…eighty mana."

"So, five health and stamina, with a few spares, and six mana each?" I muttered, working it out. "That's not bad, actually; it's better than we usually have."

"So, rather than working on making us a decent reserve, you're going to waste your time working on something totally different?" Bane asked, getting the finger as I thought.

"Nope!" I said eventually. "And not just because you're a dick, either. I'm going to work on the mana potion recipe."

He said something, but I ignored him, happily pulling ingredients out and laying them across the bench before me.

"The underside of the leaf here is the best," I mumbled, stripping the last of the labian leaves in my inventory, then spreading out the resulting fibrous mess on the bench. "So…the recipe says to boil you, but what if…"

Six hours passed in the blink of an eye, and by the time Tang and I were chased, coughing, from the alchemy room hours later by a thick, noxious smoke, I'd managed to increase my mana mastery by three points, and I'd added another point of Intelligence.

"I think that's enough of that," Oracle said firmly, coming along to collect me, leading me, still coughing, up and onto the upper deck to join the others.

"Sorry…Tenandra," I wheezed, having to force the words out as the ship changed direction slightly, doors popping open here and there to funnel the breeze of our passage into the right cabin to clear the air.

"What did you do?" Jian asked, shaking his head at me.

"Got two more points in poison patterning, apparently," I mumbled, stunned, staring at the notification before me.

Congratulations Journeyman!

You have taken further steps to a wider understanding of the art of the Alchemist!

Once again you find that a cure can be as deadly as a poison, should it be misapplied.

The Path to Poison Pattern Mastery has continued! 30/100

"Tell me that was worth it," Tang groaned. "I feel like I've been on a two-day pass without the fun."

"Sorry Tang." I banished the screen and started to cast, hitting first him, then me with Complex Healing, stunned at the sheer scope of the damage I'd managed to inflict on us both, and with only a collection of ingredients that damn well healed, as near as I could tell.

I pulled up the details for each of the ingredients over and over again, searching. Yeah, each and every one should have had clearly beneficial effects. Hell, if I'd strained out the pulp, then added water instead of boiling and reducing them, I'd have made a fairly high-level Cure Poison potion!

I genuinely didn't understand why or how that had happened, but I was going to find out, although…seeing the frown that Nerin was giving me, this wasn't the time to ask her.

"Jax," Oracle said, her voice rising in a clear warning. I sighed, admitting that, for today at least, the experimentation was over.

"What's happening up here, then?" I asked, seeing Lydia leading the others through a calm series of stretches.

"We're getting ready for a game of bulls," Yen informed me. "It's a variant on something Thomas suggested."

"And just like that, I'm out," I said. "If it's that lunatic's idea…"

"You're in!" Lydia called, pointing to a space next to her. "You know you should be training, and after hours in there, you really need it!"

"It's simple, Jax," Tenandra assured me, stepping forward and making a point of ignoring the white smoke that was still drifting out of the lower deck. "One of each team has a chalk stick. Each team has a box they draw on the deck, and you score a point by making a cross in it."

"Bulldog," I muttered. "It's a variant on bulldog." I recognized the game as one we'd played at school. Rather than the standard version, where you tried to run across a section of ground the other team defended, usually violently, the version we'd played meant you HAD to go into the middle of it all.

The school had banned it inside a week after half the players ended up in the hospital. That, quite naturally, meant that the entire school started playing it as well as a second game, which involved several kids distracting the teachers so we could play without interruption.

We separated into teams, roughly equal-sized, with a defender for the box and the rest of us out to get the attacker through the other side.

Tenandra was declared the judge. Oracle joined her, along with Nerin, while the rest of us lined up.

The deck was mostly in place now, the last few hours being all that was needed for the single complex crafter golem that Tenandra had commandeered working around the clock to finish up.

Three sections were still open to the floor below, leading into storage areas, but the rest was ready, and I faced off against Grizz, possibly the only one who was large enough to be able to stop me if I ran at him full speed, with Tang on my side, Bane on his, Jian with me, Yen standing across from him, and Sehran facing Giint.

That left us both with a single defender, Bob in our case, and Lydia in theirs. Arrin had managed to convince Lydia that he needed to meditate and improve on that skill more than anything else.

Tenandra gave a whistle, and they moved slowly, waiting and watching. I didn't. That wasn't how you won bulldog.

I sprinted right at Grizz, surprising him, then surprising him even more when I dived low, hitting him in the waist and lifting him up and over my shoulder.

He grappled at me, trying to stop me, but I was already past him, running straight at Giint, who turned and ran three steps, then kicked off the wall and leaped back at me, mouth open and ready to bite.

I smacked him aside, then got tripped by Bane, hitting the deck and rolling before grabbing Yen's leg and dragging her in close.

Then, at the last second, she realized that it wasn't me who was carrying the chalk; I was just the distraction!

It'd all been a feint, and as she shouted to watch out…Tang slid into the left of the box, coming out of stealth as he scrawled an X in the box. Lydia shot him a look that could melt glass as she realized she'd been fooled, moving out of position to stop me.

Tenandra whistled and declared a point, making me grin as I got back up, moving past Grizz and his mock anger.

"Next time, boss," he promised, and fuck, did he deliver.

The whistle was barely blown when he *threw* Giint at me.

I'd barely dodged a flying, screaming, and fucking insane gnome, who'd apparently been promised catnip if he managed to bite me, when Grizz took me out, sending me bouncing and rolling across the deck.

I grabbed a deck hatch and pulled myself to my feet, only to be hit with a low-flying Giint who bit my knee, then the whistle was blown.

I had to pry the fucker off, but when I'd managed that, and Oracle had hit me with a heal, blowing me a kiss from where she sat with Tenandra on the top of the wheelhouse, I grinned to myself, evilly.

I took a quick drink from my bag…and palmed a stick of catnip, getting ready for the next round.

As soon as it started, with Giint clearly furious that he wasn't getting his promised wonderdrug yet…I showed him the stick and threw it at Grizz.

Giint predictably went mad, trying to get at it, and bit Grizz who was trying to stop him, Sehran wiped Jian out, and Lydia took the opportunity to clothesline her. I caught Bane, pinning him to the deck, with Tang swiping Yen's leg and sending her crashing to the floor before rolling into the box and scoring again.

That was the pattern for the next two hours, leaving us exhausted, bloody, and laughing as we laid around on the deck. In the end, Grizz and Lydia beat my team, the pair starting to fight in serious tandem, with Bane covering the gaps.

Bob didn't really get into the game, wandering off at one point to stand at the fore of the ship and watch the sea passing below as the sun gradually sank in a final glittering burst of scarlet hue.

"Eight hours until we reach the Prax," Tenandra announced calmly. I groaned, shifting to look to my left at the equally wiped-out Grizz, who grinned at me, his bloody nose healed but still leaving its mark on him.

"Good game, mate," I called, forcing myself to sit up. "Good game, everyone!" I repeated louder, seeing the few crew that were aboard and not busy now sat off to one side, drinking beers and eating their evening meal.

"I still say drugging Giint was cheating," Grizz said as he clambered to his feet and offered me a hand, pulling me upright when I accepted.

"Of course it was. But you bribed him to bite me, didn't you?"

"Well, yeah, yer use what yer have ta hand, and we 'ad a mad gnome," Lydia agreed, standing and flapping her wings, smiling up at them as they shifted, finally healed fully.

"You did it?" I asked, shocked. "I thought it was Grizz!"

"Nope, all her, boss." Grizz laughed. "You don't want to know what she promised if he managed to bite your cock off."

"What?!" I gasped, horrified.

"Ah didn't, don't worry!" She assured me, glaring at Grizz, who burst out laughing.

"Sorry, boss, but fuck, the look on your face!"

"I hate you."

"Food, then bed!" Oracle called, flying down to land next to me and taking my hand. "Don't worry, Giint wouldn't dare bite off my favorite toy. He'd be swimming back if he tried!" She made sure Giint got it, getting a nod then an unstable smile from him.

I wasn't entirely sure if he was trying to assure us that he wouldn't do that, or if he was considering if he'd get drugs if he did, and I scuttled away quickly.

We ate, then sat around in companionable silence, occasionally broken with a "did you see" and "you did" and so on as we reflected on the game, generally feeling like we'd come full circle. The stress of the last few days, especially after the harp, had lifted a little.

It was a day of healing and relaxing, more or less, that we definitely needed. Despite being bruised, battered, and absolutely exhausted, I felt a hell of a lot better. When Oracle hit me with a heal, and then Scour, I felt even more human.

We had a few drinks, sitting on the deck and telling daft stories, comparing notes and suggestions on things, talking about everything from landing Tenandra in some little cove somewhere so we could all go swimming, to the need for popcorn and beers when the giant golem was finished and released into the ocean.

The occasional huge sea monster that could be seen in the distance, frequently sunning themselves in the shallow water around seamounts or chasing whale pods, meant that we knew the fucker was going to be busy.

Eventually, we all headed our separate ways, the couples and singles peeling off at little breaks as they decided that it was bedtime, be that for entertainment or rest.

Eventually, when it was just Oracle and me—with Bane no doubt hiding nearby but allowing us the illusion of privacy—we stared up at the stars, enjoying the steady breeze and a little time alone.

"Are you ready for this?" Oracle asked. I looked over at her, laid on our backs on the upper deck, our fingers entwined.

"Fatherhood, the Empire, or the Prax?" I asked, smiling gently.

"Yes?" she replied, rolling onto her stomach and looking down at me as she crossed her arms on my chest and laid her head on them.

"I'm as ready as I'll ever be to be a dad," I said. "Honestly, it was never something I'd thought about, but...I couldn't imagine having a child with anyone else, and I wouldn't want to. I love you, and while the timing isn't great...well, is it ever?" I smiled ruefully and sighed. "At least it'll keep us on our feet!"

"And the Empire?"

"I'm getting used to that. It still seems a bit weird that people look up to me. I used to be a barman and bouncer, unofficially at least, but…"

"You did those jobs, my love, but they were never what defined you."

I grinned at her, looking back at my last night as a free man on Earth. Covered in blood, barely coherent from blood loss, and leaving bloody hand and footprints everywhere in the damn local late-night supermarket. I remembered going to Lou's house, finding the clothes all over, and then that she was in bed with Martin, her 'friend' from work.

I remembered seeing her in the sexy underwear that I'd bought her, yet never seen her wear for me, and this time I felt…nothing.

No regret about it ending, no hate for her or him. I didn't know when it'd happened, but at some point the hate and hurt, the outrage, and the distrust…the determined belief that "that's what happens when you trust someone," all of it had gone.

I had a partner now who would stand by my side as I kicked the gates of hell in and pissed into Satan's breakfast cereal, cheering me on and standing with me should I rise or fall.

In comparison, my ex? Hell, ALL of my exes were pathetic. Not that some weren't good people in their own rights, and we were simply wrong for each other at the time, but when you compared the ONE to anyone else, it wasn't a fair fight.

I smiled at Oracle, knowing that, while she'd not have gotten all of it, she'd have gotten enough.

"I love you," I said. "And yeah, I'm ready. I'm ready to be a dad, I'm ready to lead the Empire, as best I can, and as to the Prax?"

"Yes?"

"Let's go fuck that place up."

CHAPTER TWENTY-SEVEN

Tenandra had offered to slow and circle the Prax, giving us the chance to land and explore in daylight, but considering we all had DarkVision or some variant of it now, and once inside, it'd be pitch black anyway, it seemed pointless.

The cruiser that had been sent ahead had landed close to where *Dreadnought* had been landed originally, a great swath of destroyed trees and more. As we approached, it became clear that, regardless of our hopes, something was very wrong.

"The engines are dead," Tenandra said, as we watched the images she projected on the wheelhouse cabin walls. "They've been shut down, and from the look of it, it was done properly, meaning by the captain or engineer by choice."

"Why?" I asked.

"Why shut them down, or why do you think it was by the engineer or captain?" she replied.

"Yeah, both."

"They'd shut her down if they believed they were entirely safe, or logically if the engineer or captain felt that they had to ground the ship to keep it from being taken or used against the Empire, perhaps. The engines show signs of being properly shut down, as they neither give off any signs of overload or stress, nor have they exploded and left a crater in the Prax."

"Fair enough…I take it only the captain or the engineer could do that?"

"More or less. You might get lucky and manage to deactivate one or two without a nova, but that cruiser has six engines. The chances of successfully shutting them down without a mistake six times?"

"Well, Oracle managed it once, but she had some pointers from Oren at the time," I agreed. "Okay, where the hell is the crew, then? And the golems?"

"No sign of them," Tenandra said. "The ship appears deserted, there are no lights, no movement, and no signs of a struggle…or at least, not from here."

"Then we go down and check it out," I said. "Tenandra, get us closer, and Lydia, Sehran, and I will ferry people to the ground. I don't want you actually landing, just in case, but be ready if we need you."

"That's a point. If you drop a few of us off, then fly back up for more, that leaves only three people on the ground, easily overrun…" Grizz pointed out. Tenandra nodded, speaking up quickly.

"I could make it a fast landing? Literally stop long enough for you all to jump clear, then launch again, hard? It'd be faster than you could ferry people down."

"Shit, yeah, good point, that's a better idea," I agreed.

"And I could send my flesh body with you…"

"That's probably *not* a good idea," I countered, shaking my head. "If they capture you, and things go badly down there, we're fucked. Better that, if the shit hits the fan, you can run and get reinforcements."

"I could do that anyway," Tenandra pointed out. "As a central being, I belong to the ship more than anything now, residing in part in the power core and in part in the ship itself as a distributed entity. The aspect of me that stands here speaking to you, my flesh body, could be replaced, if I needed it to be. Also, with my body with you, I could ensure that my ship body is where you most need me to be."

"I don't think it's a good idea," Oracle said. "It has definite advantages, such as having Tenandra able to share an active manapool and use spells, much as I did at first with you, Jax, but ultimately, the risk to having her flesh body captured? It would provide a conduit to the ship. I can reach out and communicate should we need it."

"Okay, thank you, Tenandra, but I agree, best if you stay here for now, please."

"Of course, Prince," she said formally, turning to the screens again. "It looks like this entrance was used heavily, and it shows signs of the golems being used to open it up." Tenandra showed us all locations on the walls, but as she spoke, I only listened with half an ear.

"Why were you against Tenandra coming?" I asked Oracle, getting a *wait* sense sent to me.

I focused on the wall, trusting her, then pointed to another entrance off to one side, in a small clearing.

"What about here?" I asked, "Can you fit and get back out at speed?"

"Yes, although it would need to be a steep insert and climb. You would need to be moving as soon as I reached the low point, as if I took this point at speed…"

"We can do that, literally dive in, we jump. Nerin, I'll help you, then Tenandra is gone again."

"I understand," Tenandra said. "Are you sure…"

"Definitely. This is going to be ridiculous if there's nothing wrong and everyone's just inside for…fuck knows, a birthday party or whatever. But if something took the crew, powered the ship down, or scared the crew to the point that they powered it down fully? I don't want you down long enough to be at risk."

"Of course," she replied, again with a little edge of frost in her voice, but accepting my decision.

I winced, knowing I'd upset her, but it was for the reasons I'd said, just not *only* for them. I trusted Oracle, and if she was saying no, especially after the conversations we'd had so recently about her making decisions for me?

It was going to be for a good reason.

"So," I said, gesturing to the door. "Time to gear up, people!"

"We're already ready?" Giint pointed out, mystified, making me sigh and scratch at my chin as I waited for almost a full minute before speaking again.

"Fine. I want a word with Tenandra and Oracle alone before we go, so everyone fuck off, okay?" I growled, seeing people wince as they realized they'd totally missed the subtle hint.

Nerin moved first, shooing the others out. In thirty seconds, the three of us were the only ones left in the wheelhouse and control area.

"You think I'm a risk because I want to regain control of the Prax," Tenandra said to Oracle without preamble.

"Yes," Oracle said frankly. "If I were cut off from the Hall of Memories then forced to travel through it for hours and possibly days on end? I'd be tempted constantly."

"I can control myself," Tenandra replied calmly. "I'm not the Wisp you first met so long ago."

"No, you're not," I agreed. "If you were, I'd sure as shit have not even considered it. Truthfully Tenandra? I trust you. I think you'd be tempted to, shit, but you'd be careful and you'd probably be totally fine."

"Then why?"

"Because it's a risk we don't need," I said, speaking over her. "The advantage of having you there? It's down to your knowledge of the Prax and possibly being able to give covering magic in a fight. You don't know the Prax as it is now, just as it was centuries ago, and you'd need to learn to fight as part of the unit. You could do it, and yes, knowing you, you'd fit in well. But if something has taken the crew and the damn golems here?" I paused, shaking my head.

"We don't know what else they could do. There's no need to risk you and the ship. If you lose contact with us, and we don't reestablish it, inside a full day? You're to leave. Burn full speed to Himnel and report to Augustus. He'll put together a team with Tommy, and they'll come back for us, but HE, Augustus I mean, is NOT to be part of it."

I saw the surprise on her face as I said that.

"It's not that I don't trust Augustus," I said quickly, holding up one hand to stop the question. "It's because I do. If we are taken out, be that killed or captured, he is either to fall back to the Tower and surround himself with the Legion, or if he feels he's best staying in Himnel, then he stays there, but he is to work on recovering the Empire, not me."

"Thomas will not accept that," Tenandra said, watching me.

"I know. That's where you come in. You will collect Thomas and anyone he wants to bring, and you'll come back and kick the living shit out of whoever has taken us captive."

"Or rescue us if we just got lost," Oracle added in a conspiratorial voice.

"Yeah, that, too. I'm sorry Tenandra, but that's the real reason."

"Why not just say that?" she asked.

I paused, not sure how to go on. "Basically, because I'd not put it all together straight away. I was still considering things when you asked to come, and I needed time to make a plan. Honestly, Tenandra? I trust you. Oracle and I trust you, and we trust you to make the hard decision and leave us, as well as Jian and Sehran behind, possibly to die. The Empire has to be the priority, and now that there is a clear chain of succession? Your responsibility is to that, not to me personally." I paused, rubbing at my chin, biting my lip as I searched for the words I needed, cursing that I was always so crap with them.

"It's one thing for you to say that you understand and you'll wait above us, but if you feel Jian or Sehran die? I know you love them; it's been obvious for a long time now how close you're all getting. It's a beautiful thing. Each of you needs the others in a lot of different ways, but I also know that, despite what you might feel and want, I can trust you to carry out those orders."

"And you don't want me down there, in case something happens and I see Jian or Sehran or any of you, die. You think that it might override my loyalty to the Empire," Tenandra finished shrewdly.

"Well, yeah, there's that," I admitted. "If you can see it, as well as feel it, yeah, I'd not blame you for losing control. At least this way, you'll only have the feeling, rather than a fragment of you being there and watching it, maybe convinced you could stop it."

"Will you ever trust me to come with you?" she asked quietly. I reached out, putting one hand on her shoulder and staring into her eyes as I spoke.

"I trust you, Tenandra. Massively so. I trust you to make the hardest decision of all. I also know that, if it was reversed, I couldn't trust myself to be strong enough to not just wait one more minute or land. I trust you, and I need you to do this."

"I understand." Tenandra forced herself to straighten up and smile politely at me, despite being clearly torn by my words. "Do you have any other orders, my Prince?"

"No," I said sadly, knowing that for now at least, she understood but didn't agree. She wanted to be with those she loved.

"Then I'll begin landing. I assume you want us down fast, so they don't have the chance to predict our landing area?" I nodded, and she turned, ostensibly to look away from me and at a misty screen.

"Thank you, Tenandra." I said, before leading Oracle out and onto the deck, where the others were checking gear and trying to look busy.

"Okay, you fuckers!" I called, forcing a bit of cheerfulness into my voice as I moved up to them. "Basically, all that was about was me making sure that, if the shit hits the fan and Tenandra loses contact with us for any reason, after twenty-four hours, she is to leave us behind."

"Reinforcements?" Grizz asked when I paused.

"Yes and no. She'll go for Thomas and his squad, not Augustus and the others. I want the Legion to be consolidating our gains. Let's face it, if we can't beat the shit out of whatever's down there, then the Legion as it is won't, either."

"So, considering that we can feel her through our bond," Jian said, before Sehran rested a hand on his shoulder and cut him off.

"If something happens that means she loses the link with us, and Oracle can't reach her, then they're right. She needs to leave us and go for help."

"Help that's a few days away, at the least," Grizz pointed out, nodding his understanding as well.

"Yeah, so if the nobles are down there, and they've captured the crew, or the SporeMother has gone all out and it's not just a brain-dead one like the others were?" I replied, looking around at them all. "Then we kill them all, we clear the Prax, or we die. Last chance to stay behind."

"And I take it I'm supposed to be pleased about this?" Nerin asked me, having been mainly silent and keeping to herself since we boarded the ship.

"No," I replied. "Truthfully, when I dragged you along, it was to heal the gnomes and help to save as many as we could. Now? If you want to stay on the ship, you can. Hell, it's probably a better idea that you do." I grunted, looking around at the ship then down at the overgrown jungle that hit the remains of the Prax.

I could have used a skilled healer like her, but she was probably right, the Empire needed...

"I'll come with you," Nerin said.

"Huh?" I replied with all the eloquence at my disposal.

"You'll be getting injured, probably all of you, and where else would a healer be?"

"You just said...?"

"Oh, don't get me wrong, boy, I'm far from pleased about the situation! But I'm a healer, and more than that, I'm the Empire's healer; there's no way I could be anywhere else. Besides that, there's going to be a lot of gnomes who need my help, not to mention the crew of that ship."

"Thank you," I said, meaning it.

"And besides, judging from everything I've seen recently, we need to start talking again and more often."

"Fuck."

"Quite," she replied with a faint smile. "Now, we're all ready for this, are you?"

"Yeah, point," I muttered, quickly checking my gear and nodding my thanks to Lydia as she stepped up, grabbing my right pauldron and checking the connections.

It was a fast check, but we tightened a handful of straps and interlocking connections, and as always, having a friend check them made the process faster.

"How long?" I asked Jian, getting a grin as he pointed ahead.

"Here...we...go!" he called out to us, as Tenandra dipped the bow, making it feel like being on a roller coaster as the ground seemed to suddenly rush toward us, with my breakfast suddenly trying to make a reappearance.

"What the hell is this!" Nerin shouted, grabbing onto the railing as everyone started to slide backward, the engines firing to drive us down even faster. "This is your fault!" she snapped.

I couldn't help it, seeing the mixed elation and fear on their faces.

"Oh shit, we're all gonna die!" I shouted, before grabbing onto a section of railing and holding on for dear life as I grinned uncontrollably.

"WHAT?" Nerin screeched.

I tightened my grip, my cheeks hurting I was smiling so much.

Half the squad were on the verge of panic. The others...Jian was clinging on with one hand and holding tight to Sehran with the other. Giint was chewing frantically on something, which meant he was probably going to be fuck all use for a while, but as he'd prioritized that over holding on...

I laughed as he rolled past, picking up speed on his way to the stern of the ship.

Ronin was visibly terrified, Lydia was loving it, and the rest fell somewhere in between, with a sudden splintering of the deck to my right giving away Bane's position as he either used his claws or daggers to dig in and secure himself.

"I love this shit!" I shouted, suddenly feeling it so strong it was insane.

No matter what, the years of waking up in my bed, covered in blood from the dreams and dealing with the pain and all the rest...apart from losing Tommy, the worst part of all of it, including catching Lou and Martin, was knowing that I was stuck back on Earth.

Knowing that, tomorrow, I had to go be nice to people, to smile, when all I wanted was to kick their teeth in.

And now?

Now I was on the far side of reality, about to go dungeon diving, surrounded by monsters, evil creatures of the night, insane and absolutely feral—as well as drugged up—gnomes.

I fucking loved every second of it.

I reached out, unthinkingly, instinctually, and felt her hand slip into my gauntlet. I looked over at Oracle and knew I was the luckiest man alive.

She twisted around, leaning against me, and I wrapped my arm around her, holding her close as she stared up into my eyes.

"Let's go kill everything, loot the shit out of it, then get back on here and screw each other's brains out," she sent to me, her wide, brilliant smile making the edges of her eyes crinkle.

Totally perfect for me.

Tenandra lifted her bow at what felt like the last second, making us all feel ten times heavier as she fired her engines on full power, burning the trees that we passed over but shedding speed like a politician trying to hide their mistresses.

Ten seconds later, we were leaping over the sides, Nerin holding onto me for grim life as I flew us down. The engines already flaring with power and pushing Tenandra, who barely touched the ground at all, back upward as the others leaped free as well.

The only notable exceptions were Ronin, who'd asked Sehran for a lift down and had been grabbed by the scruff of the neck by Lydia…and Giint.

Grizz had grabbed the now unconscious gnome by the scruff of the neck and tossed him over the side. Judging by the sound of breaking branches, he was probably stuck in a tree.

I landed gently, setting Nerin down and getting a nod of thanks as well as a promise that I'd "pay for that." The ship was pushing back up through the trees nearby as stray branches, snapped by the ship's entry, rained down behind it.

The clearing was barely ten meters wider and longer than Tenandra's hull, and as she vanished into the sky, I had to shake my head in wonder.

She was a hell of a pilot or ship or whatever. More and more, I was coming around to the idea of getting the Prax cleared out and repaired, then having her bind herself to it.

I was going to need to have a proper conversation with her soon, her and the other Wisps, and make sure they were happy to continue. As much as Seneschal was the Tower, Heph was the golems, and Tenandra was the ship, I couldn't imagine how they'd unbind themselves if they decided they wanted to leave.

Oracle had been different. She was bound, but in a minor way; she'd been a subsidiary part of a room of the Tower, rather than spread throughout the actual Tower itself, the way that Seneschal was.

I banished the thought–we were on the ground and had no time for that now.

The others had spread out already, weapons drawn, helms locked in place, shields at the ready. Bane and Tang were already gone. Grizz was standing square between me and the entrance to the Prax, Lydia by his side. Ronin waited behind them, the opening notes of "Luck's My Mistress" already filling the air.

Jian had both swords unsheathed, while Sehran stood with one hand clutching her whip and the other bare, ready to begin casting.

Yen stood tall by Arrin, the pair of them having taken the support role to heart now. A solid spread of Magic Missiles popped into golden life, glimmering gently above Arrin's fingertips as Yen waited, picking her spell, likely not wanting to start with her most powerful shot before we'd even laid eyes on an enemy.

I moved up, striding to the front. Grizz and Lydia stepped up to take their places on either side of me as Oracle and Nerin took up their place between Yen and Arrin, Bob dropping the still-unconscious and now retrieved Giint at Nerin's feet.

She started healing him, muttering about teaching him about the proper time and place for recreational substances as I slid my naginata free of the bag and stood ready.

In less than thirty seconds, she had him back on his feet, swaying and confused as he stared at the sky then at his feet.

"Giint not dead?" he mumbled, confused.

"Yeah, we're all dead," Grizz told him in a low voice. "This is the afterlife."

"Oh," Giint agreed, rubbing his head, then shrugged, apparently delighted that, in the next life, he still had his bags. "We fight soon?"

"Yeah, we're going into the cave." Grizz pointed ahead.

"Good."

That was apparently all we were getting, so I grinned to myself, wondering how long it'd take Giint to figure out he wasn't dead.

"Clear ahead," Tang reported, appearing from the depths of the cave and waving us forward.

We started running, those with spells ready letting them dissipate, absorbing the mana back into themselves as we closed in.

"What have we got?" I asked Tang, my voice low and terse.

"Signs of movement, a few days old, though, about thirty came out of this one then headed north, probably for the ship. They didn't come back in this way."

"Let's hope it's not sealed, then," I replied.

Tang fell in at the back of the column, ready to take anyone following us by surprise.

The cavern was old, likely having been used off and on over the centuries. I guessed at it being the remains of a much taller building once, especially judging from the remains of fallen columns long buried by the dirt and exposed only in sections.

The roof, once probably magnificent, peaked, and supported, possibly even covered with the local equivalent of the Sistine Chapel, was now barely three feet above our heads.

Fractal patterns of shattered stone barely held together by the roots of trees now laid crumbling on all sides. The piled dirt, mixed with centuries of rust and animal remains, filled the rest.

The path was narrow, muddy earth, freshly wet by the recent rains, splashed underfoot as we hurried along, the path growing narrow enough that we were reduced to single-file before opening out as it sloped downwards.

A shattered staircase, ancient marble showing through here and there with banisters that looked like they belonged in a fancy museum, appeared ahead. We took it, descending into the lower floors. The jingle and clink of our armor and weapons rang out, but the dirt on all sides meant that the sound didn't travel far.

The stairway led down almost thirty feet, a faint light filtering down from a crack high overhead to illuminate a small pool, plants and stunted trees surrounding it even as something dived in, a faint splash and ripples the only evidence of its passing.

"Which way?" I asked quietly as we reached the bottom. Tang slid up next to me to examine the paths before pointing out the second of three ahead.

"That one," he said. "The majority of footprints come from the right, but Bane went that way."

"We follow Bane, then," I confirmed, Tang standing aside and letting Yen move up to take her station next to me.

"I might not live and breathe stealth like those mad buggers, but I'll be able to keep you on track," she promised, making me smile as she took the lead.

I fell in behind her, slowing from the speed I'd been leading us at and taking the subtle hint from her in the way she crouched and moved as silently as possible.

Ten minutes passed in virtual silence, only broken by the occasional clink or clatter or Giint complaining that he didn't think the afterlife was supposed to be like this and that it made him think of home.

He was shushed each time, subsiding into grumbles, but it kept the mood a lot lighter than it could have been until Bane finally reappeared.

"How bad?" I asked him when he returned, jogging out of a side passage ahead.

"Bad," he reported. "Very bad."

"How…"

He shook his head. "Bad enough that you need to consider falling back and leaving. The nobles are here. They've got control of the gnomes and what must be the Imperial golems."

"Fuck!" I snarled. "Ours or the dead ones from here?"

"I think ours, and a handful of much older ones, considering they're covered in dirt and debris. There's a collection of lines that connect our people to the golems, some kind of wire."

"Our people?" I interrupted with a growl.

"It looks like they've been captured and put to work, used as mana barrys."

"Barrys?"

"You know, the storage devices, the mana barrys you were talking about."

"Fucks sake, batteries!" I corrected him, unable to help my grin then wincing as I realized what he meant. "They're using our people as mana batteries to bring the golems to life, building an army."

"Exactly."

"How many and how many golems?"

"I counted twelve golems, but there may be more out of sight or in the other rooms, but the people?"

"Yeah?"

"There's easily the entire crew and twenty of the gnomes chained up, being drained. Another ten gnomes were working on a single golem, doing something with it."

"Shit, now there's a concern with those crazy fuckers," I grumbled, a general rise of agreement sounding around me.

"Then there's the enemy," Bane said. "I counted twenty, nowhere near the numbers we've faced before, but all at least level fifteen and higher. They've clearly been training their whole lives for this."

"Well, so have we," I replied. "Talk to me about layout; give me options."

"This passage leads to a collapsed section. At the bottom of the slope is a domed building, probably part of the original upper decks, considering the way it's laid out. It's tilted to one side, and there's a lot of devastation around it, but it's more or less intact. Three openings lead inside, that I could sense, anyway, only one uncovered.

"The room it's in is a large cavern, several floors having fallen into each other, giving a lot of places to hide, but..."

"But?"

"But they know that," he said firmly. "I was careful with my Worldsense, and I picked up seven hidden around the room, watching over it. They're hidden well, and they're armed."

"What with?"

"Something that appears like a spear...but the way they hold it? It makes no sense."

"It'll be ranged." I muttered, wondering if they'd managed to get spearguns through. If so, not only would that fucking suck for us attacking them, but if we could capture them? That'd be a game-changer. "Okay, think you can reach any of them undetected?"

"Probably one, maybe two, but I couldn't get to all of them before being spotted." Bane squatted down and drew a rough outline in the dirt of the floor. "They're set out in a rough circle around the building."

"Wish we had Tenandra to tell us what it was," Jian muttered to Sehran.

"It'd change nothing," I disagreed. "What the room was seven hundred years ago is less important than what it is now. All we know is that it holds our people and..."

"No," Bane interrupted.

"What?"

"The building isn't holding them. The golems are standing guard on either side of the entrance. Others are clearing the debris away, but our people are out the front, they're not inside."

"Right," I muttered, looking at the rough sketch and rubbing my chin in thought. "If Tang went with you, could you both take the ones on overwatch?"

"If we both went in different directions, maybe, but I doubt it," Bane said. "There's too many, and too great a distance to reach them, also..." He marked points around the outer wall of his drawing. "This is where they are."

"That's not making a great deal of sense," Yen interrupted. "If they're laid out like that, there's three close by each other here and a big gap there." She gestured to the gaps in the markings.

"Exactly." He nodded. "I think there's more than I could sense."

"Okay, give me options, people."

"We could go back up, loop around, and see if we can find a way behind them?" Ronin suggested.

"Might be a waste of time but is there another path?" I asked Bane, figuring that he might know.

"There's at least one other. Farther back at the crossing behind us, there's a path that leads straight to them, and there's two openings that lead off away from the cavern, but they could take hours or days to get there or even be dead ends. Also, there must be at least one other, as the crew of the ship weren't taken down the route we came."

"Fuck, good point." I growled, pulling my helm off and scratching at my beard as I thought. "That route goes straight there, you say?" I jerked my thumb over my shoulder.

"It does, but it's a single corridor that leads up to the entrance across some damaged sections. I'd recommend NOT trusting the ground; there's two dead at the bottom of a collapsed section."

"An' marching up to the front door would be stupid, anyway." Lydia added.

"Oh definitely," I agreed, starting to smile. "Say, what kinda gear are they wearing?"

"Oh fuck," Oracle whispered seeing my smile. "He's got a plan."

"I've got a plan," I agreed. "So, Bane, how high is the cavern, and that gear?"

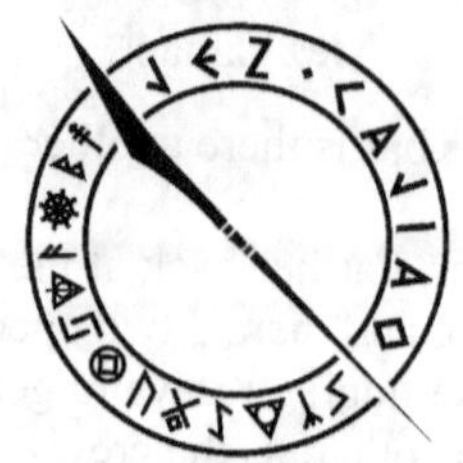

CHAPTER TWENTY-EIGHT

"**Y**ou sure about this, boss?" Grizz whispered, bracing himself on my arm as I struggled to maintain my flight, Jian and Bob having already passed across the crumbling section.

"Just watch your feet," I hissed back, trying to keep myself steady as he took another step, then launched himself off, jumping to land on the more solid section ahead.

I flew across, cutting my ability and dropping onto the floor with a groan of relief. "Tell me we're clear."

"All clear, boss," Jian's voice came back. "And no movement on their side. They think this path is fucked."

"I hoped that was the case," I whispered, sitting up and hitting myself with a heal, banishing the little drop in health I'd suffered for the flight.

Bob had been by far the worst to get across, moving slowly and steadily, as well as weighing a shitload, but he was necessary for the plan.

"Plan" was probably being generous though, even I had to admit.

"How long 'til the others are in place?" Grizz asked.

I frowned, reaching out to Oracle, even as Jian did the same to Sehran.

"My love?" I asked, getting a quick response.

"I'm with Lydia and Yen; we're ready to move when Sehran and the others are in place."

"Can you see them?"

"No, but that's a good thing."

"Yeah, but this is Arrin we're talking about."

"I think they made him wait behind until they're ready...wait, yes, I see him!"

Oracle shared a vision of the cavern from above. I blinked, adjusting my mental angle to make sure it all worked.

It was roughly circular, with a big V of collapsed wall and upper sections at the back, leading up to the building we suspected the noble was hiding in. On either side of the entrance to the building were two golems, war variants, of course, and a half dozen servitors wandering around removing sections of fallen wall and replacing them with repaired parts.

One entire section of the wall already looked like it'd be able to shrug off a bloody Challenger tank, and I had to assume they were working around the outside to repair it all.

In the middle of the room, directly before the entrance to the domed building—which was sunken into the floor and shattered, yet looked like it'd been important once—were the prisoners.

Dozens of them, both gnomes and the crew of the airship were laid there, ropes and chains securing them. The lines that led from them were, as Bane had described, like wire. But to Oracle's vision, creature of mana as she was, they blazed like a sun of silver.

Mana was being dragged from the unwilling victims and fed into the bodies of three war golems, lying cold and dead nearby.

She focused on them, and I felt the buildup of mana that was slowly recovering the stone creations to life, before she looked back to the people. The gnomes were in the worst state, covered in blood, having clearly already been beaten into submission before they were chained up. The crew were all unconscious, suffering from mana deprivation.

All around the prisoners and the slumbering golems were piles of equipment, some still in wooden packing and transport crates, others unboxed and stacked. Here and there, they were heavily reinforced lead-lined cases covered in runes. They might have been to transport something valuable or guns. I didn't know which, but I didn't like it one bit.

Most of it was neat, but here and there were random piles of cans and more, dumped. I froze, tracking back and focused in, the mixture of Oracle's vision and my own Perception permitting me a zoom that worked wonders as I read the labels on several of the empty bottles, one of which had been tossed aside and left to drain into the dirt.

Rum.

Damn good bottles of rum, and one had been dumped, half-drank, and left to run out and be wasted. Well, I was always going to kill these fuckers, but now? Now it was clear that not only were they assholes, but they had no goddamned taste!

The floor–well, the ground I supposed was more accurate, as some dickbags liked to argue over that terminology, but either way I didn't care–The *floor* was a mixture of dirt, mud, and general filth that partially covered the shattered stone. It left some sections clear while others looked like a marsh or forest floor.

I pulled back my focus, seeing the whole room from Oracle's point of view as she slowly climbed, using her abilities to make herself as invisible as possible, shifting her skin and clothing to match the walls around her as she slowly flew upward.

Lydia and Yen crouched hidden below her, and off to the right-hand side…

Yeah, there was Arrin.

Fuck, that guy needed to spend some time on stealth training.

He was creeping along, hurrying from shadow to shadow, pausing then rushing again.

Fast movements draw the eye, that was one of the simplest things you learned in stealth training, any kind of fast movement, hell, spiders, evolutionarily designed to fucking hide in plain sight?

When they ran across your living room carpet in jerky stop-start bursts, everyone went onto full on murder-mode. If they just strolled calmly across the floor? Set themselves up in the corner? Stayed the hell out of the way? I'd be all "evenin', Keith, good day mate?" Instead of "kill it with fucking fire!"

But there was Arrin, practically wearing a flashing neon sign and screaming he was here to fix the fridge or play hide the sausage with the noble's wife while he was at work.

I cut the connection with a burst of mental swearing that Oracle echoed.

"Okay, Arrin is going to be seen in literally half a second, if we don't distract them. We need to move, now," I growled. The others set off running without any further explanation.

I was at the back of the group, suddenly racing to catch up, and Grizz dashed into the lead, Jian barely ahead of me as we struggled to leap over collapsed sections of stone and metal, Bob falling back as we'd planned.

"Help!" Grizz shouted, the sound echoing off the tight confines, closely followed by Jian.

"They've killed the rest of the squad!"

"Help!" I shouted as well, dipping a hand into my pocket and making damn sure I had the bloodstone to hand, as well as the standard spare legion sword Grizz had given me. My own naginata was stashed away, it being too distinctive a weapon.

Bob deliberately let us draw ahead a bit, and I focused, reaching out to him.
"Are you okay?"
"I am functional."
"That's not what I meant, are you...oh fuck it, look we'll talk later, okay?"
"Yes."

I cut the connection, knowing damn well that Bob had something he needed to talk about or communicate or whatever. I'd been getting the sense for the last few hours that there was something going on there, but I'd just not had the time and kept getting distracted. This time, after this fight, we'd speak, I vowed to myself.

We took the next right, then a left, Grizz bellowing again as I slapped my sword hard against a metal stanchion, making it ring out, the steel-on-steel hanging in the air even over the thunder of feet.

"You're nearly there. They can hear you; they're forming up," Oracle sent.

I grinned self-consciously; this was either going to be awesome, or a seriously short fight.

I took the final corner, the flicker of firelight reflecting off the wall ahead, then my DarkVision was washed out in a flare of bright light, and the cavern was before us.

"Help!" Grizz shouted, waving behind us. "They're coming!"

He ran to one, as if expecting to be welcomed with open arms, before turning and digging his feet in, sending a great spray of filthy water flying as he turned his back on them and faced back the way we came.

Jian and I raced in behind him, doing the same, weapons drawn and facing the dark corridor as Bob came into sight.

"Get ready!" Grizz barked at them. "You two! Get that side, there's hundreds of them!" he roared at a confused pair to his right, even as I gestured to the men on my left.

"You! Grab those shields, form a wall, or we're all dead!" I ordered, injecting as much right of command into my voice as I could.

I'd been trying to remember the Voice of Command that Amon had used with the Dark Hunter-werewolf cross in the throne room when we captured Himnel. I used my best attempt at that that, combined with my utter belief that they WOULD obey.

There was a split second's hesitation, then Bob emerged more fully from the darkness, his eyes glowing and the bones that he was constructed from becoming clear.

"Fuckin' 'ell!" one of the men shouted in a terrified cockney accent. I felt my stomach, frozen with fear that this wasn't going to work, suddenly lighten as they grabbed shields and ran to stand alongside us.

"Take my slot!" I barked at the cockney. "I'll get the golems!"

"They don't listen to nobody!" he shouted after me. But as I moved, he stepped into the space, glancing at Jian nervously, until Grizz barked orders at them, forming a shallow box formation.

"Snipers!" I barked, facing up at the cavern over me as I strode up to the golems. "Get ready!"

I looked away from them as if confident they'd obey, even as the golems stirred to life, their eyes glowing as they fixated on me.

They were both old school designs, ornate but working creations, massive maces that could destroy an armored car lifting, even as shields were moved into place.

"Halt." They both barked as one, clearly about to attack if I didn't obey.

"By the right of my bloodstone, I order you to obey me and only me. All those in authority over you previously are removed. I am Jax Amon, Scion and Prince of the Empire." I extended my left hand and showed them the gleaming bloodstone.

The pair of them froze, standing stock still as they assessed the bloodstone, before suddenly moving again, maces lifting to chest height, shields held steady.

Their maces tapping lightly against the shield, they saluted then spoke as one.

"The right of Imperial Authority is confirmed. Awaiting orders."

"I claim this structure for the Empire. Kill the trespassers," I ordered.

"'Ere, what'd 'e just say?" Cockney asked, confused, before Grizz turned and punched him in the face, sending him reeling. Jian spun as well, blades spearing out to take the men next in line. Bob raced forward, and screams rose from higher up in the cavern, as Bane and Tang attacked.

Yen and Arrin stood in their respective places, hands lighting with spells, even as Lydia launched into the air, her winged magnificence drawing the eye of any Earthborn with shock.

"Throw down yer weapons!" she roared, her wings beating steadily and holding her there where everyone could see her.

There was a long moment of silence while Bane and Tang held their targets prisoner, blades to their throats. Arrin held hands aloft with glowing darts pulsing and ready, while Yen filled the air above her with a huge spear that rippled with fire.

Grizz faced off against five men and women, weapons held ready, his massive Legion Knight sword and shield heavier than most men could even lift.

He rolled his wrist, sending the massive blade whooshing through a figure eight before them, the razor-sharp metal practically tearing a path through reality as it went.

Jian faced four on his side, blades held at the ready, red blood dripping from them to fall onto the unmoving pair he'd just killed with a single blow each.

Bob had hefted the massive ice dragon's thighbone that I'd altered into a hammer and was clearly ready to make pâté from his targets when the golems burst into action.

They ran at full tilt into the two groups, maces swinging and shields battering, and the twenty or so enemy soldiers spread out across the cavern were suddenly about to be cut down, both in number and literally.

One of the soldiers lifted his shield to take the blow from the mace and made what I expected to be the last and most fatal of all his mistakes in life.

I was wrong.

The golem's mace came down like the hammer of the Gods, whistling through the air…then was hurled backwards with a detonation that tore the mace apart, destroying the golem's arm in the process.

The soldier that had held the shield was sent flying as well, screaming in pain, the shield shattered, along with his arm, but the golem?

It was reeling, clearly off-balance, and a new voice boomed from the interior of the structure the golems had been guarding.

"Up, you maggots! They're stone and dumb as shit! Kill them all!"

At the sound of that voice, I spun around, having turned to face the fight. I swore as I saw the man striding out of the entrance, tossing what appeared to be a spent RPG launcher aside.

He was tall, physically fit, and, on a side note, almost offensively handsome. He was the kind of guy who could never be cast in any film, unless it were a porno, as a supporting character, and I hated him instantly.

He was dressed, not unlike the others, in seemingly updated versions of our armor. The main chest, upper shoulders and thighs, as well as calves and forearms were clad in seemingly solid steel.

The rest, however, was a composite mesh of rippling scales that made me think of graphite or that insanely expensive body armor they could never get right on Earth.

Mind you, here, they'd not be facing many bullets, if any at all, so it probably was that stuff.

He was armed with a hammer in his left hand that he tugged free of a belt loop and a shield in his right. He leapt forward, seemingly expecting to sweep me aside.

"Golems!" I barked as I took a quick step back, slapping his swing aside with my sword and lashing it back across his shield in a shower of sparks. "Kill those soldiers."

I blocked his second swing, seeing the way he suddenly crouched behind his shield, and I grinned, knowing what was coming.

I tossed my sword in the air, spinning between us, the light of fires reflecting off the blade with each revolution. "Catch!" I bellowed, my left hand dipping into my bag, dropping the bloodstone in and grabbing my naginata, yanking it free.

He ignored the blade, shouting Bull-Rush and blurring across the short distance between us, aiming to smash me from my feet with the shield.

I was ready, though. Instincts hard-bought through long hours of battles–be that practices against Flux and the others or in true life and death combat–rose to save me. I jumped, planting both feet on the shield and riding it back, triggering Soaring Majesty.

The result was me practically flying backward, pushed by his ability, but taking no more than a handful of points of damage.

Had I not seen it coming, though? I'd have had my bell rung, at the very least.

I flipped over, landing, cutting the ability and grinning as I finished drawing the naginata, taking it in both hands as I stalked him.

His cold stare regarded me as more of an opponent than he had at first as he alternated between watching me and attacking with short, probing blows.

I held my weapon in both hands, keeping the blade moving constantly, seeing the way he watched me, not it.

"So…come here often?" I asked, then leaped forward, the blade stabbing down low, driving at his ankle, only to have him shift his feet, backing up and dipping his shield, trying to trap my weapon between it and the ground.

"More than I'd like!" he snarled, swinging his hammer at me and twisting it! I'd pulled back, thankfully, so he missed, but he'd tried to hook the head behind my shaft, the cunning bastard.

He took the chance to rush me again, this time without an ability, hammer blurring as he went for me over and over. His hammer swung with a roar, and I sidestepped, not needing the dead arms I'd get trying to stop it, not when I could just dodge.

I did that twice, then the third time…

"Watch out," Oracle sent from her position overhead. *"He's driving you toward a central point."*

"Or the snipers, I'd bet." I grinned despite myself, knowing that Bane and Tang would soon have them slaughtered.

I triggered Mana-Overdrive and slapped his next strike aside, wrapping my blade behind the head of his hammer and shoving as hard as I could, my altered state enabling me to drive it toward the ground at a hell of a speed.

His eyes widened in realization at the last second. Then I was twisting around, turning my back to him as I built momentum. The end of the naginata howled through the air, aimed right for the side of his head.

He abandoned the hammer, diving sideways, hitting the ground with a shoulder and rolling with a grunt to come to his feet, facing me.

"Fire!" he roared, pointing at me, and from high overhead, three flashes of light showed the locations of snipers Bane and Tang hadn't reached yet. "Ogun! Use the artifact!"

I spun, diving to my left and rolling in turn shoving my naginata back into my bag as I did. I bounded to my feet and was briefly surprised that there'd been no sounds of gunshots.

Then the fucking RPGs landed.

I was thrown through the air in an explosion of epic magnitude, the structure around creaking wildly as the floor gave way, and I spun into a wall head-first, my helm keeping my brains inside, but definitely scrambled.

Walls crumbled, the superstructure around us creaking then roaring as sections that had barely survived centuries of rust and neglect, not to mention the original impact, tore free.

Oracle was screaming, Lydia barking orders, Grizz roaring in fury. Cries rose, both of terror and pain, and I fell, an entire section of wall shifting over to come down atop me.

I smashed into the floor, the back of my head banging off it this time, before a mass of steel and stone fell on me. I curled up into as tight a ball as I could, the clatter and boom or falling structure combining with the impacts to rob me of all sense.

CHAPTER TWENTY-NINE

I laid there, blinking, my ears ringing, feeling my pulse in my head with every beat of my heart and the damn slow and steady leaking of blood from my nose running over my cheek and to the back of my helm.

"Fuck's sake," I growled, lifting a hand to my face, only to feel the pain of a broken wrist as it clanged against a section of the structure.

I took a long breath, then exhaled and forced myself to look around.

I was buried, not heavily, but enough that I couldn't see a way out. The sections that had fallen atop me were fairly large and solid, and I was pinned under them, trapped in a dark corner. I'd not be for long though, so that was all right, I just had to…

Oracle.

I reached out to her, wondering why she'd not come to me already, why she'd not been going mad over yet another of my brilliant plans going utterly tits-up, and…and nothing.

Cold dread filled me as I laid there, feeling nothing. Nothing at all! I tried to pull up my screen, looking for the tell-tale symbols of the others, searching for information on them all…and NOTHING!

My heart raced as my breathing sped up massively. I bit down on the need to physically call out, to scream Oracle's name.

"No," I whispered. No, this wasn't possible, I couldn't have lost my abilities, magic…I started casting, and I felt…. something.

There was definitely something there, but it was distant, like a massive wall stood between me and my abilities. I focused and dug deep and achieved absolutely nothing beyond the beginning of a migraine.

"Okay, Jax, just think, just think," I mumbled. "You're under the level that they were on, and it's all fucking black."

I'd not realized it, not with everything else going on, but the light was so dim I could barely see, and it was coming from somewhere below me.

My DarkVision should have kicked in automatically, but it didn't.

I swallowed hard. Just because I'd lost my abilities, that didn't mean the others weren't okay.

Hell, Grizz was a man-mountain of muscle. Even if his abilities were suppressed somehow, he could still kick their asses!

I forced myself not to think about Oracle, knowing that she'd been flying near the ceiling of the cavern.

All I could do right now was get myself out of here. I could get myself out and get up there, then I'd find Oracle and the others. They'd fix whatever was wrong with me, and it'd all be all right again.

I heard muffled and distant sounds, shouts it sounded like, but they were echoing down to where I was, and none of them were clear enough to tell anything from.

I forced my mind away from that and put my arms under the slab that was holding my lower legs in place, twisting my legs as much as I could to get them braced as well.

My ankle grated in my boot. Something had gotten in there, into the gap between my skin and the metal, a stone or something. I needed to rotate my ankle to brace my foot, and it was stopping me.

I left it, shifting my arms and knee and pushing against the slab.

It held its place, seemingly unconcerned by my attempts. I hissed in pain, my broken wrist flaring with agony as I jammed that arm in and heaved, feeling a slight shift.

It wasn't a good one.

Somewhere, I'd shifted something that was holding it all up, and it hadn't been just resting on me, as I'd thought.

The sudden increase in massive pressure made me gasp as the "I can do this, might take a few attempts, but I can do this" mentality changed.

This was a case of "escape now, or I'm fucked." My arms were at a shitty angle to use my strength, but they were positioned the best I was going to get.

I pushed, heaving until spots appeared before my eyes. and I felt like I was going to break my back or shit myself, and it still wasn't enough!

I could feel it. I was going to lose this one. The solid mass of metal and stone was going to pin me and…

"Fuuuuuuuck!" I ground out, knowing what I had to do.

I had no time to work myself up to it, nor come up with a better plan, so I just did it.

The space that my left leg was in, and the way the stone was somehow trapped inside my goddamn boot against my lower ankle, meant that, if I wanted to use my legs in this fight, I had only one choice.

I twisted and rammed my knee against the underside of the slab, heaving with all my might, using the pain of breaking my own fucking ankle to drive myself harder.

It seemed to hesitate for a second as the slabs tried to fight back, but this was my only chance, and I damn well knew it.

My right leg was still trapped, and I needed that as well, and I was damn well getting out of here, if it was the last thing I did!

I imagined the nobles laughing, finding me trapped here. I imagined what they'd do to Oracle, to the others. I forced myself to think of Oracle, lying broken and bloody somewhere far above me. Then I screamed as I fought against whatever blockage it was, hammering and beating my mind against the scant hair-thick barrier that was keeping me from my mana.

I forced my mind against it, feeling something shifting infinitesimally, then realizing it wasn't just in my mind! I might not have my mana, but I damn well had my massive fucking muscles!

The slab shifted, rising, and other rocks slid off it as it rose.

With each rock that fell, with each clatter and slide of sheets of metal and every goddamn grain of dirt that fell free, the weight lessened, and it rose that fraction of a bit easier.

I heaved it upward with a roar of triumph, rolling to the right as soon as my right leg was free. The slab that had been pinning me fell back, smashing into the gap I'd filled with a boom that echoed off the walls.

I collapsed backward, lying there in the dim light, panting as I tried to get myself under control before forcing myself to look down at my ankle.

"Yup…that's fucked." I groaned, looking away from the sideways-facing foot and the dripping blood that was running free of the bottom of my leg armor.

Worst of all, I could feel my enhanced healing starting up.

Normally, that'd be a great thing, especially knowing that, while nothing else might be working, if that was, then there had to be a reason.

The problem was that the healing wasn't magical, not in the way that my spells were. The enhanced healing wouldn't make sure the bone was in its right place or that the veins were all correct, that the nerves were right, none of it.

It was just like my normal human ability from childhood, hell, it was the same as everyone else's, just much, *much* faster.

If I wanted to walk on that damn foot anytime soon, I needed to set it. I needed to fix my goddamn ankle, and the only way I could do that was…

"Fuck this shit!" I gasped, suddenly remembering that I had healing potions! I sighed, reaching into my bag and…

And feeling something I never had before.

The bottom of the bag.

I froze, then looked down in panic, seeing that it was indeed the right one, my Bag of Spatial Folding, not just an accidental normal bag I'd picked up somewhere.

I started panicking then, shoving at the bottom of the bag until my mind screamed a warning at me. If, and I was praying that it was an if, this was just a special room or something that stopped all magic, then me ripping the bottom out of the bag in my panic would mean that I was fucked when I got outside of the room as well.

I had to hold it together, keep my shit under control, and it'd all be all right.

I made myself stop, slowly removing my hand, and looking down at my bags.

I checked each of them, finding them as empty as the first. Whatever magic created the alternative dimensions of the bags was not functioning.

I forced myself to stop again, releasing the bags and sitting upright. Reaching down, popping the connections on my left leg, I freed the lower leg armor and the boot, then slid them off with a muted cry of agony.

The blood I'd felt running was from a bone that had poked through the surface, and the foot…

It wasn't supposed to be that color. I knew that much.

I had to hope my healing would fix it, because I'd gotten out of the habit of carrying anything in my pockets since I'd gotten used to the bags. That meant I had literally fuck all that was going to be of any use to me right now.

I took a deep breath and pressed on the bone that was jutting out, letting loose an involuntary whimper as I pushed it back inside, gritting my teeth against the little wiggle in my flesh as it tried to follow the original path.

I felt it grate against something else.

Another fragment of bone.

That wasn't good.

I felt that fragment move, grating against other bits, and I fought down my bile. It was one thing to go through this knowing that, in a minute it'd all be healed, but going through it and not knowing?

Fuck. I was practically back to a mere human and living on Earth again, judging by the uncertainty I felt.

I forced that down along with all the rest and gripped that ankle with my half-useless left hand. It was more of a drunken fumble than a grip, and not the way that I liked it, but that was life.

I held it as tight as I could bear with that hand, and I poked and prodded the sections of bone back into place as best I could, pausing when I had them about as good as I could for now.

Then I grabbed my foot with my right hand, and I twisted it around to face in the right direction.

That time, my control wasn't enough.

I threw back my head and roared out my pain, my anger, and everything between, hearing it echo off the walls, reaching upward and into the darkness on all sides.

When it was done, and I couldn't have said another word if my life depended on it, I let my head sag, and I sat there, holding my goddamned foot and ankle.

It seemed like forever as I sat there, breath hissing between clenched teeth as I probed and pushed the fragments of bone into place, but in reality, it was only a few minutes. By the end of it, I could feel strength returning to my left hand.

I let go of the ankle, lifting that hand and trying to rotate the wrist, wincing in pain but finding it was better than it had been, and by a lot.

I gave myself five minutes. I hated it.

Five minutes could be a lifetime. Hell, it could be the difference between all of my team living and them all being dead, but that wasn't something I couldn't deal with right now.

I had a broken ankle, a broken wrist, and probably more. I had no weapons, no healing potions, nothing, I…

I was being stupid.

I took a deep breath, in and out, and forced myself to look at myself. I wasn't doing well.

I'd taken forever to remember about the potions, when it should have been the first thing I did. Now it was weapons. Yes, my naginata was stuck wherever the fuck it was between realities that functioned as the realm of storage devices, but I had my swords on my back, a dagger on either hip, and my goddamn razor wire.

I *had* weapons.

That meant that I wasn't thinking right.

I made myself work logically through things. I wasn't thinking clearly. That could be from the impacts, in which case it'd get better once I was out of here.

It could be from a spell or something. Hell, I remembered the guy I'd been fighting shouting something about an artifact, so maybe that was involved?

It could be from a poison or a gas that I couldn't sense. It could just be from the magic pixies who were pissed that I'd just landed on their houses and they were no longer going to deliver the internet to people back home down the magic pipes, for all I knew.

I'd never really understood what the internet was, really, not how it worked, so maybe it was that...

And I'd gone off on a tangent.

I shook my head and waited as the world slowly resolved again, seemingly on a two-second delay, before nodding. Something was definitely wrong, and...

I froze.

I'd reached up, unthinking to rub at a feeling of discomfort, high on the right side of my head. It was a bit stupid, really, considering I was rubbing at the outside of my helm, but I'd felt something.

I let my fingers, encased in the gauntlets, gently prod, and I gritted my teeth. There was a dent in the helm.

I tugged it up and off, letting out a long breath as pain I'd not noticed I was ignoring was suddenly lessened.

It was difficult to see in the darkness, but there was definitely a dent in the top of the helm. I winced at the thought of whatever had done that, and what it would have been done to my head if I'd not been wearing it.

I rolled my wrist again, evaluating it, and nodded to myself.

It was definitely better. It wasn't good, fuck no, not by any sense of the word, but it wasn't as fucked as it had been, and that meant that my ankle would be the same.

I checked around, finding the finger of stone that had ended up in the bottom of my leg armor. Taking what I really hoped was the most shitty of the bags I had, an old one that was empty and winced as I replaced the stone gently, hoping that it wouldn't do anything weird as I tore the mouth of the bag open.

It ripped with a jerk, a sudden tingling flaring up my arms then vanishing, making me sigh in relief. I used it quickly, wrapping the material around my ankle and using it as a makeshift bandage and with the finger of stone as a splint.

That done, and when I stopped whispering swear words, I pulled my armor back on, followed by my boot, tasting blood in my mouth as I bit down hard on my cheek at the pain.

Less than a minute later, I was dragging myself to my feet and crossing to the wall, staring up into the shadowy recesses. It was a hell of a job, but as the minutes passed, and I slowly limped around the small room I found myself in, I started to really curse.

The room was a triangle, roughly. There was a name for it, I knew, but I didn't remember, and I cared even less. It had one long side and two shorter ones, and the fallen stone and metal had sealed it like a goddamn tomb.

The higher areas, even if I could get to them, were pretty solid, with the walls intact. But the roof itself had been smashed through and was mainly filled by rubble. Rubble that, as I looked at it, seemed to shift ominously. While the majority of the mass overhead was solid, the section that was directly over the hole was most definitely *not*.

There was no door anywhere that I could find, which meant it was a sealed room with a magic door, I guessed, or the door was buried under the multiple tons of fallen debris.

That, in turn, meant that either I was royally fucked, or…I turned back to the faint light that was shining up, and I moved back to it.

The light was coming from a crack in the floor, gleaming upward, and was blue-white in color, making me think of the runes on the mana engines on the ships. I pressed my eye to the crack, seeing something on the other side, and I gasped in shock.

Below, far enough that I knew it was going to royally suck getting down there, was another floor. And, while this one was as shattered as the rest, it was also inhabited.

Light reflected off the water, a lot of goddamn water, and movement. I could barely make that out; the crack was narrow enough that I had only a tiny sliver of sight of the floor below, but still.

I couldn't get out by going *up*, so maybe it was time to go down?

I pushed myself back up, looking around the room and making sure of everything as I saw it. There were sections of almost clear space and others that were entirely buried. Where I'd lain, against the far wall, only a small amount of the debris had reached it.

The other end of the room, though, had a massive girder driven deep into the floor with a load of stone and structural crap gathered around it. The crack I'd been looking through was one of several that radiated out from the impact of that girder. While the section it'd punched into might be solid enough to hold it, the surrounding area might only need a little bit of pressure to set it off.

That gave me another option.

Sure, I could set off a landslide of debris, the mass that was even now precariously held overhead, but after that? If I could brace myself somewhere out of the way, then I'd have a choice! I could climb down, I hoped, or I might be able to climb up, once the rubble had gone!

Also, and I was seriously hoping for this one, the Prax had to have facilities to hold prisoners originally. Logically, to hold magical beings, you needed magical prisons.

Maybe the problem wasn't me. Maybe I'd just found one of the prisons? Thomas had mentioned being held in a magical dampening field in Himnel prison; he'd have kicked their asses and slaughtered his way free otherwise.

Hell, if there weren't such places, then mages would be killed at the first offense, because there'd be no way to restrain them otherwise.

I nodded to myself. That was it. This was some kind of mage prison, and when I got out of here, I'd be fine again.

Hell, maybe if I fell, I'd be able to get Soaring Majesty working again. As soon as I made it out of here.

Fuck it, I was going to have to find out.

The room was piled high with debris, but there was a small, and I mean *small*, gap directly underneath and behind the girder, where the wall of the room formed a little area I tentatively pegged as my safe zone.

I hurried around the room, checking everything to make sure, then moved into the narrow gap that I was seriously hoping would be safe. Bracing myself, digging my feet in, and pushing with all my might, I stifled a scream as my broken ankle made its presence known.

The girder held for a long minute, then just as spots were exploding across my vision, I felt the smallest shift. It was tiny where I was, but to the hundreds of tons resting atop the girder, it was anything but minor.

The creaking and sudden cascade of dust was all the warning I was going to get, and I threw myself behind the girder, curling myself up in as small a space as I could manage.

I laid there, a handful of pebbles clattering down around me, and I wondered if that was it. Was I going to have to try again, or come up with a new plan?

Then the first large section shifted.

I stared up, unable to look away as it moved with glacial slowness, sliding forward, seeming about to stop at any second, until the mass reached tipping point and tilted forward. It was as if someone had hit fast-forward, as suddenly everything was in motion, hundreds of tons of stone and metal roaring downward, impacting the ground on the other side of the girder, inexorably guided away from me as I stared in amazement that I'd moved all that.

Then a section of steel landed, edge-first, on the crack, and a bright, blazing light shone upward from the far side of the room, before being snuffed out by the mass that hit it next.

I rolled back into a ball, wincing as more and more debris clattered down, bouncing off and hitting me.

"Fucking idiot! Helms help!" I snarled, unwilling to uncurl from my ball to get my damaged helm, but knowing I should damn well be wearing it right now!

Ten seconds more of rattling booms and crashes rang out before a hesitant silence returned. I slowly raised my head, coughing on all the dust in the air as I grabbed the helm and dragged it close, forcing it back on and wincing in pain as the healing section of my head flared with pain from the damn dent.

I took it back off, attaching it to a loop on my belt, then looked around.

The room was brighter than it had been, as now, from somewhere far overhead, firelight shone down. From below, the eerie blue glow reached up.

Firelight!

"Jenae?" I whispered hopefully, feeling a horrible dip in my stomach when nothing happened. "It's okay, she just can't hear me without magic...I've got this..." I muttered to myself.

I uncurled myself, moving slowly but dragging myself around a huge block that sat three inches from my head. I refused to consider what would have happened if that had landed ever so slightly farther over.

It was a little higher than I was tall, but squared off with carvings on one side. I grabbed a corner, using the carvings as footholds, climbing up slowly, freezing as the first creaks rang out, then moving faster.

Distant sounds whispered from far overhead. I stood carefully, then grabbed onto the girder, feeling rough carved patches that were good grips, and started to climb. Pulling myself around the girder to look upward, I got a good look at the room I'd fallen from for the first time.

I winced as the strangeness of the angles in the room I was leaving suddenly made sense.

This section of the city wasn't as well-connected as the rest was, the overall city itself having been like a burger in shape, with levels of meat and cheese, but the lower levels?

When the city had crashed, landing atop the seamount, some of it had stayed neatly stacked, sagged a little, or even been lifted, depending on the rocks below.

Other sections of the city, however, had come down where there was nothing below for some distance, peeling free and falling sideways. I was climbing as much along as up, when comparing my position to the original layout.

Whatever this section had been designed for originally was beyond me, but it had a fuckload of individual rooms and crossing corridors, most of which were long reduced to slag.

Some sections were flooded, running water, well, fucking *cascading* water actually could be heard nearby, it sounded like a goddamn waterfall in fact.

I just had to hope that the water was going somewhere else and wasn't about to pour over the edge above and drown me.

I *really* wasn't dressed for swimming.

I dragged myself up the girder, hand over hand, passing out of the room I was in, and kept going a few extra meters for good measure. Then I swore under my breath when, instead of getting better, the feeling of being cut off from my mana got worse!

I clambered farther up, one meter, two, five…Climbing steadily, one hand, one foot, one hand, one foot, moving like my right hand and left foot were joined by a chain. As one lifted and braced, the other did.

An ex once told me that that was the secret to rock climbing, as I lay knackered on a mat in an indoor climbing center, staring up at the massive artificial wall above me.

"Just don't stop." I whispered it over and over, climbing higher, seeing the lip of the next room ahead and deciding that was my target.

I'd get there and then…

…the girder shifted.

I froze, then looked back up. It was five, maybe six meters. I could do it.

I started moving, and the girder shifted again, and the faster I moved, the more it did, too.

"Come on, you fucker!" I snarled, ignoring the constant pain from my ankle and wrist as I went, not having the time to be careful, not anymore.

I raced across the last few meters, the girder shifting with every movement, and I tried not to think about what *that* meant, considering the base was rammed into what I'd thought was the solid section of the floor.

I reached up. The lip was within a meter of my hand, then the girder slipped.

It slid downward, slowly but steadily, more of the curve that arced out of sight through the doorway overhead coming into view as the bottom seemingly slid through the ground. I threw caution to the wind, rushing to reach the lip.

Hand over hand, feet scrambling, I made it to less than six inches, literally fucking just out of range, when the base slid again.

This time, it didn't go slowly or stop.

It was like a fire ladder in reverse, vanishing downward as I frantically threw myself forward…and missed.

"Oh shiiit!!" I cried, tumbling away from the girder.

I had one chance, I knew that instinctively, as I ripped a dagger free from my hip, slamming it into the wall that flashed past, trying to catch something, *anything…*

The blade sank into a section of wall, carving a deep furrow and slowing me. For a split second, I had hope.

Then whatever it was my blade had embedded in ended, and the blade was ripped out of my hand. The softer material gave way to hard stone again, and I fell in a shower of sparks, the blade tumbling after me, snapped in two.

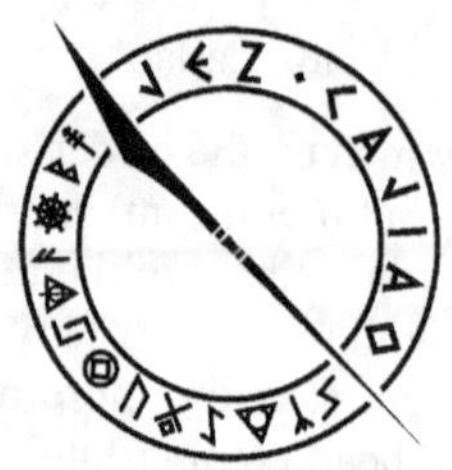

CHAPTER THIRTY

I landed briefly on a section of stone with a crash of armor, banging my head and leaving a smear of blood behind from my temple. Then I was falling again, sliding down the angled slabs, the world rushing past in a blur.

I hit the next one then slid in the opposite direction, picking up speed as I tried to grab anything. More and more debris fell from sight at the bottom as the light grew brighter.

Dozens of blocks were falling, sections of wall cracking and tumbling free as I tried to catch myself on something.

At the last second, I managed to get my boot under me and leaped forward, somehow clearing the tumbling blocks and the hole, landing on a tiny section of solid ground on the far side against the wall.

I grabbed it, hanging on tight to a couple of slight bumps and looking into a filthy crystal sheet that looked vaguely familiar.

I stared at it, my brain stunned as I saw a faint glow of blue beyond it, diffracted through the crystal doorway.

"A door oooh shit. Don't think 'open'," I whispered, but like trying not to imagine an elephant with pink ears, I thought it, and the section I was braced against vanished, letting me tumble through.

I caught the edge of the door frame with one outstretched hand, swinging myself through the gap. Bringing my feet up, I twisted my body and grabbed onto the doorframe.

For a long few seconds, I clung to it, terrified that the door would reform and cut me in half. But whatever remnants of mana had powered it were long gone now, the suppression field preventing it from reforming presumably.

I hung there, clinging to the edge of the doorframe. My options were down to jump…or hang on, then fall when I got too tired.

I wished I'd thought to look at the floor for a damn door, hidden under the inches of goddamn dirt, rather than the wall, but considering I was dangling over the edge, and my options were down to fuck all I wanted to go with, that wasn't really helpful.

I heard a shout from somewhere up high and in the distance, followed by the ringing sound of metal on stone, then metal, and I cursed.

The others were up there, and it damn well sounded like they were getting hammered right now. I took a couple of deep breaths to nerve myself up, working it out in my mind, before I did what I knew I had to do.

The room I was in was clearly *not* the source of the magic dampening field, not after I'd been up there and felt it getting steadily worse the higher I climbed.

Looking down at the distant lower sections, I could see a mixture of what looked like a twisted forest, a cave system and…

I blinked, trying to make sense of it.

There was a section that had clearly flooded a long time ago, with bloody coral and everything growing in there, lit by the reflection of a series of massive crystals held haphazardly in a shattered cradle.

The water was being held back, literally, by something the crystals were doing, with a shield or something forcing it into a rippling wall of water.

I stared into it, seeing figures moving around, watching me. I winced, looking down at the collection of fallen debris that covered part of the floor.

"Shit, I hope there's nobody under there." I shook my head and forced myself to ignore it all.

That shit wasn't important, not right now.

What was important was that there was magic down there.

The crystal doorway had some mana in it, until I'd opened it, like a dick.

Whatever was fucking the magic up must be up *there*, not below me. Logically, anyway.

Admittedly, I'd gotten a Wisp, a creature entirely made of magic and a different species from me pregnant, at the other end of reality. I was having the literal God of Death's skull made into a goblet, so maybe logic wasn't a great yardstick to measure my life by.

Either way, the facts I knew for sure were down to a scant few important ones.

Oracle and the others were above me and needed my help.

I couldn't climb up, and I couldn't do magic, not here.

There was active magic below me, though, and it was keeping the sea back without any apparent issue. Either I was right, and the farther I got from the upper levels, the more mana I'd have, or this rescue was going to end really badly.

I took two more deep breaths, then I let go and fell backward into the vast, open gulf underneath me.

The floor above receded, picking up speed as I fell. I spammed Soaring Majesty over and over again…feeling absolutely fuck all.

Seconds passed as the wind whipped by, my hair and beard being tugged this way and that. I suddenly found that I really, *really* needed a bathroom break, as I twisted around awkwardly, seeing the floor below coming up to meet me.

It was getting closer by the second, trees reaching up toward me and light growing stronger. I started to panic, thinking I'd literally just committed suicide by stupidity, when I felt something.

It wasn't my ability, not fully, but it was something. A flicker of my usual vision, my health bars, my notifications appeared, fading slowly into view as the ground raced toward me.

I felt the tingling sensation of my Ability, like an all-over body shiver, then I felt it.

It was there!

I pushed, and I damn well pushed *hard*, aiming to counter my fall…and I kept going!

I was moving too fast, my ability still recovering and…and there were creatures scuttling out of the water section!

They burst through, shaking the water free, letting it fall as they raced toward me on multiple limbs, crablike, but massive, heavily armed, and covered in spikes.

Their faces were nightmarish, all multiple eyes, feelers, and clacking jaws. Fuck, they made Horkesh look attractive…no, scratch that, she was still terrifying in the dark.

They raced forward, pincers and claw-tipped hands reaching clearly, expecting a feast, and finally, *finally*, Soaring Majesty activated.

I twisted around, punching down with my right fist, even as I shoved upward with the tiny amount of mana I had…and I slammed into the ground in a perfect superhero three-point pose.

The sound of my impact was lost in the frenzied rush, the clattering of claws and chitinous mandibles, screeches of challenge and warning to others. I looked up, an evil grin stretching my cheeks.

"Daddy's home!"

I moved before they could process the strange words, lunging at the nearest of the creatures. I had no mana, a blinding mana-migraine, and a healing wrist and ankle, but this was a fight I knew how to handle.

These were beasts—they might be semi-sentient; they might be totally bestial— but the one thing they clearly understood was prey and predator.

They thought they were the predators, seeing each other as competition for the tasty morsel of prey that had fallen into their midst.

They needed to understand that they were wrong.

They were the prey, and I was the alpha predator.

The nearest of them reared up, clearly overjoyed that the prey was racing toward it. It was a little taller than me, the upper body encased in an armored bulk, like a bell-shaped crab's body. Four arms jointed from that, the upper two of them much larger than the lower, meant for battling their own kind.

The left arm was bigger again than the right, blunt-ended and thick, while the right was narrower, slightly longer. It looked savagely sharp, with two much smaller arms below the head, probably meant to feed food into the mouth.

I had to assume that, like a lobster's, the larger claw gripped and crushed while the smaller cut, and the pair held the prey steady for the little arms to feed sections into its mouth.

The waist was small, barely a point of flex, while the lower section had four legs, spaced around a short triangle of armored flesh, ending with a short, stabbing tail.

It was a well-developed predator, no doubt, but it was also reaching out for me, not understanding that I was a threat.

I dove, rolling under it, then coming to my feet bracing my shoulders and back under it, in the middle of all four legs, and *heaving*.

It flipped, landing on its face with stunning force, the massively muscled arms trapped under its bulk, the smaller ones shattering.

The tail was short and stubby as a means to defend the back, but it wasn't armored the way the rest was.

I grabbed it behind the stinger and forced it back on itself with a crunch of chitin, tearing it free before discarding it and grabbing a leg in either hand, bracing my foot against its underside and roaring as I pulled with all my might.

The legs tore off in a jet of blood as the creature, just recovering its wits, screamed in agony, crippled.

I twisted, knowing the others were closing, but now…I had weapons.

I pointed at one of the incoming things and triggered Lunge, covering the distance before it realized, ramming the sharp-tipped leg of its companion through its face to skewer its brain. I ducked and pivoted, twisting away as its arms instinctively closed in.

The creatures were slow to understand, still looking for me where I'd been, only just now looking to the side, and I used that. I ran into the next in line, hitting it where it couldn't see and stabbing the chitinous leg into its narrow waist over and over until it hit something, nerves spasming and dying as the creature collapsed.

I jumped to the right, going on instinct, the clack of a claw closing behind me, making me roll then leap to my feet again. I grinned at them all, seeing dozens closing in from all sides, and I tossed the cracked and ichor-coated claw tip aside as I dipped a hand into my Bag of Spatial Folding, grinning as no bottom met my questing fingers. Instead, a ten-by-ten grid materialized.

I dismissed it, as usual, summoning what I wanted with a thought.

The mana potion was a powerful one, and I licked the minty taste from my lips as I tossed the empty vial aside. One hand came up, and flames danced as I summoned a Fireball, even as my other hand popped a health potion, downing that next.

It took three seconds to build, layering weaves of mana that became clearer to me with each discovery I made in magic. Then it was done, the creatures mere feet away as I slammed the spell into the ground, aiming it behind five of them on my left side.

It cut through the air with a high-pitched whistle then detonated as the outer ball ruptured on impact.

The first thing to escape was the ring of napalm-like fire that sat behind the containment sphere, flooding out, riding the expanding shockwave of the detonation like a surfer at a competition.

The flames coated everything in a five-meter radius–everything, that is, that wasn't blocked from view by the creatures themselves.

Then the shockwave picked them up and threw them through the air. Limbs shattered, burning napalm coating their bodies and seeping into unarmored folds, eating away at the beasts.

I was already running, leaping toward the others closing in from my right, but now I was surrounded by flying, burning, and screaming murder-lobsters.

Those facing me hesitated, stunned, then I was too close.

I leaped at the nearest, planting a foot on a lower arm and flipping myself over the head, landing on its back and spinning around, grabbing the larger arms and triggering Mana-Overdrive. My strength rocketed through the roof, and the arms that were so strong at grasping and closing were weak when pulled back and locked into place.

I planted a foot on the back of its carapace, then braced, heaving. There was a second's hesitation as chitin cracked and crumpled, stress fractures radiating out. Then, with a roar of triumph, I ripped the arms free.

The one I was standing atop screeched in terrified agony, collapsing as it went into shock. High-pressure blood jetted free to bathe the area in a stinking mess, even as it, along with the others I'd been fighting already, released a cloud of hormones into the air.

I scowled. The smell was awful, like hot eggs and burned metal, but I saw the effect on the others.

Whatever they'd been thinking, if they thought at all, that hormone was a clear "we're fucked" sign, causing the others to spin and race frantically for the water, diving through the rippling barrier and fleeing.

I threw the arms aside, the sounds of their flight dying away as they ran. Silence returning as I cut Mana-Overdrive and healed the effects away with a tired hand.

Glancing around, I examined the area, looking for an obvious way up and finding nothing. There were remnants of walls here and there on either side. The bottom of the shaft where I stood was a mess of piled debris, covered gradually by mud and more, presumably tracked in by the various beasts of the deep as they explored this strange interloper to their world.

There were trees and even moss in place of grass, but they grew in the direction of the giant crystals, not upward towards the sky. That made a lot of sense, I supposed, considering there wasn't a sun down here to give any need to reach towards it.

I moved towards the crystals curiously, checking my mana then triggering my examination spell.

Greater Manastone	Further Description *Yes/No*		
Details:	Weighing in excess of half a metric ton, greater manastones are exceedingly rare, being created when huge numbers of manastones are compressed together over long centuries. Greater manastones are self-accumulating, even after harvesting, and should they not be fully drained, will recover over time. Greater manastones will continue to grow unless their power is regularly siphoned away, and when full, will frequently release bursts of undirected mana into the local area, with often unexpected results.		
Rarity:	**Magical:**	**Durability:**	**Charge:**
Legendary	Yes	100/100	10,000/10,000

"Well paint me red and spank my arse," I mumbled, wondering how the hell I was going to get the damn things out of here.

They were huge, and I mean *huge*, easily twice my size with a flat, angular, multifaceted appearance, like the way I'd seen crystals on TV in caves, instead of the more rounded, thumbnail to finger-length ones I was used to.

Four of them were pressed tight together, two sharing a base that appeared to have grown across the metal and stone stand they'd sat atop once.

The other two were laid nearby with long fingers of growth leading from one toward the other as they all slowly grew into each other.

I studied the slow movements of light within the crystals then forced myself to look away. It was mesmerizing, and I needed them, but I needed to go to my people more.

These could be recovered, or not, later. Oracle and the others were my priority, and while they weren't showing in my secondary vision as injured, they were just…missing.

I shook my hands, unthinkingly splattering the crystals in ichor and turned away, pausing only long enough to use a rock to shatter a few of the fingers of growth free, figuring that, if I could get them to Oracle, maybe she could use them somehow.

I paused, rubbing the surface of the crystal, a steady tingle emanating from them. I couldn't decide if it felt like it was draining mana from me or pushing additional into me, but it felt…*good.*

Worried that I'd encounter the mana disruption field again and not wanting to lose them in my bags, I slid a fragment inside each forearm bracer, between the cushioning material and the metal of the armor. Just in case.

Then I turned my back on the greater manastones and searched the distant walls.

Where I was felt like the bottom of a well, staring up at the floor above, well over a hundred meters at the closest. There was no way I was going to get up there fast.

To my left, as I stood, was a steep slope that climbed up toward the floor overhead, leading to where the floors had originally joined. To my right was a wall that arched slowly back on itself leading up sharply overhead. In front was the water barrier, and behind, more of the twisted jungle and the wall.

Where there should have been holes leading out, there still were, like this one that had the watery barrier across it, but the sections where the side of the structure had clearly come away? There was…something else.

I frowned, focusing and grunting as I saw it. There was a sand-like texture to the space between the shattered original and the new sections, clearly delineated along stress points.

I could see sections of jagged and original steel or whatever meshed with the new structure, and I guessed that the crystals must be responsible.

Something, and I had to assume it was them had enforced a sort of repair, like the tower did, but instead of it being guided by a Wisp, the different segments blending seamlessly, this was rougher, clearly powerful, but unskilled and almost certainly unguided.

I grunted, even more determined to get those damn crystals home with me, but for now, my priority was clear.

The forest of twisted trees were black and gray, almost camouflage in color, and they climbed steadily away from the crystals until it became too steep for them to gain purchase. From there to the ceiling, mold took over. Here and there, small movements in the trees suggested life hiding in there. I cursed, knowing damn well that I would regret it if I tried to go that way.

I shrugged, crouching, then leaped into the air, feeling an instant dip in my connection to my mana the higher I went. As I twisted around, flying across the tops of the trees instead of directly upward? It lessened massively. I wanted my naginata, hell I knew I'd damn well need it, but I couldn't carry everything I actually wanted to, not without my bags of holding, so I would make do with my remaining dagger, the razor wire, and the swords over either shoulder.

If I took out the naginata, then lost magic, not being able to use the bags? I'd have to carry it. Normally, that'd not be a problem, but I was going to have to climb, and soon, and that would almost certainly mean dropping it.

I considered carrying potions as well, toting them in my hands until I lost magic, then using the bags as, well, bags.

Then I remembered that the potions were literally liquid spells. There was no way a strawberry fuckin' daquiri would heal a broken bone after all. Remove the magic? Remove the point.

I grimaced, deciding I'd be fine with what I had, noting the steady dip of my mana and health from the flight and feeling the dying connection to my mana as well.

I'd covered maybe half of the distance diagonally up the side of the structure when I felt the first stuttering cut in my ability, no longer flying but slowing and starting to dip. I damn well focused hard, having been waiting for it.

I was about thirty meters up from the crystals, even if I was a fair bit along as well. That made me think of a circle of effect, with the side rising here, but all of that was academic, as I was also only three or four meters above the goddamn trees at this point, and I came down hard.

I went from flying gracefully to falling, arms and legs windmilling wildly, swearing.

I aimed for a patch of ground, feeling my ability stuttering to life then dying, and I frantically just tried to lower myself gently.

It was going well. I was slowing, the headlong descent becoming more manageable, until my foot caught a particularly spindly branch, and I was half-flipped forward to crash through thin upper limbs and black leaves, the trees shuddering as if physically pained by my unwitting damage, until I was through them, falling into the black mulch and mold that covered the ground around the base of the trees.

I hit hard, skidding across the mess, tearing a line of scoured earth and rendering my armor filthy before I stopped, but eventually, I did.

I lay there, eyes wide, staring at the twisted tree trunk less than two inches from my face, panting as I tried to get over the fact I'd practically head-planted the ground from flying, was armored everywhere except my head, yet I was still alive.

"Damn, I've got to get that helm fixed." I shook my head and pushed myself up, clambering to my feet as I dragged muck from the joints of my armor, flicking it to the ground with a disgusted sigh.

The mana-exclusion zone, because whatever it was, that was what I was going to call it, was clearly higher than my head again. While the HUD wasn't very clear, it was definitely back again, as was my mana.

I forced myself to sit on a low branch, spitting some mud onto the floor that had made it into my mouth somehow and pulled out a coffee, taking a deep drink to get rid of the taste. Before putting it back, I cast a healing spell to recover the lost health, while I still could. I wanted to run, to power through all of this and get back to Oracle and the others…but I had to be realistic; they were well over an hour, probably two or three, from here, even if I knew the way.

I didn't know the damn way, though, not even slightly so I needed to pace myself and pay attention. I pulled some random dried meat from my bag and chewed on that while I set off jogging again toward the upper level.

It wasn't long before a hand reaching into my bag for another bit met only cloth, and I growled, hoping that whatever the interlopers–as I was by now sure it was those fuckers–had done, they'd turn it off soon.

The ground was a little slippery, angled as it was and covered in mold, but here and there, sections stood proud, jagged breaks that had begun to flourish with life.

I passed caves, or so they seemed, sections where rooms had collapsed and walls were laid to create overhangs, with centuries' worth of muck and debris, exploring amphibious creatures and more having died and contributed to both the ground covering, and the damn smell…

The farther I went, the stronger the smell of the hormones became. I gagged, wishing I could just run back down to get my magic back and Scour the shit away.

At first, it'd not been bad. Yeah, the first whiff was strong, but then it died away, and I thought it was all right, and hey, it might even keep things clear of me.

Instead, the higher I went, the more movement I saw out of the corner of my eyes.

Just here and there, a shift or a tree, a clicking of stones being knocked by something in passing, and it became clear I was being stalked.

It might have nothing to do with the smell, but the farther I went, the more movement there was, and a horrible thought occurred to me.

I started to worry that maybe, just maybe, the hormonal spray wasn't intended to warn the crustacean things away.

Maybe it was a general "fuck you" to whatever was feeding on them, and instead of warning other creatures away…it *attracted* them, creating a battlefield that the crustaceans could return to later and pick off the weakened survivors.

I swore as I saw more and more things appearing, and I picked up the speed, moving from a steady uphill jog to a full-on run, feeling the steady burn from my thighs and calves that running in full armor always brought. I grinned to myself. Finally, all those hours of Restun screaming at me and making me run up the Tower might pay off.

A fight broke out somewhere behind me, and rather than look back or let myself get bogged down, I ignored it, moving even faster.

I was racing up the hill now, the angle increasing by the second as I burst out of the real tree cover and into the intermittent sections, where an occasional tree remained. But now they were the abnormality, rather than the norm.

More noises were rising behind me, and as I jumped, grabbing onto the lip of a section of stone jutting out ahead and pulling myself up, it was clear it was coming closer.

I got my elbows over the edge, scrabbling with my feet and dragged the rest of me up, rolling onto the flattened surface and ignoring the squelch of the damn mosses and fungi as I crushed them.

I rolled onto my front, hands pressed into the mulch, and started to push to my feet, when I saw the words and froze.

…and goodbye, my love…

-Anderson

The rest of it was indecipherable, but it had been scratched into a section of the surface, obviously cleared beforehand, with something sharp, the majority of it lost to the encroaching biological crap.

I paused briefly, wondering who Anderson was. It sounded like they were from my world–hell, that might mean there was another survivor down here somewhere, and they might not be a complete cockwaffle...

My thoughts were cut off by a roar and a sudden spray of spittle, making me look up and practically shit myself.

There was something that looked like a troll–all bumpy skin and general bad temper, three eyes and pointed teeth–had spent the night in an ill-advised sexual liaison with a servitor golem.

The result was at least nine feet tall, hence the head that was poking over the lip I'd just climbed, had four arms, spaced equally around its torso, and was pulling itself up to come and say "hi."

Behind it was a trail of devastation as easily a dozen other creatures raced at each other, claws, fangs and spines jutting aggressively, and behind them...

"Fuck that shit, nope!" I shouted, seeing the creature that was climbing up behind them all.

It was a spider, or not, but looking like it lived at the bottom of the sea normally, possibly giving megalodons nightmares.

It was at least three meters at the shoulder, had a bulbous back that was covered in dozens of its young, and was letting loose with a whistling noise that was building, while dozens of eyes picked out targets.

Those targets were grabbed and dragged, by tentacles no less, into the fucker's slavering maw, and the face? It just...no. It was all teeth and mandibles, and worst of all was the almost-human eyes in the middle, locking onto me.

"NOPE!" I shouted, my instinctive aversion to spiders getting a whole new lease on life as I ripped my swords off my back. For once, the fuckers didn't get caught, and I slashed them across the rock monster's face.

It roared in fury, eyes bursting, the fury turning to anguished squeals as I blinded it, then started hacking at the hands holding it on the rock, sending green, thick blood spurting free.

The fingers were as thick as my wrist, and the skin hard. Hell, the repeated blows to the fingers were causing just as much damage to the non-magical swords, as it would have if I'd been hacking at a statue.

The fingers came free eventually, though, and it screamed, bracing itself with one arm and blindly swiping at me with the remaining ones. I leaped upwards, tucking my legs under me as the arm, leaking blood, passed underneath. I stabbed it in the face again, my right blade digging deep.

It screeched, falling back, hands going to the face and ripping my sword free as it fell backward.

The THING was still coming, pausing only to grab more of the free meat fighting around it before resuming its journey.

"Nope. No. Nope, fuckity fucking fuck, no!" I shouted, turning my back as I slid my remaining sword into its sheath, awkwardly changing my grip as I seated it, stumbling a few steps before running again.

The section I'd climbed onto was flat, having landed and created a plateau, but there was less than twenty meters before the wall was there, and it wasn't looking good.

There was a section ahead and above with a stairwell, leading up into darkness, which was just *great* without DarkVision, and while it looked too small for fuckin' *Shelob* behind me, it was also a good fifteen meters to the side of where I could climb up, meaning I had a precarious run over the remains of sagging girders to get to it.

I gritted my teeth, sprinting across the flat section before jumping and grabbing onto a protruding part of the wall, dragging myself upward and reaching for the next handhold.

If I'd had my way, I'd have flown around the big fucker and fireballed it into the next time zone, but fighting it on foot with no magic?

Hell to the no.

I grabbed the next handhold, feeling it sag slightly, and shifted my grip quickly. Moving up hand over hand, quickly reaching the level of the floor above, I stood on the edge of one of the rooms.

It was intact, and the next room over had an open door leading into it, a veritable maze starting just out of sight. But I also knew that it would get darker the further in I went, and for all I knew, that was Shelob's nest or larder, and there was no way up from there.

Or…

I turned, seeing the huge goddamn thing was twenty meters and closing with nothing between us now, and the damn stairwell that I could see, that definitely existed and was almost within reach, was just an unsupported race across rusty girders.

I put one foot on the edge of one, feeling it give slightly as a cascade of rusted flakes fell away, and the damn creature picked up speed.

There were a dozen struggling bodies on its back now, all being bound up and fed upon by the little ones, and fuck me, that was a hell of an incentive.

I took two quick steps back, then ran for it.

Even from the first foot landing on the girder, I decided I'd made a mistake.

The damn thing shook like crazy, and with each pounding step, it shifted more.

I saw connections ahead working loose and ran harder.

I jumped, going from a girder that ran straight ahead to one that it joined to, barely catching my balance, silently thanking my insane Agility as they moved underfoot, and I kept going.

The next section was a diagonal, running across and outward from the section of flooring I needed to reach, but the one after corrected, angling back.

As I ran, below I heard screeching and slobbering, and something on the edge of awareness that made my skin prickle as I almost, *almost* understood the creature.

I jumped, and not a second too soon, as the girder under my feet suddenly slid sideways, vanishing downward. I grabbed onto the edge of the floor and found a smooth surface, liberally coated in the goddamn fungus!

"Shit, shit, shit!" I snarled, my gauntlets filling the air with the sound of scratching metal as I slid backward. I scrabbled at it, desperately grabbing and finding mulch and nothing solid, save the smooth surface of the floor.

My legs were dangling, kicking wildly, the floor and the wall it was attached to shuddering as massive limbs grabbed onto it from below.

I had a vision of the tentacles grabbing me and ripping me backward. Of everything ending here, killed by a fucking beast and my own stupidity, when something hit me in the face, and I batted it aside, frantically trying to hook my fingers into something…

"Grab the fucking rope, you idiot!" a voice screamed at me. I froze, looking up, wide-eyed, seeing a wizened old man braced against the edge of the stairwell, one end of the rope in his hands, and the other…

I'd just slapped it aside!

I lunged for it, almost falling off the edge, but managed to get it with one hand and brace with the other.

"You'll have to climb! I can't pull you up!" he gasped.

He was half my size, if that, literally skin and bones, and even if he'd been close to healthy, the weight of me in full armor…

I braced my arm, nearly dragging him free, then forced my elbow over, slid slightly, then felt him tugging on the rope, helping a tiny bit.

It was enough, though, as I managed to get myself up onto both elbows, leaning forward and rolling myself onto the floor.

"Quick!" he shouted, waving at me to move. "Quick! Sara won't give you a chance! You have to run!"

"Wha…?" I mumbled, looking up, and the entire section shook as a waving tentacle appeared by the wall. "Fuuuuuck!" I screamed, hands, knees and feet scrabbling on the muck as I forced myself across the floor, leaping for the edge of the stairwell and dragging myself into it, then running up the stairs frantically.

I caught up with the old man a single revolution up, panting and shaking, each step clearly more than he could manage, yet he was still going.

I grabbed him, tossing him over my shoulder, and ran blindly upward into darkness.

CHAPTER THIRTY-ONE

I ran up two revolutions, the old man gasping something that I couldn't make out…until I ran face-first into a low section of rock and almost knocked myself out, loosening two teeth and sending both of us crashing to the floor.

He, thankfully, managed to twist aside so he didn't end up half under me, as I'd probably have killed him. Instead, the pair of us slid back down the stone steps. While he managed to stop himself, I picked up speed, as stunned as I was.

I hit the wall, scraping along it, and sending a shower of sparks flying from my armor, rolling over and over. I came to myself and frantically grabbed at anything and everything, barely slowing my speedy descent.

In a handful of seconds, I was back at the bottom, where a nest of tentacles were stabbing into the stairwell, desperately searching for the meat it could sense but not see yet.

I slid to a halt, feet braced against the backside of a tentacle, feeling the rubber-like consistency as I crushed it, blinking as I tried to make sense of the still-reeling world around me.

A tentacle directly above me came loose from the wall where it'd been crawling and hovered over me. I rolled to the side just as it smashed down, and I stared in horror at the sharp, hooked claws that ran the length of the damn thing.

"NOPE!" I screamed, scrabbling at the stone and pushing off the one under my feet, feeling it retract before I could get any real purchase.

I slid and scraped my way back into the stairwell, making it less than a meter before something smacked into the back of my armor, trying to drag me backward.

It scraped down, leaving a fresh set of gouges and scratches in the metal, but missing anything to catch onto as I made it onto the next step. A rough and cracked section of wall greeted my fingers underhand, and I gripped it, pulling myself forward even as I started to run back up the stairs.

I made it two more steps before the first tentacle managed to get a grip, wrapping around my left knee and tugging, sending me staggering, nearly falling.

I was damn lucky to have a hold on the wall, or I'd have been dragged out already. But I still half-fell, the crash of my armor filling the stairwell again as I managed to get both hands on the edge of the wall, bracing myself and clawing my way upward.

The tentacle tugged, hard, and I slid back before heaving on the wall and starting to drag the beast up with me.

For a few seconds, as I braced myself and found another grip, heaving again, I thought I was going to do it, to drag the beast up and kill it by crushing it into the wall…

Then the second, third, and fourth tentacles hit me.

One got my shoulder, the very edge hitting the back of my neck, the claws tearing the skin as I kept dragging myself ahead. The others got my left leg, below the knee, sliding down and wrapping around my foot, tugging hard, and scraped down my right calf, almost getting a grip, but not quite.

As more grabbed onto me, I heaved, now lifted off the ground and literally hanging sideways in the air, only managing to stay where I was thanks to my ridiculous amount of points in strength as I hissed in pain, the weight increasing.

The damn thing must have braced itself and was using both its own weight and the strength of its tentacles and legs to fight me.

It wasn't a fight I was likely to win, especially as it was a fucking enormous monster, and I was clinging to a section of damaged passageway by my fingers.

I gritted my teeth and heaved, gaining maybe an inch, then I started to slide back, my arms straightening against my will as every single damn inch they straightened, I lost both leverage and distance.

More tentacles slapped onto me, climbing higher, wrapping around my waist and thighs, then another went over my shoulder, this time resting against my neck, and I hissed in pain as the claws slid into the side of my neck, cutting deep.

They tore into the skin, the muscle, and I felt sudden terror as I realized they might hit the main nerves or the jugular?

I was boned either way.

"Fuuuuuck!" I hissed, looking up and seeing the wide eyes of the old man. He fumbled with a bundle of rags a few stairs ahead of me. He was dancing from foot to foot, looking at me, at the tentacles, then down at the mess in his arms and back again.

"Help!" I roared, and he jumped, whimpered, then frantically dragged something across a stone, blowing on it, rather than helping me. I opened my mouth, about to call him an asshole, then let go. I was planning on going down fighting, not being paralyzed by severed nerves and eaten, when a tiny spark flashed to life, floating into the bundle of rags.

We both watched it, time seeming to stop as it landed, his last breath granting it a tiny surge in growth as it bloomed, the strands of fabric and dried fuel around it catching, and the red lines of heat and fire spreading with almost glacial slowness.

He blew on it once more, then took two steps, throwing it over my shoulder, presumably out toward the creature.

"I'm sorry!" he screamed, but not to me, to the fucking creature!

Then he spun, tears flowing down his cheeks as he told me to close my eyes.

I stared at him in disbelief as he wrapped his arms around his head and ran blindly back up the stairs…

A new sun flared to life right behind me. I screwed my eyes shut, late, but better than not at all. Even through them, I screamed as the light seemed to sear into my brain, before being drowned out by an almighty screech of agony from somewhere below.

The tentacles released me all at once, and I crashed to the floor, curling into a ball and covering my eyes, barely aware as I slid slowly down the steps to rest on the little section of stone at the bottom. The insanely bright light found its way in, somehow, even around my tightly wrapped arms and screwed-shut eyes.

I twisted, blindly, feet searching and forced myself back into the stairwell, clambering to my feet and hurrying up as pained howl and screams followed me.

I was blinded, my eyes feeling like I'd been staring at the sun nonstop for an hour, and I'd been facing away, with it going off somewhere behind and presumably below me.

The effect on the damn creature must have been horrific indeed, especially considering how many goddamn eyes it'd had.

I couldn't hear anything over its screams, but a dozen feet up, I stumbled over something that moved, and when I reached out, I felt the old man.

I dragged him to his feet, and, far more cautiously, we climbed blindly up the stairs again.

This time, when we had made another revolution, he shook his arm free of my grasp and led me to one side, saying something about ducking my head in a croaky voice.

I did as he said, the light slowly vanishing, but my eyes saw nothing but an afterimage that seemed to have burned into my retinas.

I reached out, feeling a solid wall, but the lower I reached, the more obvious a half-buried passage became.

I had to practically kneel as I ducked under, and despite everything, the screams from below, the worries about Oracle and the others, and the goddamn blindness and pain, I worried that I was getting set up, medieval style.

A memory of an ex pointing out that the really old castles had such small and tight doorways that you *had* to duck your head, making it easier for defenders to lop it off, came to mind. I just hoped I hadn't been set up to be killed and robbed, or eaten, or…

If it was the or? I'd be fine with being killed and eaten as an alternative, I decided. I raised an arm, ready to block, or at least try to defend myself, but felt nothing coming and reached up instead, finding myself in a larger space.

"You're safe," a voice ahead rasped. I turned in its direction instinctively.

"I can't see," I whispered, unthinkingly, then cleared my throat and repeated it louder. "I can't see."

"I heard." the old man replied, before the sound of water being poured came to me. "Give it an hour or so, and you'll recover. You looked healthy enough, from what I saw."

"An hour?" I asked, aghast. "I can't wait an hour! My friends, they…" I paused, shaking my head and trying again. "Look. I have friends farther up; can you show me the way? Guide me maybe?"

"Hah!" he responded bitterly. "You think I'd be here, living in the dark and drinking my own piss if there was a choice? There's no way up, and even if there was, the creatures…"

"I'll fight them," I said firmly.

"Like you did Sara?" he snapped back in contempt. "She'll never forgive me using that on her, not now." His voice trailed away in a mumble, and I stood there, confused, rubbing at my eyes.

"You called that thing Sara before."

"She's not a thing!" he snarled. "She's just not well!"

"She's a giant fucking spider thing that could scare the Gods in a dark room!" I shot back. "Fuck's sake, she looks like she's Australian!"

"She's African!"

I froze, eyes wide. "What?"

"She's African, or her mother was," he repeated, before pausing as well. "Wait, you know what that means?"

"Yeah."

"Tell me!" he hissed, scuttling forwards, the sound of his hands and feet on the floor more animal than man. "You know of her world? Tell me!"

"I'm from there," I whispered, stunned. "Her mother was?"

"YES!" he howled, his hands and feet pattering around as he performed a mad little caper in the darkness. "She'll talk to me! She'll forgive me, she'll understand, yes she will, she couldn't eat you, not straight away! She needs to know more!"

Silence fell as I took a step backward, one hand reaching out and patting the wall of rubble behind me, clogging the corridor that led to the stairs.

"NO!" he snapped, his voice suddenly strong and demanding. "No! You can't leave; you have to tell me–you have to explain!"

"What is she?" I asked, my mind racing.

"She's not well, that's all!"

"Yeah, yeah she didn't look it. When I saw her, I thought that..." I kept patting around the wall, searching for the damn exit, wanting to make sure of where it was, when a roar from behind me, and back down the stairwell rang out, as well as sudden clatters and bangs, the sounds of stone and metal being battered and smashed around making it clear that Sara there wasn't very happy.

"Uh, who are you?" I asked into the sudden silence of the room.

He giggled. "She called me Anderson because I had no name, and my father was Ander. It was clever, that–she's smart, smarter than me, but that's okay. She feeds me, keeps me safe."

"She keeps you safe?" I asked slowly, "And...wait, she feeds you? What the fuck does she feed you?"

"What she can catch," he said happily. "We have to stay down here, where the magic is strongest. She protects it...it changed her, *blessed* her...but sometimes, sometimes she forgets, sometimes she's sick, and she needs to be left alone."

"Yeah...and that thing you threw at her?" I asked slowly.

"She made it, said it would protect me from her, if I needed it. Sometimes she gets angry, when she remembers what she was, and what happened."

"What did happen?" I was getting annoyed with the clearly batshit guy. "Can she get up here?" I asked as the noises built in volume.

"Sometimes."

I stared around in the oppressive darkness, horrified, imagining having to fight that thing in here.

"What do you fucking mean sometimes?!" I waved my arms, trying to catch the little fucker, before wincing as I tore open the wounds in my neck that were only just starting to heal.

"Sometimes," he repeated, then giggled, the sound coming from my left. As I spun that way, I heard a scuffing sound behind me, making me crouch instinctively, hunching my shoulders and ducking my head.

Something clanged off the back of my armor, the majority of it missing my neck and head, but there was enough of a blow, with all the rest combined, that I grunted in pain.

Then I kicked out, instinctively going from low to high in a spin kick that connected and sent the diminutive figure flying. There was a clatter, similar to the sound a bowling ball made when smashing through pins, and a groan, followed by a whimper as I turned, staring blindly around the room.

I reached out, finding one wall then following it, finding the next, then following that one until I found the fellow who had both saved my life and tried to attack me.

I crouched, grabbing him and roughly searching him, finding a single bag, much like my own, apparently a bag of holding, although, also like mine, there was a bottom instead of a magical pouch.

I pulled it free, starting to dump it into one of mine, until I felt a strange dissonance, a resistance. I hesitated, then tried it with my biggest and best bag. It accepted it, making me suspect that, while the manafield was still suppressed, it wasn't as strong as it had been, perhaps.

I banished the thought, taking him by the throat and hauling him upright, staring fixedly at the darkness and cursing the lack of magic for the umpteenth time.

"Why?" I asked him flatly.

"She'll want you," he repeated.

"Not good enough! She's a creature, she wants to kill me, hell she'd have killed *you*!"

"She loves me."

"Dude your sex life is disgusting," I retorted before I could think better of it. "She's a creature; she's a fucking giant spider-thing, and…"

"She protects me!" he snapped, bringing a hand across and driving a concealed dagger into the sternum of my armor.

There were a few sparks as it failed to do more than scratch the heavy metal, and I slapped his wizened forearm aside with my armored one, then wrapped it around his and twisted as I straightened it.

Instead of an arm bar, as I'd intended, locking the arm straight and holding it tight under pressure, preventing him from moving, he screamed as the weakened elbow joint hinged open unnaturally.

I heard a clatter as the dagger hit the stone, and I shook him, closing my fist around his throat.

"I've no time for this!" I snarled. "Where is the way up? Think very carefully, because if you don't tell me? I'll throw you to Sara!" There was a brief pause before he whispered back to me.

"She loves me."

"Yeah. With fucking ketchup!" I snarled, twisting and throwing him in the general direction of the hole that led down to her.

I heard a wet slap of flash hitting stone and him hitting the floor, then silence beyond the steady destruction of the passage outside as his beloved tried to reach us both.

No doubt wanting to have us for dinner.

I stood, hesitating, before finding the dagger then turning and checking the walls. I almost felt bad about leaving him; hell, I thought seriously about taking him with me. But in the end, he was clearly batshit, and I was going to need to climb, something I couldn't do with that dick as he was.

He'd rescued me, then tried to kill me, had clearly wanted to help, but he also apparently wanted to stab me and feed me to his girlfriend.

Maybe, once all of this was sorted out, I'd bring Nerin down, and we'd see what could be salvaged, but right now, without magic, and with only the barest hope that all was all right?

Fuck no. He could get eaten, as far as I was concerned.

I walked quickly, the dagger in one hand, extended at head height, and the other arm holding onto the wall as I followed the corridor.

After a few minutes, both of utter darkness and of slowly fading sounds, a new one rang out, as Sara apparently expressed her displeasure with Anderson.

I swallowed hard, then picked up the pace, feeling guilty for leaving him, but more importantly, worrying that if she could get inside somehow, compacting her body to squeeze up and into there, then maybe, just maybe, she was now following me.

I picked up the pace, the blood having dried on my neck. My insane healing was taking over, making the needed changes.

The minutes passed in silence, barring the occasional distant noise behind me. Each time I heard it, and I was never sure if it was a real noise or not, I picked up my speed, darting farther and faster.

Occasionally, I came across debris, collapsed walls, or more, laid broken across the floor and sections that bulged inward, or dips in the floor, causing me to stumble and fall in the darkness.

Sometimes, I passed sections where faint light filtered down through cracks or reflected sections. Despite my desires, I hurried on, not wanting to lose the tiny amount of darkness adjusted vision I had that might save me later, despite how ruined my eyes were.

Even rarer, fortunately, were the sections of the floor that were plain missing.

The first one of those I found was almost the last as my left foot failed to find the floor, and I fell forward, barely managing to catch myself on a support beam. I clung to it for long seconds, the taste of blood in my mouth from where I'd bitten through my lip.

I slowly forced myself back up, climbing out into the corridor and patting the ground all around.

I found that there were only a few small sections that had fallen through. While more were ready to fall, there were strong sections left as well, and between the support stanchions and the remaining sections, I could make it across the gap.

The most nerve-wracking was knowing that there may well be no end.

There was, though, and after only a few desperate minutes, I was back on solid ground. I drew my sword after that, knowing I was damaging the edge, and laid it against the floor as I hurried ahead.

That way, I found several more sections of missing floor, and without killing myself in the process. But the longer it went on, the more concerned I became that I was running in a big circle.

I had visions of reaching the same place I'd left, of Sara waiting in the darkness for me, laughing, and of Oracle and the others dead or dying while I played hide and seek with a giant spider-troll.

I had entire minutes of terror and fury-filled introspection where I looked at my decisions so far, wondering if one of them had cost me the life of the woman I loved and our unborn child. I cursed myself over the loss of my friends and those that would die because of my actions in the future, and I went on, forcibly banishing the thoughts over and over again.

I had no choice.

To give in, to allow myself to wallow in the belief that Oracle, our child, and, or, the others were all dead, was meaningless. Until I physically found them, I saw their bodies and held them in my arms, I couldn't give in.

I could yet find them, I could yet save them, and no matter what…

Something hit me from the side, driving me into the wall with powerful claws and foul breath.

I hit the wall and rebounded, swinging wildly with the sword and feeling it catch, then come free, barely injuring whatever had attacked me, even as hissing rage made her identity clear.

"Hey Sara," I whispered, eyes forced as wide as they'd go, searching the sheer darkness for anything and everything.

I moved back slowly, knowing that putting my back against the wall behind me limited my mobility options. But I was also blind as fuck right now and had been attacked from my right.

I had been headed in a rough circle, or so I'd guessed, but I sure as shit hadn't covered enough ground to loop all the way around to be back to near where I started, not considering the size of the damn island. Hell, I couldn't have made it even halfway. That meant that this fucker could see in here to be able to intercept me this easily.

That meant I had one choice.

I couldn't run, I'd only end up dying tired or falling down a hole. I couldn't reason with it; hell, I didn't know if it could reason.

I had to kill it, and as always, when the world boiled down to just this space, just this situation, and just a single, binary solution, I felt better.

There were two options here. I lived, or it died. There was no other solution I'd accept.

The corridor was silent, utterly so. I crouched there, sword held out before me, across my chest, ready to slash in any direction, as I tried to hear anything and everything.

For something so huge, it was strangely silent. As the seconds passed, and still nothing, I started to doubt myself. Had it been in my mind? Had I been so preoccupied with the creature catching me that I'd run into a stanchion and decided it was her?

No…I sniffed and almost gagged, the sudden foul odor that filled the corridor telling me I wasn't alone. I'd been so focused on my eyes…

I closed my eyes, using my nose and ears alone, weaving my sword through the air in little patterns, a figure eight over and over again, making the pattern as predictable as possible, and a little noise, hoping I wasn't making a terrible mistake.

I waited and waited, then I opened my eyes and stepped, stabbing frantically, hoping that she'd taken the bait.

Spoiler: she hadn't.

The blade glanced off the corner of a connecting corridor, and the brief shower of sparks showed her to me, attached to the ceiling overhead, crawling ever so slowly like a monstrous slug.

In that one terror-filled glance, I saw that she'd changed.

To fit into the section to visit Anderson, she'd discarded her exoskeleton like a hermit crab that no longer wanted its shell. She'd abandoned it, and the body that remained…

Much of it was the same–the long legs, the tentacles that hung from her back, the face of nightmare and the teeth, the multitude of eyes, many of which were burned and scarred now, some popped and blistered, others missing entirely.

The thing that was different, beyond the sudden lack of her young on her back, was that the massive abdomen that had been covered by them and bobbing with every step was more like something from a leech.

It was long, with a dozen or more little pseudopods anchoring it to the roof of the corridor. It pulsed and flared, shaking with every beat of the massive heart pulsing inside.

I stared at Sara in horrified realization, before she dropped from the ceiling.

She was lighter than I expected, but she was also a giant spider with a soft and flaccid back half, long legs and tentacles, and she landed atop me, driving me into the floor face-first.

She twisted and rolled, having not expected to have to attack that way yet, and not being ready, and I did the same.

Partially, I rolled to get my weapon to bear, and partially out of instinct, because I was seriously being traumatized by this shit. Her body was warm, tough, wet, and slimy, leaving a sticky residue behind as we rolled.

She managed to get the first attack in, teeth clamping down hard on the back of my thigh, denting the armor, even as she wrapped her legs around me. A stinger, similar to the crustaceans' butthole stinger, slammed into my left forearm.

The armor held, again, but only just, and I went wild trying to get free as the legs wrapped around me, tentacles starting to drag something sticky and strong onto me.

I reached up and back as I forced myself over, pinning her momentarily under me, then I grabbed at the base of her body, left hand gripping the stinger before it could stab at me again. I returned the favor, ramming the sword blade into her ass and ripping it sideways.

She'd clearly not been a fan of backdoor action, as me ramming it deep didn't go down well. A momentary need to shout "bite the pillow, I'm going in dry" came to mind.

I ripped the blade back and forth as she bit and clawed. A great gout of blood and fluids gushed over me before I was sprayed with something else.

Whatever it was, it must have been to do with the stuff she was binding things with, because it both burned and stuck itself to my skin.

I tried to ignore it, keeping my eyes closed, stabbing her again and again. But after a few seconds, when I felt it hardening, I realized I'd made a terrible mistake.

It was webbing, or something similar. Hell, it was like that PVA glue that we'd all played with at school, liquid for a little bit, then hardening and forming a plastic-like coating!

I couldn't breathe!

I twisted and stabbed, then when the blade got caught on something, I abandoned it, releasing her butt-dagger as well, as I frantically scrabbled at my face.

I couldn't find an edge!

The sticky morass was just everywhere, and without an edge…I grabbed the dagger I'd taken from Anderson, barely managing to get it free from webs that were holding it in place, and I lifted it, knowing this was going to suck.

I stabbed it into toward my face at an angle, trying to just get it the upper layer of the weblike substance and finding it harder than I could believe.

I pushed, and pushed hard, until the mess suddenly gave up and the blade plunged deep into my cheek!

I gritted my teeth, pain from her claw tipped legs digging into my armor, from her teeth as she buckled and began to chew her way into my leg, numbness spreading from her bite, and now I'd started to cut my own face off.

Or so it felt.

I sawed upward, careful to avoid my eyes, arcing around the bone, whimpering as I felt tendons and flesh springing free, until finally I could grab an edge with my other hand and pull.

It was supposed to be the edge of the glue-like shit, but my skin came with it, and I screamed as soon as my mouth was free, before sucking in a huge breath.

The edges of the mess, clutched in my gauntleted hand, twitched, and I realized, horrified, that it wasn't just a random fluid.

It was a part of her, and alive.

Questing tendrils reached out, searching for my skin…trying to push up into my nose and down into my mouth. My eyelids were being slowly pried apart, and I roared, horror filling me, terror blooming as I genuinely started to see the end coming.

I'd lost the sword, the dagger was fuck-all use. Hell, I'd hacked at everything within reach and she'd basically ignored me, each burst of fluids now revealed not as me winning, but her!

And I panicked even more.

I reached for my bags, fingers finding only cloth. My remaining dagger on my opposite hip was webbed in place. The damn creature was shifting around, forcibly turning me, starting to bind me with its web, packaging me as a tasty treat for later, while I suffocated…

Lethargy flowed through me, a desire to just give in, to rest for just a few heartbeats, then I'd do more, I'd be able to fight it, if I just gave up for now…

My fingers closed on something, my hands being pushed back towards my chest as I was rolled over and over. It was something uncomfortable, something sharp-edged edged that was stuck in the gaps between my vambraces and sleeves, making it hurt. It kept me from sinking deeper into myself.

I pulled it free, a sudden light catching at my eyes, even through the webbing.

I flinched. A sudden cold rush flooded me, pouring up my arm from my fingers, making my arm tingle all over again. I felt it and remembered the first time I'd felt it.

So long ago, sitting in a chair with Madame Xiao, reading a spellbook and learning…

"Firebolt…" I sub-vocalized to myself, remembering the freedom of the new spell, of being able to do magic. It'd evolved later, becoming a go-to spell for me, but I instinctively followed through with it, fingers twitching as, despite their restraints, they tried to follow the same patterns.

My mouth was gummed shut, but it hadn't gotten all the way down my throat, not yet.

The memory was wonderful, and even as I slid slowly into the forever sleep, I drew it up and enjoyed the burning heat and wash of power…

As well as the pain and the screams!

Searing pain flashed across my skin, the strands that held me so tight, like handcuffs at night, vanished in a sudden flash of all-consuming flame!

My eyes fluttered awake, hair singed as the burning mass evaporated. Whatever it was, it was seriously flammable, like thin-stretched sulfur, and when the flame passed? All that was left were floating wisps of smoke.

I rolled away from the creature, frantically, as she screamed, the flame flashing along the webbing that covered me and led…

…and led straight up from me and into her!

The flames flowed, the corridor suddenly brightly lit, my HUD and everything else still dead, but the glowing manastone fragment in my left hand?

It was dimming slowly, steadily. But in my right?

I held a glowing Fireball!

It rolled slowly, a sea of greens and whites, blues, reds, and yellow, and it begged to be put to use.

I forced myself upright, left leg barely working, the right one stiff, blood leaking from a dozen places, half my face torn off. I stared down at the rolling, howling creature.

I could see the fire inside her, little globs of burning liquid ran from wounds and orifices. Her abdomen looked like it was going to explode, swelling as liquids boiled and pressure built.

Her legs, attached to what was presumably her torso further up, latched onto the abdomen as one and started stabbing at it, trying to tear it free, reminding me of that bitch getting free to come after Ripley.

I grabbed her head by one of the mandibles that clacked and shuddered.

There was a second of frozen time as we stared at each other, her all-too-human eyes in the middle of her face, apparently the only ones to survive so far, illuminated by the glowing blue crystal in my hand.

Then I rammed the Fireball into her maw and released it.

The explosion, going off right in front of me, sent me flying backward, even as it literally blew her insides out.

The corridor was illuminated in a mess of dripping flames, and here and there, as I twisted around, trying to put myself out, I saw twitching sections of meat.

I forced myself to my feet, still holding the manastone fragment tight in my hand, and stared at the mess before bending over and being violently sick at the memory of that shit creeping into my mouth and toward my throat.

Bile splashed across the floor, putting a few flames out, washing more smoldering bits aside. For a second, I thought I was all right, until the miniature tsunami rolled an eyeball over, and it seemed to stare up at me accusingly.

I washed that away in a fresh spray, before straightening and wiping at my face with a shaking hand.

It was barely cleaner than my face had been, but when you're that bad, anything's a step up.

I looked around, making damn sure she was dead, unable to see the notifications that I hoped against hope were actually just suppressed still.

I had a few seconds of fear that the suppression might be damaging my ability to use magic, then I glanced at the sheer power in my hand.

The manastone was glowing happily, a significant portion of its power having been used in the fireball, but the rest was still available.

I had a chance.

I should save the power, and I would, I promised myself, but even now, my eyes were barely able to focus, and the amount of blood and more I'd lost?

I tried to cast Complex Healing and felt nothing.

I tried again, and again, confused, then forced myself to go back to the last few seconds of horror, ignoring the need to scrub at myself again, and instead focused on the *feeling*.

I'd pulled the magic down my arm, or…

No. That wasn't right.

I'd not been conscious of it. I'd not pulled anything, I'd just stopped keeping it *out*. I didn't know how or why my skin was resisting the flow, but when I consciously opened myself to the fragment in my palm, the power flowed.

My HUD flickered but didn't seem capable of coming back, the light of the fragment dimming instantly. I cast my healing spell, almost panicking as I did it, then cursing as the stone shattered, the last sweet rush of power flowing into me, even as the spell roared onward.

I stood there, shaking and gasping. My face felt like snakes were writhing around under the skin, meeting up and reconnecting. The dozens of small holes in my flesh that had been cut and torn were mending, my face rearranging slightly as my skin flowed back into the correct place, my eyes burning and tingling.

Overall, it was a waste of the power, but…but had my eyes been right when I'd been in the corridor before, I'd have seen the damn glow coming off my arm where the second manastone was still stuffed out of sight.

I pulled it free, seeing the corridor by the reflected light it gave off. I grunted, seeing how Sara had tracked me so easily.

I was literally holding a damn torch in the darkness.

I growled to myself, searching around, and quickly gathered up my weapons along with one of her legs. It was seven feet long, slightly curved, and had a wickedly sharp tip, with a serrated backside, and it was going to be all kinds of useful to me as I sheathed my other weapons.

Freshly healed, and with a way to see at last, as well as what was, at best, two spells to my name from the crystal, with darkness as my only friend thereafter, I started off again, this time jogging down the corridor with a weapon in hand and a light held high.

CHAPTER THIRTY-TWO

I'd started jogging, but now that I could see, I picked up speed quickly. I hobbled along, the armor around my left thigh bent and battered. I passed two more connecting corridors, having no clue if I should take them or not, but the one Sara had come out of had to lead back to the lower floor.

The third time I passed a connecting corridor, I cursed and took it, not really knowing why. I'd been jumping collapsed sections for a little while, and clearly I was getting into a section that was considerably more broken, judging from the debris laid about.

I'd also passed a LOT of dead bodies.

I'd stopped for the first one, then the next two, finding that the insects that had managed to get aboard from somewhere had enjoyed themselves. The bodies were broken by more than time, the weapons…well. The sword was seemingly welded into a leather scabbard that was, in turn, only slightly softer than the rock around it.

I wasn't getting that out, and the other items weren't much better.

There was a tang of salt in the air now, the sea below and all around seeping in here and there, making sure that nothing looked like it should.

Without a spell to identify it all, I'd be wasting my time, and I left the shit-encrusted rings and more on the ground where they'd fallen.

Occasionally, I found groups, a dozen bodies all together. Sometimes, the corpses were more or less intact, other times there were literal piles of bones mixed haphazardly with filth-encrusted armor.

The corridor I was following now wasn't as busy as many had been. There were bodies laid here and there, as if this was where they'd stood in life. They'd fallen, remaining at attention before certain doors.

I slowed as I followed the corridor, paying more attention as I went and trying to make the map in my head, rough as it was, correspond to the one Tenandra had shown us.

I shook my head quickly; it just didn't make sense.

Here and there, I passed set buildings, strange as this was, as if rather than making standard rooms with all the walls connected, as most of the structure I'd passed was, they decided to make a village as the roof lifted higher and higher.

The deeper I went, the more individual houses I found, until eventually I found a single building that rose to the roof. This one was massive with a contingent of bodies outside on marble steps that led up to a pillared colonnade.

If I was going to find a way up anywhere, it would be here.

I passed the bodies, pausing as I went, more than a little convinced that these were legionnaires, considering their placing. I remembered the stories that I'd been told in passing about the sunken city, that the revenants had patrolled and hunted down intruders, bound to the structure by their beliefs that they'd failed the Empire, determined to carry out the last order they could, protecting it from all who would plunder the depths.

If that was true, and when I'd freed those spirits, then the bodies they'd been inhabiting would have fallen wherever they'd been, at that point.

That made a kind of sense. Legionnaires would have been at their duty stations, be that guarding a location, as many of the bodies seemed to suggest, or performing patrols.

I'd not passed any golems, but that could be just blind luck. I'd only explored a tiny fraction of the facility, after all.

Also, when they crashed, anything that survived would have attempted to repair the Prax, I suspected. Looking at some of the buildings around me, the delicate fluted columns and more, I guessed that this was evidence of that, at least.

I forced myself to go on after only a brief check of the bodies. Their armor was more or less intact. My left thigh and the connecting plates were damaged and making it harder and harder to make any real speed, as they were rubbing the inside of my leg raw, having carved through the padded underclothes already.

Soon, I'd have to decide between stripping it off and reducing the integrity of my armor, or having it start to cut through my flesh and possibly sever an artery.

That wasn't a good choice to make, but considering the state of this armor and that laid around me, swapping that section out wasn't an option, here at least.

I continued up the stairs, passing inside, the echo of my boots on the marble surface ringing in the air as I passed the remnants of banners.

The walls had mold growing on them, but it was notably less than there had been elsewhere, suggesting that these sections had been cared for longer than the rest.

I passed through an ornate foyer. The remains of the carpeting had made a banquet for moths and who knew what else, with a massive spiral staircase in the center of the room.

I hurried up, wincing with each step and determined that I'd check the next body more carefully, when I heard the first sound in seemingly ages.

It was a clicking noise, followed by a grumble and a handful of low voices rising in argument. In seconds, I heard a shout, then more voices ringing out, before a new one snarled something over the top of them, the tone of a command unmistakable, then voices fell silent again.

I stood stock still, listening, and when nothing else was said, I took the landing I was closest to, rather than continuing higher up, limping down the corridor as I searched the rooms on either side.

I started to find scattered debris, the remains of meals, broken items, and general filth, before moving closer to a door and hearing a low argument start up again inside.

The voices were slurred, unclear, but there were several, and as well as the voices rising in argument...

I pushed the door open slowly, the voices inside falling dead as I did so. I stepped inside, makeshift spear at the ready...and froze at the sight of more than a dozen gnomes, filthy, exhausted, and lying around the room, clearly trying to recover.

"Shit." I muttered, stunned by the condition of them. They looked like they'd been through the grinder then flushed into the sewers. Hell, they smelled like it as well, and…

One of their number tried to get to his feet, pulling a killstick in either hand and flicking the activation lever. When they did nothing, he sagged, then forced himself to move, stepping between us while two others joined him.

"Ruuuuun…" he whispered, groggily, barely able to keep on his feet. A long and clearly very badly infected cut ran from his right knee to his ankle, with the flesh around it blackened and oozing pus.

"Don't be so bloody stupid," I said, shaking my head. "Where did you come from?"

"Wha?" He stared at me, blinking muzzily, and I looked from him to the killstick and his people behind him.

"You power those things with manastones, right?" I asked, realizing that I'd never asked where the hell the gnomes, who were insane about using that kinda shit up, were getting enough to keep going until I found them.

There had to be another crystal!

"So?" one of the others muttered, stepping to my left and holding a hand up, even as he gestured to the others, completely unsubtly. "You want this?" He quickly disassembled the stick and held up a tiny nugget of manastone.

"Yeah, I do," I said, pretending to ignore the way that the other two were moving, getting ready to attack, while the rest, clearly refugees who were fleeing something, tried to gather up children and various bits and bobs. They were slowed by injuries, exhaustion, and quite frankly, terror. I glanced up, seeing the hole they'd used to climb though into this room from what I assumed was the next level up, and the way the battered gnomes were looking for another way out.

"Look, it's all right," I said softly, sliding the manastone I'd been carrying into the back of my bracer again and drawing a dagger. They tensed, getting ready to fight, until I tossed the dagger, hilt-first, onto the floor next to the one who'd disassembled his killstick.

"What's that for?" he asked after a few seconds.

"Can I sit down?" I jerked my head back behind me, in the direction of the corner of the room. "Without these two attacking me, I mean? I'd really prefer not to have to kill them, but I will if they make me."

The one with the bad leg growled, and I looked at him, seeing the metal teeth and the unfocused look in his eyes.

"Badunka rider, right?" I asked him. He took a step back in shock, his leg giving out, and his friend having to catch him.

"Look, you're all on your last fucking legs, can we just take a minute here? I need manastones, you need healing. I can heal you, and you can get me back up higher in the ruin, deal?" I suggested, getting glares, followed by the nearest one, who'd been holding his friend up, suddenly shoving him aside as he leaped for me, a small dagger clutched in one hand.

I backhanded him, sending him flying, the dagger barely managing to leave a scratch on my damn armor, followed by his friend pushing himself up and staggering toward me.

He didn't even have a weapon, the killsticks having both failed to start up, and so he was reduced to using them like clubs.

I swapped my makeshift spear to my left hand and put my right on his forehead, keeping him at an arm's length, while he swung desperately at me like a drunken toddler. I turned back to the other one that I'd passed Anderson's dagger to, and I spoke calmly but coldly.

"My friends and the woman I love are somewhere up there. I'll give you a minute to think about this, then the deal is off, and I'll be leaving. Anyone attacks me again, I'll kill them."

There was a long minute of silence, broken only by the huffs of the injured and infected badunka rider who was still swinging his clubs at my arm, with absolutely no effect beyond adding to the mass of scratches.

Finally, the one that seemed to be in charge proved me wrong, by turning to the group and having an older gnome wave to him that it was alright.

This one I recognized, vaguely.

"You," I said, glaring at him.

"Me?" He blinked in confusion.

"Yeah, we offered you the chance to go with us, and you attacked us!"

"Eh?" He glared at me, before being elbowed by a female gnome next to him who whispered furiously in his ear. Over the general mutterings, shifting, and clattering, the crying of two small ones, and several noisy farts by a few gnomes who started high-fiving each other over the volume and stench, I only made a few words out.

"…swear…Giint…airship."

"You!" he barked eventually. "You stole our airship and left us!"

"No, I took an abandoned airship after rescuing a load of its old crew," I corrected, all the while realizing that I'd commandeered the airship, and they were right. It'd been sitting there, and I'd grabbed it and basically dared anyone to complain.

"It was ours!" he snarled. "We went to get it after gathering all the others who needed a home or weren't around when you gave them the chance, and you'd gone!"

"There were SporeMothers coming."

"Not coming! Here!" the little bastard shouted, spittle flying. "We lost good gnomes to that thing, and…"

"Good?" I asked. He paused, momentarily stopping his tirade.

"Well, well no, actually they were assholes, good-for-nothing badunka riders, but it gave us the time to run, and we've been running ever since!"

"Isn't he a badunka rider?" I asked, looking down at the panting figure I still held at arm's length, as he weakly hit my arm with the dead killstick.

"Yeah. He look particularly sane to you?" the older gnome asked gruffly.

"Nope."

"Exactly. We feed him and give him clean water; he protects us, but once he gets a thought in his head, well, can't get it out until something else comes along to replace it."

"You said you came to the ship?" I asked after a brief pause while we all watched him slowly hit my arm again, the brief *tink* of the metal on metal apparently all we were getting.

"It were our ship!" he snarled.

"This whole place?" I said, gesturing around with my other hand. "It belongs to the Empire. We built it; I've reclaimed it. You've been stripping its corpse forever, so how about we forget about who owned what, unless you want me to start charging you rent?"

"What's rent?"

"It's…fuck it, it means you'd owe me more than I owe you, that's all you need to know. So, you were coming to join us?" I asked, confused.

"Not like there were many choices," he muttered.

"That's a fair point, so…you were coming to join us after you attacked us?" I paused, waiting for an apology, and he just stared at me, confused. "Shit, forgot you're all mad," I muttered. "So, what've you been doing since we left?"

"Fighting!"

"Fucking!"

"Drugs!"

"Running away!"

"Everything!"

"Gstupth!"

That last came from a gnome who slowly toppled over after speaking and prompted a pile on by all the nearby gnomes to search him for his stash.

"He's eaten it!" one of them complained, sounding annoyed, while another tried to pry his jaws apart with a crowbar, making me wonder if that's how so many of them ended up with metal teeth.

"Fucking gnomes," I muttered, before shoving the one under my hand over, letting him collapse to the floor. "Look, you said you were running and hiding. Who from?"

"That human!" the leader growled, and I looked at him quizzically. "A few days back, a bunch of humans came out of the old tower, said they were in charge, and we served or died."

"And what did you do?"

"We killed them."

"Okay, and…?"

"Then the whole place just exploded, really good one, too, not too much sulfur, just a pinch of nitric acid…lots of leviathan piss," he mumbled, rubbing his filthy chin as I blinked at him.

I'd given up on wondering which side knowledge had originally come from. I'd heard once that all our legends about creatures that I had found in the UnderVerse were from people, normal people, on Earth making a momentary connection across the realities. Usually, it was in dreams.

I guessed that if it could go one way, it could go the other, but why the fuck was it the gnomes who had learned about chemical explosives? And specifically, the most unstable ones?

Hell, maybe it was why they were so unstable. Dreaming of Earth would probably do that.

"I told you! It's not piss, it just smells like it!" one of the others snapped, and several more joined in what was clearly a popular argument.

"So?" I said after a brief pause. "You were attacked?"

"Oh!" He grunted, apparently having totally forgotten about me as the argument had started a conversation on chemical properties, and about using their own shit. "Yeah, big explosion, then a load more humans came out, and we ran. Some of us got caught, and were made to serve them, some went down into the depths, and others went up, trying to get around the SporeMother."

"It's still alive?" I asked grimly.

"It got about fifty Gnomes and some humans, has a section over to the north, mid-ring."

"Mid-ring?"

"Mid-dle-of-the-ring," he pronounced carefully, as if talking to an idiot. "Mid-ring."

"And the ring?" I asked, getting a sign as he gestured for one of the others to show me something.

She pulled a tattered map out of a bag after several seconds of searching and passed it over, before asking in a low voice if I had any good shit.

I reached into a bag automatically, then cursed, hitting cloth and realizing that I was still in the magic exclusion zone. The Gnomes, however, had all heard her and were fixated on me like Quagmire in heat.

I removed my hand slowly, showing it was empty, like I used to for my ex's dog, and got a growl from her as she tried to get at my pouch.

That started a mad scramble which I had to stop by a mixture of kicks, punches, and picking two of the most feral up and smacking their heads together.

"Stop it, you bloody idiots!" I snarled, throwing them aside, then doing the only thing I could think of. I mimed grabbing something from the bag and held it up. "This is too strong!" I lied desperately. "Its super strength, it was too strong even for Giint!"

That got everyone's attention, and they froze, watching my hand unblinkingly.

"If you want it, we need to free my friends," I said. "They've got the rest, and this won't work unless we get the…" I searched around for inspiration. "The cumofsumyunggai?"

It was an old chef's joke, sending the buyer to a random store to ask for it, knowing they'd end up saying it slowly and carefully while the staff stared at them in amusement. It was all I could think of, though, and fortunately, it seemed to work.

"Why?" The one I'd tentatively pegged as the chief asked, watching my hand like all the rest. I shook it slightly, watching their heads bobble up and down, following it as I responded.

"It needs something they have, it's a chemical…won't work without it."

"I could try it," one offered helpfully.

I snorted, making a point of shaking the hand again as I spoke. "It'd kill you…but if you're *sure* you want it? And the super, super strength stuff? You need to help me free my friends," I said, shaking my hand again, making a point of putting it back in my bag and 'leaving' it there.

I regretted that instantly, because I now had nearly twenty insane gnomes essentially staring at my crotch and baring mainly metal teeth.

"So!" I said quickly. "There are two options, if I can make this work. You all give me your manastones, and I'll heal you, one stone should heal one person…I think…and then we attack."

"What's the other option?"

"You don't give me the stones, I don't heal you, and if you want the drugs, you still have to attack, but you'll probably all die," I replied honestly.

"Why you want the stones?" one of them asked.

"The magic," I said. "They've done something. It's drained the magic away, and I can pull more from the stones, but…"

"Wait 'til tomorrow," one of them grunted, and the others nodded in agreement.

"What?"

"Tomorrow. The suppressor can only ever be turned on for a short burst. Uses too much mana to run. They'll run out by tomorrow."

"We could try the drugs while we wait," another suggested, smiling in what they clearly thought was a winning way.

It made me think of a honey badger on acid.

"How about fuck no?" I suggested brightly. "Look, you want the drugs? You want healing and to be free and safe?" I paused, having seen the way they all reacted as I was speaking.

"The drugs," I repeated, tapping my bag as I went on. "If you want the *drugs*, well I've only got a little here, because I only brought enough for Giint. He fights for me, and he gets *all the drugs he wants*," I lied.

The effect on them was insane. The entire room, including gnomes I would have said were on the verge of being put in a box, perked up.

"If you swear the Oath to me, and you'll serve me and the Empire, I'll heal you all," I said. "Then you help me to free my friends. We'll go kill some assholes that need it, then we all fuck off from here and get some drugs."

It was possibly the dodgiest speech I'd ever given, but damn, it went down better than most of them, with a collection of smiles and clumsily crossed fingers.

"Me swear!"

"Already sweared, drugs now?"

"Swear at who?"

"Who's Oath? Why we all swearing at them?"

"I swear! Honest!"

"Fuck's sake!" I snarled as several crowded in close trying to get their hands in my bag, setting off a veritable tsunami of druggie gnomes struggling to their feet, thinking they were missing out.

"NO!" I snapped, and smacked a particularly insistent Gnome that was halfway up my leg on the nose with two fingers. "Bad Gnome!" I shook him or her off my leg. "If you want to be healed, and you want to take the Oath, you need to give me the stones!"

That made them pause for a few minutes as they apparently thought that through, then fights broke out over the stones and who had what.

I watched the majority gleefully pounding on each other when a little one, maybe a third smaller than the rest, sidled up to me and offered me a pouch. I reached down and took it, opening it and freezing in awe at the sight of literally a dozen manastones glittering up at me, their light spilling free.

"You take me and my mum?" she asked. I looked at her, stunned.

She was both smaller and slighter built than the rest. Where a lot of them looked like they'd been dragged through the hedge backward and had used fingers coated in honey and treacle to do their hair and beards, if they'd put that much effort in, she looked…almost sane.

She was dressed in grimy, but serviceable overalls, clearly several sizes too big, that had been cut and sewn to fit her. Her cloak that pulled down low, covering most of her head and allowing only a brief glimpse inside, and her hands…

Her hands were covered in lumps and scaled, the way she held herself suddenly clicking in my mind, as I crouched down, reaching out and brushing her cloak hood back.

The face that stared up at me was covered in small marks and blemishes, growths and more. The others stayed clear of her, not nastily, not sneering or worse, but they were clearly keeping their distance, and her eyes were red-rimmed and glistened with pain.

"Who are you?" I saw the way she shied away, and her small hands lifted to tug the cloak back up. "It's all right," I assured her, despite everything, feeling that she was used to being pushed aside or ignored.

"Daana," she replied, her voice low. "You'll take me and my mum?" I nodded. "Can you…can you heal us?"

"What is it?" I asked, looking at the growth of the scales on her hands, the dangling tumors and more.

"Nobody knows," she whispered. "The plague…"

"The plague did it," a second voice said as an older, hunched-over gnome shuffled out of the mass, the others moving back from her and letting her pass.

I'd seen her at the back and assumed she was too tired to fight through the rest. But judging from the way the others separated to let her through, I'd been wrong.

"Where the others either died, or got better, we were changed…the others like us, the old master ate…"

"They…*ate* them?" I asked, remembering the Skinwalker suddenly and wondering where that fucker had gotten to. This place was a goddamned nightmare at times.

"They said we were different…will you eat us?" the older gnome asked calmly. I frowned, shaking my head.

"Fuck, no," I assured her. "Okay, give me a second, and be ready to swear the Oath. I don't know how long I can hold the mana…" I took the smallest of the stones in my hand, focusing and deliberately relaxing barriers I'd only just discovered.

I felt the tingle from the manastones, well aware that I was probably wasting more than ninety percent of the power, hell, probably ninety-nine point nine, if I had any real clue of the amount of magic needed to keep an airship aloft compared to the amount I used in a spell. I focused hard, and with difficulty, and without a screen to reference, I pushed the Oath out to them all.

"Okay everyone," I groaned. "Swear quickly, and parents swear for their children."

There was a ragged start to the Oath, but within a few seconds, I relaxed, relieved, as the manastones' massive output temporarily overrode the suppression field around the room.

"I swear to obey Prince Jax and those he places over me; I will serve to the best of my ability, speak no lie to him when commanded otherwise, and treat all other citizens as family.

"I will work for the greater good, being a shield to those who need it, a sword to those who deserve it, and a warden to the night."

"I will stand with my family, helping one another to reach the light, until the hour of my death or my lord releases me from my Oath.

"Lastly, I will not be a dick!"

I knew less than half had taken the Oath, judging from the crossed fingers, knowing grins and winks that a fair few were exchanging, clearly thinking I was fucking idiot, but that was fine.

"So, thank you to those who chose to take the Oath. Did anyone not?" I asked, damn well knowing the truth, but nodding as if I believed them when everyone declared they had.

"I'm glad, because this spell, the one that will heal those who have sworn to me, will rip the life from anyone who hasn't and use that to heal the others."

I let that hang in the air for a few seconds, seeing the change on the faces on several and asked again. "Now, did anyone think that maybe they didn't make the Oath properly? Maybe they want to try again?"

Three came forward, and I took the manastones they offered begrudgingly, smiling grimly as I pushed it out again, discarding the drained first stone and using a second.

It galled me, using these goddamn stones this way, and the time this was wasting as well. But I knew what vicious bastards Gnomes could be, and if they were useful as a distraction, that might be the difference that got me to Oracle and the others.

Once that was done, and the second stone was discarded, crumbling to dust that I shook free of my gauntlet, I cast the first spell.

Frostfire Circle of Cleansing spread out from me a few seconds later, the entire spell warping badly as it activated and was suppressed, then activated and was suppressed over and over again.

I felt the connection from me to the circle being tugged on, and I pulled out another stone, feeding the mana for that into the mass as well.

It drained quickly, far quicker than I'd hoped, but as soon as the spell activated, the screams began.

I'd positioned it over me as the center of the circle, leaving half of the room free of the flames. If the little fuckers who had lied got a little singed in escaping it, well, that was their problem, not mine.

Those like the badunka rider, whose wounds were heavily infected, were the worst. He screamed in shock and pain, as the flames burst to life and then converged on him, burrowing into the flesh. The skin around the wound was the first to go, blackening, the edges, already green, pus-covered and black in places, smoldered away, breaking down into floating ash carried away on the breeze, as he screamed and rolled, beating at the flames.

They dug deeper, the flesh bubbling and crisping as the impurities and infections were rooted out. He bellowed and slapped at them, hissing in fury and reaching out, trying to drag himself to me.

I moved, darting closer and grabbing his arms, staring into his eyes as he shouted curses, screaming about how he'd kill me and how I'd pay.

The seconds turned to minutes as the spell drained the second, then the third stone, before dying as the available mana was extinguished.

He gradually slowed, his shouts and curses growing lower and lower in volume, less inventive, and more confused, as his eyes took in the others standing nearby, silently.

I released his hands, letting him drop them to his leg, feeling for what he expected to be a burned wreck…and instead was healthy skin.

"How…?" He grunted after a minute, looking back at me, as I stood taller, seeing the marked line between those who had sworn and those who hadn't.

Those closer to me were suddenly looking around at the world with new eyes, standing straighter, and were more or less sane, to some degree.

The others were markedly less. The feral glimmer in their eyes, the challenge and confusion as their fellows–many of whom they'd have stabbed happily, had they something they wanted a few weeks and months ago–were now looking at them with pity and horror.

"Last chance for those who want to actually swear," I said sadly. "The spell is designed to heal those who are in my party. If you won't swear, it won't heal you, and I won't waste more time on you."

This time, they all stepped forward, handing the manastones over without complaint, and ten minutes later, the entire group were shuddering from the aftereffects.

"Now, I need *your* help," I said. "The woman I love is up there, as well as my friends. The humans who drove you out and attacked you are my enemies, and I need to kill them all and free my people."

I looked around, seeing the expressions on their faces as they rubbed at missing wounds.

"What am I missing here?" I asked after a brief pause, and the young girl who had brought me the stash of manastones spoke up.

"We don't know how to help."

"Why not? You're Gnomes, and you know this place, right?"

"Not really," she said. "We escaped down the drainage system. You can't get back up it; it's too small, we barely fit."

"Okay, then you lead me to another way up."

"We don't know of one. Not that we can fit in."

"There has to be," I replied grimly. "I've wasted an hour or more here, wasted manastones I needed!"

"And we're grateful," she firmly, looking up at me as she slowly pushed her hood back, exposing her face to the room which suddenly filled with stunned gasps.

Before, she was covered in scaled growths, and her skin looked more reptilian than mammal. The scales were ridged and coarse, the flesh almost entirely buried behind it all. Now, though? She was entirely different. Her hair was patchy, clearly having grown in areas that would permit it, while clumps were entirely missing.

Her eyes were different colors, one blue and one green, while her skin was pale as fresh cream. Her pointed ears were small and dainty. While I thought she looked fairly pretty, for a gnome, clearly others felt that she was more than that.

Gasps rolled around the room again as her mother stood, throwing her own hood back and exposing an older, but clearly attractive woman as she started to speak.

"We aren't fighters," she explained. "We can't fight, not won't, we can't. We've no weapons that work, no magic, and we have no skill there."

"But, but I've fought your people! You're fucking insane!" I said, twisting to look at the badunka rider, who ducked his head and looked at the floor in shame.

"We're inventors, creators. Not warriors," she pointed out. I hesitated, reviewing the fights I'd had with them.

She was right.

I'd found them and thought they'd be useful, that I could send them at the nobles' forces, and they would draw their attention while I closed in…

But I also had the image of the fight I'd had with them in that ruined house. They'd piled in on me in their dozens and possibly hundreds.

I'd run out of weapons, and I'd used their friends, literally, as clubs. I'd beaten them to death with bare hands, and suddenly the fight I'd had took on a new light.

I'd basically beaten a shitload of mentally ill people to death. They were lethal opponents when they could build a weapon, or when they mobbed a target, but beyond that?

I remembered the stories of the slave raids on the gnome villages that Lucian had told us about, of the dozens of small bodies that were left behind for every one of their attackers who was killed.

And Giint?

Giint was awesome, and he was my friend, but he was also a freak of nature, physically a bit bigger than the average gnome. After all the healing magic that had been used on him, he was a lethal motherfucker.

He was the exception to the rule, the way he'd worked in the storm, the way he'd braved the worst of the elements, determined not to fail, while the others had collapsed and broken down in terror.

He didn't give two shits at the best of times, stealing anything not nailed down, and the nails as well if it was, but he was driven and brave.

He was more unique than I'd thought, and these people…

They weren't. Sadly. They were normal people, and right now, they were crafters who couldn't make their creations work. I looked at her again, and I spoke quietly.

"The manastones won't power your creations, will they?"

"Not now. The suppressor was a gnomish invention, from the records," the older woman replied, sighing. "It was designed to stop not only spells but the way that the manastones work to power things."

"I can use them for spells."

"Don't know why. What I know of the suppressor says you shouldn't be able to." She shook her head, clearly searching for the words she lacked. "We were driven out, my daughter Daana and I, with our condition. We were in the outer ring. We hid from Naga and their badunkas, the dead, and everything else. We searched for a way down for years. That tunnel is the only way."

"It's not now, then," I said. "They used the explosives you mentioned." I gestured to the older male gnome. "And they blew the ground apart. They missed me, but I was knocked senseless and fell down the hole."

"So there's a hole now? Makes sense," he grunted.

"Why does it make sense?"

"The Naga went mad, attacked us, the humans did, the…*everyone* attacked us. They probably think the place is sinking. Or that they can get out," he snarled, plopping himself down on the filthy floor and looking around the small room as if seeing it for the first time and being disgusted by it.

"We used to be respected. We helped design these places, we made the airships, the cannons, a thousand wonderful creations, and now?" He spat at the floor before looking down at grubby hands and refusing to meet anyone else's eyes.

"Can you help me?" I asked the room in general, sensing the defeat, the depression, and knowing I was asking more of them than I had any right to ask.

"We can't fight."

"I cannnnn," the badunka rider said, clambering awkwardly to his feet.

"Posstoss!" one of the others snapped. I looked at him, thinking he was swearing. "You're no better at fightin' than I am!"

"Then yer caaan heeelp," he growled, making me nod to him in respect. He sounded like Giint had at first as he adjusted, learning to speak again. The spell I'd used on them all was far more powerful and comprehensive than that original one had been, and it'd helped them massively.

That brought its own issues, though, as I suddenly remembered Giint collapsing as soon as his internal system was restored. Glancing around, I swore under my breath as I realized that, in healing them and saving their lives, I'd made them useless to me in the coming fight.

If I managed to destroy the suppressor, then these gnomes would collapse and start to gain all the points they'd been denied all their lives as their mana system rebooted and came back together.

They'd be utterly useless and defenseless as they collapsed and their bodies adjusted, something that had taken Giint several hours. Frankly, that little bastard was unreliable in the extreme as any kind of yardstick to measure his race.

If I'd known him better at the time, I'd have kicked him a few times to make sure he hadn't just found some drugs and decided that in the middle of a fight was a good time to try them out.

Either way, there was no way I could expect them to fight now, and apart from the manastones I'd gained from them, I'd wasted this time.

I checked the bag, seeing I had eleven stones, each roughly the size of my thumbnail, and one crystal down the back of my left bracer that was about the size of my pinky finger.

That gave me approximately twelve spells.

I suspected that any spell I 'fired', like I did a Fireball, would unravel before it could go very far. The circle had needed a horrific amount of mana to keep going. It'd used up a handful of stones, and when I'd repaired the Tower…

Well. A half dozen stones had turned shattered stone to liquid and had rebuilt staircases, walls, and floors, replaced glass and more. Hundreds of stones, yeah, bigger and better-grade, whatever that meant, but hundreds had *literally* rebuilt the Great Tower, a structure that was nearly three miles high, doing probably fifty years' worth of heavy construction.

Probably three hundred and fifty years' worth, if it was a government project with tea breaks added in.

I shook myself and straightened as Posstoss grabbed a handful of other gnomes, dragging them to their feet and kicking them when they tried to argue.

"We're wiiiith youuu." He grinned maniacally at me

"Look, I want the help, seriously I do, but if the way you came down is too small for me, and there's no other way up?" I shook my head. "You'll not be able to help me," I grumbled, pissed at the way all of this had worked out.

"Youuu want helpppp orrr nottt?" he growled.

"I do, but if you can't get back up…"

"Cannn get tooo prisonnn," he suggested, teeth gleaming in the dim light of the manastones. "Prisonnnn has tooo lead somewherrrre."

"Prison?" I asked, latching onto the word and the way everyone else winced. "What prison?"

"Prisonnn that theyyy use," he said, shrugging. "Theyyy keep prisonerrrrs therrre."

"Fuck's sake, are you kidding me?" I snarled. "I'm literally telling you that I need to free my friends who were taken prisoner, and you don't tell me there's a fucking *prison*?"

"You won't be able to get to it," Daana said quickly. "It's thirty across, and maybe ten karr up from here…"

"Kar?"

"Karr," she corrected, drawing in imaginary line and walking a short distance. "About this long."

"A meter, or close enough, anyway, and it's that close?" I felt hope surge in me until she shook her head.

"It is, but the pipes we'd need to crawl along…we can do it, and we will," she added hastily, seeing the look on my face. "But it'll take at least an hour to travel that distance."

"Nearly two," her mother corrected. "It's up, not down; takes longer."

"Whatever." I shrugged. "Why didn't you mention this before?"

"Because it's insane," she said. "The pipes lead underneath it, and we could get out there, probably, but the people in the prison are in cages, and there's no way we could get them into the pipes. Not even all of the gnomes, never mind if your friends are there, and your size."

"How many are there?" I asked. "How many gnomes? How many prisoners overall? And would they have taken my people there?"

"That where they keep everyone when they're not being used to wake the golems or rebuild the city," she replied. "They're used over and over, drained to the point that they might never recover, then dumped in there while others are used."

"Mana batteries," I muttered. "You said the gnomes and possibly others; did you see others?"

"No, but we heard them when we passed. They're sewer pipes; they run under everything, but if we try to get out." She paused, clearly thinking about how to put it.

"We smash toilets. Cover everything in shit," Posstoss added helpfully. "You want us break toilet?"

"There's toilets?" I asked, eyes wide, having never noticed them before. We'd been doing our business wherever we could with any degree of privacy here, but that made a lot of sense, really. You couldn't be taking a shit out of the window or in a corner of the corridor normally, not back when this was a working and *flying* city. Although, the pigeons would be in for some harsh justice if I could.

"We smash?" Posstoss asked again.

I paused, thinking. "Let's start this again," I suggested. "You all crawled down here through the toilets, right?"

"A maintenance hatch," Daana's mother corrected.

"Okay, so you all got into a maintenance hatch, but it's too small for me?"

"Definitely," she replied, eyeing me. "Two of us were too big and went last."

"Where are they?"

"In the pipes."

"Wait, they're stuck in there? Abandoned?"

"Can't get to them." She shrugged. "Better to leave two than the entire group. That's why they went last."

"Fuck, that's cold. Okay, so if they couldn't fit and got stuck, then I sure as shit can't, but you passed the prison? How did you know if you were in a sewer pipe?"

"One of the guards used the pipe," one of the gnomes muttered. I glanced at him, seeing the color of his overalls and...my mind blanked, resetting as I shuddered with the conclusion he wasn't saying.

"Okay, so...you know it was the prison because...?"

"They were talking, and the others have a toilet in a cell."

"Okay!" I said, pointing to Daana as she said that. "That's a good point. So there's a toilet in the cell; can you get into that one?"

"Maybe, can't tell much except for listening, so will have to guess, and it might take a while."

Why?"

"Without access to our inventions?" She shrugged, and Posstoss lifted a small hammer and the dagger, miming tapping the back of the dagger with the hammer, like he was using a chisel.

"Fuck," I growled. "Okay, you said it was on the next level up?"

"Yes, but no stairs."

"There's stairs back there." I jerked my thumb over my shoulder.

"No way out," she said, shaking her head. "We checked it, I went up personally. The next floor has collapsed and buried it all, no way out."

"Goddamn it. Okay, I'll look for another..."

"Unless you broke the windows," another gnome added in helpfully.

"Oh, yeah, if you broke the glass, but that's *old.*"

"What?"

"The glass in the windows," Daana pointed out, smiling. "There's two windows that aren't buried."

"There's fucking windows up there that lead out to the prison?" I gestured back toward the corridor and the stairs leading up. They all nodded, beginning to comment on how nice the windows were. "Is there anything else here?" I asked, my voice a low hiss through gritted teeth as I tried unsuccessfully to keep my temper, reminding myself that these were gnomes, and until recently, at least half mad.

"Nope."

"Nothing."

"Nothing at all."

"Except the armory."

"Well, yeah, except for that."

"Yeah, nothing at all."

I stared at the barrage of random talking, and in the case of one, arguing, apparently with himself, as I searched out a voice I'd just heard.

"You," I said finally, pointing at him. "You said the armory?"

"Oh yeah, old armory from the people who used to live here. No use, though."

"Why not?" I asked, sagging slightly.

"It's locked away, some kind of crystal door."

"WHERE IS IT?" I snapped, trying to keep my voice steady.

"Bottom of the stairs, it's on the left," he offered.

I was off, running before he'd even finished speaking.

I made it out of the door, then into the hall before the crumpled armor reminded me exactly why I needed to replace that section, making me wince as the dented plates tore skin loose all over again.

I hobbled down the corridor, limping down the stairs, spotting a pair of ancient bodies next to one of the doors nearby. The doorway was large, boasting two metal-clad single doors. One of the heavy doors had cracked away, hanging loose with a hinge that had given way at some point.

I pushed inside, pausing at the crystal doorway that greeted me just inside, the dull reflective surface sparking occasionally with a room beyond them, dull shapes reflecting the light.

I reached out, my hand resting against the cool crystal, and I focused, ordering it to open, using my Imperial Authority. Even after all these long centuries, the crystal was active, and as soon as it felt me, tasted me, and recognized me, however it worked—it dissipated, the solidity breaking apart into mist and flowing back into the frame, laying the room before me bare.

Holding the manastone high, staring around at the treasure before me, I shook my head over the fact they were all complaining they had no weapons while this was below them.

There was a full armory protected from the ravages of time by the crystal doorway and the solid walls. This section of the building must have been specially constructed, much like the Hall of Memories had been.

I understood why Jenae hadn't mentioned it before now, when we'd been desperately searching for magic and more, while this was frankly mundane...

"Recover Mundane Materials," I muttered to myself, shaking my head in memory. The mundane section She'd added to the quest, and I'd thought it had been to reference the damn bits and bobs, storerooms of repair materials and more, but it must have been this as well.

The room was filled with row upon row of armor, helms by the dozen, breastplates...shit.

I stepped forward, taking three quick steps to a quartet of armored suits that stood complete on their own stands.

They were gleaming as if freshly oiled and set aside only yesterday. Matching undergarments and more were folded next to them, along with a selection of weapons, but the armor…

This wasn't *standard* legion armor. This had to be…I reached out, touching it reverently and shaking my head in amazement.

This was a hell of a find, and it'd have Thorn on her knees weeping in reverence if she were here.

This was Legion Praetorian armor, original, and made by the armorers of old, protected from the ravages of time and sealed away here.

Four complete sets.

I wasn't worthy.

I knew I wasn't, and that it'd be years before I was truly worthy of this armor. Hell, I had divine armor that Thorn was working on, but this? This, as the Prince, as a member of the Legion, and frankly as the man who'd made the God of Death my bitch, was something I could wear right now.

I looked down at my scratched, scuffed, and badly dented legion plate, then back up at the armor before me. I heard the gnomes entering the room, looking about and muttering about how everything was made for giants rather than real people before grabbing a few armfuls of daggers.

"Go," I said quietly to them. "Grab what you need and go, climb the pipe, get into the prison, and smash your way through. Take extra daggers for my people."

Posstoss took a minute to grab a small hammer as well before leaving. Daana looked from me to the armor and back again, seeing me starting to disassemble my own and pausing to nod respectfully to me before leaving, trying to tug the door closed on her way out.

It was huge and had a broken hinge. It barely moved at all, but I understood the respectful gesture she was making.

I stripped quickly, standing in my underwear as I thought about it, then cursed as I did it, feeling it was a waste, but also not. I used almost a third of a manastone on a full-body Scour, unwilling to countenance putting such a magnificently made suit on without doing that first.

The undergarments were stiff at first, hell, as I unfolded them, I winced, wondering if they'd be all right to wear, as even though they'd escaped most of the damage that time should have wrought, it was still over seven hundred years since they'd been folded up.

They creaked a bit, but after some experimental prodding and shaking, they folded out fine. At least they weren't coated in gunk and bits of creature like my old padding and armor was.

The padding was a bit tight in places, and it took two changes to get a full set that fit me comfortably, meaning I had to remove sections from the other armors to assemble a full set that fit me.

I disassembled the armor carefully, taking the legs and waist from the first stand, the arms from the second, and the chest and helm from the fourth, but once it was done?

The armor that was spread out before me was amazing.

The connected sections had spring-loaded joints, weighted slides and latches, the connections were smooth as silk, and hell, *everything* was amazing.

It wasn't to the level Thorn could achieve with the help of the gnomes, and even with them helping, it'd never be the level of my divine plate over my conjured dragon scale armor, but as normal armor?

Even for elite troops, it was magnificent.

I stepped into the boots, feeling the click as the ankles closed, reaching down and flicking the latches, twisting a small, almost impossible to see section three times. The bolts connected and locked. The lower legs, knees, and the upper legs came next. Section by section, the gleaming scalemail, the plate, the waist and more, assembling as I went, automatically connected sections to hooks built into the under-armor padding.

I did it thanks to the practice I'd had until now, assembling each bit as I went, and where there were differences–my armor before had been good, but it was legion scout then standard legion armor–this was the top level, and the alterations were easily understandable.

I worked smoothly, knowing that sending the gnomes into the prison was *a* solution, but if this wasn't where they were holding the others, I was back to square one.

I had to believe that Oracle and the others were alive still, otherwise, there was no point in living, as far as I was concerned.

Not beyond revenge.

I needed the armor to be ready, the equipment here, to make sure I had the best chance possible. They had rocket-propelled grenades. I'd not seen guns, but I seriously doubted that at least some of them wouldn't have them.

If they'd used some trick to bring the RPGs through, then I couldn't see them leaving a couple of rifles behind, rather than stuffing them down the sides of the box or something.

Either Oracle and the others would be okay or they wouldn't, in which case I'd tear this place apart with my bare hands and bathe in the blood of my enemies.

That meant I needed armor that could keep me alive long enough to achieve that. I needed to give the gnomes time to get into position and be the distraction.

It also meant I was probably sending those brave, utterly batshit gnomes off to be slaughtered.

I hated that, and it went against every instinct. I had no right to demand they give up their lives to protect me and my friends. But they'd offered, and I wasn't turning them aside.

All I needed to do was take out the suppressor, then my own magic would turn the tables, especially when powered by the stones.

I continued to dress, working my way up and adding section by section. The chest fit nicely, with the shoulders being a little loose, but adjusting straps helped massively, then it was the arms, the bracers, the gauntlets.

As each section clicked and was adjusted, I grew more and more determined. Lydia couldn't make use of this; she needed her own specialist Valkyrie armor, but Grizz? Then probably Jian and definitely Restun. They'd get the other sets.

I shifted, bending and straightening, performing a few quick lunges and twists.

The armor fit like it'd been made for me, aside from tightening a section here and there. It was perfect the first time, and when I was done…

There was a cloak.

It wasn't just a hood and cloak, which was fairly common here for bad weather, no this was a cloak, or more accurately, a fucking cape.

It looked like something I should be wearing with pointed ears on my armor and driving cool cars with. It was sodding amazing, and I loved it.

I loved that it connected to my armor with something like magnets as well; they held comfortably in set grooves, but they also broke away with a sharp tug, meaning that I wasn't at risk from jet aircraft intakes or assholes pulling on it.

I looked the armor over once it was on, a mirror of polished brass on one side of the room clearly intended for this.

I looked fucking terrifying.

The Dark Legion had clearly copied the Praetorian armor's color scheme, as where the Imperial Legion was all silver and highlights of red or gold, this was as black as pitch. The under-armor itself was, anyway.

The actual armor plates were a deep, blood red, and atop the black, with a black cape, it just looked awesome. I lifted the helm, finding it was a similar design to the Imperial Right one I'd been wearing, and that had evolved thanks to the Gods' help.

It wasn't as cool, and it was missing the bladed ridge that let me stab people while headbutting them, but that was fine.

The eye slots were familiar, and as I slid the helm on, it rested comfortably, not moving as I shook my head from side to side to test it.

I dumped the makeshift spear on the floor, attaching a pair of short swords to a back sheath, finding that they worked even with the cape attached!

I was so keeping this fucker after I'd freed the others, I decided, refusing to consider any other outcome but that I'd be successful.

I reached for the weapons rack again as a sudden pain tore through me, gripping my heart and making me stagger, hissing.

The world changed, all at once. Suddenly, mana was back, and it came back with the force of a speeding semi, making me groan as my vision flared, not only my HUD returning, not only my mana coming back, but Oracle and the others, they were there! I could feel them, somewhere above me, farther away than I'd hoped, but…

But those fuckers up above would know where they were. There'd be a path, there had to be! I grimaced, feeling the pain that Oracle and Sehran had been filled with, and Bob! Fuck's sake, Bob had been reduced to inanimate! He lived, if lived was the right word, but his body…his heart and the center of his being was intact, but he'd been reduced to a pile of fucking bones by the mana theft.

Oracle—as much as I cared for Bob, and he was a friend, he wasn't Oracle. I sensed her finally seeming to draw a shuddering breath, a massive influx of mana as she frantically checked something. I felt her hitting Sehran with her mana, flooding it into her as well, as she tried to help and…

And they were gone suddenly, the sense of them distant, miles so, possibly thousands of miles traveled in a second, and…

"A portal!" I hissed in fury, right before the mana was ripped from the world again, and I fell to my knees, gasping, the world shrinking back to a much smaller place, a tiny fraction of what it had been.

They were alive. Oracle, and possibly the others, had been suddenly taken from me. Bob was alive but reduced to a pile of bones. Sehran, my friend and the love of Jian's life, had been starved of mana, and fuck knows how she was even here still. I'd been so focused on Oracle that I'd not considered it.

Worst of all, I'd felt Oracle's panic and her desperate drawing on the mana of the realm. I'd felt the way she'd not reached out to me, but in and down toward a faint, flickering spark of life.

To our baby.

The cold took me over, flooding me, as all emotion save a furious hatred was suppressed.

They'd taken them from me.

They'd stolen them, but I'd get them back. I'd take them all back, all those who'd been taken, and when I was done? People would shit themselves a thousand years from now over what I was going to do with the thieves.

I forced myself to move calmly to pick out a spear, adding a dagger on either hip, checking to make sure that all the weapons were easily reachable. Then I picked a shield from the rack, hefting it and nodding in satisfaction with the weight.

The only issue was that, if I carried a shield, I couldn't hold the damn manastones. I needed to hold them to draw the mana out, so after a long breath, I put the shield down again. Magic was going to make all the difference in what was to come.

I assessed myself, knowing that the gnomes were moving, that they needed time, or I'd never make it to Oracle. I'd waited this long; I needed to be patient. Everything fit, nothing was too heavy or too light, and clearly the original Praetorian Legionnaires had been of similar levels, if not higher than I was, judging from the weight of everything.

I paused, thinking about how Amon had literally had an entire Praetorian Legion, five thousand men and women that were, at their minimum, my equals.

Most were so far beyond me, I could barely imagine it.

The thought of what I could achieve with that…

I shook it free, leaving the hall without looking back at the discarded gear.

I'd shifted my bags and manastones and so on over, but beyond that, I'd left the rest in a pile of discarded gear, knowing that the crystal door, once opened, was now used up and couldn't be closed.

I strode out, my left leg chafing and uncomfortable, but infinitely better now that it wasn't being ground to bits with every step.

I climbed the stairs steadily, a cold weight in my chest as I faced the fact that soon, one way or another, I'd know what happened to Oracle and the others.

Either I'd rescue them all, or I'd see them again when I, too, passed through the veil.

CHAPTER THIRTY-THREE

I stood at the top of a nearby dome, watching out of the narrow windows a short time later as I waited, wishing I had a damn clock, or better yet, a fucking radio.

I was waiting for the gnomes to cause a kind of ruckus. After all, a gang of those mad bastards smashing their way out of the toilet, regardless of which toilet they exited, would wreak unimaginable havoc, I was sure.

Where I stood, I could see the front of the building across and below, a goddamned freestanding *building*, rather than a room or suite of rooms, which made no damn sense to me. The dome of the building *I* stood in now was the top of the building I'd entered a floor below, and was clearly the center of this new level. Staring down from it, the wide, squat building off to the side was what I assumed was the prison they were using.

I frowned at the thought of the floor below me that housed the lower section of this building and wondered just how many damn ways there were up, as well as if there was a way down in the prison.

Fuck it, it didn't matter.

A single guard sat against the wall that I could see, a steadily burning torch set in a wall sconce above him, lighting the entrance.

He was there to see, but also to be seen, as I'd spotted two others so far, one hidden in the upper floor of a building next to the one he was sitting outside of, and the other was slowly patrolling the walls.

All three looked like they were bored to tears, but they also appeared to be professionals. Timing the one who stomped around the outer wall of the building gave me a different time every loop, as he was clearly trying to mix it up, rather than be predictable.

Similarly, the one who sat outside, seemingly utterly bored, was checking his surroundings regularly. A sword was laid across his knees, and while he had food, he was clearly on guard, rather than napping, judging from the regular movements, the checks, and the way his head swiveled.

I guessed that they were professionals on Earth, and here their paranoia was helping and fairly understandable, considering the mad shit they must have seen.

The darkness of the lower floors was lessened here, with the torch just adding to the sun that shone down through cracks in the overhead sections, illuminating the cavernous expanse of shattered buildings in shifting light and shadow.

There were trees here, entire sections of dappled shade, ponds that showed signs of life to my experienced eyes, even from this distance.

Sections stood out to my eyes, places I'd expect Bane or Tang to be, and I watched for the slightest hint of anyone else that might be hiding.

After half an hour, a horrific amount of time waiting that I managed only by constantly reminding myself that to run screaming at the building now, without my distraction, would at best result in a far longer time for me to reach Oracle and the others. I forced myself to spend most of it staring, eyes slightly unfocused, at the middle of the prison, letting my mind process everything, highlighting little details here and there.

By the time the first distant crash, followed by screams, finally rang out, I was desperately ready.

As soon as the sounds filled the air, the guard at the front was on his feet, sword gripped tight and point held low, the one who had been walking the walls sprinted for the stairs that led down from there and into the courtyard. One more appeared from the shadows, making me curse that I'd not spotted them until then.

The last one, still in the building on overwatch, stayed put.

I'd hoped he'd go as well, but to be fair, if they had any real sense, they'd be watching outward as well, still, and they blatantly weren't.

Be thankful for small mercies, and all that.

I'd spent some of the time while I was waiting with a dagger, carefully cutting away at the edge of the window and exposing the housing of the glass.

Unlike the Great Tower, this place was mainly metal with a thin veneer of stone across it to make it look nice. As such, the windows, hell, most of the place, was easily taken apart if you had a little time, especially after all these centuries.

This place had been *constructed*, not grown, and it showed in a thousand little ways.

I'd stripped the thin coating from the edge of the glass, then sliced steadily down, cutting a little way into the wood they'd used to secure it in here.

The glass slid out easily, and I set it aside before I stepped out onto the ledge, crouching, then pulling the first burst of mana into me from a stone. The stone crumbled to dust, then I was leaping forward, fucking praying silently to Jenae that this was going to work.

Soaring Majesty triggered!

…more or less.

I felt the sudden pull as the mana was ripped from me, the second and third stones crumbling as well. By then, I was already landing atop the roof of the building the overwatch was in, and it was too late for them.

I cut the ability, landing as lightly as I could and ran. The roof was flat; clearly there was no need to accommodate rainwater runoff in here, and the door that led down from the large balcony area the roof had been turned into was missing.

I took the stairs two and three at a time, racing down them, knowing damn well that, unless they were utterly deaf, there was no way I was sneaking up on someone in all this gear.

The stairs ended in a hall. Two doors to my right and left were open, both showing large and what had probably been pleasant-looking rooms.

They were also markedly empty.

Lucky number three, however, was directly ahead, and I slammed into it at full speed, taking the door off its hinges as I jumped and straight-kicked it.

The door was rigged, a grenade or something having been attached to the back of the door, presumably to surprise someone sneaking in.

Instead, it was sent flying along with the door, landing on the floor between me and the overwatch with a crash.

I stepped back, spinning and ducking out of the room, even as he hefted a rifle, a pair of suppressed shots tearing through the air.

One hit the stairs, ricocheting upwards and out of sight, while the other hit the wall next to the door.

Unfortunately for the shooter, he'd neglected to consider that the walls were stone over metal, and his bullets were…shit, really.

It pinged around, making him duck, which was followed by a brief scream of horror, then a boom as his grenade trap reminded him of its presence.

I was off and running, knowing that every second I wasted out here was a second I wasn't freeing Oracle and the others, as well as giving the local assholes time to get ready for me.

I took the room in, all in one go, seeing the poor grenaded sod on the floor, frantically trying to staunch the blood loss from a truncated leg that now ended at the knee.

Racing through the room, I slashed his throat as I passed, before I leaped through the already shattered window, triggering Soaring Majesty with another stone. It crumbled, and even as I rocketed upwards, I knew I needed more.

I triggered a second and a third, leaving myself with only five regular stones and the finger-length crystal. I didn't care, though—no matter what else happened, I was getting to Oracle now.

The look on the guard's face as he turned was tremendous, I had to admit. The house I'd just left was filled with smoke and fire. Then there I was, flying like an avatar of death straight out of the shattered window, cape billowing behind me in full-on plate mail armor that they had to know was heavy as fuck.

I powered my flight all the way through the air to land literally three meters from him, landing lightly and already running.

The guy, to give him credit, did raise his sword to try and stop me. The tip was shaking like a shitting dog, but he tried.

I smacked it aside with the haft of my spear, then punched him in the face, not even slowing as I raced through the front gate and into the courtyard.

He practically flew backward, the back of his head hitting the wall and sending him rebounding to the floor, unconscious and possibly dead, considering the force behind the blow.

I paid him no further mind, having seen the main door of the building ahead of me, and I was racing for it.

The main building, surrounded on two sides by smaller wings, which were surrounded in turn by a fence, was three stories tall, close to the ceiling of this cavernous floor and easily twenty meters wide at the front.

There were fires inside, reflecting the light through cracked and dusty windows, weeds and small bushes grew up through the courtyard here and there, and more dangled from the upper balcony and down one wall. The building had the appearance of a moss and ivy-encrusted tomb, and I half expected a guard to pop up and start telling me that he used to be an adventurer, too, until an arrow met his knee and ended it all.

I raced through the door, shouldering it aside. It hit something or *someone,* more accurately, and I heard the grunt of pain as it bounced back.

I'd been expecting to be backstabbed, rogues being the scumbags they are, but the loud clang of the ricochet that announced it was a bullet, instead of a dagger, pissed me off even more.

I twisted around, finding a woman dressed in standard-issue, military-grade body armor, her nose broken, now missing two front teeth, and blood pouring down from both nose and mouth in a scarlet flood. She shakily raised the gun, having seen that the bullet to my armor did nothing, yet was still determined to try.

I didn't have time for it.

I batted the gun aside and stabbed out, the spear taking her in the chest, cutting clear through the bone and bisecting her heart.

Her eyes went wide, gun clattering to the floor as her hands came inward, shocked at how easily my spear had pierced her fancy body armor and sternum, but I was already moving.

There were shouts coming from the right and the left. The right was mixed voices, different tones echoing. The left was the sound of a group shouting things to bolster themselves, like "come on," "let's get them," and "oh my god, we're all going to fucking die."

That last one was accurate, at least. I grabbed a grenade from the woman's body, pulling the pin and flinging it down the left side of the corridor underarm before turning and running to the right.

Voices got closer, then started screaming, just as the grenade went off with a blast that echoed down the corridor. I ignored them as I raced past dozens of doors.

I dismissed them, for the most part, following the sound of screaming coming from up ahead, occasionally glancing in as I went, seeing empty rooms with bedrolls laid out, a cooking setup, and boxes of gear. In the next one, a collection of golems slumped over in death or deactivation.

I continued onward, recognizing and ignoring the risk of a sneaky son of a bitch hiding in a room and popping out after I'd passed.

The handgun and the rifle I'd seen might have been little risk to me in this armor, but that didn't mean I'd shrug off a .50 caliber fired into the back of my skull.

I wasn't risking some bright fucker deciding the only chance they had was the prisoners, though, and when I came to a special section at the back, I knew I'd found it.

There were two soldiers, both in the same body armor and both with spears, jabbing them into the room beyond, backs to me as I turned the corner at the end of the corridor.

They didn't notice me at first, one of them catching a glimpse at the last second and looking sideways, his mouth opening to shout a warning, when I plowed into him and his friend, shoulder-first.

I picked them both up and slammed them into the wall, pinning them between my armored bulk and the stone covering. A crunch of shattering bones and the gush of blood from one's mouth made it clear neither were in the fight any longer. I found an unfamiliar and unkempt woman with a dagger in either hand, surrounded by easily fifty gnomes, half a dozen of whom were covered in shit, marking them as my lunatics who had climbed up the toilet.

"We did it!" one of them screamed upon seeing me.

"We won!"

"Drugs now?"

"Hooray!"

"Who the hell are you?"

That last one was from the woman, clearly military, I'd guess from her clothing, hairstyle, and the way she held herself, one dagger extended and one held back, ready for a fight.

"Where are they!" I roared at her, ignoring the Gnomes and leveling my spear at her. "Where is *she*!"

"Who?" She backed up, the Gnomes going silent as they turned to regard her, then back to me.

"We not done?" Posstoss asked.

I growled at him, considering the open cell doors I'd passed and wondering if there were more hidden as I spoke.

"No!" I snapped absently. "She's not one of mine!"

"Oh okay, we kill?" he suggested, pointing the dagger at her happily. I shook my head as her eyes widened farther, and she shook her head.

"Not yet."

"I'm not on their side!" she said quickly, pointing at the figures on the floor behind me.

"Good. Doesn't mean you're on mine," I growled.

She bit her lip. "Look, where I'm from, we have a saying, 'the enemy of my enemy…'"

"Is my enemies' enemy. Nothing more and nothing less," I finished for her, replacing the traditional quote with another I'd heard bandied around on the internet for years.

"You…you're from Earth?" she asked, stunned, then straightened up and patted herself on the chest. "I'm…ow." She stopped, having clearly forgotten she was holding a dagger in each hand and nearly cutting a tit off.

"You're from Earth," I said in a dull tone. "So are all these dickheads, note the fact that they're bleeding out on the floor? You came here to fight me, to try and take my home, so explain yourself and fucking quickly."

"No!" she said quickly, then glanced around. "Look, if I put the knives down, will you stop pointing that thing at me? And tell the Dwarves to leave me alone as well?"

"What Dwarves?" I asked, frowning, then grunting as she glanced around, confused. "Fuck's sake. These are Gnomes."

"How can you tell the difference?" she asked.

"Easy," I replied straightening. "Hey, you fuckers!" I called to the Gnomes. "Don't touch the things that look like strange eggs, and don't kill anyone who surrenders, but these guys and their friends might have drugs in their pockets."

There was a frozen silence, then the entire room, bar myself and the woman, were fighting to get out of the single small door.

"Remember! No touching the eggs!" I shouted after them, before looking back at her and growling. "Dwarves are short but broad, bearded, and generally a lot more sane. Gnomes are smaller, probably smarter, but utterly batshit. If you're in doubt: drink and drugs. Gnomes are all druggies given a chance, dwarves like their booze.

There's probably an exception to that somewhere, but I don't care. Now, where the fuck are my people!" I snapped, leveling the spear at her chest again.

"I don't know!" she replied quickly spreading her hands again and clearly trying to speak in a calming way. "Look, I was locked away here a couple of days back. They come and dump some gnomes here and take others away, that's it, that's all I know! The lord's son was left in charge while he went through the portal, and…"

"Which portal? Where'd he go?"

"I don't know!" she growled back at me, clearly getting angry. "I was a scout, okay? I was forced to come to this shithole, then kicked through another fucking portal and told to search the damn place! We were slaughtered! I barely escaped. I told that dickbag of a lord that there was an ambush, and he still led everyone else through. He had me locked up and left his son, who let me just tell you is a fucking *idiot*, to watch over the place!" She paused for breath, clearly furious and about to go on, when I lowered my spear.

"How long?"

"What?"

"How long ago!" I replied through gritted teeth, glaring at her.

"Oh, umm, four, five days? No more than a week?"

"Which is it, four days or a week?" I snapped.

"I don't know, okay!" she replied hotly. "I've been here in the goddamn dark, surrounded by those lunatics who keep trying to strip me and who knows what, and…"

"They're not rapists," I said, the base of the spear hitting the floor with a chime of metal.

"What?"

"The Gnomes, they're not, well, those I know are basically totally uninterested in sex beyond it being a requirement to get new gnomes. Except for Giint, who's just fucked up in too many ways to count, but definitely not a rapist. Shit, look, what I'm trying to say is that they were probably looking for any drugs you had stashed."

"Why the hell is there a race of druggies?!" she hissed. "That's not right, and it's not evolutionarily viable, either!"

"Fucked if I know, fucked if I care," I snapped. "These Gnomes were trapped here and forced to drink and eat contaminated stuff; it fucked with their brains. Look, the suppressor…where is it?"

"Is it a magic thing?" she asked. I nodded. "No clue but there were some artifacts they found here, but that's *all* I know. Maybe in the tower?"

"And where the fuck is the Tower?" I growled.

"Oh!" She winced. "Um, it was near the gnome village place?"

"Great, and to make this as clear as possible, where the fuck is that from here!" I snapped, circling my hand in a gesture of 'get to the fucking point'.

"Aren't you from here?" she asked.

"No! No I'm not from the sunken, ruined fucking shithole of a Prax! It's a ruin! I came here because you dickheads invaded. Now, last goddamned chance – tell me where my friends are, or I swear I'll poke you with this, and I'm not buying you a drink first!" I snarled, waving the spear at her.

"Whoa, okay, just calm down, I'm a…" She shook her head and changed tack. "Your accent–you're from the north, right? Up near Newcastle? I was a copper from Manchester; how about we both just calm down and…"

"The woman I love is in danger, as are my closest friends. I've had the magic ripped from me, and my unborn child might be dying right now. Do you really think 'calm down' is going to work?" I growled.

"I'll show you!" she wailed. "I'm not being a dick. I didn't know any of that, and I was brought here *days* ago, after spending most of my time in this world on the other side of the portal. They released me from the Oath because they were going to kill me, all right?"

"Whatever."

"Give me a second," she said, moving around me gingerly, watching to see if I was going to attack her. Once she reached the bodies on the floor, she quickly went through the discarded mess the gnomes had left behind, taking a grenade and a handgun, checking them over and making sure both were fully functional.

"Don't get your hopes up with those," I warned her.

"What?"

"The guns." I nodded. "Bet you didn't bring much ammo."

"No, it needed to be in special crates, and they came after the rest of us, one at a time. One of them exploded, as well, so only three crates made it through." She shrugged. "Still better than a spear, though. Bet you've wanted these since you got here!" She hefted the gun and grinned at me.

"Do you see me taking them?" I asked flatly. "Most of the creatures I've fought wouldn't even notice you using that popgun on them. Those who would? They'd just be pissed off. Take the spear."

"I had two lessons with a spear, that's it. I was armed response for nine months before…"

"I don't care. Lead the way," I ordered. "And what? Before what?"

"I shot a rapist piece of shit in the back of the head," she said, standing and walking out into the corridor ahead of me, gun at the ready. "We arrested him. I saw the girls, and he played the 'mad not bad' card. Despite *everything* we'd done, the jury decided there wasn't enough evidence to convict. He was laughing as we escorted him out of the courthouse. We were there as protection *for him*. Having to protect that sack of shit from the public, seeing the families of those girls in the crowd was the last straw. I pulled my gun out, aimed, pulled the trigger, then unloaded and surrendered my gun, got down on the floor, and let Pete, my partner, arrest me."

"Bet the papers loved that." I grunted. "Killer cop."

"They did," she said flatly, hurrying down the corridor, then pausing to pick up a rifle from a nearby body, checking it and flicking the safety back on the handgun, sticking it down the back of her pants. "They praised me, or at least the public did. The entire legal system was starting to fall apart. And me, someone who was required to uphold it, having to let shits like that go loose because some lawyer wanted their name in the paper for some fucking high score?"

"The whole system was fucked," I agreed, following her as she ran from cover to cover, my armor clicking and clattering as I ran up the middle, ignoring the cover entirely. "How many sniper rifles?"

"What?"

"Sniper rifles, the high-powered kind, how many did they bring through?" I repeated, thinking back to the figure that had been on overwatch, and wondering if he'd had one or not.

"Oh, two I think, maybe fifty rounds?"

"Two of them, great."

"They'd have taken one with them, the one who carried it was part of the lord's own squad. His personal death squad of losers."

"What?" I asked, running by her side as she gave up on the cover, leading me to the right and away from the building, toward the outer ring on the right-hand side as near as I could tell.

The buildings around us were intact for a short while before changing from the individual ones that I'd passed back in the center, into a ring around the outside.

The majority here was as I'd seen with the gnomes and on the last visit, a solid section that was more like the inside of a sailing ship. Rooms were separated by corridors and laid out side by side, with larger or smaller ones, depending on the function.

"His loser squad, that's what we all called them. He's some ultimately powerful wizard guy, right? So why the hell does he need a squad of personal followers? He doesn't. They're just a bunch of assholes who suck up to him and act all amazed when he pulls off some magic trick. He basically keeps them around to keep everyone in check, apart from the Oath thingy he used on us all; nobody except his close group ever saw him do magic. He didn't need them, not if he was really able to do the shit he claimed."

"Well-figured-out," I replied laconically. "You sure you know where you're going?"

"The outer ring," she said. "The maps we found show there's a staircase up every four corridors."

We turned to the left, running along a corridor that seemed to loop as if in a ring, taking the second connecting corridor and racing down that, a wide stairwell appearing in the distance, lit by a crack in the wall that let sunlight filter down through swaying leaves.

"Fuck's sake, every four corridors?" I asked, getting a nod from her. I'd passed I didn't know how many corridors when I was half-blinded, and then fuck knows how long I'd run past them, not knowing that the stairs were just out of sight.

The map the gnomes had shared with me…it wasn't accurate. I genuinely had no clue what it was of, possibly a stylized version of the Prax or something. Hell, maybe it was meant as a recruitment tool, but it looked a lot prettier than the functional war machine that Tenandra had shown us.

The central sections looked like the drawing, a small city complete with houses with roofs and open pathways. That was what the gnomes had shared. The majority, though? It was a shattered and ruined mess of twisted steel and stone.

I banished it all from my mind, watching the running figure ahead of me and hearing the panting, tired breaths. "Who are you?" I asked bluntly. "And why are you helping me?"

"I'm Morgana," she said, glaring back. "My dad was into the Arthurian legends, all right?"

"Don't care. I have a bodyguard called Bane; he doesn't wear a mask and act like a dick…well, not most of the time."

"Okay, well, I'm helping you because, well…" she hesitated, and I forced myself not to shout at her.

"Out with it."

"I'm on my own, all right?" she snapped back. "I've got fuck-all to my name, I had the choice of prison–and as a copper, I'd be dead in there–or take a job with this asshole as a bodyguard. I took it, and the next thing I know, I'm a fucking soldier again, I'm halfway across the galaxy, or realm or universe or whatever, and I'm running from things that want to eat my face and possess people. Then I'm in prison, and there's gnomes smashing the shitter apart!"

She waved one arm as she spoke, getting more and more animated.

"There's people going nuts, crazy fuckers bursting out of toilets, and the only person who hasn't tried to stab me with a dagger or their cock or strip search me for drugs is a massive fucker in shiny armor, and you're killing *everyone*! You've obviously got a plan, you know what you're doing here, and I…I need some of that, all right? As long as you're not an asshole, I'll help you. Give me a chance, some food, and some money, maybe some clothes and weapons, point me in the direction of the nearest town, and give me a few pointers, maybe?"

I looked at her, hearing the ragged edge to her voice, the way she was running and barely staying upright, the fear she tried to hide.

"I'll give you a chance," I agreed grudgingly. "After this, but you fuck with me, and I will *kill* you."

"Story of my fucking life," she muttered. "Might as well send me back to high school."

"What?" I asked, then spoke again quickly. "Slow down, get ready."

The stairway was wide, but halfway up it split, going to the left and the right. Both sections were clear, apart from the tree roots that had worked their way in, and the shallow pools that took up most of the middle of the stairs, pouring down to vanish into a crack halfway down.

We splashed through the shallow water, Morgana leading the way up the stairs to the right, rifle raised, moving in a crouch. I jogged out in the open, left hand holding a manastone and the right holding my spear.

We climbed the second flight of stairs slower, the sight that greeted us making me grunt in recognition.

There was a doorway ahead, more of a hatch than anything else, and it had been levered open, leading into a huge, cavernous expanse that was filled with the undead.

Now they were the re-dead, though, as I recognized the bodies of the creatures the necromancer Barry had created. I slowed, orienting myself with the room before pointing across to the far side.

"That way."

"How'd you know?" Morgana asked, before hissing at me as I started off. "You need to avoid the bodies!"

"Why?" I asked, nonplussed.

"They said they might wake up. This is the remnants of some long-ago battle, but the dead here sometimes wake up, and you don't want to wake them, all right?" She gestured at the piles of bodies, getting a grunt from me.

"No time for fucking around. Do what you want," I told her, running across the middle of the floor, and hearing a few seconds later her faltering steps behind me.

"What if they?"

"They're dead." I called back. "Properly dead. We made sure of that the last time we were here, and even if they weren't? The suppressor means they'll stay dead; no mana for them to leech to power their bodies."

"Oh," she said after a second. "Wait, you said *you* did this?"

"Me and my team," I replied absently, instincts screaming that something was wrong. I started checking the dead, wondering what the hell was triggering my paranoia. "What…"

A shot rang out, hitting my left pauldron and ricocheting off into the cavernous expanse overhead.

My head snapped around, glaring in the direction of the hole in the floor we were headed to, even as Morgana threw herself down and returned fire with a three-round burst.

The bullets sparked off a pillar to one side of the far end, and I finally spotted the little bastard. I'd been fixated on the collapsed section that led downward, the hole in the floor being the way we'd come up into this area, and I'd missed the hidden guard who even now was peppering me with bullets.

Bullets that were sparking off in all directions and barely scratching the lacquered plates of my armor.

I ran toward him, growling under my breath, clenching the manastone as I started casting.

The fireball that appeared in that hand, hovering above the manastone it drew the power for its creation from, was almost blisteringly hot. The mana condensed fast and hard as the stone collapsed to dust.

I'd powered it far too much, but I needed to know what was going to happen, and I fired it off with a snarl of hatred.

The spell started to break up even as it left my hand, the outer edge of the compressed ball seeming to float away into smoke.

With every meter it crossed, the spell came apart more and more. Despite the high-pitched whine of its passage, it was obvious, to me at least, that it'd never reach the hidden guard.

Fortunately, the guard didn't know that, and judging from the way he ran out of cover, firing wildly, "anywhere else" was his plan of where to be.

He managed five steps before a bullet hit him high in the left shoulder, spinning him around and sending him to the floor, as my fireball vanished in the air between us.

It would have basically blow-dried his hair, *slightly*, had he stayed where he was.

"Motherfucker!" I ran on. "Come on!" I called back to her, ignoring whether she had listened or not.

The earlier gunshots on the floor below might not have carried up to here, as few of them as there had been, but the latest exchange of shots sure as hell would have carried a lot farther.

I leaned into the run, outdistancing Morgana easily as I leaped down the hole in the floor, then raced left and right, up and down, passing along corridors I had only the barest memories of. Every so often, I'd pass the faded scratches Bane had made on the walls, and I'd snarl to myself at the thought of my people and what could be happening to them.

It wasn't long, and yet it seemed like *forever* by the time I burst out of the doorway ahead, the gnomes cavern suddenly coming into clear view.

The first time we'd arrived it had been filled with industry, screaming and insane gnomes, and masses of fungus being grown to feed the population, now it was eerily quiet.

I raced onward, feet sending up splashes of mud, oil, and general filth as I fixated on the landmark ahead.

The tower reared drunkenly in the distance; between us lay the wreck of the huge creation that had held and fired the badunkas. It was a shattered pile of steel and stone now, wooden beams and more that had clearly been scavenged and burned, and nearby…

A long, low house had begun construction, looking more like a northern European longhouse than anything else. It was half-built, then had been abandoned, the piles of scavenged building materials left where they'd fallen, half in and out of pools of stagnant water. Nearby, a new well had overflowed.

The entire cavern, the nearest houses and the gardens, the paths, and the lower sections of the tower, looked like it'd been under reconstruction, and here and there lay golems as well.

The massive creations had fallen suddenly, clearly in the middle of working, marching back and forth or on guard; it'd made no difference. I grinned to myself, picking up speed as I raced onward, hearing shouted words distantly, as well as the crack of more firearms coming from the tower.

The golems must have fallen when the assholes triggered the suppressor, then not having the mana to reactivate them, they'd not dared to turn the suppressor off again.

Now, someone was fighting them, though, and for all I knew…

I growled to myself. I didn't have enough manastones to cover the distance to the tower; hell, if I drained them all, I might have enough to get two thirds of the distance. But then I'd have nothing left to fight with, and I'd have fuck all as a reserve.

So instead?

I ran. I *ran* as fast as I could, weaving in and out of piled materials, jumping over stacks of ingots that had been dropped when the golems carrying them were drained of mana.

I passed between houses, and jumped over the remains of picket fences. I passed burned and blackened badunkas and houses that had their front door painted recently, small patches of garden that had been cleared and planted, with fungus now roaming wild, covering half the entrance.

I took each twist and turn, racing across in the most direct route I could see until I got to the bottom of the hill that led up to the old master's tower.

Whatever the building had been intended as, we'd never really gotten, something that the gnomes had taken and worked on, repairing and refurbishing it until it must have become the center of their community.

Then the Master had come and had taken over, killing them, poisoning them and treating them as slaves. They'd been transformed from innocent people, beleaguered on all sides, but trying to live their lives as they could, here, trapped in the Prax. They'd been reduced to the state of feral animals feeding on and killing each other.

Then I'd shown up with my party, and in the process of looting and burning half the Prax to the waterline, I'd basically slaughtered a load of seriously unwell people trying to defend their homes, and that didn't sit well with me.

They were feral, though, and they'd started it, which was all the excuse I would accept.

I raced up the switchback, passing the remains of my stolen and burned-out badunka, and ran in the gaping hole in the wall that still hadn't been entirely fixed.

Even for me, running that distance, in full armor, especially armor that while it was brilliant and better than anything I'd worn before that wasn't divine, was still a hell of a distance.

My breath was coming heavily, my heart hammering as I ran through the first ring of rooms, skidding on a collection of shattered tiles, before righting myself, and taking fire.

I cursed myself again for not taking the goddamn shield as bullets slammed into me. Rather than the hit or two from low-powered rifles and handguns, these were on full auto and at close range.

As I staggered backward, I saw the trio positioned halfway up the stairs, the bodies of naga strewn all around the lower floor, leaking blood.

I'd clearly made enough noise that they'd heard me coming. The fuckers were crouched behind the low wall that ran up the stairs, half-hidden as they poured fire on me.

I spun to the side, bullets following me as I dove behind a carved and fluted pillar, the edges of the marble shattering as bullets hit it, chewing divots deep and sparking off the walls.

I held my spear close, waiting, breathing deep and slow, trying to get my heart rate back under control. The fuckers couldn't afford to waste ammunition, not the way they were right now.

The best I could hope for was that they'd be dumb enough to keep this up until they ran out of ammo, then...

A grenade clanked off the wall nearby, flung hard enough and with enough skill that it rebounded toward me. I swore, scrambling around the damn edge of the pillar...and right into the waiting hail of gunfire.

I was hit in the chest, the shoulders, the legs. The bullets chewed the overlapping scalemail apart, hit by hit. While the main plates were fine, every hit on the scale that covered the sections without plate left painful bruises, damaging it over and over.

I didn't have long; the scale could maybe take two hits in a close area, an inch or so apart before the scales would break and fall apart, but...

The grenade went off behind me. Clearly, the fuckers had pulled the pin and waited before throwing it. As I was hit from behind with a blast of concussive force, the shrapnel punching into me and tearing red-hot lines of pain where it overcame the armor, the voice of an old sarge came back to me.

"When his pin has been removed, Mr. Grenade is no longer your friend!"

I landed hard, sliding across the floor in a crash of steel, coughing and spitting some blood that dripped out of the gap in my helm and into the dust before me as the guns overhead ran dry, my armor chewed, dented, and scarred, but still functional.

As was I.

I growled, pushing myself up to my hands and knees then my feet and looking up at the stunned guards. One had frozen entirely, staring wide-eyed at me, while the other two were frantically trying to seat a fresh magazine into their rifles.

I snatched up my spear, took two quick steps back, then threw it, before grabbing a handful of the stones in the pouch, halving them. I crouched, then leaping upward, I activated Soaring Majesty.

The spear hit one of the men. The one who'd been gaping at me, having shouted a warning, had ducked, but it was too late for his friend. He'd just seated the magazine, looked up, and the spear took him in the chest, the point punching easily through the anti-ballistic material, the razor-sharp tip sinking deep enough it relieved him of all other concerns.

He fell backward as his other friend dropped his magazine, snatching it from the air, fumbling it, then locking it in place with a relieved grin.

I landed before him, backhanding the rifle aside, then I grabbed him by the front of his armored jerkin and ripped him off the balcony in one smooth motion, sending him screaming headfirst, arms windmilling, over the side.

It was less than twenty meters here, hell it was probably only fifteen, but falling fifteen feet onto marble, head-first, wasn't something a normal human could do twice.

The last man started babbling an apology trying to assure me, in some outrageously posh Southern accent, that it wasn't his choice, and he was sorry.

He did it while still holding his rifle in one hand, the slide locked back, and a grenade in the other.

I reached out, grabbed the grenade, closing my fist around his, and pulled the pin with my other hand. Then I ripped it free of him and dropped it over the side after his friend, who may or may not have survived his fall.

"Where are they?" I growled, gripping him by the throat and yanking him close, staring into his eyes.

The grenade went off a second later, the boom echoing up in the enclosed tower, even as Morgana apparently arrived at the bottom. She hadn't made it out of the connecting rooms and into real danger range, but she still screamed as fragments went whizzing by her.

To her credit, she ran back out a second later, rifle raised and ready…to spot me dangling my victim over the balcony with one hand.

He was talking, pleading, as he explained that some of the group were up above us, held in cages, ready to be killed if anything happened to the new lord.

I threw him backward over the edge, screaming, before I ripped the spear from the body on the ground next to me.

Then I was off, running faster and harder than any normal human could have achieved, let alone in full armor.

I raced up the stairs. They flew by underfoot, barely seeming to slow me as I landed and pushed off, launching myself time and again, circling the tower as I approached the top, firm in my belief that the only chance I had was speed.

I burst out onto the top floor, seeing a completely repaired and stunning room ahead as I smashed through the door. The figure that had been hiding behind it took the door full to the face and slumped unconscious to the floor, leaving a smear of blood on the wall behind him.

I took in the room in one go.

It was the same as we'd seen before, just repaired. A master bedroom with a huge balcony was on the left through a connecting door, and the room ahead was a mixture of command center, sitting room, and portal facility.

It was circular, surrounded by cabinets and display cases, and while they'd been empty before, now they were full. There were slabs of metal on the walls that I vaguely remembered seeing before, positioned by seats that ringed the wall, placed between these desks and cabinets.

I recognized them as being similar to the screens Tenandra used to project the outside world onto the interior of her cabin, and in the center was the portal itself.

It stood atop a ring of runes carved into the floor and ascending its twisted sides. As always, the portal grabbed the eyes, a twisted triangle of stone that lifted into the air, a single side visible that rolled around. Yet, if you tried to follow that side, even with a finger, you'd find it only had one edge.

It was like a real life mobius strip, yet a fucking triangle. It did my head in and gave me a headache just looking at it.

More importantly, though, were the other occupants in the room.

Three cages stood on either side of the portal, where once only one had stood. My friends were there, but as soon as I saw them, I was filled with both relief and utter fury.

They were naked, all of them, and unarmed, trapped inside the cages, waiting, wounded, and exhausted, and...

Oracle wasn't there. Neither Oracle nor Sehran were! I knew it in my heart; I'd felt it, but...

I stopped dead, seeing the beaten, broken state of my friends, and the way they were drained almost to death, and the crew of the airship by their side in a third cage, with several of them...

They were dead.

The cages had a loop of silvery metal connected to them, then running all around the bars inside, so there was no way to avoid touching it.

The metal ran from the cages to an almost innocuous device, a pair of gleaming silver balls that were housed in a small ring.

The balls rolled, steadily, around the inside of the ring, keeping it and a collection of gems flowing around.

It made no sense to me, and yet I knew it as soon as I saw it, a memory springing to mind of this and a half dozen others, all being used to trap something.

They'd been attached to the outside of a massive cage, then sunk in the ocean, creating a mana dead zone that became the Whirlpool of Styx.

It was a memory of Amon's, one of the many that I'd received when he'd shared his mind with me close to the end, and that I'd had no frame of reference for until now.

They would, in theory, keep something imprisoned there until the end of time.

I didn't care.

Three figures faced me. One was tall, blond, and scruffy-looking, with a generally bewildered look on his face, the other two having been arguing with him, facing the portal.

He screamed, spinning and smashing a hand down hard on the suppressor, a flash of purple and red light erupting and blinding us all.

I was moving already, running forward. The roars of approval from my friends made it clear they'd seen me, and they either recognized that it was me or thought the Praetorian Guard had come back.

"You're all *fucked* now!" I heard Grizz roar triumphantly as I closed the distance, eyes still blinded, but confident of where they'd been.

There was a crackle of power and sudden, overwhelming nausea ripped into me as a sensation like a meat hook being driven into my guts. I was yanked forward.

Then the world was tumbling, as my expected footfall didn't land on the deck as I'd known it should have.

Instead, I fell several feet, my heel catching the edge of a step as I lunged.

I instinctively rolled, turning my spear sideways so I didn't embed it or stab myself. I hit a few last steps, then rolled to a halt. Hungry cries lifted into the air on all sides, and still, *still* I was blind!

"Jax!" I heard Sehran roar, and I twisted around, blinking furiously. I could see her in my augmented vision, her image and identity. I could see them all in that vision, Oracle included, though her health and her body...she looked...no she felt...she was being hurt!

I felt the wrongness of Oracle's situation, even as I felt the downdraft of Sehran's wingbeat, grunting as a Complex Healing hit me, washing away the various aches, pains, and the blindness.

The world slammed back into focus. I was under attack. There were creatures on all sides, closing in. Some stumbled, their eyes vacant, others stared hungrily. Some were, or had until recently, been human and were dressed in the expensive-looking armor I'd seen the asshole earlier wearing, although many weren't.

I spun, seeing Sehran dressed in tattered rags, wheeling overhead, her claws flashing as she tried to drive the creatures back, to give me the time I needed, even as I felt her mana and her health dropping.

Then I saw it.

The portal that stood behind me at the top of a flight of steps.

The place I stood in was a city, seemingly, one with odd architecture that was just slightly off, arches and doorways that were just too wide or tall, stairs too shallow to be right to the human mind.

I saw the rough stone walls of the cavern that climbed to meet overhead and directionless, seemingly omnipresent light, the trees that swayed in a breeze that couldn't have existed, and I felt the hunger.

I was surrounded on all sides by the dead, but unlike the dead I'd fought before, these were infected with black veins, their eyes and mouths were pits of shadow, and they were coming for me.

I took one look back up, seeing the self-satisfied sneer of the noble prick and his two guards standing *on the other side of the portal*. He reached out to something, even as he stepped back within range of Grizz, who grabbed him from behind, one arm snaking around his neck and ripping him back against the cage.

And the portal winked out, like a candle snuffed.

A hollow laugh rang out somewhere in the distance. The creatures around me closed in, followed by Oracle's scream of pain, then the lights began to dim as the laughter rose higher.

CHAPTER THIRTY-FOUR

"**O**racle!" I screamed into the air, even as the mass closed in around me, hands reaching.

The majority looked dead, gaping wounds making it clear they'd not gone peacefully. But here and there, a horrified and pain-wracked face, covered in slowly spreading lines of infection, showed that not all were free of this world's cares.

Screams of hunger rose, as well as cries for mercy, peace, and help.

Distant screams and cries echoed across the buried city, and I swore. They were too close, too fast, and the only way I was getting out of here…I saw both Oracle and Sehran's health meters in my peripheral vision. Oracle's was fluctuating wildly, her mana the same as she fought with something.

Sehran's, though…

"Bond to me!" I roared, backhanding a creature that leaped at me, claws and teeth reaching hungrily.

"But Jian!" she wailed, arcing above me, her wings beating desperately as she tried to stay aloft, the wave of undead racing in from all directions.

"He'll understand!" I shouted, stabbing out with the spear then ripping it sideways, using it more as a club, thanks to the bodies leaping unheedingly atop it, than a spear. "Just fucking do it, Sehran!" I pulled the spear in close, three bodies skewered already.

I shoved as hard as I could, driving them and the creatures on that side of them staggering backward, falling in a heap of limbs and flashing teeth.

Hands grasped, scraping over me from behind from the right and now the left. They raced in, hurdling the prone bodies, and I cursed at seeing the way the fallen leaned aside to clear the path for their brethren.

I had mana again, that was true, but I'd had it for seconds. Literally. It'd take at least a few minutes to build up to a level I could do something useful with it, and…

"I bind myself to thee, my master!" Sehran called out. I swore as my tiny amount of mana dropped almost to the red line. A prompt opened, and I just approved it, needing to be able to damn well see and trusting her.

A second later, I felt it, a sudden ripping as something forced its way into my mana channels, a leech of sorts, diving in and feeding hungrily, even as she fell from the air, stunned.

"Fuck!" I screamed, right hand dipping into the pouch on my waist and ripping it apart in my haste to free the manastones inside.

I fumbled them, two of the remaining three tumbling from my grasp as my arm was yanked sideways. A creature that looked like a humanoid bat wrapped itself around the limb and chewed on the pauldron.

The last one, the last manastone was in my hand, and I held to it with a desperation that I'd never have believed mere hours earlier.

I opened myself to it, relaxing as much as I could, and gritted my teeth, an evil smile coming to my face inside my helm as I heard Sehran's full-throated scream of joy as mana flooded into me, then her.

I didn't have long, the way she was sucking on it. I couldn't hold anything back, and in seconds, she'd have it all. I needed to do what I had to right now.

My left hand was gripped tight by something—I had no way to see what, as the bodies piled atop me—but I didn't care. I could move my fingers, and a little flexing of the fingers was all it'd take.

Well, that and some subvocalizations.

The Fireball that flared to life in my left hand terminally ruined the day of whatever the fuck was trying to chew on me, the grip on that side releasing as the body fell away.

I twisted the hand back and fired the Fireball point-blank into the nearest body, feeling the flames bloom, the concussive blast lifting me and shoving me through the air, bodies blown free as I landed atop the pile that was attempting to restrain Sehran.

Flames rolled all around us, my innate fire resistance from being the Chosen of Jenae and Sehran being a demon helped us both.

Then it was down to the press of bodies.

Before they could recover, and whatever controlled them could shift them again, I'd torn them from her, finding a wildly grinning, scratched, and bitten succubus at the bottom of the pile, claws ripping gleefully into her attackers.

"Fly, you fool!" I roared, picking her up and throwing her into the air as the stunned and burning creatures around me…screamed, flailing wildly.

I twisted and spun. I was burning. Hell, yes, I was burning. No matter the situation here, no matter that it was my own damn spell, this was still a fuck load of fire, and while I was resistant, I wasn't Jenae Herself.

But it was bearable, mainly thanks to my armor, my anger, and my resistances beating it down to a manageable level. I sucked air through my teeth, hissing in pain as I threw bodies back, reaching into my Bag of Spatial Folding and grinning as my naginata leaped into my hand.

I pulled it free, clambering over thrashing and screaming bodies. The creatures around me on all sides backed up. For a second, I thought it was me, that they'd seen me and knew they were fucked…then I realized that they weren't even watching me.

They were staring fixedly at the flames, hissing in hatred.

I stabbed down, skewering a crawling body as I realized the burning ones were forcing themselves close to each other, minimizing the spread of flames even as they burned.

I opened my mouth to say something, until Sehran shouted to me.

"By your feet!"

I looked down, seeing a black, oily substance flowing away, leaking from the bodies, from anywhere not ablaze, this tar-like sludge flowing desperately away from the fire.

The creatures around me shifted, reaching for it, trying to protect it, and I acted predictably.

"Fuck that!" I snarled, stabbing a burning corpse and flipping it over, an outstretched hand splashing down into the mass and setting it alight.

It was like a petrol fire. The sudden race of the flame across the black mass, and the screams of outrage and hatred from all sides made it clear that whatever *was* in charge was not a happy bunny.

"Oracle!" I shouted as loud as I could. "It's afraid of fire!"

Sehran landed next to me, grabbing a corpse and twisting at the hip, hurling it out into the waiting crowd.

"We need to fly," she panted through ruby red lips. "Together! We can get to Oracle and…"

"Go!" I snapped at her. "Go and help Oracle. I'll take care of this."

"But…"

"GO!" I roared, seeing more bodies running in to join the swelling mass around me.

The flames were spreading, but slowly, as sacrificial bodies leaped atop the writhing ones, pinning them down and stopping the spread as fast as I could throw more of the burning mess onto the burning ones.

The new bodies moved through the crowd, and those that surrounded me stepped aside, moving with military precision to let them through…and the newcomers were armed.

Swords, flails, spears, and hammers, crossbows, and more, all were held ready as I spun to face them.

"Well fuck, looks like it's time to dance," I muttered *sotto-voce*, reaching out and grabbing the naginata. "On the other side, though." I grinned. "I've still got a little mana."

It was an overstatement. I didn't have a little mana, I practically had fuck-all mana. Compared to my normal amount of twenty-one hundred mana when I was full, the thirty-eight points I had left in the tank was nothing, and that was vanishing rapidly, draining to Sehran by the second.

It was enough to send a lick of flames rolling down my naginata, though. The creatures took a collective step back.

Then I attacked.

I went for the frenzied 'death by a thousand cuts' method, literally stabbing and slashing, twisting and moving constantly. I barely interacted with the weapons they carried, slapping them aside, dodging, and parrying when I absolutely had to and couldn't move out of the way quick enough.

The mass of bodies before me numbered in the hundreds, though, and as one they seemed to reach a decision, the controlling sentience going from an act of containment and restriction to one of slaughter.

The bodies before me dropped their weapons, hunching slightly as others behind them stepped up, arms spreading to the sides to interlock, heads of the second rank under the arms of the first.

They moved into a pattern I recognized from years of playing rugby. The full-on scrum style they were adopting wasn't good, not at all, and more weapons were discarded as the ring around me tightened.

Then they were moving.

Again, as one, they lunged on all sides, ignoring me as I frantically stabbed and slashed. Wounds that would have incapacitated a living creature, a slash across the face ruining eyes and carving deep, arteries in throats being opened and more, were barely noticed.

The blood that flowed sluggishly free was more black than red, and while the flames of the naginata set them ablaze, the bodies simply screamed and lunged ahead anyway, determined to stop me.

I was buried under an avalanche of burning flesh, bodies leaping onto the tip of my naginata and ramming themselves down it to take it out of commission.

Grabbing faces, I released it, snapping necks sideways, feeling the dry crack as I broke them, the heads sagging…as the bodies continued regardless.

I cursed and swore, punching and kicking as they latched onto me, hands grabbing at my legs, my knees, and my ankles, pulling even as more reached around me from behind, yanking backward.

I tottered, trying to keep my feet, screaming in fury and outrage as these fuckers dared to do this…

Then I was gone, lifted as others moved underneath me.

My arms and legs were each clasped by a dozen hands, pulled out straight. I was hoisted atop a kneeling, burning mass of bodies that shifted to ensure that I could gain no solid surface to push against.

I was pulled and pinned, fingers scrabbling at the connections of my armor, worming their way into the front of my helm and underneath, latching on and tugging it free.

I blinked as it was yanked roughly back, and I saw the next row of waiting bodies.

They'd picked up the discarded weapons their brethren had left and were advancing, blades held high, hammers ready, and they were all staring at my immobilized head.

"Join us…or die."

The threat rose into the air from a hundred voices at once, the mass of overlapping voices making it difficult to understand, and I hesitated, then spoke, mind whirling as I tried to figure out what the hell I was doing, trying to find a way free.

"What?" I called out, playing for time.

"Join us…or die," the massed voices repeated.

"I can't understand you!" I shouted. "My helm hurt my ears when you took it off…"

There was silence for a handful of seconds, then a single voice rang out. A body in bloodied combat armor from Earth stepped forward, glaring down at me, its eyes pits of shadow.

"Join us," it said, a single voice this time.

There was a long pause as it lifted both hands, the left filled with the black sludge-like material, and the right clutching a mace.

"Accept our gift, or receive our displeasure."

I stared at it, something about the way they spoke, the timbre and the underground setting…"Malthus?" I asked confused. It wasn't right; hell, the tiny fraction of the city I'd seen so far didn't look like his city, but it was all I could think of.

The word hung in the air for a long second as the body moved closer, resting its left hand on my armored chest, the gunk flowing free and starting to crawl upward.

"How do you know that name?" It hissed. I licked my lips, thinking fast.

"Stop the gunk, and I'll tell you," I bargained.

"Once you join us, we will know," it countered.

"Kill me, and you'll never find out!" I tried. It sneered, the face becoming more animated as others nearby mimicked the expression.

"Wrong. We will tear the knowledge from your body." It sounded firm on that, and I bucked, arching my back and heaving for all I was worth, trying to free myself.

I twisted, yanking hard on my captors, managing to move them bare inches back and forth as more and more notifications flashed in the corner of my vision.

"Fucking read it!" a scream from the distance rang out in exasperation. I blinked, recognizing Sehran's voice as the bodies turned, looking toward the far end of the courtyard.

I blinked, leaning my head right back, trying to increase the distance between me and the mass that was seeping its way up my chest as I pulled the notifications up, discarding my kill counts and more as multiples of the same one. I pulled it forward, filling my view.

Your bonded slave Sehran requests her freedom to bind to another...do you wish to release her?

Yes/No

I hit yes, frantically, then cried out as a second burst of pain raged through me as Sehran was torn from my mana channels.

It was like having a wedge driven into a block, splitting it wide open, then the wedge being removed all at once. The mana that had been drawn into her, into feeding her and keeping her going, was suddenly released and available again, what was left of it, anyway.

Two hundred mana sat there, and I started casting as fast as I could, fingers barely able to make the movements required as they were grabbed and bent backward, some breaking under the strain.

I subvocalized the words as the mass poured around the upper lip of my chest piece and onto my throat, racing higher. It was warm, hot almost, and I knew instinctively that this was the creature I faced, the thing that was puppeting the bodies around me.

It flowed up, passing over my bobbing Adam's apple as I spoke quickly, before rolling through my beard. I snapped my mouth shut, determined not to allow it in...and it flowed over and around my lips, pouring over my nostrils, collecting over my eyes.

I felt tiny tendrils extending sharp prickles as they sank into the skin around my lips and eyes, digging in deep and levering the resisting flesh apart.

It poured deeper up into my nose and into my mouth, across my eyeballs and into my ears, driving toward my brain as a second, new awareness blooded in my mind.

It was filled with a terrible hunger and hatred for those who trespassed in its realm, and a determination to tear the knowledge of the location of Malthus from my brain.

I felt the desperate need to find that wayward excavata, knowing that the ameboid creature had been spread far and wide long ago, before being partially cleansed in…*in the War of the Gods.*

I saw the memories of this thing, just as it rifled through mine, and I felt small and pathetic in the face of a creature that had literally come from the dawn of time.

It had endured millennia, being forcibly evolved by others, by the environment, and it was still here! The first Gods, beings that made Jenae and her kin clear as poor, distant imitations had fought a war with this…a single creature that had existed forever, and they'd won…but in doing so, they'd lost as well.

Tiny fragments of it had survived and had burrowed deep, finding the darkness at the heart of the realms and slowly growing again, needing nothing but time.

Centuries had passed as the Gods, who were once allies against a common foe, fought and squabbled. The God of Magic, a being that was all the Gods and none, in some way I couldn't figure, was killed outright as the others fought to gain its power for themselves.

The strands of power that fell were taken up, and more and more were used in new ways. Fire, Earth, Air, and Water were the first to form, followed by Light, Darkness, Life, and Death. Time and Invention came later, as beings never intended to wield such powers impressed their will upon the wildness or reality, even as the true Gods faded, their wars having drained them beyond measure.

They fell into the sleep of eons, their powers slowly seeping free and transforming the barren realm around them into one saturated with possibilities. New beings rose, feeding on that energy.

They took the strands of power, such as they could understand, and they in turn guided and raised up new forms, until they saw the creations of others and regarded their strands with jealous eyes.

Through it all, this *thing*, a creature literally older than time, spun out fragments and colonies, attempting to regain all it had lost.

I saw the discovery of the cities. Of creatures that had built the original ones, blind and simple beings that wished for a home before later beings would find them ages in the future and add refinements.

They evolved, and the hatred this thing had for them for daring to change, to grow, and to become *more*…grew with them. I saw its hatred of both life and death, of the inevitability of its rise, and…

A fresh scream of pain from Oracle rang out somewhere in the distance, and the world came crashing back. I was walking, released, head slumped but body upright, in the mass of beings.

No longer was I restrained, instead the part that was me? I was separate, riding inside my body as it was led across the city, heading toward the screams.

I wasn't sure if I could break free of the control. In fact, I was fairly sure I couldn't, not with this thing in me. I could feel it throughout my body, a tingling, shifting morass that had bound itself around my nerves and spinal column.

It was making me move, and there was nothing I could do about it. I should just accept that. I should just rest, sleep, and let my cares drift away. There was nothing I could do, after all.

All this thing seemed to fear was fire, and it wasn't as if I could use my magic now.

My magic.

I could feel my mana pool still, quiescent, slowly refilling, ignored and unwanted. I felt the disgust and hatred that emanated from my parasite at the mana channels that ran through me, and yet...

There was a hunger as well.

It wanted magic, it *wanted* it, and it *hated* it with all its being. It knew it was a path to unlimited power, and yet, it was also its destruction time and time again.

Entire colonies had been severed and burned free. The Malthus extension–an attempt at creating a separate colony that could be sacrificed, should it be discovered, as it searched for magic to augment the greater being–had been rooted out and destroyed eons ago.

Or so it had thought.

Now it had found the memories in my meat brain and was examining them, distracted as it relived my meeting with what had pretended to be an administrator of a hidden city.

That meant I had a short while as it was distracted, and I damn well needed to use it.

Magic.

I blocked out Oracle's anguished screams and the sense of approaching doom from Sehran as the mana she'd taken to sustain herself here was burned through.

I focused only on magic.

I knew there were secrets there to be had. I knew there were so many, literally before me, and I also knew, from the brief glimpse I'd had, that this creature held the hints that would enable me to unlock them.

Doing so, though, submerging myself in its mind, its memories, and more, was the path to dissolution. I'd be lost as it colonized my brain, eating me as it spread out more.

The only reason I still had a chance was because it needed my brain intact. It needed to be sure it'd learned all it could before it absorbed me.

That meant I had precious seconds, and that was all.

Magic.

What was magic? It was...

No.

That wouldn't help me; that was the wrong path.

Amon.

He'd been a master of mana. He could do things that weren't *possible*, from everything I'd been taught of magic. That meant what I'd been taught was wrong.

It couldn't be that you just learned something new, that you reached a new level in your understanding, then pop! You suddenly didn't need to do certain things anymore. That made no sense.

I thought about the spells I used, like Fireball. I thought of the motions, the words, the...

Why the hell did moving my fingers or speaking words—regardless of it being subvocalized or aloud—make any damn difference to the spell, anyway?

I'd been told before that it was about forcing control onto the mana, making sure it had to do what I wanted and nothing else, but that didn't make any goddamn sense, either.

Mana wasn't fucking listening and going "oh, all right, mate, no worries, I'll just go toast that fucker for you" when I cast a Fireball, after all.

No this was wrong, and I knew it.

I remembered Amon clicking his fingers and consuming a mage who was trying to fight us in the throne room of Himnel. I remembered the total lack of a gesture, beyond the obvious *watch this, you dicks* one of the finger snap.

I had been in him, we had been one, and I'd felt his determination that this was simply how it would be.

Then it had been.

I'd felt that power myself as I wiped the Dark Legion practically from existence. I'd used that power to change Grizz from dead to alive.

I'd forced my will on reality, using Amon's ability. It'd still worked. I'd literally made him alive rather than dead, and now that I looked at it, I knew how, although I couldn't replicate it again, not at this point.

I'd literally ripped the death mana from him, replacing it with life. I'd forced reality to bend to my will, and while I no longer had the kind of power I needed to do that, I still had power.

Mana and magic.

Mana was *my* magic, it was the amalgamation of magic given form, created in a way that I could manipulate.

It was the way that the UnderVerse interacted with us all. It allowed us to interact with the UnderVerse, to change it, using its own building blocks.

The spells I was learning, the weaves of a touch of this and a hint of that, the structure I used, they were all creations of people. Of beings who learned to assemble things in a certain order to get a certain result.

I knew my go-to spells like Fireball or the original Cleansing Fire so well I'd altered them by using them again and again, and yet I'd done it subconsciously.

I'd done something similar when I'd been using Amon's Master of Mana ability, and yet…did that mean that the abilities didn't exist? Were they just the way that our minds used the mana of the UnderVerse, the way that we processed the fact we could do it?

Some of the rules had to be real, surely?

I couldn't just decide that I could fly, then fly, after all. I'd had to learn the Ability, and I sacrificed both mana and health to power it.

Kids who didn't know they couldn't fly didn't just fly away.

That meant that some rules were real, like gravity, until we learned to overcome them.

That meant…

My mind shuddered as the logical step was taken then retreated from.

A sudden glimpse of the path to Godhood lay before me, a path I wasn't ready for yet, no matter what I wanted or others did, as I saw a brief hint of a realm where *everything* was malleable. Where the rules literally were what we made them.

I had a second to wonder if this reality, where I was now, was the starter zone, and that was simply the next level up for those who could learn it, and I closed off that line of thought as well.

It needed to be addressed, to be considered, but not now.

Time was running out, so back to basics.

Mana and magic.

If magic was the reality around us bending to our will, and mana was a way that our will was trained to do that without being broken in turn…if the spells I had learned were literally codified bullshit to keep me from adding in things that didn't work, and that was all?

If the gestures, the words, and more were me adding components to the spells mentally and just affirming them in a way that I'd believed I required before now…

I blinked, my wandering feet having led me up a stairwell to a room high in the tower that overlooked the city.

The room was filled with dust-covered treasures, maps of places that had long since crumbled to dust, while the diamond carved maps remained pristine, forgotten here.

In the center of it all though, was Oracle.

She was pinned to an altar, a veritable mass of the black sludge holding her in place and stabbed into her through multiple wounds.

Her skin writhed as it tried to force its way through to…

Her abdomen was bulging, shaking as the creature tried to reach our baby, and I suddenly saw it all, feeling this creature's desperate hunger.

Our baby would be the first of its kind, a true creation of both worlds, the physical that I was rooted in and the magical that Oracle had come from.

It would be born with the Imperial Rights I possessed by my blood, all of the magical innate gifts that Oracle had, and the strength of a child blessed by the Gods.

It would be the bridge that the sludge creature needed to truly embrace mana, to become the one being that was all.

It would use our baby to become a Greater God, a true force of omnipotence, and it would use that power to rend reality until there was only it and nothing else.

I saw it all, the determination, and read hints of the plans it had.

I saw the way that our child would need to be altered, fed and in turn fed upon, fragments of its soul torn free and changed by artifacts long forgotten by the worlds of men and light, things that sat on shelves gathering dust in Imperial museums and lost at the bottom of oceans.

I sensed the movements of this creature as it spun off other colonies, thousands of miles away and more, sending them after these things, diverting resources to begin the cleansing of areas to make them ready…

I saw it all, and I saw the love of my life in the middle of it, being ripped apart as she frantically held onto life to protect our baby.

I felt her, her love, her need for me, and I realized the reason I'd felt nothing from her guiding me was that she was lost in her own personal hell as she tried to survive and keep our baby alive.

I saw and sensed it all in a split second, as well as finally seeing the counter to its attack. I spoke the words.

"No more."

They hung in the air, barely heard above the agonized screaming, but the creature heard them and it knew it'd made a mistake. It had permitted me to live, to recover as it had been distracted.

"Aegis."

The ability that had been granted to me months ago by the dragon Tuthic-Amon flared to life, sealing and protecting my mind from invasion, somehow doing the same for my meat-based reality as well, burning health, stamina, and mana to do so.

It granted me precious seconds, though, segregating me from my body as I did what I had to do.

I didn't cast the spell, I *created* it.

Cleansing Flames had grown and changed, the latest version that Oracle had created being recent enough that I held it strongly in my mind. Without fanfare, without words or gestures, the spell rolled out, Frostfire Circle of Cleansing slammed into the floor beneath me, surrounding Oracle and me in a white-hot explosion of twinned rage.

The flames roared to life, semi-sentient as they burrowed into us both, searing the contamination free of our bodies. Oracle's infection was both better and worse than my own, her body having been pierced in multiple places and deeply, the skin torn and rent as more and more sludge was pumped into her.

It had been focused, though, wrapped around her womb, which in turn was protected by her magic and her abilities to alter herself, an unending battle of growth and decay that had been steadily losing ground.

Now that flames rooted the infection free, as each second passed and the secondary effect of the healing repaired the damage wrought, Oracle grew less and less frenzied, coming back to reality as she recovered.

I was more obvious in my pain, collapsing and howling as the flames literally burrowed into me, searing through the same paths the sludge had entered by, even as I held the line and maintained the spell.

Fire melted and reconstructed my eyes, burrowing along optical nerves that were regrown directly behind the cleansing flames.

My auditory and nasal passages were scoured, my mouth and throat, hell I was seared from the inside out. My heart crisped and gave out before restarting, lungs quaking under the onslaught as I was ripped apart and rebuilt, all the time focusing on maintaining the spell.

I left the intrusion when Sehran landed then collapsed inside the ring, the flames sealing over her wounds and going to work on repairing them, even as she starved for the mana she so desperately needed, her organs shutting down.

Oracle stirred, coming back from the desperate place she'd buried herself, protecting our child. Sehran's hand reached out, desperately trying to protect and reassure us both as she consumed her final mana potion.

When I opened my eyes, they were black with fury.

I forced myself to my feet, looking first to Oracle then to Sehran, seeing the pain, the fear and the acceptance on their faces. At least now and here, we were together.

My teeth drew back in a furious snarl as I turned from them, the circle having kept the creatures back, but little else.

A huge concentration of the sludge-thing, a being I still didn't have a damn name for, had been burned away, and it was furious, but this was a creature that had faced Gods.

It had survived millennia of purging, slinking back as its enemies let their guard down.

It stood there, staring at me from the faces of a dozen beings clustered around the edge of the flames, waiting.

It simply had to wait, it knew.

No living creature would use such magics, after all that had happened, without them being a last resort. Eventually, I would give in, I would rest, and it would have us. If need be, it would wait weeks until we starved or died of dehydration in mere days, even.

I canceled my *Aegis*, feeling the stirring of the creatures around us as I did it and hissed as the flames healed me.

"Are you..." I dimly heard Sehran whisper, before being cut off by Oracle, who had recognized the state I was in.

I felt only cold fury and determination, staring into the eyes of shadow that stared back.

We faced each other, its multiple forms standing there in the doorway of the circular tower staring back at me patiently, quite content to wait me out...

Until I raised a hand, and a fireball bloomed to life in it.

The packed bodies that had filled the stairwell hurriedly backed away as I threw it over their heads and into the stairwell behind them.

The concussive blast threw several of the bodies forward and into the circle, allowing the patrolling spells to catch them, latching on and spreading wildly. The stairwell quickly became an inferno, bodies collapsing where they stood, rather than risk carrying the terrible flames elsewhere.

In seconds, beyond the popping of crisping fats from the dead, silence filled the room. I walked back to Oracle and Sehran, seeing the relieved look on Sehran's face and the exhausted, but triumphant one on Oracle's.

"You've bonded to her?" I asked Oracle, and she nodded, lifting her arms to me in mute request. I took her into my arms, holding her close and kissing the top of her head, then her cheek as she wrapped her arms around my neck, sobbing as I held her.

"The...baby..."

I froze, unable to speak as my heart turned to ice.

"It's okay," she said, having felt the change and the horror in me. "It's okay," she repeated, pulling back and looking me in the eyes, resting her forehead against mine before closing them again as tears started to leak out. "But I don't know for how long."

"I will rain fucking *hellfire* on this place," I swore as she opened her eyes and looked at me. "*Believe me*. Our baby will get back home safely. If I have to make the Cataclysm look like a fucking Sunday stroll, I'll do it." I felt the resonance from her, and distantly, weirdly, from Sehran, as I set Oracle down.

"I can feel you," I said softly, looking down at Sehran, who grinned tiredly and waggled her eyebrows, making me grunt a laugh.

"Usually when a man says that, there's a lot less clothing involved." She groaned, taking my hand as I reached down and she climbed to her feet. "Anyway...my poor loves will be wondering what the hell is going on. I had to sever our bond, and I swore to only do that if I was in real danger."

"We were."

She nodded. "But then I bound myself to you, then to Oracle, and our bonding…" She winced, then shook her head.

"What?" I asked.

"A bonding is generally two directional, but with one side in clear ascendance," Oracle explained softly. "Our bond is that you are the master, and I the servant, and…"

"What?" I growled, and she shook her head.

"Don't worry, it's not that kind of a bond. While you could enforce your will on me, like you did in the forest when we were being hunted by the Dark Legion, and you sent me away, I trust you. Also, in our relative positions, it's necessary. Trust me on that. Sehran's customary bond, on the other hand, is usually based more on…fun."

"There's a lot less emotional sharing and a lot more physical twinning of sensations, so when I…"

"I think he gets it," Oracle interrupted Sehran quickly, looking at me. Sehran moved out of sight of Oracle slightly and winked at me, lifting one finger to her lips before slipping a hand inside her top, manipulating her nipple with a sly smile. "So, it means that Sehran is feeling the emotional…side…of…things…stop that!" Oracle scolded the succubus, who pulled her hand back out of her top, laughing.

"Sorry!" Sehran said, holding both hands up and shaking her head. "I just realized that, as I'm experiencing the emotional side much more strongly than I'm used to, then you'd be doing the same with the physical, as open as our bond is."

"Actually, we always feel it." Oracle smiled. "I feel Jax, and he me, normally…"

"Then why did my playing with my nipple get that effect?" Sehran asked, smiling.

"Because his nipples are…how did you put it?" she asked me.
I grinned despite myself, feeling more human as I fed more mana into the spell, keeping the room clear of the creatures. "My nipples are for decoration; yours are for fun?" I asked.

She nodded. "Exactly. I'm used to feeling his sensations, and he's used to feeling mine, but I'm not used to feeling another set of female sensations, and it kind of put me off."

"Or on." Sehran winked.

"Sehran, you know you don't have to do that, right?" I asked her seriously. "Acting all horny all the time? You're a member of the team, and we value you as you are, you don't have to…"

"And I'm not," Sehran said, holding a hand up. "Seriously, I'm not offering to fuck you both here on the table, as much as the distraction from all *that* would be welcome right now. I'm very happy with Jian and Tenandra, and I'm proud to only be with them, but…"

"But?"

"But…as a succubus, I don't have the kind of hang-ups on sexuality that most others do. For me, touching myself for a joke is perfectly normal, as is stripping naked for a distraction or when I am, touching…"

"And we're stopping this conversation right there," I said.

Sehran grinned at me. "I felt that! You like the idea of me touching my…"

"Sehran, dear, that's enough." Oracle laughed. I glared at the pair of them, knowing that I was being deliberately distracted as much as anything else.

"I don't think this is really the place for these games." I jerked my thumb toward the door.

"Are you kidding?" Sehran grunted, most of the humor dropping from her demeanor as she moved to the window, staring out and down at the massed bodies below. "Personally, I think this is the perfect time for some distraction."

Oracle and I joined her at the window, staring down at them, and I felt that black fury returning at the unmoving challenge in their eyes.

There were almost a hundred of them in the courtyard below, and I almost started fireballing them, until I realized that was exactly what they wanted.

They knew I was low on mana. Hell, they had to have been sensing my slow accumulation of it as I was puppeted around. They knew Oracle hadn't been able to fight them for long, and as for Sehran...I had no clue how she'd survived so long.

"How did you survive until I bonded you?" I asked Sehran suddenly.

"I had some mana from Jian, and he'd been giving me blood...the others, too," she whispered, suddenly ashamed.

"Blood?"

"I'm a demon. I need to drain the life of others to stay here, and while Jian was feeding me mana, it was okay, great even, as mana is literally the lifeblood of the realm but when he didn't have any left, he made me take his blood. I held off as long as I could, literally, the mana lasted me hours, then a little blood. Just a bite and a little drink..."

"We all agreed," Oracle said. "You're one of our family; if you get dragged back to the demon realm kicking and screaming, then just sit and wait, because we'll be opening a portal to get you back."

"The Kings of Hell won't like that," Sehran said softly, her cheeks reddening as she looked at her hands.

"They won't get a choice," I said. "If I can bitch-slap the God of Death, you think a demon is going to stop me?"

Sehran winced. "The Kings of Hell are a bit more powerful than I think you realize."

"Then I'll get some levels," I said. "You're part of our family now, so don't worry. Anyway, you survived on the other side, I get that. The others are fine; it's their bodies, I'd have done the same, and..."

"Ronin even asked if it had to be blood or if other 'fluids of life' might help," Oracle pointed out. I sighed, rubbing the bridge of my nose.

"Fucking bards...is there anything more unstoppable than a horny bard?"

"Probably not, though I think his self-image might have been permanently damaged. He was in a cage with Grizz, Giint, and Arrin, and they're all a LOT bigger than he is."

"Arrin isn't that...oh." I stopped, seeing the waggled eyebrows. "Fuck's sake!" I laughed, despite myself. "Okay, okay! Moving on from that mental image, how did you survive HERE?" I asked.

Sehran winced. "When Oracle and I got here, she bonded me; we knew it was our only chance. Then when Oracle was captured, and I was preventing her from using her mana, I got her to release me," Sehran explained, one claw scratching idly at the stone windowsill as she looked down at the figures below.

"Once she released me, I survived on a handful of mana potions I managed to snag from several bodies," she explained, shrugging. "That's also where I got the clothes."

I glanced at the clothing and shook my head. She was wearing bloodstained body armor, clearly meant for someone that was both smaller in height and presumably chest than her, as she was literally falling out. I grunted, dipping a hand into my bag and pulling some of my spare clothing free.

"Here, I think that'll fit you a little better, but..."

"Thank you!" she said, sighing, before shrugging herself free of...everything. I forced myself to look aside. I mean, I'd seen it all before; we'd shared baths and washed in damn rivers and more, but seeing a friend who was also stunningly beautiful and literally a succubus stripping fully naked is distracting at the best of times.

Especially when you know that, not only would she not *mind* you looking, but she'd also actively enjoy it.

That didn't mean it was right, though. I was with Oracle, and the old saying about it being okay to look, but not to touch...well, I was with Oracle, and Sehran was with Jian and Tenandra, and that was enough.

"So, why were you wearing all that, then? Considering it was too small?" I asked, knowing it definitely wasn't body-modesty.

"It was armor," she said simply, shrugging. "The body that I took it from had lost the head, so I think that, besides burning them, that must kill them as well, as they'd left it lying there. Also, I needed something to attach the pouches to, and unless I was going to pierce my nipples for it?" She shrugged.

"Makes sense," I agreed, leaning out of the window overlooking the stone and parks. "How big is the city?"

"Not as big as Himnel or Narkolt," Sehran replied, her voice muffled as she pulled a top over her head. "It may be on par with twice the size of the keep and courtyard of Himnel, a hundred or so buildings, each with a front or back that opens out onto a park or garden."

"Okay, and the outer wall?"

"Solid, as near as I can tell," Oracle interjected, her magical senses giving her a different perspective. "Or, more specifically, it's intact. The wall goes all around the outside of the cavern, with stone rising upward from the top of the wall to enclose us over our head, and that mist that generates the light gathers up there."

"What's the difference between solid and intact?" I asked, watching more and more of the figures clambering onto rooftops and moving in to surround the tower we were in.

"The wall is intact in that I can't see any entrances or exits. It's solid, in that it's not damaged, but...but I don't think it's fully solid."

"Why not?"

"There's no way in or out. If that's the case, and the walls are worked stone, then a cavern wall that rises directly from the top of them. Why?"

"Why make the walls if the cavern is there?" I agreed.

"I think the city was made first, then it was either sunk into the ground, creating the cavern, or the stone of the cavern was created around it."

"Malthus grew that pagoda building out of the ground as an exit," I said. "It made me climb the stairs as it opened the way out, but thinking about it, if it was growing it, it could have made a damn chair and lifted me all the way, no doubt."

"Probably," Oracle agreed.

"So is this city like the other one?" Sehran asked curiously. "Like Malthus and Peleth's View, I mean?"

"Similar. That one didn't look quite as alien as this does. The doorways were a better size and the stairs closer to our natural size, but yeah, the light, the parks, the walls…all of it is damn similar."

"Is it like a hermit crab, then?" Oracle suggested, plucking a creature from my mind she knew I'd be familiar with. "Is the creature creating the city as a home or a lure, then killing anyone who enters it?"

"I don't think so." I frowned as I tried to remember the memories I'd read while I was part of the gestalt.

"I think…I think it found the city. I think there's a hell of a lot of shit like this out there, places abandoned millennia ago, lost and forgotten. The Empire was only the latest version to fall."

"It wants our baby, I know that much," Oracle said softly, arms wrapped defensively around the now-visible bulge of our child.

"They're growing," I said softly, putting one arm around her shoulders and pulling her in close.

"They are," she agreed. "I know humans take a lot longer to gestate than Wisps; we take a few hours to a few days, depending on how many have joined, but this is…this is different from both. At this rate, they'll be here in a few weeks at most. Certainly less than a third of a human gestation."

"Shit," I muttered, feeling even more on edge. "Well, regardless, we can talk about this shithead's plans later; first, we need to get out."

As we'd been talking, I'd searched everywhere I could, gaze roaming up and down, and so far, all I could damn well see was the solid-seeming stone and the mass of assholes that stood atop it, watching and waiting.

"Why aren't they attacking?" I muttered. "Just waiting until we starve do you think?"

Oracle replied, "I don't think they realize what we are, not really."

"Besides amazingly skilled and sexy?" Sehran quipped. I grunted, smiling at her.

"I mean, they know we have access to magic, but not how much. They don't really seem to understand it," Oracle clarified.

"They were thinking they'd just wait us out if need be," I remembered.

"That's…terrible news, and it'll probably work." Oracle said, before looking at Sehran then at me. *"I think we should be careful what we say aloud; if the creature is part of the city, it can probably hear everything we say."*

"Okay, so, you really think it's that dumb?" I asked through our bond.

"I do. I think it's been buried for a long time; it's probably not sure about what we are or what we can do. When it was in your mind, did it see much of your abilities?"

"No...no, it was only interested in Malthus," I replied, rubbing my chin as I thought. *"The Malthus entity is an offshoot of this, and one that this one thought was killed off; now it knows it's alive..."*

"That's its focus, that and our baby," Oracle replied grimly. *"That's a mistake."*

"Very much so. Think you can keep them back with a circle while I meditate?"

"We'd need to alternate for Sehran; she needs the mana."

"I can hold my breath. Okay, it's not quite like that, not really, but I can survive for a bit?" Sehran added in, her connection faint and distant.

"You said you can survive on blood?" I asked. She hesitated, sending a mixture of unhappiness and desire.

"I can. I...it's part of being a demon; we can survive on the blood of others, but it'll weaken you..."

"But it'll mean I can recover my mana," I pointed out. *"Oracle can use that mana to keep the circle going, generate some water for us all, and make sure we're as healed and ready as possible. Once we're ready, she can heal me, and you can bond to her again, then I'll tear this fucking place apart."*

"Then that's the plan," Oracle agreed. *"Sehran, dear, you need to be at your best, but please try not to drain him too much."*

"I will, and both of you? Thank you," she said, sending both her relief and her guilt at us needing to do this for her.

I reached out, not looking around, distantly feeling her through the bond as I searched for her. I pulled her in close, feeling her arms wrap around my waist, Oracle on the other side as the three of us stood there, my arms around their shoulders as they both clung to me.

We stood that way for a long minute, enjoying the closeness that physical contact brought, before we separated, moving to the back of the room, farthest from the window as I sat on an old stone seat that was close enough to my dimensions it wasn't too uncomfortable.

"What do you need?" I asked Sehran as I readied myself to meditate.

"A finger?" she suggested hesitantly. "I need to be able to draw blood, but with the mana that Oracle gave me already, a little blood, but frequently, will sustain me longer, and I won't need the mana, so it can be kept in reserve?"

"Of course," I agreed, disconnecting a gauntlet and offering her my left hand. "And...let's not tell Jian about me sticking something in your mouth to suck on, all right?" I grinned at her, and Oracle as Sehran sat on a seat next to me.

"Men...such children!" Oracle sighed, playing along, but I sensed the humor from her. There was a second of thinking, as any healthy male would, about replacing my finger in her mouth with something else, until her teeth lengthened, showing off the points of her pearly-whites.

That killed that thought instantly, and I couldn't help but wince as they pierced the skin, the sudden feeling of gentle pressure and of sucking not dissimilar to a mixture of a passionate kiss combined with donating blood.

Then Sehran looked up and winked at me, and those thoughts rose up again.

I forced myself to close my eyes, seeking that calm center inside myself as I meditated, creating the walls around myself and drawing deeply.

The sensation of Sehran's feeding grew fainter and fainter as I buried myself down deep, opening myself to the mana all around me.

Time passed in a blur, and soon Oracle was shaking me, making me stand, groggily, as she slumped into the seat in my place.

"*It's close,*" she whispered to me inside my mind. "*Sehran and I are as full as we can be, of mana, to be clear.*" She smiled tiredly at me. "*You're full as well, and...*"

"*And as soon as you've rested, it's time to begin,*" I said.

"*Definitely.*"

I looked down at the small wound on my finger, even now closing up as the flames of the circle expanded their last on it. I looked over to Sehran, who stood nearby, seemingly healthy and hale, even if I could feel the guilt and shame in her that she'd needed to stoop to feeding on me.

"Don't worry," I repeated to her, stepping forward and putting a hand on her shoulder. "You're part of the family, and we'd all do anything for you."

"Thank you," she whispered, blinking away tears as she looked up at me before stepping in close and wrapping her arms around my chest, head ducked into my armor as I patted her back awkwardly.

Her wings fluttered slightly as she spoke, and I stroked the back of her neck. "Thank you for seeing more than a toy, more than I let myself show, for the blood, and for understanding."

"You earned it," I said softly.

"We trust you, Sehran; you'll be trusted with our baby, as well, if you want to help us with them?"

"Please," Sehran whispered, nodding gently. "I'd like that..."

"Then how about we tear this place apart and go home?" I suggested, getting a nod as she stepped back, wiping at her eyes. "*When it all begins, you use the naginata. You're a demon, so I'd imagine you have access to fire?*" When she nodded, I grinned and went on. "*Use that and protect the stairwell; stab any fucker who comes up, and let them burn.*"

"Jax, before we start," Oracle said suddenly. I twisted around to look at her, seeing the distant look, the thousand-yard stare that suggested she was seeing something else.

"Yeah?"

"Notifications, you need to read them. Your mana pool is bigger than it should be. Did you examine the armor when you put it on?"

"No. I didn't have access to my magic."

"You might want to check it out then," she whispered, clearly seeing something I couldn't.

CHAPTER THIRTY-FIVE

nodded, pulling the notifications up and grimacing. There were a handful of the usual crap ones detailing injuries, poisoning notifications, broken bones, and influences ignored. I dismissed them all, scouting for the ones that I knew must be in there

Congratulations!

You have raised your skill Medium Armor to level 20.

You may now choose your Second evolution of this skill.

Congratulations!

You have raised your skill Medium Armor to its second evolution.

You must now pick a new path to follow.

Will you choose to invest further into your bond with your armor, enabling greater speed and doubling the force of the impact granted through BULL'S BURST or will you dedicate yourself to understanding your armor more with the path of SECOND SKIN?

Choose carefully, as this choice cannot be undone.

Bull's Burst:
You have learned to move gracefully in medium armor, training your body to lock the armor you wear into place, forming an impenetrable shield of steel. Now you can choose to double down on that skill, embracing the Ability: Bull's Burst!

Gain the Ability: Bull's Burst. Once per fight, you may force 100 stamina into your body, overcharging your muscles and driving yourself forward at tremendous speeds. Where others would use petty abilities such as Shield Bash, you use Bull's Burst, tearing through a defensive shieldwall like gossamer!

Note: Bull's Burst is an evolution of your current Ability: Stampede

Second Skin:
Over hundreds of hours of training and fighting, living in your metal cocoon, you have adjusted, learned and evolved as an armored warrior. You now move more gracefully in medium armor than ever before, and have gained the passive Ability: Second Skin!

Gain the permanent Ability: Second Skin. Any medium armor you wear will now fit you better, as the thousand little adjustments you know to make instinctively when dressing in your armored shell combine to grant you a permanent boost to your Dexterity and Agility of +2

I looked them both over, seeing the advantages of both, I'd been using Lunge more than Stampede all this time, mainly because Stampede launched me in a single direction and felt unalterable.

It left me with the impression that I could essentially throw myself directly at a target, but it was only useful in a short distance, and it locked my armor in place.

If my target suddenly extended a spear or stepped aside, revealing a cliff's edge, I was fucked.

I'd started to use Lunge, alternatively because it covered the same short distance, but could be used in any direction, and while I still had to extend a blade, and it locked me into that movement, I felt I could change it, at the cost of stamina, if I needed to.

As with everything here, the game mechanics that I knew about back on Earth and through the descriptions, were only half the story. The other half was the reality of it, gifted to me in hints and feelings, the unsaid mattering as much as the said.

Bull's Burst would give me the charging power of a bull, smashing through obstacles. While that was great, it came with the problems I'd already felt. If someone had a pike leveled at me, I couldn't adjust, I couldn't stop, and my own ability would kill me.

It could be great, but it just wasn't.

Alternatively, Second Skin, well, normally I'd have taken that in a heartbeat. The boost to Agility and Dexterity might be minor, but that was a set change, boosting them both by that outright, while also making my armor fit me better.

That in itself would reduce the weight of it, reducing the drain on my stamina, the injuries and the chafing.

My gods, the chafing!

If the padding wasn't on right? Kiss your balls goodbye. Literally, in this case, and not only was the padding monstrously hot at the best of times, creating a situation of swamp balls within minutes, in many situations, it also wore through in places.

This new set was great, but the thought of this armor doing that…

That also added a minor detail.

This was *heavy armor*, meaning that the skill gain for medium must have happened before I found this, and it'd been suppressed by the mana exclusion field.

This armor was better crafted and didn't feel much heavier, I had to admit, but realistically, it was. Sections on the last one that were lighter, covered with leather or thinner chainmail were now either solid metal in rings to enable flexibility or scale mail.

That meant the bonus for the armor…wouldn't work.

Fuck.

I paused for a few seconds, knowing the others would alert me if they needed to, before cursing and selecting Second Skin. I knew I could gain more with the Bull's Rush, for a start it'd be an actual ability, rather than getting nothing for now.

It could also be lethal to me or those around me though, and taking Second Skin…most of my skills and abilities were synergistic after all, and I felt like this would be the same. Selecting this now, would hopefully help to guide the first evolution of heavy armor in this direction.

At the very least, it couldn't fucking hurt.

I chose that then moved on.

Congratulations!

You have raised your spell Fireball to its Second Evolution!

You must now pick a path to follow.

Will you choose to keep it ranged, with Pyroclastic Blast or make it up close and personal with Dragonfire?

Choose carefully, as this choice cannot be undone.

Pyroclastic Blast:
Pyroclastic Blast is a massively effective weapon, combining all the most fun parts of a volcano's eruption with the ability to reach out and say "You see that guy? Fuck him, and fuck all his friends!"

Concussive effect is tripled within the first five feet of the impact site, dropping by 10% per two feet of distance while radiating outwards. Chance to inflict secondary fire damage is increased to a 60% Pyroclastic flow that impacts anyone will proceed to do massive situational damage until it cools.

Pyroclastic Blast costs 400 mana per casting.

Dragonfire:
You've felt the effects on your enemies as you've reached deep into your latent draconic capabilities, but now you have the chance to survive doing it at will! Dragonfire will be directed from the specified eruption point across a four meter distance in a flexible stream, costing 350 mana to cast and 100 mana per second active!

Well, that was a much harder choice. Instead of wanting neither, I wanted them both! Pyroclastic Blast was basically a lava-filled, napalm-upgraded version of Fireball, which I already loved. Dragonfire, though, could basically be me walking through these dickheads with impunity.

Hell, if I could find some mana potions like Sehran had, I could literally vomit flames across them like a flamethrower, chug a potion, and do it all over again!

I really wanted them both!

I hesitated, chewing my lip in thought, before cursing and selecting Pyroclastic Blast. Dragonfire was awesome. Fuck, it really was. But it wasn't ranged.

I had up-close and personal covered with the circles and with imbuing my naginata with my powers. If I gave up Pyroclastic Blast and took Dragonfire, then I was fucked when it came to distance for fire spells.

Yes, I'd have other options, and that was cool and all, Lightning and Magic Missile both being awesome. But fuck it, I really *liked* Fireball.

I nodded as the spell altered in my mind, paying attention as I felt Oracle doing the same, pathways solidifying as the spell evolved and half sensed hints became clearer as the spells unlocked knowledge somehow dormant in me.

I took a deep breath, then nodded as the next notification popped up. This one, at least, I'd been expecting.

Congratulations!

You have killed the following:

- 11x Human Guards of various levels for a total of 26,110xp

- 77x Xenefier's Blood Contaminated Beings of various levels for a total of 35,124xp

A party under your command killed the following:

- 37x Human Guards of various levels for a total of 58,950xp

- 26x Xenefier's Blood Contaminated Beings of various levels for a total of 11,140xp

Total party experience earned: 70,090xp

As party leader, you gain 25% of all experience earned

Progress to level 49 stands at 4,475,881/6,455,000

I paused, frowning as I wondered where all the other kills were, then cursed as I realized that the damn kills had started to show up when I was hunting for the notification from Sehran, and I'd dismissed it.

Fuck it, knowing how much I earned for a kill wasn't particularly helpful at the minute anyway, besides knowing that these contaminated creatures that stood around this tower were fuck all use for levelling.

Whatever they were, the system that worked all this shit out clearly thought they were worth bugger-all. Thinking about how many I'd killed, I was inclined to agree. Seventy-seven of them and most of that was without my magic. Hell, it'd be in the hundreds if I'd had access to that earlier.

I dismissed the screens, before pausing and focusing on my wrists, then legs, pulling my helm off and checking that, as Oracle, seeing what I was doing, joined in, getting the sections I couldn't clearly see from where I was.

Dark Tide Rising

Congratulations!

You have equipped a full set of Praetorian Guard Heavy Armor.

For equipping eight out of eight set pieces, you have an increase of 40% to all physical damage resistances, +10 to physical damage and +200 to your mana pool.

Cuirass of the Praetorian Guard		Further Description *Yes/No*	
Details:		This chest armor includes attached pauldrons and is made of horizontal strips of Darksteel attached to a scale mail undergarment. It gives a bonus of +10 to resisting physical damage.	
Rarity:	**Magical:**	**Durability:**	**Charge:**
Highly Rare	Yes	97/100	N/A

Revebrace of the Praetorian Guard		Further Description *Yes/No*	
Details:		This armor covers the upper arms and connects to both the vambraces and the pauldrons. It is made of interlocked plates of Darksteel laid over scale mail. It gives a bonus of +5 to resisting physical damage.	
Rarity:	**Magical:**	**Durability:**	**Charge:**
Highly Rare	Yes	97/100	N/A

Vambraces of the Praetorian Guard		Further Description *Yes/No*	
Details:		This armor covers the lower arms and connects to both the revebraces and the gauntlets. It is made of interlocked plates of Darksteel laid over scale mail. It gives a bonus of +5 to resisting physical damage.	
Rarity:	**Magical:**	**Durability:**	**Charge:**
8	Yes	93/100	N/A

Culet of the Praetorian Guard		Further Description *Yes/No*	
Details:		This armor covers the groin and connects to both the cuirass and the cuisse. It is made of interlocked plates of Darksteel laid over scale mail, with larger, solid sections in place to cover vital areas. It gives a bonus of +8 to resisting physical damage.	
Rarity:	**Magical:**	**Durability:**	**Charge:**
Highly Rare	Yes	99/100	N/A

Helm of the Praetorian Guard		Further Description *Yes/No*	
Details:		This helmet is made of Darksteel and formed into a solid shape with high cheeks and a thin section for ventilation. It gives a bonus of +8 to resisting physical damage and +200 to your mana pool.	
Rarity:	**Magical:**	**Durability:**	**Charge:**
Highly Rare	Yes	98/100	N/A

Gauntlets of the Praetorian Guard		Further Description *Yes/No*	
Details:		These gauntlets connect to the vambraces to form a fitting seal and are constructed of individual sections of Darksteel, with a mixture of scales and plate construction for added protection. They grant a bonus of +8 to resisting physical damage.	
Rarity:	Magical:	Durability:	Charge:
Highly Rare	Yes	96/100	N/A

Greaves of the Praetorian Guard		Further Description *Yes/No*	
Details:		These armored greaves are made of Darksteel and are constructed to be both protective and comfortable. They grant a bonus of +8 to resisting physical damage.	
Rarity:	Magical:	Durability:	Charge:
Highly Rare	Yes	99/100	N/A

Sabatons of the Praetorian Guard		Further Description *Yes/No*	
Details:		These armored boots are made of Darksteel and are constructed to be both protective and comfortable, and grant a bonus of +6 to resisting physical damage.	
Rarity:	Magical:	Durability:	Charge:
Highly Rare	Yes	99/100	N/A

The cape apparently was just cool as fuck, as it granted no bonuses, but I didn't give two shits. I was keeping it. I'd lost my swords and the spear, and…and the daggers, at some point, which was more than a little annoying, but that was fine. I still had the good shit.

Next was a nice surprise with a few earned bonuses to my stats from my efforts.

Congratulations!

Through hard work and perseverance, you have increased your stats by the following:

Agility +1

Charisma +1

Strength +1

Continue to train and learn to increase this further.

There weren't a whole hell of a lot of changes, but hey, any improvements were welcome. I pulled my stat sheet up next, unable to help myself, having seen all the improvements with my armor, and whistled softly.

Name: Jax Amon				

Title: Godslayer				

Class: Sorcerer II			Renown: Imperial Scion, Prince of Dravith, Master of Himnel and Narkolt	
Level: 48			Progress: 4,475,881/6,455,000	
Patron: Jenae, Goddess of Fire and Exploration			Points to Distribute: 0 Meridian Points to Invest: 0	

Stat	Current points	Description	Effect	Progress to next level
Agility	81	Governs dodge and movement.	+710% maximum movement speed and reflexes.	4/100
Charisma	61 (56)	Governs likely success to charm, seduce, or threaten	+51% success chance in interactions with other beings	11/100
Constitution	120 (118)	Governs health and health regeneration	2400 health, regen 160 points per 600 seconds, (each point invested now worth 20 health)	N/A
Dexterity	92	Governs ability with weapons and crafting success	+82% to weapon proficiency, +92% to the chances of crafting success	84/100
Endurance	70 (67)	Governs stamina and stamina regeneration	2100 stamina, regen 52 points per 30 seconds, (each point invested now worth 30 stamina)	66/100
Intelligence	201	Governs base mana and number of spells able to be learned	2210 mana, spell capacity: 102 (100 + 2, +200 mana from items)	N/A
Luck	70	Governs overall chance of bonuses	+60% chance of a favorable outcome	84/100
Perception	70 (60)	Governs ranged damage and chance to spot traps or hidden items	+60% ranged damage, +60% chance to spot traps or hidden items	69/100
Strength	76 (73)	Governs damage with melee weapons and carrying capacity	+76 damage with melee weapons, +76% maximum carrying capacity	11/100
Wisdom	100 (90)	Governs mana regeneration and memory	+1350% mana recovery, 15 points per minute,	N/A

I winced as I saw that my Wisdom, Constitution, and Intelligence were all flatlined now, no longer evolving as I worked, but that was…fine…I guessed.

I'd gained new abilities, and it was damn well time to start using them. The genetic storage would help me no end once I started investing my mana into it. As it stood, I'd drain my pool and have twenty-one health to show for it, when I really needed it.

Meh. I'd start using that one *soon*.

The same with the ability to make solidified mana crystals of whatever type that I needed.

That was going to be awesome, crucibles that boiled without flames, knives that cauterized as they cut, hell, potion bottles that slowly purified the mix, maybe?

I shook myself free of all that, looking out across the silent city, seeing the bodies of men and women who had, until recently, been worried about paying mortgages and more, now standing, possessed and puppeted by a sentient sludge in a realm far from the one they were born to.

All in all, I almost felt sorry for the things I was about to do to them…then I remembered that they signed up to follow an asshole noble, taking his money as bodyguards and more. Sure there were probably some like Morgana in there, conned, and some like West, who were good guys who had made a mistake, but most were probably dicks, and I was improving the overall IQ of the species by slaughtering them.

No, I was going to use what I hoped was the mainstay of my new Ability, Mana-Manipulation.

I interlocked my fingers, twisted them around, and stretched, cracking my knuckles and allowing myself a small smile as I picked my helm up, settling it back in place and resting my naginata against the wall, setting a mana potion down and taking a deep breath.

"So, where to start," I murmured. "Oracle, you ready for this?"

"I'm *so* ready for this." She smiled grimly.

"Sehran?"

"Very much so!" she agreed as she reached out hesitantly to the naginata. "Are you sure about this?"

"Definitely," I said, smiling, even though all she could see through my armored helm was a quirk of my lips. "You think I'd trust you with my firstborn and my back, but not my weapon? That's just crazy."

She gripped the naginata tightly, lifting it free of the wall and checking the weight and balance, making a few clumsy stabs and reminding me that her main weapons were her tits, ass and her whip. Not necessarily in that order.

"Are you going to be all right with that?" I asked her, getting an earnest nod as she stepped across to the stairwell. "Okay…well, shout if you need help." I glanced at Oracle.

"I'll watch over her, my love, until I'm too deep. Then I'll need you to take over and hold the shield…release it too soon, and we'll regret it," Oracle said into my mind as I let out an agreeing breath.

"Yeah, for the rest of our lives…both seconds of it. Okay then," I muttered, frowning as I examined the cityscape before me. "So, what do I need?" I reached out, triggering Mana-Manipulation and smiling as the world around me changed.

I'd discovered that my own mana could be manipulated without all the crap that was required by standard spellcasting now, but…I needed to really know the spell, at least as new to it as I was.

Using this Ability, though…

The world before me had changed. There was still the drab gray and dirty cream stone, the bodies that stood, cold and still, and the pulsing mist that granted the light the plants needed.

But overlaying it all was a new universe.

Strands of mana floated across my vision, much as it had when I manipulated the fragment of the divine soul. I saw death hovering across most of the creatures that stood on silent watch, others I saw life and death in equal measure, while a rare few pulsed with more life than death.

I saw heat in literal form as fire mana radiated outward from beating hearts, each pulse flooding the body, while water, tinged with death, showed me the cold of the grave as the bodies began to break down.

Air moved sluggishly, filtering down through small breaks in the stone, clearly permitted access, and bringing a taste of…of fire with it?

Fire and earth flowed down through cracks along with the air, while the solidity of earth pressed in from all sides.

Time was everywhere, pressed into the very bedrock of this new world, but invention was massively lacking. I suspected that, while time and invention were the terms people used these days for those aspects, perhaps change and perfection would be closer, or evolution and stability.

None of those terms were right, I knew, those Gods covered so much more, but then Jenae was known as the Lady of Fire, rather than the Lady of Nuclear Fusion and Shit, so admittedly it was all down to interpretation.

Even here, I could feel Sint's touch as light and order kept the realm together and darkness enveloped it all.

I smiled, knowing that while this…*thing* had existed forever, it was known to one of the Gods at least, and probably several, even if they'd been too busy to pay it attention.

Tamat and Cruit would know about it, I guessed, but banished that thought as it appeared.

I sensed all the strands of mana here, as well as more as the various strands interacted, forming new variants that had additional aspects.

I reached out, feeling them, and I started to weave.

The first few attempts were clumsy, the magical equivalent of a toddler trying to grab a reflection, the light spreading across the floor as they wondered at their own shadow.

Each time I did it, though, I felt a little change, the strands floating through my fingers as I tried to manipulate them at a distance, rather than the mana that was in me at all times.

I was doing this wrong, I realized, frowning. I was ignoring what I had, trying to touch that bit, right over…there!

No wonder it wasn't damn well working.

I focused, not trying to do anything with my mana, just swirling it around in my body, reaching out with it, feeling it altering as I reached for the fire mana, figuring that was likely the best mana to try this with, my affinity for it having been increased with worshiping Jenae.

The strand I reached out with split, the other kinds falling away as only a finger of fire remained. When the fire touched the fire, I felt an immediate reaction. The heat in the air shifted, following my questing thread.

I frowned as I shifted it sideways and back and forth. It formed eddies in the overlapping *mélange* of mana before me as more and more fire mana shifted, following the thread I was guiding out to it.

I nodded, satisfied that I could do it, and snipped the thread loose to flicker free, rising to mingle with the rest.

I checked my mana, grunting at the nearly seventy mana that experiment had cost me.

It was a hell of a risk, this, considering I might not be able to do it at all, but…but that fucker was out there, spread everywhere. For all I knew, I could kill everything in here, and it'd just close the tiny fractures that led up to the surface, starving us of air.

Then, when we collapsed, it'd infiltrate us all.

The mere thought of that terrified me, and I resolved to make damn sure that didn't happen. If need be, I'd pick up Oracle and run through the fuckers to the portal. I might not make it, but surely the chance was better than none at all.

I took a deep breath, then brought up what I knew about the new Pyroclastic Blast spell, mentally shortening its damn name to Pyro, because there was fuck-all chance I was calling it that from now on.

I examined the weaves, finding them woven in and around the spell as I called it up, holding it before my eyes and diving in mentally.

The ball of smoldering hellfire got an immediate reaction from the possessed sludge creatures out and around the tower as soon as they saw it. One in three stayed where they were, while the rest moved quickly, if jerkily, out of sight.

I grinned at the sight of several of them falling off rooftops in their haste, landing with painful crunches on the stone below, then I winced as they stood back up, leaving blood and teeth behind as the puppets were marched from sight.

"Can you see it?" I asked Oracle, showing her what I had in mind and feeling her amusement as she started picking it apart and reconstructing it.

"I've no idea how you managed to make this before," she told me with the mental equivalent of a sigh of resignation. *"If you made it like this, it should have blown up in your face."*

"Yeah, I had no clue," I admitted. "The fact it worked at all, I think, was down to the excessive amount of mana I forced into it."

*"You **did** drain the entire area for miles around. I mean it; there was a massive mana dip for about ten miles."*

"It worked…more or less."

"You basically forced a shit ton of mana to do what you wanted. A third of the mana you used would have done more devastation, had you made it more gracefully," Oracle pointed out, even as weaves before me were snipped free, floating away on unseen winds, while others formed, woven into the mass before me.

In less than a minute and some three hundred mana later, it formed, pulsing, and twisting gently flowing as we stared at it.

"Will it work?" I asked Oracle in a hushed mental tone, getting a hopeful shrug in return. I blew out a long breath, then nodded to her.

"Let's begin, then," I said. I felt the sentience all around us as it heard that, having been expecting that whatever we were doing was all of it.

It wasn't.

It was the *seed*, the kernel of power that would either rid this tower and the city below of our enemies or kill us all in a roaring configuration of epic proportions. Either way, it was going to be fucking awesome.

I lifted both hands, spreading them slowly apart as the spell before me stretched thin, the mana manipulation allowing me to see connections where none could have existed before. Oracle, through me, reached out, teasing more and more strands free of the world around us.

As they snapped, the natural consequence of the spell before us being pulled literally apart, she added in fresh connections, a strand of earth reaching out to snag a floating morass here, a hint of water there, pulling the strands in close and connecting them to the ones before us.

As each connected, we felt the other ends reaching out as this broken strand connected to that, the far end would seek another, connecting to it and flowing onward, consuming and absorbing.

Seconds turned to minutes as the spell before us blossomed into a miniature sun, a ball of sheer nuclear fury hanging in the air before us, radiating heat and power as it grew.

I took the strands Oracle had prepared, even as she reached out, linking the spell to more and more strands. Quickly, I popped a mana potion, barely tasting the spearmint flavor as I knocked it back, slipping the glass vial into a bag without looking.

The shield Oracle had constructed and held ready for me was a weird thing, basically guiding the strands of mana away from the window, rather than anything actually solid.

"Uh, Oracle…are you sure…?" I said, eyes widening as I saw that there was literally no shield component for this spell, as near as I could tell.

In fact, apart from the guiding away of the mana, it…it did *nothing!*

"Yes Jax!" Oracle hissed, her voice strained as she focused on the hundreds of weaves she was manipulating, making it clear that now was not the time for my concerns. "It'll work, okay?"

"I was just a bit worried, that's all," I finished lamely, staring wide-eyed over the roiling mass of threads that mixed and flowed.

"Probably," Oracle added under her breath, even as the distant sounds of running feet could be heard in the stairwell.

"Sehran?" I called and glanced over to her, seeing the succubus as she stepped into the doorway of the stairwell, the door itself having long since vanished.

Sehran leveled the naginata at the darkness and focused, her lips drawing back to expose gleaming white teeth and long incisors. The naginata didn't respond at first, remaining dead and black in her hands, a lethal weapon, but only a sharpened piece of steel, for all that. But as the first body appeared from the darkness, she grinned.

It wasn't a welcoming smile, more like the kind of a smile you'd get from a honey badger when you were trapped in its lair, restrained, and it'd heard you'd been insulting its parentage.

The flowing pattern of the Damascus steel changed first, the simple gray and silvery metal starting to glow from within. Then the patterns that made up the blade shifted and flowed like liquid.

They twisted around, the blade heating from a simple silver-gray to a cherry red in seconds. As the first foot fell on the top step, she stabbed out.

The blade dipped into an exposed throat, the skin old and leathery, yet parting like silk on a scalpel as it slid inside, the heat crossing that final threshold as flames burst to life along its length.

Sehran pulled back, the blade sliding free even as the body fell. Flames spread across the corpse as the sludge caught light, smoke and worse lifting as the body fell backward, tumbling from sight into the mass of onrushing bodies.

"Jax!" Sehran called, her eyes widening as more and more raced up the stairwell. "There's a lot of them!" She stabbed out again and again, sending the bodies tumbling back, but she was forced to slowly retreat.

At first a single step, then two, then three, as the frenzied bodies clambered over each other, and our spell continued to build.

"Two more minutes!" I called to her, using the shield spell to basically scoop the mana out of the room, feeling the loss as I did it.

"I'll try!" she grunted, stabbing and thrusting, the naginata held loosely in her left and tight in her right, guiding it as she stabbed out, running it between her fingers.

The blade punched through the flesh effortlessly. As each blow landed, a fresh conflagration would begin, the blade sliding back out as spurts of flaming sludge leaped free as well.

The stairwell was quickly becoming a literal descent into hell as more and more bodies fell, their sludge feeding the flames as more and of their kind clambered across the bodies, others yanking their flailing comrades aside to make room for the bodies that replaced them.

I looked out and cursed.

I'd been focused on the ones inside, but out there…

"Incoming!" I shouted, seeing the creature as it folded its wings in, aiming for the window.

I yanked Oracle aside, clotheslining a flying creature that looked like a cross between a bat and an Alkyon, sending the thing flipping over as its neck broke, and it slammed into the table behind us.

More and more were coming, as well as the creatures that were…yup…climbing the fucking outside of the tower.

"Oracle! Now would be a great time!"

"I'm trying to fill every room in the entire city!" she hissed, her eyes glaring into the mass of weaves before her fixedly. "Do you want to do this?"

"Just do it quicker!" I snapped, having to keep the shield or not I supposed was more accurate, going, as I grabbed the flying thing and dragged it back to the window.

Its neck was broken, along with half its bones and certainly the right wing, but that made no difference whatsoever to the fucker's determination to gut me.

Screeches filled the air as sharp claws carved lines across the armor of my stomach, paint falling free as I grabbed the little bastard and flipped it over, smacking it down face-first on the floor, planting an armored boot between its shoulders and snapping both arms back.

I twisted, then released, grabbing it by the back of the head and the base of the wings, lifting and flinging it back out of the window, still hanging on mentally to the net I was holding over the window, filtering out the mana that constantly floated around us.

As the body passed back through the window, three more dive bombed me, and I swore, a split second's hesitation before I planted my feet and stayed exactly where I was.

I was about to dodge, but that would have let them in, and besides…I was wearing heavy armor.

Fuck that shit.

The first one hit me full speed, flipping over to kick out at the last second, just as I grabbed onto the windowsill and braced myself.

There was a loud succession of snapping bones, then it was tumbling backward, even as I grunted and braced myself again, shifting minutely to take the next on my chest.

The pain as they slammed into me at full speed wasn't minor. Hell, it broke their bodies, so they were clearly coming off worse, but damn.

The last impact was the worst, tumbling free as its momentum was spent, tearing several free of the wall below as they climbed. Oracle gasped and called out quickly.

"I'm nearly there!"

"Fuck my life," I whispered, shaking my arms and flexing fingers, frantically sliding the mental net around the room to separate out the last strands that had made it inside from the stairwell's inferno.

"Everyone, back from the window!" Oracle called, her hands twisting and spiraling around a ball of fire that seemed to make a nuclear core look tame by comparison.

Flames were bursting out in desperate arcs, while something black as pitch roiled in the center, lightning coated the surface, racing constantly, then…

…then Oracle dipped both hands into the blazing inferno that hovered before her, stepping up to the window and seeming to tear it apart, tossing its guts out across the city.

The weaves raced free, dozens multiplying into hundreds as they streamed out, becoming visible regardless of your magical competence, bringing a bright and terrible light to the underground city.

The streams flashed across the sky and dipped to the ground, floating weaves of fire and earth mingling, water flooding the earth and transforming it with life and death, forming falling oil that set light to the air.

The entire city seemed to detonate all at once as the first stage went active. The raining oil coated everything, seeping into corners and running down stairwells, pooling in out of the way corners as it brought light and terrible heat to the forgotten places.

The second phase went active as the first continued, the air filling with a mixture similar to a fuel-air explosive, igniting and sending a massive shockwave blasting through the entire city.

The creatures battling to reach us were torn apart. The blast of horrific heat and a terrible burning smell, erupted like I'd imagine from the devil's arsehole after a curry, punching into the tower we were huddled in and washing over us, despite my removal of all the mana I could.

Without the mana to convert and feed on, the spell raced elsewhere, but the backlash alone that we suffered would have killed lesser beings.

As it was, Sehran had run from the stairwell, leaping atop Oracle and wrapping her wings around the Wisp. I'd then folded myself around them both, huddled into the small area in the corner of the room while the world detonated around us.

I hissed in pain as the flames washed across me, superheating my armor, paint peeling free, crisping my padding and making me flinch as the back of my neck was burned, exposed by the angle of my head.

I released the weave, unable to hold it any longer before disconnecting a gauntlet and offering a shaking finger to Sehran, knowing she was suffering from the flames as much as I was.

She bit down hungrily, sucking blood out as Oracle started casting, no longer having to reserve her mana and frantically surrounding us in a fresh circle.

Seconds turned to minutes as outside the conflagration grew, and the heat increased. The air was getting harder to breathe, and I looked at Sehran and Oracle, the former releasing my finger so I could replace my gauntlet.

"We have to get out!" Oracle projected to us both. I nodded, Sehran joining in emphatically a second later.

"How?" she asked, and I straightened up, wincing as I looked out over the windowsill and saw the entire city was ablaze.

Pools of burning oil flowed across the plazas and courtyards. The trees were transformed into torches that blazed in terrible celebration of their energy.

The buildings were alight, rivulets of flame rolling down them, bodies staggered around, livening, and unliving torches that filled the air with their screams and billowing smoke.

The walls of the city cracked and shifted, dust cascading from above, and in the distance…

A sudden mental screech of pain and fury stabbed into our minds, sending all three of us to the floor, clutching our heads and hissing, crying out in pain.

"We have to run!" Sehran sent, forcing herself upright, grabbing at Oracle and my hands, and we joined her. I cast around frantically, sweeping up the naginata and dumping it in my bag, fairly sure that the dangers we would face on the way out wouldn't be affected by a sharp bit of metal.

"Downstairs!" I shouted above the roar of the flames, coughing as the smoke entered my lungs and doubling over, hacking and spitting.

"We need to go down!"

We ran, Sehran leading, Oracle in the middle, as much flying as running, staying low, with me lumbering along at the back.

The stairwell was circular, spiraling around and around as we raced on, coming to the ground floor and hesitating as we saw the piled bodies, the blazing pools, and the still-falling rain.

"How long will it last?" I asked, staring out across what looked like an antechamber to hell.

"I don't know!" Oracle replied, a hint of desperation in her sending. *"I tied it to the mana in the air, but that should have run out by now!"*

"The table!" Sehran sent. I spun around, following her pointing finger to a stone oblong table in one corner of the room, dripping burning oil. *"Can you carry it?"*

I didn't bother to answer, knowing it was our best damn chance, and instead ran to it, tipping it onto one side to drain most of the oil off, then hoisting it onto my shoulders and turning back around to face them.

It was heavy, my gods it was heavy, an inch or more thick and solid stone, two meters at least wide by three long, and even with my strength, I grunted. The damn thing had to be close on a metric ton or more.

With my strength as it was, lifting it was awkward, but doable. The real issue was running with it.

"Get…under!" I snapped, hoisting it and adjusting it on my shoulders and back, half-stooped as Oracle and Sehran ducked underneath.

"I could," Sehran offered, reaching up and about to try and take some of the weight.

"No!" I barked, shifting it and huffing out a breath. "You two…guide me…I'll carry!"

"This way!" Oracle sent, tugging the left leg slightly. I turned in the direction, edging it out of the door and onward.

The worst part was the bouncing as we rushed on. Each footfall made the table bounce, and I felt the strain in my neck, back, shoulder, and more. Every step grew harder, and when Oracle or Sehran had to stop me, directing me left or right, or even back on ourselves, guiding us around areas that were simply too thick with flame and smoke to continue…it grew worse.

We paused, resting in a small courtyard under a lean-to, as Oracle summoned a fountain for us all, then drenched the cloth that Sehran tore apart. We wrapped it around our faces, covering our mouths and noses as the fire continued to spread.

Minutes were lost as we backtracked again and again, looping around certain areas before suddenly, the ground shook.

The entire city quaked, cracks racing up and down the walls, great sections of the ceiling tumbling free and shattering on the floor, smaller stones hitting my makeshift shield and making me grunt in pain as the table was knocked this way and that.

"Wait here!" Sehran shouted, darting out from under the table and hissing in pain as the falling oil burned her skin.

She launched herself into the air before looping higher and higher, dodging falling sections.

"We're trapped!" she cried out seconds later as she returned, falling to the ground under the table and gasping as Oracle healed her. "The plaza, the *entire* plaza is alight. The portal has fallen, shattered on the floor, and to the north, the biggest building…it's got flames shooting out of every window and door!"

"Fuck!" I cursed, looking around desperately, trying to think of a way out.

"I'm sorry!" Oracle sent to us both, and inward as well, I suddenly knew. She was apologizing to our unborn child as much as to us. *"I'm so sorry! I went too far, and now…"*

Too far…far…

My mind spun as I wondered just how deep underground we actually were.

"Sehran!" I barked, looking at her. "The walls, are there cracks big enough for us?"

"For us…?" she asked, breaking off to cough from the smoke that was forcing its way into our lungs past the rapidly drying cloth masks.

"For us to pass through!" I clarified. "Is there a way up and out!"

"I…" She hesitated, then scrambled to her feet, running to the side and out from under the protection of the table, leaping into the air even as burning oil seared holes in her wings.

A long minute passed before I sensed her reaching out, guiding us to her, her mind a mess of pain.

"Let's go!" I called to Oracle, knowing she was already preparing a healing spell as we started to run, bent over, the table braced on my shoulders to protect us as best we could.

Three streets over, we turned, guided by Sehran as she limped out from under a low-hanging shattered section of wall that had protected her, shuddering as Oracle hit her again and again with healing before binding Sehran to her again.

"Two more streets over, there's a section of wall that's collapsed. It leads through to somewhere, but it's too dark to see, and my wings…" She glanced down at them, seeing the skin slowly regrowing as Oracle's spell healed her. "I couldn't get close enough. It might be nothing."

"Or it might be a way out!" I declared. "We're dead if we stay here, so move!" I ordered, starting to lumber along again, the table bouncing and jarring with every step as they were forced to keep under its protection.

Inside, I cursed myself, my own damn stupidity, in my swearing to rain down hellfire on this city.

It was *literally* what we'd done.

The ground shook again, and buildings closer to the center that we could see towering above the nearby buildings were suddenly covered in spider-webbing cracks.

They shuddered and twisted, starting to fall as more and more buildings sent massive plumes of flames into the air.

"Run!" I screamed, sending the table clattering onto the floor, legs breaking as Oracle and Sehran raced ahead.

The ground shook, cobbled floors rippling and popping as they rolled. The sound of shattering stone filled the air as the mental screams continued, a burgeoning hatred and determination to get us, to kill us in as horrifically painful a way as possible, and to possess our child, flooded the mental ether.

We ran on, slipping, scrabbling as the floor suddenly tilted, lifting, and falling, buildings toppling.

"Left, then right!" Sehran screamed, dragging Oracle. I grunted, kicking off a wall, then scooped them both up, an arm around each waist.

I lined up on the wall ahead, the edge of a massive black crack just in sight as I formed a blade with my right hand and triggered Lunge.

It sent us blurring across the gap, my boots carving a trail of sparks as we landed, shifting direction and running the last dozen feet.

The crack was about half a meter wide, three tall, and radiated out in all directions, with loose stonework falling from it as the city shook, but beyond…

"Go!" I called, shoving Sehran and Oracle ahead of me. Rain ran down my armor and seeped into the gaps, blistering and burning my skin as I braced myself, waiting for them.

They dove in; no matter what was ahead, at least it wasn't this fucking place, and I forced myself to wait as they wriggled out of sight.

"Come!" Oracle sent to me, the relief in her sending clear as I twisted, and forced myself into the gap.

Unlike them, with their softer bodies and more malleable flesh, my damn armor wasn't built with any give in it, and after only a handful of seconds, I was stuck.

I tried to back up, unable to, then go ahead again, but it was no good. I was wedged tight.

"Move back!" I bellowed to them, checking my mana and hissing at how low it was.

I had one chance.

Mana-Overdrive would either get me stuck fast, or get me free, and the way the wall was shaking…

I activated it, the doubling and redoubling of my strength making it literally possible for me to rip sections of the wall free…even as others started to fall, plummeting toward my head.

I ripped at the stones, forcing some aside, even as the walls shook others free, stone slipping and sliding away to clatter against each other as I heaved and swore.

At first, I could barely make it a few inches, and even here, the spell was starting to spread, the strands of mana flowing in from the darkness ahead, bringing in fuel that quickly shifted into fresh falling rain.

I got a grip on a section of stone, yanking it backward.

The stone didn't come out, but it turned. The stone that held it above and below shifted in turn as the entire section began to crumble.

I braced both hands on the wall, gripping sections that wouldn't move, no matter the effort I put in, and instead I dragged myself through, the screech of metal on stone filling the air…followed by a solid *boinggg* as a section of my cuirass deformed inwards.

I grunted in pain, but ahead of me, I could see Oracle and Sehran, and the weave that Oracle was using. Sehran was once again set adrift to "hold her breath" as Oracle worked to stop the spread of the spell.

It took me several more seconds, and that was with Sehran bracing both feet on the wall and grabbing my arm, adding her not inconsiderable strength to it. But eventually, I fell free, clattering to the floor, as Oracle sealed the wall, cutting off the flow of mana as we all collapsed to the floor, spent.

CHAPTER THIRTY-SIX

I shifted—sometime later—on the stone floor, wincing as I rose back to full consciousness, a pain in my right side making it awkward to breathe fully. Blinking in the dim corridor as my DarkVision activated, I saw Oracle and Sehran sitting nearby, Oracle looking pale and wan, Sehran speaking softly as they discussed, of all things, baby names.

"Hey," I whispered, shifting, and filling the air with the creak and groan of stressed armor plates, as I got up.

"Hey you," Oracle said, taking a deep breath, and I knew what was coming.

"I'm sorry," I said quickly, speaking before she could. "I'm sorry that *my* spell, that you tried to fix, went this mad."

"No Jax, I changed it, I made it work, and…"

I shook my head, looking from her to Sehran. "You took my spell, and you tried to fix it, and it did all of that still? That was amazing." I pointed out, trying to take a deep breath and wincing. "Are we safe here?" I looked around. "Also, where *is* here?"

"The wall collapsed inward a while ago, and since then, well, about an hour after we made it out, it went silent," Oracle said, looking around at the dusty cavern.

There was a rockslide where we'd come through earlier, and on the other side, a narrow and clearly ancient path led away, the rusted remains of wall sconces to hold torches leaving red streaks on the stone.

"Looks like we've got a little space," I said. "Help me out of this, will you?" I asked, gesturing to my cuirass and getting questing and helpful fingers a few seconds later.

It took nearly ten minutes, all told, to get the cuirass and remaining upper body armor off, take a large rock and hammer the dent until it popped back out, then redress, but by the time I'd managed it, I was feeling a lot better.

I'd also taken the time to have a drink and some food, and with the appearance of a fresh pot of good coffee, the world was a better place for all three of us.

That however had opened us up to the real concern that we couldn't sense the others any more.

Well, we *could*. I could anyway, and through me Oracle could, Sehran was having issues sensing anything, but if it was down to me being the one who'd set up the group, or because I was the Scion, or hell, because I had a really fancy fucking cape, I didn't know.

All I knew was that the others were alive, and they were far away. I guessed that could mean that we were on the west of the continent somewhere, that'd explain why I couldn't feel any others sworn to me nearby, but still.

We talked it out as best we could, then decided that for now, we knew they were alive, and that had to be enough. We'd get to the surface, we'd find a way goddamn home, and I'd even put up with the ear-bashing I was sure to get from Romanus and Restun for losing my guards again.

As long as everyone was okay, I didn't care.

Shortly after that, we were armored up again, or I was anyway, with no spare gear beyond the clothing I had in my bag. Sehran was unfortunately unarmored for the foreseeable future. The body armor that she'd looted earlier had been discarded in favor of the gloom silk clothing I'd given her, and while I had to admit it made perfect sense, it killed me to cut sections of the top apart to let her wings move more comfortably.

Before now, the top had been diagonally down from the top of her wings, acting as a partial 'push-up' bra as well as any covering, considering it'd been looped under her norks.

Now it was cut, then adjusted, letting her wings have free movement, as well as massively improving her comfort level…and reducing the risk of a black eye or her being knocked unconscious if we needed to run again.

The path we took, striding along with me in the lead, my naginata leveled and ready, was narrow and clearly unused for a long time.

Here and there were the occasional signs of ancient activity, rusted rings in the walls, occasional bracing in areas where the roof had presumably been dodgy in the past, that sort of thing.

It was a full hour of walking before we found the first separation in the road.

A T junction lay ahead, with a path leading left and right, both directions appearing equally unused and abandoned, covered in fallen stone from what had apparently been an attempt to block off the passageway leading this way.

"Any ideas?" I asked the other two, getting a head shake from both. "Left it is, then." I said, trying to pretend confidence.

"Why left?" Oracle asked as we set off. I reached out, taking her hand in mine as I smiled down at her.

"First of all, the ground looks like it's going up rather than down, and secondly…"

"Yes?"

"Total guess."

"Do you think the Gods would help?" Sehran asked, making me pause before shaking my head in negation.

"Honestly, they probably *could*, but from what I understand, if we ask for their help, and they give it, then that frees up the Dark Wanker and his dickheads to act as well. That portal could have taken us a few miles…or tens of thousands. We might be directly below His new main cathedral, for all we know, and I think if we reached out to shout at the Gods across space and time, it might be overheard."

"For now, there's no point," Oracle said, one hand in mine, the other gently caressing her bump. "Until we make it out of the caves and can see the sun, or we can't find our way out, we're better off not running the risk, I think."

"Makes sense." Sehran sighed. "I really can't wait to be home, though…"

"Home?" I asked, wondering, and she smiled.

"Aboard Tenandra," she clarified. "The cabin is perfect for us, just the right size, enough privacy that we could do anything we want, with the thrill of knowing someone might come in at any time and catch us all, and the swing…"

"Please," I whispered, shaking my head. "It's been literally days, don't get me thinking about that."

"Oh, I'm sure Tenandra and Jian wouldn't mind if you wanted to try it out!" Sehran said quickly. "It's the perfect height and means you can brace yourself."

"Nope!" I said quickly, shaking my head. "Lalalalalalala."

"You know she's teasing you, don't you?" Oracle sent to me, and I nodded slightly as I responded.

"It makes her happy."

"And the thought of me in that swing makes you happy," Oracle pointed out with a wicked grin.

"Not you, too!" I shook my head as Oracle sent me mental images and the occasional sensation, trying to distract us both from worrying over the others, even as we'd all decided that the last sight I'd had of Grizz meant they were probably free by now.

Both she and I got so distracted after a while, sending each other mental images, that we were both utterly flummoxed when Sehran sent one to us both.

It involved her closing the door and leaving us with two of her sisters to play. The sudden burst of amusement as we both staggered, reminding us that not only was she bonded to Oracle again and had access to her mana pool, but she also had access to her mind and bodily sensations.

A little tweak had Oracle blushing furiously, even as I grinned and tried to calm myself down, realizing belatedly that in the images we'd been sharing unwittingly, we'd shared a lot of information about what we liked, as well as memorized images.

We drew a line under it and talked about inconsequential things, realizing how silent Oracle and I had become as we sent each other the mental equivalent of filthy texts.

The three of us were walking along quite happily, talking and joking, when Sehran suddenly hissed, reaching out and grabbing us both, yanking us back as we were about to step into the crossing corridor, following a random rule of whichever path seemed to lead upwards was the one taken.

"What's…"

"Ahead…life," she said mentally, making me nod as I shifted into the middle of the corridor.

I crept forward for a short distance before being tapped on the shoulder, and Sehran slipped past me, pausing only to whisper.

"You sound like a collapsing ironworks," she said. "Wait here."

I grunted, but yeah, stealth wasn't exactly my strongest suit, and in this armor, awesome as it was, the clanking and clattering that was reflected off the walls nearby, not to mention the stones and more I knocked aside…

"Okay," I muttered, stepping up to the edge and waiting there, peering carefully around into the next path.

It was the same as the last as far as I was concerned, hell, I couldn't hear or sense anything, but when Oracle reached out, and I felt the interest in her mind, I did the same.

Triggering Mana-Manipulation allowed me to see the mana of the realm all around us, and as I focused…

There was significantly more life mana flowing from that direction, as well as other things, some death, some water…fire, and air…

I glanced in the other direction, seeing noticeably less, and that what there was both weaker and…and *drifting,* I decided was the best way to describe it.

It didn't seem to be doing anything, just floating along, but to the left, it seemed to be propelled, stirred up.

"See anything?" I sent to Sehran, getting a non-committal response, and was forced to wait several long minutes as she crept closer.

Eventually, though, she responded, and it was with a sense of wonder.

"You have to see this," she sent back.

"Is it safe?"

"Probably not, but there's…there's no way I can describe this," she replied.

Oracle and I took a quick look at each other before releasing the ability and setting off, hurrying along the corridor as quickly and quietly as we could.

Two minutes later, as I stopped next to Sehran, I saw exactly what she meant.

Before us, in a massive underground cavern and a good distance away, surrounded on all sides by a moat with a raised central section, was what could only be described as a goddamn *castle.*

Or it would be, if termites had made one.

Weirdest of all, was that it sat in daylight.

The cavern was bathed in strong sunlight, reflected down from however far overhead by a series of crystals and what looked, at this distance, to be mirrors.

The castle sat in the middle of developed farmland, complete with animals, and encircling the farmland was, as I'd thought before, a series of moats.

Each of them had liquid filling them, and the castle or keep. or whatever it was, appeared to be closer to a fortified mound rather than a classical castle. The sides were rounded, dotted with dozens of small windows and lit by…

Lit by glyphs and runes!

The entire fucking place fairly reeked of magic, and all around it were towers, small walls and more. The moats were deep, and here and there, tiny thanks to the distance, I could see short, fat creatures wandering around.

"Gnomes?" I asked Oracle and Sehran hopefully, thinking that if this was indeed a gnomish hidden village or city, not only would they be able to get us home, but they could probably solve the damn population crisis Baant was so worried about.

"No," Sehran whispered, frowning as she watched them. "They're too big."

"Damn…what are they then?" I asked slowly, crouching down next to her and staring across the distance, watching as the figures waddled here and there, their movements vaguely familiar.

"Xon'dike," came a voice from behind me, even as the haft of an axe was laid across my right shoulder, the head angled inward towards my neck. "We are the Xon'dike, and you are our prisoners."

"Fuck."

There was a moment of silence as we all paused, wondering who was going to move first.

"So…you going to move that axe?" I asked eventually, waiting a half second before triggering Mana-Overdrive and twisting left, coming to my feet and wrapping my left hand around the haft, clamping it tight.

The figure before me tried to pull his axe back, surprising me when he almost managed it, then I yanked hard, dragging him closer, kicking out with a front snap kick.

It landed hard in the center of its carapace, staggering him backward. I yanked again, twisting the weapon free of its grip.

The Xon'dike stumbled and fell, landing on its back and cursing, pulling its arms and legs in, then twisting, rolling itself left then right, clearly trying to get back to its feet.

I paused, setting the haft down on the ground and glancing at it, then the Xon'dike, then all around.

"Sehran, are we alone?" I asked and she hesitated.

"I think so," she eventually replied. "But I thought we were before, as well."

"Oracle?"

"Probably?" she suggested.

"Well, best we can manage, I suppose. Do you want a hand?" I asked the Xon'dike, just as the figure managed to build up enough speed to roll over.

He landed on all fours, crouched, then straightened as far as he could, holding both arms ready to fight and blowing a thin crest up on either side of his neck, some kind of glands throbbing visibly.

"Here," I said, tossing the axe back, the head upright and haft extended vertically. The weapon was more of a halberd than an axe. But regardless, when it hit him and bounced off, his hands closing just a little too late in his surprise, it made it clear that whatever else he'd expected, me returning his weapon wasn't it.

"Why?" he asked after a long minute, the crest sagging slightly as the protruding glands on either side of the neck deflated.

"Why what?"

"Why give me back my weapon?"

"It's crap," I said honestly. "Mine's a lot better, and even if it weren't, honestly, we just want to get back to the surface. I figure giving your weapon back demonstrates that we're not looking to fight you."

"The surface?" he asked, confused. "You say you're from the surface?"

"That a problem?" I asked, glancing him over as he hesitantly picked his weapon up and looked at me, head cocked to one side.

He looked kind of like an armadillo wearing armor for fuck's sake, a long snout, huge black eyes, a finely-crafted but clearly damn old helm that had been patched and repaired so much it was as much patch as original parts now.

The massive half-circle carapace that covered his back, which had almost turtled it, was made up of ridged armor, with a metal breastplate covering his softer underbelly.

The lower legs were wide-splayed, and the upper arms ended in sharp claws, the limbs heavily muscled from carrying its bulk, but…but the grip was weak, judging from the way I'd ripped the weapon free.

All in all, it gave the impression of a figure who was playing at being a guard.

"Oracle, you said the Xon'dike were the soldiers of the Prax, didn't you?" I asked, frowning as I tried to remember what she'd said in the middle of the damn fight with the undead months ago.

"They were the more basic guardians. Essentially, the Prax's first line of defense was the Legion, but then as well as its resident crew, there were the Xon'dike, both in terms of engineers and warriors." Oracle replied slowly. "They were…" She hesitated, and I nodded, understanding her point as she left it unsaid. Frankly, if I boarded an enemy vessel and found this fucker waiting for me, I'd barely slow down as I cut through them.

"You mean the Sect of War and the Sect of Artificers," the Xon'dike cut in slowly. "You know of them?"

"Yeah," I replied slowly, sliding the naginata into my Bag of Spatial Folding as it became clear that he wasn't likely to attack us now. "Are you all from a Prax, or a village that supplied one, or something?"

"Best to speak to the elders," he replied after a few seconds. "But…" He glanced back at the passage we'd come from, then back at us, clearly uncertain.

"What's up?"

"I'm not permitted to leave my post," he admitted. "The Path to the Dark must be watched at all times." He shuffled forward a few steps and pointed to the side where a wide, well-maintained path sloped downward, leading to the ground level of the cavern. "Take that path; you will be met by others."

"Will we have to fight them?"

"No, they know you're here and that I've let you pass. But they'll need to test you."

"Test?"

"To make sure you're not infected by the Darkness."

"That creature back there?" I asked, jerking a thumb to the passageway. He nodded, eyes widening.

"You know of it?"

"Did you feel the ground shaking?" Oracle asked, smiling.

"Yes?"

"That's what's left of it. Locally at least," Sehran added in. "Oracle lost her temper, and she always says Jax is the one that has no self-control."

"I did NOT lose my temper!" Oracle argued, turning to stare at Sehran, apparently offended. "I was the soul of self-control!"

"You destroyed the city."

"It was old and practically falling apart!"

"Not until you arrived, it wasn't," Sehran threw back, grinning as Oracle spluttered.

"And she says I'm the one with no self-control," I said, waving at the guard as I started down the path, seeing four larger creatures waddling along from what looked to be a checkpoint in the distance. "Seriously? This is the woman who shrinks down, then climbs into my pocket to tease me?"

"Really?"

"Oh, yeah, she used to do that shit all the time," I assured Sehran.

"You were wearing the Drow pants!" Oracle wailed. "They had an easy-access hole!"

"Never heard it called that before," Sehran quipped, winking at Oracle.

"Also, have you worked with the Drow much?" I asked Sehran as we left the guard at the passage, strolling down the path side-by-side.

"Gods, no," Sehran said with feeling. "Well, once. Most of us do *once*."

"Why only once?"

"Well, what was it you called them again?"

"A race of whisky-dicked, overcompensating assholes?" Oracle asked. I shrugged, considering all the names I'd called the Drow.

"Well, let's just say it's accurate. As much as succubai are demons, we kinda still have standards, and well, we *like* our job. We get summoned to this realm fairly irregularly, so when we do get the chance to come and play? Regardless of the increase in power we gain, it's generally a fun time. We all sit around and reminisce when we go home. Our brothers and sisters gather round when one of us first returns, and we celebrate, listen to their stories, and when it's been a Drow summoning, we usually laugh. A lot."

"I thought they'd be pretty kinky fuckers," I muttered.

"Oh, they are, but they're just a bit shit at it as well. Think of your first ever sexual experience, how skilled were you?"

"Not very," I admitted, wincing. "There was a lot more…*enthusiasm*…than skill."

"Exactly. Well, imagine that you'd managed it only once or twice and were having performance issues, while all those around you were swearing blind that *they* didn't. While recommending all sorts of weird things you should try."

"So…so they're all limp-dicked and lying about it to each other?" I asked.

"Most of the time I was summoned by that Drow was spent listening to them explaining that it wasn't their fault, then walking around in public having me pretending to be exhausted. Or me sitting and reading a book in his quarters while occasionally shouting out things like 'it's so big' and 'please be gentle' to anyone who might be listening while the summoner sulked in the corner."

She snorted, shaking her head. "Honestly, all succubai have a time limit in our contracts that we can extend or cut short. I, like most of my sisters, didn't even bother to add it in when Jian summoned me. I used the standard one with him. The Drow contract? It's sixteen pages long, hundreds of clauses."

"Bet they read it all as well." I grunted.

"They DO!" Sehran agreed, looking scandalized. "They read the entire thing!"

"Fucking limp-dicked lawyers," I muttered, shaking my head.

"When the summoning circle appears for us, and we see it's a Drow? It usually gets opened to the rest of the clan, if we don't want to go. Occasionally, we ignore it entirely until it runs out of mana and closes," Sehran admitted, shrugging and making me grin.

"Man, that's cold, when an actual sex demon turns your entire species down as not worth the effort?" I shook my head, letting loose a low whistle as I considered the mental damage that'd do.

"Usually as part of the deal with summoning us, we arrange a second book toward the end of the visit, if we've had fun. Makes it possible to summon us again."

"Right?"

"I don't know of anyone, well, besides Triana, who has ever given one to a Drow."

"Who's Triana?"

"She's a bit of a strange one, not really into the whole sex thing. Loves to read, though. She lets the Drow summon her every few centuries."

"I thought you couldn't come too regularly?" I asked, and Sehran winked at me.

"Oh, I can, a lot!" She giggled, before shaking her head. "But seriously. We have a limit, that's all. The more powerful we become, the more likely we are to be stopped returning. Our realm is all about balance of power. If we grow too powerful, wars break out. Instead, we try to limit things. As one of the few demon species that gets summoned more than once, we tend to grow in power quickly. Often quicker than we grow in sense."

"You said…we can talk about this later." I said, breaking off as the four creatures ahead broke into a run, dropping to all fours and picking up speed.

"Yeah, maybe we should have waited with the friendly guard," Sehran mumbled, squinting at the oncoming group.

"Oracle, think they'd freak out if we cast a circle?" I asked.

She snorted. "They will if they step into it."

"More or less than if I kill one of them if they attack?"

"Probably less; it'd make them pause at least," she admitted.

"Then let's do that." I reached out with my right hand. I was about to start casting, as I normally did, but forced myself to take the time to do it without the crutch of the words and gestures.

I stared at the floor of the cavern all around us, focusing, and telling the mana that was what it should be. A Frostfire Circle of Cleansing, surrounding us.

Predictably, fuck all happened.

CHAPTER THIRTY-SEVEN

"**P**erformance issues, dear?" Oracle quipped after a few seconds. I narrowed my eyes at her before lifting a single finger to Sehran. "Not one word!" I warned her, getting a pout as my response.

"Perhaps soon?" Oracle suggested, and I waved that hand at her distractedly, focusing on the feeling of the spell, on the way the mana reacted.

When I'd been working with Amon's power, I didn't need to do any of this; I'd simply made reality be what I wanted it to be, within reason.

Since then, I'd been able to mimic it on a very small scale with spells I knew really well, mainly because I was in the zone and operating on instinct as much as anything else.

Now, though, I was having to do it more carefully, focusing and doing it, making it happen while people watched.

I suddenly wondered if this was what porn stars had to put up with, having an entire crew sitting around eating their lunch and doing various jobs while they had to spring to attention and bang on demand.

That image completely buggered my attempt, and I cursed, before going back to the usual way of doing it and casting the goddamn spell.

I barely managed to get the damn spell in place before they reached us, skidding to a halt and spreading out around the edge of the circle.

One stepped into it, then hissed and leaped back, glaring at us while shaking its leg, the flames dying as it limped back, hissing something at the others.

"So, that's not a very friendly greeting!" I called to them, looking from one to another.

"You're still trespassers," came a call from above. I looked back behind us, and up at where the bugger we'd left on guard had stepped up to the edge to shout down.

"You asshole! We told you we only want to talk!" I shouted back.

"And you can…once you give up your weapons," one of the others said, his voice deeper.

I turned away, dismissing the guard as I looked at the figures before me.

"Sect of War, right?" I asked, pointing at them and seeing the look they exchanged at my words.

The difference between these and the guard was clear. Not only were they significantly bigger and wearing much better maintained and fitted gear, they also had what looked to be natural spikes growing out of their carapace.

Their faces were shorter. Rather than long snouts, they were wide, flatter-faced, with larger mouths filled with sharp teeth. Their limbs were much heavier muscled, and their carapace–as well as the spikes that were everywhere on them, their carapace had three long lines down it, ridged plates of bone that looked to have been sharpened.

"You know of us?" one asked after a minute, its voice, like the first, deeper and gravelly.

"Yeah. Well, a little. We've come across your dead on a Prax, and Oracle remembers you as well," I said, nodding in her direction.

"Look, we're not interested in fighting you; we're trying to make it to the surface. That wanker up there…" I paused, jerking a thumb up toward the guard. "He said we should speak to your elders; now he's saying we're trespassing."

"Do you have permission from the elders to be here?" the leader of the group asked.

"Nope."

"Then you are trespassing, yes?"

"More like an uninvited guest," I suggested. "We're passing through on our way to the surface; we need to get back home, that's all. We're happy to meet your elders, but we're not giving up our weapons."

"Then you're not entering the city."

"Fine by me; bring the fuckers out to talk." I shrugged.

"The elders never leave the city."

"Then we're at a bit of an impasse. We're going to the surface. If you don't want to talk to us, fine, point us in the right direction, and we'll go."

"You cannot leave," another snapped, his weapons a pair of hooked swords that looked fucking painful to fight.

"Let's not be silly here," I said, when Oracle stepped forward, clearly having had enough of their shit as she lifted both hands, a glowing ball of Pyro appearing above each palm.

"Get out of our way, or you'll regret it," she snapped.

I stared at her, stunned, feeling the waves of anger and irritation that rolled off her.

"Okay!" I said, knowing damn well that Oracle, who was currently sustaining Sehran, was using my manapool to cast the damn spells. "How about we all calm the fuck down for a minute? We just destroyed that city back there, and while I'd prefer not to do that here…" I left the threat unsaid as I looked at the creatures before me.

"You visited the city of darkness?" the leader asked grimly.

"Yeah, your guy up there said you'd want to test us?"

"Test?" he rumbled. "There is a test…"

"Okay…"

"You need to enter the city."

"Well, let's…"

"You must surrender your weapons."

"Fuck's sake," I growled. "Look, that's not happening, all right? Add to that, we have *magic*! Giving you the damn weapons is pointless when we have magic, right? I give you a dagger, and I can't stab you, right? How do you stop me ramming a fireball up your ass?!"

"We have ways…"

"Fine." I growled. "Fuck it. Oracle, calm the hell down; we're taking that path over…" I frowned looking around the cavern, then picking the most heavily guarded, assuming that would be the way that led upward.

"That one!" I declared, pointing at it and gesturing around. "Now, you want to talk to us, come chat, you want to bring your elders? Great, bring their happy asses over to join in. You want to stop us? Take our weapons and our magic? Fuck no." I paused, frowning, feeling the change as Oracle absorbed the spells and instead shifted the circle, recasting it and tethering it to me, rather than to the ground we stood atop.

I grinned and took a step forward.

The circle shifted, blurring as the original stayed where it was, cut off from my mana, but still running through the little it had left. The new one, though, flowed forward, rolling across the ground and sending all four backing away, cursing as they were burned.

"Heal them please, Oracle," I said, glaring at them as they readied to fight us.

"They…"

"They're defending their home, and this is the last chance they get." I maintained eye contact with the leader. "They were burned trying to cross the line, then again when I moved. Now they understand that, to fight us, they have to come close enough, that before they even have to try and fight us, they'll be being burned to death. I think that's a valuable lesson right there. Heal them, then we're leaving."

With that, I took another slow step forward and another, starting to walk slowly but steadily, cutting across the cavern in the direction of the most heavily guarded of the exits.

"Move," the leader snapped to the others, backing up and giving me room, staring at me with glossy black eyes that showed nothing of what he was thinking.

They moved around the outside, healing spells flying out from Oracle one after another to hit them, making them hiss and shudder.

The leader, clearly about to object, had tried to dodge the spell, then hissed in pain as the spell made adjustments on the fly to them.

Seconds passed, then he slumped, glaring at us, panting as he flexed fingers and watched us passing.

He gestured to one of the others, drawing them in close, then speaking rapidly before sending them running in the direction of the city, then jerking his head to the other two and following along behind us.

I glared at him, then shrugged, striding along, Oracle's hand in mine as we went.

"What happened there?" I asked Oracle, getting a growl as I looked from her to Sehran.

"Sorry," Sehran said before Oracle could. "I'm trying to suppress it as much as possible…"

"What?"

"I *am* a demon," she pointed out. "We're not exactly pictures of calm and restraint. Believe me, it takes a while to learn not to act on our impulses."

"And Oracle is feeling them," I realized, nodding and remembering the way we both were at first until we learned to balance our emotions.

"She is, also hormones," Sehran said.

"Why hormones?" I asked, frowning and looking down at Oracle, who responded.

"SHE doesn't particularly enjoy being talked about like she's not here!" Oracle glared as we both grinned at her. "And I'm not hormonal OR having anger issues! Okay?" she snapped, seeing our grins and grinding her teeth as she shook her head.

"Oh, okay, clearly not," I agreed, humoring her.

"Picture of calmness," Sehran agreed.

"Totally didn't nearly start a war or anything," I pointed out.

"You do that all the time!" Oracle shot back.

I frowned. "Hey, I did that once!"

"You picked a fight with a God."

"He's a dick!"

"You conquered two cities."

"They were shitholes." I shrugged.

"Wiped out goblins and stole their homes?"

"They're goblins!" I pointed out quickly. "Practically fucking vermin."

"Destroyed another city?" She suggested, gesturing back behind us.

"That was totally your fault."

"Wiped out hundreds of gnomes?"

"They started it."

"Beat a SporeMother to death with your bare hands?"

"I was wearing gauntlets." I held my hands up as proof, looking down at them. "Although, had I been wearing this shit, I'd probably have been fine. It's *nice*."

"It is," Oracle agreed with a sigh. "Sorry, I'm a bit on edge, that's all. So where did you get that armor, then? And you know Thorn is going to kill you if it's an original?"

"It is," I said, glancing down at the mess of it. It was covered in dried blood, burns, scratches, dents, and more, and comparing it to the original when I'd first put it on…

"She's going to kill you."

"There're a few sets in the armory," I said. "She can have one of them to compare to her own work…and wait, didn't she say she had to make a set to prove herself, anyway?"

"She did; she and the others made the most basic, unenchanted version. You're wearing one that was made for the actual Praetorian Guard, around seven to eight hundred years ago, and polished and ready for a parade. She's going to have a breakdown when she sees it."

"Fuck," I muttered, stepping off the path and getting a growl from behind us as I stepped into the field of knee-high crops. I glanced back, and the leader of the interception group gestured for me to walk along the path instead of cutting across their fields.

Being the subtle man I am, I contemplated telling him to go fuck himself, to suck a barrel of dicks, and that I hoped he developed a case of super-gonorrhea.

After a second, though, I stepped back onto the path, muttering under my breath and led the others around the edge of the small field.

"Good boy," Oracle murmured.

The next few minutes passed in silence as the three of us walked around the edges of several small fields, making it clear that, from a distance, while most of the cavern appeared to be cultivated, it was in dozens, if not hundreds of damn patches, rather than two or three massive fields, as we would have done it at home.

"Why do you do this?" I asked the leader who was marching behind me, eventually losing my patience.

"What?" he growled.

"Break the damn land up into tiny parcels like this!"

"It's the farmer' land," he declared as if that made it clear.

"A single farmer?" I asked, frowning.

"A family."

"You're shitting me."

"No."

"You're seriously telling me that this," I gestured to the dozens upon dozens of patches that surrounded us on all sides. "...all of this is broken up into individual farmers' fields?"

"Of course."

"Fucking idiots."

"Watch yourself."

"Or fucking what?" I snapped, turning around and glaring at him. "I've had a seriously shitty couple of days, pal! I got blown up, shot, stabbed, shit on by monsters, had to climb my fucking way up a Prax, deal with goddamn gnomes that had just crawled out a fucking toilet, and now I've left my friends behind, thanks to some knob-jockey opening a goddamn portal! We've had to destroy a city of sludge fucking monsters, then on top of all that, we're lost, and some asshole is wasting my fucking time expecting me to walk around a million tiny fields!"

"It kept you busy," he grunted, gesturing to the right where a group of another thirty of the soldier caste or whatever they were hurried toward us from the city.

"Really," I snapped, folding my arms. "You really want to fucking do this?"

"You cannot leave; the Darkness cannot be allowed to escape." He hefted his weapon and licked his lips as he worked himself up to attack.

"The darkness? That sludge thing that I already told you we killed?"

"It cannot die."

"It damn well can when you burn the fucker with fire."

"It has been tried."

"Well you didn't try hard enough, did you?" I snarled.

"Jax..." Oracle said slowly, her voice rising in clear warning.

"What?!" I rounded on her, seeing the way she was looking in the other direction, at the distant passage that the majority of the guards were clustered around, as hoots and whistles rang out, the shrill sounds carried on the still air, answered in seconds by bells from the city ringing out in iron warning.

"INCURSION!" The leader screamed, eyes widening, turning to the incoming group from the city. "S'barrr incursion!"

The incoming group had switched direction as they heard the bells, turning and trampling the nearby crops until they were on a new path that ran straight and true toward the far passage.

I looked at him, then Oracle and Sehran, wondering what the hell was going on.

"You want a chance to prove yourself?" the leader asked me suddenly. I turned back to him.

"Not really. I stopped giving a shit about you all a while ago," I replied rudely.

"Then leave! Run and hide like the cowards you are!" he spat, snapping something I missed to the remaining two. They stared at him, then us, but stayed watching us, even as he ran around the edge of the circle and in the direction of the guarded passage.

"He has a point," Sehran said after a minute.

"I'm a coward?" I asked, stunned.

"Ha! No, that's something you could never be accused of. No, if we want a chance to prove ourselves, to speak to their elders and more, we could help?"

"Oracle?" I asked, not wanting to admit it made sense. Despite these assholes being unfriendly so far, I couldn't really argue with them being that, all things considered.

"We…should," she admitted, sighing. "Sehran, dear, you are insanely distracting, and yes, both because of the emotions and the desires, it's all I've been able to do not to strip off and jump on you both all the way here!"

"Honestly, the first fifty or so years? That's all we do," Sehran admitted with a toothy grin. "We just fuck like crazy."

"We are never coming to visit," Oracle said. "Jax!"

"Yeah?" I responded as the sudden thought of dozens of women like Sehran jumping on each other all day long derailed my brain for a split second.

"I am extremely frustrated right now. Go work our frustration out, please."

"Yes, ma'am!" I grinned as I sensed the unspoken promise that, when we were alone again soon, Oracle was going to work out some other frustrations for us both.

I cut the circle spell, no longer powering it and feeling it fade already, knowing that Oracle and Sehran could damn well fly if they needed to. I crouched, unable to do this without the style points being added, like doing superhero landings.

Then I punched upward, activating Soaring Majesty and rocketing into the sky. I flashed over the lumbering figure of the squad leader below, then seconds later passed over the path the reinforcements were taking.

I'd covered maybe half the distance, squinting at the entrance to the passage perhaps a mile away, as the distant figures of the Xon'dike broke and started to run.

The passage came apart suddenly, wood shattering and making it clear that what had looked like a normal-sized passage from here was a much bigger one and had been artificially narrowed by wood and stone.

The creature that broke through, sending a hardier last few defenders reeling and biting down on them, was a thing of nightmares.

It stood around ten meters tall and was perhaps eighteen long from nose to twitching, barbed tail.

It stood atop two massive hind legs, with four more on either side of its chest, currently reaching out and greedily snatching at the defenders, yanking them in close as the head darted down and bit, feeding messily on the Xon'dike.

The arms grabbed the Xon'dike victims' arms and legs. holding them immobile and stretched out, even as the head, covered in a chitinous shell, drove forward.

It had no eyes, I noted, details jumping out to me as I closed the distance, pushing harder at the pitiful screams of the fleeing figures.

Instead, the mouth appeared to make up the majority of the head, with something like a spider's pedipalps spread out around the head.

As it lunged forward, the pedipalps dragged back the chitin, exposing the mouth and presumably the softer bits, enabling it to feed. Then it discarded the Xon'dike, now an empty carapace, dripping with gore and filled with torn flesh, the pedipalps released, and the chitin closed over the head again.

Bolts from crossbows shattered against the chitin as more and more of the defenders formed up, massive hammers like the squad leader carried hefted and held ready.

"They need to shatter it," I grunted, speaking aloud unconsciously as I closed the distance. "Shatter the chitin, then the crossbows can hurt it."

The creature threw back its head and roared, reminding me of nothing so much as a T-Rex, with extra arms, chitin armor cladding, and a goddamn stinger for a tail.

I banished that thought, realizing that yeah, okay, it was fucking big and stood on two legs with a long tail and a massive toothy maw, but the rest?

It was like a horror film maker had been tripping balls and decided to give spiders nightmares.

I checked my mana, seeing that, with the recent steady casting and the flight so far, I was down to a quarter of my mana…but that was still nearly seven hundred mana.

More than enough to fuck this shit up.

I doubled down, mana and health leaking from me like wine from a broken bottle. The creature twisted, sensing one of the figures near it.

It stepped forward, stamping down hard, crushing the Xon'dike beneath a taloned foot, then taking a step to the left and half-spinning, smashing its tail into two more that ran in from that side, pikes raised.

The weapons barely had time to pierce the skin before their wielders were sent flying, one rolling to its feet awkwardly, the other unmoving, either out cold or dead.

I picked up speed, reaching into my bag and pulling an old, battered shield free.

This was going to hurt, but being realistic, if the chitin was hard enough, my naginata could get pretty fucked up by the impact. Also, this was going to look cool as fuck.

As I closed the distance, I braced myself and held one hand against the back of the shield, focusing on it, forming it into a blade of bone. Then, as the creature grew huge before me, I dismissed my flying ability and triggered Lunge.

I was using it more as a Shield-Bash, but fuck it, whatever reality governed this shit, it still worked.

I was already travelling at a horrific speed when I triggered it, and when I impacted the side of its head, just as it started to roar out a challenge again, it shut the fucker right up.

I screamed, hitting it and being deflected off to the side, colliding with the ground at around ninety miles an hour and carving a deep furrow through three of the small fields before I stopped, lying there dazed, the shield snapped in two and lost somewhere along the way.

The creature, the S'barrr, as they'd called it, hit the floor as well–the equivalent of a God's fist smacking it in the side of the head at speed and out of the blue tends to do that.

It'd hit the ground with an almighty crash, the chitinous armor that surrounded the head shattered and leaked fluids, the creature itself stunned and the side of the jaw broken and unhinged.

I blinked slowly, lifting my hands up and looking at them, the mangled fingers making it clear that, while yes, the gauntlets had survived, the fingers…not so much.

I tried to cast healing without the spell, doing it on instinct and just make it so, but the way my mind was reeling from the impact…

I tried once, then just cast it normally, hissing in pain as my armored gauntlets popped and creaked as the fingers were forced straight, dragging the displaced sections back into place.

I blinked, letting out a long breath and grunted at the handle, all that was left with me of the shield, still held in one hand, and tossed it aside as I clambered awkwardly to my feet.

I reached into my bag as I walked forward, then changed my mind, sliding the naginata, which had only just started to appear, back in, picking up one of the hammers the fleeing Xon'dike had left scattered around instead.

The local guard had raced back in once the fucker was knocked to the ground, and they were busily mutilating it as I hefted the hammer consideringly, closing the distance.

"Who are you, stranger?" a voice called. I turned, seeing a tall local figure striding closer as the others of his species stepped aside, giving him room.

"Just a friend passing through," I called back.

"Well, *friend*, I like your sense of timing. Do you wish to claim the kill?"

"What?"

"The S'barrr, do you wish to kill it? It was your blow that took it down."

I shook my head. "Nah, it's fine. You can kill it if…"

I broke off as a fresh roar echoed down the nearby passage, making the nearest Xon'dike curse.

"Kill it, quickly!" the figure called to the others, gesturing to the still-stunned creature and moving closer to me, standing almost as tall as I was and clad in much better-crafted armor than most of his fellows. "I am Rathore, Leader of the Sect of War."

"Jax, Prince of the Empire," I said unthinkingly, feeling the sudden pause as those around me froze.

"Hmmm," Rathore replied after a few seconds, gesturing to the others who had frozen nearby to get back to work. "Well, *Jax*, what brings you to my little settlement?"

"A trick," I said honestly, looking down the passageway and figuring that there was no point in hiding it, even as I wondered at the sudden disapproval I was sensing from him. "I was stupid and was tricked into a portal when I was trying to save my people. Landed in a city filled with sludge creatures a few hours' walk from here."

"The City of Darkness." Rathore nodded, his fingers curling and tightening on the haft of his hammer, clearly watching me for any sign of threat.

"Yeah, your friends called it that." I nodded to the others in the distance.

He glanced over at the hurrying reinforcements, nodding and looking back to me as his people started cutting into the S'barrr, severing arteries and tendons as it began to come round, flopping weakly as it was rendered immobile.

"And when you reached that city? They just let you go?" he asked carefully.

"No, we burned it to the ground."

"There was an earthquake recently…"

"My partner lost her temper," I said. "The city might have two stones still standing atop one another, but you'd have to look carefully to find them."

"And its inhabitants?"

"They really didn't like fire." I smiled. "Shouldn't have fucked with me."

"Indeed," he agreed, nodding his head once. "Before you are permitted into the city, you must be tested. Will you agree to this?"

"I'd said I would, but your people basically said that I was to be stripped of my weapons and restrained, and that I couldn't leave, nor could I speak to your elders."

"I think…given the circumstances…" He paused, looking at the S'barrr that was being butchered to one side, with the bellows and distant roars echoing down to us. "Yes. I think exceptions might be made."

"Appreciate that. Don't suppose you've got any cold beer?"

"I think not. Our food and drink is…generally not well received by our trading partners."

"Well, that sucks."

"And we have outlawed alcohol and mood-altering substances."

"What do you do when you're not fighting?"

"We work, we pray, and we discuss philosophy."

"No wonder you all want to fight giant monsters," I muttered. "No booze, all work and praying, I'd want to die, too."

"There is more to life than serving our own desires," he corrected me sharply.

"Yeah, but it does no harm to enjoy yourself now and then," I pointed out. He shook his head, speaking quietly.

"A word of advice if you will? From one warrior to another, knowing that we neither may survive what is coming, and as such perhaps it may be forgotten?"

"Go for it," I said, as the first of the creatures smashed through the hanging remains of the barrier, lifting its head and screaming in triumph at the meat it sensed nearby.

"Claiming to be a Prince of the Holy Empire is something easily verified and heavily punishable. It would be a claim best not made again and certainly not repeated where others could hear it."

"The holy…?" I muttered, looking at him, my eyes widening. Then the second and third S'barrr broke free of the passage, roaring and racing toward us. "Hold that thought." I turned back to the charging creatures.

CHAPTER THIRTY-EIGHT

I watched them for a second, seeing the way they ran, reminding me of the T-rex chasing the jeep in the movies, two-legged, with the tail used for balance as much as anything.

"I'll take the middle and right," I said. "You can have the one on the left."

"I was about to say the opposite. We'll take the left and middle…"

"Whoever kills theirs first gets the spare," I countered.

"Done," he agreed, barking out orders as his companions, who'd closed the distance to us, spread out in a semicircle.

"C'mere, you fucker," I growled, fingers dancing as I used a significant part of my remaining mana to cast Explosive Compression.

It lumbered forward, a dozen meters closer, the pedipalps dragging the chitin back to expose the mouth. I grinned, shifting my aim.

I'd planned on taking its ankle out, intending to fuck it up that way, but hey, when life gives you lemons…

The spell ripped free of my hands, tearing across the space between us with a crack as it broke the sound barrier, hitting the creature's front teeth as they were exposed, and the containment sphere detonated.

There was a second where I wondered if I'd powered it too far, thinking it might rip out of the back, as the chitin slammed back down, protecting the head.

Then it bloomed, and the entire skull was ripped inward.

The body dropped like a sack of shit, the head almost entirely missing as it was compressed into a tiny marble of bone, flesh, and blood. The body hit the floor while the gravitational field clung to all it had grabbed, the flesh around the edge of its reach tearing under the sudden differential shear of forward momentum and upward gravity, combined with the sheer mass of the body below.

The neck, spurting blood and powered along by momentum, slid a few more meters toward me, pumping its life out across the floor.

"Spare's mine," I called into the stunned silence, before hefting the hammer in one hand and striding toward the oncoming 'spare'.

Rathore cleared his throat into the silence, having to cough to get control of his voice before shouting to his troops.

"That's it! Don't you dare show me up! Our guest has killed one and helped with another! If you've not killed ours before he's done with that, I'll…" He coughed again. "I'll…I'll be very upset," he finished lamely, making me grin inside my helm.

The S'barrr closed the last few meters, lunging, mouth driving down for me as I triggered Mana-Overdrive and took two quick steps to the right, dodging the bite.

It was close enough I practically felt the passage of the air as the massive head slid past me, jaws snapping closed literally inches from my shoulder.

I took another step, drawing the hammer back and swinging as hard as I could at the ankle as the foot landed nearby.

The hammer impacted the foot just as it started to lift again, landing atop the junction of the bones in the elbow and foot, and they shattered.

The leg continued to rise, or it tried to, the motion thrown off entirely as the hammer, swung with several tons of force dragged the foot back down, pulverizing the bones.

The hammer's shaft snapped about halfway, the head flashing past me, spiraling over and over as the S'barrr screamed and faceplanted the ground, teeth smashing as it hit a rock, the chitin that protected the head splitting under the impact and fracturing.

I dropped the broken haft, shaking my hands as they flared in pain. The force that transferred along them made me hiss, even as the S'barrr started to squeal.

"Mother-fuc…" I whimpered, spinning in a circle and shaking my hands out before fumbling in my bag and pulling free my naginata.

I checked my mana overdrive and my current mana levels, deciding that, just in case the Xon'dike became aggressive afterwards, I'd better save it.

I cut the ability, awkwardly casting Complex Healing and sighing as my hands stopped ringing, finally able to hold the damn weapon without having to watch to make sure it didn't fall from numb fingers.

That done, I looked to the S'barrr. It was thrashing around, the leg I'd hit utterly fucked. The foot was a mess of blood and protruding bones, as was the ankle. The beast thrashed around wildly, blood spraying as it squealed and kicked, head half buckled in like a motorbike helmet hit by a sledgehammer.

All in all, as I looked at it, shifting to lean on my naginata as I did so, the only real risk it posed now was if it rolled over someone accidentally.

The landing had buggered at least two of its lower arms, and clearly they were blind, so…

"Hey, Rathore!" I called over at the stunned warrior who was watching the fight, directing his people as they ran in and hammered at the legs and tail before darting back from the one they faced.

"What?" he shouted back, clearly a bit nonplussed at the whole "friendly conversation over deadly enemies" thing I was starting.

"Do you want your people to kill this one? It's a bit fucked now, no real threat, so…?"

"Don't discount them; they're terrible foes," he called back. I shrugged, stepping up and waiting. The S'barrr rolled to the left, then the right, then the left, claws scrabbling at the floor as it tried to turn itself over, and I struck.

I stabbed the naginata into the base of its spine where the legs met the lower back, a trickle of Fire fed into the weapon, causing it to flare bright.

The tip punched deep, sliding across a bone then finding the gap I'd been hoping for and cutting deep into the spinal column.

The legs went out from under it, tail slamming down hard and laying still as the creature let loose a pathetic mewl of panic.

I ripped the naginata free, the wound cauterized by the fire, and stepped back to glance at them as they fought the last one, calling out after a few seconds.

"Hey, you need a little help?"

"No!" Rathore snapped back, "In now!" he roared, and both sides ran in while I watched.

The Xon'dike were clearly used to fighting these fuckers, and after a few blows to slow them down and make the things cautious, they seemed to kill them easily enough.

They worked in trios, a hammer wielder racing in and smashing it down, working over and over to cripple its movement, while two pike-wielding companions jabbed at its head and chest, driving it back and keeping it from savaging the hammer.

Every so often, it would spin and try to attack the other side or trample over the gnats attacking it.

That, or it would plant its legs and try to use its tail, stabbing the barbed end out at them to skewer a victim.

They dodged the attempts easily enough, though, and both sides rushed in, pikes stabbing and forcing it to back up, even as the hammers fell.

The one on the right landed true, overstressing already damaged bones and sending the beast reeling, screaming and falling to the ground.

After that, it was all over but the slaughter, and Rathore ordered his people with short clear commands, guiding them as they darted in and out, bleeding the things from a thousand cuts, before he stepped in personally and landed a massive overhead blow on its head, cracking the chitin and exposing the softer flesh beneath to the pikes.

He stepped back, letting his warriors kill it before moving closer to me and gesturing at the crippled one in question.

"They're worth practically fuck-all in terms of experience," I said. "Back home, I'd usually call for anyone nearby who needed a few levels to bleed the fucker dry, so they all got some experience, but this one is a gift for a friend."

"What kind of a friend would appreciate such a gift?" he asked, before turning as Oracle and Sehran landed nearby.

"Sehran?" I called to her, gesturing to the S'barrr and getting a grin from her as she ran over to examine it.

"Any good to you?" I asked. She nodded quickly.

"Probably only a point, maybe; it's not actually a thinking creature with a soul, but it's still alive!" she assured me, nodding.

"Enjoy, then." I said, shrugging. "Oh, Rathore…" I gestured to him, then the girls. "This is Oracle, my partner and love, and Sehran, our companion and friend."

"Welcome," he said, inclining his head. "I am Rathore, First Warrior of the city, Leader of the local Sect of War."

"Good to meet you. So, you want to talk to us then, or are we going to have to fight you?" I asked, getting a groan from Oracle.

"Rathore, I'm sorry, Jax is terrible at polite conversation," she apologized.

"No I'm not," I replied, frowning. "I was well-behaved before, and they threatened to drag us all off to prison or whatever?"

"They didn't exactly say that," Oracle corrected me, before turning back to Rathore. "He does have a point; however, we were happy to speak to your elders, then were informed that we were to be stripped of our weapons and taken prisoner for trespassing."

"I think allowances can be made," Rathore replied dryly, before pausing as Sehran fell on the massive beast, sinking her teeth into its throat and feasting on its lifeblood. "Perhaps."

"Don't mind Sehran," I said. "Yes, she's a demon, but her bonded partner was left behind accidentally. She needs life and mana to survive, so to be clear, if you make allowances then trigger some kind of mana trap? You'll hurt her and really, really piss us off."

"I have no intention of…"

"And that's great, I'm just a little low on trust right now." I cut him off. "So, I'm laying it out nice and straight. I already had to burn your troops back there as a warning."

"Burn?" he asked, glancing at the squad leader from earlier as he huffed his way up a small incline to join us.

"First Warrior," he panted, dropping to one knee, a fist clenched to his chest in salute as he tried to catch his breath.

"Rise, Squad leader," he responded, returning the salute and jerking his head.

"These trespassers…"

"Are guests." Rathore interrupted. "This one killed a S'barrr outright and crippled two more with little effort. I believe the restraint shown so far makes it clear we'd rather they were friends than enemies. We've precious few of those of late."

"Y…yes, First Warrior," he replied, ducking his head.

"Rejoin your squad."

With that, the Xon'dike staggered upright, looked around, then sighed and set off stumbling across the ground on his way back, without another word, and Rathore turned to Oracle and me.

"We have little that would be edible for your kind, but what we have, you are welcome to," he offered, and I nodded my thanks.

"Your people prefer water, I believe?" Oracle asked, getting a confused nod, until she summoned two fountains, one after the other.

"They won't last long," I explained. "But if you have any who are injured drink from the fountains, it'll help them to heal and grant them an increase to their stamina regeneration."

"Then I thank you," he said. "We have several injured; do you have access to healing magic?"

"We do," Oracle said.

"We can heal a few if you need it, but we'll need time to recover mana in between each," I said, getting a nod from Oracle as well. "Don't you have healers?"

"Our species has little aptitude for magic," Rathore told us. "There were several healers aboard the Holy City, but we were banished long ages past."

"What?" I asked confused. "You're from the Prax?" I paused, looking around and wondering where the hell we could be in relation to the Sunken City. It didn't make much sense that we were close enough that they'd been banished from it, not considering how far out to sea it was, yet…"Wait, I thought everyone was killed in the crash?"

"The Crash?" he asked, eyes opening wide. "You know of the Holy City and its fall from the Heavens?"

The emphasis as he spoke were a clear warning that this wasn't a minor thing to them. I remembered the way he'd reacted to my name and title, making me bite my lip before I responded.

"Look, perhaps we should talk, and Oracle could heal your people?" I suggested, wondering if, with the quiet warning he'd given me already, we might have found someone I could at least get some advice from before meeting the elders.

"Of course, and perhaps…" he said, when the bells rang out again and everything stopped. The warriors that were cutting into the S'barrr clambered down, and the First Warrior and others turned, moving in unison and dropping to one knee, facing the distant wall of the cavern, their voices rising in a practiced cadence as they repeated the same words over and over again.

"Holy Empire, Master of Reality, and God above all Gods, We, your servants, swear our lives to you, in this realm and the next, our souls to serve, our blood to sustain, we exist to obey."

They repeated it over and over again, until after a few minutes, Sehran fell off the side of the S'barrr, hiccupped and staggered, then vomited blood over the nearest two Xon'dike.

They looked up in horror, breaking their chant and saw Sehran's face, her eyes glowing bright blue, cheeks stretched in a wide grin and blood covering her as she looked down at them.

They panicked, screaming something I didn't catch, and leaped sideways, knocking ours over. The mood changed from one of religious fervor…to fury as more and more realized we'd not joined in with the chanting.

Rathore hissed something, and the others dropped to a knee. They began chanting again, but it was clear that, in not joining in, we'd made a mistake.

Oracle and I moved to the back, grabbing Sehran and checking her out, finding her unsteady, with what appeared to a massive alcohol debuff.

"She's drunk," Oracle said, stunned. "The blood of that thing…"

"She's not drunk, you are!" Sehran mumbled, then smiled and reached out for Oracle, stroking her cheek. "So pretty…we could have such fun!"

"Scour?" I asked Oracle, who shook her head.

"Not a good idea. It's in her stomach and bloodstream; if we strip her of the various things in there that aren't strictly to her genetics, a cold might kill her."

"So…"

"She's already thrown most of it up; I'd say we make her drink a lot of water, and let her body come out of it on its own." She broke off as Sehran giggled and wrapped her arms around Oracle's neck, leaning in to whisper something in her ear that made her eyes widen and her cheeks grow hot. "Or, maybe we heal her now anyway, see if that would help!"

"You know you want me to," Sehran slurred, sliding a hand down Oracle's chest, fingers slipping inside the edge of the material and cupping her breast. "And no one will know…"

"I don't know who or what you are," Rathore stomped up as the chanting fell away, only to find Oracle looking shocked, her top opened before she could stop it, Sehran clearly touching her and grinning as she started to shrug out of her own clothing as well. "What is this!" he hissed in disbelief.

"We're the Emmmm-pire!" Sehran half sang at him as Oracle and I tried to think of how to deal with this. Oracle quickly reformed her clothing as she stepped out of Sehran's reach, nearly making her fall over. "He's the Prince! Prince Jax of the Empire!" she called out, loud enough that everyone nearby could hear.

"The Prince?" Rathore repeated. Lines of bright red appeared on his cheeks, arms and throat as a wide hood like that of a cobra spread out from his neck, emerging from slits cut into his helm for it. "You dare…I warned you, and still you *dare* to blaspheme! You've claimed to be the Prince to your fellow adventurers?!"

"It's not blasphemy," Oracle said quickly, holding her hands up as we backed away. "Jax is the Prince of the Empire, the Scion, named by Amon, the Eternal Emperor…"

"Heretic!" one of the other Xon'dike screamed, leveling a shaking claw at her. "Kill the heretic!"

"Oracle!" I snarled, stepping between her and Sehran and the others as they started to spread out, weapons clutched.

"Got it!" Oracle replied, and I took three quick steps back, grimacing at how low my manapool was still, as she cast quickly, surrounding us with a circle.

"You dare attack us!" Rathore snarled, slamming down his helm and glaring through the eye slits, clearly ready for battle.

"Don't fucking do this, Rathore!" I warned him, looking around at them all as Sehran hissed behind me, the flames burning the alcohol from her. "This won't end well!"

"Kill the heretics!" another of them screamed. Rathore hefted his hammer, glowering at me from the edge of the circle.

"You said you didn't have enough mana to heal all my people," he pointed out. "You won't have the mana to maintain this for long."

"This is a warning," I said. "To give you time to come to your fucking senses. Step inside the circle, and you'll burn."

"And when it runs out?" he hissed.

"We're leaving." I said after a second's thought. "Clearly this isn't going to work, us and you, so we'll go our separate ways and…"

"Kill the heretics!"

"Burn them!"

The shouts rose from all of them, and the group that had been sent as reinforcements, having stopped not far away to pray along with seemingly every other Xon'dike, lumbered toward us at the signs of tension.

Those with crossbows, leveled them at us, and I pointed at one.

"Don't you fucking do this, Rathore," I warned him. "That's just going to piss me off, and then I'll have to kill them."

"You can't kill us all," he hissed, and I shook my head, glaring at him.

"The fuck I can't. We just wiped that city of darkness out, slaughtered hundreds if not thousands of the fucking possessed creatures it led, and there's not even a fraction of that here!"

"Surrender," he growled. "You must be tried by the elders and taken before the prophet."

"Don't do this, Rathore," Oracle said as Sehran stood finally on her own, shoving her hair back and shaking her head, cursing as she realized what she'd done.

"I…I blasphemed, not my companions!" Sehran called out. "Let them go, and I will…"

"You'll damn well leave with Oracle right now," I snapped at her, cutting her off. "The passage that those big fuckers came down, go, and now!"

"But, Jax," she said, only to be cut off by hisses of fury from those nearby.

"The Oaths!" Oracle snapped, clicking her fingers. "If we could reactivate the bond…" She broke off, staring at something nobody but us could see.

Our manapool was massively depleted, and it'd take three hours to recover it fully, three hours we damn well didn't have. As it was, we had maybe one more casting of this circle left, and that was it. There was nowhere near enough to activate the Oaths and claim them as my own.

Even if there was, there was no saying if these fuckers would have spoken the oaths, considering that butchered prayer they were saying before. Even if they'd intended to swear it, it might have been done wrong.

I didn't even have any more mana or health potions, and Oracle knew it as well as I did. Our stupid desire to help these fuckers, casting the fountains, using magic to kill the S'barrr and to show off a little hadn't proven, as I'd hoped, that we could be allies.

Instead, it'd cemented us as enemies they couldn't permit to live.

"Ready!" Rathore called, his people moving in closer, crossbows aimed at us.

"Fly!" I frantically sent to Oracle.

It was faster than walking, and she knew it, as did Sehran. Neither argued as I took two quick steps forward, bringing the edge of the circle into contact with the Xon'dike. They screamed as flames attacked them, throwing off their aim.

"Fire!" Rathore screamed, hammer raised overhead and already swinging.

I dodged to the left, then right, bolts flying past, two delivering glancing blows to my armor, one redirected almost straight up, the other hitting the dirt.

Rathore and two others closed with me, others only a few steps behind as they raced inward.

Pikes were stabbed at me and I cursed, twisting around and grabbing one of them behind the head, yanking hard and pulling the warrior off-balance before I released it.

I slapped the other aside on my left, deflecting it downward and stamped on it, the blow landing just behind the metal head where it joined the wooden haft.

It snapped, splinters sent flying, but before I could capitalize on it, Rathore was there, hammer swinging for my helm.

I leaped aside, landing awkwardly as he used his momentum to follow, twisting his body and bringing the hammer around again.

I rolled to my feet, a pike from behind glancing off my armored pauldron and making me hiss, then dodge again instead of counterattacking.

The hesitation cost me, the hammer coming too close, and I was forced to smack it aside, left-handed.

It was enough, just, to deflect the blow, but it damn well cost me. Pain roared up the arm, and the numbness made it clear I wasn't going to be doing that again.

I took another step to the right, then ran to the left, the circle dragging with me across the floor and attacking them all with questing flames that threw off their attacks.

"We're clear!"

As soon as Oracle sent that, I twisted around again, ducking low on my right knee, the hammer being drawn back. I leaped into the air, triggering Soaring Majesty and flashing past him before the hammer could land.

I twisted around, damn sure that I didn't have the time to waste. I had about three seconds of flight time before it came to an abrupt end, and I'd be blinded by the mana-migraine to boot.

I lined up on the exit to the cavern, seeing Oracle and Sehran racing down the passageway, and shoved the mana into my ability, rocketing into the passage as the lights went out, losing my DarkVision as I ran out of even enough mana to power that.

CHAPTER THIRTY-NINE

I landed hard, hell, I didn't so much land as tear a furrow in the packed dirt of the passage with my face at about seventy miles an hour.

If I'd been a human from Earth, well, if I'd been as I was when I first arrived from Earth, I'd have been killed on impact.

Instead, I was stunned, had broken several fingers, *again,* sustained a mild concussion, and had to spit out what felt like half a field. It had forced its way onto the gap in my helm, into my mouth, up my nose, and into my eyes.

I forced myself to my feet, coughing and spitting, shaking my helm to get it out, blinded by the crap that was in my eyes. I ran into a wall, bouncing off and falling, stunned.

I could feel and hear, sort of, Oracle calling to me, telling me this way, but over the migraine, the impacts, and the goddamn state of me generally, I couldn't make head nor tails of what direction she meant and actually got to my feet and started lumbering in the wrong direction at first.

Once she'd got it through my head that I was going in the opposite direction, I stopped and started running again, tripping and stumbling as I hit the divot I'd dug with my face, then stabilizing and picking up speed as Oracle kept directing me with "left a bit, now right" as practically all I had.

Nearly a minute later, as I was putting my helm back on, having had to remove it to clean it and my eyes out, DarkVision was flickering to life, and I could just make out the curve of the passage ahead as it took a kink to the right.

Oracle and Sehran were waiting at the corner. I threw my arm up defensively as a crossbow bolt hit the wall nearby, sending sparks flying from exposed flint.

Two more bolts almost made it to us when the fourth hit the back of my knee, the distance robbing it of the force it needed to fully penetrate the armor, but it made me stagger and shout out in pain.

I fell, hitting the floor and cursing as I tried to get back up, another two bolts hitting the wall nearby, as distant shouting echoed down toward us.

The race was on.

I forced myself back to my feet, limping around the turn and out of sight of the crossbow wielders, accepting Sehran's shoulder as she ducked under that arm, helping me to move on.

"A few minutes," Oracle said. "Another few minutes, and I'll be able to heal you…"

"I'll heal fast enough. Nothing's broken, just fucking hurts, and we'll need the mana to fight."

"We could collapse the tunnel?" Sehran suggested. "Explosive Compression, I've got nearly enough…maybe two more minutes, or I could heal you?"

"Take the tunnel down," I ordered after a few seconds' thought. "They might have been great allies."

"I'm sorry."

"You didn't know that damn thing had booze for blood, did you?" I asked. She shook her head.

"Then don't apologize."

"It tasted weird, and I thought…I don't know."

"Don't worry about it," I grunted, as I looked at Sehran, making sure she knew I didn't blame her for this. "Yes, they *might* have been great allies, considering they'd made some damn runes glow around their city and more, but for all we know, they were fucking cannibals or would have swarmed us when they found out who we really were, anyway. Religious fanatics don't tend to make good friends."

"Especially not when they'd have found out that you were the focus of the religion…I mean, can you imagine the statues?" Oracle quipped, trying to distract me.

"Damn right I can!" I replied, going along with it, wincing as I forced myself to keep going. "Me replacing David in a museum, just with a much bigger knob."

"Wrong word, not you *have*…you *are* a big knob," she replied, laughing.

"Meh, details, details!"

"Who is David?" Sehran asked, confused.

"Nobody," I said. "It's just a joke about a statue of a man called David in a museum back home, with a little pecker and naked. The Greeks did that kinda thing a lot."

"What?"

"Make statues of naked people…usually in public places."

"Why?"

"Because they didn't have the internet, I guess. Had to get their kicks somewhere, and the printing press hadn't been invented yet, so no cheap photos."

"Ignore it, Sehran," Oracle advised. "I could explain it all, but honestly, it's not worth it; most of the time I just nod and smile. I bet you've done it before."

"Oh!" She nodded to Oracle. "I understand what you mean, don't worry." She looked up at me and fluttered her eyelashes. "It's the biggest I've ever seen!" she said, with just a hint of awe in her voice, before looking over at Oracle. "Like that?"

"Perfect!" Oracle grinned. "Okay, are you ready to bring the tunnel down?"

"Okay, just a second…" she said, before smiling genuinely at me as I braced on the wall and stretched my knee out. "You can tell me more about it soon," she promised, again in an awestruck and now clearly fake voice.

"I hate you two," I muttered, wincing as I flexed my knee.

"You know you don't, really," Oracle whispered, hitting me with a heal and making me gasp in relief as something in the back of my knee shifted. The painful fluid buildup I'd been trying to ignore was soothed away in seconds.

"I know," I said, sighing and keeping my eyes closed as the migraine flared viciously.

"I know you said no to healing, to save it," she said. I shook my head.

"It was worse than I thought," I agreed. "I couldn't have kept going much longer. Thank you." I pulled the helm off and kissed Oracle, long and deep, then held her to me as a sudden boom rang out, then a rumble of collapsing stone from behind us, accompanied by a blast of dirt and noise.

"Sorry," Sehran said, hurrying back to us a few seconds later. "I went around the last corner to make sure it'd not reach us here."

"Good choice," I said. "Come on, then…I can't see again now, so…"

"We'll guide you," Oracle agreed, taking one hand, as Sehran took my other, leading me onward.

Twenty minutes passed, the first few minutes with them leading me, then when my vision returned and the migraine died away, I released them and hurried alongside the pair, until at last a forking in the passage gave us a choice of ahead or right.

"Which way?" I asked, and Oracle pointed ahead.

"There's more air that way, but…"

"But?"

"But a lot less water, and more fire and death."

"Oh joy."

"Why go that way, then?" Sehran asked. I shrugged as we moved on.

"More air, more likely to be a way out to the surface," I said, getting a nod from Oracle.

Another half an hour passed, the heat steadily rising as we alternated between running and walking, five minutes of each, before the path took a sudden twist to the left, narrowing massively as it passed through a different kind of rock, then switching back on itself and climbing sharply, narrowing here and there.

We followed it, seeing places where the S'barrr must have had to squeeze through, sections of rock rubbed bloody, piles of discarded flesh and hairy chitin.

A minute later, the answer to the question of why the hell anything would be that desperate to get underground was answered, as we reached the mouth of a cave, moving up to stare out across the surface before us.

The heat that had been climbing was suddenly explained as I swore, blinking out at the bright light and furnace-like heat…of an open desert.

We stared out across miles upon miles of golden dunes that shimmered in the merciless heat, only to see a crumbling city in the distance, more than half-buried and clearly long-abandoned.

"It can't be!" Oracle hissed in shock, shaking her head.

"What?"

"The city…" she whispered, lifting one shaking hand to point at it. "The Dome of Truth."

I frowned, looking again, and seeing a dust-whipped dome, similar to one I'd seen in movies of the U.S. Capitol, towering over many of the other nearby buildings.

It was surrounded by fallen buildings, crumbling, with a line of Romanesque pillars leading up to the dome. Most were fallen, mounds covered by the encroaching desert, but here and there they still stood, showing what must have been a wide walkway leading up to the building.

"The Dome of Truth. I saw images of it, in the city of Romesh, and less than a hundred miles from the edge of the Great Altan," Oracle said, stunned. "We're in the Altan…it must have spread, engulfed the city and…" She shook her head, stepping forward and out into the full glare of the sun, horrified as she pieced together the things she was seeing.

"The where?" I asked, not recognizing the name.

"The Great Altan Desert. The second largest desert in the Empire, and thousands of miles from Dravith." Tears tracked down her cheeks as she turned to me. "We're lost, my love, and we're halfway around the realm from everyone who would want to help us."

"Well, fuck."

EPILOGUE

"What the hell do you mean they're not here?" Thomas roared at Grizz, who stood at attention, facing the brother of his Prince.

"I mean they're not here, sir!" Grizz replied, the internal fury that had driven him for the last few days, ever since he'd managed to kill that fucker of a lord and free them all, rising as he stared into Thomas' eyes.

"Then where the hell is he?"

"We don't know," Lydia said before Grizz could reply, marching tiredly up the slope of the fallen building to reach the others. "He went through a portal, a portal we now can't activate, and he was with Oracle and Sehran. They're all alive, but that's all we know."

"So, what?" Thomas groaned. "He could be anywhere in the fucking realm now? Hell, all of the realms?!"

"No." Grizz said. "The Portal led to a city, one that was buried underground, apparently, and that they'd been going to and from already. The survivors of the lord's guard on this side told us about it, after a little persuasion."

"And?"

"And they were tricked into going through, then attacked. There's something living on the other side, something that's able to take over the people it catches. No idea how or why, but once it's in them, they can't go back through the portal. They'd come up to the edge, apparently, and try anything to get the guys on this side to go through, but they wouldn't step over themselves."

"Sounds dodgy."

"Very. The son was left in charge of the lord's guard here; he'd been opening it and trying to find his father, or to connect to anywhere else. Apparently, the father went through and took the rest of the keys with him. Something about needing to know where you're going means that, without the right key, you could end up anywhere. Then we attacked, and he panicked, thinking the possessed ones had gotten through somehow. He triggered the mana null field and wiped out all magic on this side. We were hit by some powerful weapons from your home. Jax was lost. He fell down a hole to a lower level." Grizz reported, still standing at attention.

"He's down below? You said…"

"No," Lydia snapped, looking around. "D' ye think we'd be 'ere otherwise? They used some gas on us, and lightning sticks that knocked us out, then when we wake up, we were naked, in cages."

"We were trying to get free, then Jax appears, in new full armor and looking seriously pissed. He ran at them, and the dickhead noble triggered the portal, sending him through and closing it after him."

"So, you let yourselves get fucking captured, then my brother, who came to rescue you all, *his guards*, ended up being kicked through a portal to some buried shithole?" Thomas snapped. "He could be fucking anywhere and…"

"He's there," Tenandra interrupted, staring off into the distance over the rolling leaden sea. "I can sense him, although not Oracle or Sehran, not properly. I can feel my bond to him as my master, though, and the Scion…"

"Where?" the others all said at almost the same time, spinning and looking out to see, ignoring the rain that was being driven in and the heavy storm clouds.

"Far, far away in that direction," she said. "Weeks of travel possibly…maybe more."

"Fuck!" Thomas cursed, turning and walking away, rubbing at his chin as people streamed past, both his squad going to help Jax's, and the crew going to help the crew of the other ship.

"Can you use the portal?" Lydia asked Tenandra. "You were the Prax's Wisp, could you activate the portal? Get us through to him?"

"Perhaps, but…what about the key? That would be linked to the destination; it should be easy to…" Tenandra said, before Lydia shook her head, cutting her off.

"We've tried. It will no' connect…the asshole who 'ad it snapped it, and now…"

"If the key was broken, it's useless," Tenandra said, thinking quickly. "Without the key, we would need to repair and activate the command center, and the work needed to repair the pathways and reconnect the portal would be weeks alone."

"And if we do that, and you can't get the portal working, we've wasted weeks of time," Thomas growled, stepping back in close. "Weeks we could have been flying to Jax."

"Exactly."

"But we could get halfway, or more, then Jax could use the portal on his end, get himself back through, and the only way we'd know is if you felt it," Lydia said, looking at Tenandra.

"True." Tenandra turned to Thomas. "I was ordered by Jax that, if I lost contact with him and the others for twenty-four hours, then I was to leave and return with you."

"You left as soon as you were cut off from them," Thomas said. "I already told you that was the right choice."

"It was, but it was also hard, because I didn't want to. I wanted to land and help; I wanted to save the ones I loved and be involved in that, not simply wait while I flew to get help."

"What's your point?"

"You face the same decision now," Tenandra said. "Jax has ordered the Empire to remain here, in Dravith. If he is lost, even if only for a short time, then the Empire is to pull in and consolidate. The Legion are to train the next generation, and we are to go on without him."

"I won't abandon my brother!" Thomas snapped. "He came to this fucking shithole of a realm for me, started a war with the Dark Dickhead, and you think I should…"

"No," Lydia said, having seen what Tenandra was aiming for. "No, she don't mean yer give up, she means yer need to stay here."

"Here?!?" Thomas looked around at the ruined Prax. "Why the hell would I…"

"If *you* stay here, you can recover the golems, you can lead the Gnomes and clear out the lower reaches of the Prax." Tenandra's gaze grew distant. "As more and more golems are recovered and reactivated, you can repair the most basic functions of the Prax, providing power to the systems and beginning recovery. As more sections are repaired, you'll be able to activate the portal, and with the control facilities, you can connect to any portal in its records, rather than using keys."

"No, you could do that better than me," Thomas said, glancing at Tenandra.

"I'll be with the others, flying straight at Jax. I'm the only one who can both sense and fly an airship to him."

"Then I'll come with you."

"That's a decision you'll have to make, Thomas. If you come with us, then the Prax will stay as it is. If, for some reason, like not having the right damn key, Jax can't reopen the portal from his side, then he's trapped there."

"You said the dickhead's son is here and had the key, so he can make another one, right?"

"He did, but as Lydia said, it was snapped in the fight," Grizz said. "We can't get it to connect, the portal powers up, draining us all to do it, but fails at the last point. Arrin and Giint think it's the key not working, but it could be anything, or…"

"Or?"

"Or the portal might be broken."

"Then I'm wasting my fucking time here!" Thomas snapped.

"No, only one with Imperial Right can command the golems. If, when they're woken up, they go into an attack mode or refuse to listen? Then the only one who can make them obey is you, Thomas. If you come with us, then you make it so that Jax can't come back this way without us finding him by ship."

"Can the golems fix the portal?" Thomas asked after a long few seconds of chewing his knuckle.

"Perhaps," Tenandra hedged. "If the golem is a high enough level crafter, complex at least, then it could fix it, a servitor, maybe. But if they can't?"

"Yeah?"

"There was a second portal in storage."

"Where?"

"In the main hold."

"So maybe at the bottom of the fucking sea?"

"Maybe, but Grizz, you said that Jax turned up in new armor?"

"Yeah, a full set of Praetorian Guard armor. It was beautiful," he said softly.

"Then the armory is intact, or reachable at least. It was near to the storage area. Thomas, you have two choices to make. I have to go to him; only I can find him. You can come with me and accept that, if he finds a working portal, then he can make it back on his own to the continent, but not here, or…"

"Or I can repair enough of the Prax to power the portal and the control center, then we can go to him," Thomas whispered, closing his eyes. "I stay here and do fucking housekeeping, repair shit, and babysit the goddamn crazy fucking Gnomes while we just hope he makes it back to us."

"It's a shitty choice, either way," Lydia admitted. "We can't go and get more of the Legion, so it's just us, flying to another continent and hoping we can find him before the locals kill us or our food runs out, or we stay here and wait for him to sort it out himself."

"This is the best chance we can give him, Thomas, you know that," Belladonna said, striding up and laying her hand on his shoulder, her elven ears having let her listen in as she'd approached.

"I know," he said slowly. "I just don't like it."

"You don't have to like it," she said. "You just have to do it. We don't get to choose the way we serve; we're soldiers. You can give him the best chance at surviving by staying here. Tenandra and his squad can go to him. We can cross-load as much food and other supplies as we can to her now, and she can leave immediately. The other ship can return to Himnel and give Duke Augustus a full report. Maybe he'll overrule us, but until then, and until they come back with those orders and more food, you have the responsibility to choose."

"Lydia," Thomas snapped after a few seconds of thought. "Strip anything and everything you need from here; you leave in an hour. Go find my goddamn brother."

"Yes sir!" she barked, fist crashing against her breastplate in salute, before she spun and shouted out orders to the others, sending them running.

"Hold on, bro…they're coming," Thomas whispered, staring out and feeling Bella's hand as it shook his pauldron gently, sharing her presence.

They stood there, watching the sea birds wheel in the rapidly darkening sky, the call of an albatross hanging in the air as it sailed past. Far out to sea, the motion of something under its surface sent a V shaped wake half a mile long rolling out behind it.

"Maybe that's not all we can do," Thomas said, watching the wake as it faded, the massive form slipping back into the deeps. "Maybe we can send more help his way, after all…"

"What do you…"

"Move it, people!" he shouted, turning on his heel and running for the second ship, the captain attempting to restart the engines and scratching his head as mainly feral Gnomes clambered over them.

"You!" Thomas snapped, pointing to two of them. "I need you both and that golem."

THE END
OF
BOOK SEVEN

SEHRAN

WELL NOW!

Okay, so I know that one or two of you are going to be demanding more and soon, as well as the occasional person who complains about the cliffhanger. I can tell you first of all it's for a good reason that I finished it here, basically my intention is to write books 8&9 towards the end of next year, with them both releasing close together.

That's because the end of book 8 will result in me getting murdered if I don't do 9 straight afterwards! I tend to spend around 6 months in a world at a time, as more than that drives me crazier than normal, so next up is Age of Steel, then Age of Glass for the Rise of Mankind, followed by a few months of a side project and then Arise 3&4…by which time I'll be back to UnderVerse hopefully!

Even with the cliffhanger though, I hope you enjoyed the book? If so, please, please remember to leave a review, its massively important, as not only does it let others know about the book, it also tells Amazon that the book is worth promoting, and makes it more likely that more people will see it.

That in turn will hopefully keep me able to keep writing full time, while listening to crazy German bands like the Grailknights screaming in my ears, and frankly, I kinda really like that!

If you want to spread the good word, that'd be amazing, and if you know of any stores or libraries that might be interested in stocking my books, I'm happy to reach out and send them samples, but honestly, if you enjoy my madness, that's massive for me.

Thank you.

AGE OF STEEL

Rise of Mankind Book 4

14th February 2023

The rising wave of the undead has been stilled, the Lich Lord Daedalus defeated, and the dungeon is safe…for now.

Now comes a time of growth, of peace and restructuring as the dungeon upgrades and the new alliances settle, but not all is peace and love.

The gangs are rising, the asuras spread, and the dead never truly rest…

The Age of Steel has begun….

https://mybook.to/AgeofSteel

REVIEWS

Hey! Well, I hope you enjoyed the book? If so, please, please remember to leave a review, its massively important, as not only does it let others know about the book, it also tells Amazon that the book is worth promoting, and makes it more likely that more people will see it.

That in turn will hopefully keep me able to keep writing full time, while listening to crazy German bands screaming in my ears, and frankly, I kinda really like that!

If you want to spread the good word, that'd be amazing, and if you know of anyone that might be interested in stocking my books, I'm happy to reach out and send them samples, but honestly, if you enjoy my madness, that's massive for me.
Thank you.

FACEBOOK AND SOCIAL MEDIA

If you want to reach out, chat or shoot the shit, you can always find me on either my author page here:

www.facebook.com/JezCajiaoAuthor

OR

We've recently set up a new Facebook group to spread the word about cool LitRPG books. It's dedicated to two very simple rules, 1; lets spread the word about new and old brilliant LitRPG books, and 2: Don't be a Dick!
They sound like really simple rules, but you'd be amazed…
Come join us!

https://www.facebook.com/groups/litrpglegion

I'm also on Discord here: **https://discord.gg/u5JYHscCEH**

Or I'm reaching out on other forms of social media atm, I'm just spread a little thin that's all!

You're most likely to find me on Discord, but please, don't be offended when I don't approve friend requests on my personal Facebook pages. I did originally, and several people abused that, sending messages to my family and being generally unpleasant, hence, the author page:

https://www.facebook.com/JezCajiaoAuthor

I hope you understand.

PATREON!

Okay then, now for those of you that don't know about Patreon, its essentially a way to support your favorite nutcases, you can sign up for a day or a month or a year, and you get various benefits for it, ranging from my heartfelt thanks, to advance access to the books, to signed books, naming characters and more.

At the time of me writing this, the advanced Patreon readers are getting a sneak peek at Age of Steel, and are voting on the next batch of Character Art as well, so yeah, you get plenty for the support!

There's three wonderful supporters out there that I have to thank personally as well; ASeaInStorm, Leighton, and Nicholas Kauffman, you utter legends you. Thank you all and as promised, the characters are in the works.

www.patreon.com/Jezcajiao

RECOMMENDATIONS

I'm often asked for personal recommendations, so if this book has whetted your appetite for more LitRPG, please have a look at the following, these are brilliant series by brilliant authors!

Ascend Online by Luke Chmilenko

The Land by Aleron Kong

Challengers Call by Nathan A Thompson

SoulShip also by Nathan

Endless Online by M H Johnson

Silver Fox and the Western Hero, also by M H Johnson

The Good Guys/Bad Guys by Eric Ugland

Condition: Evolution by Kevin Sinclair

Space Seasons by Dawn Chapman

The Wayward Bard by Lars M

LITRPG!

To learn more about LitRPG, talk to other authors including myself, and to just have an awesome time, please join the LitRPG Group

www.facebook.com/groups/LitRPGGroup

FACEBOOK

There's also a few really active Facebook groups I'd recommend you join, as you'll get to hear about great new books, new releases and interact with all your (new) favorite authors! (I may also be there, skulking at the back and enjoying the memes…)

www.facebook.com/groups/LitRPGsociety/

www.facebook.com/groups/LitRPG.books/

www.facebook.com/groups/LitRPGforum/

www.facebook.com/groups/gamelitsociety/

9 781915 617026